A VISIT TO THE CHESAPEAKE BAY SAGA IS A VISIT TO THE UNFORGETTABLE FAMILY KNOWN AS THE QUINNS . . .

For the first time, the final two novels of Nora Roberts's breathtaking Chesapeake Bay Saga are together in one volume, bringing "a welcome crescendo to the story-symphony that is the family Quinn in all its boisterous, loving resonance" (*BookPage*).

INNER HARBOR

As Phillip Quinn struggles to draw his new brother into his life, he must deal with a beautiful woman who has secrets that will affect them all—a woman who needs both his trust and his heart . . .

"With bright dialogue and lots of heart, Roberts provides a safe harbor for Phillip . . . and for her many fans."   —*Publishers Weekly*

CHESAPEAKE BLUE

When world-renowned artist Seth Quinn returns to his home on Maryland's Eastern Shore, he finds the woman of his dreams. But someone from his past is determined to destroy his newfound happiness . . .

"Roberts . . . delivers luscious prose."   —*The Boston Globe*

DON'T MISS
THE QUINN BROTHERS,
FEATURING SEA SWEPT AND RISING TIDES

D0189403

NORA ROBERTS

THE QUINN LEGACY

BERKLEY BOOKS, NEW YORK

THE BERKLEY PUBLISHING GROUP
Published by the Penguin Group
Penguin Group (USA) Inc.
375 Hudson Street, New York, New York 10014, USA
Penguin Group (Canada), 90 Eglinton Avenue East, Suite 700, Toronto, Ontario M4P 2Y3, Canada
(a division of Pearson Penguin Canada Inc.)
Penguin Books Ltd., 80 Strand, London WC2R 0RL, England
Penguin Group Ireland, 25 St. Stephen's Green, Dublin 2, Ireland (a division of Penguin Books Ltd.)
Penguin Group (Australia), 250 Camberwell Road, Camberwell, Victoria 3124, Australia
(a division of Pearson Australia Group Pty. Ltd.)
Penguin Books India Pvt. Ltd., 11 Community Centre, Panchsheel Park, New Delhi—110 017, India
Penguin Group (NZ), Cnr. Airborne and Rosedale Roads, Albany, Auckland 1310, New Zealand
(a division of Pearson New Zealand Ltd.)
Penguin Books (South Africa) (Pty.) Ltd., 24 Sturdee Avenue, Rosebank, Johannesburg 2196,
South Africa

Penguin Books Ltd., Registered Offices: 80 Strand, London WC2R 0RL, England

PRINTING HISTORY
Berkley trade paperback one-volume edition / February 2006

Berkley trade paperback ISBN: 0-425-20815-X

This book has been cataloged with the Library of Congress

PRINTED IN THE UNITED STATES OF AMERICA

10   9   8   7   6   5   4   3   2   1

CONTENTS

INNER HARBOR

For Elaine and Beth, such devoted sisters—
even if they won't wear blue organdy and sing

PROLOGUE

Phillip Quinn died at the age of thirteen. Since the overworked and underpaid staff at the Baltimore City Hospital emergency room zapped him back in less than ninety seconds, he wasn't dead very long.

As far as he was concerned, it was plenty long enough.

What had killed him, briefly, were two .25-caliber bullets pumped out of a Saturday night special shoved through the open window of a stolen Toyota Celica. The finger on the trigger had belonged to a close personal friend—or as near to a close personal friend as a thirteen-year-old thief could claim on Baltimore's bad streets.

The bullets missed his heart. Not by much, but in later years Phillip considered it just far enough.

That heart, young and strong, though sadly jaded, continued to beat as he lay there, pouring blood over the used condoms and crack vials in the stinking gutter on the corner of Fayette and Paca.

The pain was obscene, like sharp, burning icicles stabbing into his chest. But that grinning pain refused to take him under, into the release of unconsciousness. He lay awake and aware, hearing the screams of other victims or bystanders, the squeal of brakes, the revving of engines, and his own ragged and rapid breaths.

He'd just fenced a small haul of electronics that he'd stolen from a third-story walk-up less than four blocks away. He had two hundred fifty dollars in his pocket and had swaggered down to score a dime bag to help him get through the night. Since he'd just been sprung from ninety days in juvie for another B and E that hadn't gone quite so smoothly, he'd been out of the loop. And out of cash.

Now it appeared he was out of luck.

Later, he would remember thinking, Shit, oh, shit, this *hurts*! But he couldn't seem to wrap his mind around another thought. He'd gotten in the way. He knew that. The bullets hadn't been meant for him in particular. He'd caught a glimpse of the gang colors in that frozen three seconds before the gun had fired. His own colors, when he bothered to associate himself with one of the gangs that roamed the streets and alleys of the city.

If he hadn't just popped out of the system, he wouldn't have been on that corner at that moment. He would have been told to stay clear, and he wouldn't now be sprawled out, pumping blood and staring into the dirty mouth of the gutter.

Lights flashed—blue, red, white. The scream of sirens pierced through human screams. Cops. Even through the slick haze of pain his instinct was to run. In his mind he sprang up, young, agile, street-smart, and melted into the shadows. But even the effort of the thought had cold sweat sliding down his face.

He felt a hand on his shoulder, and fingers probed until they reached the thready pulse in his throat.

This one's breathing. Get the paramedics over here.

Someone turned him over. The pain was unspeakable, but he couldn't release the scream that ripped through his head. He saw faces swimming over him, the hard eyes of a cop, the grim ones of the medical technician. Red, blue, and white lights burned his eyes. Someone wept in high, keening sobs.

Hang in there, kid.

Why? He wanted to ask why. It hurt to be there. He was never going to escape as he'd once promised himself he would. What was left of his life was running red into the gutter. What had come before was only ugliness. What was now was only pain.

What was the damn point?

He went away for a while, sinking down below the pain, where the world was a dark and dingy red. From somewhere outside his world came the shriek of the sirens, the pressure on his chest, the speeding motion of the ambulance.

Then lights again, bright white to sear his closed lids. And he was flying while voices shouted on all sides of him.

Bullet wounds, chest. BP's eighty over fifty and falling, pulse thready and rapid. In and out. Pupils are good.

Type and cross-match. We need pictures. On three. One, two, three.

His body seemed to jerk, up then down. He no longer cared. Even the dingy red was going gray. A tube was pushing its way down his throat and he didn't bother to try to cough it out. He barely felt it. Barely felt anything and thanked God for it.

BP's dropping. We're losing him.

I've been lost a long time, he thought.

With vague interest he watched them, half a dozen green-suited people in a small room where a tall blond boy lay on a table. Blood was everywhere. His blood, he realized. He was on that table with his chest torn open. He looked down at himself with detached sympathy. No more pain now, and the quiet sense of relief nearly made him smile.

He floated higher, until the scene below took on a pearly sheen and the sounds were nothing but echoes.

Then the pain tore through him, an abrupt shock that made the body on the table jerk, that sucked him back. His struggle to pull away was brief and fruitless. He was inside again, feeling again, lost again.

The next thing he knew, he was riding in a drug-hazed blur. Someone was snoring. The room was dark and the bed narrow and hard. A backwash of light filtered through a pane of glass that was spotted with fingerprints. Machines beeped and sucked monotonously. Wanting only to escape the sounds, he rolled back under.

He was in and out for two days. He was very lucky. That's what they told him. There was a pretty nurse with tired eyes and a doctor with graying hair and thin lips. He wasn't ready to believe them, not when he was too weak to lift his head, not when the hideous pain swarmed back into him every two hours like clockwork.

When the two cops came in he was awake, and the pain was smothered under a few layers of morphine. He made them out to be cops at a glance. His instincts weren't so dulled that he didn't recognize the walk, the shoes, the eyes. He didn't need the identification they flashed at him.

"Gotta smoke?" Phillip asked it of everyone who passed through. He had a low-grade desperation for nicotine even though he doubted he could manage to suck on a cigarette.

"You're too young to smoke." The first cop pasted on an avuncular smile and stationed himself on one side of the bed. The Good Cop, Phillip thought wearily.

"I'm getting older every minute."

"You're lucky to be alive." The second cop kept his face hard as he pulled out a notebook.

And the Bad Cop, Phillip decided. He was nearly amused.

"That's what they keep telling me. So, what the hell happened?"

"You tell us." Bad Cop poised his pencil over a page of his book.

"I got the shit shot out of me."

"What were you doing on the street?"

"I think I was going home." He'd already decided how to play it, and he let his eyes close. "I can't remember exactly. I'd been . . . at the movies?" He made it a question, opening his eyes. He could see Bad Cop wasn't going to buy it, but what could they do?

"What movie did you see? Who were you with?"

"Look, I don't know. It's all messed up. One minute I was walking, the next I was lying facedown."

"Just tell us what you remember." Good Cop laid a hand on Phillip's shoulder. "Take your time."

"It happened fast. I heard shots—it must have been shots. Somebody was screaming, and it was like something exploded in my chest." That much was pretty close to the truth.

"Did you see a car? Did you see the shooter?"

Both were etched like acid on steel in his brain. "I think I saw a car— dark color. A flash."

"You belong to the Flames."

Phillip shifted his gaze to Bad Cop. "I hang with them sometimes."

"Three of the bodies we scraped off the street were members of the Tribe. They weren't as lucky as you. The Flames and the Tribe have a lot of bad blood between them."

"So I've heard."

"You took two bullets, Phil." Good Cop settled his face into concerned lines. "Another inch either way, you'd have been dead before you hit the pavement. You look like a smart kid. A smart kid doesn't fool himself into believing he needs to be loyal to assholes."

"I didn't see anything." It wasn't loyalty. It was survival. If he rolled over, he was dead.

"You had over two hundred in your wallet."

Phillip shrugged, regretting it as the movement stirred up the ghosts of pain. "Yeah? Well, maybe I can pay my bill here at the Hilton."

"Don't smart-mouth me, you little punk." Bad Cop leaned over the bed. "I see your kind every fucking day. You're not out of the system twenty hours before you end up bleeding into the gutter."

Phillip didn't flinch. "Is getting shot a violation of my parole?"

"Where'd you get the money?"

"I don't remember."

"You were down in Drug City to score."

"Did you find any drugs on me?"

"Maybe we did. You wouldn't remember, would you?"

Good one, Phillip mused. "I could sure as hell use some now."

"Ease off a little." Good Cop shifted his feet. "Look, son, you cooperate and we'll play square with you. You've been in and out of the system enough to know how it works."

"If the system worked I wouldn't be here, would I? You can't do anything to me that hasn't been done. For Christ's sake, if I'd known something was going down I wouldn't have been there."

The sudden disturbance out in the hall took the cops' attention away. Phillip merely closed his eyes. He recognized the voice raised in bitter fury.

Stoned, was his first and last thought. And when she stumbled into the room, he opened his eyes and saw that he'd been right on target.

She'd dressed up for the visit, he noted. Her yellow hair was teased and sprayed into submission, and she'd put on full makeup. Under it, she might have been a pretty woman, but the mask was hard and tough. Her body was good, it was what kept her in business. Strippers who moonlight as hookers need a good package. She'd peeled on a halter and jeans, and she clicked her way over to the bed on three-inch heels.

"Who the hell do you think's gonna pay for this? You're nothing but trouble."

"Hi, Ma, nice to see you, too."

"Don't you sass me. I got cops coming to the door 'cause of you. I'm sick of it." She flashed a look at the men on either side of the bed. Like her son, she recognized cops. "He's almost fourteen years old. I'm done with him. He ain't coming back on me this time. I ain't having cops and social workers breathing down my neck anymore."

She shrugged off the nurse who hustled in to grab her arm, then leaned over the bed. "Why the hell didn't you just die?"

"I don't know," Phillip said calmly. "I tried."

"You've never been any good." She hissed at Good Cop when he pulled her back. "Never been any damn good. Don't you come around looking for a place to stay when you get out of here," she shouted as she was dragged out of the room. "I'm done with you."

Phillip waited, listening to her swearing, shouting, demanding papers to sign to get him out of her life. Then he looked up at Bad Cop. "You think you can scare me? I live with that. Nothing's worse than living with that."

Two days later, strangers came into the room. The man was huge, with blue eyes bright in a wide face. The woman had wild red hair escaping from a messy knot at the nape of her neck and a face full of freckles. The woman took his chart from the foot of the bed, scanned it, then tapped it against her palm.

"Hello, Phillip. I'm Dr. Stella Quinn. This is my husband, Ray."

"Yeah, so?"

Ray pulled a chair up to the side of the bed and sat down with a sigh of pleasure. He angled his head, studied Phillip briefly. "You've got yourself into a hell of a mess here, haven't you? Want to get out of it?"

ONE

Phillip loosened the Windsor knot in his Fendi tie. It was a long commute from Baltimore to Maryland's Eastern Shore, and he'd programmed his CD player with that in mind. He started out mellow with a little Tom Petty and the Heartbreakers.

Thursday-evening traffic was as bad as predicted, made worse by the sluggish rain and the rubberneckers who couldn't resist a long, fascinated goggle at the three-car accident on the Baltimore Beltway.

By the time he was heading south on Route 50, even the hot licks of vintage Stones couldn't completely lift his mood.

He'd brought work with him and somehow had to eke out time for the Myerstone Tire account over the weekend. They wanted a whole new look for this advertising campaign. Happy tires make happy drivers, Phillip thought, drumming his fingers on the wheel to the rhythm of Keith Richards's outlaw guitar.

Which was a crock, he decided. Nobody was happy driving in rainy rush-hour traffic, no matter what rubber covered their wheels.

But he'd come up with something that would make the consumers think that riding on Myerstones would make them happy, safe, and sexy. It was his job, and he was good at it.

Good enough to juggle four major accounts, supervise the status of six lesser ones, and never appear to break a sweat within the slick corridors of Innovations, the well-heeled advertising firm where he worked. The firm that demanded style, exuberance, and creativity from its executives.

They didn't pay to see him sweat.

Alone, however, was a different matter.

He knew he'd been burning not a candle but a torch at both ends for months. With one hard slap of fate he'd gone from living for Phillip Quinn to wondering what had happened to his cheerfully upwardly mobile urban lifestyle.

His father's death six months before had turned his life upside down. The life that Ray and Stella Quinn had righted seventeen years ago. They'd walked into that dreary hospital room and offered him a chance and a choice. He'd taken the chance because he'd been smart enough to understand that he had no choice.

Going back on the streets wasn't as appealing as it had been before his chest had been ripped open by bullets. Living with his mother was no longer an option, not even if she changed her mind and let him buy his way back into the cramped apartment on Baltimore's Block. Social Services was taking a hard look at the situation, and he knew he'd be dumped into the system the minute he was back on his feet.

He had no intention of going back into the system, or back with his mother, or back to the gutter, for that matter. He'd already decided that. He felt that all he needed was a little time to work out a plan.

At the moment that time was buffered by some very fine drugs that he hadn't had to buy or steal. But he didn't figure that little benefit was going to last forever.

With the Demerol sliding through his system, he gave the Quinns a canny once-over and dismissed them as a couple of weirdo do-gooders. That was fine with him. They wanted to be Samaritans, give him a place to hang out until he was back to a hundred percent, good for them. Good for him.

They told him they had a house on the Eastern Shore, which for an inner-city kid was the other end of the world. But he figured a change of scene couldn't hurt. They had two sons about his age. Phillip decided he wouldn't have to worry about a couple of wimps that the do-gooders had raised.

They told him they had rules, and education was a priority. School didn't bother him any. He breezed his way through when he decided to go.

No drugs. Stella said that in a cool voice that made Phillip reevaluate her as he put on his most angelic expression and said a polite *No, ma'am.* He had no doubt that when he wanted a hit, he'd be able to find a source, even in some bumfuck town on the Bay.

Then Stella leaned over the bed, her eyes shrewd, her mouth smiling thinly.

You have a face that belongs on a Renaissance painting. But that doesn't make you less of a thief, a hoodlum, and a liar. We'll help you if you want to be helped. But don't treat us like imbeciles.

And Ray laughed his big, booming laugh. He squeezed Stella's shoulder and Phillip's at the same time. It would be, Phillip remembered he'd said, a rare treat to watch the two of them butt heads for the next little while.

They came back several times over the next two weeks. Phillip talked with them and with the social worker, who'd been much easier to con than the Quinns.

In the end they took him home from the hospital, to the pretty white house by the water. He met their sons, assessed the situation. When he learned that the other boys, Cameron and Ethan, had been taken in much as he had been, he was certain they were all lunatics.

He figured on biding his time. For a doctor and a college professor they hadn't collected an abundance of easily stolen or fenced valuables. But he scoped out what there was.

Instead of stealing from them, he fell in love with them. He took their name and spent the next ten years in the house by the water.

Then Stella had died, and part of his world dropped away. She had become the mother he'd never believed existed. Steady, strong, loving, and shrewd. He grieved for her, that first true loss of his life. He buried part of that grief in work, pushing his way through college, toward a goal of success and a sheen of sophistication—and an entry-level position at Innovations.

He didn't intend to remain on the bottom rung for long.

Taking the position at Innovations in Baltimore was a small personal triumph. He was going back to the city of his misery, but he was going back as a man of taste. No one seeing the man in the tailored suit would suspect that he'd once been a petty thief, a sometime drug dealer, and an occasional prostitute.

Everything he'd gained over the last seventeen years could be traced back to that moment when Ray and Stella Quinn had walked into his hospital room.

Then Ray had died suddenly, leaving shadows that had yet to be washed with the light. The man Phillip had loved as completely as a son could love a father had lost his life on a quiet stretch of road in the middle of the day when his car had met a telephone pole at high speed.

There was another hospital room. This time it was the Mighty Quinn lying broken in the bed with machines gasping. Phillip, along with his brothers, had made a promise to watch out for and to keep the last of Ray Quinn's strays, another lost boy.

But this boy had secrets, and he looked at you with Ray's eyes.

The talk around the waterfront and the neighborhoods of the little town of St. Christopher's on Maryland's Eastern Shore hinted of adultery, of suicide, of scandal. In the six months since the whispers had started, Phillip felt that he and his brothers had gotten no closer to finding the truth. Who was Seth DeLauter and what had he been to Raymond Quinn?

Another stray? Another half-grown boy drowning in a vicious sea of neglect and violence who so desperately needed a lifeline? Or was he more? A Quinn by blood as well as by circumstance?

All Phillip could be sure of was that ten-year-old Seth was his brother as much as Cam and Ethan were his brothers. Each of them had been snatched out of a nightmare and given a chance to change their lives.

With Seth, Ray and Stella weren't there to keep that choice open.

There was a part of Phillip, a part that had lived inside a young, careless thief, that resented even the possibility that Seth could be Ray's son by blood, a son conceived in adultery and abandoned in shame. It would be a betrayal of everything the Quinns had taught him, everything they had shown him by living their lives as they had.

He detested himself for considering it, for knowing that now and then he studied Seth with cool, appraising eyes and wondered if the boy's existence was the reason Ray Quinn was dead.

Whenever that nasty thought crept into his mind, Phillip shifted his concentration to Gloria DeLauter. Seth's mother was the woman who had accused Professor Raymond Quinn of sexual harassment. She claimed it had happened years before, while she was a student at the university. But there was no record of her ever attending classes there.

The same woman had sold her ten-year-old son to Ray as if he'd been a package of meat. The same woman, Phillip was certain, that Ray had been to Baltimore to see before he had driven home—and driven himself to his death.

She'd taken off. Women like Gloria were skilled in skipping out of harm's way. Weeks ago, she'd sent the Quinns a not-so-subtle blackmail letter: If you want to keep the kid, I need more. Phillip's jaw clenched when he remembered the naked fear on Seth's face when he'd learned of it.

She wasn't going to get her hands on the boy, he told himself. She was going to discover that the Quinn brothers were a tougher mark than one softhearted old man.

Not just the Quinn brothers now, either, he thought as he turned off onto the rural county road that would lead him home. He thought of family as he drove fast down a road flanked by fields of soybeans, of peas, of corn grown taller than a man. Now that Cam and Ethan were married, Seth had two determined women to stand with him as well.

Married. Phillip shook his head in amused wonder. Who would have thought it? Cam had hitched himself to the sexy social worker, and Ethan was married to sweet-eyed Grace. And had become an instant father, Phillip mused, to angel-faced Aubrey.

Well, good for them. In fact, he had to admit that Anna Spinelli and
Grace Monroe were tailor-made for his brothers. It would only add to their
strength as a family when it came time for the hearing on permanent
guardianship of Seth. And marriage certainly appeared to suit them. Even if
the word itself gave him the willies.

For himself, Phillip much preferred the single life and all its benefits. Not
that he'd had much time to avail himself of all those benefits in the past few
months. Weekends in St. Chris, supervising homework assignments, pounding a hull together for the fledgling Boats by Quinn, dealing with the books
for the new business, hauling groceries—all of which had somehow become
his domain—cramped a man's style.

He'd promised his father on his deathbed that he would take care of
Seth. With his brothers he'd made a pact to move back to the Shore, to share
the guardianship and the responsibilities. For Phillip that pact meant split-
ting his time between Baltimore and St. Chris, and his energies between
maintaining his career—and his income—and tending to a new and often
problematic brother and a new business.

It was all a risk. Raising a ten-year-old wasn't without headaches and
fumbling mistakes under the best of circumstances, he imagined. Seth De-
Lauter, raised by a part-time hooker, full-time junkie, and amateur extor-
tionist, had hardly come through the best of circumstances.

Getting a boatbuilding enterprise off the ground was a series of irksome
details and backbreaking labor. Yet somehow it was working, and if he dis-
counted the ridiculous demands on his time and energy, it was working
fairly well.

Not so long ago his weekends had been spent in the company of any
number of attractive, interesting women, having dinner at some new hot
spot, an evening at the theater or a concert, and if the chemistry was right, a
quiet Sunday brunch in bed.

He'd get back to that, Phillip promised himself. Once all the details were
in place, he would have his life back again. But, as his father would have
said, for the next little while . . .

He turned into the drive. The rain had stopped, leaving a light sheen of
wet on the leaves and grass. Twilight was creeping in. He could see the light
in the living room window glowing in a soft and steady welcome. Some of
the summer flowers that Anna had babied along were hanging on, and early
fall blooms shimmered in the shadows. He could hear the puppy barking,
though at nine months Foolish had grown too big and sleek to be considered
a puppy anymore.

It was Anna's night to cook, he remembered. Thank God. It meant a real meal would be served at the Quinns'. He rolled his shoulders, thought about pouring himself a glass of wine, then watched Foolish dash around the side of the house in pursuit of a mangy yellow tennis ball.

The sight of Phillip getting out of his car obviously distracted the dog from the game. He skidded to a halt and set up a din of wild, terrified barking.

"Idiot." But he grinned as he pulled his briefcase out of the Jeep.

At the familiar voice, the barking turned into mad joy. Foolish bounded up with a delighted look in his eyes and wet, muddy paws. "No jumping!" Phillip yelled, using his briefcase like a shield. "I mean it. Sit!"

Foolish quivered, but dropped his rump on the ground and lifted a paw. His tongue lolled, his eyes gleamed. "That's a good dog." Gingerly Phillip shook the filthy paw and scratched the dog's silky ears.

"Hey." Seth wandered into the front yard. His jeans were grubby from wrestling with the dog, his baseball cap was askew so that straw-straight blond hair spiked out of it. The smile, Phillip noted, came much more quickly and easily than it had a few months before. But there was a gap in it.

"Hey." Phillip butted a finger on the bill of the cap. "Lose something?"

"Huh?"

Phillip tapped a finger against his own straight, white teeth.

"Oh, yeah." With a typical Quinn shrug, Seth grinned, pushing his tongue into the gap. His face was fuller than it had been six months before, and his eyes less wary. "It was loose. Had to give it a yank a couple of days ago. Bled like a son of a bitch."

Phillip didn't bother to sigh over Seth's language. Some things, he determined, weren't going to be his problem. "So, did the Tooth Fairy bring you anything?"

"Get real."

"Hey, if you didn't squeeze a buck out of Cam, you're no brother of mine."

"I got two bucks out of it. One from Cam and one from Ethan."

Laughing, Phillip swung an arm over Seth's shoulders and headed toward the house. "Well, you're not getting one out of me, pal. I'm on to you. How was the first full week of school?"

"Boring." Though it hadn't been, Seth admitted silently. It had been exciting. All the new junk Anna had taken him shopping for. Sharp pencils, blank notebooks, pens full of ink. He'd refused the *X-Files* lunch box she'd wanted to get him. Only a dork carried a lunch box in middle school. But it had been really cool and tough to sneer at.

He had cool clothes and bitching sneakers. And best of all, for the first time in his life, he was in the same place, the same school, with the same people he'd left behind in June.

"Homework?" Phillip asked, raising his eyebrows as he opened the front door.

Seth rolled his eyes. "Man, don't you ever think about anything else?"

"Kid, I live for homework. Especially when it's yours." Foolish burst through the door ahead of Phillip, nearly knocking him down with enthusiasm. "You've still got some work to do on that dog." But the mild annoyance faded instantly. He could smell Anna's red sauce simmering, like ambrosia on the air. "God bless us, every one," he murmured.

"Manicotti," Seth informed him.

"Yeah? I've got a Chianti I've been saving just for this moment." He tossed his briefcase aside. "We'll hit the books after dinner."

He found his sister-in-law in the kitchen, filling pasta tubes with cheese. The sleeves of the crisp white shirt she'd worn to the office were rolled up, and a white butcher's apron covered her navy skirt. She'd taken off her heels and tapped a bare foot to the beat of the aria she was humming. *Carmen*, Phillip recognized. Her wonderful mass of curling black hair was still pinned up.

With a wink at Seth, Phillip came up behind her, caught her around the waist, and pressed a noisy kiss onto the top of her head. "Run away with me. We'll change our names. You can be Sophia and I'll be Carlo. Let me take you to paradise where you can cook for me and me alone. None of these peasants appreciate you like I do."

"Let me just finish this tube, Carlo, and I'll go pack." She turned her head, her dark Italian eyes laughing. "Dinner in thirty minutes."

"I'll open the wine."

"Don't we have anything to eat now?" Seth wanted to know.

"There's antipasto in the fridge," she told him. "Go ahead and get it out."

"It's just vegetables and junk," Seth complained when he pulled out the platter.

"Yep."

"Jeez."

"Wash the dog off your hands before you start on that."

"Dog spit's cleaner than people spit," Seth informed her. "I read how if you get bit by another guy it's worse than getting bit by a dog."

"I'm thrilled to have that fascinating tidbit of information. Wash the dog spit off your hands anyway."

"Man." Disgusted, Seth clomped out, with Foolish slinking after him.

Phillip chose the wine from the small supply he kept in the pantry. Fine wines were one of his passions, and his palate was extremely discriminating. His apartment in Baltimore boasted an extensive and carefully chosen selection, which he kept in a closet he'd remodeled specifically for that purpose.

At the Shore, his beloved bottles of Bordeaux and Burgundy kept company with Rice Krispies and boxes of Jell-O Instant Pudding.

He'd learned to live with it.

"So how was your week?" he asked Anna.

"Busy. Whoever said women can have everything should be shot. Handling a career and a family is grueling." Then she looked up with a brilliant smile. "I'm loving it."

"It shows." He drew the cork expertly, sniffed it and approved, then set the bottle on the counter to breathe. "Where's Cam?"

"Should be on his way home from the boatyard. He and Ethan wanted to put in an extra hour. The first Boat by Quinn is finished. The owner's coming in tomorrow. It's finished, Phillip." Her smile flashed, brilliant and glowing with pride. "At dock, seaworthy and just gorgeous."

He felt a little tug of disappointment that he hadn't been in on the last day. "We should be having champagne."

Anna lifted a brow as she studied the label on the wine. "A bottle of Folonari, Ruffino?"

He considered one of Anna's finest traits to be her appreciation for good wine. "Seventy-five," he said with a broad grin.

"You won't hear any complaints from me. Congratulations, Mr. Quinn, on your first boat."

"It's not my deal. I just handle the details and pass for slave labor."

"Of course it's your deal. Details are necessary, and neither Cam nor Ethan could handle them with the finesse you do."

"I think the word they use, is 'nagging.' "

"They need to be nagged. You should be proud of what the three of you have accomplished in the last few months. Not just the new business, but the family. Each one of you has given up something that's important to you for Seth. And each one of you has gotten something important back."

"I never expected the kid to matter so much." While Anna smothered the filled tubes with sauce, Phillip opened a cupboard for wineglasses. "I still have moments when the whole thing pisses me off."

"That's only natural, Phillip."

"Doesn't make me feel any better about it." He shrugged his shoulders in dismissal, then poured two glasses. "But most of the time, I look at him and think he's a pretty good deal for a kid brother."

Anna grated cheese over the casserole. Out of the corner of her eye she watched Phillip lift his glass, appreciate the bouquet. He was beautiful to look at, she mused. Physically, he was as close to male perfection as she could imagine. Bronze hair, thick and full, eyes more gold than brown. His face was long, narrow, thoughtful. Both sensual and angelic. His tall, trim build seemed to have been fashioned for Italian suits. But since she'd seen him stripped to the waist in faded Levi's she knew there was nothing soft about him.

Sophisticated, tough, erudite, shrewd. An interesting man, she mused.

She slipped the casserole into the oven, then turned to pick up her wine. Smiling at him, she tapped her glass on his. "You're a pretty good deal too, Phillip, for a big brother."

She leaned in to kiss him lightly as Cam walked in.

"Get your mouth off my wife."

Phillip merely smiled and slid an arm around Anna's waist. "She put hers on me. She likes me."

"She likes me better." To prove it, Cam hooked a hand in the tie of Anna's apron, spun her around, and pulled her into his arms to kiss her brainless. He grinned, nipped her bottom lip and patted her butt companionably. "Don'cha, sugar?"

Her head was still spinning. "Probably." She blew out a breath. "All things considered." But she wiggled free. "You're filthy."

"Just came in to grab a beer to take into the shower." Long and lean, dark and dangerous, he prowled over to the fridge. "And kiss my wife," he added with a smug look at Phillip. "Go get your own woman."

"Who has time?" Phillip said mournfully.

⟨⟨⟩⟩

After dinner, and an hour spent slaving over long division, battles of the Revolutionary War, and sixth-grade vocabulary, Phillip settled down in his room with his laptop and his files.

It was the same room he'd been given when Ray and Stella Quinn had brought him home. The walls had been a pale green then. Sometime during his sixteenth year he'd gotten a wild hair and painted them magenta. God knew why. He remembered that his mother—for Stella had become his mother by then—had taken one look and warned him he'd have terminal indigestion.

He thought it was sexy. For about three months. Then he'd gone with a stark white for a while, accented with moody black-framed, black-and-white photographs.

Always looking for ambience, Phillip thought now, amused at himself. He'd circled back to that soft green right before he moved to Baltimore.

They'd been right all along, he supposed. His parents had usually been right.

They'd given him this room, in this house, in this place. He hadn't made it easy for them. The first three months were a battle of wills. He smuggled in drugs, picked fights, stole liquor, and stumbled in drunk at dawn.

It was clear to him now that he'd been testing them, daring them to kick him out. Toss him back. Go ahead, he'd thought. You can't handle me.

But they did. They had not only handled him, they had made him.

I wonder, Phillip, his father had said, *why you want to waste a good mind and a good body. Why you want to let the bastards win.*

Phillip, who was suffering from the raw gut and bursting head of a drug and alcohol hangover, didn't give a good damn.

Ray took him out on the boat, telling him that a good sail would clear his head. Sick as a dog, Phillip leaned over the rail, throwing up the remnants of the poisons he'd pumped into his system the night before.

He'd just turned fourteen.

Ray anchored the boat in a narrow gut. He held Phillip's head, wiped his face, then offered him a cold can of ginger ale.

"Sit down."

He didn't so much sit as collapse. His hands shook, his stomach shuddered at the first sip from the can. Ray sat across from him, his big hands on his knees, his silvering hair flowing in the light breeze. And those eyes, those brilliant blue eyes, level and considering.

"You've had a couple of months now to get your bearings around here. Stella says you've come around physically. You're strong, and healthy enough—though you aren't going to stay that way if you keep this up."

He pursed his lips, said nothing for a long moment. There was a heron in the tall grass, still as a painting. The air was bright and chill with late fall, the trees bare of leaves so that the hard blue sky spread overhead. Wind ruffled the grass and skimmed fingers over the water.

The man sat, apparently content with the silence and the scene. The boy slouched, pale of face and hard of eye.

"We can play this a lot of ways, Phil," Ray said at length. "We can be hard-asses. We can put you on a short leash, watch you every minute and bust your balls every time you screw up. Which is most of the time."

Considering, Ray picked up a fishing rod, absently baited it with a marshmallow. "Or we could all just say that this little experiment's a bust and you can go back into the system."

Phillip's stomach churned, making him swallow to hold down what he didn't quite recognize as fear. "I don't need you. I don't need anybody."

"Yeah, you do." Ray said it mildly as he dropped the line into the water. Ripples spread, endlessly. "You go back into the system, you'll stay there. Couple of years down the road, it won't be juvie anymore. You'll end up in a cell with the bad guys, the kind of guys who are going to take a real liking to that pretty face of yours. Some seven-foot con with hands like smoked hams is going to grab you in the showers one fine day and make you his bride."

Phillip yearned desperately for a cigarette. The image conjured by Ray's word made fresh sweat pop out on his forehead. "I can take care of myself."

"Son, they'll pass you around like canapés, and you know it. You talk a good game and you fight a good fight, but some things are inevitable. Up to this point your life has pretty much sucked. You're not responsible for that. But you are responsible for what happens from here on."

He fell into silence again, clamping the pole between his knees before reaching for a cold can of Pepsi. Taking his time, Ray popped the top, tipped the can back, and guzzled.

"Stella and I thought we saw something in you," he continued. "We still do," he added, looking at Phillip again. "But until you do, we're not going to get anywhere."

"What do you care?" Phillip tossed back miserably.

"Hard to say at the moment. Maybe you're not worth it. Maybe you'll just end up back on the streets hustling marks and turning tricks anyway."

For three months he'd had a decent bed, regular meals, and all the books he could read—one of his secret loves—at his disposal. At the thought of losing it his throat filled again, but he only shrugged. "I'll get by."

"If all you want to do is get by, that's your choice. Here you can have a home, a family. You can have a life and make something out of it. Or you can go on the way you are."

Ray reached over to Phillip quickly, and the boy braced himself for the blow, clenched his fists to return it. But Ray only pulled Phillip's shirt up to expose the livid scars on his chest. "You can go back to that," he said quietly.

Phillip looked into Ray's eyes. He saw compassion and hope. And he saw himself mirrored back, bleeding in a dirty gutter on a street where life was worth less than a dime bag.

Sick, tired, terrified, Phillip dropped his head into his hands. "What's the point?"

"You're the point, son." Ray ran his hand over Phillip's hair. "You're the point."

Things hadn't changed overnight, Phillip thought now. But they had begun to change. His parents had made him believe in himself, despite himself.

It had become a point of pride for him to do well in school, to learn, to re-make himself into Phillip Quinn.

He figured he'd done a good job of it. He'd coated that street kid with a sheen of class. He had a slick career, a well-appointed condo with a killer view of the Inner Harbor, and a wardrobe that suited both.

It seemed that he'd come full circle, spending his weekends back in this room with its green walls and sturdy furniture, with its windows that over-looked the trees and the marsh.

But this time, Seth was the point.

Two

Phillip stood on the foredeck of the yet-to-be-christened *Neptune's Lady*. He'd personally sweated out nearly two thousand man-hours to take her from design to finished sloop. Her decks were gleaming teak, her bright work glinted in the yellow September sun.

Belowdecks her cabin was a woodworker's pride, Cam's for the most part, Phillip mused. Glossy cabinets were fashioned of natural wood, hand-fitted and custom-designed with sleeping room for four close friends.

She was sound, he thought, and she was beautiful. Aesthetically charming, with her fluid hull, glossy decks, and long waterline. Ethan's early decision to use the smooth-lap method of planking had added hours to the labor but had produced a gem.

The podiatrist from D.C. was going to pay handsomely for every inch of her.

"Well . . . ?" Ethan, hands in the pockets of his faded jeans, eyes squinting comfortably against the sun, left it an open-ended question.

Phillip ran a hand over the satin finish of the gunwale, an area he'd spent many sweaty hours sanding and finishing. "She deserves a less clichéd name."

"The owner's got more money than imagination. She takes the wind." Ethan's lips curved into one of his slow, serious smiles. "Good Christ, she goes, Phil. When Cam and I tested her out, I wasn't sure he was going to bring her back in. Wasn't sure I wanted him to."

Phillip rubbed a thumb over his chin. "I've got a friend in Baltimore who paints. Most of the stuff he does is strictly commercial, for hotels and restaurants. But he does terrific stuff on the side. Every time he sells one, he bitches about it. Hates to let a canvas go. I didn't really understand how he felt until now."

"And she's our first."

"But not our last." Phillip hadn't expected to feel so attached. The boat-building business hadn't been his idea, or his choice. He liked to think his brothers had dragged him into it. He'd told them it was insane, ridiculous, doomed to fail.

Then, of course, he'd jumped in and negotiated for the rental of the building, applied for licenses, ordered the necessary utilities. During the construction of what was about to become *Neptune's Lady,* he'd dug splinters out of his fingers, nursed burns from hot creosote, soaked muscles that wept after hours of lifting planks. And had not suffered in silence.

But with this tangible result of long months of labor swaying gracefully under his feet, he had to admit it was all worth it.

Now they were about to start all over again.

"You and Cam made some headway this week on the next project."

"We want to have the hull ready to turn the end of October." Ethan took out a bandanna and methodically polished Phillip's fingerprints off the gunwale. "If we're going to keep to that killer schedule you worked up. Got a little bit more to do on this one, though."

"This one?" Eyes narrowed, Phillip tipped down his Wayfarers. "Damn it, Ethan, you said she was ready to go. The owner's coming in to take her. I was about to go in and work up the last of the papers on her."

"Just one little detail. Have to wait for Cam."

"What little detail?" Impatient, Phillip checked his watch. "The client's due here any minute."

"Won't take long." Ethan nodded toward the cargo doors of the building. "Here's Cam now."

"She's too good for this yahoo," Cam called out as he came down the narrow dock with a battery-operated drill. "I'm telling you we should get the wives and kids and sail her off to Bimini ourselves."

"She's good enough for the final draw he's going to give us today. Once he gives me that certified check, he's the captain." Phillip waited until Cam stepped nimbly aboard. "When I get to Bimini I don't want to see either of you."

"He's just jealous because we've got women," Cam told Ethan. "Here." He shoved the drill into Phillip's hand.

"What the hell am I supposed to do with this?"

"Finish her." Grinning, Cam pulled a brass cleat out of his back pocket. "We saved the last piece for you."

"Yeah?" Absurdly touched, Phillip took the cleat, watched it wink in the sun.

"We started her together," Ethan pointed out. "Seemed only right. It goes on the starboard."

Phillip took the screws Cam handed him and bent over the markings on the rail. "I figured we should celebrate after." The drill whirled in his hands. "I thought about a bottle of Dom," he said, raising his voice over the noise, "but figured it'd be wasted on the two of you. So I've got three Harps chilling down in the cooler."

They would go well, he thought, with the little surprise he was having delivered later that afternoon.

❦

It was nearly noon before the client had finished fussing over every inch of his new boat. Ethan had been elected to take the man out for a shakedown sail before they loaded the sloop onto its new trailer. From the dock, Phillip watched the butter-yellow sails—the client's choice—fill with the wind.

Ethan was right, he thought. She moved.

The sloop skimmed toward the waterfront, heeled in like a dream. He imagined the late-summer tourists would stop to watch, point out the pretty boat to each other. There was, he thought, no better advertising than a quality product.

"He'll run her aground the first time he sails her on his own," Cam said from behind him.

"Sure. But he'll have fun." He gave Cam a slap on the shoulder. "I'll just go write up that bill of sale."

The old brick building they rented and had modified for the boatyard didn't boast many amenities. The lion's share was a vast open space with fluorescent lights hanging from the rafters. The windows were small and always seemed to be coated with dust.

Power tools, lumber, equipment, gallons of epoxy and varnish and bottom paint were set up where they could be easily reached. The lofting platform was currently occupied by the bare skeleton of the hull for the custom-designed sport's fisher that was their second job.

The walls were pitted brick and unfinished Sheetrock. Up a steep flight of iron stairs was a cramped, windowless room that served as the office.

Despite its size and location, Phillip had it meticulously organized. The metal desk might have been a flea market special, but it was scrubbed clean. On its surface was a Month-at-a-Glance calendar, his old laptop computer, a wire in/out box, a two-line phone/answering machine and a Lucite holder for pens and pencils.

Crowded in with the desk were two file cabinets, a personal copier, and a plain-paper fax.

He settled in his chair and booted up the computer. The blinking light on the phone caught his eye. When he punched it for messages, he found two hang-ups and dismissed them.

Within moments, he'd brought up the program he'd customized for the business, and found himself grinning at the logo for Boats by Quinn.

They might be flying by the seat of their pants, he mused as he plugged in the data for the sale, but it didn't have to look that way. He'd justified the high-grade paper as an advertising expense. Desktop publishing was second nature to him. Creating stationery, receipts, bills was simple enough—he simply insisted that they have class.

He shot the job to the printer just as the phone rang.

"Boats by Quinn."

There was a hesitation, then the sound of throat clearing. "Sorry, wrong number." The voice was muffled and female and quickly gone.

"No problem, sweetheart," Phillip said to the dial tone as he plucked the printed bill of sale from the machine.

⚭

"There goes a happy man," Cam commented an hour later when the three of them watched their client drive off with the trailered sloop.

"We're happier." Phillip took the check out of his pocket and held it out. "Factoring in equipment, labor, overhead, supplies . . ." He folded the check in half again. "Well, we cleared enough to get by."

"Try to control your enthusiasm," Cam muttered. "You got a check for five figures in your hot little hand. Let's crack open those beers."

"The bulk of the profits have to go right back into the business," Phillip warned as they started inside. "Once the cold weather hits, our utility bill's going to go through the roof." He glanced up at the soaring ceiling. "Literally. And we've got quarterly taxes due next week."

Cam twisted the top off a bottle and pushed it at his brother. "Shut up, Phil."

"However," Phillip continued, ignoring him, "this is a fine moment in Quinn history." He lifted his beer, tapped the bottle to both Cam's and Ethan's. "To our foot doctor, the first of many happy clients. May he sail clean and heal many bunions."

"May he tell all his friends to call Boats by Quinn," Cam added.

"May he sail in Annapolis and keep out of my part of the Bay," Ethan finished with a shake of his head.

"Who's springing for lunch?" Cam wanted to know. "I'm starving."

"Grace made sandwiches," Ethan told him. "They're out in my cooler."

"God bless her."

"Might want to put off lunch just a bit." Phillip heard the sound of tires on gravel. "I think what I've been waiting for just got here." He strolled out, pleased to see the delivery truck.

The driver leaned out the window, worked a wad of gum into his cheek. "Quinn?"

"That's right."

"What'd you buy now?" Cam frowned at the truck, wondering how much of that brand-new check was flying away.

"Something we need. He's going to need a hand with it."

"You got that right." The driver huffed as he climbed out of the cab. "Took three of us to load her up. Son of a bitch weighs two hundred pounds if it weighs an ounce."

He hauled open the back doors. It lay on the bed on top of a padded cloth. It was easily ten feet long, six high, and three inches thick. Carved in simple block letters into treated oak were the words BOATS BY QUINN. A detailed image of a wooden skiff in full sail rode the top corner.

Lining the bottom corner were the names Cameron, Ethan, Phillip, and Seth Quinn.

"That's a damn fine sign," Ethan managed when he could find the words.

"I took one of Seth's sketches for the skiff. The same one we use for the logo on the letterhead. Put the design together on the computer at work." Phillip reached in to run a thumb along the side of the oak. "The sign company did a pretty good job of reproducing it."

"It's great." Cam rested his hand on Phillip's shoulder. "One of the details we've been missing. Christ, the kid's going to flip when he sees it."

"I put us down the way we came along. Works out alphabetical and chronological. I wanted to keep it clean and simple." He stepped back, his hands sliding into his pockets in an unconscious mirroring of his brothers' stances. "I thought this fit the building and what we're doing in it."

"It's good." Ethan nodded. "It's right."

The driver shoved at his gum again. "Well, you guys gonna admire it all day, or you want to get this heavy bastard out of the truck?"

They made a picture, she thought. Three exceptional specimens of the male species engaged in manual labor on a warm afternoon in early September. The building certainly suited them. It was rough, the old brick faded and pitted, the grounds around it scrabbly—more weeds than grass.

Three different looks as well. One of the men was dark, with his hair long enough to pull back in a short ponytail. His jeans were black, fading to gray. There was something vaguely European about his style. She decided he would be Cameron Quinn, the one who'd made a name for himself on the racing circuit.

The second wore scuffed work boots that looked ancient. His sun-streaked hair tumbled out of a blue-billed ball cap. He moved fluidly and lifted his end of the sign with no visible effort. He would be Ethan Quinn, the waterman.

Which meant the third man was Phillip Quinn, the advertising executive, who worked at the top firm in Baltimore. He looked gilded, she thought. Wayfarers and Levi's, she mused. Bronzed hair that must be a joy to his stylist. A long, trim body that must see regular workouts at the health club.

Interesting. Physically they bore no resemblance to each other and through her research she knew they shared a name but not blood. Yet there was something in the body language, in the way they moved as a team, that indicated they were brothers.

She intended simply to pass by, to give the building where they based their business a quick look and evaluation. Though she'd known that at least one of them would be there, since he'd answered the phone, she hadn't expected to see them outside, as a group, to have this opportunity to study them.

She was a woman who appreciated the unexpected.

Nerves shimmered in her stomach. Out of habit, she took three slow breaths and rolled her shoulders to relax them. Casual, she reminded herself. There was nothing to be uneasy about. After all, she had the advantage here. She knew them, and they didn't know her.

It was typical behavior, she decided as she crossed the street. A person strolling along and seeing three men working to hang an impressive new sign would display curiosity and interest. Particularly a small-town tourist, which was, for this purpose, what she was. She was also a single female, and they were three very attractive men. A mild flirtation would be typical as well.

Still, when she reached the front of the building, she stood back. It seemed to be difficult and precarious work. The sign was bolted to thick black chains and wrapped in rope. They'd worked out a pulley system, with the ad exec on the roof guiding and his brothers on the ground hauling. Encouragement, curses, and directions were issued with equal enthusiasm.

There were certainly a lot of muscles rippling, she observed with a lift of her brow.

"Your end, Cam. Give me another inch. Goddamn." Grunting, Phillip dropped onto his belly and squirmed out far enough that she held her breath and waited for gravity to do its work.

But he managed to balance himself and snag the chain. She could see his mouth working as he fought to loop the heavy link around a thick hook, but she couldn't hear what he was saying. She thought that might be for the best.

"Got it. Hold it steady," he ordered, rising to tightwalk his way across the eaves to the other end. The sun struck his hair, gleamed over his skin. She caught herself goggling. This, she thought, was a prime example of sheer male beauty.

Then he was bellying over the edge again, grabbing for the chain, hauling it into place. And swearing ripely. When he rose, he scowled at the long tear down the front of his shirt where she supposed it had caught on something on the roof.

"I just bought this sucker."

"It was real pretty, too," Cam called up.

"Kiss my ass," Phillip suggested and tugged the shirt off to use it to mop sweat off his face.

Oh, well, now, she thought, appreciating the view on a purely personal level. The young American god, she decided. Designed to make females drool.

He hooked the ruined shirt in his back pocket, started for the ladder. And that's when he spotted her. She couldn't see his eyes, but she could tell by the momentary pause, the angle of the head, that he was looking at her. The evaluation would be instinctive, she knew. Male sees female, studies, considers, decides.

He'd seen her all right and, as he started down the ladder, was already considering. And hoping for a closer look. "We've got company," Phillip murmured, and Cam glanced over his shoulder.

"Hmmm. Very nice."

"Been there ten minutes." Ethan dusted his hands on his hips. "Watching the show."

Phillip stepped off the ladder, turned and smiled. "So," he called out to her, "how's it look?"

Curtain up, she thought and started forward. "Very impressive. I hope you don't mind the audience. I couldn't resist."

"Not at all. It's a big day for the Quinns." He held out a hand. "I'm Phillip."

"I'm Sybill. And you build boats."

"That's what the sign says."

"Fascinating. I'm spending some time in the area. I hadn't expected to stumble across boatbuilders. What sort of boats do you build?"

"Wooden sailing vessels."

"Really?" She turned her easy smile toward his brothers. "And you're partners?"

"Cam." He returned the smile, jerked a thumb. "My brother Ethan."

"Nice to meet you. Cameron," she began, shifting her gaze to read from the sign. "Ethan, Phillip." Her heartbeat accelerated, but she kept the polite smile in place. "Where's Seth?"

"In school," Phillip told her.

"Oh, college?"

"Middle. He's ten."

"I see." There were scars on his chest, she saw now. Old and shiny and riding dangerously close to his heart. "You have a very impressive sign, Boats by Quinn. I'd love to drop by sometime and see you and your brothers at work."

"Anytime. How long are you staying in St. Chris?"

"Depends. It was nice to meet you all." Time to retreat, she decided. Her throat was dry, her pulse unsteady. "Good luck with your boats."

"Drop by tomorrow," Phillip suggested as she walked away. "Catch all four Quinns at work."

She shot a look over her shoulder that she hoped revealed nothing more than amused interest. "I might just do that."

Seth, she thought, careful now to keep her eyes straight ahead. He'd just given her the open door to see Seth the following day.

Cam gave a quiet and male hum. "I gotta say, there's a woman who knows how to walk."

"Yes, indeed." Phillip hooked his hands in his pockets and enjoyed the view. Slim hips and slender legs in breezy maize-colored slacks, a snug little shirt the color of limes tucked into a narrow waist. A sleek and swinging fall of mink-colored hair just skimming strong shoulders.

And the face had been just as attractive. A classic oval with peaches-and-cream skin, a mobile and shapely mouth tinted with a soft, soft pink. Sexy eyebrows, he mused, dark and well arched. He hadn't been able to see the eyes under them, not through the trendy wire-framed sunglasses. They might be dark to match the hair, or light for contrast.

And that smooth contralto voice had set the whole package off nicely.

"You guys going to stand there watching that woman's butt all day?" Ethan wanted to know.

"Yeah, like you didn't notice it." Cam snorted.

"I noticed. I'm just not making a career out of it. Aren't we going to get anything done around here?"

"In a minute," Phillip murmured, smiling to himself when she turned the corner and disappeared. "Sybill. I sure hope you hang around St. Chris for a while."

She didn't know how long she would stay. Her time was her own. She could work where she chose, and for now she'd chosen this little water town on Maryland's southern Eastern Shore. Nearly all of her life had been spent in cities, initially because her parents had preferred them and then because she had.

New York, Boston, Chicago, Paris, London, Milan. She understood the urban landscape and its inhabitants. The fact was, Dr. Sybill Griffin had made a career out of the study of urban life. She'd gathered degrees in anthropology, sociology, and psychology along the way. Four years at Harvard, postgraduate work at Oxford, a doctorate from Columbia.

She'd thrived in academia, and now, six months before her thirtieth birthday, she could write her own ticket. Which was precisely what she'd chosen to do for a living. Write.

Her first book, *Urban Landscape*, had been well received, earned her critical acclaim and a modest income. But her second, *Familiar Strangers*, had rocketed onto the national lists, had taken her into the whirlwind of book tours, lectures, talk shows. Now that PBS was producing a documentary series based on her observations and theories of city life and customs, she was much more than financially secure. She was independent.

Her publisher had been open to her idea of a book on the dynamics and traditions of small towns. Initially, she'd considered it merely a cover, an excuse to travel to St. Christopher's, to spend time there on personal business.

But then she'd begun to think it through. It would make an interesting study. After all, she was a trained observer and skilled at documenting those observations.

Work might save her nerves in any case, she considered, pacing her pretty little hotel suite. Certainly it would be easier and more productive to approach this entire trip as a kind of project. She needed time, objectivity, and access to the subjects involved.

Thanks to convenient circumstance, it appeared she had all three now.

She stepped out onto the two-foot slab that the hotel loftily called a terrace. It offered a stunning view of the Chesapeake Bay and intriguing glimpses of life on the waterfront. Already she'd watched workboats chug into dock and unload tanks of the blue crabs the area was famous for. She'd watched the crab pickers at work, the sweep of gulls, the flight of egrets, but she had yet to wander into any of the little shops.

She wasn't in St. Chris for souvenirs.

Perhaps she would drag a table near the window and work with that view. When the breeze was right she could catch snippets of voices, a slower, more fluid dialect than she heard on the streets of New York, where she'd based herself for the last few years.

Not quite Southern, she thought, such as you would hear in Atlanta or Mobile or Charleston, but a long way from the clipped tones and hard consonants of the North.

On some sunny afternoons she could sit on one of the little iron benches that dotted the waterfront and watch the little world that had formed here out of water and fish and human sweat.

She would see how a small community of people like this, based on the Bay and tourists, interacted. What traditions, what habits, what clichés ran through them. Styles, she mused, of dress, of movements, of speech. Inhabitants so rarely realized how they conformed to unspoken rules of behavior dictated by place.

Rules, rules, rules. They existed everywhere. Sybill believed in them absolutely.

What rules did the Quinns live by? she wondered. What type of glue had fashioned them into a family? They would, of course, have their own codes, their own short-speak, with a pecking order and a reward and discipline standard.

Where and how would Seth fit into it?

Finding out, discreetly, was a priority.

There was no reason for the Quinns to know who she was, to suspect her connection. It would be better for all parties if no one knew. Otherwise, they could very well attempt, and possibly succeed in blocking her from Seth altogether. He'd been with them for months now. She couldn't be sure what he'd been told, what spin they might have put on the circumstances.

She needed to observe, to study, to consider, and to judge. Then she would act. She would not be pressured, she ordered herself. She would not be made to feel guilty or responsible. She would take her time.

After their meeting that afternoon, she thought it would be ridiculously simple to get to know the Quinns. All she had to do was wander into that big brick building and show an interest in the process of creating a wooden sailboat.

Phillip Quinn would be her entrée. He'd displayed all the typical behavioral patterns of early-stage attraction. It wouldn't be a hardship to take advantage of that. Since he only spent a few days a week in St. Chris, there was little danger of taking a casual flirtation into serious territory.

Wrangling an invitation to his home here wouldn't present a problem. She needed to see where and how Seth was living, who was in charge of his welfare.

Was he happy?

Gloria had said they'd stolen her son. That they'd used their influence and their money to snatch him away.

But Gloria was a liar. Sybill squeezed her eyes shut, struggling to be calm, to be objective, not to be hurt. Yes, Gloria was a liar, she thought again. A user. But she was also Seth's mother.

Going to the desk, Sybill opened her Filofax and slid the photograph out. A little boy with straw-colored hair and bright blue eyes smiled out at her. She'd taken the picture herself, the first and only time she'd seen Seth.

He must have been four, she thought now. Phillip had said he was ten now, and Sybill remembered it had been six years since Gloria showed up on her doorstep in New York with her son in tow.

She'd been desperate, of course. Broke, furious, weepy, begging. There'd been no choice but to take her in, not with the child staring up with those huge, haunted eyes. Sybill hadn't known anything about children. She'd never been around them. Perhaps that was why she'd fallen for Seth so quickly and so hard.

And when she'd come home three weeks later and found them gone, along with all the cash in the house, her jewelry, and her prized collection of Daum china, she'd been devastated.

She should have expected it, she told herself now. It had been classic Gloria behavior. But she'd believed, had needed to believe, that they could finally connect. That the child would make a difference. That she could help.

Well, this time, she thought as she tucked the photo away again, she would be more careful, less emotional. She knew that Gloria was telling at least part of the truth this time. Whatever she did from this point on would depend on her own judgment.

She would begin to judge when she saw her nephew again.

Sitting, she turned on her laptop and began to write her initial notes.

The Quinn brothers appear to have an easy, male-pattern relationship. From my single observation I would suspect they work together well. It will take additional study to determine what function each provides in this business partnership, and in their familial relations.

Both Cameron and Ethan Quinn are newly married. It will be necessary to meet their wives to understand the dynamics of this family. Logically one of them will represent the mother figure. Since Cameron's wife, Anna Spinelli Quinn, has a full-time career, one would suspect that Grace Monroe Quinn fulfills this function. However, it's a mistake to generalize such matters and this will require personal observations.

I found it telling that the business sign the Quinns hung this afternoon contained Seth's name, but as a Quinn. I can't say if this disposal of his legal name is for their benefit or his.

The boy must certainly be aware that the Quinns are filing for custody. I can't say as yet whether he has received any of the letters Gloria has written him. Perhaps the Quinns have disposed of them. Though I sympathize with her plight and her desperation to get her child back, it's best that she remain unaware that I've come here. Once I've documented my findings, I'll contact her. If there is a legal battle in the future, it's best to approach the matter with facts rather than raw emotion.

Hopefully the lawyer Gloria has engaged will contact the Quinns through the proper legal channels shortly.

For myself, I hope to see Seth tomorrow and gain some insight into the situation. It would be helpful to determine how much he knows about his parentage. As I have only recently become fully informed, I've not yet completely assimilated all the facts and their repercussions.

We will soon see if small towns are indeed a hotbed of information on their inhabitants. I intend to learn all I can learn about Professor Raymond Quinn before I'm done.

THREE

The typical venue for socializing, information gathering, and mating rituals, small town or big city, Sybill observed, was the local bar.

Whether it was decorated with brass and ferns or peanut shells and tin ashtrays, whether the music was whiny country or heart-reeling rock, it was the traditional spot for gathering and exchanging information.

Shiney's Pub in St. Christopher's certainly fit the bill. The decor here was dark wood, cheap chrome, and faded posters of boats. The music was loud, she decided, unable to fully identify the style booming out of the towering amps flanking the small stage where four young men pounded away at guitars and drums with more enthusiasm than talent.

A trio of men at the bar kept their eyes glued to the baseball game on the small-screen TV bracketed to the wall behind the bar. They seemed content to watch the silent ballet of pitcher and batter while they nursed brown bottles of beer and ate fistfuls of pretzels.

The dance floor was jammed. There were only four couples, but the limited space caused several incidents of elbow rapping and hip bumping. No one seemed to mind.

The waitresses were decked out in foolish male-fantasy outfits—short black skirts, tiny, tight V-neck blouses, fishnet stockings, and stiletto heels.

Sybill felt instant sympathy.

She tucked herself into a wobbly table as far away from the amps as humanly possible. The smoke and noise didn't bother her, nor did the sticky floor or the jittery table. Her choice of seating afforded her the clearest view of the occupants.

She'd been desperate to escape her hotel room for a couple of hours. Now she was set to sit back, enjoy a glass of wine, and observe the natives.

The waitress who approached was a petite brunette with an enviable bustline and a cheery smile. "Hi. What can I get you?"

"A glass of Chardonnay and a side of ice."

"Coming right up." She set a black plastic bowl filled with pretzels on the table and picked her way back to the bar, taking orders as she went.

Sybill wondered if she'd just had her first encounter with Ethan's wife. Her information was that Grace Quinn worked at this bar. But there had been no wedding ring on the little brunette's finger, and Sybill assumed that a new bride would certainly wear one.

The other waitress? That one looked dangerous, she decided. Blond, built, and brooding. She was certainly attractive, in an obvious way. Still, nothing about her shouted newlywed either, particularly the way she leaned over an appreciative customer's table to give him the full benefit of her cleavage.

Sybill frowned and nibbled on a pretzel. If that was Grace Quinn, she would definitely be scratched from mother-figure status.

Something happened in the ball game, Sybill assumed, as the three men began to shout, cheering on someone named Eddie.

Out of habit she took out her notebook and began to record observations. The backslapping and arm punching of male companions. The body language of the females, leaning in for intimacy. The hair flipping, the eye shifting, hand gesturing. And of course, the mating ritual of the contemporary couple through the dance.

That was how Phillip saw her when he came in. She was smiling to herself, her gaze roaming, her hand scribbling. She looked, he thought, very cool, very remote. She might have been behind a thin sheet of one-way glass.

She'd pulled her hair back so that it lay in a sleek tail on her neck and left her face unframed. Gold drops studded with single colored stones swung at her ears. He watched her put her pen down to shrug out of a suede jacket of pale yellow.

He had driven in on impulse, giving in to restlessness. Now he blessed that vaguely dissatisfied mood that had dogged him all evening. She was, he decided, exactly what he'd been looking for.

"Sybill, right?" He saw the quick surprise flicker in her eyes when she glanced up. And he saw that those eyes were as clear and pure as lake water.

"That's right." Recovering, she closed her notebook and smiled. "Phillip, of Boats by Quinn."

"You here alone?"

"Yes . . . unless you'd like to sit down and have a drink."

"I'd love to." He pulled out a chair, nodding toward her notebook. "Did I interrupt you?"

"Not really." She shifted her smile to the waitress when her wine was served.

"Hey, Phil, want a draft?"

"Marsha, you read my mind."

Marsha, Sybill thought. That eliminated the perky brunette. "It's unusual music."

"The music here consistently sucks." He flashed a smile, quick, charming, and amused. "It's a tradition."

"Here's to tradition, then." She lifted her glass, sipped, then with a little hmmm began transferring ice into the wine.

"How would you rate the wine?"

"Well, it's basic, elemental, primitive." She sipped again, smiled winningly. "It sucks."

"That's also a proud Shiney's tradition. He's got Sam Adams on draft. It's a better bet."

"I'll remember that." Lips curved, she tilted her head. "Since you know the local traditions, I take it you've lived here for some time."

"Yeah." His eyes narrowed as he studied her, as something pushed at the edges of his memory. "I know you."

Her heart bounded hard into her throat. Taking her time, she picked up her glass again. Her hand remained steady, her voice even and easy. "I don't think so."

"No, I do. I know that face. It didn't click before, when you were wearing sunglasses. Something about . . ." He reached out, put a hand under her chin and angled her head again. "That look right there."

His fingertips were just a bit rough, his touch very confident and firm. The gesture itself warned her that this was a man used to touching women. And she was a woman unused to being touched.

In defense, Sybill arched an eyebrow. "A woman with a cynical bent would suspect that's a line, and not a very original one."

"I don't use lines," he murmured, concentrating on her face. "Except originals. I'm good with images, and I've seen that one. Clear, intelligent eyes, slightly amused smile. Sybill . . ." His gaze skimmed over her face, then his lips curved slowly. "Griffin. *Doctor* Sybill Griffin. *Familiar Strangers*."

She let out the breath that had clogged in her lungs. Her success was still very new, and having her face recognized continued to surprise her. And, in this case, relieve her. There was no connection between Dr. Griffin and Seth DeLauter.

"You are good," she said lightly. "So, did you read the book or just look at my picture on the dust jacket?"

"I read it. Fascinating stuff. In fact, I liked it enough to go out and buy your first one. Haven't read it yet though."

"I'm flattered."

"You're good. Thanks, Marsha," he added when she set his beer in front of him.

"Y'all just holler if you need anything." Marsha winked. "Holler loud. This band's breaking sound records tonight."

Which gave him an excuse to edge his chair closer and lean in. Her scent was subtle, he noted. A man had to get very close to catch its message. "Tell me, Dr. Griffin, what's a renowned urbanite doing in an unapologetically rural water town like St. Chris?"

"Research. Behavioral patterns and traditions," she said, lifting her glass in a half toast. "Of small towns and rural communities."

"Quite a change of pace for you."

"Sociology and cultural interest aren't, and shouldn't be, limited to cities."

"Taking notes?"

"A few. The local tavern," she began, more comfortable now. "The regulars. The trio at the bar, obsessed with the ritual of male-dominated sports to the exclusion of the noise and activities around them. They could be home, kicked back in their Barcaloungers, but they prefer the bonding experience of passive participation in the event. In this way they have companionship, partners with whom to share the interest, who will either argue or agree. It doesn't matter which. It's the pattern that matters."

He found he enjoyed the way her voice took on a lecturing tone that brought out brisk Yankee. "The O's are in a hot pennant race, and you're deep in Orioles' territory. Maybe it's the game."

"The game is the vehicle. The pattern would remain fairly constant whether the vehicle was football or basketball." She shrugged. "The typical male gains more enjoyment from sports if he has at least one like-minded male companion with him. You have only to observe commercials aimed primarily at the male consumer. Beer, for instance," she said, tapping a finger on his glass. "It's quite often sold by showcasing a group of attractive men sharing some common experience. A man then buys that brand of beer because he's been programmed to believe that it will enhance his standing with his peer group."

Because he was grinning, she lifted her eyebrows. "You disagree?"

"Not at all. I'm in advertising, and that pretty much hit the nail."

"Advertising?" She ignored the little tug of guilt at the pretense. "I wouldn't think there would be much call for that here."

"I work in Baltimore. I'm back here on weekends for a while. A family thing. Long story."

"I'd like to hear it."

"Later." There was something, he thought, about those nearly translucent blue eyes framed by long, inky lashes that made it nearly impossible to look anywhere else. "Tell me what else you see."

"Well . . ." It was a fine skill, she decided. A masterwork. The way he could look at a woman as if she were the most vital thing in the world at that one moment. It made her heart bump pleasantly. "You see the other waitress?"

Phillip glanced over, watched the frivolous bow on the back of the woman's skirt swivel as she walked to the bar. "Hard to miss her."

"Yes. She fulfills certain primitive and typical male-fantasy requirements. But I'm referring to personality, not physicality."

"Okay." Phillip ran his tongue around his teeth. "What do you see?"

"She's efficient, but she's already calculating the time until closing. She knows how to size up the better tippers and play to them. She all but ignores the table of college students there. They won't add much to her bill. You'd see the same survival techniques from an experienced and cynical waitress in a New York bar."

"Linda Brewster," Phillip supplied. "Recently divorced, on the prowl for a new, improved husband. Her family owns the pizza place, so she's been waitressing off and on for years. Doesn't care for it. Do you want to dance?"

"What?" Then that's not Grace either, she thought and struggled to tune back in. "I'm sorry?"

"The band's slowed it down if they haven't turned it down. Would you like to dance?"

"All right." She let him take her hand to lead her through the tables to the dance floor, where they shoehorned themselves into the crowd.

"I think this is supposed to be a version of 'Angie,' " Phillip murmured.

"If Mick and the boys heard what they're doing to it, they'd shoot the entire band on sight."

"You like the Stones?"

"What's not to like?" Since they could do no more than sway, she tilted her head back to look at him. It wasn't a hardship to find his face so close to hers, or to be forced to press her body firmly to his. "Down-and-dirty rock and roll, no frills, no fuss. All sex."

"You like sex?"

She had to laugh. "What's not to like? And though I appreciate the thought, I don't intend to have any tonight."

"There's always tomorrow."

"There certainly is." She considered kissing him, letting him kiss her. As an experiment that would certainly include an aspect of enjoyment. Instead, she turned her head so cheeks brushed. He was entirely too attractive for an impulsive and uncalculated risk.

Better safe, she reminded herself, than stupid.

"Why don't I take you to dinner tomorrow?" Skillfully, he slid a hand up her spine, back down to her waist. "There's a nice place right in town. Terrific view of the Bay, best seafood on the Shore. We can have a conversation in normal tones, and you can tell me the story of your life."

His lips had brushed her ear, sending a shocking ripple of reaction down to her toes. She should have known, she thought, that anyone who looked like he did would be damn good at sexual maneuvers.

"I'll think about it," she murmured and, deciding to give as good as she got, skimmed her fingertips over the back of his neck. "And let you know."

When the song ended, and the next picked up on a blast of sound and speed, she eased away. "I have to go."

"What?" He leaned down so she could shout in his ear.

"I have to go. Thanks for the dance."

"I'll walk you out."

Back at the table, he pulled out some bills while she gathered her things. The first step outside into the cool and quiet air made her laugh. "Well, that was an experience. Thank you for adding to it."

"I wouldn't have missed it. It's not very late," he added, taking her hand.

"Late enough." She pulled out the keys to her car.

"Come by the boatyard tomorrow. I'll show you around."

"I might just do that. Good night, Phillip."

"Sybill." He didn't bother to resist, simply brought her hand to his lips. Over their joined fingers, his eyes locked with hers. "I'm glad you picked St. Chris."

"So am I."

She slipped into her car, relieved that she had to concentrate on the task of switching on the lights, releasing the brake, starting the engine. Driving wasn't second nature to a woman who had depended on public transportation or private car services most of her life.

She focused on reversing, on putting the car in drive to make the turn onto the road. And she firmly ignored the faint echo of pressure on her knuckles where his lips had touched.

But she didn't quite resist glancing in the rearview mirror and taking one last look at him before she drove away.

Phillip decided that going back into Shiney's would be absurdly anticlimactic. He thought about her as he drove home, the way her eyebrows arched when she made a point or enjoyed a comment. That subtle and intimate scent she wore that told a man that if he'd gotten close enough to catch a whiff, maybe, just maybe, he'd have a chance to get closer.

He told himself she was the perfect woman for him to invest some time in getting closer to. She was beautiful; she was smart; she was cultured and sophisticated.

And just sexy enough to make his hormones stand at attention.

He liked women, and missed having time for conversations with them. Not that he didn't enjoy talking with Anna and Grace. But let's face it, it wasn't quite the same as talking with a woman when you could also fantasize about taking her to bed.

And he'd been missing that particular area of male-female relationships just lately. He rarely had time to do more than stumble into his apartment after a ten- or twelve-hour workday. His once interesting and varied social calendar had taken some large hits since Seth had come to the family.

The week was dedicated to his accounts and consultations with the lawyer. The fight with the insurance company on payment of his father's death benefits was coming to a head. The resolution of permanent guardianship of Seth would be decided within ninety days. The responsibility of dealing with the mountain of paperwork and phone calls that sprang from those actions was his. Details were his strong point.

Weekends were consumed by household duties, the business, and whatever had slipped through the cracks during the week.

When you added it all up, he mused, it didn't leave much time for cozy dinners with attractive women, much less the ritual of slipping between the sheets with those women.

Which explained his recent restlessness and moodiness, he supposed. When a man's sex life virtually vanished, he was bound to get a little edgy.

The house was dark but for the single beam of the porch light when he pulled into the drive. Barely midnight on Friday night, he thought with a sigh. How the mighty have fallen. There would have been a time when he and his brothers would have been out cruising, looking for action. Well, he and Cam would have dragged Ethan along, but once they'd hounded him into it, Ethan would have held up his end.

The Quinn boys hadn't spent many Friday nights snoozing.

These days, he thought as he climbed out of the Jeep, Cam would be upstairs cozied up to his wife and Ethan would be tucked into Grace's little house. Undoubtedly they both had smiles on their faces.

Lucky bastards.

Knowing he wouldn't be able to sleep, he skirted the house and walked to where the edge of the trees met the edge of the water.

The moon was a fat ball riding the night sky. It shed its soft white light over the dark water, wet eelgrass, and thick leaves.

Cicadas were singing in their high, monotonous voices, and deep in those thick woods, an owl called out in tireless two-toned notes.

Perhaps he preferred the sounds of the city, voices and traffic muffled through glass. But he never failed to find this spot appealing. Though he missed the city's pace, the theater and museums, the eclectic mix of food and people, he could appreciate the peace and the stability found right here day after day. Year after year.

Without it, he had no doubt he would have found his way back to the gutter. And died there.

"You always wanted more for yourself than that."

The chill washed through him, from gut to fingertips. Where he had been standing, staring out at the moonlight showering through the trees, he was now staring at his father. The father he'd buried six months before.

"I only had one beer," he heard himself say.

"You're not drunk, son." Ray stepped forward so that the moonlight shimmered over his dramatic mane of silver hair and into the brilliant blue eyes that were bright with humor. "You're going to want to breathe now, before you pass out."

Phillip let out his breath in a *whoosh*, but his ears continued to ring. "I'm going to sit down now." He did, slowly, like a creaky old man, easing himself down onto the grass. "I don't believe in ghosts," he said to the water, "or reincarnation, the afterlife, visitations, or any form of psychic phenomenon."

"You always were the most pragmatic of the lot. Nothing was real unless you could see it, touch it, smell it."

Ray sat beside him with a contented sigh and stretched out long legs clad in frayed jeans. He crossed his ankles, and on his feet were the well-worn Dock-Sides that Phillip himself had packed into a box for the Salvation Army nearly six months before.

"Well," Ray said cheerfully, "you're seeing me, aren't you?"

"No. I'm having an episode most likely resulting from sexual deprivation and overwork."

"I won't argue with you. It's too pretty a night."

"I haven't reached closure yet," Phillip said to himself. "I'm still angry over the way he died, and why, and all the unanswered questions. So I'm projecting."

"I figured you'd be the toughest nut of the three. Always had an answer for everything. I know you've got questions, too. And I know you've got anger. You're entitled. You've had to change your life and take on responsibilities that shouldn't have been yours. But you did it, and I'm grateful."

"I don't have time for therapy right now. There's no place on the schedule to fit sessions in."

Ray let out a hoot of laughter. "Boy, you're not drunk, and you're not crazy either. You're just stubborn. Why don't you use that flexible mind of yours, Phillip, and consider a possibility?"

Bracing himself, Phillip turned his head. It was his father's face, wide and lined with life and filled with humor. Those bright-blue eyes were dancing, the silver hair ruffling in the night air. "This is an impossibility."

"Some people said when your mother and I took you and your brothers in, that it was an impossibility we'd make a family, make a difference. They were wrong. If we'd listened to them, if we'd gone by logic, none of you would have been ours. But fate doesn't give a horse's ass about logic. It just is. And you were meant to be ours."

"Okay." Phillip shot out a hand and jerked it back in shock. "How could I do that? How could I touch you if you're a ghost?"

"Because you need to." Casually, Ray gave Phillip's shoulder a quick pat. "I'm here, for the next little while."

Phillip's throat filled even as his stomach tightened into knots. "Why?"

"I didn't finish. I left it up to you and your brothers. I'm sorry for that, Phillip."

It wasn't happening, of course, Phillip told himself. He was probably in the first stages of a minor breakdown. He could feel the air against his face, warm and moist. The cicadas were still shrilling, the owl still hooting.

If he was having an episode, he thought again, it seemed only right to play it out. "They're trying to say it was suicide," he said slowly. "The insurance company's fighting the claim."

"I hope you know that's bullshit. I was careless, distracted. I had an accident." There was an edge to Ray's voice now, an impatience and annoyance that Phillip recognized. "I wouldn't have taken the easy way. And I had the boy to think about."

"Is Seth your son?"

"I can tell you that he belongs to me."

Both his head and his heart ached as he turned to stare out at the water again. "Mom was still alive when he was conceived."

"I know that. I was never unfaithful to your mother."

"Then how—"

"You need to accept him, for himself. I know you care for him. I know you're doing your best by him. You have that last step to take. Acceptance. He needs you, all of you."

"Nothing's going to happen to him," Phillip said grimly. "We'll see to that."

"He'll change your life, if you let him."

Phillip let out a short laugh. "Believe me, he already has."

"In a way that will make your life better. Don't close yourself off to those possibilities. And don't worry too much about this little visit." Ray patted him companionably on the knee. "Talk to your brothers."

"Yeah, like I'm going to tell them I sat outside in the middle of the night and talked to . . ." He looked over, saw nothing but the moonlight on the trees.

"Nobody," he finished and wearily laid down on the grass to stare up at the moon. "God, I need a vacation."

Four

It wouldn't do to appear too anxious, Sybill reminded herself. Or to get there too early. It had to be casual. She had to be relaxed.

She decided not to take her car. It would look more like a careless visit if she walked down from the waterfront. And if she included the visit to the boatyard in an afternoon of shopping and wandering, it would appear more impulsive than calculated.

To calm herself, she roamed the waterfront. A pretty Indian-summer Saturday morning drew tourists. They poked and strolled along as she did, dropping into the little shops, pausing to watch boats sail or motor on the Bay. No one seemed to be in a particular hurry or have a specific destination.

That in itself, she mused, made an interesting contrast to the usual urban Saturday when even the tourists seemed to be in a rush to get from one place to the next.

It would be something to consider and analyze and perhaps theorize over in her book. And because she *did* find it interesting, she slipped her mini recorder out of her bag and murmured a few verbal notes and observations.

"Families appear to be relaxed rather than harried or desperately seeking the entertainment they've traveled to find. The natives seem to be friendly and patient. Life is slow to reflect the pace set by the people who make their living here."

The little shops weren't doing what she'd term a bustling business, yet the merchants didn't have that anxious and sly-eyed look prevalent among the vendors where the crowds were thick and the wallets tightly guarded.

She bought a few postcards for friends and associates in New York, then, more out of habit than need, selected a book on the history of the area. It would help her in her research, she imagined. She lingered over a pewter fairy with a teardrop crystal hanging from her elegant fingers. But she resisted it, firmly reminding herself that she could purchase any sort of foolishness she wanted in New York.

Crawford's appeared to be a popular spot, so she strolled in and treated herself to an ice cream cone. It gave her something to do with her hands as she walked the few blocks to Boats by Quinn.

She appreciated the value of props. Everyone used them in the continuing play of living, she thought. A glass at a cocktail party, a paperback book on the subway. Jewelry, she realized when she caught herself twisting her necklace around her nervous fingers.

She dropped the chain, and concentrated on enjoying her scoop of raspberry sherbet.

It didn't take long to walk to the outskirts of town. She calculated that the waterfront area ran for barely a mile from end to end.

The neighborhoods ran west from the water. Narrow streets with tidy houses and tiny lawns. Low fences designed as much for backyard gossiping, she mused, as for boundary lines. Trees were large and leafy, still holding the deep, dark green of summer. It would be, she thought, an attractive sight when they turned with autumn.

Kids played in yards or rode bikes along the sloping sidewalks. She saw a teenage boy lovingly waxing an old Chevy compact, singing in a loud, just-out-of-tune voice to whatever played through his headphones.

A long-legged mutt with floppy ears rushed a fence as she passed, barking in deep, rusty clips. Her heart did a quick dance when he planted his huge paws on the top of the fence. And she kept walking.

She didn't know much about dogs.

She spotted Phillip's Jeep in the pothole-filled parking lot beside the boatyard. An aging pickup truck kept it company. The doors and several of the windows of the building were wide open. Through them came the buzz of saws and the Southern rock beat of John Fogerty.

Okay, Sybill, she thought and took a deep breath as she carefully swallowed the last of her cone. Now or never.

She stepped inside and found herself momentarily distracted by the look of the place. It was huge, and dusty and bright as a spotlighted stage. The Quinns were hard at work, with Ethan and Cam fitting a long, bent plank into place on what she assumed was a hull in progress. Phillip stood at a big, dangerous-looking power saw, running lumber through it.

She didn't see Seth.

For a moment she simply watched and wondered if she should slip back out again. If her nephew wasn't there, it would be more sensible to postpone the visit until she was sure he was.

He might be away for the day with friends. Did he have any friends? Or he could be home. Did he consider it his home?

Before she could decide, the saw switched off, leaving only John Fogerty crooning about a brown-eyed, handsome man. Phillip stepped back, pushed up his safety goggles, turned. And saw her.

His smile of welcome came so quickly, so sincerely, that she had to clamp down on a hard tug of guilt. "I'm interrupting." She raised her voice to compete with the music.

"Thank God." Dusting his hands on his jeans, Phillip started toward her. "I've been stuck with looking at these guys all day. You're a big improvement."

"I decided to play tourist." She jiggled the shopping bag she carried. "And I thought I'd take you up on the offer of a tour."

"I was hoping you would."

"So . . ." Deliberately, she shifted her gaze to the hull. It was safer, she decided, than looking into those tawny eyes for any length of time. "That's a boat?"

"It's a hull. Or will be." He took her hand, drew her forward. "It's going to be a sport's fisher."

"Which is?"

"One of those fancy boats men like to go out on to act manly, fish for marlin, and drink beer."

"Hey, Sybill." Cam shot her a grin. "Want a job?"

She looked at the tools, the sharp edges, the heavy lumber. "I don't think so." It was easy to smile back, to look over at Ethan. "It looks like the three of you know what you're doing."

"We know what we're doing." Cam wiggled his thumb between himself and Ethan. "We keep Phillip around for entertainment."

"I'm not appreciated around here."

She laughed and began to circle the hull. She could understand the basic shape but not the process. "I assume this is upside down."

"Good eye." Phillip only grinned when she cocked an eyebrow. "After she's planked, we'll turn her and start on the decking."

"Are your parents boatbuilders?"

"No, my mother was a doctor, my father a college professor. But we grew up around boats."

She heard it in his voice, the affection, the not-quite-settled grief. And hated herself. She'd intended to ask him more about his parents in some detail, but couldn't. "I've never been on a boat."

"Ever?"

"I imagine there are several million people in the world who haven't."

"Want to?"

"Maybe. I've enjoyed watching the boats from my hotel window." As she studied it, the hull became a puzzle she needed to solve. "How do you know where to begin to build this? I assume you work from a design, blue-prints or schematics or whatever you call it."

"Ethan's been doing the bulk of the design work. Cam fiddles with it. Seth draws it up."

"Seth." Her fingers tightened on the strap of her purse. Props, she thought again. "Didn't you say he was in middle school?"

"That's right. The kid's got a real talent for drawing. Check these out."

Now she heard pride and it flustered her. Struggling for composure, she followed him to a far wall, where drawings of boats were roughly framed in raw wood. They were good—very, very good. Clever sketches done with pencil and care and talent.

"He . . . A young boy drew these?"

"Yes. Pretty great, huh? This is the one we just finished." He tapped a hand on the glass. "And this one's what we're working on now."

"He's very talented," she murmured around the lump in her throat. "He has excellent perspective."

"Do you draw?"

"A little, now and then. Just a hobby." She had to turn away to settle herself. "It relaxes me, and it helps in my work." Determined to smile again, she tossed her hair over her shoulder and aimed a bright, easy one at Phillip. "So, where's the artist today?"

"Oh, he's—"

He broke off as two dogs raced into the building. Sybill took an instinctive step back as the smaller of the two made a beeline in her direction. She made some strangled sound of distress just as Phillip jabbed out a finger and issued a sharp command.

"Hold it, you idiot. No jumping. No jumping," he repeated, but Fool-ish's forward motion proved too much for all of them. He was already up, already had his paws planted just under Sybill's breasts. She staggered a bit, seeing only big, sharp teeth bared in what she took for fierceness rather than a sloppy doggie grin.

"Nice dog," she managed in a stutter. "Good dog."

"Stupid dog," Phillip corrected and hauled Foolish down by the collar. "No manners. Sit. Sorry," he said to Sybill when the dog obligingly plopped down and offered his paw. "He's Foolish."

"Well, he's enthusiastic."

"No, Foolish is his name—and his personality. He'll stay like that until you shake his paw."

"Oh. Hmm." Gingerly she took the paw with two fingers.

"He won't bite." Phillip angled his head, noting there was a good deal more distress than irritation in her eyes. "Sorry—are you afraid of dogs?"

"I . . . maybe a little—of large, strange dogs."

"He's strange, all right. The other one's Simon, and he's considerably more polite." Phillip scratched Simon's ears as the dog sat calmly studying Sybill. "He's Ethan's. The idiot belongs to Seth."

"I see." Seth had a dog, was all she could think as Foolish offered his paw yet again, eyeing her with what appeared abject adoration. "I don't know very much about dogs, I'm afraid."

"These are Chesapeake Bay retrievers—or Foolish mostly is. We're not sure what else he is. Seth, call off your dog before he slobbers all over the lady's shoes."

Sybill lifted her head quickly and saw the boy just inside the doorway. The sun was streaming at his back, and it cast his face into shadows. She saw only a tall, slightly built boy carrying a large brown bag and wearing a black-and-orange ball cap.

"He doesn't slobber much. Hey, Foolish!"

Instantly, both dogs scrambled to their feet and raced across the room. Seth waded through them, carrying the bag to a makeshift table fashioned from a sheet of plywood laid over two sawhorses.

"I don't know why I have to always go up for lunch and stuff," he complained.

"Because we're bigger than you," Cam told him and dived into the bag. "You get me the cold-cut sub loaded?"

"Yeah, yeah."

"Where's my change?"

Seth pulled a liter of Pepsi out of the bag, cracked the top and guzzled straight from the bottle. Then he grinned. "What change?"

"Look, you little thief, I've got at least two bucks coming back."

"Don't know what you're talking about. You must've forgotten to add on the carrying charges again."

Cam made a grab for him, and Seth danced agilely away, hooting with laughter.

"Brotherly love," Phillip said easily. "That's why I make sure I only give the kid the right change. You never see a nickel back otherwise. Want some lunch?"

"No, I . . ." She couldn't take her eyes off Seth, knew she had to. He was talking with Ethan now, making wide, exaggerated gestures with his free hand while his dog took quick, playful leaps at his fingers. "I had something already. But you go ahead."

"A drink, then. Did you get my water, kid?"

"Yeah, fancy water. Waste of money. Man, Crawford's was packed."

Crawford's. With a sensation she couldn't quite define, Sybill realized they might have been in the store at the same time. Might have walked right by each other. She would have passed him on the street without a clue.

Seth glanced from Phillip to Sybill, studied her with mild interest. "You buying a boat?"

"No." He didn't recognize her, she thought. Of course he wouldn't. He'd been hardly more than a baby the only time they'd seen each other. There was no stunned familial awareness in his eyes, any more than there would have been in hers. But she knew. "I'm just looking around."

"That's cool." He went back to the bag and pulled out his own sandwich.

"Ah . . ." Talk to him, she ordered herself. Say something. Anything. "Phillip was just showing me your drawings. They're wonderful."

"They're okay." He jerked a shoulder, but she thought she saw a faint flush of pleasure on his cheeks. "I could do better, but they're always rushing me."

Casually—she hoped it was casually—she crossed to him. She could see him clearly now. His eyes were blue, but a deeper, darker blue than hers or her sister's. His hair was a darker blond than the little boy's in the picture she carried. He'd been nearly a towhead at four, and now his hair was a richer blond and very straight.

The mouth, she thought. Wasn't there some resemblance around the mouth and chin?

"Is that what you want to be?" She needed to keep him talking. "An artist?"

"Maybe, but that's mostly for kicks." He took a huge bite of his sandwich, then talked through it. "We're boatbuilders."

His hands were far from clean, she noted, and his face wasn't much better. She imagined such niceties as washing up before meals went by the wayside in a household of males. "Maybe you'll go into design work."

"Seth, this is Dr. Sybill Griffin." Phillip offered Sybill a plastic cup of bubbling water over ice. "She writes books."

"Like stories?"

"Not exactly," she told him. "Like observations. Right now I'm spending some time in the area, observing."

He wiped his mouth with a swipe from the back of his hand. The hand Foolish had enthusiastically licked, before and after, Sybill noted with an inward wince.

"You going to do a book about boats?" he asked her.

"No, about people. People who live in small towns, and right now people who live in small towns by the water. How do you like it—living here, I mean?"

"I like it okay. Living in the city sucks." He picked up the soft drink bottle, glugged again. "People who live there are nuts." He grinned. "Like Phil."

"You're a peasant, Seth. I worry about you."

With a snort, Seth bit into his sandwich again. "I'm going out on the dock. We got some ducks hanging out."

He bounced out, dogs trailing behind him.

"Seth's got very definite opinions," Phillip said dryly. "I guess the world's pretty black and white when you're ten."

"He doesn't care for the urban experience." Nerves, she noted, had been drowned out by sheer curiosity. "Has he spent time with you in Baltimore?"

"No. He lived there for a while with his mother." His tone had darkened, making Sybill raise an eyebrow. "Part of that long story I mentioned."

"I believe I mentioned I'd enjoy hearing it."

"Then have dinner with me tonight, and we'll exchange those life stories."

She looked toward the cargo doors. Seth had gone out through them, very much at home. She needed to spend more time with him. Observing. And, she decided, she needed to hear what the Quinns had to say about the situation. Why not start with Phillip?

"All right. I'd like that."

"I'll pick you up at seven."

She shook her head. He seemed perfectly safe, perfectly fine, but she knew better than to take chances. "No, I'll meet you there. Where's the restaurant?"

"I'll write it down for you. We can start the tour in my office."

⟨⟨⟨⟩⟩⟩

It was easy enough, and she had to admit it was interesting. The tour itself didn't take long. Other than the huge work area, there was little to the boatyard—just Phillip's closet-size office, a small bathroom, and a dark, dingy storeroom.

It was obvious even to the untrained eye that the work center of the operation was its heart and soul.

It was Ethan who patiently instructed her on smooth-lap planking, about waterlines and bow shapes. She thought he would have made an excellent teacher, with his clear, simple phrasing and willingness to answer what must have been very basic questions.

She watched, genuinely fascinated, as the men held timber in a box and pumped out steam until the plank bowed into the shape they desired. Cam demonstrated how the ends were rabbeted together to form the smooth joints.

Watching Cam with Seth, she was forced to admit there was a definite bond between them. If she had come across them knowing nothing, she would have assumed they were brothers, or perhaps father and son. It was all in the attitude, she decided.

Then again, they had an audience, she mused, and were likely on their best behavior.

She would see how they acted once they became used to her.

Cam let out a long, low whistle when Sybill left the building. He wiggled his eyebrows meaningfully at Phillip. "Very nice, bro. Very nice, indeed."

Phillip flashed a grin, then lifted his bottle of water to his lips. "Can't complain."

"She going to be around long enough to, ah . . ."

"If there's a God."

Seth laid a plank down by the saw, let out a huff. "Shit, you mean you're going to start poking at her? Is that all you guys think about?"

"Other than pounding on you?" Phillip whipped off Seth's hat and bopped the boy over the head with it. "Sure, what else?"

"You guys are always getting married," Seth said in disgust and tried to grab his hat.

"I don't want to marry her, I just want to have a nice, civilized dinner with her."

"Then bounce on her," Seth finished.

"Christ. He gets that from you," Phillip accused Cam.

"He came that way." Cam wrapped an arm around Seth's neck. "Didn't you, brat?"

The panic didn't come now, as it used to whenever Seth was touched or held. Instead he wriggled and grinned. "At least I think of something besides girls all the time. You guys are really lame."

"Lame?" Phillip put Seth's hat on his own head to free his hands, then rubbed them together. "Let's toss this runt fish off the dock."

"Can you do that later?" Ethan asked while Seth shouted in wild and delighted objection. "Or do I have to build this damn boat by myself?"

"Later, then." Phillip leaned down until he and Seth were nose to nose. "And you won't know when, you won't know where, you won't know why."

"Man, I'm shaking now."

⟨⟐⟩

I *saw Seth today.*
     At her laptop, Sybill gnawed her bottom lip, then deleted the first sentence she'd typed.

I made contact with the subject this afternoon.

Better, she decided. More objective. To approach this situation properly, it would be best if she thought of Seth as the subject.

There was no recognition on either side. This is, of course, as expected. He appears to be healthy. He's attractive, slimly built yet sturdy. Gloria was always thin, so I suspect he's inherited her basic body type. He's blond, as she is—or was when I last saw her.

He seemed to be comfortable with me. I'm aware that some children are shy around strangers. That doesn't appear to be the case here.

Though he was not at the boatyard when I arrived, he came in shortly after. He'd been sent to the store for lunch. From the ensuing complaints and conversation, I can assume he is often expected to run errands. This could be construed two ways. One that the Quinns take advantage of having a young boy available and use him accordingly. Or two, that they are instilling a sense of responsibility.

The truth likely resides in the middle.

He has a dog. I believe this to be a usual, even traditional occurrence for a child living in suburban or rural areas.

He also has a talent for drawing. I was somewhat taken by surprise by this. I have some talent for it myself, as does my mother. Gloria, however, never showed any skill or interest in art. This shared interest may be a way to develop a rapport with the boy. It will be necessary to have some time alone with him to assist me in choosing the correct course to take.

The subject is, in my opinion, comfortable with the Quinns. He seems to be content and secure. There is, however, a certain roughness, a mild crudeness in him. Several times during the hour or so I spent with him, I heard him swear. Once or twice he was rather absently corrected, otherwise his language was ignored.

He was not required to wash his hands before eating, nor did any of the Quinns correct him for speaking with his mouth full or for feeding the dogs bits of his lunch. His manners are by no means appalling, but they are far from strictly polite.

He mentioned preferring living here to the city. In fact, he was most disdainful of urban life. I have agreed to have dinner with Phillip Quinn tonight and will urge him to tell me the facts of how Seth came to be with the Quinns.

How those facts agree with, and differ from, the facts I received from Gloria will help me assimilate the situation.

The next step will be to obtain an invitation to the Quinn house. I'm very interested to see where the boy is living, to see him and the Quinns on this stage. And to meet the women who are now a part of his foster family.

I hesitate to contact Social Services and identify myself until I have completed this personal study.

Sybill sat back, tapping her fingers on the desk as she skimmed over her notes. It was so little, really, she thought. And her own fault. She'd thought she was prepared for that first meeting, but she wasn't.

Seeing him had left her dry-mouthed and sad. The boy was her nephew, her family. Yet they were strangers. And wasn't that nearly as much her fault as it was Gloria's? Had she ever really tried to make a connection, to bring him into her life?

True, she had rarely known where he was, but had she ever gone out of her way to find him, or her sister?

The few times Gloria had contacted her over the years for money, always for money, she had asked about Seth. But hadn't she simply taken Gloria's word that the child was fine? Had she ever demanded to speak with him, to see him?

Hadn't it simply been easier for her to send money over the wire and forget about them again?

Easier, she admitted. Because the one time she had let him in, the one time she had let herself open her home and her heart, he'd been taken away. And she had suffered.

This time she would do something. She would do whatever was right, whatever was best. She wouldn't allow herself to become too emotionally involved, however. After all, he wasn't her child. If Gloria retained custody, he would still move out of her life again.

But she would make the effort, take the time, see that he was situated well. Then she would get on with her life and her work.

Satisfied, she saved the document and shifted to another to continue her notes for her book. Before she could begin, the phone on her desk rang.

"Yes. Dr. Griffin."

"Sybill. It took me a great deal of time and trouble to track you down."

"Mother." On a long sigh Sybill closed her eyes. "Hello."

"Would you mind telling me what you're doing?"

"Not at all. I'm researching a new book. How are you? How's Father?"

"Please, don't insult my intelligence. I thought we'd agreed you would stay out of this sordid little affair."

"No." As it always did when faced with a family confrontation, Sybill's stomach pitched. "We agreed that you would prefer I stay out of it. I decided I prefer not to. I've seen Seth."

"I'm not interested in Gloria, or her son."

"I am. I'm sorry that upsets you."

"Can you expect it to do otherwise? Your sister has chosen her own life and is no longer a part of mine. I will not be dragged into this."

"I have no intention of dragging you into this." Resigned, Sybill reached into her purse and found the small cloisonné box she used to store aspirin. "No one knows who I am. And even if I'm connected to Dr. and Mrs. Walter Griffin, that hardly follows to Gloria and Seth DeLauter."

"It can be followed, if anyone becomes interested enough to pursue it. You can't accomplish anything by staying there and interfering in this situation, Sybill. I want you to leave. Go back to New York, or come here to Paris. Perhaps you'll listen to your father if not to me."

Sybill washed down the aspirin with water, then dug out antacids. "I'm going to see this through. I'm sorry."

There was a long silence ripe with temper and frustration. Sybill closed her eyes, left them closed, and waited.

"You were always a joy to me. I never expected this kind of betrayal. I very much regret that I spoke with you about this matter. I wouldn't have if I'd known you would react so outrageously."

"He's a ten-year-old boy, Mother. He's your grandson."

"He is nothing to me, or to you. If you continue this, Gloria will make you pay for what you see as kindness."

"I can handle Gloria."

There was a laugh now, short and brittle as glass. "So you always believed. And you were always wrong. Please don't contact me, or your father, about any of this. I'll expect to hear from you when you've come to your senses."

"Mother—" The dial tone made Sybill wince. Barbara Griffin was a master at having the last word. Very carefully, Sybill set the receiver on the hook. Very deliberately, she swallowed the antacid.

Then, very defiantly, she turned back to her screen and buried herself in work.

FIVE

Since Sybill was always on time and nearly everyone else in the world, as far as she was concerned, never was, she was surprised to find Phillip already sitting at the table he'd reserved for dinner.

He rose, offered her a killer smile and a single yellow rose. Both charmed her and made her suspicious.

"Thank you."

"My pleasure. Sincerely. You look wonderful."

She'd gone to some trouble in that area, but more for herself than for him. The call from her mother had left her miserably depressed and guilty. She'd tried to fight off both emotions by taking a great deal of time and putting a great deal of effort into her appearance.

The simple black dress with its square neck and long, snug sleeves was one of her favorites. The single strand of pearls was a legacy from her paternal grandmother and much loved. She'd swept her hair up in a smooth twist and added sapphire cabochon earrings that she'd bought in London years before.

She knew it was the sort of feminine armor that women slipped into for confidence and power. She'd wanted both. "Thank you again." She slid into the booth across from him and sniffed the rose. "And so do you."

"I know the wine list here," he told her. "Trust me?"

"On wine? Why not?"

"Good." He glanced toward the server. "We'll have a bottle of the number 103."

She laid the rose beside the leather-bound menu. "Which is?"

"A very nice Pouilly Fuisse. I remember from Shiney's that you like white. I think you'll find this a few very important steps up from what you had there."

"Almost anything would be."

He cocked his head, took her hand. "Something's wrong."

"No." Deliberately she curved her lips. "What could be wrong? It's just as advertised." She turned her head to look out the window beside her, where the Bay stretched, dark blue and excitingly choppy under a sky going rosy with sunset. "A lovely view, a pretty spot." She turned back. "An interesting companion for the evening."

No, he thought, watching her eyes. Something was just a little off. On impulse he slid over, cupped her chin in his hand, and laid his lips lightly on hers.

She didn't draw away, but allowed herself to experience. The kiss was easy, smooth, skilled. And very soothing. When he drew back, she raised an eyebrow. "And that was because?"

"You looked like you needed it."

She didn't sigh, but she wanted to. Instead, she put her hands in her lap. "Thank you once again."

"Any time. In fact . . ." His fingers tightened just a little on her face, and this time the kiss moved a bit deeper, lasted a bit longer.

Her lips parted under his before she realized that she'd meant it to happen. Her breath caught, released, and her pulse shivered as his teeth scraped lightly, as his tongue teased hers into a slow, seductive dance.

Her fingers were linked and gripped tight, her mind just beginning to blur when he eased away.

"And that was because?" she managed.

"I guess I needed it."

His lips brushed over hers once, then again, before she found the presence of mind to lay a hand on his chest. A hand, she realized, that wanted to ball into a fist on that soft shirt and hold him in place rather than nudge him away.

But she nudged him away. It was simply a matter of handling him, she reminded herself. Of staying in control.

"I think as appetizers go, that was very appealing. But we should order."

"Tell me what's wrong." He wanted to know, he realized. Wanted to help, wanted to smooth those shadows out of her incredibly clear eyes and make them smile.

He hadn't expected to develop a taste for her so quickly.

"It's nothing."

"Of course it is. And there can't be anything much more therapeutic than dumping on a relative stranger."

"You're right." She opened her menu. "But most relative strangers aren't particularly interested in someone else's minor problems."

"I'm interested in you."

She smiled as she shifted her gaze from the entrées to his face. "You're attracted to me. That's not always the same thing."

"I think I'm both."

He took her hand, held it as the wine was brought to the table, as the label was turned for his approval. He waited while a sample was poured into his glass, watching her in that steady, all-else-aside way she'd discovered he had. He lifted it, sipped, still looking at her.

"It's perfect. You'll like it," he murmured to her while their glasses were being filled.

"You're right," she told him after she sipped. "I like it very much."

"Shall I tell you tonight's specials?" their waiter began in a cheerful voice. While he recited, they sat, hands linked, eyes locked.

Sybill decided she heard about every third word and didn't really give a damn. He had the most incredible eyes. Like old gold, like something she'd seen in a painting in Rome. "I'll have the mixed salad, with the vinaigrette, and the fish of the day, grilled."

He kept watching her, his lips curving slowly as he drew her hand across the table to kiss her palm. "The same. And take your time. I'm very attracted," he said to Sybill as the waiter rolled his eyes and walked away. "And I'm very interested. Talk to me."

"All right." What harm could it do? she decided. Since, sooner or later, they would have to deal with each other on a different sort of level, it might be helpful if they understood one another now. "I'm the good daughter." Amused at herself, she smiled a little. "Obedient, respectful, polite, academically skilled, professionally successful."

"It's a burden."

"Yes, it can be. Of course, I know better, intellectually, than to allow myself to be ruled by parental expectations at this stage of my life."

"But," Phillip said, giving her fingers a squeeze, "you are. We all are."

"Are you?"

He thought of sitting by the water in the moonlight and having a conversation with his dead father. "More than I might have believed. In my case, my parents didn't give me life. They gave me *the* life. This life. In yours," he considered, "since you're the good daughter, is there a bad daughter?"

"My sister has always been difficult. Certainly she's been a disappointment to my parents. And the more disappointed they've become in her, the more they expect from me."

"You're supposed to be perfect."

"Exactly, and I can't be." Wanted to be, tried to be, couldn't be. Which, of course, equaled failure. How could it be otherwise? she mused.

"Perfect is boring," Phillip commented. "And intimidating. Why try to be either? So what happened?" he asked when she only frowned.

"It's nothing, really. My mother is angry with me just now. If I give in and do what she wants . . . well, I can't. I just can't."

"So you feel guilty and sad and sorry."

"And afraid that nothing will ever be the same between us again."

"As bad as that?"

"It could be," Sybill murmured. "I'm grateful for all the opportunities they gave me, the structure, the education. We traveled quite a bit, so I saw a great deal of the world, of different cultures, while I was still a child. It's been invaluable in my work."

Opportunities, Phillip thought. Structure, education, and travel. Nowhere had she listed love, affection, fun. He wondered if she realized she'd described a school more than a family. "Where did you grow up?"

"Um. Here and there. New York, Boston, Chicago, Paris, Milan, London. My father lectured and held consultations. He's a psychiatrist. They live in Paris now. It was always my mother's favorite city."

"Long-distance guilt."

It made her laugh. "Yes." She sat back as their salads were served. Oddly enough, she did feel a little better. It seemed slightly less deceptive to have told him something about herself. "And you grew up here."

"I came here when I was thirteen, when the Quinns became my parents."

"Became?"

"It's part of that long story." He lifted his wineglass, studying her over its rim. Normally if he brought up that period of his life with a woman, what he told was a carefully edited version. Not a lie, but a less-than-detailed account of his life before the Quinns.

Oddly enough, he was tempted to tell Sybill the whole, the ugly and unvarnished truth. He hesitated, then settled on something between the two.

"I grew up in Baltimore, on the rough side. I got into trouble, pretty serious trouble. By the time I was thirteen, I was headed for worse. The Quinns gave me a chance to change that. They took me in, brought me to St. Chris. Became my family."

"They adopted you." She'd had that much information, from researching everything she could find on Raymond Quinn. But it didn't give her the why.

"Yeah. They already had Cam and Ethan, and they made room for one more. I didn't make it easy for them initially, but they stuck with me. I never knew either of them to back off from a problem."

He thought of his father, broken and dying in a hospital bed. Even then Ray's concerns had been for his sons, for Seth. For family.

"When I first saw you," Sybill began, "the three of you, I knew you were brothers. No real physical resemblance, but something less tangible. I'd say you're an example of how environment can offset heredity."

"More an example of what two generous and determined people can do for three lost boys."

She sipped her wine to soothe her throat before she spoke. "And Seth."

"Lost boy number four. We're trying to do for him what my parents would have done, what our father asked us to do. My mother died several years ago. It left the four of us floundering some. She was an incredible woman. We couldn't have appreciated her enough when we had her."

"I think you did." And moved by the sound of his voice, she smiled at him. "I'm sure she felt very loved."

"I hope so. After we lost her, Cam took off for Europe. Racing—boats, cars, whatever. He did pretty well at it. Ethan stayed. Bought his own house, but he's locked into the Bay. I moved back to Baltimore. Once an urbanite," he added with a quick smile.

"The Inner Harbor, Camden Yards."

"Exactly. I came down here off and on. Holidays, the occasional weekend. But it's not the same."

Curious, she tilted her head. "Would you want it to be?" She remembered her secret thrill when she'd gone off to college. To be on her own, not to have every movement and word weighed and judged. Freedom.

"No, but there were times, are times, I miss the way it was. Don't you ever think back to some perfect summer? You're sixteen, your driver's license is shiny and new in your wallet, and the world is all yours."

She laughed, but shook her head. She hadn't had a driver's license at sixteen. They'd been living in London that year, as she recalled. There had been a uniformed driver to take her where she'd been allowed to go, unless she managed to slip out and ride the Tube. That had been her small rebellion.

"Sixteen-year-old boys," she said, while their salad plates were removed, their entrées served, "are more emotionally attached to their cars than sixteen-year-old girls are."

"It's easier for that boy to get himself a girl if he has wheels."

"I doubt you had any trouble in that area, with or without a car."

"It's tough to neck in the backseat until you've got one."

"True enough. And now you're back here, and so are your brothers."

"Yeah. My father had Seth through complicated and not entirely clear circumstances. Seth's mother . . . well, you'll hear talk if you stay in the area for any length of time."

"Oh?" Sybill cut into her fish, hoping that she could swallow it.

"My father taught English lit at the university, the Eastern Shore campus of Maryland. A little less than a year ago a woman came to see him. It was a private meeting, so we don't have the details, but from all accounts it wasn't pleasant. She went to the dean and accused my father of sexual harassment."

Sybill's fork clattered onto her plate. As casually as she could, she lifted it again. "That must have been very difficult for him, for all of you."

"Difficult isn't quite the word for it. She claimed to have been a student here years back and said that at that time he had demanded sex for grades, intimidated her, had an affair with her."

No, she couldn't swallow, Sybill realized, gripping her fork until her fingers ached. "She had an affair with your father?"

"No, she said she did. My mother would still have been alive," he said half to himself. "In any case, there was no record of her ever attending the university. My father taught on that campus for more than twenty-five years, without a whisper of improper behavior. She took a shot at destroying his reputation. And it left a smear."

Of course there'd be no truth to it, Sybill thought wearily. It was Gloria's usual pattern. Accuse, damage, run. But she herself still had a part to play. "Why? Why would she do that?"

"Money."

"I don't understand."

"My father gave her money, a great deal of it. For Seth. She's Seth's mother."

"You're saying that she . . . she traded her son for money?" Not even Gloria could do something so appalling, she told herself. Surely, not even Gloria. "That's difficult to believe."

"Not all mothers are maternal." He jerked a shoulder. "He had a check for several thousand made out to Gloria DeLauter—that's her name—and he went away for a few days, then came back with Seth."

Saying nothing, she picked up her water glass, cooled her throat. *He came and got Seth*, Gloria had sobbed to her. *They've got Seth. You have to help me.*

"A few months later," Phillip continued, "he drew almost all his savings out into a cashier's check. He was on his way back from Baltimore when he had an accident. He didn't make it."

"I'm so sorry." She murmured the words, recognizing their inadequacy.

"He hung on until Cam got in from Europe. He asked the three of us to keep Seth, to look out for him. We're doing everything we can to keep that promise. I can't say it wasn't rough for a while," he added, smiling a little now. "But it's never been dull. Moving back here, starting the boat business, not such a bad deal. Cam got a wife out of it," he added with a grin. "Anna is Seth's caseworker."

"Really? They couldn't have known each other very long."

"I guess when it hits, it hits. Time doesn't factor in."

She'd always believed it did, vitally. To be successful, marriage took planning and dedication and a strong, solid knowledge of one's partner, an assurance of compatibility, an assessment of personal goals.

Then again, that portion of the Quinn dynamics wasn't her concern.

"That's quite a story." How much was true? she wondered, sick at heart. How much was slanted? Was she supposed to believe that her sister had sold her own son?

Somewhere in the middle, she decided. The real truth could generally be found somewhere between two opposing stories.

Phillip didn't know, she was sure of that now. He had no clue what Gloria had been to Raymond Quinn. When that single fact was added to the mix, how did it change everything else?

"At this point it's working out. The kid's happy. Another couple of months and the permanent guardianship should be wrapped. And this big brother stuff has its advantages. Gives me somebody to boss around."

She needed to think. She had to put emotion aside and think. But she had to get through the evening first. "How does he feel about that?"

"It's a perfect setup. He can bitch to Cam or Ethan about me, to me about Cam or Ethan. He knows how to play it. Seth's incredibly smart. They did placement tests when my father enrolled him in school here. He's practically off the charts. His final report card for last year? Straight A's."

"Really?" She found herself smiling. "You're proud of him."

"Sure. And me. I'm the one who got roped into being homework monitor. Until recently I'd forgotten how much I hate fractions. Now that I've told you my long story, why don't you tell me what you think of St. Chris?"

"I'm just getting my bearings."

"Does that mean you'll be staying a while yet?"

"Yes. A while."

"You can't really judge a water town unless you spend some time on the water. Why don't you go sailing with me tomorrow?"

"Don't you have to get back to Baltimore?"

"Monday."

She hesitated, then reminded herself that this was exactly why she was here. If she was to find that real truth, she couldn't back away now. "I'd like that. I can't guarantee what kind of sailor I'll be."

"We'll find out. I'll pick you up. Ten, ten-thirty?"

"That'll be fine. All of you sail, I imagine."

"Right down to the dogs." He laughed at the expression on her face. "We won't bring them along."

"I'm not afraid of them. I'm just not used to them."

"You never had a puppy."

"No."

"Cat?"

"No."

"Goldfish?"

She laughed, shook her head. "No. We moved around quite a bit. Once I had a schoolmate in Boston whose dog had puppies. They were darling." Odd, she thought, to have remembered that now. She'd wanted one of those pups desperately.

It had been impossible, of course. Antique furniture, important guests, social obligations. Out of the question, her mother had said. And that had been the end of it.

"Now I move around quite a bit. It's not practical."

"Where do you like best?" he asked her.

"I'm flexible. Wherever I end up tends to suit me, until I'm somewhere else."

"So right now it's St. Chris."

"Apparently. It's interesting." She gazed out the window, where the rising moon glittered light onto the water. "The pace is slow, but it's not stagnant. The mood varies, as the weather varies. After only a few days, I'm able to separate the natives from the tourists. And the watermen from everyone else."

"How?"

"How?" Distracted, she looked back at him.

"How can you tell one from the other?"

"Just basic observation. I can look out of my window onto the waterfront. The tourists are couples, more likely families, occasionally a single. They stroll, or they shop. They rent a boat. They interact with each other, the ones in their group. They're out of their milieu. Most will have camera, map, maybe binoculars. Most of the natives have a purpose for being there. A job, an errand. They might stop and say hello to a neighbor. You can see them easing back on their way as they end the conversation."

"Why are you watching from the window?"

"I don't understand the question."

"Why aren't you down on the waterfront?"

"I have been. But you usually get a purer study when you, the observer, aren't part of the scene."

"I'd think you'd get more varied and more personal input if you were."
He glanced up as the waiter arrived to top off their wine and offer them
dessert.

"Just coffee," Sybill decided. "Decaf."

"The same." Phillip leaned forward. "In your book, the section on isolation as a survival technique, the example you used of having someone lying
on the sidewalk. How people would look away, walk around. Some might
hesitate before hurrying past."

"Noninvolvement. Disassociation."

"Exactly. But one person would eventually stop, try to help. Once one
person broke the isolation, others would begin to stop, too."

"Once the isolation is breached, it becomes easier, even necessary for
others to join. It's the first step that's the most difficult. I conducted that
study in New York and London and Budapest, all with similar results. It follows the urban survival technique of avoiding eye contact on the street, of
blocking the homeless out of our line of sight."

"What makes that first person who stops to help different from everyone
else?"

"Their survival instincts aren't as well honed as their compassion. Or
their impulse button is more easily pushed."

"Yeah, that. And they're involved. They're not just walking through, not
just there. They're involved."

"And you think that because I observe, I'm not."

"I don't know. But I think that observing from a distance isn't nearly as
rewarding as experiencing up close."

"Observing's what I do, and I find it rewarding."

He slid closer and kept his eyes on hers, ignoring the waiter who tidily
served their coffee. "But you're a scientist. You experiment. Why don't you
give experiencing a try? With me."

She looked down, watched his fingertip toy with hers. And felt the slow
heat of response creep into her blood. "That's a very novel, if roundabout,
way of suggesting that I sleep with you."

"Actually, that wasn't what I meant—though if the answer's yes, I'm all
for it." He flashed her a grin as she shifted her gaze warily to his. "I was going to suggest that we take a walk on the waterfront when we've finished our
coffee. But if you'd rather sleep with me, we can be in your hotel room in,
oh, five minutes flat."

She didn't evade when his head lowered to hers, when his lips slid lazily
into a lovely fit over hers. The taste of him was cool, with an underlying
promise of heat. If she wanted it. And she did. It surprised her how much,

just at that one moment, she wanted the flash and burn—the demand that would override the tension inside her, the worry, the doubts.

But she'd had a lifetime of training against self-indulgence, and now she laid a hand lightly on his chest to end the kiss, and the temptation.

"I think a walk would be pleasant."

"Then we'll walk."

He wanted more. Phillip told himself he should have known that a few tastes of her would stir up the need. But he hadn't expected that need to be quite so sharp, quite so edgy. Maybe part of it was sheer ego, he mused as he took her hand to walk with her along the quiet waterfront. Her response had been so cool and controlled. It made him wonder what it would be like to peel that intellect away, layer by layer, and find the woman beneath. To work his way down to pure emotion and instinct.

He nearly laughed at himself. Ego, indeed. For all he knew, that formal, slightly distant response was precisely all that Dr. Sybill Griffin intended to give him.

If so, that made her a challenge he was going to have a very difficult time resisting.

"I see why Shiney's is a popular spot." She slanted him a smiling look. "It's barely nine-thirty and the shops are closed, the boats are moored. A few people strolling along, but for the most part everything here is tucked in for the night."

"It's a little livelier during the summer. Not much, but a little. It's cooling off. Are you warm enough?"

"Mmm. Plenty. It's a lovely breeze." She stopped to look out at the swaying masts of boats. "Do you keep your boat here?"

"No, we have a dock at home. That's Ethan's skipjack."

"Where?"

"It's the only skipjack in St. Chris. There are only a couple of dozen left on the Bay. There." He gestured. "The single mast."

To her untrained eye, one sailboat looked very much the same as the next. Size varied, of course, and gloss, but essentially they were all boats. "What's a skipjack?"

"It evolved from the flat-bottomed bay-crabbing skiffs." He drew her closer as he spoke. "They were enlarged, designed with a V-shaped hull. Had to be easily and inexpensively built."

"So they go out crabbing in them."

"No, mostly the watermen use motor-powered workboats for crabbing.

The skipjack is for oysters. Back in the early 1800s they passed a law in Maryland that allowed only sail-powered vessels to dredge for oysters."

"Conservation?"

"Exactly. The skipjack came out of that, and it still survives. But there aren't many of them. There aren't many oysters either."

"Does your brother still use it?"

"Yeah. It's miserable, cold, hard, frustrating work."

"You sound like the voice of experience."

"I've put in some time on her." He stopped near the bow and slipped an arm around Sybill's waist. "Sailing out in February, with that wind cutting through you, bouncing on the high chop of a winter storm . . . all in all, I'd rather be in Baltimore."

She chuckled, studying the boat. It looked ancient and rough, like something out of an earlier time. "Without having set foot on it, I'm going to agree with you. So why were you bouncing on the high chop of a winter storm instead of in Baltimore?"

"Beats the hell out of me."

"I take it this isn't the boat you invited me out on tomorrow."

"No. That one's a tidy little pleasure sloop. Do you swim?"

She arched an eyebrow. "Is that a statement on your sailing abilities?"

"No, it's a suggestion. The water's cool, but not so cold you couldn't take a dip if you like."

"I didn't bring a bathing suit with me."

"And your point is?"

She laughed and started walking again. "I think a sail's enough for one day. I've got some work I want to finish up tonight. I enjoyed dinner."

"So did I. I'll walk you to your hotel."

"There's no need. It's just around the corner."

"Nonetheless."

She didn't argue. She had no intention of allowing him to walk her to her door, or to talk his way into her suite. All in all, she felt she was handling him, and a difficult, confusing situation, very well. An early night, she mused, would give her time to sort out her thoughts and feelings before she saw him again the next day.

And since the boat was docked at his home, the odds were good that she would see Seth again, too.

"I'll come down in the morning," she began as she stopped a few feet from the lobby entrance. "Ten or so?"

"Fine."

"Is there anything I should bring? Besides Dramamine?"

He shot her a grin. "I'll take care of it. Sleep well."

"You, too."

She prepared herself for the easy and expected good-night kiss. His lips were soft, undemanding. Pleased with both of them, she relaxed, started to back away.

Then his hand cupped the back of her neck firmly, his head changed angles, and for one staggering moment, the kiss went hot and wild and threatening. The hand she'd laid on his shoulder curled into a fist, gripping his jacket, hanging on for balance as her feet all but swept out from under her. Her mind went blank as her pulse leapt to roar in her spinning head.

Someone moaned, low and deep and long.

It lasted only seconds, but it was as shocking and burning as a brand. He saw the stunned arousal in her eyes when they opened and stared into his. And he felt that basic need claw to a new level inside him.

Not a cool, controlled, and distant response this time, he decided. One layer down, he mused, and skimmed his thumb along her jawline.

"I'll see you in the morning."

"Yes—good night." She recovered quickly and sent him a smile before turning. But she pressed an unsteady hand to her jittery stomach as she slipped into the lobby.

She'd miscalculated that one, she admitted, fighting to take slow, even breaths as she walked to the elevator. He wasn't as smooth, polished, and harmless as he appeared on the surface.

There was something much more primitive and much more dangerous inside that attractive package than she'd realized.

And whatever it was, she found it entirely too compelling for her own good.

Six

It was like riding a bike. Or sex, Phillip mused as he tacked, threading through the light traffic on the Bay toward an available slip on the waterfront. It had been a while since he'd done any solo sailing, but he hadn't forgotten how. If anything, he'd forgotten how much he enjoyed being out on the water on a breezy Sunday morning, with the sun warm and the water blue and the wicked screams of gulls echoing on the air.

He was going to have to start finding time for simple pleasures again. Since this was the first full day he'd taken off in more than two months, he intended to make the most of it.

He certainly intended to make the most of a few golden hours on the Bay with the intriguing Dr. Griffin.

He looked over at the hotel, idly trying to calculate which window might be hers. From what she'd told him, he knew it faced the water, giving her a view of the life that pulsed there and enough distance for her research.

Then he saw her, standing on a tiny balcony, her glossy, mink-colored hair sleeked back and haloed in the sunlight, her face aloof and unreadable from so far away.

Not so aloof close up, he thought, replaying their last sizzle of a kiss in his mind. No, there'd been nothing aloof in that long, throaty moan, nothing distant in that quick, hard tremble her body had made against his. That instinctive, involuntary signal of blood calling to blood.

Her eyes, that water-clear blue, hadn't been cool; nor had they been intriguingly remote when he'd lifted his mouth from hers and looked into them. Instead, they'd been just a little clouded, just a little confused. And all the more intriguing.

He hadn't quite been able to get her taste out of his system, not on the drive home, not through the night, not now, seeing her again. And knowing she stood and watched him.

What, he wondered, do you observe, Dr. Griffin? And what do you intend to do about it?

Phillip flashed her a quick smile, snapped her a salute to let her know he'd seen her. Then he shifted his attention away from her and maneuvered into dock.

His brows lifted in surprise as he saw Seth standing on dock waiting to secure the lines. "What're you doing here?"

Expertly, Seth looped the bow line over the post. "Playing errand boy again." There was a hint of disgust in the tone, but Seth had to work to put it there. "They sent me down from the boatyard. Donuts."

"Yeah?" Phillip stepped nimbly onto the dock. "Artery cloggers."

"Real people don't eat tree bark for breakfast," Seth sneered. "Just you."

"And I'll still be strong and good-looking when you're a wheezing old man."

"Maybe, but I'll have more fun."

Phillip tugged Seth's ball cap off, batted him lightly with it. "Depends, pal, on your definition of fun."

"I guess yours is poking at city girls."

"That's one of them. Another is hounding you over your homework. You finish *Johnny Tremaine* for your book report?"

"Yeah, yeah, yeah." Seth rolled his eyes. "Man, don't you ever take a day off?"

"What, when my life is devoted to you?" He grinned at Seth's snort. "So, what'd you think of it?"

"It was okay." Then he jerked a shoulder, a purely Quinn movement. "It was pretty good."

"We'll put together some notes for your oral report later tonight."

"Sunday night's my favorite night of the week," Seth said. "It means you'll be gone for four days."

"Come on, you know you miss me."

"Shit."

"You count the hours until I come home."

Seth barely suppressed a giggle. "Like hell." Then he did giggle as Phillip snagged him around the waist for a tussle.

Sybill heard the bright, happy sound as she walked toward them. She saw the wide grin on Seth's face. Her heart did a long, slow roll in her chest. What was she doing here? she asked herself. What did she hope to accomplish?

And how could she walk away until she found out?

"Good morning."

Distracted by her voice, Phillip glanced over, dropping his guard just long enough for Seth's elbow to slip through and into his gut. He grunted, wrapped an arm around Seth's neck, and leaned down. "I'll have to beat you up later," he said in a stage whisper. "When there aren't any witnesses."

"You wish." Flushed with pleasure, Seth settled his cap securely on his head and feigned disinterest. "Some of us gotta work today."

"And some of us don't."

"I thought you were going with us," Sybill said to Seth. "Would you like to?"

"I'm just a slave around here." Seth looked longingly at the boat, then shrugged. "We got a hull to build. Besides, Pretty Boy here will probably capsize her."

"Smart-ass." Phillip made a grab, but Seth danced laughingly out of reach.

"Hope she can swim!" he called out, then raced away.

When Phillip looked back at Sybill, she was gnawing her bottom lip. "I'm not going to capsize her."

"Well . . ." Sybill glanced toward the boat. It seemed awfully small and fragile. "I can swim, so I suppose it's all right."

"Christ, kid comes along and completely smears my rep. I've been sailing longer than the brat's been alive."

"Don't be angry with him."

"Huh?"

"Please, don't be angry with him. I'm sure he was just joking with you. He didn't mean to be disrespectful."

Phillip just stared at her. She'd actually gone pale, and her hand was nervously twisting the thin gold chain she wore around her neck. There was active and acute distress in her voice. "Sybill, I'm not mad at him. We were just fooling around. Relax." Baffled, he rubbed his knuckles lightly over her jaw. "Razzing each other is just our clever male way of showing affection."

"Oh." She wasn't certain whether to be embarrassed or relieved. "I guess that shows I didn't have any brothers."

"It would have been their job to make your life a living hell." He leaned down, touched her lips lightly with his. "It's traditional."

He stepped onto the boat, held out a hand. After the briefest of hesitations, she let him take hers.

"Welcome aboard."

The deck rocked under her feet. She did her best to ignore it. "Thank you. Do I have an assignment?"

"For now, sit, relax, and enjoy."

"I should be able to manage that."

At least she hoped so. She sat on one of the padded benches, gripping it tightly as he stepped out again to release the lines. It would be fine, she assured herself. It would be fun.

Hadn't she watched him sail into port, or dock, or whatever you would call it? He'd seemed very competent. Even a bit cocky, she decided, the way he'd scanned the hotel until he saw her standing out on her balcony.

There had been something foolishly romantic about that, she thought now. The way he had sailed across the sun-splashed water, searching for her, finding her. Then the quick smile and wave. If her pulse had bumped a little, it was an understandable and human response.

He made such a picture, after all. The faded jeans, the crisp T-shirt tucked into them as blindingly white as the sails, that gilded hair, and the warmly tanned, sleekly muscled arms. What woman wouldn't feel a bump at the prospect of spending a few hours alone with a man who looked like Phillip Quinn?

And kissed like Phillip Quinn.

Though she had promised herself she wouldn't dwell on that particular talent of his. He'd shown her just a little too much of that skill the night before.

Now with the sails lowered, he motored gently away from the dock. She found some security in the low rumble of the engine. Not that different from a car, really, she supposed. This vehicle just happened to drive over water.

Nor were they really alone. Her hands relaxed their death grip on the bench as she watched other boats skim and glide. She saw a boy who was surely no older than Seth, tucked into a tiny boat with a triangular red sail. If it was an activity considered safe for children, surely she could handle it.

"Hoisting sails."

She turned her head, smiled absently at Phillip. "What did you say?"

"Watch."

He moved gracefully over the deck, working the lines. Then suddenly the sails rose, snapped in the wind, filled with it. Her heartbeat skipped and scrambled, and her fingers tightened once more on the bench.

No, she'd been wrong, she saw that now. This was nothing at all like a car. It was primitive and beautiful and thrilling. The boat no longer seemed small, or fragile, but powerful, just a little dangerous. And breathtaking.

Very much like the man who captained her.

"It's lovely from down here." Though she kept her hands firmly locked on the bench, she smiled over at Phillip. "They always look pretty when I watch from the window. But it's lovely to see the sails from below."

"You're sitting," Phillip commented as he took the wheel. "And you're enjoying, but I don't think you're relaxing."

"Not yet. I might get there." She turned her face to the wind. It tugged and teased at her hair, trying to free it from the band. "Where are we going?"

"Nowhere in particular."

Her smile warmed and widened. "I rarely have a chance to go there."

She hadn't smiled at him just that way before, Phillip thought. Without thinking, without weighing. He doubted she realized how that easy smile transformed her coolly beautiful face into something softer, more approachable. Wanting to touch her, he held out a hand.

"Come on up here, check out the view."

Her smile faded. "Stand up?"

"Yeah. There's no chop today. It's a smooth ride."

"Stand up," she repeated, giving each word separate weight. "And walk over there. On the boat."

"Two steps." He couldn't stop the grin. "You don't want to just be a bystander, do you?"

"Actually, yes." Her eyes widened when he stepped away from the wheel. "No, don't." She stifled a scream when he laughed and snagged her hand. Before she could dig in, he'd pulled her to her feet. Off balance, she fell against him and held on in terror and defense.

"Couldn't have planned that one better," he murmured and holding her, stepped back to the wheel. "I like getting close enough to smell you. A man has to get almost right here . . ." He turned his head, nuzzled his lips on her throat.

"Stop." Thrills and fears raced through her. "Pay attention."

"Oh, believe me"—his teeth caught and nipped her earlobe—"I am."

"To the boat. Pay attention to the boat."

"Oh, yeah." But he kept one arm snug around her waist. "Look out over the bow, to port. The left," he explained. "That little swash there goes back into the marsh. You'll see herons and wild turkey."

"Where?"

"Sometimes you have to go in to find them. But you can catch sight of them now and then, the herons standing like a sculpture in the high grass or rising up from it, the turkeys bobbling their way out of the trees."

She wanted to see, she discovered. She hoped she would see.

"In another month, we'll have geese flying over. From their view this area wouldn't look much different from the Everglades."

Her heart was still jumping, but she inhaled slowly, exhaled deliberately. "Why?"

"The marshland. It's too far from the beaches for the developers to be very interested. It's largely undisturbed. Just one of the Bay's assets, one of the factors that makes it an estuary. A finer one for watermen than the fjords of Norway."

She inhaled again, exhaled. "Why?"

"The shallows, for one thing. A good estuary needs shallows so the sun can nourish aquatic plants, plankton. And the marshlands, for another. They add the tidal creeks, the coves. There." He brushed a kiss over the crown on her head. "Now you're relaxing."

With some surprise, she realized she wasn't simply relaxing. She'd already gotten there. "So, you were appealing to the scientist."

"Took your mind off your nerves."

"Yes, it did." Odd, she thought, that he would know so quickly which switch to throw. "I don't think I have my sea legs yet, but it is a pretty view. Still so green." She watched the passing of big, leafy trees, the deep pockets of shadows in the marsh. They sailed by markers topped with huge, scruffy nests. "What birds build those?"

"Osprey. Now they're experts at those disassociation techniques. You can sail right by one when it's sitting on its nest, and it'll look right through you."

"Survival instinct," she murmured. She'd like to see that, too. An osprey roosting on that rough circular nest, ignoring the humans.

"See those orange buoys? Crab pots. The workboat putting down that gut? He's going to check his pots, rebait. Over there, to starboard." He nudged her head to the right. "The little outboard. Looks to me like they're hoping to catch some rockfish for Sunday dinner."

"It's a busy place," she commented. "I didn't realize there was so much going on."

"On and under the water."

He adjusted the sails and, heeling in, skimmed around a thick line of trees leaning out from shore. As they cleared the trees, a narrow dock came into view. Behind it was a sloping lawn, flower beds just starting to lose their summer brilliance. The house was simple, white with blue trim. A rocker sat on the wide covered porch, and bronze-toned mums speared out of an old crockery tub.

Sybill could hear the light, drifting notes of music floating through the open windows. Chopin, she realized after a moment.

"It's charming." She angled her head, shifting slightly to keep the house in view. "All it needs is a dog, a couple of kids tossing a ball, and a tire swing."

"We were too old for tire swings, but we always had the dog. That's our house," he told her, absently running his hand down her long, smooth ponytail.

"Yours?" She strained, wanting to see more. Where Seth lived, she thought, struck by dozens of conflicting emotions.

"We spent plenty of time tossing balls, or each other, in the backyard. We'll come back later and you can meet the rest of the family."

She closed her eyes and squashed the guilt. "I'd like that."

He had a place in mind. The quiet cove with its lapping water and dappled shade was a perfect spot for a romantic picnic. He dropped anchor where the eelgrass gleamed wetly, and the sky canopied in unbroken autumnal blue overhead.

"Obviously my research on this area was lacking."

"Oh?" Phillip opened a large cooler and retrieved a bottle of wine.

"It's full of surprises."

"Pleasant ones, I hope."

"Very pleasant ones." She smiled, raising a brow at the label on the wine he opened. "Very pleasant."

"You struck me as a woman who'd appreciate a fine dry Sancerre."

"You're very astute."

"Indeed I am." From a wicker hamper he took two wineglasses and poured. "To pleasant surprises," he said and tapped his glass to hers.

"Are there more?"

He took her hand, kissed her fingers. "We've barely started." Setting his glass aside, he unfolded a white cloth and spread it on the deck. "Your table's ready."

"Ah." Enjoying herself, she sat, shaded her eyes against the sun, and smiled up at him. "What's today's special?"

"Some rather nice paté to stir the appetite." To demonstrate, he opened a small container and a box of stoned wheat crackers. He spread one for her and held it to her lips.

"Mmm." She nodded after the first bite. "Very nice."

"To be followed by crab salad à la Quinn."

"Sounds intriguing. And did you make it with your own two hands?"

"I did." He grinned at her. "I'm a hell of a cook."

"The man cooks, has excellent taste in wine, appreciates ambience, and wears his Levi's very well." She bit into the paté again, relaxed now, the ground familiar and easily negotiated. "You appear to be quite a catch, Mr. Quinn."

"I am indeed, Dr. Griffin."

She laughed into her wine. "And how often have you brought some lucky woman to this spot for crab salad à la Quinn?"

"Actually, I haven't been here with a woman since the summer of my sophomore year in college. Then it was a fairly decent Chablis, chilled shrimp, and Marianne Teasdale."

"I suppose I should be flattered."

"I don't know. Marianne was pretty hot." He flashed that killer grin again. "But being callow and shortsighted, I threw her over for a pre-med student with a sexy lisp and big brown eyes."

"Lisps do weaken a man. Did Marianne recover?"

"Enough to marry a plumber from Princess Anne and bear him two children. But, of course, we know she secretly yearns for me."

Laughing, Sybill spread a cracker for him. "I like you."

"I like you, too." He caught her wrist, holding it as he nibbled at the cracker she held. "And you don't even lisp."

When his fingers continued to nibble, at the tips of her fingers now, it wasn't quite as easy to breathe. "You're very smooth," she murmured.

"You're very lovely."

"Thank you. What I should say," she continued, and eased her hand out of his, "is that while you're very smooth, and very attractive, and I'm enjoying spending time with you, I don't intend to be seduced."

"You know what they say about intentions."

"I tend to hold to mine. And while I do enjoy your company, I also recognize your type." She smiled again and gestured with her glass. "A hundred years ago, the word 'rogue' would have come to mind."

He considered a moment. "That didn't sound like an insult."

"It wasn't meant to be. Rogues are invariably charming and very rarely serious."

"I have to object there. There are some issues that I'm very serious about."

"Let's try this." She peeked in the cooler and took out another container. "Have you ever been married?"

"No."

"Engaged?" she asked as she opened the lid and discovered a beautifully prepared crab salad.

"No."

"Have you ever lived with a woman for a consecutive period of six months or more?"

With a shrug, he took plates out of the hamper, passed her a pale-blue linen napkin. "No."

"So, we can theorize that one of the issues about which you are not serious is relationships."

"Or we can theorize that I have yet to meet the woman I want a serious relationship with."

"We could. However . . ." She narrowed her eyes at his face as he scooped salad onto the plates. "You're what, thirty?"

"One." He added a thick slice of French bread to each plate.

"Thirty-one. Typically, by the age of thirty a man in this culture would have experienced at least one serious, long-term, monogamous relationship."

"I wouldn't care to be typical. Olives?"

"Yes, thanks. Typical is not necessarily an unattractive trait. Nor is conformity. Everyone conforms. Even those who consider themselves the rebels of society conform to certain codes and standards."

Enjoying her, he tilted his head. "Is that so, Dr. Griffin?"

"Quite so. Gang members in the inner city have internal rules, codes, standards. Colors," she added, selecting an olive from her plate. "In that way they don't differ much from members of the city council."

"You had to be there," Phillip mumbled.

"Excuse me?"

"Nothing. What about serial killers?"

"They follow patterns." Enjoying herself, she tore a chunk off her slice of bread. "The FBI studies them, catalogs them, profiles them. Society wouldn't term them standards certainly, but in the strictest sense of the word, that's precisely what they are."

Damned if she didn't have a point, he decided. And found himself only more fascinated. "So you, the observer, size people up by noting what rules, codes, patterns they follow."

"More or less. People aren't so very difficult to understand, if you pay attention."

"What about those surprises?"

She smiled, appreciating the question as much as she appreciated that he would think to ask it. Most laymen she'd socialized with weren't really interested in her work. "They're factored in. There's always margin for error, and for adjustments. This is wonderful salad." She sampled another bite. "And the surprise, a pleasant one, is that you would have gone to the trouble to prepare it."

"Don't you find that people are usually willing to go to some trouble for someone they care for?" When she only blinked at him, he tilted his head. "Well, well, that threw you off."

"You barely know me." She picked up her wine, a purely defensive gesture. "There's a difference between being attracted to and caring for. The latter takes more time."

"Some of us move fast." He enjoyed seeing her flustered. It would be, he decided, a rare event. Taking advantage of it, he slid closer. "I do."

"So I've already observed. However—"

"However. I like hearing you laugh. I like feeling you tremble just slightly when I kiss you. I like hearing your voice slide into that didactic tone when you expand on a theory."

At the last comment she frowned. "I'm not didactic."

"Charmingly," he murmured, skimming his lips over her temple. "And I like seeing your eyes in that moment when I start to confuse you. Therefore, I believe I've crossed over into the care-for stage. So let's try your earlier hypothesis out on you and see where that leaves us. Have you ever been married?"

His mouth was cruising just under her ear, making it very difficult to think clearly. "No. Well, not really."

He paused, leaned back, narrowed his eyes. "No or not really?"

"It was an impulse, an error in judgment. It was less than six months. It didn't count." Her brain was fogged, she decided, trying to inch away for some breathing room. He only scooted her back.

"You were married?"

"Only technically. It didn't . . ." She turned her head to make her point, and his mouth was there. Right there to meet hers, to urge her lips to part and warm and soften.

It was like sliding under a slow-moving wave, being taken down into silky, shimmering water. Everything inside her went fluid. A surprise, she would realize later, that she'd neglected to factor into this particular pattern.

"It didn't count," she managed as her head fell back, as his lips trailed smoothly down her throat.

"Okay."

If he'd taken her by surprise, she'd done exactly the same to him. At her sudden and utter surrender to the moment, his need churned to the surface, thrashing there. He had to touch her, to fill his hands with her, to mold those pretty curves through the thin, crisp cotton of her blouse.

He had to taste her, deeper now, while those little hums of shock and pleasure sounded in her throat. As he did, as he touched and as he tasted, her arms came around him, her hands sliding into his hair, her body turning to fit itself against him.

He felt her heart thud in time with his own.

Panic punched through pleasure when she felt him tug at the buttons of her blouse. "No." Her own fingers shook as she covered his. "It's too fast." She squeezed her eyes shut, struggling to find her control, her sense, her purpose. "I'm sorry. I don't go this fast. I can't."

It wasn't easy to check the urge to ignore the rules, to simply press her under him on the deck until she was pliant and willing again. He put his tense fingers under her chin and lifted her face to his. No, it wasn't easy, he thought again as he saw both desire and denial in her eyes. But it was necessary.

"Okay. No rush." He rubbed his thumb over her bottom lip. "Tell me about the one that didn't count."

Her thoughts had scattered to the edges of her mind. She couldn't begin to draw them together while he was looking at her with those tawny eyes. "What?"

"The husband."

"Oh." She looked away, concentrated on her breathing.

"What are you doing?"

"Relaxation technique."

Humor danced back and made him grin at her. "Does it work?"

"Eventually."

"Cool." He shifted until they were hip to hip and timed his breathing to hers. "So this guy you were technically married to . . ."

"It was in college, at Harvard. He was a chemistry major." Eyes shut, she ordered her toes to relax, then her arches, her ankles. "We were barely twenty and just lost our heads for a short time."

"Eloped."

"Yes. We didn't even live together, because we were in different dorms. So it wasn't really a marriage. It was weeks before we told our families, and then, naturally, there were several difficult scenes."

"Why?"

"Because . . ." She blinked her eyes open, found the sun dazzling. Something plopped in the water behind her, then there was only the lap of it, kissing the hull. "We weren't suited, we had no feasible plans. We were too young. The divorce was very quiet and quick and civilized."

"Did you love him?"

"I was twenty." Her relaxation level was reaching her shoulders. "Of course I thought I did. Love has little complexity at that age."

"So spoken from the advanced age of what twenty-seven, twenty-eight?"

"Twenty-nine and counting." She let out a last long breath. Satisfied and steady, she turned to look at him again. "I haven't thought of Rob in years. He was a very nice boy. I hope he's happy."

"And that's it for you?"

"It has to be."

He nodded, but found her story strangely sad. "Then I have to say, Dr. Griffin, that using your own scale, you don't take relationships seriously."

She opened her mouth to protest, then wisely, shut it again. Casually, she picked up the wine bottle and topped off both glasses. "You may be right. I'll have to give that some thought."

SEVEN

Seth didn't mind running herd on Aubrey. She was kind of his niece now that Ethan and Grace were married. Being an uncle made him feel adult and responsible. Besides, all she really wanted to do was race around the yard. Every time he threw a ball or a stick for one of the dogs, she went into gales of laughter. A guy couldn't help but get a kick out of it.

She was pretty cute, too, with her curly gold hair and her big green eyes that looked amazed at everything he did. Spending an hour or two on a Sunday entertaining her wasn't a bad deal.

He hadn't forgotten where he had been a year ago. There'd been no big backyard that fell off into the water, no woods to explore, no dogs to wrestle with, no little girl who looked at him like he was Fox Mulder, all the Power Rangers and Superman rolled into one.

Instead, there'd been grungy rooms three flights up from the street. And those streets had been a dark carnival at night, a place where everything had its price. Sex, drugs, weapons, misery.

He'd learned that no matter what went on in those grungy rooms, he shouldn't go out after dark.

There'd been no one to care if he was clean or fed, if he was sick or scared. He'd never felt like a hero there, or even very much like a kid. He'd felt like a thing, and he'd learned quickly that things are often hunted.

Gloria had ridden all the rides in that carnival, again and again. She'd brought the freaks and the hustlers into those rooms, selling herself to whoever would pay the price of her next spin.

A year ago Seth hadn't believed his life would ever be any different. Then Ray came and took him to the house by the water. Ray showed him a different world and promised he would never have to go back to the old one.

Ray had died, but he had kept his promise all the same. Now Seth could stand in the big backyard with water lapping at its edges and throw balls and sticks for the dogs to chase while an angel-faced toddler laughed.

"Seth, let me! Let me!" Aubrey danced on her sturdy little legs, holding up both hands for the mangled ball.

"Okay, you throw it."

He grinned while she screwed up her face with concentration and effort. The ball bounced inches away from the toes of her bright-red sneakers.
Simon snapped it up, making her squeal with delight, then politely offered
it back.

"Oooh, good doggie." Aubrey batted the patient Simon on either side of
his jaw. Angling for attention, Foolish nudged his way in, shoved her down
on her butt. She rewarded him with a fierce hug. "Now you," she ordered
Seth. "You do it."

Obliging her, Seth winged the ball. He laughed as the dogs raced after it,
bumping their bodies like two football players rushing downfield. They
crashed into the woods, sending a pair of birds squawking skyward.

At that moment, with Aubrey bouncing with giggles, the dogs barking,
the fresh September air on his cheeks, Seth was completely happy. A part of
his mind focused on it, snatched at it to keep. The angle of the sun, the brilliance of light on the water, the creamy sound of Otis Redding drifting
through the kitchen window, the bitchy complaints of the birds, and the rich
salty scent of the bay.

He was home.

Then the putt of a motor caught his attention. When he turned he saw
the family sloop angling in toward the dock. At the wheel, Phillip raised a
hand in greeting. Even as Seth returned the wave, his gaze shifted to the
woman standing beside Phillip. It felt as if something brushed over the nape
of his neck, light and cagey as the legs of a spider. Absently he rubbed at it,
shrugged his shoulders, then took Aubrey firmly by the hand.

"Remember, you have to stay in the middle of the dock."

She gazed up at him adoringly. "Okay. I will. Mama says never, never go
by the water by myself."

"That's right." He stepped onto the dock with her and waited for Phillip
to come alongside. It was the woman who, awkwardly, tossed him the bow
line. Sybill something, he thought. For a moment, as she balanced herself, as
their eyes met, he felt that sly tickle on the nape of his neck again.

Then the dogs were bounding onto the dock and Aubrey was laughing
again.

"Hey, Angel Baby." Phillip helped Sybill step onto the dock, then
winked down at Aubrey.

"Up," she demanded.

"You bet." He swung her onto his hip and planted a smacking kiss on
her cheek. "When are you going to grow up and marry me?"

"Tomorrow!"

"That's what you always say. This is Sybill. Sybill, meet Aubrey, my best girl."

"She's pretty," Aubrey stated and flashed her dimples.

"Thank you. So are you." As the dogs bumped her legs, Sybill jolted and took a step back. Phillip shot out a hand to grab her arm before she backed her way off the dock and into the water.

"Steady there. Seth, call off the dogs. Sybill's a little uneasy around them."

"They won't hurt you," Seth said with a shake of his head that warned Sybill she'd just dropped several notches in his estimation. But he snagged both dogs by the collar, holding them back until she could ease by.

"Everybody inside?" Phillip asked Seth.

"Yeah, just hanging until dinner. Grace brought over a monster chocolate cake. Cam sweet-talked Anna into making lasagna."

"God bless him. My sister-in-law's lasagna is a work of art," he told Sybill.

"Speaking of art, I wanted to tell you again, Seth, how much I liked the sketches you've done for the boatyard. They're very good."

He shrugged his shoulders, then bent down to scoop up two sticks to toss and distract the dogs. "I just draw sometimes."

"Me, too." She knew it was foolish, but Sybill felt her cheeks go warm at the way Seth studied her, measured and judged. "It's something I like to do in my spare time," she went on. "I find it relaxing and satisfying."

"Yeah, I guess."

"Maybe you'll show me more of your work sometime."

"If you want." He pushed open the door to the kitchen and headed straight to the refrigerator. A telling sign, Sybill mused. He was at home here.

She took a quick scan of the room, filing impressions. There was a pot simmering on what seemed to be an ancient stove. The scent was impossibly aromatic. Several small clay pots lined the windowsill over the sink. Fresh herbs thrived in them.

The counters were clean, if a bit worn. A pile of papers was stacked on the end beneath a wall phone and anchored with a set of keys. A shallow bowl was centered on the table and filled with glossy red and green apples. A mug of coffee, half full, stood in front of a chair under which someone had kicked off shoes.

"Goddamn it! That ump ought to be shot in the head. That pitch was a mile high."

Sybill arched an eyebrow at the furious male voice from the next room.

Phillip merely smiled and jiggled Aubrey on his hip. "Ball game. Cam's taking this year's pennant race personally."

"The game! I forgot." Seth slammed the refrigerator door and raced out of the kitchen. "What's the score, what inning is it, who's up?"

"Three to two, A's, bottom of the sixth, two outs, a man on second. Now sit down and shut up."

"Very personally," Phillip added, then set Aubrey down when she wiggled.

"Baseball often becomes a personal challenge between the audience and the opposing team. Especially," Sybill added with a sober nod, "during the September pennant race."

"You like baseball?"

"What's not to like?" she said and laughed. "It's a fascinating study of men, of teamwork, of battle. Speed, cunning, finesse, and always pitcher against batter. In the end it all comes down to style, endurance. And math."

"We're going to have to take in a game at Camden Yards," he decided. "I'd just love to hear your play-by-play technique. Can I get you anything?"

"No, I'm fine." More shouts, more cursing burst out of the living room. "But I think it might be dangerous to leave this room as long as your brother's team is down a run."

"You're perceptive." Phillip reached out to curve his hand over her cheek. "So, why don't we stay right here and—"

"Way to go, Cal!" Cam shouted from the living room. "That son of a bitch is amazing."

"Shit." Seth's voice was cocky and smug. "No stinking California outfielder's going to blow one by Ripken."

Phillip let out a sigh. "Or maybe we should head out back and take a walk for a few innings."

"Seth, I believe we've discussed acceptable word usage in this house."

"Anna," Phillip murmured. "Coming downstairs to lay down the law."

"Cameron, you're supposed to be an adult."

"It's baseball, sugar."

"If the pair of you don't watch your language, the TV goes off."

"She's very strict," Phillip informed Sybill. "We're all terrified of her."

"Really?" Sybill considered as she glanced toward the living room.

She heard another voice, lower, softer, then Aubrey's firm response. "No, Mama, please. I want Seth."

"She's okay, Grace. She can stay with me."

The easy, absent tone of Seth's voice had Sybill considering. "It's unusual, I'd think, for a boy Seth's age to be so patient with a toddler."

Phillip shrugged his shoulders and walked to the stove to start a pot of fresh coffee. "They hit it off right away. Aubrey adores him. That has to boost the kid's ego, and he's really good with her."

He turned, smiling as two women walked into the room. "Ah, the ones who got away. Sybill, these are the women my brothers stole from me. Anna, Grace, Dr. Sybill Griffin."

"He only wanted us to cook for him," Anna said with a laugh and held out a hand. "It's nice to meet you. I've read your books. I think they're brilliant."

Taken by surprise, both by the statement and the lush and outrageous beauty of Anna Spinelli Quinn, Sybill nearly fumbled. "Thank you. I appreciate you tolerating a Sunday-evening intrusion."

"It's no intrusion. We're delighted."

And, Anna thought, incredibly curious. In the seven months she'd known Phillip, this was the first woman he'd brought home to Sunday dinner.

"Phillip, go watch baseball." She waved him toward the doorway with the back of her hand. "Grace and Sybill and I can get acquainted."

"She's bossy, too," Phillip warned Sybill. "Just yell if you need help, and I'll come rescue you." He gave her a hard, firm kiss on the mouth before she could think to evade it, then deserted her.

Anna gave a long, interested hum, then smiled brightly. "Let's have some wine."

Grace pulled out a chair. "Phillip said you were going to stay in St. Chris a while and write a book about it."

"Something like that." Sybill took a deep breath. They were just women, after all. A stunning dark-eyed brunette and a cool lovely blonde. There was no need to be nervous. "Actually, I plan to write about the culture and traditions and social landscapes of small towns and rural communities."

"We have both on the Shore."

"So I see. You and Ethan are recently married."

Grace's smile warmed, and her gaze shifted to the gold band on her finger. "Just last month."

"And you grew up here, together."

"I was born here. Ethan moved here when he was about twelve."

"Are you from the area, too?" she asked Anna, more comfortable in the role of interviewer.

"No, I'm from Pittsburgh. I moved to D.C., wandered down to Princess Anne. I work for Social Services, as a caseworker. That's one of the reasons I was so interested in your books." She set a glass of deep-red wine in front of Sybill.

"Oh, yes, you're Seth's caseworker. Phillip told me a little about the situation."

"Mmm," was Anna's only comment as she turned to take a bib apron from a hook. "Did you enjoy your sail?"

So, Sybill realized, discussing Seth with outsiders was off-limits. She ordered herself to accept that, for now. "Yes, very much. More than I'd expected to. I can't believe I've gone so long without trying it."

"I had my first sail a few months ago." Anna set a huge pot of water on the stove to boil. "Grace has been sailing all her life."

"Do you work here, in St. Christopher's?"

"Yes, I clean houses."

"Including this one, thank the Lord," Anna put in. "I was telling Grace she ought to start a company. Maids Are Us or something." When Grace laughed, Anna shook her head. "I'm serious. It would be a terrific service, to the working woman in particular. You could even do commercial buildings. If you trained two or three people, word of mouth alone would get it going."

"You think bigger than I do. I don't know how to run a business."

"I bet you do. Your family's been running the crab house for generations."

"Crab house?" Sybill interrupted.

"Picking, packing, shipping." Grace lifted a hand. "Odds are, if you've had crab while you've been here, it came to you via my father's company. But I've never been involved in the business end."

"That doesn't mean you couldn't handle your own business." Anna took a chunk of mozzarella out of the refrigerator and began to grate it. "A lot of people out there are more than willing to pay for good, reliable, and trustworthy domestic services. They don't want to spent what little free time they might have cleaning the house, cooking meals, separating laundry. Traditional roles are shifting—don't you agree, Sybill? Women can't spend every spare second of their time in the kitchen."

"Well, I would agree, but . . . well, here you are."

Anna stopped, blinked, then threw back her head and laughed. She looked, Sybill thought, like a woman who should be dancing around a campfire to the sound of violins rather than cozily grating cheese in a fragrant kitchen.

"You're right, absolutely." Still chuckling, Anna shook her head. "Here I am, while my man lounges in front of the TV, deaf and blind to anything but the game. And this is often the scene on Sundays around here. I don't mind. I love to cook."

"Really?"

Hearing the suspicion in Sybill's voice, Anna laughed again. "Really. I find it satisfying, but not when I have to rush in from work and toss something together. That's why we take turns around here. Mondays are leftovers from whatever I've cooked Sunday. Tuesdays we all suffer through whatever Cam cooks, because he's simply dreadful in the kitchen. Wednesdays we do takeout, Thursdays I cook, Fridays Phillip cooks, and Saturdays are up for grabs. It's a very workable system when it works."

"Anna's planning on having Seth take over as chef on Wednesdays within the year."

"At his age?"

Anna shook back her hair. "He'll be eleven in a couple of weeks. By the time I was his age, I could make a killer red sauce. The time and effort it takes to teach him and to convince him he's still a male if he knows how to make a meal will be worth it in the end. And," she added, sliding wide, flat noodles into the boiling water, "if I use the fact that he can outdo Cam in any area, he'll be an A student."

"They don't get along."

"They're wonderful together." Anna tilted her head as the living room exploded with shouts, cheers, stomping. "And Seth likes nothing more than to impress his big brother. Which means, of course, they argue and prod each other constantly." She smiled again. "I take it you don't have any brothers."

"No. No, I don't."

"Sisters?" Grace asked and wondered why Sybill's eyes went so cool.

"One."

"I always wanted a sister." Grace smiled over at Anna. "Now I've got one."

"Grace and I were both only children." Anna squeezed Grace's shoulder as she walked by to mix her cheeses. Something in that easy, intimate gesture stirred a tug of envy inside Sybill. "Since we fell in with the Quinns, we've been making up rapidly for coming from small families. Does your sister live in New York?"

"No." Sybill's stomach clenched reflexively. "We're not terribly close. Excuse me." She pushed away from the table. "Can I use the bathroom?"

"Sure. Down the hall, first door on the left." Anna waited until Sybill walked out, then pursed her lips at Grace. "I can't decide what I think about her."

"She seems a little uncomfortable."

Anna shrugged her shoulders. "Well, I guess we'll have to wait and see, won't we?"

In the little powder room off the hall, Sybill splashed water on her face. She was hot, nervous, and vaguely sick to her stomach. She didn't understand this family, she thought. They were loud, occasionally crude, pieced together from different origins. Yet they seemed happy, at ease with each other, and very affectionate.

As she patted her face dry, she met her own eyes in the mirror. Her family had never been loud or crude. Except for those ugly moments when Gloria had pushed the limits. Just now she couldn't honestly say for certain if they had ever been happy, ever been at ease with each other. And affection had never been a priority or something that was expressed in an overt manner.

It was simply that none of them were very emotional people, she told herself. She had always been more cerebral, out of inclination, she decided, and in defense against Gloria's baffling volatility. Life was calmer if one depended on the intellect. She knew that. Believed that absolutely.

But it was her emotions that were churning now. She felt like a liar, a spy, a sneak. Reminding herself that she was doing what she was doing for the welfare of a child helped. Telling herself that the child was her own nephew and she had every right to be there, to form opinions, soothed.

Objectivity, she told herself, pressing her fingertips against her temples to smother the nagging ache. That's what would get her through until she'd gathered all the facts, all the data, and formed her opinion.

She stepped out quietly and took the few steps down the hall toward the blaring noise of the ball game. She saw Seth sprawled on the floor at Cam's feet and shouting abuse at the set across the room. Cam was gesturing with his beer and arguing the last call with Phillip. Ethan simply watched the game, with Aubrey curled in his lap, dozing despite the noise.

The room itself was homey, slightly shabby, and appeared comfortable. A piano was angled out from the corner. A vase of zinnias and dozens of small-framed snapshots crowded its polished surface. A half empty bowl of potato chips sat at Seth's elbow. The rug was littered with crumbs, shoes, the Sunday paper, and a grubby, well-gnawed hunk of rope.

The light had faded, but no one had bothered to switch on a lamp.

She started to step back, but Phillip glanced over. Smiled. Held out a hand. She walked to him, let him draw her down to the arm of his chair. "Bottom of the ninth," he murmured. "We're up by one."

"Watch this reliever kick this guy's sorry ass." Seth kept his voice down, but it rang with glee. He didn't even flinch when Cam slapped him on the head with his own ball cap. "Oh, yeah! Struck him *out!*" He leaped up, did a victory boogie. "We are number one. Man, I'm starving." He raced off to the kitchen and soon could be heard begging for food.

"Winning ball games works up an appetite," Phillip decided, absently kissing Sybill's hand. "How's she doing in there?"

"She appeared to be on top of things."

"Let's go see if she made antipasto."

He pulled her into the kitchen, and within moments it was crowded with people. Aubrey rested her head on Ethan's shoulder and blinked like an owl. Seth stuffed his mouth with tidbits from an elaborate tray and did a play-by-play of the game.

Everyone seemed to be moving, talking, eating at the same time, Sybill thought. Phillip put another glass of wine in her hand before he was drafted to deal with the bread. Because she felt slightly less confused by him than by the others, Sybill stuck to his side as chaos reigned.

He cut thick slices of Italian bread, then doctored them with butter and garlic.

"Is it always like this?" she murmured to him.

"No." He picked up his own glass of wine, touched it lightly to hers. "Sometimes it's really loud and disorganized."

By the time he drove her back to her hotel, Sybill's head was ringing. There was so much to process. Sights, sounds, personalities, impressions. She had survived complex state dinners with less confusion than a Sunday dinner with the Quinns.

She needed time, she decided, to analyze. Once she was able to write down her thoughts, her observations, she would align them, dissect them, and begin to draw her initial conclusions.

"Tired?"

She sighed once. "A little. It was quite a day. A fascinating one." Blew out a breath. "And a fattening one. I'm definitely going to make use of the hotel's health club in the morning. I enjoyed myself," she added as he parked near the lobby entrance. "Very much."

"Good. Then you'll be willing to do it again." He climbed out, skirted the hood, then took her hand as she stepped onto the curb.

"There's no need for you to take me up. I know the way."

"I'll take you up anyway."

"I'm not going to ask you to come in."

"I'm still going to walk you to your door, Sybill."

She let it go, crossing with him to the elevators, stepping inside with him when the doors opened. "So, you'll drive to Baltimore in the morning?" She pushed the button for her floor.

"Tonight. When things are fairly settled here, I drive back Sunday nights. There's rarely any traffic, and I can get an earlier start on Mondays."

"It can't be easy for you, the commute, the demands on your time, and the tug-of-war of responsibilities."

"A lot of things aren't easy. But they're worth working for." He caressed her hair. "I don't mind putting time and effort into something I enjoy."

"Well . . ." She cleared her throat and walked out of the elevator the minute the doors opened. "I appreciate the time and effort you put into today."

"I'll be back Thursday night. I want to see you."

She slipped her key card out of her purse. "I can't be sure right now what I'll be doing at the end of the week."

He simply framed her face with his hands, moved in and covered her mouth with his. The taste of her, he thought. He couldn't seem to get enough of the taste of her. "I want to see you," he murmured against her lips.

She'd always been so good at staying in control, at distancing herself from attempts at seduction, from resisting the persuasions of physical attractions. But with him, each time she could feel herself slipping a little farther, a little deeper.

"I'm not ready for this," she heard herself say.

"Neither am I." Still, he drew her closer, held her tighter and took the kiss toward desperation. "I want you. Maybe it's a good thing we both have a few days to think about what happens next."

She looked up at him, shaken, yearning, and just a little frightened of what was happening inside her. "Yes, I think it's a very good thing." She turned, had to use both hands to shove the key card into its slot. "Drive carefully." She stepped inside, closed the door quickly, then leaned back against it until she was certain her heart wasn't going to pump its way out of her chest.

It was insane, she thought, absolutely insane to get this involved this quickly. She was honest enough with herself, scientist enough not to skew the results with incorrect data, to admit that what was happening to her where Phillip Quinn was concerned had nothing whatsoever to do with Seth.

It should be stopped. She closed her eyes and felt the pressure of his mouth still vibrating on her lips. And she was afraid it couldn't be stopped.

EIGHT

It was probably a chancy step to take. Sybill wondered if it could possibly be illegal. Loitering near St. Christopher's Middle School certainly made her feel like some sort of criminal, no matter how firmly she told herself she was doing nothing wrong.

She was simply walking on a public street in the middle of the afternoon. It wasn't as though she was stalking Seth, or planning to abduct him. She only wanted to talk to him, to see him alone for a little while.

She'd waited until the middle of the week, watching from a careful distance on Monday and Tuesday to gauge his routine, and the timing. Habitually, she now knew, the buses lumbered up to school several minutes before the doors opened and children began pouring out.

Elementary first, then middle, then the high school students.

That alone was a lesson in the process of childhood, she mused. The compact little bodies and fresh round faces of the elementary children, then the more gangling, somewhat awkward forms of those who hovered around puberty. And last, the astonishingly adult and more individual young people who strolled out of the high school.

It was a study in itself, she decided. From dangling shoelaces and gaptoothed smiles to cowlicks and ball jackets to baggy jeans and shining falls of hair.

Children had never been a part of her life, or her interests. She'd grown up in a world of adults and had been expected to acclimate, to conform. There had been no big yellow school buses, no wild rebel yells when bursting out of the school doors into freedom, no lingering in the parking lot with some leather-jacketed bad boy.

So she observed all those things here like an audience at a play and found the mix of drama and comedy both amusing and informative.

When Seth hurried out, bumping bodies with the dark-haired boy she'd decided was his most usual companion, her pulse quickened. He whipped his ball cap out of his pocket and put it on his head the moment he was through the doors. A ritual, she thought, symbolizing the change of rules.

The other boy fished in his pocket and pulled out a fistful of bubblegum. In seconds it was wadded into his mouth.

The noise level rose, making it impossible for her to hear their conversation, but it appeared to be animated and included a great deal of elbow jabbing and shoulder punching.

Typical male affection pattern, she concluded.

They turned their backs on the buses and began to walk down the sidewalk. Moments later, a smaller boy raced up to them. He bounced, Sybill noted, and seemed to have a great deal to say for himself.

She waited a moment longer, then casually took a path that would intersect with theirs.

"Shit, man, that geography test was nothing. A bozo could've aced it." Seth shrugged to distribute the weight of his backpack.

The other boy blew an impressive candy-pink bubble, popped it, then sucked it in. "I don't know what's the big damn deal about knowing all the states and capitals. It's not like I'm going to live in North Dakota."

"Seth, hello."

Sybill watched him stop, adjust his train of thought, and focus on her. "Oh, yeah, hi."

"I guess school's done for the day. You heading home?"

"The boatyard." There was that little dance on the nape of his neck again. It irritated him. "We got work."

"I'm going that way myself." She tried a smile on the other boys. "Hi, I'm Sybill."

"I'm Danny," the other boy told her. "That's Will."

"Nice to meet you."

"We had vegetable soup for lunch," Will informed everyone grandly. "And Lisa Harbough threw up *all over*. And Mr. Jim had to clean it up, and her mom came to get her, and we couldn't write our vocabulary words." He danced around Sybill as he relayed the information, then shot her an amazingly innocent, wonderfully bright smile that she was helpless to resist.

"I hope Lisa's feeling better soon."

"Once when I threw up I got to stay home and watch TV all day. Me and Danny live over there on Heron Lane. Where do you live?"

"I'm just visiting."

"My Uncle John and Aunt Margie moved to South Carolina and we got to visit them. They have two dogs and a baby named Mike. Do you have dogs and babies?"

"No . . . no, I don't."

"You can get them," he told her. "You can go right to the animal shelter and get a dog—that's what we did. And you can get married and make a baby so it lives in your stomach. There's nothing to it."

"Jeez, Will." Seth rolled his eyes, while Sybill only managed to blink.

"Well, I'm going to have dogs and babies when I grow up. As many as I want." He flashed that hundred-watt smile again, then raced away. " 'Bye."

"He's such a geek," Danny said with the shuddering disdain of older brother for younger. "See you, Seth." He bounded after Will, turned briefly to run backward and flipped a wave toward Sybill. " 'Bye."

"Will's not really a geek," Seth told Sybill. "He's just a kid, and he's got diarrhea of the mouth, but he's pretty cool."

"He's certainly friendly." She shifted her shoulder bag, smiled down at him. "Do you mind if I walk the rest of the way with you?"

"It's okay."

"I thought I heard you say something about a geography test."

"Yeah, we took one today. It was nothing."

"You like school?"

"It's there." He jerked his shoulder. "You gotta go."

"I always enjoyed it. Learning new things." She laughed lightly. "I suppose I was a geek."

Seth angled his head, narrowing his eyes as he studied her face. A looker, Phillip had called her, he remembered. He guessed she was. She had nice eyes, the light color a sharp contrast to the dark lashes. Her hair wasn't as dark as Anna's, nor light like Grace's. It was really shiny, he noted, and the way she pulled it back all smooth and stuff left her face right out there.

She might be cool to draw sometime.

"You don't look like a geek," Seth announced just as Sybill felt heat begin to rise into her cheeks under his long, intense study. "Anyway, that would be a nerd."

"Oh." She wasn't sure if she'd just qualified for nerd status and decided not to ask. "What do you like studying best?"

"I don't know. Mostly it's just a bunch of—stuff," he decided, quickly censoring his opinion. "I guess I like it better when we get to read about people instead of things."

"I've always liked to study people." She stopped and gestured toward a small two-story gray house with a trim front yard. "My theory would be that a young family lives there. Both husband and wife work outside the home and they have a preschooler, most likely a boy. Odds are that they've known each other a number of years and have been married less than seven."

"How come?"

"Well, it's the middle of the day and no one's home. No cars in the drive, and the house looks empty. But there's a tricycle there and several large toy trucks. The house isn't new, but it's well kept. Most young couples both work today in order to buy a home, have a family. They live in a small community. Younger people rarely settle in small towns unless one or both of them grew up there. So I'd theorize that this couple lived here, knew each other, eventually married. It's likely they had their first child within the first three years of marriage and the toys indicate he's three to five."

"That's pretty cool," Seth decided after a moment.

However foolish it was, she felt a surge of pride that she might have avoided nerddom after all. "But I'd want to know more, wouldn't you?"

She'd caught his interest. "Like what?"

"Why did they choose this particular house. What are their goals? What is the status of their relationship? Who handles the money, which indicates the disposition of power, and why? If you study people, you see the patterns."

"How come it matters?"

"I don't understand."

"Who cares?"

She considered. "Well, if you understand the patterns, the social picture on a large scale, you learn why people behave in certain manners."

"What if they don't fit?"

Bright boy, she thought on another, deeper wave of pride. "Everyone fits some pattern. You factor in background, genetics, education, social strata, religious and cultural roots."

"You get paid for that?"

"Yes, I suppose I do."

"Weird."

Now, she concluded, she had definitely been relegated to nerd status. "It can be interesting." She racked her brain to come up with an example that would salvage his opinion of her. "I did this experiment once in several cities. I arranged for a man to stand on the street and stare up at a building."

"Just stare at it?"

"That's right. He stood there and stared up, shading his eyes from the sun when he had to. Before long someone stopped beside him and stared up at the same building. Then another and another, until there was a crowd of people, all looking up at that building. It took much longer for anyone to actually ask what was going on, what were they looking at. No one really wanted to be the first to ask because that was an admission that you didn't see what you assumed everyone else was seeing. We want to conform, we want to fit in, we want to know and see and understand what the person beside us knows and sees and understands."

"I bet some of them thought someone was going to jump out of a window."

"Very likely. The average time an individual stood, looking, interrupting their schedule, was two minutes." She believed she'd caught his imagination again, and so she hurried on. "That's actually quite a long time to stare at a perfectly ordinary building."

"That's pretty cool. But it's still weird."

They were coming to the point where he would have to veer off to go to the boatyard. She thought quickly and in a rare move went with impulse. "What do you think would happen if you conducted the same experiment in St. Christopher's?"

"I don't know. The same thing?"

"I doubt it." She sent him a conspirator's smile. "Want to try it?"

"Maybe."

"We can head over to the waterfront now. Will your brother worry if you're a few minutes late? Should you go tell him you're with me?"

"Nah. Cam doesn't keep me on a leash. He cuts me some slack time."

She wasn't sure how she felt about the loose discipline in that area, but at the moment she was happy to take advantage of it. "Let's try it, then. I'll pay you in ice cream."

"You got a deal."

They turned away from the boatyard. "You can pick a spot," she began. "It's necessary to stand. People don't generally pay attention to someone who's sitting and looking. They often assume the person is simply daydreaming or resting."

"I get it."

"It's more effective if you look up at something. Is it okay if I video-tape?"

He raised his eyebrows as she took a neat compact video recorder out of her bag. "Yeah, I guess. You carry that around all the time?"

"When I'm working, I do. And a notebook, and a micro audio tape recorder, backup batteries and tapes, extra pencils. My cell phone." She laughed at herself. "I like being prepared. And the day they make a computer small enough to fit in a purse, I'm going to be the first in line."

"Phil likes all that electronic stuff, too."

"The baggage of the urbanite. We're desperate not to waste a minute. Then, of course, we can't get away from anything because we're plugged in every second of the day."

"You could just turn everything off."

"Yes." Oddly she found the simplicity of his statement profound. "I suppose I could."

Pedestrian traffic was light on the waterfront. She saw a workboat unloading the day's catch and a family taking advantage of the balmy afternoon by splurging on ice cream sundaes at one of the little outdoor tables. Two old men, their faces nut brown and deeply seamed, sat on an iron bench with a checkerboard between them. Neither seemed inclined to make a move. A trio of women chatted in the doorway of one of the shops, but only one of them carried a bag.

"I'm going to stand over there." Seth pointed to his spot. "And look up at the hotel."

"Good choice." Sybill stayed where she was as he strolled off. Distance was necessary to keep the experiment pure. She lifted the camera, zoomed in as Seth moved away. He turned once, shot her a quick, cocky smile.

And when his face filled her view screen, emotions she hadn't been prepared for flooded her. He was so handsome, so bright. So happy. She struggled to pull herself back from a dangerous edge that she was afraid was despair.

She could walk away, she thought, pack up and leave, never see him again. He would never know who she was or what they were to each other. He would never miss whatever she could bring into his life. She was nothing to him.

She'd never really tried to be.

It was different now, she reminded herself. She was making it different now. Deliberately she ordered her fingers to relax, her neck, her arms. She was causing no harm by getting to know him, spending some time studying his situation.

She taped him as he settled on his spot, lifted his face. His profile was finer, more angled than Gloria's, Sybill decided. Perhaps his bone structure had come from his father.

His build wasn't Gloria's either, as she'd first assumed, but more like her own, and her mother's. He would be tall when he finished growing, mostly leg, and on the slim side.

His body language, she saw with a slight jolt, was typical Quinn. Already, he'd taken on some of the traits of his foster family. That hip-shot stance, hands tucked into pockets, head angled.

She fought back an annoying spurt of resentment and ordered herself to focus on the experiment.

It took just over a minute for the first person to stop beside Seth. She recognized the big woman with the gray-streaked hair who manned the counter at Crawford's. Everyone called her Mother. As expected, the woman shifted her gaze, tilted her face up to follow Seth's line of sight. But after a quick scan, she patted Seth on the shoulder.

"What're you looking at, boy?"

"Nothing."

He muttered it so that Sybill edged closer to try to pick up his voice on the tape.

"Well, hell, you stand there for long looking at nothing, people're going to think you're pixilated. Why aren't you down to the boatyard?"

"I'm going in a minute."

"Hey, Mother. Hi, Seth." A pretty young woman with dark hair stepped into the frame, glanced up at the hotel. "Something going on up there? I don't see anything."

"Nothing to see," Mother informed her. "Boy's just standing looking at nothing. How's your mama, Julie?"

"Oh, she's a little under the weather. She's got a sore throat and a little cough."

"Chicken soup, hot tea and honey."

"Grace brought some soup over this morning."

"You see she eats it. Hey, there, Jim."

"Afternoon." A short, stocky man in white rubber boots clumped over, gave Seth a friendly swat on the head. "What you staring at up there, boy?"

"Jeez, can't a guy just stand around?" Seth turned his face to the camera, rolled his eyes for Sybill and made her chuckle.

"Stand here long, gulls'll light on you." Jim winked at him. "Cap'n's in for the day," he added, referring to Ethan. "He gets to the boatyard before you, he's gonna want to know why."

"I'm going, I'm going. Man." Shoulders rounded, head down, Seth stalked back to Sybill. "Nobody's falling for it."

"Because everyone knows you." She switched off the camera, lowered it. "It changes the pattern."

"You figured that would happen?"

"I theorized," she corrected, "that in a closely knit area where the subject was known, the pattern would be that an individual would stop. They would probably look first, then question. There's no risk, no loss of ego when questioning a familiar person, and a young one at that."

He frowned over toward where the trio continued to chat. "So, I still get paid."

"Absolutely, and you'll likely rate a section in my book."

"Cool. I'll take a cookie dough cone. I've got to get to the boatyard before Cam and Ethan hassle me."

"If they're going to be angry with you, I'll explain. It's my fault you're late."

"They won't be pissed or anything. Beside, I'll tell them it was, like, for science, right?" When he flashed that grin she had to resist an unexpected urge to hug him.

"That's exactly right." She risked laying a hand on his shoulder as they started toward Crawford's. She thought she felt him stiffen and casually let her hand drop away. "And we can always call them on my cell phone."

"Yeah? Way cool. Can I do it?"

"Sure, why not?"

Twenty minutes later Sybill was at her desk, fingers racing over her keyboard.

Though I spent less than an hour with him, I would conclude that the subject is extremely bright. Phillip informed me that he achieves high grades academically, which is admirable. It was satisfying to discover that he has a questioning mind. His manners are perhaps a bit rough, but not unpleasant. He appears to be considerably more outgoing socially than his mother or I were at his age. In that, I mean he seems quite natural with relative strangers without the polite formality that was stressed in my own upbringing. Part of this may be due to the influence of the Quinns. They are, as I have noted previously, informal, casual people.

I would also conclude from watching both the children and the adults with whom he interacted today, that he is generally well liked in this community and accepted as part of it. Naturally I cannot, at this early stage, conclude whether or not his best interest would be served by remaining here.

It's simply not possible to ignore Gloria's rights, nor have I attempted, as yet, to discover the boy's wishes as concern his mother.

I would prefer that he grow accustomed to me, feel comfortable around me, before he learns of our family connection.

I need more time to . . .

She broke off as the phone rang and, scanning her hastily typed notes, picked up the receiver.

"Dr. Griffin."

"Hello, Dr. Griffin. Why do I suspect I've interrupted your work?"

She recognized Phillip's voice, the amusement in it, and with a flare of guilt lowered the top of her computer. "Because you're a perceptive man. But I can spare a few minutes. How are things in Baltimore?"

"Busy. How's this? The visual is a handsome young couple, beaming smiles as they carry their laughing toddler to a mid-size sedan. Caption: 'Myerstone Tires. Your family matters to us.'"

"Manipulative. The consumer is led to believe that if he or she buys another brand, the family doesn't matter to that other company."

"Yeah. It works. Of course, we're hitting the car mags with a different image. Screaming convertible in kick-ass red, long, winding road, sexy blonde at the wheel. 'Myerstone Tires. You can drive there, or you can BE there.'"

"Clever."

"The client likes it, and that takes a load off. How's life in St. Chris?"

"Quiet." She bit her lip. "I ran into Seth a bit ago. Actually, I drafted him to help me with an experiment. It went well."

"Oh, yeah? How much did you have to pay him?"

"An ice cream cone, double scoop."

"You got off cheap. The kid's an operator. How about dinner tomorrow night, a bottle of champagne to celebrate our mutual successes?"

"Speaking of operators."

"I've been thinking about you all week."

"Three days," she corrected and, picking up a pencil, began to doodle on her pad.

"And nights. With this account settled, I can get out a little earlier tomorrow. Why don't I pick you up at seven?"

"I'm not sure where we're going, Phillip."

"Neither am I. Do you need to be?"

She understood that neither of them was speaking of restaurants. "It's less confusing that way."

"Then we'll talk about it, and maybe we'll get past the confusion. Seven o'clock."

She glanced down, noticed that she'd unconsciously sketched his face on her notepad. A bad sign, she thought. A very dangerous sign. "All right." It was best to face complications head-on. "I'll see you tomorrow."

"Do me a favor?"

"If I can."

"Think of me tonight."

She doubted she had any choice in the matter. "'Bye."

I n his office fourteen stories above the streets of Baltimore, Phillip pushed
back from his slick black desk, ignored the beep on his computer that signaled an interoffice e-mail and turned toward his wide window.

He loved his view of the city, the renovated buildings, the glimpses of
the harbor, the hustle of cars and people below. But just now he didn't see
any of it.

He literally couldn't get Sybill out of his mind. It was a new experience
for him, this continual tug on his thoughts and concentration. It wasn't as if
she was interfering with his routine, he reflected. He could work, eat, brainstorm, do his presentations as skillfully as he had before he'd met her.

But she was simply there, he decided. A tickle at the back of his mind
through the day, that inched forward to the front when his energies weren't
otherwise occupied.

He wasn't quite sure if he enjoyed having a woman demand so much of his
attention, particularly a woman who was doing very little to encourage him.

Maybe he considered that light sheen of formality, that cautious distance
she tried to maintain, a challenge. He thought he could live with that. It was
just another of the entertaining and varied games men and women played.

But he worried that something was happening on a level he'd never explored. And if he was any judge, she was just as unsettled by it as he.

"It's just like you," Ray said from behind him.

"Oh, Jesus." Phillip didn't spin around, didn't goggle. He simply shut
his eyes.

"Pretty fancy office you got here. Been a while since I got in." Ray
prowled the room casually, pursing his lips at a black-framed canvas
splashed with reds and blues. "Not bad," he decided. "Brain stimulator. I'd
guess that's why you put it in your office, get the juices going."

"I refuse to believe that my dead father is standing in my office cri-
tiquing art."

"Well, that wasn't what I wanted to talk about anyway." But he paused
by a metal sculpture in the corner. "But I like this piece, too. You always had
high-class taste. Art, food, women." He grinned cheerfully as Phillip turned.
"The woman you've got on your mind now, for instance. Very high-class."

"I need to take some time off."

"I'd agree with you there. You've been up to and over your head for
months. She's an interesting woman, Phillip. There's more to her than you
see, or than she knows. I hope when the times comes you'll listen to her, really listen to her."

"What are you talking about?" He held up a hand, palm out. "Why am I asking you what you're talking about when you're not here?"

"I'm hoping that the pair of you will stop analyzing the steps and stages and accept what is." Ray shrugged, slipped his hands into the pockets of his Orioles fielder's jacket. "But you have to go your own way. It's going to be hard. There's not much time left before it gets a lot harder. You'll stand between Seth and what hurts him. I know that. I want to tell you that you can trust her. When it's down to the sticking point, Phillip, you trust yourself, and you trust her."

A new chill skidded down his spine. "What does Sybill have to do with Seth?"

"It's not for me to tell you that." He smiled again, but his eyes didn't match the curve of his lips. "You haven't talked to your brothers about me. You need to. You need to stop feeling you have to control all the buttons. You're good at it, God knows, but give a little."

He drew in a deep breath, turned a slow circle. "Christ, your mother would've gotten a kick out of this place. You've done a hell of a job with your life so far." Now his eyes smiled. "I'm proud of you. I know you'll handle what comes next."

"You did a hell of a job with my life," Phillip murmured. "You and Mom."

"Damn right we did." Ray winked. "Keep it up." When the phone rang, Ray sighed. "Everything that happens needs to happen. It's what you do about it that makes the difference. Answer the phone, Phillip, and remember Seth needs you."

Then there was nothing but the ringing of the phone and an empty office. With his gaze locked on where his father had been, Phillip reached for the phone.

"Phillip Quinn."

As he listened, his eyes hardened. He grabbed a pen, and began to take notes on the detective's report on the most recent movements of Gloria De-Lauter.

NINE

"She's in Hampton." Phillip kept his eyes on Seth as he relayed the information. He watched Cam lay a hand on the boy's rigid shoulder, an unspoken sign of protection. "She was picked up by the police—drunk and disorderly, possession."

"She's in jail." Seth's face was white as bone. "They can keep her in jail."

"She's there now." How long she would stay there, Phillip thought, was another matter. "She probably has enough money to post bond."

"You mean she can pay them money and they'll let her go?" Beneath Cam's hand, Seth began to tremble. "No matter what?"

"I don't know. But for now we know exactly where she is. I'm going down to talk to her."

"Don't! Don't go there."

"Seth, we've talked about this." Cam massaged the shaking shoulder as he turned Seth to face him. "The only way we're going to fix this for good is to deal with her."

"I won't go back." It was said in a whisper, but a furious one. "I'll never go back."

"You won't go back." Ethan unhitched his tool belt, laid it on the workbench. "You can stay with Grace until Anna gets home." He looked at Phillip and Cam. "We'll go to Hampton."

"What if the cops say I have to? What if they come while you're gone and—"

"Seth." Phillip interrupted the rising desperation. He crouched, took Seth's arms firmly. "You have to trust us."

Seth stared back at him with Ray Quinn's eyes, and those eyes were glazed with tears and terror. For the first time, Phillip looked into them and felt no shadowy resentment, no doubts.

"You belong with us," he said quietly. "Nothing's going to change that."

On a long, shuddering breath Seth nodded. He had no choice, could do nothing but hope. And fear.

"We'll take my car," Phillip stated.

"Grace and Anna will calm him down." Cam shifted restlessly in the passenger seat of Phillip's Jeep.

"It's hell being that scared." From the backseat, Ethan glanced at the speedometer and noted that Phillip was pushing eighty. "Not being able to do anything but wait and see."

"She's fucked herself," Phillip said flatly. "Getting arrested isn't going to help her custody case, if she tries to make one."

"She doesn't want the kid."

Phillip spared a brief glance at Cam. "No, she wants money. She isn't going to bleed any out of us. But we're going to get some answers. We're going to end it."

She'd lie, Phillip thought. He had no doubt that she would lie and wheedle and maneuver. But she was wrong, dead wrong, if she thought she could get past the three of them to Seth.

You'll handle what comes next, Ray had said.

Phillip's hands tightened on the wheel. He kept his eyes on the road. He'd handle it, all right. One way or the other.

With her head throbbing, her stomach rolling, Sybill walked into the small county police station. Gloria had called her, weeping and desperate, begging her to send money for bail.

For bail, Sybill thought now, fighting off a shudder.

Gloria said it was a mistake, she reminded herself, a terrible misunderstanding. Of course, what else could it have been? She'd nearly wired the money. She still wasn't sure what had stopped her, what had pushed her to get into her car and drive.

To help, of course, she told herself. She only wanted to help.

"I'm here for Gloria DeLauter," she told the uniformed officer who sat behind a narrow, cluttered counter. "I'd like to see her, if possible."

"Your name?"

"Griffin. Dr. Sybill Griffin. I'm her sister. I'll post her bond, but I'd . . . I'd like to see her."

"Can I see some ID?"

"Oh, yes." She fumbled in her purse for her wallet. Her hands were damp and shaky, but the cop simply watched her with cool eyes until she offered identification.

"Why don't you have a seat?" he suggested, then scraped back his own chair and slipped into an adjoining room.

Her throat was dry and desperate for water. She wandered the small waiting area with its grouping of hard plastic chairs in industrial beige until she found a water fountain. But the water hit her tortured stomach like frigid balls of lead.

Had they put her in a cell? Oh, God, had they actually put her sister in a cell? Is that where she would have to see Gloria?

But under the sorrow, her mind was working coolly, pragmatically. How had Gloria known where to reach her? What was she doing so close to St. Christopher's? Why was she accused of having drugs?

That was why she hadn't wired the money, she admitted now. She wanted the answers first.

"Dr. Griffin."

She jolted, turned to the officer with her eyes wide as a doe's caught in headlights. "Yes. Can I see her now?"

"I'll need to take your purse. I'll give you a receipt."

"All right."

She handed it over to him, signed the log where he indicated, accepted the receipt for her belongings.

"This way."

He gestured toward a side door, then opened it into a narrow corridor. On the left was a small room furnished only with a single table and a few chairs. Gloria sat at one, her right wrist cuffed to a bolt.

Sybill's first thought was that they'd made a mistake. This wasn't her sister. They'd brought the wrong woman into the room. This one looked far too old, far too hard, with her bony body, the shoulders like points of wings, the contrast of breasts pressing against a tiny, snug sweater so hard that the nipples stood out in arrogant relief.

Her frizzed mass of straw-colored hair had a dark streak shooting up the center, deep lines dug in around her mouth, and the calculation in her eyes was as sharp as those shoulders.

Then those eyes filled, that mouth trembled.

"Syb." Her voice cracked as she held out an imploring hand. "Thank God you've come."

"Gloria." She stepped forward quickly, took that shaking hand in her own. "What happened?"

"I don't know. I don't understand any of it. I'm so scared." She laid her head on the table and began to weep in loud, racking sobs.

"Please." Instinctively Sybill sat and draped her arm around her sister as she looked over at the cop. "Can we be alone?"

"I'll be right outside." He looked back at Gloria. If he thought what a change this was from the screaming, cursing woman who'd been pulled in a few hours ago, his face revealed nothing.

He stepped out, shut the door, and left them alone.

"Let me get you some water."

Sybill rose, hurried over to the water jug in the corner, and filled a thin triangle of paper. She cupped her hands around her sister's, holding it steady.

"Did you pay the bail? Why can't we just go? I don't want to stay here."

"I'll take care of it. Tell me what happened."

"I said I don't know. I was with this guy. I was lonely." She sniffed, accepting the tissue that Sybill passed her. "We were just talking for a while. We were going to go out to lunch, then the cops came up. He ran away and they grabbed me. It all happened so fast."

She buried her face in her hands. "They found drugs in my purse. He must have put them there. I just wanted someone to talk to."

"All right. I'm sure we'll straighten it all out." Sybill wanted to believe, to accept, and she hated herself because she couldn't. Not quite. "What was his name?"

"John. John Barlow. He seemed so sweet, Sybill. So understanding. I was feeling really low. Because of Seth." She lowered her hands and her eyes were tragic. "I miss my little boy so much."

"Were you coming to St. Christopher's?"

Gloria lowered her gaze. "I thought, if I just had a chance to see him."

"Is that what the lawyer suggested?"

"The—oh . . ." The hesitation was brief, but it set off warning bells in Sybill's head. "No, but lawyers don't understand. They just keep asking for money."

"What's your lawyer's name? I'll call him. He may be able to help straighten this out."

"He's not from around here. Look, Sybill, I just want to get out of here. You can't believe how horrible it is. That cop out there?" She nodded toward the door. "He put his hands on me."

Sybill's stomach began to pitch again. "What do you mean?"

"You know what I mean." The first hint of annoyance sliced through. "He felt me up, and he said he'd be back later for more. He's going to rape me."

Sybill shut her eyes, pressed her fingers to them. When they were teenagers, Gloria had accused more than a dozen boys and men of molesting her, including her high school counselor and principal. Even their own father.

"Gloria, don't do this. I said I would help you."

"I'm telling you that bastard put his hands all over me. As soon as I'm out of here, I'm filing charges." She crumpled the paper cup, heaved it. "I don't give a damn if you believe me or not. I know what happened."

"All right, but let's deal with now. How did you know where to find me?"

"What?" A dark rage had been sliding over her brain, and she had to struggle to remember her role. "What do you mean?"

"I didn't tell you where I was going, where I would be. I said I would contact you. How did you know to call me at the hotel in St. Christopher's?"

It had been a mistake, which Gloria had realized shortly after making the call. But she'd been drunk and furious. And damn it, she didn't have the cash on her to make bail. What she had left was safely tucked away. Until the Quinns added to it.

She wasn't thinking when she called Sybill, but she'd had time to think since. The way to play sister Sybill, she knew, was to tug on the guilt and responsibility strings.

"I know you." She offered a watery smile. "I knew that when I told you what happened with Seth, you'd help. I tried your apartment in New York." Which she had, more than a week ago. "And when your answering service said you were out of town, I explained how I was your sister and there was an emergency. They gave me the number of the hotel."

"I see." It was plausible, Sybill decided, even logical. "I'll take care of the bail, Gloria, but there are conditions."

"Yeah." She gave a short laugh. "That sounds familiar."

"I need the name of your lawyer so I can contact him. I want to be brought up to date on the status of this situation with Seth. I want you to talk to me. We'll have dinner and you can explain to me about the Quinns. You can explain to me why they claim Ray Quinn gave you money for Seth."

"The bastards are liars."

"I've met them," she said calmly. "And their wives. I've seen Seth. It's very difficult for me to equate what you told me with what I've seen."

"You can't put everything all neat and tidy into reports. Christ, you're just like the old man." She started to get up, snarled at the jerk of the cuff on her wrist. "The two eminent Dr. Griffins."

"This has nothing to do with my father," Sybill said quietly. "And everything, I suspect, to do with yours."

"Fuck this." Gloria twisted her lips into a vicious smile. "And fuck you. The perfect daughter, the perfect student, the perfect goddamn robot. Just pay the fucking bail. I got money put by. You'll get it back. I'll get my kid back without your help, sister dear. My kid. You want to take the word of a bunch of strangers over your own flesh and blood, you go right ahead. You always hated me anyway."

"I don't hate you, Gloria. I never have." But she could, she realized, as the ache began in her head and heart. She was afraid she very easily could. "And I'm not taking anyone's word over yours. I'm just trying to understand."

Deliberately Gloria turned her face away so Sybill wouldn't see her smile of satisfaction. She'd found the right button to push after all, she decided. "I need to get out of here. I need to get cleaned up." She made certain her voice broke. "I can't talk about this anymore. I'm so tired."

"I'll go deal with the paperwork. I'm sure it won't take long."

As she rose, Gloria grabbed her hand again, pressed it to her cheek. "I'm sorry. I'm so sorry I said those things to you. I didn't mean them. I'm just upset and confused. I feel so alone."

"It's all right." Sybill pulled her hand free and walked to the door on legs that felt as brittle as glass.

Outside, she downed two aspirin and chased them with antacids as she waited for the bail to be processed. Physically, she thought, Gloria had changed. The once astonishingly pretty girl had hardened, toughened like dried leather. But emotionally, Sybill feared, she was exactly the same unhappy, manipulative, and disturbed child that had taken dark joy in disrupting their home.

She would insist that Gloria agree to therapy, she decided. And if drug abuse was part of the problem, she would see to it that Gloria went into rehab. Certainly the woman she'd just spoken with wasn't capable of taking custody of a young boy. She would explore the possibilities of what was best for him until Gloria was back on track.

She would need to see a lawyer, of course. First thing in the morning she would find a lawyer and discuss Gloria's rights and Seth's welfare.

She would have to face the Quinns.

The thought of that had her stomach clutching again. A confrontation was inevitable, unavoidable. Nothing left her feeling more miserable and vulnerable than angry words and hateful emotions.

But she would be prepared. She would take the time to think through what had to be said, anticipate their questions and demands so she would have the proper responses. She would, above all, remain calm and objective.

When she saw Phillip walk into the building, her mind went blank. Every ounce of color drained out of her face. She stood frozen when his gaze whipped to hers, when it narrowed and hardened.

"What are you doing here, Sybill?"

"I . . ." It wasn't panic that spurted through her but embarrassment. Shame. "I had business."

"Really?" He stepped closer, while his brothers stood back in speculative silence. He saw it in her face—guilt and more than a little fear. "What kind of business would that be?" When she didn't answer, he angled his head. "What's Gloria DeLauter to you, Dr. Griffin?"

She ordered herself to keep her gaze steady, her voice even. "She's my sister."

His fury was ice cold and deadly. He balled his hands into his pockets to keep from using them in a way that was unforgivable. "That's cozy, isn't it? You bitch," he said softly, but she flinched as if he had struck her. "You used me to get to Seth."

She shook her head, but she couldn't voice the denial. It was true, wasn't it? She had used him, had used all of them. "I only wanted to see him. He's my sister's son. I had to know he was being cared for."

"Then where the hell have you been for the last ten years?"

She opened her mouth, but swallowed the excuses and explanations as Gloria was led out.

"Let's get the hell out of here. You buy me a drink, Syb." Gloria hitched a cherry-red shoulder bag over her arm, aimed an invitational smile at Phillip. "We'll talk all you want. Hi, there, handsome." She shifted her weight, put a fist on her hip, and let the smile spread to the other men. "How's it going?"

Under other circumstances the contrasts between the women might have been laughable. Sybill stood pale and quiet, her glossy brown hair brushed smoothly back, her mouth unpainted, her eyes shadowed. She exuded simple elegance in a tailored gray blazer and slacks and a white silk blouse, while Gloria offered sharp bones and overblown curves poured into black jeans and a snug T-shirt that plunged between her breasts.

She'd taken the time to repair her makeup, and her lips were as slickly red as her handbag, her eyes darkly lined. She looked, Phillip decided, like precisely what she was: an aging whore looking for an angle.

She fished a cigarette out of a crumpled pack in her bag, then wiggled it between her fingers. "Got a light, big guy?"

"Gloria, this is Phillip Quinn." The formal introduction echoed hollowly in her ears. "His brothers, Cameron and Ethan."

"Well, well, well." Gloria's smile went sharp and ugly. "Ray Quinn's wicked trio. What the hell do you want?"

"Answers," Phillip said shortly. "Let's take this outside."

"I got nothing to say to you. You make one move I don't like, I'll start screaming." She jabbed with the unlit cigarette. "There's a houseful of cops in here. We'll see how you like spending some time in a cage."

"Gloria." Sybill put a restraining hand on her arm. "The only way to straighten this out is to discuss it rationally."

"They don't look like they want a rational discussion to me. They want to hurt me." She shifted tacks skillfully, throwing her arms around Sybill, clinging to her. "I'm afraid of them. Sybill, please help me."

"I'm trying to. Gloria, no one's going to hurt you. We'll find a place where we can all sit down and talk this through. I'll be right there with you."

"I'm going to be sick." She yanked back, wrapped her arms around her stomach, and dashed into the bathroom.

"Quite a performance," Phillip decided.

"She's upset." Sybill linked her hands together, twisted her fingers. "She's not in any shape to deal with this tonight."

He shifted his gaze back to Sybill's, and it was ripe with derision. "Do you want me to believe you bought that? Either you're incredibly gullible, or you think I am."

"She spent most of the afternoon in jail," Sybill snapped back. "Anyone would be upset. Can't we discuss all of this tomorrow? It's waited this long, surely it can wait one more day."

"We're here now," Cam put in. "We'll deal with it now. Are you going to go in there and bring her out, or am I?"

"Is that how you plan to resolve this? By bullying her. And me?"

"You don't want to get me started on how I plan to resolve this," Cam began, and shrugged off Ethan's calming hand. "After what she put Seth through, there's nothing we can do to her that she hasn't earned."

Sybill glanced uncomfortably behind her at the uniformed officer manning the desk. "I don't think any of us want to cause a scene in a police station."

"Fine." Phillip took her arm. "Let's just step outside and cause one."

She held her ground, partly out of fear, partly common sense. "We'll meet tomorrow, at whatever time is convenient for you. I'll bring her to my hotel."

"You keep her out of St. Chris."

Sybill winced when Phillip's fingers tightened on her arm. "All right. Where do you suggest?"

"I'll tell you what I suggest," Cam began, but Phillip held up a hand.

"Princess Anne. You bring her into Anna's office at Social Services. Nine o'clock. That keeps everything official, doesn't it? Everything aboveboard."

"Yes." Relief trickled through her. "I can agree to that. I'll bring her. You have my word."

"I wouldn't give you two cents for your word, Sybill." Phillip leaned in slightly. "But if you don't bring her, we'll find her. Meanwhile, if either of you tries to get within a mile of Seth, you'll both be spending time in a cell." He dropped her arm and stepped back.

"We'll be there at nine," she said, resisting the urge to rub her aching arm. Then she turned and went into the bathroom to get her sister.

"Why the hell did you agree to that?" Cam demanded as he stalked outside behind Phillip. "We've got her, here and now."

"We'll get more out of her tomorrow."

"Bullshit."

"Phillip's right." As much as he detested it, Ethan accepted the change of plans. "We keep it in official surroundings. We keep our heads. It's better for Seth."

"Why? So his bitch of a mother and his lying auntie have more time to put their heads together? Christ, when I think Sybill was alone with Seth for a good hour today, I want to—"

"It's done," Phillip snapped. "He's fine. We're fine." With fury bubbling through his blood, he slammed into the Jeep. "And there are five of us. They won't get their hands on Seth."

"He didn't recognize her," Ethan pointed out. "That's funny, isn't it? He didn't know who Sybill was."

"Neither did I," Phillip murmured and shoved the Jeep into gear. "But I do now."

 ❧

Sybill's priority was to get Gloria a hot meal, keep her calm, and question her carefully. The little Italian restaurant was only a few blocks from the police station, and after a hurried glance, Sybill decided it would fill the bill.

"My nerves are shot to hell." Gloria puffed greedily on a cigarette while Sybill maneuvered into a parking spot. "The nerve of those bastards, coming after me like that. You know what they'd have done if I'd been alone, don't you?"

Sybill only sighed and stepped out of the car. "You need to eat."

"Yeah, sure." Gloria sniffed at the decor the minute they stepped inside. It was bright and cheerful, with colorful Italian pottery, thick candles, striped tablecloths, and decorative bottles of herbed vinegars. "I'd rather have a steak than Wop food."

"Please." Forcing back irritation, she took Gloria's arm and requested a table for two.

"Smoking section," Gloria added, already pulling out another cigarette as they were led to the noisier bar area. "Gin and tonic, a double."

Sybill rubbed her temples. "Just mineral water. Thank you."

"Loosen up," Gloria suggested when the hostess left them alone. "You look like you could use a drink."

"I'm driving. I don't want one anyway." She shifted away from the smoke Gloria blew toward her face. "We have to talk, seriously."

"Let me get some lubrication, will you?" Gloria smoked and scanned the men at the bar, toying with which one she'd pick up if she didn't have her deadly dull sister along.

Christ, Sybill was a bore. Always had been, she mused, drumming her fingers on the table and wanting her goddamn drink. But she was useful, and always had been. If you played her right, laid on plenty of tears, she came through.

She needed a hammer with the Quinns, and Sybill was the perfect choice. Upstanding, fucking respectable Dr. Griffin. "Gloria, you haven't even asked about Seth?"

"What about him?"

"I've seen him several times, spoken with him. I've seen where he's living, where he goes to school. I met some of his friends."

Gloria clicked into the tone of her sister's voice, adjusted her attitude. "How is he?" She worked up a shaky smile. "Did he ask about me?"

"He's fine. Really wonderful, actually. He's grown so much since I saw him."

Ate like a horse, Gloria remembered, and was always growing out of his clothes and shoes. Like she was made of fucking money or something.

"He didn't know who I was."

"What do you mean?" Gloria snatched up her drink the minute it was set on the table. "You didn't tell him?"

"No, I didn't." Sybill glanced up at the waitress. "We need a few more minutes before ordering."

"So you were poking around incognito." Gloria let out a long, hoarse laugh. "You surprise me, Syb."

"I thought it best that I observe the situation before changing the dynamics."

Gloria snorted. "Now that sounds just like you. Man, you don't change. 'Observe the situation before changing the dynamics,'" she repeated in her imitation of a snooty voice. "Christ. The situation is those sons of bitches have my kid. They threatened me, and God knows what they're doing to him. I want some dough to work on getting him back."

"I sent you money for the lawyer," Sybill reminded her.

Gloria clinked ice against her teeth as she drank. And the five thousand had come in handy, she thought now. How the hell could she have known how fast the money she'd bled out of Ray would slip away? She had expenses, didn't she? She'd wanted to have some fun for a change. Should have demanded twice as much from him, she decided.

Well, she'd get it out of those bastards he'd raised.

"You got the money I wired for your lawyer, didn't you, Gloria?"

Gloria took another deep drink. "Yeah, well, lawyers suck you dry, don't they? Hey!" She called out, signaling to the waitress and pointing at her empty glass. "Hit me again, will you?"

"If you drink like that and you don't eat, you're going to be sick again."

Like hell, Gloria sneered as she snatched up her menu. She didn't intend to stick her finger down her throat again. Once was more than enough. "Hey, they got steak Florentine. I can handle that. Remember when the old man took us off to Italy that summer? All those hot-looking dudes on motorbikes. Holy God, I had a hell of a time with that guy, what was his name. Carlo or Leo or whatever. I snuck him into the bedroom. You were too shy to stay and watch, so you slept in the parlor while we did the deed half the night."

She snatched up her fresh glass, lifted it in toast. "God bless the Italians."

"I'll have the linguini with pesto and the insalada mista."

"Give me the steak, bloody." Gloria held out the menu without looking at the waitress. "Skip the rabbit food. Been a while, hasn't it, Syb? What, four, five years?"

"Six," Sybill corrected. "It's been just over six since I came home to find you and Seth gone, along with a number of my personal possessions."

"Yeah, sorry about that. I was messed up. It's tough raising a kid on your own. Money's always tight."

"You never told me very much about his father."

"What's to tell? Old news." She shrugged it off and rattled the ice in her glass.

"All right, then, let's deal with current events. I need to know everything that happened. I need to understand it in order to help you and to know how to handle our meeting with the Quinns tomorrow."

The gin and tonic thudded onto the table. "What meeting?"

"We're going in to Social Services tomorrow morning to air out the problems, discuss the situation, and try to reach a solution."

"The hell I am. The only thing they want is to fuck me over."

"Keep your voice down," Sybill ordered sharply. "And listen to me. If you want to straighten yourself out, if you want your son back, this has to be done calmly and legally. Gloria, you need help, and I'm willing to help you. From what I can see, you're not in any shape to take Seth back right now."

"Whose side are you on?"

"His." It came out of her mouth before she realized that it was the absolute truth. "I'm on his side, and I hope that puts me on yours. We need to resolve what happened today."

"I told you I was set up."

"Fine. It still needs to be resolved. The courts aren't going to be very sympathetic to a woman who's facing charges of possession."

"Great, why don't you get on the witness stand and tell them how worthless I am? That's what you think anyway. That's what all of you always thought."

"Please, stop it." Lowering her voice to a murmur, Sybill leaned over the table. "I'm doing everything I know how to do. If you want to prove to me you want to make this work, you have to cooperate. You have to give something back, Gloria."

"Nothing's ever been free with you."

"We're not talking about me. I'll pay your legal fees, I'll talk to Social Services, I'll work to make the Quinns understand your needs and your rights. I want you to agree to rehab."

"For what?"

"You drink too much."

She sneered, deliberately gulping down more gin. "I've had a rough day."

"You had drugs in your possession."

"I said they weren't fucking mine."

"You've said that before," Sybill said, coolly now. "You get counseling, you get therapy, you get rehab. I'll arrange it, I'll foot the bill. I'll help you find a job, a place to stay."

"As long as it's your way." Gloria tossed back the rest of her drink. "Therapy. You and the old man used that to solve everything."

"Those are the conditions."

"So you're running the show. Jesus, order me another drink. I've gotta piss." She swung her purse over her shoulder and strode past the bar.

Sybill sat back and closed her eyes. She wasn't going to order Gloria another drink, not when her sister's words were already beginning to slur. That would be another bitter little battle, she imagined.

The aspirin she'd taken had failed miserably. Pain was drumming at both temples in a sick and consistent rhythm. Across her forehead was a squeez-ing band of iron. She wanted nothing quite so much as to stretch out on a soft bed in a dark room and sink into oblivion.

He despised her now. It made her ache with regret and shame to remem-ber the contempt she'd seen in Phillip's eyes. Maybe she deserved it. At that moment she simply couldn't think clearly enough to be sure. But she was sorry for it.

More than that, she was furious with herself for letting him and his opin-ion of her come to matter so much in such a short time. She'd known him for only a matter of days and had never, never intended to allow his emotions or hers to become entangled.

A casual physical attraction, a few mutually enjoyable hours in each other's company. That was all it was supposed to be. How had it become more?

But she knew when he'd held her, when he'd sent her blood swimming with those long, intimate kisses, she'd wanted more. Now she, who had never considered herself particularly sexy or overly emotional, was a frus-trated, pitiful wreck because one man had jiggled a lock he was no longer in-terested in opening.

There was nothing to be done about it, she reminded herself. Certainly, considering the circumstances, she and Phillip Quinn had never been meant to develop a personal relationship of any kind. If they managed to have one now, it would be because of the child. They would both be adult, coldly po-lite, and—in the end, she hoped—reasonable.

For Seth's sake.

She opened her eyes as the waitress served her salad and hated the pity she saw on a stranger's face.

"Can I get you anything else? More water?"

"No. I'm fine, thank you. You could take that," she added, indicating Gloria's empty glass.

Her stomach rebelled at the thought of food, but she ordered herself to pick up her fork. For five minutes she toyed with the salad, poking at it while her gaze drifted regularly toward the rear of the restaurant.

She must be ill again, Sybill thought wearily. Now she would have to go back, hold Gloria's head, listen to her whining, and mop up the mess. One more pattern.

Battling both resentment and the shame that trickled from it, she rose and walked back to the ladies' room.

"Gloria, are you all right?" There was no one at the sinks and no answer from any of the stalls. Resigned, Sybill began to nudge doors open. "Gloria?"

In the last stall she saw her own wallet lying open on the closed lid of the toilet. Stunned, she snatched it up, flipped through it. Her various identifications were there, and her credit cards.

But all her cash was gone, along with her sister.

TEN

With her mind jumbled with pain, her hands unsteady, and her system begging to shut down for the night, Sybill keyed open her hotel door. If she could just get to her migraine medication, to a dark room, to oblivion, she would find a way to deal with tomorrow.

She would find a way to face the Quinns, alone, with the shameful sting of failure.

They would believe she'd helped Gloria run away. How could she blame them? She was already a liar and a sneak in their eyes. In Seth's.

And, she admitted, in her own.

With slow deliberation, she turned the bolt, fixed the safety lock, then leaned back against the door until she could will her legs to move again.

When the light switched on, she stifled a yelp and covered her eyes in defense.

"You're right about the view," Phillip said from her terrace doors. "It's spectacular."

She lowered her hand, forced her mind to engage. He'd removed his jacket and tie, she noted, but otherwise he looked just as he had when he'd confronted her at the police station. Polished, urbane, and bitterly angry.

"How did you get in?"

His smile was cold, turning his eyes a hard, chilly gold. The color of an icy winter sun. "You disappoint me, Sybill. I'd have thought your research on your subject would have included the fact that one of my formative skills was breaking and entering."

She stayed where she was, supported by the door. "You were a thief?"

"Among other things. But enough about me." He stepped forward to settle on the arm of the sofa, like a casual friend making himself comfortable for a chatty visit. "You fascinate me. Your notes are incredibly revealing, even to a layman."

"You read my notes?" Her gaze swung toward the desk and her laptop. She couldn't quite find outrage through the prickly blanket of pain enveloping her head, but she knew it must be there. "You had no right to come in here, uninvited. To break into my computer and read my work."

So calm, Phillip thought, and rose to help himself to a beer from her mini bar. What kind of woman was she? "As far as I'm concerned, Sybill, all bets are off. You lied to me, you used me. You had it all worked out, didn't you? When you waltzed into the boatyard last week, your agenda was set."

He couldn't stay calm. The longer she stood, staring at him with no expression on her face, the higher his temper spiked. "Infiltrate the enemy camp." He slammed the beer onto the table. The crack of glass on wood split through her head like an axe. "Observe and report, pass information to your sister. And if being with me helped you slide more smoothly behind the lines, you were willing to make the sacrifice. Would you have slept with me?"

"No." She pressed a hand to her head and nearly gave in to the need to slip to the floor and curl into a ball. "I never meant for things . . ."

"I think you're lying." He crossed to her, taking her arms and drawing her up to her toes. "I think you'd have done anything. Just one more object lesson, right? And with the added benefit of helping your bitch of a sister bleed us for more money. Seth doesn't mean any more to you than he does to her. Just a means to an end for both of you."

"No, that's not—I can't think." The pain was excruciating. If he hadn't been holding her up, she would have gone to her knees and begged. "I—we'll discuss it tomorrow. I'm not well."

"You and Gloria have that in common too. I'm not falling for it, Sybill."

Her breath began to hitch, her vision to blur. "I'm sorry. I can't stand it. I have to sit down. Please, I have to sit down."

He focused in, past his fury. Her cheeks were dead pale, her eyes glassy, her breath coming fast and uneven. If she was faking illness, he decided, Hollywood had missed a major star.

Muttering an oath, he pulled her to the sofa. She all but melted onto the cushions.

Too ill to be embarrassed, she closed her eyes. "My briefcase. My pills are in my briefcase."

He picked up the soft black leather case beside the desk, riffled through it and found the prescription bottle. "Imitrex?" He looked over at her. She had her head back, her eyes closed, and her hands fisted in her lap as if she could center the pain there and squeeze it to death. "Major migraine drugs."

"Yes. I get them now and again." She had to focus, she ordered herself, had to relax. But nothing she did eased her past the vicious pain. "I should have had them with me. If I'd had them with me it wouldn't have gone this far."

"Here." He handed her a pill and water he'd taken from the mini bar.

"Thank you." She nearly bobbled the water in her rush. "It takes a while, but it's better than the injection." She closed her eyes again and prayed he would just leave her alone.

"Have you eaten?"

"What? No. I'll be all right."

She looked fragile, terrifyingly so. Part of him thought she deserved to hurt, was tempted to leave her with her misery. But he picked up the phone and asked for room service.

"I don't want anything."

"Just be quiet." He ordered up soup and tea, then began to prowl the room.

How could he have misjudged her so completely? Pegging people quickly and accurately was one of his most finely honed skills. He'd seen an intelligent, interesting woman. A classy one, with humor and taste. But beneath the glossy surface, she was a liar, a cheat, and an opportunist.

He nearly laughed. He'd just described the boy he'd worked half his life to bury.

"In your notes you say you haven't seen Seth since he was about four. Why did you come here now?"

"I thought I could help."

"Who?"

The hope that the pain would begin to recede gave her the strength to open her eyes. "I don't know. I thought I could help him, and Gloria."

"You help one, you hurt the other. I read your notes, Sybill. Are you going to try to tell me you care about him? 'The subject appears healthy.' He's not a fucking subject, he's a child."

"It's necessary to be objective."

"It's necessary to be human."

It was a dart, sharp enough to strike her heart and make it ache as well. "I'm not very good with emotions. Reactions and behavioral patterns are more my forte than feelings. I'd hoped to be able to keep a certain distance from the situation, to analyze it, to determine what was best for all involved. I haven't been doing a good job of it."

"Why didn't you do anything before?" he demanded. "Why didn't you do anything to analyze the situation when Seth was with your sister?"

"I didn't know where they were." Then she let out a breath and shook her head. It was no time for excuses, and the man staring at her with those cold eyes wouldn't accept them in any case. "I never seriously tried to find out. I sent her money now and again if she contacted me and asked for it. My connection with Gloria was usually unproductive and unpleasant."

"For Christ's sake, Sybill, we're talking about a little boy here, not your views on sibling rivalry."

"I was afraid to get attached," she snapped out. "The one time I did, she took him away. He was her child, not mine. There was nothing I could do about it. I asked her to let me help, but she wouldn't. She's been raising him all alone. My parents have disinherited her. My mother won't even acknowledge that she has a grandson. I know Gloria has problems, but it can't be easy for her."

He simply stared at her. "Are you serious?"

"She's had no one to depend on," Sybill began, then closed her eyes again as a knock sounded on the door. "I'm sorry, but I don't think I can eat."

"Yes, you can."

Phillip opened the door for the room service waiter, directed him to set the tray on the table in front of the sofa. He dispatched him quickly, with cash and a generous tip.

"Try the soup," he ordered. "You need something in your system or the medication's going to end up making you nauseous. My mother was a doctor, remember."

"All right." She spooned it up slowly, telling herself it was just more medicine. "Thank you. I'm sure you're not in the mood to be kind."

"It's harder for me to kick you when you're down. Eat up, Sybill, and we'll go a round or two."

She sighed. The leading edge of the headache was dulling. She could handle it now, she thought. And him as well. "I hope you'll at least attempt to understand my point of view on this. Gloria called me a few weeks ago. She was desperate, terrified. She told me she'd lost Seth."

"Lost him?" Phillip let out a short, sarcastic laugh. "Oh, that's rich."

"I thought abduction at first, but I was able to get some of the details out of her. She explained that your family had him, had taken him from her. She was almost hysterical, so afraid she'd never get him back. She didn't have the money to pay her lawyer. She was fighting an entire family, an entire system all alone. I wired her the money for the lawyer, and I told her I'd help. That she should wait until I contacted her."

As her system began to settle again, she reached for one of the rolls in the basket beside her bowl and broke it open. "I decided to come and see the situation for myself. I know Gloria doesn't always tell the entire truth, that she can slant things to suit her position. But the fact remains that your family had Seth and she didn't."

"Thank God for that."

She stared at the bread in her hand, wondered if she could manage to put it in her mouth and chew. "I know you're providing him with a good home, but she's his mother, Phillip. She has a right to keep her own son."

He watched her face carefully, measured the tone of her voice. He didn't know whether to be furious or baffled by both. "You actually believe that, don't you?"

Color was seeping back into her cheeks. Her eyes had cleared and now met his steadily. "What do you mean?"

"You believe that my family took Seth, that we took advantage of some poor single mother down on her luck and snatched the kid, that she wants him back. That she even has a lawyer working on custody."

"You do have him," Sybill pointed out.

"That's right. And he's exactly where he belongs and is going to stay. Let me give you some facts. She blackmailed my father, and she sold Seth to him."

"I know you believe that, but—"

"I said *facts*, Sybill. Less than a year ago, Seth was living in a set of filthy rooms on the Block in Baltimore, and your sister was on the stroll."

"On the stroll?"

"God, where do you come from? She was hooking. This isn't a whore with a heart of gold here, this isn't a desperate, down-on-her-luck unwed mother doing anything she has to to survive and keep her child fed. She was keeping her habit fed."

She only shook her head, slowly, side to side, even as part of her mind accepted everything he said. "You can't know all this."

"Yes, I can know it. Because I live with Seth. I've talked with him, I've listened to him."

Her hands went icy. She lifted the pot of tea to warm them, poured some slowly into a cup. "He's just a boy. He could have misunderstood."

"Sure. I bet that's it. He just misunderstood when she brought a john up to the place, when she got so stoned she sprawled on the floor and he wondered if she was dead. He just misunderstood when she beat the hell out of him when she was feeling testy."

"She hit him." The cup rattled into the saucer. "She hit him?"

"She beat him. No controversial yet civilized spanking, Dr. Griffin. Fists, belts, the back of the hand. Have you ever had a fist in the face?" He held his up to hers. "Figure it out. Proportionately, this would be about right, comparing a grown woman's fist to, say, a five-, six-year-old boy. Put liquor and drugs into that fist and it comes faster and harder. I've been there."

He angled his fist away, studied it. "My mother preferred smack—to the uninitiated that's heroin. If she missed her fix, you learned to stay far out of her way. I know just what it is to have a vicious, fucked-up female take her fists to me." His gaze whipped back to Sybill's. "Your sister won't ever have the chance to use them on Seth again."

"I—she needs to go into therapy. I never . . . He was fine when I saw him. If I'd known she was abusing him—"

"I haven't finished. He's a good-looking kid, isn't he? Some of Gloria's clients thought so."

The color that had come back to her cheeks fell away. "No." Shaking her head, she pushed away from him and staggered to her feet. "No, I don't believe that. That's hideous. That's impossible."

"She didn't do anything to stop it." He ignored the pale cheeks and fragility now and pushed. Hard. "She didn't do a goddamn thing to protect him. Seth was on his own there. He fought them off or hid. Sooner or later, there would have been one he couldn't fight off or hide from."

"That's not possible. She couldn't."

"She could—especially if it earned her a few extra bucks. It took months with us before he could stand to be touched in even the most casual way. He has nightmares still. And if you say his mother's name, it makes you sick to see the fear that comes into his eyes. That's your situation, Dr. Griffin."

"God. How can you expect me to accept all that? To believe she's capable of that?" She pressed a hand to her heart. "I grew up with her. I've known you less than a week, and you expect me to accept this horror story, this vileness as fact?"

"I think you believe it," he said after a moment. "I think, under it all, you're smart enough, and let's say observant enough to know the truth."

She was terrified. "If it is the truth, why didn't the authorities do anything? Why wasn't he helped?"

"Sybill, have you lived on that smooth plateau so long that you really don't know what life's like on the street? How many Seths there are out there? The system works some of the time, for the few and the lucky. It didn't work for me. It didn't work for Seth. Ray and Stella Quinn worked for me. And just under a year ago, my father paid your sister the first installment on a ten-year-old boy. He brought Seth home, he gave him a life, a decent one."

"She said—she said he took Seth."

"Yeah, he took him. Ten thousand the first time, a couple of other payments of about the same. Then last March she wrote him a letter demanding a lump-sum payment. A hundred fifty thousand, cash, and she'd walk away."

"A hundred and—" Appalled, she broke off, struggled to concentrate on verifiable facts. "She wrote a letter?"

"I've read it. It was in the car with my father when he was killed. He was on his way back from Baltimore. He'd cleaned out most of his bank accounts. I'd have to guess she's gone through a big chunk of it by now. She wrote us, demanding more money, just a few months ago."

She turned away, walked quickly to the terrace doors, and flung them open. The need for air was urgent, and she gulped it in like water. "I'm supposed to accept that Gloria has done all of this, and her primary motive is money?"

"You sent her money for her lawyer. What's his name? Why hasn't our lawyer been contacted by him?"

She squeezed her eyes shut. It wouldn't help to feel betrayed, she reminded herself. "She evaded the question when I asked her. Obviously, she doesn't have a lawyer, and it's doubtful she ever intended to consult one."

"Well, you're slow"—the sarcasm rang clearly—"but you do catch on."

"I wanted to believe her. We were never close as children, and that has to be as much my fault as hers. I'd hoped I could help her, and Seth. I thought this was the way."

"So, she played you."

"I felt responsible. My mother is so unbending on this. She's angry that I came here. She has refused to acknowledge Gloria since she ran off at eighteen. Gloria claimed to have been molested by the counselor at our school. She was always claiming to have been molested. They had a terrible row, my mother and she, and Gloria was gone the next day. She'd taken some of my mother's jewelry, my father's coin collection, some cash. I didn't hear from her for nearly five years. Those five years were a relief.

"She hated me," Sybill said quietly and continued to stare out at the lights on the water. "Always, as long as I can remember. It didn't matter what I did, whether I fought with her or stepped back and let her have her way, she detested me. It was easier for me to keep my distance. I didn't hate her, I simply felt nothing. And when I brush everything else aside right now, it's exactly the same. I can't feel anything for her. It must be a flaw," she murmured. "Maybe it's genetic."

With a weak smile, she turned around again. "It might make an interesting study one day."

"You never had a clue, did you, of what she was doing?"

"No. So much for my renowned observational skills. I'm sorry, Phillip. I'm so terribly sorry for what I've done, and haven't done. I promise you I didn't come here to harm Seth. And I give you my word I'll do whatever I can to help. If I can go into Social Services in the morning, speak with Anna, your family. If you'll allow it, I'd like to see Seth, try to explain."

"We won't be taking him to Anna's office. We're not letting Gloria near him."

"She won't be there."

His eyes flickered. "I beg your pardon?"

"I don't know where she is." Defeated, she spread her hands. "I promised I'd bring her. I meant to."

"You just let her walk? Goddamn it."

"I didn't—not intentionally." She sank down onto the sofa again. "I took her to a restaurant. I wanted to get her a meal, talk to her. She was agitated and drinking too much. I was annoyed with her. I told her we were going to straighten everything out, that we were going to have a meeting in the morning. I made ultimatums. I should have known better. She didn't like it, but I didn't see what she could do about it."

"What sort of ultimatums?"

"That she would get counseling, go into rehab. That she would get help, get herself straightened out before she tried to gain custody of Seth. She went to the ladies' room, and when she didn't come back out, I went in looking for her."

She lifted her hands, let them fall uselessly. "I found my wallet. She must have taken it out of my purse. She left me my credit cards," she added with a wry smile. "She'd know I would cancel them straight off. She only took the cash. It's not the first time she's stolen from me, but it always surprises me." She sighed, shrugged it off. "I drove around for nearly two hours, hoping I'd find her. But I didn't, and I don't know where she is. I don't know what she intends to do."

"She messed you over pretty good, didn't she?"

"I'm an adult. I can take care of myself, and I'm responsible for myself. But Seth . . . if even a part of what you've told me is true . . . he'll hate me. I understand that and I'll have to accept it. I'd like the chance to talk to him."

"That'll be up to him."

"Fair enough. I need to see the files, the paperwork." She linked her fingers together. "I realize you can require me to get a court order, but I'd like to avoid that. I'd process this better if I had it all in black and white."

"It's not as simple as black and white when you're dealing with people's lives and feelings."

"Maybe not. But I need facts, documentation, reports. Once I have them, if I'm persuaded that Seth's best interest is to remain with your family, through legal guardianship or adoption, I'll do whatever I can to help that happen."

She had to push now, she told herself. She had to push to make him give her another chance. Just one more chance. "I'm a psychologist, and I'm the birth mother's sister. I'd think my opinion would bear weight in court."

He studied her objectively. Details, he thought. He was the man who handled the details, after all. Those she was adding would only help settle everything the way he wanted it settled. "I imagine it would, and I'll discuss it with my family. But I don't think you get it, Sybill. She isn't going to fight for Seth. She's never intended to fight for him. She's just trying to use him to get more money. She's not going to get that, either, not another dime."

"So I'm superfluous."

"Maybe. I haven't decided." He rose, jingling the change in his pockets as he paced. "How are you feeling?"

"Better. Fine. Thank you. I'm sorry to have fallen apart like that, but the migraine was a full-blown one."

"You get them often?"

"A few times a year. I'm usually able to get to the medication at onset, so they're not too bad. When I left this evening I was distracted."

"Yeah, bailing your sister out of jail would be a distraction." He glanced back at her with mild curiosity. "How much did it take to spring her?"

"Bail was set at five thousand."

"Well, I'd say you can kiss that good-bye."

"Most likely. The money isn't important."

"What is?" He stopped, turned toward her. She looked exhausted and disconcertingly fragile still. An unfair advantage was still an advantage, he decided, and pressed. "What is important to you, Sybill?"

"Finishing what I've started. You may not need my help, but I don't intend to walk away until I've done what I can."

"If Seth doesn't want to see you or speak to you, he won't. That's bottom line. He's had enough."

She straightened her shoulders before they could slump. "Regardless of whether he agrees to see or speak with me, I intend to stay until the legalities are settled. You can't force me to leave, Phillip. You can make it difficult for me, uncomfortable, but you can't make me leave until I'm satisfied."

"Yeah, I can make it difficult for you. I can make it damn near impossible for you. And I'm considering just that." He leaned over, ignoring her instinctive jerk, and caught her chin firmly in his hand. "Would you have slept with me?"

"Under the circumstances, I believe that's moot."

"Not to me it isn't. Answer the question."

She kept her eyes level with his. That was a matter of pride, though she felt she had little of that or her dignity left intact. "Yes." When his eyes flared, she jerked her chin away. "But not because of Seth or Gloria. I would have slept with you because I wanted you. Because I was attracted to you and when I was around you for any length of time my priorities became blurred."

"Your priorities became blurred." He rocked back on his heels, dipped his hands into his pockets. "Jesus, you're a case. Why do I find that snotty attitude intriguing?"

"I don't have a snotty attitude. You asked a question, I answered it honestly. And, you'll note, in the past tense."

"Now I've got something else to consider. If I want to change that to present tense. Don't say it's moot, Sybill," he warned when she opened her mouth. "I'm bound to take that as a dare. If we end up in bed tonight, neither one of us is going to like ourselves in the morning."

"I don't like you very much right now."

"We're on the same curve there, honey." He jingled his change again, then shrugged. "We'll keep the meeting at Anna's office in the morning. As far as I'm concerned, you can see all the paperwork, including your sister's blackmail letters. As far as Seth goes, I don't make any promises. If you try to go around me and my family to get to him, you'll regret it."

"Don't threaten me."

"I'm not. I'm giving you facts. It's your family who likes threats." His smile was sharp, dangerous, and without an ounce of humor. "The Quinns make promises, and they keep them."

"I'm not Gloria."

"No, but we still have to see just who you are. Nine o'clock," he added. "Oh, and Dr. Griffin, you may want to look over your own notes again. When you do it might be interesting, psychologically speaking, to ask yourself why you find it so much more rewarding to observe than to participate. Get some sleep," he suggested as he walked to the door. "You're going to want to be sharp tomorrow."

"Phillip." Going with the impulse of temper, she rose and waited for him to turn around, with the door open at his back. "Isn't it fortunate that circumstances changed before we made the mistake of sex?"

He angled his head, both impressed and amused that she'd dared such a dangerous parting shot. "Darling, I'm counting my blessings."

He closed the door with a quiet snap.

ELEVEN

Seth needed to be told. There was only one way to do it, and that was straight out, as a family. Ethan and Grace would bring him home as soon as Aubrey was settled with the baby-sitter.

"We shouldn't have let her out of our sight." Cam paced the kitchen, hands jammed in his pockets, gray eyes hard as flint. "God knows where she took off to, and instead of having answers, instead of straightening her ass out, we've got nothing."

"That's not entirely true." Anna brewed coffee. It wouldn't help to settle nerves, she thought, but everyone would want it. "I'll have a police report for the file. You couldn't very well drag her out of the station house, Cameron, and force her to talk to you."

"It would've been a hell of a lot more satisfying than watching her walk."

"Momentarily, perhaps. But it remains in Seth's best interest, and ours, to handle everything in an official, by-the-book manner."

"How do you think Seth's going to feel about that?" He whirled, and the leading edge of his temper whipped out at his wife and his brother. "Do you think he's going to feel it's in his best interest that we had Gloria and did nothing?"

"You did do something." Because she understood his frustration, Anna kept her voice calm. "You agreed to meet her in my office. If she doesn't keep the appointment, it's another strike against her."

"She won't be anywhere near Social Services tomorrow," Phillip began, "but Sybill will."

"And we're supposed to trust her?" Cam snapped out. "All she's done so far is lie."

"You didn't see her tonight," Phillip said evenly. "I did."

"Yeah, and we know what part of your anatomy you're looking with, bro."

"Stop it." Anna stepped quickly between them as two pairs of fists curled, two pairs of eyes flashed. "You're not going to beat each other brainless in this house." She slapped a hand on Cam's chest, then Phillip's, found them both immovable. "It's not going to help anyone if you rip pieces off each other. We need a united front. Seth needs it," she added, pushing harder when she heard the front door open. "Now, both of you sit down. Sit down!" She hissed it, the image of those ready fists swinging over her head, adding both urgency and authority to her voice.

With their gazes still heated and locked, both men dragged out chairs and sat. Anna had time for one relieved breath before Seth came in, trailed by two dogs with cheerfully swatting tails.

"Hey, what's up?" His cheerful grin vanished immediately. A lifetime of living with Gloria's wildly swinging moods had taught him to gauge atmosphere. The air in the kitchen was simmering with tension and temper.

He took a step back, then froze as Ethan came in behind him and laid a hand on his shoulder. "Coffee smells good," he said mildly, and the hand on Seth's shoulder remained, part restraint, part support.

"I'll get some cups." Grace hurried past them to the cupboard. She knew she'd be better off with her hands busy. "Seth, do you want a Coke?"

"What happened?" His lips felt stiff and his hands cold.

"It's going to take a little while to explain it all." Anna walked to him, put her hands on his cheeks. The first order of business, she determined, was to erase the fear that had come into his eyes. "But you don't have to worry."

"Did she ask for more money again? Is she coming here? Did they let her out of jail?"

"No. Come sit down. We'll explain everything." She shook her head at Cam before he could speak and locked her eyes with Phillip's as she guided Seth toward the table. He had more firsthand information, she decided. It was best that it come from him.

Where the hell was he supposed to start? Phillip dragged a hand through his hair. "Seth, do you know anything about your mother's family?"

"No. She used to tell me stuff. One day she'd say how her parents were rich, really rolling in it, but they died and some slick lawyer stole all the money. Another day she'd say how she was an orphan and she'd run away from this foster home because the father tried to rape her. Or how her mother was this movie star who gave her up for adoption so she wouldn't lose her career. She was always changing it."

His gaze shifted around the room as he spoke, trying to read faces. "Who cares?" he demanded, ignoring the soft drink Grace set in front of him. "Who the hell cares, anyway? There wasn't anybody or she'd've tapped them for money."

"There is somebody, and it seems she did tap them for money off and on." Phillip kept his voice quiet and calm, as a person would when soothing a frantic puppy. "We found out today that she has parents, and a sister."

"I don't have to go with them." Alarm rang in his head as he surged out of his chair. "I don't know them. I don't have to go with them."

"No, you don't." Phillip took Seth's arm. "But you need to know about them."

"I don't want to." His gaze flew to Cam's, pleaded. "I don't want to know. You said I could stay. You said nothing was going to change that."

It made Cam sick to see that desperation, but he pointed to the chair. "You are staying. Nothing is going to change that. Sit down. You never solve anything by running."

"Look around, Seth." Ethan's tone was soft, the voice of reason. "You've got five people here, standing with you."

He wanted to believe it. He didn't know how to explain that it was so much easier to believe in lies and threats than in promises. "What are they going to do? How did they find me?"

"Gloria called her sister a few weeks ago," Phillip began when Seth sat again. "You don't remember her sister?"

"I don't remember anybody," Seth muttered and hunched his shoulders.

"Well, it seems she spun a tale for the sister, told her that we'd stolen you from her."

"She's full of shit."

"Seth." Anna drilled him with a look that made him squirm.

"She conned the sister out of some money for a lawyer," Phillip continued. "Said she was broke and desperate, that we'd threatened her. She needed the money to get you back."

Seth wiped his mouth with the back of his hand. "She bought it? She must be an idiot."

"Maybe. Or maybe she's a soft touch. Either way, the sister didn't buy the whole package. She wanted to check things out for herself. So she came to St. Chris."

"She's here?" Seth's head whipped up. "I don't want to see her. I don't want to talk to her."

"You already have. Sybill is Gloria's sister."

Seth's dark-blue eyes widened, and the angry flush faded from his cheeks. "She can't be. She's a doctor. She writes books."

"Nonetheless, she is. When Cam and Ethan and I drove down to Hampton, we saw her."

"You saw her? You saw Gloria?"

"Yeah, we saw her. Hold on." Phillip laid a hand over Seth's rigid one. "Sybill was there, too. She was posting bail. So it all came out."

"She's a liar." Seth's voice began to hitch. "Just like Gloria. She's a damn liar."

"Let me finish. We agreed to meet them both in the morning, in Anna's office. We have to get the facts, Seth," he added when the boy snatched his hands free. "It's the only way we're going to fix this for good."

"I'm not going."

"You can decide that for yourself. We don't think Gloria's going to show. I saw Sybill just a little while ago. Gloria had given her the slip."

"She's gone." Relief and hope struggled to beat back fear. "She's gone again?"

"It looks that way. She took money out of Sybill's wallet and split." Phillip glanced over at Ethan, judged his brother's reaction to the news as angry resignation. "Sybill will be in Anna's office in the morning. I think it would be better if you went in with us, talked to her there."

"I don't have anything to say to her. I don't know her. I don't care about her. She should just go away and leave me alone."

"She can't hurt you, Seth."

"I hate her. She's probably just like Gloria, only she pretends to be different."

Phillip thought of the fatigue, the guilt, the misery he'd seen on Sybill's face. But he said, "That's for you to decide, too. But you need to see her and hear what she has to say to do that. She said she'd only seen you once. Gloria came to New York and you stayed at Sybill's place for a little while. You were about four."

"I don't remember." His face went stony with stubbornness. "We stayed in a lot of places."

"Seth, I know it doesn't seem fair." Grace reached over to give the hands he had balled into fists on the table a quick, reassuring squeeze. "But your aunt may be able to help. We'll all be there with you."

Cam saw the refusal in Seth's eyes and leaned forward. "Quinns don't walk away from a fight." He paused until Seth's gaze shifted to his. "Until they win it."

It was pride and the fear of not living up to the name they'd given him that stiffened his shoulders. "I'll go, but nothing she says is going to mean dick to me." With eyes hot and brooding, he turned to Phillip. "Did you have sex with her?"

"Seth!" Anna's voice was sharp as a slap, but Phillip only raised a hand.

Maybe his first instinct was to tell the boy it was none of his business, but he knew how to think past the quick retort and study the whole. "No, I didn't."

Seth gave a stiff shrug. "That's something, then."

"You come first." Phillip saw the surprise flicker in Seth's eyes at the statement. "I made a promise that you would, so you do. Nothing and no one changes that."

Beneath the warm thrill, Seth felt a greasy tug of shame. "Sorry," he mumbled and stared down at his own hands.

"Fine." Phillip sipped at the coffee that had gone cold in his cup. "We'll hear what she has to say in the morning, then she'll hear what we have to say. What you have to say. We'll go from there."

She didn't know what she was going to say. She felt sick inside. The dregs of a migraine hangover fuzzed her brain, and her nerves were stretched to the breaking point at the prospect of facing the Quinns. And Seth.

They had to hate her. She doubted very much they could feel more contempt for her than she felt for herself. If what Phillip had told her was true—the drugs, the beatings, the men—she had by the sin of omission left her own nephew in hell.

There was nothing they could say to her that was worse than what she had said to herself during the endless, sleepless night. But she was sick with anticipation of what was to come as she pulled into the small parking lot attached to Social Services.

It was bound to become ugly, she thought, as she tilted her rearview mirror and carefully applied lipstick. Hard words, cold looks—and she was so pitifully vulnerable to both.

She could stand against them, she told herself. She could maintain that outward calm no matter what was happening to her insides. She'd learned that defense over the years. Remain aloof and detached, and survive.

She would survive this. And if she could somehow ease Seth's mind, whatever wounds she suffered would be worth it.

She stepped out of the car, a cool and composed woman in a elegantly simple silk suit the color of mourning. Her hair was swept up in a sleek twist, her makeup was subtle and flawless.

Her stomach was raw and burning.

She stepped inside the lobby. Already the waiting area contained a scattering of people. An infant whimpered restlessly in the arms of a woman whose eyes were glazed with fatigue. A man in a flannel shirt and jeans sat with his face grim and his fisted hands dangling between his knees. Two other women sat in a corner. Mother and daughter, Sybill deduced. The younger woman had her head cradled on the other's shoulder and wept silently out of eyes blackened by fists.

Sybill turned away.

"Dr. Griffin," she told the receptionist. "I have an appointment with Anna Spinelli."

"Yes, she's expecting you. Down this hall, second door on your left."

"Thank you." Sybill closed her hand around the strap of her purse and walked briskly to Anna's office.

Her heart plummeted to her stomach when she reached the doorway. They were all there, waiting. Anna sat behind the desk, looking professional in a navy blazer, her hair pinned up. She was scanning an open file.

Grace sat with her hand swallowed by Ethan's. Cam stood at the narrow window, scowling, while Phillip sat, flipping through a magazine.

Seth sat between them, staring down at the floor, his eyes curtained by his lashes, his mouth set, his shoulders hunched.

She gathered her courage, started to speak. But Phillip's eyes flicked up and found hers. The one long look warned her he hadn't softened overnight. She ignored her trembling pulse and angled her head in acknowledgment.

"You're prompt, Dr. Griffin," he said, and instantly all eyes were on her.

She felt scalded and pinned all at once, but she took the last step over the threshold into what she fully understood was Quinn turf. "Thank you for seeing me."

"Oh, we're looking forward to it." Cam's voice was dangerously soft. His hand, Sybill noted, had gone to Seth's shoulder in a gesture that was both possessive and protective.

"Ethan, would you close the door?" Anna folded her hands on the open file. "Please sit down, Dr. Griffin."

It wouldn't be Sybill and Anna here. All the friendly female connection that came from cozy kitchens and simmering pots was gone.

Accepting that, Sybill took the vacant seat facing Anna's desk. She set her purse in her lap, clutched it with boneless fingers, and smoothly, casually, crossed her legs.

"Before we begin, I'd like to say something." She took a slow breath when Anna nodded in agreement. Sybill shifted and looked directly at Seth. He kept his eyes on the floor. "I didn't come here to hurt you, Seth, or to make you unhappy. I'm sorry that I seem to have done both. If living with the Quinns is what you want, what you need, then I want to help see that you stay with them."

Seth lifted his head now and stared at her with eyes that were stunningly adult and harsh. "I don't want your help."

"But you may need it," she murmured, then turned back to Anna. Sybill saw speculation there, and what she hoped was an open mind. "I don't know where Gloria is. I'm sorry. I gave my word I would bring her here this morning. It's been a very long time since I'd seen her, and I . . . I hadn't realized how much she'd . . . how unstable she is."

" 'Unstable.' " Cam snorted at the term. "That's a rich one."

"She contacted you," Anna began, shooting her husband one warning look.

"Yes, a few weeks ago. She was very upset, claimed that Seth had been stolen from her and that she needed money for her lawyer, who was going to fight a custody case. She was crying, nearly hysterical. She begged me to help her. I got as much information as I could. Who had Seth, and where he was living. I sent her five thousand dollars."

Sybill lifted her hands. "I realized yesterday when I spoke with her that there was no lawyer. Gloria has always been a clever actress. I'd forgotten that, or I chose to forget that."

"Were you aware that she had a drug problem?"

"No—again, not until yesterday. When I saw her, and spoke with her, it became clear that she's not capable at this time of handling the responsibility of a child."

"She doesn't want the responsibility of a child," Phillip commented.

"So you said," Sybill responded coolly. "You indicated that she wanted money. I'm aware that money is important to Gloria. I'm also aware that she's not stable. But it's difficult for me to believe, without proof, that she's done all that you claim."

"You want proof?" Cam stepped forward, fury all but visible in waves around him. "You got it, sugar. Show her the letters, Anna."

"Cam, sit down." Anna's order was firm before she turned back to Sybill. "Would you recognize your sister's handwriting?"

"I don't know. I suppose I might."

"I have a copy of the letter found in Raymond Quinn's car when he was killed, and one of the letters sent to us more recently."

She took them out of the file and passed them over the desk into Sybill's hands.

Words and phrases leaped out at her, burned into her mind.

Quinn, I'm tired of playing nickel and dime. You want the kid so bad, then it's time to pay for him. . . . A hundred and fifty grand's a pretty good bargain for a good-looking boy like Seth.

Oh, God, was all Sybill could think. Dear God.

The letter to the Quinns after Ray's death was no better.

Ray and me had an agreement.

If you're set on keeping him . . . I'm going to need some money . . .

Sybill willed her hands to remain steady.

"She took this money?"

"Professor Quinn drew out cashier's checks to Gloria DeLauter, twice for ten thousand dollars, once for five." Anna spoke clearly and without emotion. "He brought Seth DeLauter to St. Christopher's late last year. The letter you have is postmarked March tenth. The following day Professor Quinn arranged to cash out his bonds, some stock, and he drew large sums of cash out of his bank account. On March twelfth, he told Ethan he had business in Baltimore. On his return, he was killed in a single-car accident. There were just over forty dollars in his wallet. No other money was found."

"He promised I wouldn't have to go back," Seth said dully. "He was decent. He promised, and she knew he'd pay her."

"She asked for more. From you. From all of you."

"And miscalculated." Phillip leaned back, studying Sybill. Nothing showed, he noted, but her pallor. "She won't bleed us, Dr. Griffin. She can threaten all she wants, but she won't bleed us, and she won't get Seth."

"You also have a copy of the letter I wrote to Gloria DeLauter," Anna stated. "I informed her that Seth was under the protection of Social Services, that an investigation by this office was under way on charges of child abuse. If she comes into the county, she'll be served with a restraining order and a warrant."

"She was furious," Grace spoke up. "She called the house right after she got Anna's letter. She threatened and demanded. She said she wanted money or she'd take Seth. I told her she was wrong." Grace looked over, held Seth's gaze. "He's ours now."

She'd sold her son, was all Sybill could think. It was just as Phillip had said. All of it was just as he'd said. "You have temporary guardianship."

"It'll be permanent shortly," Phillip informed her. "We intend to see to that."

Sybill laid the papers back on Anna's desk. Inside she was cold, brutally cold, but she linked her fingers lightly on top of her purse and spoke evenly to Seth. "Did she hit you?"

"What the hell do you care?"

"Answer the question, Seth," Phillip ordered. "Tell your aunt what life was like with her sister."

"Okay, fine." He bit the words off, but his sneer was wobbly around the edges. "Sure, she knocked me around when she felt like it. If I was lucky, she was too drunk or stoned for it to hurt much. I could usually get away, anyhow." He shrugged as if it didn't matter in the least. "Sometimes she got me by surprise. Maybe she hadn't been able to turn enough tricks to score. So she'd wake me up and pound on me a while. Or she'd cry all over me."

She wanted to turn away from that image, as she'd turned away from the desperate strangers in the waiting area. Instead she kept her gaze steady on Seth's face. "Why didn't you tell anyone, find someone to help you?"

"Like who?" Was she stupid, Seth thought? "The cops? She told me what the cops would do. I'd end up in juvie and some guy would use me like some of her johns wanted to. They could do whatever they wanted once I was inside. As long as I was out, I could get away."

"She lied to you," Anna said softly while Sybill tried to find words, any words. "The police would have helped."

"She knew?" Sybill managed. "About the men who tried to . . . touch you?"

"Sure, she thought it was funny. Hell, when she's stoned, she thinks most everything is funny. It's when she's drunk that she gets mean."

Could this monster the boy spoke of so casually be her sister? "How . . . Do you know why she decided to contact Professor Quinn?"

"No, I don't know anything about it. She got wired up one day, started talking about hitting a gold mine. She took off for a few days."

"She left you alone?" Why that should horrify her, after everything else she'd heard, Sybill couldn't say.

"Hey, I can take care of myself. When she came back, she was flying. Said I was finally going to be of some use. She had some money—real money, because she went out and scored a lot of dope without hooking. She stayed stoned and happy for days. Then Ray came. He said I could come with him. At first I thought he was like the guys she brought home. But he wasn't. I could tell. He looked sad and tired."

His voice had changed, she noted, softened. So, she thought, he grieves, too. Then she saw the ripe disgust come into his eyes.

"She came on to him," Seth said shortly, "and he got real upset. He didn't yell or anything, but he got real hard in the eyes. He made her leave. He had money with him, and he said if she wanted it, to leave. So she took it and went. He told me he had a house by the water, and a dog, and that I could live there if I wanted. And no one would mess with me."

"You went with him."

"He was old," Seth said with a shrug. "I figured I could get away from him if he tried anything. But you could trust Ray. He was decent. He said I'd never have to go back to the way things were. And I won't. No matter what, I won't go back. And I don't trust you." His eyes were adult again, his voice controlled and derisive. "Because you lied, you pretended to be decent. All you were doing was spying on us."

"You're right." She thought it the hardest thing she'd ever done, or would ever have to do, to meet those scornful eyes in a child's face and admit her own sins. "You have no reason to trust me. I didn't help you. I could have, all those years ago when she brought you to New York. I didn't want to see. It was easier not to. And when I came home one day and both of you were gone, I didn't do anything about that, either. I told myself it wasn't my concern, that you weren't my responsibility. That wasn't just wrong, it was cowardly."

He didn't want to believe her, didn't want to hear the regret and the apology in her voice. He balled his hands into fists on his knees. "It doesn't have anything to do with you now, either."

"She's my sister. I can't change that." Because it hurt to see the contempt in his eyes, she turned back to Anna. "What can I do to help? Can I make a statement to you? Talk to your lawyer? I'm a licensed psychologist, and Gloria's sister. I would assume that my opinion might carry some weight toward the guardianship."

"I'm sure it would," Anna murmured. "It won't be easy for you."

"I have no feelings for her. I'm not proud to say that, but it's the simple truth. I feel nothing toward her whatsoever, and the sense of responsibility I thought I should feel to her is over. As much as he may wish it otherwise, I'm Seth's aunt. I intend to help."

She rose and scanned the faces in the room while her stomach pitched and rolled. "I'm terribly sorry, for all of this. I realize an apology is useless. I have no excuse for what I did. Reasons, but no excuses. It's perfectly clear that Seth is where he belongs, where he's happy. If you'll give me a moment to gather my thoughts, I'll give you a statement."

She walked out, without hurry, and continued to the outside, where she could find air.

"Well, she went about it wrong, but she seems level right now." Cam got up, paced off some of his energy in the crowded office. "She sure doesn't shake easily."

"I wonder," Anna murmured. She, too, was a trained observer, and instinct told her there was a great deal more going on under that placid surface than any of them might guess. "Having her on our side will, without question, help. It might be best if you left the two of us alone so I can talk with her. Phillip, you'll want to call the lawyer, explain the situation, and see if he wants to depose her."

"Yeah, I'll take care of it." He frowned thoughtfully at the fingers drumming on his knee. "She had a picture of Seth in her Filofax."

"What?" Anna blinked at him.

"I went through her things before she got back to the hotel last night." He smiled a little, then shrugged as his sister-in-law closed her eyes. "Seemed like the thing to do at the time. She's got this snapshot of Seth when he was little, tucked in her Filofax."

"So what?" Seth demanded.

"So, it was the only picture I found anywhere. It's interesting." He lifted his hands, dropped them again. "On another path, it could be that Sybill knows something about Gloria's connection to Dad. Since we can't question Gloria, we ought to ask her."

"Seems to me," Ethan said slowly, "that whatever she knows would've come from Gloria. Be tough to believe it. I think she'd tell us what she knows," he continued, "but what she knows might not be fact."

"We don't know fact or fiction," Phillip pointed out, "until we ask her."

"Ask me what?" Steadier, determined now to finish it out, Sybill stepped back into the room and closed the door quietly at her back.

"The reason Gloria hit on our father." Phillip rose so their eyes were level. "The reason she knew he would pay to protect Seth."

"Seth said he was a decent man." Sybill's gaze roamed the faces of the men. "I think you're proof of that."

"Decent men don't have adulterous affairs with women half their age, then walk away from a child conceived from that affair." Bitterness coated Phillip's voice as he took another step toward Sybill. "And there's no way you're going to convince us that Ray slept with your sister behind our mother's back, then walked away from his son."

"What?" Without realizing it, Sybill shot a hand out to grip his arm, as much in shock as to keep her balance as she reeled from it. "Of course he didn't. You told me you didn't believe that Gloria and your father . . ."

"Others do."

"But that's—where did you get the idea that Seth was his son, his son by Gloria?"

"It's easy enough to hear it in town if you keep your ears open." Phillip narrowed his eyes at her face. "It's something your sister planted. She claimed he molested her, then she blackmails him, sells him her son." He looked back at Seth, into Ray Quinn's eyes. "I say it's a lie."

"Of course it's a lie. It's a horrible lie."

Desperate to do at least this one thing right and well, she went to Seth, crouched in front of him. She wanted badly to take his hand, but resisted her impulse when he leaned away from her.

"Ray Quinn wasn't your father, Seth. He was your grandfather. Gloria's his daughter."

His lips trembled, and those deep-blue eyes shimmered. "My grandfather?"

"Yes. I'm sorry she didn't tell you, so sorry you didn't know before he . . ." She shook her head, straightened. "I didn't realize there was confusion about this. I should have. I only learned about it myself a few weeks ago."

She took her seat again, prepared herself. "I'll tell you everything I know."

TWELVE

It was easier now, almost like a lecture. Sybill was used to giving lectures on social topics. All she had to do was divorce herself from the subject and relay information in a clear and cohesive manner.

"Professor Quinn had a relationship with Barbara Harrow," she began. She put her back to the window so that she could face all of them as she spoke. "They met at American University in Washington. I don't have a great many of the details, but what I do know indicates that he was teaching there and she was a graduate student. Barbara Harrow is my mother. Gloria's mother."

"My father," Phillip said. "Your mother."

"Yes. Nearly thirty-five years ago. I assume they were attracted to each other, physically at least. My mother . . ." She cleared her throat. "My mother indicated that she believed he had a great deal of potential, that he would rise up the ranks in academia quickly. Status is an essential requirement to my mother's contentment. However, she found herself disappointed in his . . . what she saw as his lack of ambition. He was content to teach. Apparently he wasn't particularly interested in the social obligations that are necessary for advancement. And his politics were too liberal for her tastes."

"She wanted a rich, important husband." Cueing in quickly, Phillip raised his eyebrows. "And she discovered he wasn't going to be it."

"That's essentially true," Sybill agreed in a cool, steady voice. "Thirty-five years ago, the country was experiencing unrest, its own internal war between youth and establishment. Colleges were teeming with minds that questioned not only an unpopular war, but the status quo. Professor Quinn, it would seem, had a lot of questions."

"He believed in using the brain," Cam muttered. "And in taking a stand."

"According to my mother, he took stands." Sybill managed a small smile. "Often unpopular with the administration of the university. He and my mother disagreed, strongly, on basic principles and beliefs. At the end of the term, she went home to Boston, disillusioned, angry, and, she was to discover, pregnant."

"Bullshit. Sorry," Cam said shortly when Anna hissed at him. "But it's bullshit. There's no way he would have ignored responsibility for a kid. No way in hell."

"She never told him." Sybill folded her hands as all eyes swung back to her. "She was furious. Perhaps she was frightened as well, but she was furious to find herself pregnant by a man she'd decided was unsuitable. She considered terminating the pregnancy. She'd met my father, and they had clicked."

"He was suitable," Cam concluded.

"I believe they suited each other." Her voice chilled. They were her parents, damn it. She had to be left with something. "My mother was in a difficult and frightening position. She wasn't a child. She was nearly twenty-five, but an unwanted and unplanned pregnancy is a wrenching episode for a woman of any age. In a moment of weakness, or despair, she confessed all of it to my father. And he offered her marriage. He loved her," Sybill said quietly. "He must have loved her very much. They were married quickly and quietly. She never went back to Washington. She never looked back."

"Dad never knew he had a daughter?" Ethan covered Grace's hand with his.

"No, he couldn't have. Gloria was three, nearly four when I was born. I can't say what the relationship between her and my parents was like in those early years. I know that later on, she felt excluded. She was difficult and temperamental, demanding. Certainly she was wild. Certain standards of behavior were expected, and she refused to meet them."

It sounded so cold, Sybill thought now. So unyielding. "In any case, she left home when she was still a teenager. Later, I discovered that both of my parents, and myself, sent her money, independently of each other. She would contact one of us and plead, demand, threaten, whichever worked. I wasn't aware of any of this until Gloria called me last month, about Seth."

Sybill paused a moment until she could compose her thoughts. "Before I came here, I flew to Paris to see my parents. I felt they needed to know. Seth was their grandchild, and as far as I knew, he'd been taken away from Gloria and was living with strangers. When I told my mother what had happened, and she refused to become involved, to offer any assistance, I was stunned and angry. We argued." Sybill let out a short laugh. "She was surprised enough by that, I think, to tell me what I've just told you."

"Gloria had to know," Phillip pointed out. "She had to know Ray Quinn was her father or she'd never have come here."

"Yes, she knew. A couple of years ago, she went to my mother when my parents were staying in D.C. for a few months. I can assume it was an ugly scene. From what my mother told me, Gloria demanded a large sum of money or she'd go to the press, to the police, to whoever would listen and accuse my father of sexual abuse, my mother of collusion in it. None of that is true," Sybill said wearily. "Gloria always equated sex with power, and acceptance. She routinely accused men, particularly men in positions of authority, of molesting her.

"In this instance, my mother gave her several thousand dollars and the story I've just told you. She promised Gloria that it was the last penny she would ever see from her, the last word she would ever speak to her. My mother rarely, very rarely, goes back on a promise of any kind. Gloria would have known that."

"So she hit on Ray Quinn instead," Phillip concluded.

"I don't know when she decided to find him. It may have stewed in her mind for a time. Now she would consider this the reason she was never loved, never wanted, never accepted as she felt she deserved to be. I imagine she blamed your father for that. Someone else is always to blame when Gloria has difficulties."

"So she found him." Phillip rose from his chair to pace. "And, true to form, demanded money, made accusations, threatened. Only this time she used her own son as the hammer."

"Apparently. I'm sorry. I should have realized you weren't aware of all the facts. I suppose I assumed your father had told you more of it."

"He didn't have time." Cam's voice was cold and bitter.

"He told me he was waiting for some information," Ethan remembered. "That he'd explain everything once he found out."

"He must have tried contacting your mother." Phillip pinned Sybill with a look. "He would have wanted to speak with her, to know."

"I can't tell you that. I simply don't know."

"I know," Phillip said shortly. "He would have done what he felt was right. For Seth first, because he's a child. But he would have wanted to help Gloria. To do that, he needed to talk to her mother, find out what had happened. It would have mattered to him."

"I can only tell you what I know or what's been told to me." Sybill lifted her hands, let them fall. "My family has behaved badly." It was weak, she knew. "All of us," she said to Seth. "I apologize for myself, and for them. I don't expect you to . . ." What? she wondered, and let it go. "I'll do anything I can to help."

"I want people to know." Seth's eyes swam when he lifted them to her face. "I want people to know he was my grandfather. They're saying things about him, and it's wrong. I want people to know I'm a Quinn."

Sybill could only nod. If this was all he asked of her, she would make certain she gave it. Drawing a breath, she looked at Anna. "What can I do?"

"You've made a good start already." Anna glanced at her watch. She had other cases and another appointment scheduled in ten minutes. "Are you willing to make the information you've given us official, and public?"

"Yes."

"I have an idea how to start that ball rolling."

The embarrassment factor couldn't be weighed, Sybill reminded herself. She could and would live with the whispers and the speculative looks that were bound to come her way once she followed through on Anna's suggestion.

⚭

She'd typed up her statement herself, spending two hours in her room choosing the right words and phrasing. The information had to be clear, the details of her mother's actions, of Gloria's, even her own.

When it was proofed and printed out, she didn't hesitate. She took the pages down to the front desk, and calmly requested that they be faxed to Anna's office.

"I'll need the originals back," she told the clerk. "And I expect a reply by return fax."

"I'll take care of this for you." The young, fresh-faced clerk smiled professionally before she slipped into the office behind the desk.

Sybill closed her eyes briefly. No turning back now, she reminded herself. She folded her hands, composed her features, and waited.

It didn't take long. And there was no mistaking from the wide eyes of the clerk that at least part of the transmission had been scanned. "Do you want to wait for the reply, Dr. Griffin?"

"Yes, thank you." Sybill held out a hand for the papers, nearly smiling as the clerk jolted, then quickly passed them across the desk.

"Are you, ah, enjoying your stay?"

Can't wait to pass on what you read, can you? Sybill thought. Typical, and totally expected human behavior. "It's been an interesting experience so far."

"Well, excuse me a moment." The clerk dashed into the back room again.

Sybill was just releasing a sigh when her shoulders tensed. She knew Phillip was behind her before she turned to face him. "I sent the fax to Anna," she said stiffly. "I'm waiting for her reply. If she finds it satisfactory,

I'll have time to go to the bank before it closes and have the document notarized. I gave my word."

"I'm not here as a guard dog, Sybill. I thought you could use a little moral support."

She all but sniffed. "I'm perfectly fine."

"No, you're not." To prove it to both of them, he rested a hand on the rigid cords in her neck. "But you put on a hell of a show."

"I prefer to do this alone."

"Well, you can't always get what you want. As the song says." He glanced over with an easy smile, his hand still on Sybill's nape, as the clerk hurried out with an envelope. "Hi, there, Karen. How's it going?"

The clerk blushed clear to the hairline, her eyes darting from his face to Sybill's. "Fine. Um . . . here's your fax, Dr. Griffin."

"Thank you." Without flinching Sybill took the envelope and tucked it into her bag. "You'll bill my account for the service."

"Yes, of course."

"See you around, Karen." Smoothly, Phillip slid his hand from Sybill's neck to the small of her back to guide her across the lobby.

"She'll have told her six best friends by her next break," Sybill murmured.

"At the very least. The wonders of small towns. The Quinns will be the hot topic of discussion over a number of dinner tables tonight. By breakfast, the gossip mill will be in full swing."

"That amuses you," Sybill said tightly.

"It reassures me, Dr. Griffin. Traditions are meant to reassure. I spoke to our lawyer," he continued as they crossed the waterfront. Gulls swooped, dogging a workboat on its way to dock. "The notarized statement will help, but he'd like to take your deposition, early next week if you can manage it."

"I'll make an appointment." In front of the bank she stopped and turned toward him. He'd changed into casual clothes, and the wind off the water ruffled his hair. His eyes were concealed behind shaded lenses, but she wasn't certain she cared to see the expression in them. "It might look less as if I'm under house arrest if I go in alone."

He merely lifted his hands, palms out, and stepped back. She was a tough nut, he decided when she strode into the bank. But he had a feeling that, once cracked, there was something soft, even delectable inside.

He was surprised that someone as intelligent, as highly trained in the human condition as she was couldn't see her own distress, couldn't or wouldn't admit that there had been something lacking in her own upbringing that forced her to build walls.

He'd nearly been fooled, he mused, into believing she was cold and distant and untouched by the messier emotions. He couldn't be sure what it was that insisted he believe differently. Maybe it was nothing more than wishful thinking, but he was determined to find out for himself. And soon.

He knew that making her family secrets accessible and so informally public would be humiliating for her, and perhaps painful. But she'd agreed without condition and was following through without hesitation.

Standards, he thought. Integrity. She had them. And he believed that she had heart as well.

Sybill offered a thin smile as she came back out. "Well, that's the first time I've seen a notary's eyes nearly pop out of her head. I think that should—"

The rest of her babbling statement was lost as his mouth rushed to cover hers. She lifted a hand to his shoulder, but her fingers only curled into the soft material of his sweater.

"You looked like you needed it," he murmured, and skimmed a hand over her cheek.

"Regardless—"

"Hell, Sybill, we've already got them talking. Why not add to the mystery?"

Her emotions were rocking, making it difficult for her to hold on to any threads of composure. "I've no intention of standing here making a spectacle of myself. So if you'll—"

"Fine. Let's go somewhere else. I've got the boat."

"The boat? I can't go out on the boat. I'm not dressed for it. I have work." I need to think, she told herself, but he was already pulling her to the dock.

"A sail will do you good. You're starting on another headache. The fresh air should help."

"I don't have a headache." Only the nasty, simmering threat of one. "And I don't want to—" She nearly yelped, so stunned was she when he simply plucked her off her feet and set her down on the deck.

"Consider yourself shanghaied, doc." Quickly, competently, he freed the lines and leaped aboard. "I have a feeling you haven't had nearly enough of that kind of treatment in your short, sheltered life."

"You don't know anything about my life, or what I've had. If you start that engine, I'm going to—" She broke off, grinding her teeth as the motor putted to life. "Phillip, I want to go back to my hotel. Now."

"Hardly anybody ever says no to you, do they?" He said it cheerfully as he gave her a firm nudge onto the port bench. "Just sit back and enjoy the ride."

Since she didn't intend to leap overboard and swim back to shore in a silk suit and Italian shoes, she folded her arms. It was his way of paying her back, she supposed, by taking away her freedom of choice, asserting his will and his physical dominance.

Typical.

She turned her head to stare out over the light chop. She wasn't afraid of him, not physically. He had a tougher side than she'd originally thought, but he wouldn't hurt her. And because he cared for Seth, deeply, she'd come to believe, he needed her cooperation.

She refused to be thrilled when he hoisted the sails. The sound of the canvas opening itself to the wind, the sight of the sun beating against the rippling white, the sudden and smooth angling of the boat, meant nothing to her, she insisted.

She would simply tolerate this little game of his, give him no reaction. Undoubtedly, he would grow weary of her silence and inattention and take her back.

"Here." He tossed something, making her jump. She looked down and saw the sunglasses that had landed neatly in her lap. "Sun's fierce today, even if the temperature's cooling. Indian summer's around the corner."

He smiled to himself when she said nothing, only slid the sunglasses primly on her nose and continued to stare in the opposite direction.

"We need a good hard frost first," he continued conversationally. "When the leaves start to turn, the shoreline near the house is a picture. Golds and scarlets. You get that deep blue sky behind them, and the water mirror-bright, that spice of fall on the air, and you could start to believe there's no place else on the planet you'd ever want to be."

She kept her mouth firmly shut, tightened the fold of her arms across her breasts.

Phillip merely tucked his tongue in his cheek. "Even a couple of avowed urbanites like you and I can appreciate a fine fall day in the country. Seth's birthday's coming up."

Out of the corner of his eye he saw her head jerk around, her mouth tremble open. She shut it again, but this time when she turned away, her shoulders where hunched defensively.

Oh, she felt all right, Phillip mused. There were plenty of messy emotions stewing inside that cool package of hers.

"We thought we'd throw him a party, have some of his pals over to raise hell. You already know Grace bakes a hell of a chocolate cake. We've got his present taken care of. But just the other day I saw these art supplies in this shop in Baltimore. Not a kid's setup, a real one. Chalk, pencils, charcoal, brushes, watercolors, paper, palettes. It's a specialty shop a few blocks from my office. Somebody who knew something about art could breeze in there and pick out just the right things."

He'd intended to do so himself, but he saw now that his instincts to tell her about it had been true. She was facing him now, and though the sun flashed off her sunglasses, he could see from the angle of her head that he had her full attention.

"He wouldn't want anything from me."

"You're not giving him enough credit. Maybe you're not giving yourself enough either."

He trimmed the sails, caught the wind, and saw the instant she recognized the curve of trees along the shore. She got unsteadily to her feet. "Phillip, however you may feel about me right now, it can't help the situation for you to push me at Seth again so soon."

"I'm not taking you home." He scanned the yard as they passed. "Seth's at the boatyard with Cam and Ethan, in any case. You need a distraction, Sybill, not a confrontation. And for the record, I don't know how I feel about you at the moment."

"I've told you everything I know."

"Yeah, I think you've given me the facts. You haven't told me how you feel, how those facts affect you personally, emotionally."

"It isn't the issue."

"I'm making it an issue. We're tangled up here, Sybill, whether we like it or not. Seth's your nephew, and he's mine. My father and your mother had an affair. And we're about to."

"No," she said definitely, "we're not."

He turned his head long enough to shoot her a glittering look. "You know better than that. You're in my system, and I know when a woman's got me in hers."

"And we're both old enough to control our more basic urges."

He stared at her another moment, then laughed. "Hell we are. And it's not the sex that worries you. It's the intimacy."

He was hitting all the targets. It didn't anger her nearly as much as it frightened her. "You don't know me."

"I'm beginning to," he said quietly. "And I'm someone else who finishes what I start. I'm coming about." His voice was mild now. "Watch the boom."

She stepped out of the way, sat. She recognized the little cove where they had shared wine and paté. Only a week ago, she thought dully. Now so much had changed. Everything had changed.

She couldn't be here with him, couldn't risk it. The idea of handling him now was absurd. Still, she could do nothing but try.

Coolly, she eyed him. Casually, she smoothed her hand over the sophisticated twist the wind had disordered. Caustically, she smiled. "What, no wine this time? No music, no neat gourmet lunch?"

He dropped the sails, secured the boat. "You're scared."

"You're arrogant. And you don't worry me."

"Now you're lying." While the boat swayed gently underfoot, he stepped forward and took the sunglasses from her. "I worry you, quite a bit. You keep thinking you have me pegged, then I don't follow the script. I imagine most of the men you've let hover around your life have been fairly predictable. Easier for you."

"Is this your definition of a distraction?" she countered. "It fits my definition of a confrontation."

"You're right." He pulled his own sunglasses off, tossed them aside. "We'll analyze later."

He moved quickly. She knew he was capable of lightning motion but hadn't expected him to snap from cynic to lover in the blink of an eye. His mouth was hot, hungry, and hard on hers. His hands gripped her arms, pressing her against him so that as the heat and the need poured out, she couldn't tell if it came from him or from herself.

He'd spoken no less than the truth when he told her she was in his system. Whether she was poison or salvation didn't seem to matter. She was in there and he couldn't stop the flow.

He jerked her back so that their lips parted, but their faces remained close. His eyes were as gold and powerful as the flare of the sun. "You tell me you don't want me, you don't want this. Tell me and mean it, and it stops here."

"I—"

"No." Impatient, suffering, he shook her until her gaze lifted to his again. "No, you look at me and say it."

She'd already lied, and the lies weighed on her like lead. She couldn't bear another. "This will only complicate things, make them more difficult."

Unmistakable triumph flashed into those tawny eyes. "Damn right it will," he muttered. "Just now, I don't give a damn. Kiss me back," he demanded. "And mean it."

She couldn't stop herself. This kind of raw, wicked need was new to her, and left her defenseless. Her mouth met his, just as hungry now, just as desperate. And the low, primal moan that escaped was an echo to the beat of desire between her legs.

She stopped thinking. Found herself swamped and spinning with sensations, emotions, yearnings. The kiss roughened, teetered toward pain as his teeth scraped and nipped. She clutched at his hair, gasping for air, shaking with shock as that skillful mouth streaked down her throat and sent wild chills over her skin.

For the first time in her life, she surrendered utterly to the physical. And craved the taking.

He pulled at her jacket, tugging the soft silk off her shoulders and tossing it heedlessly aside. He wanted flesh, the feel of it under his hands, the taste of it in his mouth. He yanked the slim ivory shell over her head and filled his hands with her trembling lace-covered breasts.

Her skin was warmer than the silk, and somehow smoother. With one impatient flick he opened her bra, then dragged it aside. And satisfied his need to taste.

The sun blinded her. Even with her eyes tightly shut, the strength of it pounded on her lids. She couldn't see, only feel. That busy, almost brutal mouth devoured her, those rough and demanding hands doing as they pleased. The whimper in her throat was a scream in her head.

Now, now, now!

Fumbling, she dragged at his sweater, finding the muscle and scars and flesh beneath as he yanked her skirt down her hips. Her stockings ended with thin bands of stretchy lace high on her thighs. Another time he might have appreciated the mix of practicality and femininity. But now he was driven to possess, and he thrilled darkly at her stunned gasp when he ripped aside the thin triangle blocking him from her. Before she could draw the next breath, he plunged his fingers into her and shot her violently over the edge.

She cried out, shocked, staggered at that vicious slap of heat. It sliced through her without warning, sending her flying, flailing.

"Oh, God. Phillip." When her head dropped weakly on his shoulder, her body going from spring-taut to limp, he swept her off her feet and pressed her down on one of the narrow benches.

The blood was pounding in his head. His loins screamed for release. His heart hammered like a dull axe against his ribs.

His breath was ragged, his vision focused on her face like a laser as he freed himself. His fingers dug into her hips as he lifted and opened them. And he plunged. Hard and deep so that his long, long groan melted into hers.

She closed around him, a tight, hot glove. Moved under him, a trembling, eager woman. Breathed his name, a breathless, aching sigh.

He drove into her again, again, strong, steady strokes that she rose to meet. Her hair escaped its pins, flowed like rich mink. He buried his face in it, lost in her scent, in her heat, in the sheer, shimmering glory of a woman aroused beyond reason.

Her nails dug into his back, her cry muffled against his shoulder as she came. Her muscles clamped around him, owned him, destroyed him.

He was as limp as she, wrecked, struggling to fill his burning lungs with air. Beneath him, her body continued to quake, the aftershock of hard, satisfying sex.

When his vision cleared, he could see the three pieces of her pretty businesswoman's suit scattered along the deck. And one black high heel. It made him grin even as he shifted just enough to nip lightly at her shoulder.

"I usually try for more finesse," he said. Slyly, he skimmed a hand down to toy with the thin lace at the top of her stocking, experimenting with textures. "Oh, you're full of surprises, Dr. Griffin."

She was floating, somewhere just above reality. She couldn't seem to open her eyes, to move her hand. "What?"

At the dreamy, distant sound of her voice, he lifted his head to study her face. Her cheeks were flushed, her mouth swollen, her hair a tumbling mass. "As an objective observation, I have to conclude you've never been ravished before."

There was amusement in his tone, and just enough male arrogance to snap her back to earth. She opened her eyes now, and saw the sleepy smile of victory in his. "You're heavy," she said shortly.

"Okay." He shifted, sat up, but pulled her up and around until she straddled his lap. "You're still wearing your stockings, and one of your shoes." He grinned and began to knead the muscles of her tight little butt. "Christ, that's sexy."

"Stop it." The heat was pouring back, a combination of embarrassment and fresh desire. "Let me up."

"I haven't finished with you yet." He dipped his head, circled his tongue lazily around her nipple. "You're still soft and warm. Tasty," he added, flicking his tongue over her stiffened nipple, sucking lightly until her breathing thickened yet again. "I want more. So do you."

Her body arched back, beautifully fluid as he trailed his mouth up to the hammering pulse in her neck. Oh, yes, yes, she wanted more.

"But this time," he promised, "it'll take a little longer."

On a yielding moan, she lowered her mouth to his. "I guess there's time."

The sun was angled low when he shifted her yet again. Her body felt golden and bruised, energized and exhausted. She'd had no idea she could claim such a sexual appetite, and now that she did, she hadn't a clue what she would do about it.

"We have to discuss . . ." She frowned at herself, draped an arm over her body. She was half naked and damp from him. And more confused than she'd ever been in her life. "We—this—can't continue."

"Not right this minute," he agreed. "Even I have my limitations."

"I didn't mean . . . This was just a diversion, as you said. Something we both apparently needed on a physical level. And now—"

"Shut up, Sybill." He said it mildly, but she caught the edge of annoyance. "It was a hell of a lot more than a diversion, and we'll discuss it to pieces later."

He scooped the hair out of his eyes, studied her. She was just beginning to feel awkward, he realized, uneasy with being naked, and with the situation. So he smiled. "Right now, we're a mess. So there's only one thing to do before we get dressed and head in."

"What?"

Still smiling, he pulled off her shoe, then scooped her up into his arms. "Just this," he said, and tossed her over the side.

She managed one scream before she hit. What surfaced was a furious woman with tangles of wet hair in her eyes. "You son of a bitch! You idiot!"

"I knew it." He stepped onto the gunwale and laughed like a loon. "I just knew you'd be gorgeous when you're angry."

He dived in to join her.

THIRTEEN

No one had ever treated her the way Phillip Quinn had treated her. Sybill couldn't decide what she thought of that, much less what to do about it.

He'd been rough, careless, demanding. He had, in his own words, ravished her—and more than once. Though she couldn't claim to have put up even what could remotely be termed a struggle, it had been a long way from a civilized seduction.

Never in her life had she slept with a man she'd known for such a short time. To do so was reckless, potentially dangerous, and certainly irresponsible. Even factoring in the overwhelming and unprecedented chemistry between them, it was foolish behavior.

Worse than foolish, she admitted, because she very much wanted to be reckless, with him, again.

She would have to consider the matter carefully, as soon as she could get her mind off her body and the incredible pleasure it had experienced under those fast, take-charge hands.

Now he was sailing her back to the waterfront at St. Christopher's, completely at ease with himself, and with her. She never would have guessed he'd just spent more than an hour engaged in wild, frantic sex.

If she hadn't been a party to it.

There was no doubt in her mind that what they'd done would further complicate an already horribly complicated situation. Both of them would have to be coldly sensible now, and carefully practical. She did her best to tidy her damp, tangled hair as the wind whipped at it.

Conversation, she decided, to bridge the gap between sex and sensibility.

"How did you get the scars?"

"Which ones?" He tossed the question over his shoulder, but he thought he knew. Most women wanted to know.

"On your chest. They look surgical."

"Mmm. Long story." This time he threw a smile back with the look. "I'll bore you with it tonight."

"Tonight?"

Oh, he just loved it when her brows buckled together, forming that little concentration line between them. "We have a date, remember?"

"But I . . . hmmm."

"I confuse the hell out of you, don't I?"

Annoyed, she slapped at the hair that insisted on blowing over her eyes. "And you enjoy that?"

"Darling, I can't begin to tell you how much. You keep trying to slip me into one of your slots, Sybill, and I'll keep sliding back out again. You figured on a fairly safe, one-dimensional urban professional who likes his wine aged and his women cultured. But that's only part of the picture."

As he entered the harbor, he dropped the sails, switched to motor. "First glance at you, I have to figure well-bred, well-educated, career-oriented city woman who likes her wine white and her men at a safe distance. But that's only part of the picture, too."

He cut the engine, let the boat bump gently at dock. Gave her hair a friendly tug before he climbed out to secure the lines. "I think we'll both be well entertained while we uncover the rest of the canvas."

"A continuation of a physical relationship is—"

"Inevitable," he finished, and offered her a hand. "Let's not waste time or energy pretending otherwise. We can call it basic chemistry for now." He tugged her to him the minute her feet hit the dock, and proved his point with one, long fiery kiss. "It works for me."

"Your family won't approve."

"Family approval's important to you."

"Of course."

"I don't discount it either. Normally, this wouldn't be any of their business. In this case, it is." It bothered him, more than a little. "But it's my family, and my concern, not yours."

"This may sound hypocritical at this point, but I don't want to do anything else that will hurt or disturb Seth."

"Neither do I. But I'm not going to let a ten-year-old take charge of my personal life. Relax, Sybill." He skimmed his fingers over her jaw. "This isn't the Montagues and the Capulets."

"I'm hardly thinking of you as Romeo," she said, so dryly that he laughed and kissed her again.

"You might, darling, if I put my mind to it. But for now, let's just be who we are. You're tired." He rubbed his thumb gently under her eye. "You've got thin skin, Sybill, the shadows show. Go take a nap. We can make do with room service later."

"With—"

"I'll bring the wine," he said cheerfully and leaped back into the boat. "I've got a bottle of Chateau Olivier I've been wanting to sample," he shouted over the motor. "No need to dress up," he added with a wicked grin as he maneuvered the boat away from the dock and out of earshot.

She wasn't sure what she would have shouted at him if she'd lost what was left of her control. Instead she stood on the dock in her wrinkled but elegant silk suit, her hair a damp mess and her dignity as shaky as her heart.

Cam recognized the signs. A fast sail on a breezy afternoon might relax a man, loosen his muscles, clear his head. But he only knew one thing that put that lazy, satisfied gleam in a man's eyes.

He recognized that gleam in his brother's eyes when Phillip slid up to the dock to toss him the lines. You son of a bitch, was his first thought.

He caught the stern line, yanked it taut. "You son of a bitch."

Phillip only lifted his eyebrows. He'd been expecting that reaction, though not quite so quickly. He'd already ordered himself to hold on to his temper, to explain his position. "Always a friendly welcome at the Quinns'."

"I figured you were past the stage where you thought with your dick."

Not quite as calm as he'd planned to be, Phillip stepped off the boat and stood facing his brother. He recognized the signs, too. Cam was spoiling for a fight. "Actually, I tend to let my dick think for itself. Though we often agree."

"You're either crazy or stupid, or you just don't give a damn. A kid's life is in the balance here, his peace of mind, his trust."

"Nothing's going to happen to Seth. I'm doing everything I can to make sure of that."

"Oh, I get it. You fucked her for his sake."

Phillip's hands shot out, and before the bright fury fully registered he had them gripped on Cam's jacket. Now their faces were close, and both were warrior hard. "You were tearing up the sheets with Anna last spring. How much were you thinking about Seth when you had her under you?"

Cam's fist rammed up, under Phillip's guard. The blow rocked his head back but didn't loosen his hold. Instinct blanked out reason as he shoved Cam back and prepared to tear in.

He swore viciously when Ethan clamped an arm around his throat from behind.

"Cool off," Ethan ordered on more of a sigh than a snarl. "Both of you—or I'll toss you in until you do." He tightened his hold on Phillip's windpipe just enough to show he meant it and scowled at Cam. "Get ahold of yourself, damn it. Seth's had a rough day. You want to add to it?"

"No, I don't want to add to it," Cam said bitterly. "This one doesn't give a good damn, but I do."

"My relationship with Sybill and my concern for Seth are two separate matters."

"Like hell."

"Let go of me, Ethan." Because Phillip's tone was cool and deliberate, Ethan released him. "You know, Cam, I don't remember you being so interested in my sex life since we both had our sights set on Jenny Malone."

"We're not in high school anymore, pal."

"No, we're not. And you're not my keeper. Either of you," he added, shifting so that he could look at both of them. He would explain himself because it mattered. Because they mattered. "I've got feelings for her, and I'm going to take the time to figure out what they are. I've made a lot of changes in my life over the last few months, and I've gone along with what the two of you wanted. But goddamn it, I'm entitled to a personal life."

"I wouldn't argue with that, Phil." Ethan glanced toward the house, hoping Seth was busy with his homework or his drawings and not spying out the window. "I don't know how Seth's going to feel about this part of your personal life."

"There's something none of you are taking into consideration. Sybill is Seth's aunt."

"That's exactly what I am taking into consideration," Cam shot back. "She's Gloria's sister, and she came in here on a lie."

"She came in here believing a lie." It was an important distinction, Phillip thought. A vital distinction. "Did you read the statement she faxed to Anna?"

Cam hissed between his teeth, hooked his thumbs in his pockets. "Yeah, I saw it."

"What do you think it cost her to put that down in black and white, to know everybody in town would be talking about it, about her, within twenty-four hours?" Phillip waited a beat, noting that the muscle in Cam's jaw relaxed, fractionally. "How much more do you want her to pay?"

"I'm not thinking about her. I'm thinking about Seth."

"And she's the best defense we've got against Gloria DeLauter."

"You think she'll stand up to it?" Ethan wondered. "When push comes to shove?"

"Yeah, I do. He needs his family, all his family. That's what Dad would want. He told me . . ." Catching himself, Phillip frowned out over the dark water.

Cam pursed his lips, exchanged a look with Ethan, and nearly smiled. "Been feeling a little odd lately, Phillip?"

"I'm fine."

"Maybe you're stressed out some." Since he'd only gotten in one punch, Cam felt entitled to enjoy himself. "I thought I saw you talking to yourself a couple of times."

"I don't talk to myself."

"Maybe you think you're talking to somebody who isn't there." He did smile now, widely and wickedly. "Stress is a killer. Eats at the mind."

Ethan didn't quite swallow a chuckle, and Phillip glared at him. "You got something to say about the state of my mental health?"

"Well . . ." Ethan scratched at his chin, "you've been looking a little tense lately."

"For Christ's sake, I'm entitled to look a little tense." He threw out his arms as if to encompass the world that too often weighed on his shoulders. "I put in ten, twelve hours a day in Baltimore, then come down here and sweat like a goddamn galley slave in the boatyard. That's when I'm not frying my brains over the books and the bills or playing housewife at the grocery store or making sure Seth doesn't slide out of his homework."

"Always was bitchy," Cam mumbled.

"You want bitchy?" Phillip took one threatening step forward, but this time Cam grinned and spread his hands.

"Ethan'll just toss you off the dock. Me, I don't feel like a swim just now."

"First few times with me, I thought I was dreaming."

Confused, unsure if he wanted to punch Cam or just sit down for a while, Phillip looked back at Ethan. "What the hell are you talking about?"

"I thought we were discussing your mental health." Ethan's tone was mild, conversational now. "It was good to see him. Hard to know you'd have to let him go again, but it was worth it."

A chill danced up Phillip's spine, and he put his suddenly unsteady hands safely in his pockets. "Maybe we should be talking about your mental health."

"We figured when it was your turn, you'd head for the therapist's couch." Cam grinned again. "Or Aruba."

"I don't know what you're talking about."

"Yes, you do." Ethan spoke calmly, then settled down on the dock, legs dangling, to take out a cigar. "It's your turn. Looks like he took us in the same order he took us in."

"Symmetry," Cam decided, dropping down beside Ethan. "He'd have liked the symmetry of it. I talked to him the first time the day I met Anna." He thought back to it, the way he'd seen her cross the back lawn with that knockout face and that ugly suit. "I guess that's a kind of symmetry, too."

The chill was still dancing, tapping fast now, up and down Phillip's spine. "What do you mean, 'talked to him'?"

"Had a conversation." Cam plucked the cigar out of Ethan's mouth and helped himself to a puff. "Of course, I figured I'd cracked." He glanced up, smiled. "You figure you've cracked, Phil?"

"No. I've just been working too hard."

"Shit, drawing pictures, coming up with jingles. Big deal."

"Kiss ass." But with a sigh, he sat on the dock. "Are the two of you trying to tell me you've talked to Dad? The one who died in March? The one we buried a few miles from here?"

In an easy gesture Cam passed Phillip the cigar. "You trying to tell us you haven't?"

"I don't believe in that sort of thing."

"Doesn't much matter what you believe when it happens," Ethan pointed out and took back his cigar. "Last time I saw him was the night I asked Grace to marry me. He had a bag of peanuts."

"Christ Jesus," Phillip murmured.

"I could smell them, the same way I can smell this cigar smoke, the water, Cam's leather jacket."

"When people die, that's it. They don't come back." Phillip paused a moment, waiting until the cigar came back down the line to him. "Did you—touch him?"

Cam angled his head. "Did you?"

"He was solid. He couldn't be."

"It's either that," Ethan pointed out, "or we're all crazy."

"We barely had time to say good-bye, and no time to understand." Cam let out a breath. His grief had eased and softened. "He bought us each a little more time. That's what I think."

"He and Mom bought us all time when they made us Quinns." He couldn't think about it, Phillip decided. Not now, at any rate. "It must have ripped him when he found out he had a daughter he'd never known."

"He'd have wanted to help her, save her," Ethan murmured.

"He'd have seen it was too late for her. But not for Seth," Cam concluded. "So he'd have done whatever he could do to save Seth."

"His grandson." Phillip watched an egret soar, then slide silently into the dark. And he was no longer cold. "He'd have seen himself in the eyes, but he would've wanted answers. I've been thinking about that. The logical step would have been for him to try to locate Gloria's mother, have her confirm it."

"It would have taken time." Cam considered it. "She's married, she's living in Europe, and from what Sybill said, she wasn't interested in contacting him."

"And he ran out of time," Phillip concluded. "But now we know. And now, we make it stick."

◌◌◌

She hadn't meant to sleep. Sybill indulged in a long, hot shower, then wrapped herself in a robe with the intention of adding to her notes. She ordered herself to drum up the courage to call her mother, to speak her mind and demand a written corroboration of her own notarized statement.

She did neither. Instead she fell face down on the bed, closed her eyes, and escaped.

The knocking at the door pulled her out of sleep into groggy. She stumbled out of bed, fumbled for the light switch. With her mind still fuzzy, she walked through the parlor and barely had the presence of mind to check the peephole.

She let out a self-directed annoyed sigh as she flipped off the locks.

Phillip took one look at her tousled hair, sleepy eyes, and practical navy terry robe, and smiled. "Well, I did tell you not to dress up."

"I'm sorry. I fell asleep." Distracted, she pushed at her hair. She hated being mussed, particularly when he looked so fresh and alert. And gorgeous.

"If you're tired, I'll take a rain check."

"No, I . . . if I sleep any more now I'll end up wide awake at three A.M. I hate hotel rooms at three A.M." She stepped back to let him in. "I'll just get dressed."

"Stay comfortable," he suggested, and used his free hand to cup the nape of her neck and bring her forward for a casual kiss. "I've already seen you naked. And a very appealing sight it was."

It appeared, she decided, that her dignity was still just out of reach. "I'm not going to claim that was a mistake."

"Good." He set the wine he carried on her coffee table.

"But," she said, with what she considered admirable patience, "neither was it wise. We're both sensible people."

"Speak for yourself, doc. I stop feeling sensible every time I get a whiff of you. What *is* that you wear?"

She leaned back when he leaned in to sniff at her. "Phillip."

"Sybill." And he laughed. "How about if I attempt to be civilized and not cart you off to bed until you're a little more awake?"

"I appreciate your restraint," she said tightly.

"And so you should. Hungry?"

"What is this almost pathological need of yours to feed me?"

"You're the analyst," he told her with a shrug. "I've got the wine. You got some glasses?"

She might have sighed, but it wouldn't have been constructive. She did want to talk to him, to put their relationship on an even footing again. To ask his advice. And, she hoped, to enlist his help in persuading Seth to accept her friendship.

She took the two short, thick glasses the hotel provided, lifting her eyebrow when Phillip sneered at them. He had a damn sexy sneer.

"They're an insult to this very delightful wine," he said, as he opened the bottle with the stainless-steel corkscrew he'd brought with him. "But if they're the best you can offer we'll just have to make do."

"I forgot to pack my Waterford."

"Next time." He poured the pretty straw-colored wine into the glasses, handed her one. "To beginnings, middles, and endings. We seem to be at all three."

"Which means?"

"The charade's ended, the teamwork is established, and we've just become lovers. I'm happy with all three aspects of our very interesting relationship."

"Teamwork?" She picked the aspect that didn't shame her or make her nervous.

"Seth's a Quinn. With your help we'll make that legal and permanent, and soon."

She stared down into her wine. "It's important to you that he have your name."

"His grandfather's name," Phillip corrected. "And it can't be nearly as important to me as it is to Seth."

"Yes, you're right. I saw his face when I told him. He looked almost awed. Professor Quinn must have been an extraordinary man."

"My parents were special. They had the kind of marriage you rarely see. A true partnership, based on trust, respect, love, passion. It hasn't been easy wondering if my father broke that trust."

"You were afraid that he had cheated on your mother with Gloria, fathered a child with her." Sybill sat down. "It was hideous of her to plant that seed."

"It was also hell living with the seeds in me that I couldn't quite stomp out. Resentment for Seth. Was he my father's son? His true son, while I was just one of the substitutes? I knew better," he added as he sat beside her. "In my heart. But it's one of those mind games that nag at you at three A.M."

If nothing else, she realized, she'd eased his mind on that one point. But it wasn't enough. "I'm going to ask my mother to corroborate my statement in writing. I don't know that she will. I doubt that she will," Sybill admitted. "But I'll ask, I'll try."

"Teamwork, see." He took her hand in his, nuzzling it, which had her turning her head to study him warily.

"Your jaw's bruised."

"Yeah." He grimaced, wiggled it. "Cam still has a damn sneaky left."

"He hit you?"

The absolute shock in her voice made him laugh. Obviously the good doctor didn't come from a world where fists flew. "I was going to hit him first, but he beat me to it. Which means I owe him one. I'd have paid him back then and there, but Ethan got me in a choke hold."

"Oh, God." Swamped with distress, she got to her feet. "This was about us. About what happened today on the boat. It should never have happened. I knew it would cause trouble between you and your family."

"Yes," he said evenly, "it was about us. And we worked it out. Sybill, my brothers and I have been pounding on each other as long as we've been brothers. It's a Quinn family tradition. Like my father's waffle recipe."

Distress continued to ripple through her. But confusion ran with it. Fists and waffles? she wondered, pulling a hand through her disordered hair. "You fight with them, physically?"

"Sure."

To try to compute it, she pressed her fingers to her temples. It didn't help a bit. "Why?"

He considered, smiled. "Because they're there?" he suggested.

"And your parents allowed this type of violent behavior."

"My mother was a pediatrician. She always stitched us up." He leaned forward to pour himself more wine. "I think I'd better explain the whole picture. You know that Cam, Ethan, and I are adopted."

"Yes. I did some research before I came . . ." She trailed off, glanced back at her laptop. "Well, you know that already."

"Yeah. And you know some of the facts, but not the meaning. You asked me about my scars. It doesn't start there," he mused. "Not really. Cam was the first. Ray caught him trying to steal my mother's car one morning."

"Her car? Steal her car?"

"Right out of the driveway. He was twelve. He'd run away from home and was planning on going to Mexico."

"At twelve he was stealing cars with plans to go to Mexico."

"That's right. The first of the Quinn bad boys." He lifted his glass to toast his absent sibling. "He'd been beaten, again, by his drunk father, and he'd figured it was time to run or die."

"Oh." She braced a hand on the arm of the sofa as she lowered herself again.

"He passed out, and my father carried him inside. My mother treated him."

"They didn't call the police?"

"No. Cam was terrified, and my mother recognized the signs of continual physical abuse. They made inquiries, arrangements, worked with the system and circumvented it. And they gave him a home."

"They just made him their son?"

"My mother said once that we were all hers already. We just hadn't found each other before. Then there was Ethan. His mother was a hooker in Baltimore, a junkie. She relieved boredom by knocking him around. And then she got the bright idea that she could supplement her income by selling her eight-year-old son to perverts."

Sybill clutched her glass in both hands and rocked. She said nothing, could say nothing.

"He had a few years of that. One night one of her customers finished with Ethan, and with her, and got violent. Since his target was her and not her kid, she objected. Stabbed him. She ran, and when the cops got there they took Ethan to the hospital. My mother was doing guest rounds."

"They took him, too," Sybill murmured.

"Yeah, that's the long and short of it."

She raised her glass, sipped slowly, watched him over the rim. She didn't know the world he was describing. Logically, she knew it existed, but it had never touched hers. Until now. "And you?"

"My mother worked the Block in Baltimore. Strip joints, turned tricks on the side. A little bait and switch now and then, some short cons." He shrugged. "My father was long gone. He did some time in Jessup for armed robbery, and when he got out he didn't look us up."

"Did she . . . did she beat you?"

"Now and then, until I got big enough, strong enough, that she worried I might hit back." His smile was thin and sharp. "She was right to worry. We didn't care for each other much. But if I wanted a roof over my head, and I did, I needed her, and I had to pull my weight. I picked pockets, lifted locks. I was pretty good at it. Hell," he said with a faint stir of pride, "I was damn good at it. Still, I stuck with small shit. The kind you turn into easy cash or drugs. If things were really tight, I sold myself."

He saw her eyes widen in shock, flick away from his.

"Survival's not always pretty," he said shortly. "Most of the time I had my freedom. I was tough, and I was mean, and I was smart. Maybe I got picked up once in a while and rattled through the system, but I always popped out again. Another few years of that life, and I'd have been in Jessup—or the morgue. Another few years of that life," he continued, watching her face, "and Seth would have gone the same way."

Struggling to absorb it, she stared into her wine. "You see your situations as similar, but—"

"I recognized Gloria yesterday," he interrupted. "A pretty woman gone brittle. Hard and sharp at the eyes, bitter at the mouth. She and my mother would have recognized each other, too."

What could she say, how could she argue when she'd seen the same thing, felt the same? "I didn't recognize her," she said quickly. "For a moment I thought there was a mistake."

"She recognized you. And she played the angles, pushed the buttons. She'd know how." He paused a moment. "She'd know exactly how. So do I."

She looked at him then, noted he was studying her coolly. "Is that what you're doing? Pushing buttons, playing angles?"

Maybe it was, he thought. They would both have to figure that out before much longer. "Right now I'm answering your question. Do you want the rest?"

"Yes." She didn't hesitate, for she'd discovered she very much wanted to hear it all.

"When I was thirteen, I thought I had it handled. I figured I was just fine. Until I found myself face down in the gutter, bleeding to death. Drive-by shooting. Wrong place, wrong time."

"Shot?" Her gaze whipped back to his. "You were shot."

"In the chest. Probably should have killed me. One of the doctors who made sure I didn't die knew Stella Quinn. She and Ray came to see me in the hospital. I figured them for weirdos, do-gooders, your basic assholes. But I played along with them. My mother was done with me, and I was going to end up solid in the system. I thought I'd use them until I was steady on my feet again. Then I'd take what I needed and cut out."

Who was this boy he described to her? And how was she to reconcile him with the man beside her? "You were going to rob them?"

"It's what I did. What I was. But they . . ." How to explain it? he wondered. The miracle of them. "They just wore that away. Until I fell in love with them. Until I'd have done anything, been anything, to make them proud of me. It wasn't the paramedics or the surgical team that saved my life. It was Ray and Stella Quinn."

"How old were you when they took you in?"

"Thirteen. But I wasn't a kid like Seth. I wasn't a victim like Cam and Ethan. I made my choices."

"You're wrong." For the first time, she reached out and, taking his face in her hands, she kissed him gently.

He lifted his hands to her wrists, had to concentrate on not squeezing her skin the way that soft kiss had squeezed his heart. "That's not the reaction I expected."

It wasn't the one she'd expected to have. But she found herself feeling pity for the boy he described to her and admiration for the man he'd made himself into. "What reaction do you usually get?"

"I've never told anyone outside the family." He managed a smile. "Bad for the image."

Touched, she rested her forehead against his. "You're right. It could have been Seth," she murmured. "What happened to you, it could have been Seth. Your father saved him from that. You and your family saved him, while mine's done nothing. And worse than nothing."

"You're doing something."

"I hope it's enough." When his mouth came to hers, she let herself slide into comfort.

FOURTEEN

Phillip unlocked the boatyard at seven A.M. The very fact that his brothers hadn't given him grief about not working the day before, or about taking a full Sunday off the previous week, had his guilt quota at peak.

He expected he had a good hour, maybe a little more before Cam showed up to continue work on the hull of the sport's fisher. Ethan would put in a morning of crabbing, taking advantage of the fall season, before heading in to work that afternoon.

So he would have the place to himself, and the quiet and solitude to deal with the paperwork he'd neglected the week before.

Quiet didn't mean silence. His first act when entering his cramped office was to hit the lights. The next was to switch on the radio. Ten minutes later, he was nose-deep in accounts and very much at home.

Well, they owed just about everybody, he concluded. Rent, utilities, insurance premiums, the lumberyard, and the ever popular MasterCard.

The government had demanded its share in the middle of September, and the bite had been just a little nasty. The next tax nibble wasn't far enough away to let him relax.

He juggled figures, toyed with them, stroked them, and decided red wasn't such a bad color. They'd made a tidy profit on their first job, the bulk of which had been poured back into the business. Once they turned the hull, they would get another draw from their current client. That would keep their heads above water.

But they weren't going to see a lot of the color black for a time yet.

Dutifully, he cut checks, updated the spreadsheet, reconciled figures, and tried not to mourn the fact that two and two stubbornly insisted on making four.

He heard the heavy door below open, then slam.

"Hiding up there again?" Cam called out.

"Yeah, having a real party."

"Some of us have real work to do."

Phillip looked at the figures dancing over his computer screen and laughed shortly. It wasn't real work to Cam, he knew, unless you had a tool in your hand.

"Best I can do," he muttered and shut the computer down. He stacked the outgoing bills on the corner of the desk, tucked the paychecks in his back pocket, then headed down.

Cam was strapping on a tool belt. He wore a ball cap backward to keep his hair out of his eyes, and it flowed beneath the down-sloped bill. Phillip watched him slide the wedding band off his finger and tuck it carefully into his front pocket.

Just as he would take it out after work, Phillip mused, and slip it back in place. Rings could catch on tools and cost a man a finger. But neither of his brothers left theirs at home. He wondered if there was some symbolism, or comfort, in having that statement of marriage on them, one way or the other, at all times.

Then he wondered why he was wondering and nudged the question, and the idea of it, aside.

Since Cam had reached the work area first, the radio wasn't tuned to the lazy blues Phillip would have chosen, but to loud, kiss-my-ass rock. Cam eyed him coolly as Phillip tugged on a tool belt of his own.

"Didn't expect to see you in so bright and early this morning. Figured you had a late night."

"Don't go there again."

"Just a comment." Anna had already chewed him out when he complained to her about Phillip's involvement with Sybill. He should be ashamed, he shouldn't interfere, he should have some compassion for his brother's feelings.

He'd rather take that brother's fist in the face any day than a hot verbal slap from his wife.

"You want to fool around with her, it's your business. She's a pleasure to look at. I'd say she's got a wide cold streak in her, though."

"You don't know her."

"And you do?" Cam lifted a hand when Phillip's eyes flashed. "Just trying to get a handle on it. It's going to matter to Seth."

"I know she's willing to do what she can so he's where he needs to be. Reading between the lines, I'd say she grew up in a repressive, restrictive atmosphere."

"A rich one."

"Yeah." Phillip strode to a pile of planks. "Yeah, private schools, chauffeurs, country clubs, servants."

"It's a little tough to feel sorry for her."

"I don't think she's looking for sympathy." He hefted a plank. "You said you wanted to get a handle on her. I'm telling you she had advantages. I don't know if she had any affection."

Cam shrugged and, deciding they'd get more accomplished working together, took the other end of the plank to fit it into place on the hull. "She doesn't strike me as deprived. She strikes me as cold."

"Restrained. Cautious." He remembered the way she reached out to him the night before. Still, it had been the first time she'd done so, the only time. He clamped down on the frustration of not being sure that Cam wasn't right. "Are you and Ethan the only ones entitled to a relationship with a woman that satisfies your hormones and your brain?"

"No." Cam lapped the ends. Deliberately he relaxed his shoulders. There was something in Phillip's voice that gave away that frustration, and something else. "No, we're not. I'll talk to Seth about her."

"I'll talk to him myself."

"All right."

"He matters to me, too."

"I know he does."

"He didn't." Phillip pulled out his hammer to nail the laps. "Not as much as he did to you. Not enough. It's different now."

"I know that, too." For the next few minutes they worked in tandem, without words. "You stood up for him anyway," Cam added when the plank was in place. "Even when he didn't matter enough."

"I did it for Dad."

"We all did it for Dad. Now we're doing it for Seth."

By noon, the skeleton of the hull had taken on the flesh of wood. The smooth-lap construction was labor-intensive, tedious and exacting. But it was their trademark, a choice that offered extreme structural strength and required great skill by the boatbuilder.

No one would argue that Cam was the most skilled of the three of them in woodworking. But Phillip thought he was holding his own.

Yeah, he thought, standing back to scan the exterior planking or skin of the hull. He was holding his own.

"You pick up any lunch?" Cam asked before he poured water from a jug into his mouth.

"No."

"Shit. I bet Grace packed Ethan one of those monster lunches of hers. Fried chicken, or thick slabs of honey-baked ham."

"You got a wife," Phillip pointed out.

Cam snorted, rolled his eyes. "Oh, yeah. I can just see me talking Anna into packing me a lunch every day. She'd smack me with her briefcase as she marched out the door to work. There are two of us," he considered. "We can take Ethan, especially if we catch him by surprise when he comes in."

"Let's go the easier route." Phillip dug into his pocket, pulled out a quarter. "Heads or tails?"

"Heads. Loser gets it, and buys it."

Phillip flipped the coin, caught it and slapped it onto the back of his hand. The eagle's beak seemed to sneer at him. "Damn it. What do you want?"

"Meatball sub, large chips, and six gallons of coffee."

"Fine, clog your arteries."

"Last I checked they don't stock any tofu at Crawford's. Don't know how you eat that crap. You're going to die anyway. Might as well go with a meatball sub."

"You go your way, I'll go mine." He reached in his pocket again for Cam's paycheck. "Here, don't spend it all in one place."

"Now I can retire to that little grass shack on Maui. You got Ethan's?"

"What there is of it."

"Yours?"

"I don't need it."

Cam narrowed his eyes as Phillip pulled on his jacket. "That's not the way it works."

"I'm in charge of the books, I say how it works."

"You put in your time, you take your share."

"I don't need it," Phillip said, with heat this time. "When I do, I'll take it." He stalked out, leaving Cam fuming.

"Stubborn son of a bitch," Cam muttered. "How am I supposed to rag on him when he pulls crap like that?"

He bitched plenty, Cam mused. He nagged his brothers to distraction over the pettiest detail. Then he handled the details, he thought as he capped the water jug. He'd back you into a corner, then he'd go to the wall for you.

It was enough to drive you nuts.

Now he was getting himself twisted up over a woman none of them knew they could trust if things got sticky. He, for one was going to keep a close eye on Sybill Griffin.

And not just for Seth's sake. Phillip might have the brains, but he was just as stupid as the next guy when it came to a pretty face.

"**A**nd young Karen Lawson who's been working down at the hotel since she hooked up with the McKinney boy last year saw it written down, in black and white. She called her mama, and as Bitty Lawson's a good friend of mine and my longtime bridge partner—though she'll trump your ace if you don't watch her—she called me right up and let me know."

Nancy Claremont was in her element, and that element was gossip. As her husband owned a sizable chunk of St. Chris, meaning she did as well, and part of that chunk was the old barn those Quinn boys—a wild bunch if you asked her—rented for their boatyard—though God knew what else went on in there—she knew it was not only her right but her duty to pass on the succulent tidbit that had come her way the previous afternoon.

Of course, she'd used the most convenient method first. The telephone. But you didn't get the pleasure of face-to-face reaction over the phone. So she'd brought herself out, dressed in her brand-new pumpkin-colored pantsuit, fresh out of the J. C. Penney catalog.

There was no point in being the most well-off woman in St. Christopher's if you didn't flaunt it a bit. And the best place to flaunt, and to spread gossip, was Crawford's.

Second-best was the Stylerite Beauty Salon over on Market, and that, as she'd made an appointment for a cut, color, and curl, was her next stop.

Mother Crawford, a fixture in St. Chris for all of her sixty-two years, sat behind the counter in her smeared butcher apron, her tongue tucked firmly in her cheek.

She'd already heard the news—not much got by Mother, and nothing got by her for long—but she disposed herself to hear Nancy out.

"To think that child is Ray Quinn's grandson! And that writer lady with her snooty airs is the sister of that nasty girl who said all those terrible things. That boy's her nephew. Her own kin, but did she say one word about it? No, sir, she did not! Just hoity-toitying around, going off sailing with Phillip Quinn, and a lot more than sailing, if you ask me. The way young people carry on today without a snap of their fingers for morals."

She snapped her own, inches from Mother's face, and her eyes glittered with malicious delight.

Since Mother sensed that Nancy was about to veer off the subject at hand, she shrugged her wide shoulders. "Seems to me," she began, knowing the scatter of people in the store had their ears bent her way, "that there are a lot of people around this town who ought to be hanging their heads after what was being passed around about Ray. Whispering about him behind his back when he was living, and over his grave when he passed on, about him cheating on Stella, God rest her, and having truck with that DeLauter woman. Well, it wasn't true, was it?"

Her sharp eyes scanned the store, and indeed, a few heads did lower. Satisfied, she beamed her gaze hard into Nancy's glittering eyes. "Seems to me you were willing enough to believe bad about a good man like Ray Quinn."

Sincerely insulted, Nancy puffed out her chest. "Why, I never believed a word of it, Mother." Discussing such matters, she thought to herself, wasn't the same as believing them. "Truth is, a blind man couldn't have missed the way that boy's got Ray's eyes. Had to be a blood relation. Why, I said to Silas just the other day, I said, 'Silas, I wonder if that boy could be a cousin or something to Ray?'"

She'd said no such thing, of course. But she might have, if she'd thought of it.

"Never thought about him being Ray's grandson, though. Why, to think Ray had a daughter all these years."

Which, of course, proved he'd done something wrong in the first place, didn't it? She'd always suspected that Ray Quinn had been wild in his youth. Maybe even a hippie. And everyone knew what *that* meant.

Smoking marijuana, and having orgies and running around naked.

But that wasn't something she intended to bring up to Mother. That little morsel could wait until she was shampooed and tucked into the styling chair at the salon.

"And that she turned out wilder than those boys he and Stella brought home," she rattled on. "That girl over to the hotel must be just as—"

She broke off when the door jingled. Hoping for a fresh ear, she was thrilled to see Phillip Quinn walk in. Better than an addition to her audience, it was one of the actors on the very interesting stage.

Phillip only had to open the door to know what subject was under discussion. Or had been, until he stepped inside. Silence fell with a clang, and eyes darted toward him, then guiltily away.

Except for Nancy Claremont's and Mother's.

"Why, Phillip Quinn, I don't know as I've seen you since your family picnic on the Fourth of July." Nancy fluttered at him. Wild or not, he was a handsome man. Nancy considered flirting one of the best ways to loosen a man's tongue. "That was a fine day."

"Yes, it was." He walked up to the counter, knowing that stares were being bulleted at his back. "I need a couple of subs, Mother Crawford. A meatball and a turkey."

"We'll fix you up, Phil. Junior!" She shouted over at her son, who jolted at her tone despite being thirty-six and the father of three.

"Yes 'um."

"You going to ring up these people or just scratch your butt the rest of the afternoon?"

He colored, muttered under his breath, and turned his attention back to the cash register.

"You working down to the boatyard today, Phillip?"

"That's right, Mrs. Claremont."

He busied himself choosing a bag of chips for Cam, then wandered back to the dairy case to decide on yogurt for himself.

"That young boy usually comes in to pick up lunch, doesn't he?"

Phillip reached in, took out a carton at random. "He's in school today. It's Friday."

" 'Course it is." Nancy laughed, playfully patting the side of her head. "Don't know where my mind is. Fine-looking young boy. Ray musta been right proud."

"I don't doubt it."

"We've been hearing that he's got some blood relations close by."

"There's never been anything wrong with your hearing, Mrs. Claremont, that I recall. I'll need a couple of large coffees to go, Mother."

"We'll fix you up there, too. Nancy, you got more than enough news to blow around for the day. You keep trying to squeeze more out of this boy, you're going to miss your hair appointment."

"I don't know what you could be meaning." Nancy sniffed, shot Mother a furious look, then fluffed at her hair. "But I have to be going. The husband and I are going to the Kiwanis dinner-dance tonight, and I need to look my best."

She flounced out, making a beeline for the beauty shop.

Inside, Mother narrowed her eyes. "The rest of you got business, Junior'll ring you up. But this ain't no lounge. You want to stand around and gawk, go stand outside."

Phillip disguised a chuckle as a cough when several people decided they had business elsewhere.

"That Nancy Claremont's got less sense than a peahen," Mother proclaimed. "Bad enough she dresses herself up like a pumpkin from head to foot, but she don't even know how to be subtle."

Mother turned back to Phillip and grinned. "Now, I won't say I don't have as much got-to-know as the next, but by God, if you can't try to jiggle a little information out of a body without being so blessed obvious, you're not just rude, you're stupid with it. Can't abide bad manners or a soft brain."

Phillip leaned on the counter. "You know, Mother, I've been thinking maybe I'd change my name to Jean-Claude, then move to the wine country of France, the Loire valley, and buy myself a vineyard."

She tucked her tongue in her cheek again, eyes bright. She'd heard this tale, or one of its variations, for years. "Do tell."

"I'd watch my grapes ripen in the sun. I'd eat bread that was hot and fresh, and cheese that wasn't. It would be a fine, satisfying life. But I've got just one problem."

"What's that?"

"It won't be any good unless you come with me." He grabbed her hand, kissing it lavishly while she roared with laughter.

"Boy, you are a caution. Always were." She gasped for breath, wiped her eyes. Then she sighed. "Nancy, she's a fool, but she's not mean, not deep down. Ray and Stella, they were just people to her. They were a lot more than that to me."

"I know that, Mother."

"People got something new to talk about, they're going to gum it to death."

"I know that, too." He nodded. "So did Sybill."

Mother's eyebrows lifted and fell as she realized the implication. "The girl's got guts. Good for her. Seth, he can be proud he's got blood kin that brave. And he can be proud a man like Ray was his granddaddy." She paused to put the finishing touches on the subs. "I think Ray and Stella would've liked that girl."

"Do you?" Phillip murmured.

"Yep. I like her." Mother grinned again as she quickly wrapped the subs in white paper. "She's not hoity-toity like Nancy wants to think. Girl's just shy."

Phillip had reached over for the subs, and now his mouth fell open. "Shy? Sybill?"

"Sure is. Tries hard not to be, but it costs her some. Now you get that meatball back to your brother before it gets cold."

❧

"Why do I have to care about a bunch of queer-os who lived two hundred years ago?"

Seth had his history book open, his mouth full of grape Bubblicious, and a stubborn look in his eye. After a ten-hour day of manual labor, Phillip wasn't in the mood for one of Seth's periodic snits.

"The founding fathers of our country were not queer-os."

Seth snorted and jabbed a finger at the full-page drawing of the Continental Congress. "They're wearing dorky wigs and girly clothes. That says queer-o to me."

"It was the fashion." He knew the kid was yanking his chain, but he couldn't seem to stop his leg from jerking on cue. "And the use of the word 'queer-o' to describe anyone because of their fashion sense or their lifestyle demonstrates ignorance and intolerance."

Seth merely smiled. Sometimes he just liked making Phillip grind his teeth the way he was doing now. "A guy wears a curly wig and high heels, he deserves what he gets."

Phillip sighed. It was another reaction Seth enjoyed. He didn't really mind the history crap. He'd aced the last test, hadn't he? But it was just plain boring to have to pick out one of the queer-os and write some dopey biography.

"You know what these guys were?" Phillip demanded, then narrowed his eyes in warning when Seth opened his mouth. "Don't say it. I'll tell you what they were. Rebels, troublemakers, and tough guys."

"Tough guys? Get real."

"Meeting the way they did, drawing up papers, making speeches? They were giving England, and most especially King George, the finger." He caught a flash of amused interest in Seth's eyes. "It wasn't the tea tax, not really. That was just the platform, the excuse. They weren't going to take any shit from England anymore. That's what it came down to."

"Making speeches and writing papers isn't like fighting."

"They were making sure there was something to fight for. You have to give people an alternative. If you want them to toss out Brand X, you have to give them Brand Y, and make it better, stronger, tastier. What if I told you Bubblicious is a rip-off?" Phillip asked, inspired as he snatched up the giant pack on Seth's desk.

"I like it okay." To prove it, Seth blew an enormous purple bubble.

"Yeah, but I'm telling you that it sucks and that the people who make it are creeps. You're not going to just toss it in the trash because I say so, right?"

"Damn straight."

"But if I gave you a new choice, if I told you about this Super Bubble Blow—"

"Super Bubble Blow? Man, you slay me."

"Shut up. SBB, it's better. It lasts longer, costs less. Chewing it'll make you and your friends, your family, your neighbors happier, stronger. SBB is the gum of the future, of *your* future. SBB is right!" Phillip added, putting a ring in his voice. "Bubblicious is wrong. With SBB you'll find personal and religious freedom, and no one will ever tell you that you can only have one piece."

"Cool." Phillip was weird all right, Seth thought with a grin, but he was fun. "Where do I sign up?"

With a half laugh, Phillip tossed the gum back on the desk. "You get the picture. These guys were the brains and the blood, and it was their job to get the people excited."

The brains and the blood, Seth thought. He liked it, and figured he could work it into his report. "Okay, maybe I'll pick Patrick Henry. He doesn't look as dorky as some of the other guys."

"Good. You can access information on him on the computer. When you hit the bibliography of books on him, print it out. The library in Baltimore's bound to have more of a selection than the one at school."

"Okay."

"And your composition for English is ready to turn in tomorrow?"

"Man, you never let up."

"Let's see what you've got."

"Jeez." Grumbling all the way, Seth dug into his binder and tugged out the single sheet.

It was titled "A Dog's Life" and described a typical day through the eyes of Foolish. Phillip felt his lips twitch as the canine narrator told of his delight in chasing rabbits, his irritation with bees, the thrill of hanging out with his good and wise friend Simon.

Christ, the kid was clever, he mused.

As Foolish ended his long, demanding day curled up on his bed, which he generously shared with his boy, Phillip handed the page back. "It's great. I guess we now know how you come by your storytelling talent naturally."

Seth's lashes lowered as he carefully slipped the composition back into place. "Ray was pretty smart and all, being a college professor."

"He was pretty smart. If he'd known about you, Seth, he'd have done something about it a lot sooner."

"Yeah, well . . ." Seth gave that Quinn shoulder jerk.

"I'm going to talk to the lawyer tomorrow. We may be able to speed things up a little, with Sybill's help."

Seth picked up his pencil to doodle on his blotter. Just shapes, circles, triangles, squares. "Maybe she'll change her mind."

"No, she won't."

"People do, all the time." He'd waited for weeks, ready to run if the

Quinns had changed theirs. When they hadn't, he'd started to believe. But he was always ready to run.

"Some people keep their promises, no matter what. Ray did."

"She's not Ray. She came here to spy on me."

"She came to see if you were all right."

"Well, I am. So she can go."

"It's harder to stay," Phillip said quietly. "It takes more guts to stay. People are already talking about her. You know what that's like, when people look at you out of the corners of their eyes and whisper."

"Yeah. They're just jerks."

"Maybe, but it still stings."

He knew it did, but he gripped his pencil more tightly, added pressure to his doodling. "You've just got a case on her."

"I might. She sure is a looker. But if I do have a case on her, that doesn't change the basic facts. Kid, you haven't had that many people give a good damn about you in your life."

He waited until Seth's eyes slid over to his, held. "It took me a while, maybe too long, to give a good damn myself. I did what Ray asked me to, because I loved him."

"But you didn't want to do it."

"No, I didn't want to do it. It was a pain in the ass. You were a pain in the ass. But that started to change, little by little. I still didn't want to do it, it was still a pain in the ass, but somewhere along the way I was doing it for you as much as for Ray."

"You thought maybe I was his kid, and that pissed you off."

So much, Phillip thought, for adults believing they kept their secrets and sins from children. "Yeah. That was one little angle I couldn't get rid of until yesterday. I couldn't accept the idea that he might have cheated on my mother, or that you might be his son."

"But you put my name on the sign anyway."

Phillip stared a moment, then let out a half laugh. Sometimes, he realized, you do what's right without really thinking about it, and it makes a difference. "It belonged there, just like you belong here. And Sybill already gave a good damn about you, and now we know why. When somebody cares, it's just plain stupid to push them away."

"You think I should see her and talk to her and stuff." He'd thought about it himself. "I don't know what to say."

"You saw her and talked to her before you knew. You could try it that way."

"Maybe."

"You know how Grace and Anna are all wired up about this birthday dinner of yours next week?"

"Yeah." He lowered his head a little more so the huge grin didn't show. He couldn't believe it, not really. A birthday dinner and he got to pick the food, then like a party with pals the next day. Not that he was going to call it a party, because that was really lame when you were turning eleven.

"What do you think of asking her if she'd like to come over for that? The family dinner deal."

The grin vanished. "I don't know. I guess. She probably wouldn't want to come anyway."

"Why don't I ask her? You could cop another present out of it."

"Yeah?" A smile came back, sly and slow. "She'd have to make it a good one, too."

"That's the spirit."

FIFTEEN

The ninety-minute appointment with the Baltimore lawyer had left Sybill jittery and exhausted. She thought she'd been prepared for it; after all, she'd had two and a half days to get ready, since she'd called first thing Monday morning and had been squeezed into his schedule on Wednesday afternoon.

At least it was over, she told herself. Or this first stage of it was over. It had been more difficult than she'd imagined to tell a perfect stranger, professional or not, the secrets and flaws of her family. And herself.

Now she had to cope with a cold, chilly rain, Baltimore traffic, and her own less-than-stellar driving skills. Because she wanted to put the traffic and the driving off as long as possible, she left her car in the parking garage and faced the rain as a pedestrian.

Fall had already pushed summer back a big step in the city, she noted, shivering as she scooted across the street at the crosswalk. The trees were starting to turn, little blushes of red and gold edging the leaves. The temperature had plummeted with the wet weather, and the wind lashed out, tugging at her umbrella as she approached the harbor.

She might have preferred a dry day, so she could have wandered, explored, appreciated the nicely rehabbed old buildings, the tidy waterfront, the historic boats moored there. But it had its appeal, even in a hard, frigid rain.

The water was stone-gray and choppy, its edges blurring into the sky so that it wasn't possible to tell where either ended. Most of the visitors and tourists had taken shelter indoors. Any who went by, went by in a hurry.

She felt alone and insignificant standing in the rain, looking at the water, wondering what the hell to do next.

With a sigh, she turned and studied the shops. She was going to a birthday party on Friday, she reminded herself. It was time she bought her nephew a present.

It took her more than an hour, comparing, selecting, rejecting art supplies. Her focus was so narrowed, she didn't note the bright glee in the clerk's eyes as she began to pile up her choices. It had been more than six years since she'd bought Seth a gift, she thought. She was going to make up for that.

It had to be just the right pencils, the perfect collection of chalks. She examined watercolor brushes as if the wrong choice would mean the end of the world as she knew it. She tested the weight and thickness of drawing paper for twenty minutes, then agonized over a case for all the supplies.

In the end, she decided simplicity was the answer. A young boy would likely feel more comfortable with a plain walnut case. It would be durable, too. If he took care, it was something he would have for years.

And maybe, after enough of those years passed, he could look at it and think of her kindly.

"Your nephew's going to be thrilled," the clerk informed her, giddy as she rang up the purchases. "These are quality supplies."

"He's very talented." Distracted, Sybill began to nibble on her thumbnail, a habit she'd broken years before. "You'll pack everything carefully and box it?"

"Of course. Janice! Would you come over and give me a hand? Are you from the area?" she asked Sybill.

"No, no, I'm not. A friend recommended your store."

"We very much appreciate it. Janice, we need to pack and box these supplies."

"Do you gift-wrap?"

"Oh, I'm sorry, we don't. But there's a stationery store in this center. They have a lovely selection of gift wrap and ribbon and cards."

Oh, God, was all Sybill could think. What kind of paper did one choose for an eleven-year-old boy? Ribbon? Did boys want ribbons and bows?

"That comes to five hundred eighty-three dollars and sixty-nine cents." The clerk beamed at her. "How would you like to pay for that?"

"Five—" Sybill caught herself. Obviously, she decided, she'd lost her mind. Nearly six hundred dollars for a child's birthday? Oh, yes, she'd absolutely gone insane. "Do you take Visa?" she asked weakly.

"Absolutely." Still beaming, the clerk held out her hand for the gold card.

"I wonder if you could tell me . . ." She blew out a breath as she took out her Filofax and flipped to the Q's in the address book. "How to get to this address."

"Sure, it's practically around the corner."

It would be, Sybill thought. If Phillip had lived several blocks away, she might have resisted.

I t was a mistake, she warned herself as she struggled back into the rain, fighting with two enormous shopping bags and an uncooperative umbrella. She had no business just dropping in on him.

He might not even be home. It was seven o'clock. He was probably out to dinner. She would be better off going back to her car and driving back to the Shore. The traffic was lighter now, if the rain wasn't.

At least she should call first. But damn it, her cell phone was in her purse, and she only had two hands. It was dark and it was raining and she probably wouldn't find his building anyway. If she didn't locate it within five minutes, she would turn around and go back to the parking garage.

She found the tall, sleekly elegant building within three and despite a case of nerves, stepped gratefully into the warm, dry lobby.

It was quiet and classy, with ornamental trees in copper pots, polished wood, a few deep-cushioned chairs in neutral tones. The familiar elegance would have relieved her if she hadn't felt like a wet rat invading a luxury liner.

She had to be crazy coming here like this. Hadn't she told herself when she'd set out for Baltimore that day that she wouldn't do this? She hadn't told him about the appointment because she hadn't wanted him to know she would be in Baltimore. He'd only try to persuade her to spend time with him.

For heaven's sake, she'd just seen him on Sunday. There was no sensible reason for this desperate urge to see him now. She would go back to St. Christopher's right now, because she had made a terrible mistake.

She cursed herself as she walked to the elevator, stepped inside, and pushed the button for the sixteenth floor.

What was wrong with her? Why was she doing this?

Oh, God, what if he was home but he wasn't alone? The sheer mortification of that possibility struck her like a blow to the stomach. They'd never said anything about exclusivity. He had a perfect right to see other women. For all she knew, he had a platoon of women. Which only proved she'd lost all common sense by becoming involved with him in the first place.

She couldn't possibly drop in on him like this, unannounced, uninvited, unexpected. Everything she'd been taught about manners, protocol, acceptable social behavior ordered her to stab the down button and leave. Every ounce of pride demanded that she turn around before she was humiliated.

She had no idea what it was that overcame all of that and pushed her out of the elevator and to the door of 1605.

Don't do this, don't do this, don't do this. The order screamed in her head even as she watched her finger depress the buzzer beside his door.

Oh, God, oh, God, oh, God, what have I done? What will I say? How can I explain?

Please don't be home, was her last desperate thought seconds before the door opened.

"Sybill?" His eyes widened in surprise, his lips curved.

Lord help her, she began to babble. "I'm so sorry. I should have called. I don't mean to—I shouldn't have . . . I had to come into the city, and I was just . . ."

"Here, let me have those. You buy out the store?" He was pulling the wet bags out of her icy hands. "You're freezing. Come inside."

"I should have called. I was—"

"Don't be silly." He dumped the bags and began to peel her out of her dripping raincoat. "You should have let me know you were coming into Baltimore today. When did you get in?"

"I—about two-thirty. I had an appointment. I was just—it's raining," she blurted out, hating herself. "I'm not used to driving in traffic. Not really used to driving at all, actually, and I was a little nervous about it."

She rambled on, while he studied her, his brows lifted. Her cheeks were flushed, but he didn't think it was from the cold. Her voice was skittish, and that was new. And interesting. She couldn't seem to figure out what to do with her hands.

Though the raincoat had protected her neat slate-gray suit, her shoes were soaked and her hair was dewed with rain.

"You're wired up, aren't you?" he murmured. He put his hands on her arms, rubbed up and down to warm them. "Relax."

"I should have called," she said for the third time. "It was rude, presumptuous—"

"No, it wasn't. A little risky, maybe. If you'd gotten here twenty minutes earlier, I wouldn't have been home yet." He drew her a little closer. "Sybill, relax."

"Okay." She closed her eyes.

Amusement flickered into his own as he watched her take slow deep breaths.

"Does that breathing stuff really work?" he asked with a chuckle.

The irritation in her voice was barely noticeable, but it was there. "Studies have proven that the flow of oxygen and mental focus relieves stress."

"I bet. I've done studies of my own. Let's try it my way." He brought his mouth to hers, rubbed gently, persuasively until hers softened, yielded, warmed. His tongue danced lightly over hers, teasing out a sigh. "Yeah, that works for me," he murmured, brushing his cheek over her damp hair. "Works just fine for me. How about you?"

"Oral stimulation is also a proven remedy for stress."

He chuckled. "I'm in danger of becoming crazy about you. How about some wine?"

She didn't care to analyze his definition of crazy just then. "I wouldn't mind one glass. I shouldn't, really. I'm driving."

Not tonight you're not, he thought, but only smiled. "Sit down. I'll be right back."

She went back to the concentrated breathing as he slipped into another room. After her nerves settled a bit, she studied the apartment.

A conversation pit in deep forest-green dominated the living area. In its center was a square coffee table. Riding over it was a large sailboat in what she recognized as Murano glass. A pair of green iron candlesticks held fat white candles.

At the far side of the room there was a small bar with a pair of black leather stools. Behind it was a vintage poster for Nuits-St.-Georges Burgundy, depicting an eighteenth-century French calvary officer sitting on a cask with a glass, a pipe, and a very satisfied smile.

The walls were white and splashed here and there with art. A framed print of a stylish poster for Tattinger champagne, with a elegant woman, surely that was Grace Kelly, in a sleek black evening gown behind a slim flute of bubbling wine, hung over a round glass table with curved steel legs. There was a Joan Miró print, an elegant reproduction of Alphonse Mucha's *Automne*.

Lamps were both sparely modern and elegantly Deco. The carpet was thick and pale gray, the uncurtained window wide and wet with rain.

She thought the room displayed masculine, eclectic, and witty taste. She was admiring a brown leather footstool in the shape of a barnyard pig when he returned with two glasses.

"I like your pig."

"He caught my eye. Why don't you tell me about what must have been a very interesting day?"

"I didn't even ask if you had plans." She noted he was dressed in a soft black sweatshirt and jeans and wasn't wearing any shoes. But that didn't mean—

"I do now." Taking her hand he led her across to the deep cushioned U-shaped sofa. "You saw the lawyer this afternoon."

"You knew about that."

"He's a friend. He keeps me up to date." And, Phillip admitted to himself, he'd been acutely disappointed when she hadn't called him to let him know she was coming to the city. "How'd it go?"

"Well, I think. He seems confident that the guardianship will go through. I couldn't persuade my mother to make a statement, though."

"She's angry with you."

Sybill took a quick swallow of wine. "Yes, she's angry, and no doubt deeply regrets the momentary lapse that allowed her to tell me what happened between her and your father."

He took her hand. "It's difficult for you. I'm sorry."

She looked down at their linked fingers. How easily he touched, she thought absently. As if it was the most natural thing in the world. "I'm a big girl. Since it's doubtful that this little incident, however newsworthy it is in St. Christopher's, will ripple across the Atlantic to Paris, she'll get over it."

"Will you?"

"Life moves on. Once the legalities are dealt with, there won't be any motive for Gloria to make trouble for you and your family. For Seth. She will, I imagine, continue to make trouble for herself, but there's nothing I can do about that. Nothing I want to do about it."

A cold streak, Phillip wondered, or a defense? "Even after the legalities are dealt with, Seth will still be your nephew. None of us would stop you from seeing him, or being part of his life."

"I'm not a part of his life," she said flatly. "And as he makes his life, it would only be distracting and unconstructive for him to have reminders of his old life. It's a miracle that what Gloria did to him hasn't scarred him more deeply. Whatever sense of security he has, it's due to your father, to you and your family. He doesn't trust me, Phillip, and he has no reason to."

"Trust has to be earned. You have to want to earn it."

She rose, walked to the dark window and looked out on the city lights that wavered behind the rain. "When you came to live with Ray and Stella Quinn, when they were helping you change your life, remake yourself, did you maintain contact with your mother, with your friends in Baltimore?"

"My mother was a part-time whore who resented every breath I took, and my friends were dealers, junkies, and thieves. I didn't want contact with them any more than they wanted it with me."

"Regardless." She turned back to face him. "You understand my point."

"I understand it, but I don't agree with it."

"I imagine Seth does."

He set his glass aside as he rose. "He wants you there on his birthday Friday."

"You want me there," she corrected. "And I very much appreciate you for persuading Seth to allow it."

"Sybill—"

"Speaking of which," she said quickly. "I found your art store." She gestured toward the bags he'd set by the door.

"That?" He stared at the bags. "*All* of that?"

Immediately she began to nibble on her thumbnail. "It's too much, isn't it? I knew it. I got caught up. I can take some of it back or just keep it for myself. I don't take enough time to draw anymore."

He'd walked over to examine the bags, the boxes inside. "*All* of this?" With a laugh, he straightened, shook his head. "He'll love it. He'll go nuts."

"I don't want him to think of it as a bribe, like I'm trying to buy his affection. I don't know what got into me. Once I started, I couldn't seem to stop."

"If I were you, I'd stop questioning my motives for doing something nice, something impulsive, and just a bit over the top." Gently he tugged at her hand. "And stop biting your nails."

"I'm not biting my nails. I never . . ." Insulted, she looked down at her hand, saw the ragged thumbnail. "Oh, God, I'm biting my nails. I haven't done that since I was fifteen. Where's my nail file?"

Phillip edged closer to her as she grabbed her handbag and took out a small manicure set. "Were you a nervous kid?"

"Hmm?"

"A nail-biter."

"It was a bad habit, that's all." Smoothly, efficiently, she began to repair the damage.

"A nervous habit, wouldn't you say, Dr. Griffin?"

"Perhaps. But I broke it."

"Not entirely. Nail biting," he murmured, moving toward her. "Migraines."

"Only occasionally."

"Skipping meals," he continued. "Don't bother to tell me you've eaten tonight. I know better. It seems to me that your breathing and concentrating isn't quite doing the job on stress. Let's try my way again."

"I really have to go." She was already being drawn into his arms. "Before it gets too late."

"It's already too late." He brushed his lips over hers once, twice. "You really have to stay. It's dark, it's cold, it's raining," he murmured, nibbling on, toying with her lips. "And you're a terrible driver."

"I'm just . . ." The nail file slipped out of her fingers. "Out of practice."

"I want to take you to bed. I want to take you to my bed." The next kiss was deeper, longer, wetter. "I want to slip you out of that lovely little suit, piece by piece, and see what's going on under it."

"I don't know how you do this." Her breath was already coming too fast, her body going too soft. "I can't keep my thoughts aligned when you're touching me."

"I like them scattered." He slid his hands under her trim jacket until his thumbs skimmed the sides of her breasts. "I like you scattered. And trembling. It makes me want to do all sorts of things to you when you tremble."

Quick flares of heat, sharp stabs of ice were already racing over her. "What sorts of . . . things?"

He made a low, delighted sound against the side of her throat. "I'll show you," he offered, and picked her up.

"I don't do this." She pushed back her hair, staring at him as he carried her into the bedroom.

"Do what?"

"Go to a man's apartment, let him carry me to bed. I don't do this."

"We'll just consider it a change in behavioral patterns then." He kissed her thoroughly before laying her down on the bed. "Caused by . . ." He paused to light a trio of candles on an iron stand in the corner. "Direct stimulation."

"That could work." The candlelight did wonders for an already impossibly handsome face. "It's just that you're so attractive."

He chuckled and slid onto the big bed to nip at her chin. "And you're so weak."

"Not usually. Actually, my sexual appetites are slightly below average, ordinarily."

"Is that so?" He lifted her just enough to slip the jacket away.

"Yes. I've found, for myself . . . oh . . . that while a sexual interlude can be pleasant . . ." Her breath caught as his fingers slowly released the buttons of her blouse.

"Pleasant?" he prompted.

"It rarely, if ever, has more than a momentary impact. Of course, that's due to my hormonal makeup."

"Of course." He lowered his mouth to the soft swell of her breasts that rose temptingly above the cups of her bra. And licked.

"But—but—" She clenched her fists at her sides as his tongue swept under the fabric and shot off shock waves.

"You're trying to think."

"I'm trying to see if I can."

"How's it going?"

"Not very well."

"You were telling me about your hormonal makeup," he reminded her, watching her face as he tugged her skirt down over her hips.

"I was? Oh, well . . . I had a point." Somewhere, she thought vaguely, a shiver going through her as he traced a fingertip over her midriff.

He saw with delight that she wore those sexy thigh-hugging stockings again, this time in sheer smoky-black. He imagined she'd considered that the black bra and panties were proper coordinates.

He thanked God for her practical mind.

"Sybill, I love what goes on under your clothes."

He moved his mouth to her belly, tasted heat and woman, felt her muscles quiver. She made a helpless little sound in her throat as her body shifted under him.

He could take her anywhere. The power of knowing that flooded him like wine. As he took her, slowly now, wanting them both to linger at each stage, he let himself sink.

He peeled those stockings down those lovely, long thighs, following the path with his mouth all the way to her toes. Her skin was creamy, smooth, fragrant. Perfect. And only more alluring when it quivered lightly under his.

He slipped fingertips and tongue beneath that silky fantasy snug over her hips in teasing strokes so that she arched, shuddered, and moaned. Heat was there. Centered just there. Wet, arousing heat.

And when the teasing drove them both mad, he stripped that barrier aside and plunged into the hot taste of her. She cried out, her body rising, her hands fisting in his hair as he spun her to peak. When she was limp and gasping he took more.

And showed her more.

He could have anything. Everything. She was powerless to deny him, to stem the tidal wave of sensations that swamped her. The world had become him, only him. The flavor of his skin in her mouth, the texture of his hair against her flesh or in her hands, the movement of his muscle beneath her fingers.

Murmurs, his murmurs, echoed in her spinning head. The sound of her own name, a whisper of pleasure. Her breath sobbed out as she found his mouth with hers, poured everything she was into that hot flood of emotion.

Again, again, again. The urgent demand circled in her head, as she clung and gave, gave, gave.

Now it was his hands that fisted, on either side of her head as the shock of feeling slammed into him, flashing against desire, melting into a need so urgent it was pain.

She opened for him, a breathless invitation. And filling her, sinking inside her, he lifted his head and watched her face in the golden shaft of candlelight.

Her eyes were on his, her lips parted as the breath trembled through them. Something clicked, a lock opening, a connection made. He found his hands groping for hers, fingers twining together.

Slow, smooth, with each movement a fresh shock of pleasure. Soft, silky, a promise in the dark. He saw her eyes glaze, felt the tension, the ripple, and closed his mouth over hers to capture the gasp as she climaxed.

"Stay with me." He murmured it as his lips roamed her face, as his body moved in hers. "Stay with me."

What choice did she have? She was defenseless against what he brought to her, helpless to refuse what he demanded in return.

The pressure built again, an internal demand that refused to be denied. When she tumbled free, he gathered her close and fell with her.

"I was going to cook," he said sometime later when she lay over him, limp and speechless. "But I think we'll order in. And eat in bed."

"All right." She kept her eyes closed, commanding herself to listen to the beat of his heart and pay no attention to the voice of her own.

"You can sleep in tomorrow." Idly he toyed with her hair. He wanted her there in the morning, badly wanted her there in the morning. It was something to think about later. "Maybe do some sight-seeing or shopping. If you hang around for most of the day, you can follow me home."

"All right." She simply didn't have the strength to assert herself. Besides, she told herself, it made sense. The Baltimore Beltway was confusing, unfamiliar ground. She would enjoy spending a few hours exploring the city. It was certainly foolish to drive all the way back tonight, in the rain, in the dark.

"You're awfully agreeable."

"You caught me in a weak moment. I'm hungry, and I don't want to face driving tonight. And I miss the city, any city."

"Ah, so it's not my irresistible charm and awesome sexual prowess."

She couldn't stop the smile. "No, but they don't hurt."

"I'll make you an egg-white omelette in the morning, and you'll be my slave."

She managed to laugh. "We'll see about that."

She was afraid she was entirely too close to a slavish condition now. The heart she was desperately trying to ignore continued to insist that she'd fallen in love with him.

That, she warned herself, would be a much bigger, more permanent mistake, than knocking on his door on a rainy evening.

Sixteen

When a twenty-nine-year-old woman changed her clothes three times before attending an eleven-year-old boy's birthday party, she was in trouble.

Sybill lectured herself on this simple fact even as she stripped off a white silk blouse—white silk, for Lord's sake, what had she been thinking of—and exchanged it for a teal turtleneck.

She was going to a simple, informal family dinner party, she reminded herself, not a diplomatic reception. Which, she admitted with a sigh, wouldn't have posed nearly as much of a social or fashion dilemma. She knew exactly what to wear, how to behave, and what was expected of her at a formal reception, a state dinner, a gala, a charity ball.

It was a pathetic statement on her narrow social experience, she concluded, that she knew neither how to dress nor how to behave at her own nephew's birthday dinner.

She slipped a long chain of silver beads over her head, took it off, cursed herself and put it on again. Underdressed, overdressed, what did it matter? She wouldn't fit in anyway. She would pretend she did, the Quinns would pretend she did, and everyone would be desperately relieved when she said her good-byes and went away.

Two hours, she told herself. She would only stay two hours. Surely she could survive that. Everyone would be polite, would avoid awkward or nasty scenes for Seth's sake.

She picked up her brush to smooth her hair back, then secured it with a clip at the nape of her neck before critically studying herself in the mirror. She looked confident, she decided. Pleasant, nonthreatening.

Except . . . maybe the color of the sweater was too vivid, too bold. Gray might be better, or brown.

Good God.

The ringing of the phone was such a welcome diversion, she all but leapt on it. "Yes, hello, Dr. Griffin."

"Syb, you're still there. I was afraid you'd taken off."

"Gloria." Her stomach plummeted to her unsteady knees. Very carefully she lowered herself to the side of the bed. "Where are you?"

"Oh, I'm around. Hey, I'm sorry I ditched you the other night. I was messed up."

Messed up, Sybill thought. It was a good term for certain conditions. From the rapid pace of Gloria's speech, she assumed her sister was messed up even now. "You stole money out of my wallet."

"I said I was messed up, didn't I? I panicked, you know, needed some cash. I'll pay you back. You talk to those Quinn bastards?"

"I had a meeting with the Quinn family, as I promised I would." Sybill uncurled the hand she'd bunched into a fist and spoke evenly. "I'd given them my word, Gloria, that both of us would meet them to discuss Seth."

"Well, I didn't give mine, did I? What'd they say? What're they going to do?"

"They say you were working as a prostitute, that you abused Seth physically, that you allowed your clients to make sexual advances toward him."

"Liars. Fucking liars. They just want to kick me around, that's all. They—"

"They said," Sybill went on, coolly now, "that you accused Professor Quinn of molesting you nearly a dozen years ago, intimated that Seth was his. That you blackmailed him, that you sold Seth to him. That he gave you more than a hundred and fifty thousand dollars."

"All bullshit."

"Not all, but part. Your part could be accurately described as bullshit. Professor Quinn didn't touch you, Gloria, not twelve years ago, not twelve months ago."

"How do you know? How the hell do you know what—"

"Mother told me that Raymond Quinn was your father."

There was silence for a moment, then only Gloria's quick breathing. "Then he owed me, didn't he? He *owed* me. Big-deal college professor with his boring little life. He owed me plenty. It was his fault. It was all his fault. All those years, he didn't give me dick. He took in scum from the street, but he didn't give me dick."

"He didn't know you existed."

"I told him, didn't I? I told him what he'd done, and who I was and what he was going to do about it. And what does he do? He just stares at me. He wants to talk to my mother. He's not going to give me a fucking dollar until he talks to my mother."

"So you went to the dean and claimed he'd molested you."

"Put the fear of God into him. Tight-assed son of a bitch."

She'd been right, Sybill thought. Her instincts when she'd walked into that room at the police station had been right after all. It was a mistake. This woman was a stranger. "And when that didn't work, you used Seth."

"Kid's got his eyes. Anybody can see that." There was a sucking noise, a hiss, as Gloria dragged on a cigarette. "Changed his tune once he got a look at the kid."

"He gave you money for Seth."

"It wasn't enough. He owed me. Listen, Sybill . . ." Her voice shifted, whined and trembled. "You don't know what it's like. I've been raising that kid on my own since he was a baby and that prick Jerry DeLauter took off. Nobody was going to help me. Our dear mother wouldn't even accept a phone call from me, and that prissy freak she married and tried to pass off as my father wouldn't either. I could've dumped the kid, you know. I could've dumped him anytime. The money Social Services doles out for a kid is pitiful."

Sybill stared out through her terrace doors. "Does it always come back to money?"

"It's easy to look down when you've got plenty of it," Gloria snapped. "You never had to hustle, you never had to worry. Perfect daughter always had plenty of everything. Now it's my turn."

"I would have helped you, Gloria. I tried to years ago when you brought Seth to New York."

"Yeah, yeah, same old tune. Get a job, straighten up, get clean, get dry. Shit, I don't want to dance to that, get it? This is my life I'm living here, baby sister, not yours. You couldn't pay me to live yours. And that's my kid, not yours."

"What's today, Gloria?"

"What? What the hell are you talking about?"

"Today is September twenty-eighth. Does that mean anything to you?"

"What the hell's it supposed to mean? It's fucking Friday."

And your son's eleventh birthday, Sybill thought and straightened her shoulders, took her stand. "You won't get Seth back, Gloria, though we're both aware that that's not your goal."

"You can't—"

"Shut up. Let's stop playing games. I know you. I haven't wanted to, I've preferred to pretend otherwise, but I know you. If you want help, I'm still willing to get you into a clinic, to pay the bill for rehab."

"I don't need your goddamn help."

"Fine, that's your choice. You won't get another penny out of the Quinns, you won't come near Seth again. I've given my deposition to their lawyer and a notarized statement to Seth's caseworker. I've told them everything, and if necessary, I'll testify in court that Seth's wishes and his best interest are served by his remaining, permanently, with the Quinns. I'll do everything I can to see that you don't use him anymore."

"You bitch." The hiss was filled with anger, but under it was shock. "You think you can screw me this way? You think you can toss me off and side with those bastards against me? I'll ruin you."

"You can certainly try, but you won't succeed. You made your deal, now it's done."

"You're just like her, aren't you?" Gloria spit the words out like bullets. "You're just like our ice cunt of a mother. Perfect society princess, and underneath you're nothing but bitch."

Maybe I am, Sybill thought wearily, maybe I'm going to have to be. "You blackmailed Raymond Quinn, who'd done nothing to harm you. It worked. At least it worked well enough for you to be paid. It won't work with his sons, Gloria. And it won't work with me. Not anymore."

"Won't it? Well, try this. I want a hundred thousand. A hundred thousand, or I'm going to the press. *National Enquirer, Hard Copy.* Let's see how fast your lousy books sell once I tell my story."

"Sales will likely increase twenty percent," Sybill said mildly. "I won't be blackmailed, Gloria. You do what you like. And think about this. You're facing criminal charges in Maryland, and there's a restraining order against you to keep you away from Seth. The Quinns have evidence. I've seen it," she continued, thinking of the letters Gloria had written. "Further criminal charges for extortion and child abuse may be brought. I'd cut my losses if I were you."

She hung up on the spew of obscenities and, closing her eyes, lowered her head between her knees. The nausea was a greasy sea in her stomach, the sneaky edge of a migraine was creeping closer. She couldn't stop the trembling. She'd held it off during the phone call, but she couldn't stop it now.

She stayed just as she was until she could control her breathing again, until the worst threat of sickness receded. Then she rose, took one of her pills to ward off the migraine and added blusher to her pale cheeks. She gathered her purse, Seth's gifts, a jacket against the chill, and left.

❧

The day had been endless. How was a guy supposed to sit through hours and hours of school on his birthday? I mean, he was double ones now, and everything. He was going to get pizza and french fries and chocolate cake and ice cream and probably even presents.

He'd never actually had a birthday present before, Seth mused. Not that he could remember, anyway. He'd probably end up with clothes and shit, but it would still be a present.

If anybody ever showed up.

"What's taking them so long?" Seth demanded, again.

Determined to be patient, Anna continued to slice potatoes for the homemade fries that Seth had requested as part of his birthday menu. "They'll be along."

"It's almost six. How come I had to come home after school instead of going to the boatyard?"

"Because," Anna said, and left it at that. "Stop poking into everything, will you?" she added as Seth opened the refrigerator, again. Shut it, again. "You're going to be stuffing your face soon enough."

"I'm starving."

"I'm making the fries right now, aren't I?"

"I thought Grace was going to make them."

Steely-eyed, Anna stared at him over her shoulder. "Are you suggesting that I can't make french fries?"

He was bored and restless enough to be pleased that he'd jabbed her ego. "Well, she makes really good ones."

"Oh." She turned completely around. "And I don't."

"You do okay. Anyway, we'll have the pizza." He nearly pulled it off, but snorted out a chuckle.

"Brat." Anna made a laughing dive at him. He danced away howling.

"That's the door, that's the door. I'll get it!" He raced off, leaving Anna grinning after him.

But the wicked laughter faded from his eyes when he yanked open the door and saw Sybill on the porch. "Oh. Hi."

Her heart sank, but she fixed on a polite smile. "Happy birthday."

"Yeah, thanks." Watching her cautiously, he opened the door.

"I appreciate you inviting me." At a loss, she held out both shopping bags. "Are you allowed to have your gifts?"

"Sure, I guess." Then his eyes widened. "All that?"

She nearly sighed. He sounded so much like Phillip had. "It all sort of goes together."

"Cool. Hey, it's Grace." Hampered by the bags, which he held now, he bumped past her onto the porch.

The joy in his voice, the quick, delighted smile on his face was such a marked contrast from the way he'd looked at her, Sybill's sinking heart cracked.

"Hey, Grace! Hey, Aubrey! I'll tell Anna you guys are here."

He darted inside again, leaving Sybill standing by the open door without a clue how to proceed. Grace got out of the car and smiled. "Sounds like he's excited."

"Yes, well . . ." She watched Grace set a bag on the hood of the car, followed by a large clear-plastic cake holder. Then she reached in to unstrap a babbling Aubrey from her car seat. "Do you need a hand?"

"Actually, I could use two. Just a minute, baby. If you keep wriggling . . ." She tossed another smile over her shoulder as Sybill walked over. "She's been wired all day. Seth is Aubrey's favorite person."

"Seth! He's got a birthday. We baked a cake."

"We sure did." Grace hauled Aubrey out, then passed her to an astonished Sybill. "Would you mind? She wanted to wear that dress, but the run from here to the house is bound to be a disaster."

"Oh, well . . ." Sybill found herself staring down into a beaming, angelic face and holding a bouncing little body dressed in party-pink ruffles.

"We're having a party," Aubrey told her and put both her hands on Sybill's cheeks to ensure her full attention. "I'll have a party next time when I'm three. You can come."

"Thank you."

"You smell pretty. I do, too."

"You certainly do." Sybill's initial stiffness couldn't stand up under that cheerfully charming smile. Phillip's Jeep pulled in behind Grace's, and most of the stiffness returned as Cam slid out of the passenger seat and shot her a cool, unmistakably warning look.

Aubrey let out a shriek of greeting. "Hi! Hi!"

"Hi, there, beautiful." Cam walked over, kissed Aubrey lightly on her comically pursed lips, then aimed those flinty eyes at Sybill. "Hello, Dr. Griffin."

"Sybill." Well able to interpret the chilly exchange, Phillip strode over, laid a supporting hand on her shoulder, and leaned in for the kiss Aubrey was offering. "Hi, there, sweetie."

"I have a new dress."

"And you look stunning in it."

In the way of females, Aubrey deserted Sybill without a glance and held out her arms to Phillip. He managed the transfer easily, settling her on his hip. "Been here long?" he asked Sybill.

"No, I just got here." She watched Cam carry three large cardboard boxes of pizza into the house. "Phillip, I don't want to cause any—"

"Let's go inside." He took her hand, pulling her along. "We've got to get this party going, don't we, Aub?"

"Seth gets presents. They're secrets." She whispered it and leaned in close. "What are they?"

"Uh-uh, I'm not telling." He set her down when they stepped into the house, gave her frilled bottom a friendly pat, and sent her off. She shouted for Seth and scrambled toward the kitchen. "She'll blab."

Determined to make it work, Sybill put her smile back in place. "I won't."

"Nope. You can just wait for it. I'm going to grab a fast shower before Cam beats me to it and uses all the hot water." He gave her a quick, absent kiss. "Anna'll get you a drink," he added as he headed upstairs.

"Great." On a huff of breath, Sybill steeled herself to deal with the Quinns alone.

The kitchen was pandemonium. Aubrey was squealing, Seth was talking a mile a minute. Potatoes were frying, with Grace manning the stove since Cam had Anna trapped against the refrigerator with a gleam of pure lust in his eyes.

"You know how I get when I see you in an apron."

"I know how you get when you see me breathe." And she hoped it would never change. Nonetheless, she narrowed her eyes at him. "Hands off, Quinn. I'm busy."

"You've been slaving over a hot stove. You really ought to take a shower. With me."

"I'm not going to—" She spotted the movement out of the corner of her eye. "There you are, Sybill." In a move that looked very practiced, and very effective to Sybill, Anna shifted and jammed her elbow into her husband's stomach. "What can I get you to drink?"

"Ah . . . the coffee smells wonderful, thank you."

"I'll take a beer." Cam snagged one out of the fridge. "And go clean up." He aimed that look at Sybill again, then strode out.

"Seth, stay out of those bags," Anna ordered as she pulled down a mug. "No gifts yet." She'd made the decision to keep him from opening Sybill's gifts until after dinner. She calculated that his aunt would make her excuses and run as quickly as she could manage it after the little ritual was complete.

"Man! Is it my birthday or what?"

"Yes, if you live through it. Why don't you take Aubrey into the other room? Entertain her for a while. We'll eat as soon as Ethan gets here."

"Well, where is he, anyway?" Grumbling, Seth stalked out with Aubrey on his heels and didn't catch the quick grin Grace and Anna exchanged.

"That goes for you dogs, too." Anna gave Foolish a nudge with her foot and pointed her finger. With canine sighs, both dogs clipped out of the kitchen.

"Peace." Anna closed her eyes to absorb it. "Momentary peace."

"Is there anything I can do to help?"

With a shake of her head, Anna passed over the mug of coffee. "I think we've got it under control. Ethan should be here any minute. In the big surprise." She walked to the window to look out through the gathering dark. "I hope you've brought an adolescent appetite," she added. "Tonight's menu consists of pepperoni-and-sausage pizza, peanut-oil fries, homemade hot fudge sundaes, and Grace's killer chocolate cake."

"We'll all be in the hospital," Sybill commented before she thought it through. Even as she winced, Anna was laughing.

"We who are about to die salute you. Uh-oh, there's Ethan." She'd lowered her voice to a stage whisper. At the stove, Grace dropped her slotted spoon with a clatter. "Did you burn yourself?"

"No, no." Chuckling weakly, Grace stepped back. "No, I'm, ah . . . I'm just going to run out and . . . help Ethan."

"All right but—hmmm," Anna finished when Grace hurried past her and out the door. "Jumpy," she muttered, then hit the outside lights. "It's not quite dark yet, but it will be by the time we finish this." She salvaged the last of the fries and switched off the stove. "Cam and Phillip better put a fire under it. Oh, God, it's cute! Can you see?"

Too curious to resist, Sybill joined her at the kitchen window. She saw Grace standing on the dock, caught in the last light of the day, and Ethan just stepping onto it. "It's a boat," she murmured. "A little sailboat."

"A ten-footer. They call it a pram." Anna's smile nearly split her face. "The three of them have been building it over at Ethan's old house—the one he rents out? The tenants let them use the shed over there so Seth wouldn't know about it."

"They built it for him?"

"Whenever they could steal an hour. Oh, he's going to love it. Well, what's this?"

"What?"

"That," Anna said and stared hard through the glass. She could see Grace talking, her hands locked together, Ethan staring at her. Then he lowered his head to hers. "I hope there's not any . . ." She trailed off as Ethan drew Grace close, buried his face in her hair and rocked. And her arms came up around him. "Oh, oh." Tears flooded Anna's eyes. "She must be—she's pregnant! She's just told him. I know it. Oh, look!" She gripped Sybill's shoulder when Ethan scooped a laughing Grace up into his arms. "Isn't that beautiful?"

The two of them were wrapped around each other, making one silhouette in the last light of day. "Yes, yes, it is."

"Look at me." Laughing at herself, Anna yanked off a paper towel and blew her nose. "I'm a mess. This is going to get to me, I know it is. I'm going to want one." She blew again, sighed. "I was so sure I could wait a year or two. I'm never going to be able to wait that long now. Not for that. I can just see Cam when I—" She stopped herself. "Sorry," she said with a watery laugh.

"It's all right. It's lovely that you're so happy for them. That you're so happy for yourself. This is really a family occasion, especially now. Anna, I really should go."

"Don't be a coward," Anna said, pointing her finger. "You're here, and you're going to have to face this nightmare of indigestion and noise just like the rest of us."

"I simply think—" All she could do was close her mouth when the door burst open. Ethan was still carrying Grace and the pair of them wore huge smiles.

"Anna, we're having a baby." Ethan made the announcement with a catch in his voice.

"What, am I blind?" She brushed Ethan aside to kiss Grace first. "I've had my nose to the window. Oh, congratulations!" Then threw her arms around both of them. "I'm so happy."

"You have to be godmother." Ethan turned his face to kiss her. "We wouldn't have gotten this far without you."

"Oh, that does it." Anna burst into tears just as Phillip walked in.

"What's going on? Why's Anna crying? Jesus, Ethan, what happened to Grace?"

"I'm fine. I'm wonderful. I'm pregnant."

"No kidding?" He plucked her out of Ethan's arms to kiss her lavishly.

"What the hell is going on in here?" Cam demanded.

Still holding Grace, Phillip grinned at him. "We're having a baby."

"Oh, yeah?" He arched his eyebrow. "How does Ethan feel about the two of you?"

"Ha-ha," was Phillip's comment as he set Grace carefully on her feet.

"You feel all right?" Cam asked her.

"I feel terrific."

"You look terrific." Cam drew her into his arms, rubbed his chin over her head. And the tenderness with which he did both had Sybill blinking in surprise. "Nice going, bro," Cam murmured to Ethan.

"Thanks. Can I have my wife back now?"

"I'm nearly done." Cam held Grace at arm's length. "If he doesn't take good care of you and the little Quinn in there, I'll beat the hell out of him for you."

"Are we ever going to eat?" Seth demanded, then stopped at the kitchen doorway and stared. "Why're Anna and Grace crying?" He swept an accusing look around the room, including Sybill in the heat. "What happened?"

"We're happy." Grace sniffled and accepted the tissue that Sybill dug out of her purse. "I'm going to have a baby."

"Really? Wow. Wow. That's cool. That's way cool. Does Aub know?"

"No, Ethan and I will tell her, in a little while. But now I'm going to go get her because there's something you need to see. Outside."

"Outside." He started for the door, but Phillip stepped neatly in his path. "Not yet."

"What is it? Come on, move. Jeez. Let me see what's out there."

"We should blindfold him," Phillip considered.

"We should gag him," was Cam's suggestion.

Ethan took care of matters by hauling Seth over his shoulder. When Grace brought Aubrey in, Ethan winked, shifted the wriggling Seth, and headed out the door.

"You're not throwing me in again!" Seth's voice rang with terrified delight and giggles. "Come on, guys, the water's really cold."

"Wimp," Cam sneered when Seth lifted his face from Ethan's back.

"If you try," Seth warned, eyes dancing with joy and challenge, "I'm taking at least one of you with me."

"Yeah, yeah, big talk." Phillip pushed Seth's face back down. "Ready?" he asked when everyone was assembled at the edge of the water. "Good. Do it, Ethan."

"Man, the water's *cold*!" Seth began, ready to scream when Ethan dropped him. But he was set on his feet and he was turned to face the pretty little wooden boat with sky-blue sails that rippled lightly in the evening wind. "What—where did that come from?"

"The sweat of our brows," Phillip said dryly while Seth gaped at the boat.

"Is it—who's buying it?"

"It's not for sale," Cam said simply.

"It . . . is it . . ." It couldn't be, he thought, while his heart thumped with nerves and hope and shock. But hope was paramount. In the past year he'd learned to hope. "Is it mine?"

"You're the only one with a birthday around here," Cam reminded him. "Don't you want a closer look?"

"It's mine?" He whispered it first, with such staggered delight and shock that Sybill felt her eyes sting. *"Mine?"* He exploded with it as he whirled around. This time the sheer joy on his face closed her throat. "To keep?"

"You're a good sailor," Ethan told him quietly. "She's a tight little boat. She's steady, but she moves."

"You built her for me." His gaze shot from Ethan's face to Phillip's to Cam's. "For me?"

"Nah, we built her for some other brat." Cam gave him a light swat on the side of the head. "What do you think? Go take a look."

"Yeah." His voice quavered as he turned. "Yeah, can I get in her? Can I sit in her?"

"For Christ's sake, she's yours, isn't she?" His voice rough with emotion, Cam grabbed Seth's hand and hauled him onto the dock.

"I think this is a guy thing," Anna murmured. "Let's give them a few minutes to pull themselves together."

"They love him so much." Sybill watched another moment as the four males made noises over a little wooden boat. "I don't think I realized it, really, until just now."

"He loves them, too." Grace pressed her cheek to Aubrey's.

⌇

And it was more, Sybill thought later as she picked at the meal in the noisy kitchen. It had been that shock on Seth's face. The utter disbelief that someone loved him, could love him enough to understand his heart's desire. And understanding, make the effort to give it.

The pattern of his life, she thought wearily, had been broken, shifted, then reformed. And all before she'd really come into it. Now it was set, the way it was meant to be set.

She didn't belong here. She couldn't stay here. She couldn't bear it.

"I really should go," she said with a well-mannered smile. "I want to thank you for—"

"Seth hasn't opened your gift yet," Anna interrupted. "Why don't we let him rip, then we'll have some cake."

"Cake!" Aubrey whacked her palms on her high chair. "Blow the candles out and make a wish."

"Soon," Grace told her. "Seth, take Sybill into the living room so you can open your gift."

"Sure." He waited for Sybill to stand, then with a jerk of his shoulder started out.

"I got it in Baltimore," she began, miserably awkward, "so if it doesn't suit, if you don't like it, Phillip could exchange things for you."

"Okay." He pulled a box out of the first bag, sat Indian-style on the floor, and within seconds was tearing the paper it had taken her untold agonies to choose to shreds.

"You could have used newspaper," Phillip told her and, chuckling, nudged her into a chair.

"It's a box," Seth said, puzzled, and Sybill's heart sank at his disinterested tone.

"Yes, well . . . I kept the receipt. So you can take it back and get whatever you'd like."

"Yeah, okay." But he caught the hard beam in Phillip's eye and made an effort. "It's a nice box." But he wanted to roll his eyes. Then he idly flicked the brass hook, flipped the top. "Holy shit!"

"Christ, Seth." Cam muttered it, glancing over his shoulder as Anna walked in from the kitchen.

"Man, look at all this stuff! It's got, like, everything. Charcoals and pastels and pencils." Now he looked at Sybill with that staggered shock. "I get to have it all?"

"It goes together." Nervous, she twisted her silver beads around her finger. "You draw so well, I thought . . . You may want to experiment with other mediums. The other box has more supplies."

"More?"

"Watercolors and brushes, some paper. Ah . . ." She eased onto the floor as Seth gleefully ripped into the second box. "You may decide you like acrylics, or pen and ink, but I lean toward watercolors myself, so I thought you might like to try your hand at it."

"I don't know how to do it."

"Oh, well, it's a simple process, really." She leaned over to take one of the brushes and began to explain the basic technique. As she spoke, she forgot her nerves, smiled at him.

The light from the lamp slanted over her face, caught something, something in her eyes that jiggled at the corners of his memory.

"Did you have a picture on the wall? Flowers, white flowers in a blue vase?"

Her fingers tightened on the brush. "Yes, in my bedroom in New York. One of my watercolors. Not a very good one."

"And you had colored bottles on a table. Lots of them, different sizes and stuff."

"Perfume bottles." Her throat was closing again, so she was forced to clear it. "I used to collect them."

"You let me sleep in your bed with you." His eyes narrowed as he concentrated on the vague blips of memory. Soft smells, soft voice, colors and shapes. "You told me some story, about a frog."

The Frog Prince. Into her mind flashed the image of how a little boy had curled against her, the bedside lamp holding back the dark for both of them, his bright-blue eyes intense on her face as she'd calmed his fears with a tale of magic and happily ever after.

"You had—when you came to visit, you had bad dreams. You were just a little boy."

"I had a puppy. You bought me a puppy."

"Not a real one, just a stuffed toy." Her vision was blurring, her throat closing, her heart breaking. "You . . . you didn't have any toys with you. When I brought it home you asked me whose it was, and I told you it was yours. That's what you called it. Yours. She didn't take it when she—I have to go."

She shot to her feet. "I'm sorry. I have to go." And bolted out the door.

SEVENTEEN

She got to her car and yanked at the door handle before she realized she'd locked it. Which was, she told herself frantically, a stupid, knee-jerk urban habit that had no more place in this pretty rural neighborhood than she did.

The next thing she realized was that she'd run out of the house without her purse, her jacket, her keys. And that she would walk back to the hotel before she would go back inside and face the Quinns again after her rude and emotional behavior.

She whirled when she heard footsteps behind her and wasn't sure if she was relieved or embarrassed to see Phillip coming toward her. She didn't know what she was, what *it* was that was bubbling up inside her, burning and swelling her heart and her throat. She only knew she had to escape it.

"I'm sorry. I know that was rude. I really have to go." In the rush to get out, the words bumped and tumbled over each other. "Would you mind getting my purse? I need my purse. My keys. I'm sorry. I hope I didn't spoil—"

Whatever was bubbling in her throat was rising higher, choking her. "I have to go."

"You're shaking." He said it gently and reached for her, but she jerked back.

"It's cold. I forgot my jacket."

"It's not that cold, Sybill. Come here."

"No, I'm leaving. I have a headache. I—no, don't touch me."

Ignoring her words, he drew her firmly against him, wrapped his arms tight around her and held on. "It's all right, baby."

"No, it's not." She wanted to scream it. Was he blind? Was he stupid? "I shouldn't have come. Your brother hates me. Seth's afraid of me. You— your—I—"

Oh, it hurt. The pressure in her chest was agony, and it was spreading. "Let me go. I don't belong here."

"Yes, you do."

He'd seen it, that connection, when she and Seth had stared at each other. Her eyes such a clear blue, his so brilliant. He'd all but heard the click.

"No one hates you. No one's afraid of you. Let go, will you?" He pressed his mouth to her temple, would have sworn he felt the pain hissing there. "Why won't you let go?"

"I'm not going to cause a scene. If you'd just get my purse, I'll go."

She was holding herself rigid as marble, but the marble was cracking, he thought, and trembling with the pressure. If she didn't let go she would explode. So he would have to push. "He remembered you. He remembered that you cared."

Through the hideous pressure there was a stab, and the stab pierced her heart. "I can't stand it. I can't bear it." Her hands gripped his shoulders, fingers clenching and unclenching. "She took him away. She took him away. It broke my heart."

She was sobbing now, her arms tight around his neck. "I know. I know it did. That's the way," he murmured, and simply picked her up, sat on the grass, and cradled her against him. "It's about damn time."

He rocked her while tears that were hot and desperate flooded out of her and soaked his shirt. Cold? he thought as the firestorm of grief whipped through her. There was nothing cold in her but the fear of emotional pain.

He didn't tell her to stop, even when the sobs shook her so violently it seemed her bones might snap. He didn't offer promises of comfort or solutions. He knew the value of purging. So he simply stroked and rocked, cradling her while she wept out the pain.

When Anna stepped out on the porch, Phillip shook his head at her, stroking still. He continued to rock her as the door shut again and left them alone.

When she'd cried herself dry, her head felt swollen and hot, her throat and stomach raw. Weak and disoriented, she lay exhausted in his arms. "I'm sorry."

"Don't be. You needed that. I don't think I've ever known anyone who needed a crying jag more."

"It doesn't solve anything."

"You know better than that." He rose and, helping her up, pulled her toward his Jeep. "Get in."

"No, I need to—"

"Get in," he repeated with just a hint of impatience. "I'll go get your purse and your jacket." He lifted her into the passenger seat. "But you're not driving." His eyes met her tired, puffy ones. "And you're not going to be alone tonight."

She didn't have the energy to argue. She felt hollowed out and insubstantial. If he took her back to the hotel, she could sleep. She'd take a pill if she had to and escape. She didn't want to think. If she started to think she might feel again. If she felt again, if any part of that flood of feeling came back, she would drown in it.

Because his face looked grim and entirely too determined when he strode out of the house with her things, Sybill accepted her own cowardice and closed her eyes.

He didn't speak, simply climbed in beside her, leaned over to secure her seat belt, then started the car. He let the blessed silence hang throughout the drive. She didn't protest when he came into the lobby with her or when he opened her purse for her key card at her door.

He took her hand again and led her directly to the bedroom. "Get undressed," he ordered. As she stared at him with those swollen, red-rimmed eyes, he added, "I'm not going to jump you, for Christ's sake. What do you take me for?"

He didn't know where the flare of temper had come from. Maybe it was looking at her like this, seeing her so utterly wrecked and defenseless. Turning on his heel, he marched into the bathroom.

Seconds later, she heard the drum of water in the tub. He came out with a glass and aspirin. "Swallow. If you don't take care of yourself, someone else has to."

The water felt like glory on her abused throat, but before she could thank him, he'd pulled the glass out of her hand and set it aside. She swayed a little, and blinked when he tugged her sweater over her head.

"You're going to take a hot bath and relax."

She was too stupefied to argue as he continued to undress her like a doll. When he laid her clothes aside, she shivered a little but didn't speak. She only stared at him when he picked her up, carried her into the bathroom and deposited her in the tub.

The water was high, and a great deal hotter than she considered healthy. Before she could get her mind around the words to mention it, he flicked off the stream.

"Sit back, shut your eyes. Do it!" he said with such unexpected force that she obeyed. She kept them closed even when she heard the door click shut behind him.

She stayed there for twenty minutes, nearly nodding off twice. Only the vague fear of drowning kept her from sinking into sleep. And the niggling idea that he would come back in, pull her out, and dry her off himself was what made her climb shakily out of the tub.

Then again, maybe he'd gone. Maybe he'd finally gotten disgusted with her outburst and left her alone. Who could blame him?

But he was standing by the terrace doors in her bedroom when she stepped out, looking out at her view of the Bay. "Thank you." She knew it was awkward, for both of them, and struggled to make the effort when he turned and stared at her. "I'm sorry—"

"You apologize again, Sybill, you're going to piss me off." He walked toward her as he spoke, laid his hands on her shoulders. He cocked his eyebrows when she jumped. "Better," he decided, running his fingers over her shoulders and neck, "but not perfect. Lie down."

He sighed, pulled her toward the bed. "I'm not after sex. I do have some small level of restraint, and I can call on it when I'm faced with an emotionally and physically exhausted woman. On your stomach. Come on."

She slid onto the bed and couldn't quite muffle the moan when his fingers began to knead along her shoulder blades.

"You're a psychologist," he reminded her. "What happens to someone who represses their feelings on a regular basis?"

"Physically or emotionally?"

He laughed a little, straddled her, then got seriously down to work. "I'll tell you what happens, doc. They get headaches, heartburn, stomach pains. If and when the dam breaks, it all floods out so hard and so fast that they make themselves sick."

He tugged the robe off her shoulders and used the heels of his hands to press the muscles.

"You're angry with me."

"No, I'm not, Sybill. Not with you. Tell me about when Seth stayed with you."

"It was a long time ago."

"He was four," Phillip prompted and concentrated on the muscles that had just tensed. "You were in New York. Same place you have now?"

"Yes. Central Park West. It's a quiet neighborhood. Safe."

Exclusive, Phillip thought. No trendy East Village for Dr. Griffin. "Couple of bedrooms?"

"Yes. I use the second as my office."

He could almost see it. Tidy, organized, attractive. "I guess that's where Seth slept."

"No, Gloria took that room. We put Seth on the living room sofa. He was just a little boy."

"They just showed up on your doorstep one day."

"More or less. I hadn't seen her in years. I knew about Seth. She'd called me when the man she'd married left her. I sent her money off and on. I didn't want her to come. I never said she couldn't, but I didn't want her to come. She's so . . . disruptive, so difficult."

"But she did come."

"Yes. I came back from a lecture one afternoon and she was waiting outside the building. She was furious because the doorman wouldn't let her in, wouldn't let her go up to my apartment. Seth was crying, and she was screaming. It was just . . ." She sighed. "Typical, I suppose."

"But you let her in."

"I couldn't just send her away. All she had was this little boy and a backpack. She begged me to let them stay for a while. She said she'd been hitchhiking. That she was broke. She started crying, and Seth just crawled onto the couch and fell asleep. He must have been exhausted."

"How long did they stay?"

"A few weeks." Her mind began to drift between then and now, sliding back and forth in time. "I was going to help her get a job, but she said she needed to rest first. She said she'd been sick. Then she said a truck driver in Oklahoma had raped her. I knew she was lying, but . . ."

"She was your sister."

"No, no." She said it wearily. "If I'd been honest, I would have admitted that that had stopped mattering years before. But Seth was . . . He hardly spoke. I didn't know anything about children, but I got a book and it indicated he should have been much more verbal."

He nearly smiled. It was so easy to picture her selecting the proper book, studying it, trying to put everything in order.

"He was like this little ghost," she murmured. "This little shadow in the apartment. When Gloria would go out for any length of time and leave him with me, he'd creep out a little. And the first night she didn't come home until morning, he had a nightmare."

"And you let him sleep with you and told him a story."

"*The Frog Prince.* My nanny told it to me. She liked fairy tales. He was afraid of the dark. I used to be afraid of the dark." Her voice was thick and slow with fatigue. "I used to want to sleep in my parents' bed when I was afraid, but I wasn't allowed to. But . . . I didn't think it would hurt him, just for a little while."

"No." Now he could see her, a young girl with dark hair and light eyes, trembling in the dark. "It wouldn't have hurt."

"He used to like to look at my perfume bottles. He liked the colors and the shapes. I bought him crayons. He always liked to draw pictures."

"You got him a stuffed dog."

"He liked to watch the dogs being walked in the park. He was so sweet when I gave it to him. He carried it around everywhere. He slept with it."

"You fell in love with him."

"I loved him so much. I don't know how it happened. It was only a few weeks."

"Time doesn't always factor in." He skimmed her hair back so he could see her profile. The curve of her cheek, the angle of her brow. "It doesn't always play a part."

"It's supposed to, but it didn't. I didn't care that she took my things. I didn't care that she stole from me when she left. But she took him. She didn't even let me say good-bye to him. She took him, and she left his little dog because she knew it would hurt me. She knew I would think about him crying for it at night, and worry. So I had to stop. I had to stop thinking about it. I had to stop thinking about him."

"It's all right. That part's all over now." He stroked gently, nudging her closer to sleep. "She won't hurt Seth anymore. Or you."

"I was stupid."

"No, you weren't." He stroked her neck, her shoulders, felt her body rise and fall on a long, long sigh. "Go to sleep."

"Don't go."

"No, I'm not." He frowned at how fragile the nape of her neck looked under his fingers. "I'm not going anywhere."

And that was a problem, he realized as he smoothed his hands down her arms, over her back. He wanted to stay with her, to be with her. He wanted to watch her sleep just the way she was sleeping now, deep and still. He wanted to be the one who held her when she cried, for he doubted that she cried often, or that she had anyone to hold her when she did.

He wanted to watch those quiet lake eyes of hers go bright with laughter, that lovely, soft mouth curve with it. He could spend hours listening to the way her voice changed tones, from warm amusement to prim formality to earnestness.

He liked the way she looked in the morning, vaguely surprised to see him beside her. And at night, with pleasure and passion flickering over her face.

She hadn't a clue how revealing that face was, he thought, as he tugged down the covers, shifting her until he could spread them over her. Oh, it was subtle, like her scent. A man had to get close, very close, before he understood. But he'd gotten close, very close, without either of them realizing it. And he'd seen the way she'd watched his family, with wistfulness, with yearning.

Always staying a step back, always the observer.

And he'd seen the way she'd watched Seth. With love, and with longing, and again from a distance.

So as not to intrude? To protect herself? He thought it was a combination of both. He wasn't quite sure exactly what went on in her heart, in her mind. But he was determined to find out.

"I think I might be in love with you, Sybill." He said it quietly as he stretched out beside her. "Damn if that doesn't complicate things for both of us."

S he woke in the dark, and for a moment, just a flash, she was a child again and afraid of all those things that lurked in the shadows. She had to press her lips together, very hard, until it hurt. Because if she cried out one of the servants would hear and might tell her mother. Her mother would be annoyed. Her mother wouldn't like it that she'd cried about the dark again.

Then she remembered. She wasn't a child. There was nothing lurking in the shadows but more shadows. She was a grown woman who knew it was foolish to be afraid of the dark when there was so much else to fear.

Oh, she'd made a fool of herself, she thought, as more memories slipped through. A terrible fool of herself. Letting herself become upset that way. Worse, letting it show until she'd had no control, none whatsoever. Instead of maintaining her composure, she'd rushed out of the house like an idiot.

Inexcusable.

Then she'd cried all over Phillip. Wept like a baby right in the front yard as if she'd . . .

Phillip.

Mortification had her moaning aloud, covering her face with her hands. She sucked in a gasp when an arm came around her.

"Ssh."

She recognized his touch, his scent even before he drew her against him. Before his mouth brushed her temple, before his body fit comfortingly to hers.

"It's all right," he murmured.

"I—I thought you'd gone."

"I said I'd stay." He slitted his eyes open, scanned the dull red glow of the bedside alarm. "Three A.M. hotel time. Should have figured it."

"I didn't mean to wake you." As her eyes grew accustomed to the dark, she could make out the sweep of his cheekbone, the ridge of his nose, the shape of his mouth. Her fingers itched to touch.

"When I wake up in the middle of the night in bed with a beautiful woman, it's hard to mind."

She smiled, relieved that he wasn't going to press her about her earlier behavior. It could just be the two of them now. No yesterday to mourn over, no tomorrow to worry about.

"I imagine you've had a lot of practice."

"Some things you want to get just right."

His voice was so warm, his arm so strong, his body so firm. "When you wake up in the middle of the night in bed with a woman, and she wants to seduce you, do you mind?"

"Hardly ever."

"Well, if you wouldn't mind . . ." She shifted, slid her body over his, found his lips with her lips, his tongue with her tongue.

"I'll let you know as soon as I start to mind."

Her laugh was low and warm. Gratitude moved through her, for what he'd done for her, what he'd come to be to her. She wanted so badly to show him.

It was dark. She could be anything she wanted to be in the dark.

"Maybe I won't stop if you do."

"Threats?" He was every bit as surprised, and aroused, by the teasing purr of her voice as he was by the deliberate, circling trail of her fingertips down his body. "You don't scare me."

"I can." She began to follow the trail with her mouth. "I will."

"Give it your best shot. Jesus." His eyes all but crossed. "Bull's-eye."

She laughed again and lapped at him like a cat. When his body quivered, and his breathing grew thick and ragged, she scraped her nails slowly up his sides and down again.

What a wonder the male form was, she thought, dreamily exploring it. Hard, smooth, the planes and angles so perfectly fashioned to mate with woman. With her.

Silky here, then rough. Firm, then yielding. She could make him want and ache just as he made her want and ache. She could give, she could take just as he did and all the wonderful and wicked things people did in the dark, she could do.

He'd go mad if she continued. He'd die if she stopped. Her mouth was hot and restless, and everywhere. Those elegant fingers had the blood raging through his veins. As their flesh grew damp, her body slipped and slid over his, a pale silhouette in the dark.

She was any woman. The only woman. He craved her like life.

Dreamlike, she rose up over him, shrugging out of her robe, arching her back, shaking her hair back. What soared through her now was freedom. Power. Lust. Her eyes gleamed, catlike against the dark, bewitching him.

She lowered herself, taking him inside her slowly, dimly aware of what effort it cost him to allow her to set the pace. Her breath caught, released on a moaning sigh of pleasure. Caught again, released again when his hands captured her breasts, squeezed, possessed.

She rocked, small movements, torturously slow, arousing herself with the power. And kept her eyes on his. He shuddered beneath her, his muscles bunched, his body tight between her thighs. Strong, she thought, he was so strong. Strong enough to let her take him as she chose.

She skimmed her hands over his chest, then lowered. Her hair curtained their faces as her mouth closed hard over his. A tangle of tongues and teeth and breath.

The orgasm rolled through her like a wave, growing, building, then sweeping her up and over. She reared back with it, body bowing, and rode it out.

Then she rode him.

He gripped her hips, his fingers digging in as she surged over him. All reckless speed and clashing light now, all heat and greed. His mind emptied, his lungs screamed, and his body climbed desperately toward release.

When he found it, it was brutal and brilliant.

She seemed to melt over him, her body as soft and hot and fluid as a pool of liquid wax. Her heart thudded hard against the frantic beat of his own. He couldn't speak, couldn't find the air to push the words free. But the ones that shimmered on his tongue were three that he'd been careful never to say to a woman.

Triumph still glowed inside her. She stretched, lazy and satisfied as a cat, then curled herself against him. "That," she said sleepily, "was exactly right."

"What?"

She chuckled softly and ended on a yawn. "I may not have scared you, but I fried your brain."

"No question." A sex-scrambled brain. Men who started thinking about love, much less bringing the word up when they were hot and naked and wrapped around a woman, just got themselves in trouble.

"First time I ever liked waking up at three A.M." Already half asleep, she pillowed her head on his shoulder. She shifted. "Cold," she muttered.

He reached down and tugged up the tangled sheets and blankets. She nipped an edge with her fingers, pulled them up to her chin.

For the second time in one night, Phillip lay awake, staring at the ceiling while she slept deep and still beside him.

Eighteen

It was barely light when Phillip crawled out of bed. He didn't bother to moan. What good would it do? Just because he'd barely slept, his mind was fogged with fatigue and worry, and he had an entire day of backbreaking manual labor ahead of him was no reason to complain.

The fact that there was no coffee was a damn good reason to complain.

Sybill stirred as he started to dress. "You have to go to the boatyard?"

"Yeah." He rolled his tongue over his teeth as he jerked up his slacks. Christ, he didn't even have a toothbrush with him.

"Do you want me to order up some breakfast? Coffee?"

Coffee. The word alone was like a siren's song in his blood.

But he grabbed his shirt. If she ordered coffee, he would have to talk to her. He didn't think it was a smart move to have a conversation when he was in such a foul mood. And why was he in a foul mood? he asked himself. Because he hadn't slept and she'd managed to sneak through his legendary defenses while he wasn't looking and make him fall in love with her.

"I'll get some at home." His voice was clipped and edgy. "I have to go back and change anyway." Which was why he was up so damn early.

The sheets rustled as she sat up. He watched her out of the corner of his eye and reached for his socks. She looked tousled and tumbled and temptingly soft.

Yeah, she was sneaky all right. Hitting him over the head like that with her vulnerability, sobbing in his arms that way and looking so damned hurt and defenseless. Then waking up in the middle of the night and turning into some sort of a sex-fantasy goddess.

Now she was offering him coffee. She had a hell of a nerve.

"I appreciate you staying last night. It helped."

"I'm here to serve," he said shortly.

"I . . ." She gnawed on her bottom lip, alerted and confused by his tone. "It was a difficult day for both of us. I suppose I'd have been wiser to stay away. I was already a little off balance after Gloria's call, and then—"

His head shot up. "What? Gloria called you?"

"Yes." And now, Sybill thought, she'd only proven why that was information best kept to herself. He was upset. Everyone was going to be upset.

"She called you? Yesterday?" With his temper simmering, he picked up his shoe, examined it. "And you didn't think that it was worth mentioning before this?"

"I didn't see any point in it." Because her hands couldn't seem to keep still, she pushed at her hair, tugged at the sheet. "I wasn't going to mention it at all, actually."

"Weren't you? Maybe you forgot, momentarily, that Seth is my family's responsibility. That we have a right to know if your sister's going to cause more trouble. A need to know," he said, rising as his anger rapidly approached flash point. "So that we can protect him."

"She won't do anything to—"

"How the hell do you know?" He exploded with it, rounding on her so that she clutched the sheets in white-knuckled fingers. "How can you know? By *observing* from ten paces back. Goddamn it, Sybill, this isn't a fucking exercise. This is life. What the hell did she want?"

She wanted to shrink, as she always did from anger. She coated her heart and her voice with ice, as she always did to face it. "She wanted money, of course. She wanted me to demand it from you, to give her more myself. She shouted at me, too, and swore at me, just as you are. It appears that staying ten paces back has put me directly in the middle."

"I want to know if and when she contacts you again. What did you tell her?"

Sybill reached for her robe, and her hand was steady. "I told her that your family would not give her anything. And neither would I. That I had spoken with your lawyer. That I had added, and would continue to add, my weight and influence to see that Seth remains a permanent part of your family."

"That's something, then," he muttered, frowning at her as she pulled on her robe.

"It's the least I can do, isn't it?" Her tone was frigid, distant and final. "Excuse me." She strode into the bathroom, shut the door.

From where he stood, Phillip heard the deliberate click of the lock. "Well, fine, that's just fine." He snarled at the door, grabbed his jacket, then got the hell out before he made matters any worse than they already were.

They didn't get any better when he arrived home to find less than half a cup of coffee left in the pot. When he discovered midway through his shower that Cam had obviously used most of the hot water, he decided that just made it all perfect.

Then he stepped into his room, a towel slung around his hips, and found Seth sitting on the side of his bed.

Definitely perfect.

"Hey." Seth eyed him steadily.

"You're up early."

"I thought I'd maybe go in with you for a couple of hours."

Phillip turned to pull underwear and jeans out of his dresser. "You aren't working today. You've got your friends coming over later for the party."

"That's not till this afternoon." Seth lifted a shoulder. "There's time."

"Suit yourself."

He'd expected Phillip to be steamed. He had a thing for Sybill, didn't he? Seth reminded himself. It had been tough to come in here, to wait, to know he'd have to say something.

So he said the single thing that was most on his mind. "I didn't mean to make her cry."

Shit, was all Phillip could think. He yanked on his Jockeys. He wasn't going to get out of this. "You didn't. She was just due for a cry, that's all."

"I guess she's pretty pissed off."

"No, she's not." Resigned to it now, Phillip pulled on his jeans. "Look, women are hard to understand under the best of circumstances. These circumstances pretty much suck."

"I guess." Maybe he wasn't so steamed after all. "I just sort of remembered some stuff." Seth stared at the scars on Phillip's chest because it was easier than looking into his eyes. And because, well, the scars were so cool. "Then she got so whacked out about it and everything."

"Some people don't know what to do with feelings." He sighed, sat on the bed beside Seth, and was bitterly ashamed of himself. He'd blasted Sybill right between the eyes because *he* hadn't known what to do with his feelings. "So they cry, or they yell, or they go off and sulk in a corner. She cares about you, but she doesn't know exactly what to do about it. Or what you want her to do about it."

"I don't know. She's . . . she's not like Gloria." His voice rose a pitch. "She's decent. Ray was decent, too, and I've got—they're like relatives, right? So I've got . . ."

Understanding came quickly and squeezed his heart. "You've got Ray's eyes." Phillip kept his voice matter-of-fact, knowing Seth would believe him if he said it right. "The color and the shape, but that something that was behind them, too. The something that was decent. You've got a sharp brain, just like Sybill. It thinks, it analyzes, it wonders. And under all that, it tries to do what's right. What's decent. You've got both of them in you." He nudged Seth's shoulder with his own. "Pretty cool, huh?"

"Yeah." The smile bloomed. "It's cool."

"Okay, scram, or we're never going to get out of here."

⌖

He arrived at the boatyard nearly forty-five minutes behind Cam and expected to get grief for it. Cam was already at the shaper, rabbeting the next run of planks. Bruce Springsteen shouted from the radio about his glory days. In defense, Phillip turned the volume down. Instantly Cam's head came up.

"I can't hear it over the tool unless it's loud."

"None of us will be able to hear if you keep blasting our ears for hours every day."

"What? Did you say something?"

"Ha-ha."

"Well, we're cheerful, aren't we?" Cam reached over and switched off the power. "So, how's Sybill?"

"Don't start on me."

Cam angled his head while Seth shifted his gaze from man to man and anticipated the entertainment value of a Quinn battle. "I asked a simple question."

"She'll survive." Phillip snatched up a tool belt. "I realize you'd prefer to see her run out of town on a rail, but you'll have to make do with the fact that I gave her a verbal bashing this morning rather than a physical one."

"Why the hell did you do that?"

"Because she pissed me off!" Phillip shouted. "Because it all pisses me off. Especially you."

"Fine, you want to try for a physical bashing, I'm available. But I asked a goddamn simple question." Cam pulled the board off the shaper and heaved it toward the stack, where it landed with a clatter. "She already took a punch in the gut yesterday. Why the hell would you add to it this morning?"

"You're defending her?" Phillip stepped forward until they were nose to nose. "You're defending her, after all the shit you've handed me over her?"

"I've got eyes, don't I? I saw her face last night. What the hell do you take me for?" He jabbed a finger into Phillip's chest. "Anybody who'd kick a woman when she's that torn up ought to have his neck snapped."

"You son of a—" Phillip's fist was clenched and halfway through the swing before he stopped himself. He would have enjoyed a few bloody rounds, especially since Ethan wasn't there to break it up. But not when he was the one who deserved to be bloodied.

He unclenched his fist, spreading his fingers as he turned away to try to find some control. He saw Seth watching him with dark, interested eyes and snarled. "Don't you start."

"I didn't say a word."

"Look, I took care of her, okay?" He dragged a hand through his hair and aimed his rationalization at both of them. "I let her cry it out, patted her hand. I dumped her into a hot tub, tucked her into bed. I stayed with her. Maybe I got an hour's sleep out of the deal, so I'm feeling just a little testy right now."

"Why'd you yell at her?" Seth wanted to know.

"Okay." He took a steadying breath, pressed his fingers to his tired eyes. "This morning she told me that Gloria had called her. Yesterday. Maybe I overreacted, but damn it, she should have told us."

"What did she want?" Seth's lips had gone white. Instinctively, Cam stepped over and laid a hand on his shoulder.

"Don't let her spook you, kid. You're beyond that now. What's the deal?" he demanded of Phillip.

"I didn't get details. I was too busy blasting Sybill for not telling me sooner. The gist of it was money." Phillip shifted his gaze to Seth, spoke directly to him. "She told Gloria to kiss ass. No money, no nothing, no how. She told her she'd been to the lawyer and was making sure you stayed just where you are."

"Your aunt's no pushover," Cam said easily, giving Seth's shoulder a quick squeeze. "She's got spine."

"Yeah." Seth straightened his own. "She's okay."

"Your brother over there," Cam continued, nodding toward Phillip. "He's an asshole, but the rest of us have sense enough to know that Sybill didn't bring up the phone call yesterday because it was a party. She didn't want anybody to get upset. A guy doesn't turn eleven every day."

"So I screwed up." Muttering to himself, Phillip grabbed a plank and prepared to beat out his frustrations with nail and wood. "I'll fix it."

Sybill needed to do some fixing of her own. It had taken her most of the day to work up both the courage and the plan. She pulled into the Quinn driveway just after four, and was relieved not to see Phillip's Jeep.

He'd be at the boatyard for another hour at least, she calculated. Seth would be with him. As it was Saturday night, they would most likely stop on the way home, pick up some takeout.

It was their pattern, and she knew her behavioral patterns, even if she didn't seem to be able to fully connect with the people who were doing the behaving.

Ten paces back, she thought, and was hurt all over again.

Annoyed, she ordered herself out of the car. She would do what she had come to do. It should take no more than fifteen minutes to apologize to Anna, for the apology to be accepted, at least outwardly. She would explain about the call from Gloria, in detail, so that it could be documented. Then she would leave.

She would be back at her hotel, buried in her work, long before Phillip arrived on the scene.

She knocked briskly on the door.

"It's open," came the response. "I'd rather kill myself than get up."

Warily, Sybill reached for the knob, hesitated, then opened the door. All she could do was stare.

The Quinn living room was usually cluttered, always appeared lived-in, but just now it appeared to have been lived in by a rampaging platoon of insane elves.

Paper plates, plastic cups, several of them dumped or spilled, littered the floor and the tables. Small plastic men were strewn everywhere as if a war had been waged, and the casualties were horrendous. Obviously fatal accidents had taken place with model cars and trucks. Shreds of wrapping paper were sprinkled over all like confetti on a particularly wild New Year's Eve.

Sprawled in a chair, surveying the damage, was Anna. Her hair was in her face, and her face was pale.

"Oh, great," she muttered, turning narrowed eyes to Sybill. "Now she shows up."

"I—I'm sorry?"

"Easy for you to say. I've just spent two and a half hours battling ten eleven-year-old boys. No—not boys," she corrected between her teeth. "Animals, beasts. Spawns of Satan. I just sent Grace home with orders to lie down. I'm afraid this experience might affect the baby. He could be born a mutant."

The children's party, Sybill remembered, her dazzled eyes scanning the room. She'd forgotten. "It's over?"

"It will never be over. I will wake up at night for the rest of my life, screaming, until they cart me off to a padded room. I have ice cream in my hair. There's some sort of . . . mass on the kitchen table. I'm afraid to go in there. I think it moved. Three boys managed to fall in the water and had to be dragged out and dried off. They'll probably catch pneumonia and we'll be sued. One of those creatures who disguised himself as a young boy ate approximately sixty-five pieces of cake, then got into my car—I don't know how he got by me, they're like lightning—and proceeded to throw up."

"Oh, dear." Sybill knew it wasn't a laughing matter. It shocked her to realize that her stomach muscles were quivering. "I'm so sorry. Can I help you, ah, clean up?"

"I'm not touching any of it. Those men—the one who claims to be my husband and his idiot brothers—they're going to do it. They're going to scrub and clean and wipe and shovel. They're going to do it all. They knew," she said in a vicious whisper. "They knew what a boy's birthday party would mean. How was I to know? But they did, and they hid themselves away down at that boatyard, using that lame excuse about contract deadlines. They left me and Grace alone with this, this unspeakable duty." She shut her eyes. "Oh, the horror."

Anna was silent for a moment, her eyes still closed. "Go ahead. You can laugh. I'm too weak to get up and belt you."

"You worked so hard to do this for Seth."

"He had the time of his life." Anna's lips curved as she opened her eyes. "And since I'm going to make Cam and his brothers clean it up, I'm feeling pretty good about it, all in all. How are you?"

"I'm fine. I came to apologize for last night."

"Apologize for what?"

The question threw her off rhythm. She was already running behind schedule, she thought, distracted by the chaos and Anna's rambling monologue. Sybill cleared her throat and began again. "For last night. It was rude of me to leave without thanking you for—"

"Sybill, I'm too tired to listen to nonsense. You weren't rude, you have nothing to apologize for, and you'll annoy me if you keep this up. You were upset, and you had a perfect right to be."

And that blew Sybill's carefully prepared speech all to hell. "I honestly don't understand why people in this family won't listen to, much less accept, a sincere apology for regrettable behavior."

"Boy, if that's the tone you use when you lecture," Anna observed with admiration, "your audience must sit at attention. But to answer your question, I suppose we don't because we so often indulge in what could be termed regrettable behavior ourselves. I'd ask you to sit down, but those are really lovely slacks and I have no idea what nasty surprises there are on any of the cushions."

"I don't intend to stay."

"You couldn't see your face," Anna said more gently. "When he looked up at you, when he told you what he remembered. But I could see it, Sybill. I could see it was a great deal more than duty or responsibility or a valiant attempt to do what was right that brought you here. It must have crushed you when she took him away all those years ago."

"I can't do this again." The burn of tears scalded the back of her eyes. "I just can't do this again."

"You don't have to," Anna murmured. "I just want you to know I understand. In my work I see so many damaged people. Battered women, abused children, men who are at the end of their ropes, the elderly we so blithely displace. I care, Sybill. I care about every one of them who come to me for help."

She sighed a little and spread her fingers. "But in order to help them, I have to hold part of myself back, be objective, realistic, practical. If I threw all my emotions into every one of my cases, I couldn't do my job. I'd burn out, burn up. I understand the need for a little distance."

"Yes." The painful tension drained out of Sybill's shoulders. "Of course you do."

"It was different with Seth," Anna went on. "Right from the first minute, everything about him pulled at me. I couldn't stop it. I tried, but I couldn't. I've thought about that, and I believe, sincerely, that my feelings for him were there, just there, even before I met him. We were meant to be a part of each other's lives. He was meant to be part of this family, and this family was meant to be mine."

Risking the consequences, Sybill eased down on the arm of the sofa. "I wanted to tell you . . . you're so good with him. You and Grace. You're so good for him. The relationship he has with his brothers is wonderful, and it's vital. That strong male influence is important for a boy. But the female, what you and Grace give him, is just as vital."

"You have something to give him, too. He's outside," Anna told her. "Drooling over his boat."

"I don't want to upset him. I really have to go."

"Running away last night was understandable and acceptable." Anna's gaze was direct, level and challenging. "Running now isn't."

"You must be very good at your job," Sybill said after a moment.

"I'm damn good at it. Go talk to him. If I manage to get out of this chair in this lifetime, I'll put some fresh coffee on."

It wasn't easy. But then Sybill supposed it wasn't meant to be. Crossing that lawn toward the boy who sat in the pretty little boat, so obviously dreaming of fast sails.

Foolish saw her first and, alerted, raced toward her, barking. She braced herself and put a hand out, hoping to ward him off. Foolish skimmed his head under it, turning the defensive gesture into a stroke.

His fur was so soft and warm, his eyes so adoring, his face so fittingly silly that she relaxed into a smile. "You really are foolish, aren't you?"

He sat, batting at her with his paw until she took it and shook. Satisfied, he raced back toward the boat, where Seth watched and waited.

"Hi." He stayed where he was, pulling on the line and making the small triangle of sail sway.

"Hello. Have you taken it out yet?"

"Nah. Anna wouldn't let me and any of the guys go out in her today." He jerked a shoulder. "Like we'd drown or something."

"But you had a good time at your party."

"It was cool. Anna's a little pissed—" He stopped and looked toward the house. She really hated it when he swore. "She's pretty steamed about Jake barfing in her car, so I figured I'd hang out here until she levels."

"That's probably very sensible."

Then silence fell, heavy, as they both looked out over the water and wondered what to say.

Sybill braced herself. "Seth, I didn't say good-bye to you last night. I shouldn't have left the way I did."

"It's okay." He shrugged again.

"I didn't think you remembered me. Or any of the time you stayed with me in New York."

"I thought I'd made it up." It was too hard to sit in the boat and look so far up. He climbed out, then sat on the dock to dangle his legs. "Sometimes I'd dream about some of it. Like the stuffed dog and stuff."

"Yours," she murmured.

"Yeah, that's pretty lame. She didn't talk about you or anything, so I thought I'd just made it up."

"Sometimes . . ." She took the risk and sat beside him. "Sometimes it was almost like that for me, too. I still have the dog."

"You kept it?"

"It was all I had left of you. You mattered to me. I know it may not seem like that now, but you did. I didn't want you to."

"Because I was hers?"

"Partly." She had to be honest, had to give him that, at least. "She was never kind, Seth. Something was twisted in her. It seemed that she could never be happy unless the people closest to her weren't. I didn't want her back in my life. I'd planned to give her a day or two, then arrange to have the two of you moved to a shelter. That way I would fulfill my family obligation and protect my own lifestyle."

"But you didn't."

"I made excuses at first. Just one more night. Then I admitted that I was letting her stay because I wanted to keep you there. If I found her a job, helped her get an apartment, worked with her to put her life back together, I could keep you close. I'd never had—you were the . . ."

She ordered herself to take one cleansing breath and just say it. "You loved me. You were the first person who ever did. I didn't want to lose that. And when I did, I pulled myself back, right back to where I'd been before you came. I was thinking much more of myself than of you. I'd like to make up for that, a little, by thinking of you now."

He looked away from her, down at the feet he was kicking back and forth over the water. "Phil said how she called and you told her to kiss ass."

"Not precisely in those words."

"But that's what you meant, right?"

"I guess it was." She nearly smiled. "Yes."

"You guys got the same mother, right, but, like, different fathers?"

"Yes, that's right."

"Do you know who my father was?"

"I never met him, no."

"No, I mean do you know who he was? She was always making up different guys and names and shit. And stuff," he corrected. "I just wondered, that's all."

"I only know his name was Jeremy DeLauter. They weren't married long, and—"

"Married?" His gaze flew back to hers. "She never got married. She was just BS-ing you."

"No, I saw the marriage license. She had it with her when she came to New York. She thought I could help her track him down and sue him for child support."

He considered a moment, absorbing the possibility. "Maybe. It doesn't matter. I figured she just took the name from some guy she lived with sometime. If he got hooked up with her, he must've been a loser."

"I could arrange for a search. I'm sure we could locate him. It would take some time."

"I don't want that." There wasn't any panic in his voice, just disinterest.

"I was just wondering if you knew him, that's all. I got a family now." He lifted his arm as Foolish nosed into his armpit, and wrapped it around the dog's neck.

"Yes, you do." Aching a little, she started to rise. She hesitated, her eye drawn toward a flash of white. She saw the heron soar, gliding over the water just at the edge of the trees. Then it was gone, around the bend, leaving barely a ripple on the air.

A lovely thing, she thought. A lovely spot. A harbor for troubled souls, for young boys who only needed a chance to become men. Perhaps she couldn't thank Ray and Stella Quinn for what they'd done here, but she could show her gratitude by stepping aside now and letting their sons finish the job with Seth.

"Well, I should go."

"The art stuff you gave me, it's really great."

"I'm glad you like it. You have talent."

"I fooled around some with the charcoal last night."

She hesitated again. "Oh?"

"I'm not getting it right." He twisted his head to look up at her. "It's a lot different than a pencil. Maybe you could show me how to do it."

She stared hard over the water because she knew he wasn't asking. He was offering. Now, it seemed, she was being given a chance, and a choice. "Yes, I could show you."

"Now?"

"Yes." She concentrated on keeping her voice even. "I could show you now."

"Cool."

NINETEEN

So, he'd been a little hard on her, Phillip told himself. Maybe he felt that she should have told him immediately that Gloria had contacted her. Party or no party, she could have taken him aside and filled him in. But he shouldn't have jumped all over her and then walked out.

Still, in his own defense, he'd felt raw and annoyed and unsettled. He'd spent the first part of the night worried about her, and the second part worried about himself. Was he supposed to be happy that she'd wormed her way through his defenses? Was he supposed to jump for joy that in a matter of weeks she'd managed to drill a hole in the highly polished shield he'd maintained so expertly for over thirty years?

He didn't think so.

But he was willing to admit that he hadn't behaved well. He was even willing to offer a peace token in the form of vintage champagne and long-stemmed roses.

He'd packed the basket himself. Two bottles of Dom, well chilled, two crystal flutes—he wasn't about to insult that brilliant French monk with hotel glasses—the beluga he'd craftily hidden, for just such an occasion, inside an empty carton of plain low-fat yogurt, knowing that no one in his family would touch it.

He'd made the toast points himself and had selected both the blush-pink roses and the vase with care.

He thought she might be a tad resistant to the visit. It never hurt to pave the way with champagne and flowers. And since he intended to do a little worming himself, they couldn't hurt. He was going to loosen her up, he decided, talk to her, and more, get her talking. He wasn't leaving until he had a much clearer view on just who Sybill Griffin was.

He rapped cheerfully on her door. That was going to be his approach—casual cheer. He shot a quick, charming smile at the peephole when he heard footsteps, saw the vague, telltale shadow.

And he stood as those footsteps receded.

Okay. Maybe more than a tad resistant, he concluded, and knocked again. "Come on, Sybill. I know you're there. I want to talk to you."

Silence, he discovered, didn't have to be empty. It could be crowded with ice.

Okay, fine, he thought, scowling at the door. She wanted to do it the hard way.

He set the basket beside the door, then marched back down the hall to the fire stairs and started down. For what he had in mind it was wiser not to be seen leaving the lobby.

"Ticked her off good, didn't you?" Ray commented as he jogged down the steps beside his son.

"Christ almighty." Phillip glared into his father's face. "Next time why don't you just shoot me in the head? It'd be less embarrassing than to die of a heart attack at my age."

"Your heart's strong enough. So, she's not speaking to you."

"She'll talk to me," Phillip said grimly.

"Bribing with bubbly?" Ray jerked a thumb behind him.

"It works."

"The flowers are a good touch. I could usually get around your mother with flowers. Quicker if I groveled."

"I'm not groveling." On that he was firm. "It was just as much her fault."

"It's never just as much their fault," Ray said with a wink. "The sooner you accept that, the sooner you'll get makeup sex."

"Jesus, Dad." He could only rub a hand over his face. "I'm not going to talk to you about sex."

"Why not? Wouldn't be the first time." He sighed as they came to the ground level. "Seems to me your mother and I talked to you plenty, and talked to you straight, about sex. Gave you your first condoms, too."

"That was then," Phillip muttered. "I've got the hang of it now."

Ray let out a rippling, delighted laugh. "I bet you do. But then again, sex isn't the prime motive here. It's always a motive," he added. "We're men, we can't help it. Lady up there, she's got you worried, though, because it's not just about sex. It's about love."

"I'm not in love with her. Exactly. I'm just . . . involved."

"Love always was a tough one for you." Ray stepped out into the windy night, zipped up the frayed sideline jacket he wore over his jeans. "When it came to females, that is. Anytime things started to head toward serious, you'd start moving fast and loose in the opposite direction." He grinned at Phillip. "Looks to me like you're moving straight ahead this time."

"She's Seth's aunt." Annoyance pricked at the back of his neck as he walked around the building. "If she's going to be part of his life, our lives, I need to understand her."

"Seth's part of it. But you slapped her back this morning because you were scared."

Phillip planted his feet, legs spread, rolled his shoulders as he studied Ray's face. "Number one, I can't believe I'm standing here arguing with you. Number two, it occurs to me that you were a hell of a lot better at letting me run my own life when you were alive than you are as a dead man."

Ray only smiled. "Well, I've got what you might call a broader point of view now. I want you happy, Phil. I'm not going to move on until I'm sure the people who matter to me are happy. I'm ready to move on," he said quietly. "To be with your mother."

"Have you—did you . . . How is she?"

"She's waiting for me." The glow slipped over Ray's face and into his eyes. "And she's never been what you could call the waiting type."

"I miss her, so much."

"I know. So do I. She'd be flattered, and annoyed, too, that under it all you've never been willing to settle for less than the kind of woman she was."

Staggered, because it was true, and a secret that he'd kept carefully locked up, Phillip stared. "It's not that, not altogether that."

"Part of that, then." Ray nodded. "You have to find your own, Phil. And make your own. You're getting there. You did a fine job with Seth today. So did she," he said, glancing up at the light shining through Sybill's bedroom window. "You make a fine team, even when you're pulling in different directions. That's because you both care, more than you might understand."

"Did you know he was your grandson?"

"No. Not at first." He sighed now. "When Gloria found me she hit me with all of it at once. I never knew about her, and there she was, shouting, swearing, accusing, demanding. Couldn't calm her down or make sense of it. Next thing I knew she'd gone to the dean with that story about how I'd molested her. She's a troubled young woman."

"She's a bitch."

Ray only moved his shoulders. "If I'd known about her sooner . . . well, that's done. I couldn't save Gloria, but I could save Seth. One look at him and I knew. So I paid her. Maybe that was wrong, but the boy needed me. It took me weeks to track down Barbara. All I wanted from her was confirmation. I wrote to her, three times. Even called Paris, but she wouldn't speak to me. I was still working on that when I had the accident. Stupid," he admitted. "I let Gloria upset me. I was angry with her, myself, everything, worried about Seth, about how the three of you would take it when I explained it all. Driving too fast, not paying attention. Well."

"We would have stood with you."

"I know that. I let myself forget it, and that was stupid, too. Stella was gone, the three of you had your own lives, and I let myself brood, and forget. You're standing with Seth now, and that's more important."

"We're nearly there. With Sybill adding her voice, the permanent guardianship's a given."

"She's adding more than her voice, and she'll add more yet. She's stronger than she gives herself credit for. Than anyone gives her credit for."

In a swift change of mood, Ray clucked his tongue, shook his head. "I guess you're going up there."

"That's the plan."

"Never quite lost that unfortunate skill. Maybe this time that's a good thing. That girl could use some surprises in her life." Ray winked again. "Watch your step."

"You're not going to come up, are you?"

"No." Ray slapped Phillip's shoulder and let out a hearty laugh. "Some things a father just doesn't need to see."

"Good. But since you're here, make it easier for me. Give me a boost up to that first balcony."

"Sure. They can't arrest me, can they?"

Ray cupped his hands, giving Phillip's foot a helpful push, then stood back to watch him make the climb. He watched, and he smiled. "I'm going to miss you," he said quietly and faded into shadows.

∞

In the parlor, Sybill concentrated fiercely on her work. She didn't give a damn if it had been petty, unreasonable behavior to ignore Phillip's knock. She'd had enough emotional upheaval for one weekend. And besides, he'd given up quickly enough, hadn't he?

She listened to the wind rattle against her windows, set her teeth, and pounded the keyboard.

The import of internal news appears to outweigh that of the external. While television, newspapers, and other information sources are as readily available in the small community as they are in large urban areas, the actions and involvements of one's neighbors take precedent when the population is limited.

Information is passed on, with varying degrees of accuracy, through

word of mouth. Gossip is an accepted form of communication. The net-
work is admirably quick and efficient.

Disattending—the pretense of not hearing a private conversation in a
public place—is not as prevalent in the small community as in the large
city. However, in transient areas such as hotels, disattending is still a con-
sistent and acceptable behavioral pattern. I would conclude that the rea-
son for this is the regular comings and goings of outsiders in this type of
area. Overt attention is paid, however, in other areas such as

Her fingers froze, her mouth dropped open, as she watched Phillip slide
her terrace door open and step inside.

"What—"

"The locks on these things are pathetic," he said. He walked to the front
door, opened it, and picked up the basket and vase of flowers he'd left there.
"I figured I could risk these. We don't get a lot of thievery around here. You
might want to add that to your notes." He set the vase of roses on her desk.

"You climbed up the building?" She could only stare at him, amazed.

"The wind's a bitch, too." He opened the basket, took out the first bottle. "I could use a drink. How about you?"

"You climbed up the building?"

"We've already established that." He opened the wine with an expert
and muffled pop.

"You can't . . ." She gestured wildly. "Just break in here, open champagne."

"I just did." He poured two glasses and discovered it didn't do his ego
any harm to have her gaping at him. "I'm sorry about this morning, Sybill."
Smiling, he offered her a glass of champagne. "I was feeling pretty rough,
and I took it out on you."

"So you apologize by breaking into my room."

"I didn't break anything. Besides, you weren't going to open the door,
and the flowers wanted to be in here. So did I. Truce?" he said and waited.

He'd climbed up the building. She still couldn't get over it. No one had
ever committed such a bold and foolish act for her. She stared at him, into
those golden angel eyes, and felt herself softening. "I have work."

He grinned because he saw the yielding. "I have beluga."

She tapped her fingers on the wrist rest of her keyboard. "Flowers,
champagne, caviar. Do you usually come so well equipped when you break
and enter?"

"Only when I want to apologize and throw myself on the mercy of a
beautiful woman. Got any mercy to spare, Sybill?"

"I suppose I might. I wasn't keeping Gloria's phone call from you, Phillip."

"I know you weren't. Believe me, if I hadn't figured that out myself, Cam would have beaten it into my head this morning."

"Cam." She blinked in shock. "He doesn't like me."

"You're wrong. He was worried about you. Can I persuade you to take a break from work?"

"All right." She saved her file, shut down the machine. "I'm glad we're not angry with each other. It only complicates things. I saw Seth this afternoon."

"So I hear."

She accepted the wine, sipped. "Did you and your brothers clean up the house?"

He gave her a pained and pitiful look. "I don't want to talk about it. I'm going to have nightmares as it is." He took her hand, drew her over to the sofa. "Let's talk about something less frightening. Seth showed me the charcoal sketch of his boat that you helped him with."

"He's really good. He catches on so quickly. Really listens, pays attention. He's got a fine eye for detail and perspective."

"I saw the one you did of the house, too." Casually, Phillip leaned forward for the bottle and topped off her wine. "You're really good, too. I'm surprised you didn't pursue art as a profession."

"I had lessons as a girl. Art, music, dance. I took a few courses in college." Desperately relieved that they were no longer at odds, she settled back and enjoyed her wine. "It wasn't anything serious. I'd always known I'd go into psychology."

"Always?"

"More or less. The arts aren't for people like me."

"Why?"

The question confused her, put her on guard. "It wasn't practical. Did you say you had beluga in there?"

There, he thought, the first step back. He'd simply have to go around her. "Mmm-hmm." He took out the container and the toast points, refilled her glass. "What instrument do you play?"

"Piano."

"Yeah? Me, too." He shot her an easy smile. "We'll have to work up a duet. My parents loved music. All of us play something."

"It's important that a child learn to appreciate music."

"Sure, it's fun." He spread a toast point, offered it. "Sometimes the five of us would kill a Saturday night playing together."

"You all played together? That was nice. I always hated playing in front of anyone. It's so easy to make a mistake."

"So what if you did? Nobody's going to cut off your fingers for hitting a sour note."

"My mother would be mortified, and that would be worse than—" She caught herself, frowned into her wine, started to set it aside. He moved smoothly, adding more to her glass.

"My mother really loved to play the piano. That's why I picked it up at first. I wanted to share something with her specifically. I was so in love with her. We all were, but for me she was everything strong and right and kind about women. I wanted her to be proud of me. Whenever I saw that she was, whenever she told me she was, it was the most amazing feeling."

"Some people strive all their lives for their parents' approval and never come close to gaining their pride." There was something bitter and cold in her voice. She caught it herself and managed a weak laugh. "I'm drinking too much. It's going to my head."

Deliberately he filled her glass again. "You're among friends."

"Overindulging in alcohol—even lovely alcohol—is an abuse."

"Overindulging on a regular basis is an abuse," he corrected. "Ever been drunk, Sybill?"

"Of course not."

"You're due." He tapped his glass to hers. "Tell me about the first time you tasted champagne."

"I don't remember. We were often served watered wine at dinner when we were children. It was important that we learn to appreciate the proper wines, how they were served, what to serve them with, the correct glass for red, the correct glass for white. I could easily have coordinated a formal dinner party for twenty when I was twelve."

"Really?"

She laughed a little, let the wine froth in her head. "It's an important skill. Can you imagine the horror if one bungles the seating? Or serves an inferior wine with the main course? An evening in ruins, reputations in tatters. People expect a certain level of tedium at such affairs, but not a substandard Merlot."

"You attended a lot of formal dinner parties?"

"Yes, indeed. First, several smaller, what you might term 'practice' ones with intimates of my parents, so that I could be judged ready. When I was sixteen, my mother gave a large, important dinner for the French ambassador and his wife. That was my first official appearance. I was terrified."

"Not enough practice?"

"Oh, I had plenty of practice, hours of instruction on protocol. I was just so painfully shy."

"Were you?" he murmured, tucking her hair behind her ear. Score one for Mother Crawford, he thought.

"So silly. But any time I had to face people that way, my stomach would seize up and my heart would pound so hard. I lived in terror that I would spill something, say something I shouldn't, or have nothing to say at all."

"Did you tell your parents?"

"Tell them what?"

"That you were afraid?"

"Oh." She waved her hand at that, as if it were the most absurd of questions, then picked up the bottle to pour more champagne. "What would be the point? I had to do what was expected of me."

"Why? What would happen if you didn't? Would they beat you, lock you in a closet?"

"Of course not. They weren't monsters. They'd be disappointed, they'd disapprove. It was horrible when they looked at you that way—tight-lipped, cold-eyed—as if you were defective. It was easier just to get through it, and after a while, you learned how to deal with it."

"Observe rather than participate," he said quietly.

"I've made a good career out of it. Maybe I didn't fulfill my obligations by making an important marriage and giving a lifetime of those beastly dinner parties and raising a pair of well-behaved, properly bred children," she said with rising heat. "But I made good use of my education and a good career, which I'm certainly more suited for than the other. I'm out of wine."

"Let's slow down a little—"

"Why?" She laughed and plucked out the second bottle herself. "We're among friends. I'm getting drunk, and I think I like it."

What the hell, Phillip thought and took the bottle from her to open it. He'd wanted to dig under that proper and polished surface of hers. Now that he was there, there was no point in backing off.

"But you were married once," he reminded her.

"I told you it didn't count. It was *not* an important marriage. It was an impulse, a small and failed attempt at rebellion. I make a poor rebel. Mmm." She swallowed champagne, gestured with her glass. "I was supposed to marry one of the sons of my father's associate from Britain."

"Which one?"

"Oh, either. They were both quite acceptable. Distant relations of the queen. My mother was quite determined to have her daughter associated by marriage with royalty. It would have been a triumph. Of course I was only fourteen, so she had plenty of time to work out the plan, the timing. I believe she'd decided I could become engaged, formally, to one or the other when I was eighteen. Marriage at twenty, first child at twenty-two. She had it all worked out."

"But you didn't cooperate."

"I didn't get the chance. I might very well have cooperated. I found it very difficult to oppose her." She brooded over that for a moment, then washed it away with more champagne. "But Gloria seduced them both, at the same time, in the front parlor while my parents were attending the opera. I believe it was Vivaldi. Anyway . . ." She waved her hand again, drank again. "They came home, found this situation. There was quite a scene. I snuck downstairs and watched part of it. They were naked—not my parents."

"Naturally."

"High on something, too. There was a lot of shouting, threatening, pleading—this from the Oxford twins. Did I mention they were twins?"

"No, you didn't."

"Identical. Blond, pale, lantern-jawed. Gloria didn't give two damns about them, of course. She did it, knowing they'd be caught, because my mother had chosen them for me. She hated me. Gloria, not my mother." Her brow knit. "My mother didn't hate me."

"What happened?"

"The twins were sent home in disgrace and Gloria was punished. Which led, inevitably, to her striking back by accusing my father's friend of seducing her, which led to another miserable scene and her finally running off. It was certainly less disruptive with her gone, but it gave my parents more time to concentrate on forging me. I used to wonder why they saw me more as creation than child. Why they couldn't love me. But then . . ." She settled back again. "I'm not very lovable. No one's ever loved me."

Aching for her, the woman and the child, he set his glass aside and framed her face gently with his hands. "You're wrong."

"No, I'm not." Her smile was soaked in wine. "I'm a professional. I know these things. My parents never loved me, certainly Gloria didn't. The husband, who didn't count, didn't love me. There wasn't even one of those kindly, good-hearted servants you read about in books, who held me against her soft, generous bosom and loved me. No one even bothered to pretend enough to use the words. You, on the other hand, are very lovable." She ran her free hand up his chest. "I've never had sex when I've been drunk. What do you suppose it's like?"

"Sybill." He caught her hand before she could distract him. "They underestimated and undervalued you. You shouldn't do the same to yourself."

"Phillip." She leaned forward, managed to nip his bottom lip between her teeth. "My life's been a predictable bore. Until you. The first time you kissed me, my mind just clicked off. No one ever did that to me before. And when you touch me . . ." Slowly she brought their joined hand to her breast. "My skin gets hot and my heart pounds, and my insides get loose and liquid. You climbed up the building." Her mouth roamed over his jaw. "You brought me roses. You wanted me, didn't you?"

"Yes, I wanted you, but not just—"

"Take me." She let her head fall back so she could look into those wonderful eyes. "I've never said that to a man before. Imagine that. Take me, Phillip." And the words were part plea, part promise. "Just take me."

The empty glass slipped out of her fingers as she wrapped her arms around him. Helpless to resist, he lowered her to the sofa. And took.

The dull ache behind her eyes, the more lively one dancing inside her temples, was no more than she deserved, Sybill decided as she tried to drown both of them under the hot spray of the shower.

She would never, as God was her witness, overindulge in any form of alcohol again.

She only wished the aftermath of drink had resulted in memory loss as well as a hangover. But she remembered, much too clearly, the way she'd prattled on about herself. The things she'd told Phillip. Humiliating, private things, things she rarely even told herself.

Now she had to face him. She had to face him and the fact that in one short weekend she had wept in his arms, then had given him both her body and her most carefully guarded secrets.

And she had to face the fact that she was hopelessly, and dangerously, in love with him.

Which was totally irrational, of course. The very fact that she believed she could have developed such strong feelings for him in such a short amount of time and association was precisely why those emotions were hopeless. And dangerous.

Obviously she wasn't thinking clearly. This barrage of feelings that had tumbled into her so quickly made it all but impossible to maintain an objective distance and analyze.

Once Seth was settled, once all the details were arranged, she would have to find that distance again. The simplest and most logical method was to begin with geographical distance and go back to New York.

Undoubtedly she would come to her senses once she'd picked up the threads of her own life again and slipped back into a comfortable, familiar routine.

However miserably dull that seemed just now.

She took the time to brush her wet hair back from her face, to carefully cream her skin, adjust the lapels of her robe. If she couldn't quite take full advantage of her breathing techniques to compose herself, it was hardly any wonder, what with the drag of the hangover.

But she stepped out of the bathroom with her features calmly arranged, then walked into the parlor, where Phillip was just pouring coffee from the room service tray.

"I thought you could use this."

"Yes, thank you." She carefully censored her gaze to avoid the empty champagne bottle and the scatter of clothing that she'd been too drunk to pick up the night before.

"Did you take any aspirin?"

"Yes. I'll be fine." She said it stiffly, accepted the cup of coffee and sat with the desperate care of an invalid. She knew she was pale, hollow-eyed. She'd gotten a good look at herself in the steamy mirror.

And she got a good look at Phillip now. He wasn't pale at all, she noted, nor was he hollow-eyed.

A lesser woman would despise him for it.

As she sipped her coffee and studied him, her muddled mind began to clear. How many times, she wondered, had he refilled her glass the night before? How many times had he refilled his own? It seemed to her there was a wide discrepancy between the two.

Resentment began to stir as she watched him generously heap jam on a piece of toast. Even the thought of food had her shaky stomach lurching.

"Hungry?" she said sweetly.

"Starving." He took the lid off a plate of scrambled eggs. "You should try to eat a little."

She'd rather die. "Sleep well?"

"Yeah."

"And aren't we bright-eyed and chipper this morning?"

He caught the tone, slanted her a cautious look. He'd wanted to take it slow, give her some time to recover before they discussed anything. But it appeared that she was recovering rapidly.

"You had a little more to drink than I did," he began.

"You got me drunk. It was deliberate. You charmed your way in here and started pouring champagne into me."

"I hardly held your nose and poured it down your throat."

"You used an apology as an excuse." Her hands began to shake, so she slammed the coffee onto the table. "You must have known I'd be angry with you, and you thought you'd just ease your way into my bed with Dom Perignon."

"The sex was your idea," he reminded her, insulted. "I wanted to talk to you. And the fact is, I got more out of you after you were buzzed than I ever would have otherwise. So I loosened you up." And damn if he was going to feel guilty over it. "And you let me in."

"Loosened me up," she whispered, getting slowly to her feet.

"I wanted to know who you are. I have a right to know."

"You—you did plan it. You planned to come in here, to charm me into drinking just a little too much so you could pry into my personal life."

"I care about you." He moved toward her, but she slapped his hand away.

"Don't. I'm not stupid enough to fall for that again."

"I do care about you. And now I know more, and understand more about you. What's wrong with that, Sybill?"

"You tricked me."

"Maybe I did." He took her arms, keeping a firm grip when she tried to pull back. "Just hold on. You had a privileged, structured childhood. I didn't. You had advantages, servants, culture. I didn't. Do you think less of me because until I was twelve I ran the streets?"

"No. But this has nothing to do with that."

"No one loved me either," he continued. "Not until I was twelve. So I know what it's like on both sides. Do you expect me to think less of you because you survived the cold?"

"I'm not going to discuss it."

"That's not going to work anymore. Here's emotion for you, Sybill." He brought his mouth down on hers, dragging her into the kiss, into the swirl. "Maybe I don't know what to do about it yet either. But it's there. You've seen my scars. They're right out there. Now I've seen yours."

He was doing it again, making her weaken and want. She could rest her head on his shoulder, have his arms come around to hold her. She only had to ask. And couldn't.

"There's no need to feel sorry for me."

"Oh, baby." Gently this time, he touched his lips to hers. "Yes, there is. And I admire what you managed to become despite it all."

"I was drinking too much," she said quickly. "I made my parents sound cold and unfeeling."

"Did either of them ever tell you they loved you?"

She opened her mouth, then sighed. "We simply weren't a demonstrative family. Not every family is like yours. Not every family shows their feelings and touches and . . ." She trailed off, hearing the trace of panicked defense in her own voice. For what, she wondered wearily. For whom?

"No, neither of them ever said that to me. Or to Gloria, as far as I know. And any decent therapist would conclude that their children reacted to this restrictive, overly formal, and demanding atmosphere by choosing different extremes. Gloria chose wild behavior as a bid for attention. I conformed in a bid for approval. She equated sex with affection and power and fantasized about being desired and forced by men in authority, including her legal and her biological fathers. I avoided intimacy in sex out of fear of failure and selected a field of study where I could safely observe behavior without risk of emotional involvement. Is that clear enough?"

"The operative word, I'd say, is 'chose.' She chose to hurt, you chose not to be hurt."

"That's accurate."

"But you haven't been able to keep it up. You risked being hurt with Seth. And you're risking being hurt with me." He touched her cheek. "I don't want to hurt you, Sybill."

It was very likely too late to prevent that, she thought, but she gave in enough to rest her head on his shoulder. She didn't have to ask for his arms to come around her. "Let's just see what happens next," she decided.

TWENTY

Fear, Sybill wrote, *is a common human emotion. And being human, it is as complex and difficult to analyze as love and hate, greed, passion. Emotions, and their causes and effects, are not my particular field of study. Behavior is both learned and instinctive and very often contains no true emotional root. Behavior is much more simple, if no more basic, than emotion.*

I'm afraid.

I'm alone in this hotel, a grown woman, educated, intelligent, sensible, and capable. Yet I'm afraid to pick up the phone on the desk and call my own mother.

A few days ago, I wouldn't have termed it fear, but reluctance, perhaps avoidance. A few days ago I would have argued, and argued well, that contact with her over the issue of Seth would only cause disruption in the order of things and produce no constructive results. Therefore, contact would be useless.

A few days ago, I could have rationalized that my feelings for Seth stemmed from a sense of moral and familial obligation.

A few days ago, I could, and did, refuse to acknowledge my envy of the Quinns with their noisy and unstructured and undisciplined interactive behavior. I would have admitted that their behavior and their unorthodox relationship were interesting, but never would I have admitted that I had a yearning to somehow slip into that pattern and become part of it.

Of course, I can't. I accept that.

A few days ago, I attempted to refute the depth and the meaning of my feelings for Phillip. Love, I told myself, does not come so quickly or so intensely. This is attraction, desire, even lust, but not love. It's easier to refute than to face. I'm afraid of love, of what it demands, what it asks, what it takes. And I'm more afraid, much more, of not being loved in return.

Still, I can accept this. I understand perfectly the limitations of my relationship with Phillip. We are both adults who have made our own pat-

terns and our own choices. He has his needs and his life, as I do mine. I can be grateful that our paths crossed. I've learned a great deal in the short time I've known him. A great deal I've learned has been about myself.

I don't believe I'll be quite the same as I was.

I don't want to be. But in order to change, truly, to grow, there are actions that must be taken.

It helps to write this out, even though the order and sense are faulty.

Phillip called just now from Baltimore. I thought he sounded tired, yet excited. He had a meeting with his attorney about his father's life insurance claim. For months now, the insurance company has refused to settle. They instigated an investigation into Professor Quinn's death and held off paying the claim over the suspicion of suicide. Financially, of course, it put a strain on the Quinns with Seth to provide for and a new business to run, but they have doggedly pursued legal action over this issue.

I don't think I realized until today how vital it is to them to win this battle. Not for the money, as I originally assumed, but to clear any shadow on their father's name. I don't believe suicide is always an act of cowardice. I once considered it myself. Had the proper note written, the necessary pills in my hand. But I was only sixteen and understandably foolish. Naturally I tore the letter up, disposed of the pills, and put the matter aside.

Suicide would have been rude. Inconvenient for my family.

Doesn't that sound bitter? I had no idea I'd harbored all this anger.

But the Quinns, I've learned, considered the taking of one's own life selfish, cowardly. They have refused all along to accept or to allow others to believe that this man they love so much was capable of such a singular selfish act. Now, it appears, they will win this battle.

The insurance company has offered to settle. Phillip believes my deposition may have swayed them toward this response. He may be right. Of course, the Quinns are, perhaps genetically, ill-suited to settlements. All or nothing, is precisely how Phillip put it to me. He believes, as does his attorney, that they will have all very shortly.

I'm happy for them. Though I never had the privilege of meeting Raymond and Stella Quinn, I feel I know them through my association with their family. Professor Quinn deserves to rest in peace. Just as Seth deserves to take the Quinn name and to have the security of a family who will love and care for him.

I can do something to ensure that all of that happens. I will have to make this call. I will have to take a stand. Oh, my hands shake just at the possibility. I'm such a coward. No, Seth would call me a wimp. That's somehow worse.

She terrifies me. There it is in black and white. My own mother terrifies me. She never raised a hand to me, rarely raised her voice, yet she shoved me into a mold of her own making. I barely struggled.

My father? He was too busy being important to notice.

Oh, yes, I see a great deal of anger here.

I can call her, I can use the very status that she insisted I achieve to gain what I want from her. I'm a respected scientist, in some small way a public figure. If I tell her I'll use that, if I make her believe I will, unless she provides a written statement to the Quinns' attorney, detailing the circumstances of Gloria's birth, admitting that Professor Quinn attempted several times to contact her for verification of Gloria's paternity, she will despise me. But she will do it.

I only have to pick up the phone to do for Seth what I failed to do years ago. I can give him a home, a family, and the knowledge that he has nothing to fear.

⁂

"Son of a bitch." Phillip wiped sweat off his forehead with the back of his hand. Blood from a nasty but shallow scrape smeared over his skin. He grinned like an idiot at the hull he and his brothers had just turned. "That's a big bastard."

"It's a beautiful bastard." Cam rolled his aching shoulders. The turning of the hull meant more than progress. It meant success. Boats by Quinn was doing it again, and they were doing it right.

"She's got a fine line." Ethan ran a calloused hand over the planking. "A pretty shape to her."

"When I start thinking a hull looks sexy," Cam decided. "I'm going home to my wife. Well, we can score her waterline and get back to work, or we can just admire her for a while."

"You score her waterline," Phillip suggested. "I'm going up and running the paperwork for the draw. It's time to hit your old racing pal up for some cash. We can use it."

"You cut the paychecks?" Ethan asked him.

"Yeah."

"Yours?"

"I don't—"

"Need it," Cam finished. "Cut one anyway, goddamn it. Buy your sexy lady some bauble with it. Blow it on some overpriced wine or lay it on the throw of the dice. But cut your check this week." He studied the hull again. "It means something this week."

"Maybe it does," Phillip agreed.

"The insurance company's going to fold their hand," Cam added. "We're going to win there."

"People are already changing their tune." Ethan rubbed a layer of sawdust off the planking. "The ones who wanted to whistle lies under their breath. We've already won there. You worked the hardest to make sure we did," he said to Phillip.

"I'm just the detail man. Either one of you tried to have more than a five-minute conversation with a lawyer . . . well, you'd nod off from boredom, Ethan, and Cam would end up punching him. I won by default."

"Maybe." Cam grinned at him. "But you skated out of a lot of the real work by talking on the phone, writing letters, zinging off faxes. It just comes down to you being secretary. Without the great legs and ass."

"Not only is that sexist, but I do have great legs and a terrific ass."

"Oh, yeah? Let's see 'em." He moved fast, diving and taking Phillip down onto that reputedly terrific ass.

Foolish scrambled up from his nap by the lumber and raced over to join in.

"Christ! Are you crazy!" Laughter prevented Phillip from rolling free. "Get off me, you moron."

"Give me a hand here, Ethan." Cam grinned, swearing as Foolish lapped eagerly at his face. Phillip struggled half-heartedly when Cam sat on him. "Come on," he urged when Ethan merely shook his head. "When's the last time you pantsed somebody?"

"Been a while." Ethan considered as Phillip began to struggle in earnest. "Maybe the last time was Junior Crawford at his bachelor party."

"Well, that's ten years ago, anyway." Cam grunted as Phillip nearly succeeded in bucking him off. "Come on, he's put on some muscle the last few months. And he's feisty."

"Maybe for old time's sake." Getting into the spirit, Ethan evaded a couple of well-aimed kicks and got a firm hold on the waistband of Phillip's jeans.

"Excuse me," was the best Sybill could manage when she walked in on air blue with curses and the sight of Phillip being held down on the beaten-wood floor while his brothers . . . well, she couldn't quite tell what they were trying to do.

"Hey." Cam avoided a fist to the jaw, barely, and grinned hugely at her. "Want to give us a hand? We're just trying to get his pants off. He was bragging about his legs."

"I . . . hmmm."

"Let him up now, Cam. You're embarrassing her."

"Hell, Ethan, she's seen his legs before." But without Ethan lending his weight, it was either let go or get bloody. It seemed simpler, if less fun, to let go. "We'll finish up later."

"My brothers forgot they're out of high school." Phillip got to his feet, brushing off his jeans and his dignity. "They were feeling a little rambunctious because we turned the hull."

"Oh." She shifted her attention to the boat, and her eyes widened. "You've made so much progress."

"It's got a ways to go yet." Ethan studied it himself, visualizing it complete. "Deck, cabin, bridge, belowdecks. Man wants a damn hotel suite in there."

"As long as he's paying for it." Phillip crossed to Sybill, ran a hand down her hair. "Sorry I got in too late to see you last night."

"That's all right. I know you've been busy with work and the lawyer." She shifted her purse from hand to hand. "Actually I have something that may help. With the lawyer, with both situations. Well . . ."

She reached into her purse and took out a manila envelope. "It's a statement from my mother. Two copies, both notarized. I had her overnight them. I didn't want to say anything until they'd arrived, and I'd read them to see . . . I think they'll be useful."

"What's the deal?" Cam demanded as Phillip quickly skimmed the neatly typed two-page statement.

"It confirms that Gloria was Dad's biological daughter. That he was unaware of it and that he attempted to contact Barbara Griffin several times during a period from last December to this March. There's a letter from Dad written to her in January, telling her about Seth, his agreement with Gloria to take custody."

"I read your father's letter," Sybill told him. "Perhaps I shouldn't have, but I did. If he was angry with my mother, it didn't show in the words. He just wanted her to tell him if it was true. He was going to help Seth anyway, but he wanted to be able to give him his birthright. A man who worried that much about a child would hardly have taken his own life. He had too much to give, and was too ready to give it. I'm so sorry."

" 'He just needs a chance, and a choice,' " Ethan read when Phillip passed the letters to him, then cleared his throat. " 'I couldn't give one to Gloria, if she's mine, and she won't take it now. But I'll see that Seth has both. Whether he's mine by blood or not, he's mine nonetheless now.' It sounds like him. Seth should read this."

"Why did she agree to this now, Sybill?" Phillip asked her.

"I convinced her that it was best for all concerned."

"No." He caught her chin in his hand, lifted her face to his. "There's more. I know there is."

"I promised her that her name, and the details, would be kept as private as possible." She made a restless little movement, then let out a breath. "And I threatened to write a book telling the entire story if she didn't do this."

"You blackmailed her," Phillip said with stunned admiration.

"I gave her a choice. She chose this one."

"It was hard for you."

"It was necessary."

Now he put both of his hands on her face, gently. "It was hard, and brave, and brilliant."

"Logical," she began, then shut her eyes. "And yes, hard. She and my father are very angry. They may not forgive me. They're capable of not forgiving."

"They don't deserve you."

"The point is Seth deserves you, so . . ." She trailed off as he closed his mouth over hers.

"Okay, move aside." Cam elbowed Phillip away and took Sybill by the shoulders. "You did good," he said, then kissed her with a firmness that made her blink.

"Oh," was all she managed.

"Your turn," Cam stated, then gave her a gentle nudge toward Ethan.

"My parents would have been proud of you." He kissed her in turn, then patted her shoulders when her eyes filled.

"Oh, no, don't let her do that." Instantly, Cam took her arm and pulled her back to Phillip. "No crying in here, no crying allowed in the boatyard."

"Cam gets jittery when women cry."

"I'm not crying."

"They always say that," Cam muttered, "but they never mean it. Outside. Anybody who cries has to do it outside. It's a new rule."

Chuckling, Phillip pulled Sybill toward the door. "Come on. I want a minute alone with you anyway."

"I'm not crying. I just never expected your brothers to . . . it's not usual for me to be—" She stopped herself. "It's very nice to be shown you're appreciated and liked."

"I appreciate you." He drew her close. "I like you."

"And it's very nice." She indulged in the luxury of both. "I've already spoken with your attorney and with Anna. I didn't want to fax the papers from the hotel as I did give my word the contents would be kept private. But both of them agree that this last document should move everything along. Anna believes that your petition for permanent guardianship will go through as early as next week."

"That soon?"

"There's nothing in the way of it. You and your brothers are Professor Quinn's legal sons. Seth is his grandchild. His mother agreed, in writing, to transfer custody. Reneging on that might stall the decree, but no one believes at this point that it would change it. Seth is eleven, and at his age his desires would be taken into account. Anna's going to push for a hearing early next week."

"It seems strange, it all coming together like this. All at once."

"Yes." She looked up as a flock of geese swept overhead. Seasons change, she thought. "I thought I would walk down to the school. I'd like to talk to him, tell him some of this myself."

"I think that's a good idea. You timed it well."

"I'm good at schedules."

"How about scheduling a family meal tonight at the Quinns, to celebrate?"

"Yes, all right. I'll walk him back here."

"Great. Hold on a minute." He went back inside, returning moments later with a very energetic Foolish on a red leash. "He could use a walk, too."

"Oh, well, I . . ."

"He knows the way. All you have to do is hold on to this end." Amused, Phillip stuck the leash in her hand, then watched her eyes go wide as Foolish made his dash. "Tell him to heel," Phillip shouted as Sybill trotted after the dog. "He won't, but it'll sound like you know what you're doing."

"This is not funny." She muttered it as she jogged awkwardly after Foolish. "Slow down. Heel! God."

He not only slowed, but stopped, burying his nose in a hedge with such determination she was terrified he would race through it and take her with him. But he only lifted his leg and looked immensely pleased with himself.

By her count, he lifted his leg eight times before they turned the corner down from the school and she caught sight of the buses. "What kind of a bladder do you have?" she demanded, looking hopefully for Seth while she struggled to cling to the leash and prevent Foolish from rocketing toward the crowd of children pouring out of the building. "No. Sit. Stay. You might bite someone."

Foolish slanted her a look that seemed to say, Please, get serious. But he sat, smacking her heels rhythmically with his tail. "He'll be along in a minute," she began, then let out a yelp as Foolish leaped up and raced forward. He'd spotted Seth first and was running on love.

"No, no, no, no," Sybill panted uselessly just as Seth caught sight of them. He let out a yelp himself, of pure joy, and dashed toward the dog as if they'd been cruelly separated for years.

"Hey! Hi!" Seth laughed as Foolish made one adoring leap and bathed his face. "How's it going, boy? Good dog. You're a good dog." Belatedly, he looked over at Sybill. "Hey."

"Hey, yourself. Here." She shoved the leash into his hand. "Not that he pays any attention to it."

"We've kind of had trouble with leash training."

"No kidding." But she managed a smile now to include Seth and Danny and Will when they hurried up behind him. "I thought I'd walk back to the boatyard with you. I wanted to talk to you."

"Sure, that's cool."

She stepped determinedly out of Foolish's path, then quickly back again as a bright-red sports car screamed up to the curb and stopped with a wild squeal of brakes. Before she could snarl at the driver that he was in a school zone, she saw Gloria in the passenger seat.

Sybill's movement was fast and instinctive. She put Seth protectively behind her.

"Well, well, well," Gloria drawled and eyed them both out of the window.

"Go get your brothers," Sybill ordered Seth. "Go right now."

But he couldn't move. He could only stand and stare while the fear settled in his stomach like balls of ice. "I won't go with her. I won't go. I won't."

"No, you won't." She took his hand firmly in hers. "Danny, Will, run to the boatyard right now. Tell the Quinns we need them. Hurry. Go straight there."

She heard the smack of running sneakers on the sidewalk but didn't look. She kept her eyes trained on her sister as Gloria slipped out of the car.

"Hey, kid. Miss me?"

"What do you want, Gloria?"

"Everything I can get." She fisted a hand on the hip of her lipstick-red jeans and winked at Seth. "Wanna go for a ride, kiddo? We can do some catching up."

"I'm not going anywhere with you." He wished he had run. He had a place in the woods, a place he'd picked out and fixed up. A hiding place. But it was too far away. Then he felt Sybill's hand, warm and strong on his. "I'm not ever going with you again."

"You'll do what the hell I tell you." Fury flashed in her eyes as she started forward. For the first time in his life, Foolish bared his teeth and growled a vicious threat. "Call off that fucking dog."

"No." Sybill said it simply, quietly, and felt a surge of love for Foolish. "I'd keep my distance, Gloria. He'll bite." She scanned the car, the leather-jacketed man behind its wheel, beating a rhythm on the dash to the blasting radio. "It looks like you landed on your feet."

"Yeah, Pete's okay. We're heading out to California. He's got connections. I need cash."

"You're not going to get it here."

Gloria pulled out a cigarette, smiling at Sybill as she lit it. "Look, I don't want the kid, but I'm going to take him unless I get a stake. The Quinns'll pay to get him back. Everybody's happy, no harm done. If you mess with me on this, Syb, I'm going to tell Pete to get out of the car."

Foolish shifted from growling to snarling. Sharp canine teeth bared. Sybill raised a brow. "Go ahead. Tell him."

"I want what's due me, goddamn it."

"You've had more than your due all your life."

"Bullshit! It was you who got everything. The perfect daughter. I hate your fucking guts. I've hated you all my life." She grabbed Sybill by the front of her jacket and all but spit in her face. "I wish you were dead."

"I know that. Now take your hands off me."

"You think you can make me?" With a laugh, Gloria shoved Sybill back a step. "You never had the guts before, did you? You'll take it, and you'll take it, and you'll give me what I want, just like always. Shut that dog up!" she shouted at Seth as Foolish strained at the leash and snapped wildly. "Shut him up and get in the goddamn car before I—"

Sybill didn't see her own hand come up, didn't realize the order had gone from her brain to her arm. But she felt her muscles tighten, her rage erupt, and then Gloria was sprawled on the ground gaping at her.

"You get in the goddamn car," she said evenly, not even looking at the Jeep that screeched up to the curb. Not blinking when Foolish dragged himself and Seth closer and growled low in his throat at the woman on the ground. "You go to California, or you go to hell, but you stay away from this boy, and you stay away from me. Keep out of this," she snapped at Phillip as he and his brothers burst out of the Jeep.

"Get in the car and go, Gloria, or I'll pay you back right now for everything you ever did to Seth. Everything you ever did to me. Get up and go, or when the cops get here to take you in for jumping bail, when we add charges of child abuse and extortion, there won't be much left of you to put in a cell."

When Gloria didn't move, Sybill reached down and, with a strength born of fury, hauled her to her feet. "Get in the car and go, and don't ever try to get near this boy again. You won't get through me, Gloria. I swear to you."

"I don't want the damn kid. I just want some money."

"Cut your losses. I'm not going to bother holding that dog or the Quinns back after another thirty seconds. Want to take all of us on?"

"Gloria, are you coming or not?" The driver flicked his cigarette out the car window. "I don't have all day to hang around this bumfuck town."

"Yeah, I'm coming." She tossed her head. "You're welcome to him. All he ever did was slow me down and get in my way. I'm going to score big in L.A. I don't need anything from you."

"Good," Sybill murmured as Gloria climbed back in the car. "Because you'll never get anything from me again."

"You knocked her down." Seth wasn't shaking, nor was he pale now. As the sports car shrieked away, the look he sent Sybill was filled with gratitude, and with awe. "You knocked her down."

"I guess I did. Are you all right?"

"She never even looked at me, really. Foolish was going to bite her."

"He's a wonderful dog." When he leaped on her now, she pressed her face into the warmth of his neck. "He's a fabulous dog."

"But you knocked her down. Sybill knocked her right on her butt," he shouted as Phillip and his brothers walked over.

"So I saw." Phillip put a hand to her cheek. "Nice going, champ. How do you feel?"

"I feel . . . fine," she realized. No cramping, no chills, no sick headache. "I feel just fine." Then she blinked as Seth threw his arms around her.

"You were great. She's never coming back. You scared the shit out of her."

The bubbly little laugh that rose into her throat caught her by surprise. Leaning down, she buried her face in Seth's hair. "Everything's just the way it's supposed to be now."

"Let's go home." Phillip slid his arm around her shoulders. "Let's all go home."

⟨∞⟩

"He's going to be telling that story for days," Phillip decided. "Weeks."
"He's already embellishing on it." Amazingly serene, Sybill walked with Phillip by the water's edge while the heroic Foolish romped in

the yard behind them with Simon. "The way he tells it now, I beat Gloria to a pulp and Foolish lapped up the blood."

"You don't sound all that displeased by it."

"I never knocked anyone down before in my life. Never stood my ground that way. I wish I could say I did it all for Seth, but I think part of it was for me, too. She won't come back, Phillip. She lost. She is lost."

"I don't think Seth will ever be afraid of her again."

"He's home. This is a good place." She turned in a circle to take in the trim house, the woods going deep with twilight, the last sparkle of the sun on the water. "I'll miss it when I'm back in New York."

"New York? You're not going for a while yet."

"Actually, I'm planning on going back right after the hearing next week." It was something she'd made up her mind on. She needed to resume her own life. Staying longer would accomplish nothing but adding to the emotional mess.

"Wait. Why?"

"I have work."

"You're working here." Where did the panic come from? he wondered. Who pushed the button?

"I have meetings with my publisher that I've put off. I need to get back. I can't live in a hotel forever, and Seth's settled now."

"He needs you around. He—"

"I'll visit. And I'm hoping he'll be allowed to come see me occasionally." She'd worked it all out in her head, and now she turned to smile at him. "I promised to take him to a Yankees game next spring."

It was as if it were already done, he realized, struggling against that panic. As if she were already gone. "You've talked to him about it."

"Yes, I thought I should let him know."

"And this is how you let me know?" he shot back. "It's been nice, pal, see you around?"

"I'm not sure I'm following."

"Nothing. Nothing to follow." He walked away. He wanted his own life back, too, didn't he? Here was his chance. End of complications. All he had to do was wish her well and wave good-bye. "That's what I want. It's always been what I wanted."

"Excuse me?"

"I'm not looking for anything else. Neither one of us was." He whirled back to her, temper glinting in his eyes. "Right?"

"I'm not sure what you mean."

"You've got your life, I've got mine. We just followed the current, and here we are. Time to get out of the water."

No, she decided, she wasn't following him. "All right."

"Well, then." Assuring himself that he was fine with it, he was calm. He was even pleased. He started back toward her.

The last of the sun shimmered over her hair, into those impossibly clear eyes, shadowed the hollow of her throat above the collar of her blouse. "No." He heard himself say it, and his mouth went dry.

"No?"

"A minute, just one minute." He walked away again, this time to the edge of the water. He stood there, staring down like a man contemplating diving in well over his head. "What's wrong with Baltimore?"

"Baltimore? Nothing."

"It's got museums, good restaurants, character, theater."

"It's a very nice city," Sybill said cautiously.

"Why can't you work there? If you have to go into New York for a meeting, you can hop the shuttle or the train. Hell, you can drive it in under four hours."

"I'm sure that's true. If you're suggesting I relocate to Baltimore—"

"It's perfect. You'd still be living in the city, but you'd be able to see Seth whenever you wanted."

And you, she thought, yearning toward the picture. But she shook her head. It would kill her to go on this way. And she knew it would spoil the happiness she'd had, the new self she'd discovered. "It's just not practical, Phillip."

"Of course it's practical." He turned around, strode back to her. "It's perfectly practical. What's impractical is going back to New York, putting up that distance again. It's not going to work, Sybill. It's just not going to work."

"There's no point in discussing it now."

"Do you think this is easy for me?" he exploded. "I *have* to stay here. I have commitments, responsibilities, to say nothing of roots. I've got no choice. Why can't you bend?"

"I don't understand."

"I have to spell it out? Damn it." He took her by the shoulders, gave her a quick, impatient shake. "Don't you get it? I love you. You can't expect me to let you walk away. You have to stay. The hell with your life and my life. Your family, my family. I want *our* life. I want *our* family."

She stared at him, the blood ringing in her ears. "What? What?"

"You heard what I said."

"You said . . . you said you loved me. Do you mean it?"

"No, I'm lying."

"I . . . I've already knocked one person down today. I can do it again." Just then, she thought she could do anything. Anything at all. It didn't matter if there was fury in his eyes, if his fingers were digging into her arms. If he looked fit to kill. She could handle this. She could handle him. She could handle anything.

"If you meant it," she said, her voice admirably cool. "I'd like you to say it again. I've never heard it before."

"I love you." Calming, he touched his lips to her brow. "I want you." To each temple. "I need you to stay with me." Then her mouth. "Give me more time to show you what we'll be like together."

"I know what we'll be like together. I want what we'll be like together." She let out a shuddering breath, resisted the urge to close her eyes. She needed to see his face, to remember it exactly as it was at this moment, with the sun sinking, the sky going peach and rose, and a flock of birds winging overhead. "I love you. I was afraid to tell you. I don't know why. I don't think I'm afraid of anything now. Are you going to ask me to marry you?"

"I was about to muddle my way through that part." On impulse, he pulled out the simple white band holding back her hair and tossed it over her shoulders where the dogs gave loud and delighted chase. "I want your hair in my hands," he murmured, threading his fingers through the thick, rich brown. "All my life I said I would never do this because there would never be a woman who would make me need to or want to. I was wrong. I found one. I found mine. Marry me, Sybill."

"All my life I said I would never do this because there would never be a man who'd need me or want me, or matter enough to make me want. I was wrong. I found you. Marry me, Phillip, and soon."

"How does next Saturday strike you?"

"Oh." Emotion flooded her heart, poured into it, out of it, warm and smooth and real. "Yes!" She leaped, throwing her arms around him.

He spun her in a circle, and for a moment, just for a flash, he thought he saw two figures standing on the dock. The man with silver hair and brilliantly blue eyes, the woman with freckles dancing over her face and wild red hair blowing in the evening breeze. Their hands were linked. They were there, then they were gone.

"This one counts," he murmured, holding her hard and close. "This one counts for both of us."

CHESAPEAKE BLUE

There is a destiny that makes us brothers;
None goes his way alone:
All that we send into the lives of others
Comes back into our own.
EDWIN MARKHAM

Art is the accomplice of love.
RÉMY DE GOURMONT

ONE

He was coming home.

Maryland's Eastern Shore was a world of marshes and mudflats, of wide fields with row crops straight as soldiers. It was flatland rivers with sharp shoulders, and secret tidal creeks where the heron fed.

It was blue crab and the Bay, and the watermen who harvested them.

No matter where he'd lived, in the first miserable decade of his life, or in the last few years as he approached the end of his third decade, only the Shore had ever meant home.

There were countless aspects, countless memories of that home, and every one was as bright and brilliant in his mind as the sun that sparkled off the water of the Chesapeake.

As he drove across the bridge, his artist's eye wanted to capture that moment—the rich blue water and the boats that skimmed its surface, the quick white waves and the swoop of greedy gulls. The way the land skimmed its edge, and spilled back with its browns and greens. All the thickening leaves of the gum and oak trees, with those flashes of color that were flowers basking in the warmth of spring.

He wanted to remember this moment just as he remembered the first time he'd crossed the Bay to the Eastern Shore, a surly, frightened boy beside a man who'd promised him a life.

He'd sat in the passenger seat of the car, with the man he hardly knew at the wheel. He had the clothes on his back, and a few meager possessions in a paper sack.

His stomach had been tight with nerves, but he'd fixed what he thought was a bored look on his face and had stared out the window.

If he was with the old guy, he wasn't with *her*. That was as good a deal as he could get.

Besides, the old guy was pretty cool.

He didn't stink of booze or of the mints some of the assholes Gloria

brought up to the dump they were living in used to cover it up. And the couple of times they'd been together, the old guy, Ray, had bought him a burger
or pizza.

And he'd talked to him.

Adults, in his experience, didn't talk to kids. At them, around them, over
them. But not to them.

Ray did. Listened, too. And when he'd asked, straight out, if he—just a
kid—wanted to live with him, he hadn't felt that strangling fear or hot panic.
He'd felt like maybe, just maybe, he was catching a break.

Away from her. That was the best part. The longer they drove, the farther away from her.

If things got sticky, he could run. The guy was really old. Big, he was
sure as shit big, but old. All that white hair, and that wide, wrinkled face.

He took quick, sidelong glances at it, began to draw the face in his mind.

His eyes were really blue, and that was kind of weird because so were
his own.

He had a big voice, too, but when he talked it wasn't like yelling. It was
kind of calm, even a little tired, maybe.

He sure looked tired now.

"Almost home," Ray said as they approached the bridge. "Hungry?"

"I dunno. Yeah, I guess."

"My experience, boys are always hungry. Raised three bottomless pits."

There was cheer in the big voice, but it was forced. The child might have
been barely ten, but he knew the tone of falsehood.

Far enough away now, he thought. If he had to run. So he'd put the cards
on the table and see what the fuck was what.

"How come you're taking me to your place?"

"Because you need a place."

"Get real. People don't do shit like that."

"Some do. Stella and I, my wife, we did shit like that."

"You tell her you're bringing me around?"

Ray smiled, but there was a sadness in it. "In my way. She died some
time back. You'd've liked her. And she'd have taken one look at you and
rolled up her sleeves."

He didn't know what to say about that. "What am I supposed to do
when we get where we're going?"

"Live," Ray told him. "Be a boy. Go to school, get in trouble. I'll teach
you to sail."

"On a boat?"

Now Ray laughed, a big booming sound that filled the car and for reasons the boy couldn't understand, untied the nerves in his belly. "Yeah, on a boat. Got a brainless puppy—I always get the brainless ones—I'm trying to housebreak. You can help me with that. You're gonna have chores, we'll figure that out. We'll lay down the rules, and you'll follow them. Don't think because I'm an old man I'm a pushover."

"You gave her money."

Ray glanced away from the road briefly and looked into eyes the same color as his own. "That's right. That's what she understands, from what I can see. She never understood you, did she, boy?"

Something was gathering inside him, a storm he didn't recognize as hope. "If you get pissed off at me, or tired of having me around, or just change your mind, you'll send me back. I won't go back."

They were over the bridge now, and Ray pulled the car to the shoulder of the road, shifted his bulk in the seat so they were face-to-face. "I'll get pissed off at you, and at my age I'm bound to get tired from time to time. But I'm making you a promise here and now, I'm giving you my word. I won't send you back."

"If she—"

"I won't let her take you back," Ray said, anticipating him. "No matter what I have to do. You're mine now. You're my family now. And you'll stay with me as long as that's what you want. A Quinn makes a promise," he added, and held out a hand, "he keeps it."

Seth looked at the offered hand, and his own sprang damp. "I don't like being touched."

Ray nodded. "Okay. But you've still got my word on it." He pulled back onto the road again, gave the boy one last glance. "Almost home," he said again.

Within months, Ray Quinn had died, but he'd kept his word. He'd kept it through the three men he'd made his sons. Those men had given the scrawny, suspicious and scarred young boy a life.

They had given him a home, and made him a man.

Cameron, the edgy, quick-tempered gypsy; Ethan, the patient, steady waterman; Phillip, the elegant, sharp-minded executive. They had stood for him, fought for him. They had saved him.

His brothers.

⬥

The gilded light of the late-afternoon sun sheened the marsh grass, the mudflats, the flat fields of row crops. With the windows down he caught the scent of water as he bypassed the little town of St. Christopher.

He'd considered swinging into town, heading first to the old brick boat-yard. Boats by Quinn still custom made wooden boats, and in the eighteen years since the enterprise had started—on a dream, on guile, on sweat—it had earned its reputation for quality and craftsmanship.

They were probably there, even now. Cam cursing as he finished up some fancywork in a cabin. Ethan quietly lapping boards. Phil, up in the office conjuring up some snazzy ad campaign.

He could go by Crawford's, pick up a six-pack. Maybe they'd have a cold one, or more likely Cam would toss him a hammer and tell him to get his ass back to work.

He'd enjoy that, but it wasn't what was drawing him now. It wasn't what was pulling him down the narrow country road where the marsh still crept out of the shadows and the trees with their gnarled trunks spread leaves glossy with May.

Of all the places he'd seen—the great domes and spires of Florence, the florid beauty of Paris, the stunning green hills of Ireland—nothing ever caught at his throat, filled up his heart, like the old white house with its soft and faded blue trim that sat on a bumpy lawn that slid back into quiet water.

He pulled in the drive, behind the old white 'Vette that had been Ray and Stella Quinn's. The car looked as pristine as the day it had rolled off the showroom floor. Cam's doing, he thought. Cam would say it was a matter of showing proper respect for an exceptional machine. But it was all about Ray and Stella, all about family. All about love.

The lilac in the front yard was smothered with blooms. That was a matter of love, too, he reflected. He'd given Anna the little bush for Mother's Day when he was twelve.

She'd cried, he remembered. Big, beautiful brown eyes flooded with tears, laughing and swiping at them the whole time he and Cam planted it for her.

She was Cam's wife, and so that made Anna his sister. But inside, he thought now, where it counted, she was his mother.

The Quinns knew all about what was inside.

He got out of the car, into the lovely stillness. He was no longer a scrawny boy with oversized feet and a suspicious eye.

He'd grown into those feet. He was six-one with a wiry build. One that could go gawky if he neglected it. His hair had darkened and was more a bronzed brown than the sandy mop of his youth. He tended to neglect that as well and, running a hand through it now, winced as he recalled his intention to have it trimmed before leaving Rome.

The guys were going to rag on him about the little ponytail, which meant he'd have to keep it for a while, out of principle.

He shrugged and, dipping his hands into the pockets of his worn jeans, began to walk, scanning the surroundings. Anna's flowers, the rockers on the front porch, the woods that haunted the side of the house and where he'd run wild as a boy.

The old dock swaying over the water, and the white sailing sloop moored to it.

He stood looking out, his face, hollow-cheeked and tanned, turned toward the water.

His lips, firm and full, began to curve. The weight he hadn't realized was hanging from his heart began to lift.

At the sound of a rustle in the woods, he turned, enough of the wary boy still in the man to make the move swift and defensive. Out of the trees shot a black bullet.

"Witless!" His voice had both the ring of authority and easy humor. The combination had the dog skidding to a halt, all flopping ears and lolling tongue as it studied the man.

"Come on, it hasn't been that long." He crouched, held out a hand. "Remember me?"

Witless grinned the dopey grin that had named him, instantly flopped down and rolled to expose his belly for a rub.

"There you go. That's the way."

There had always been a dog for this house. Always a boat at the dock, a rocker on the porch and a dog in the yard.

"Yeah, you remember me." As he stroked Witless, he looked over to the far end of the yard where Anna had planted a hydrangea over the grave of his own dog. The loyal and much-loved Foolish.

"I'm Seth," he murmured. "I've been away too long."

He caught the sound of an engine, the sassy squeal of tires from a turn taken just a hair faster than the law allowed. Even as he straightened, the dog leaped up, streaked away toward the front of the house.

Wanting to savor the moment, Seth followed more slowly. He listened to the car door slam, then to the lift and lilt of her voice as she spoke to the dog.

Then he just looked at her, Anna Spinelli Quinn, with the curling mass of dark hair windblown from the drive, her arms full of the bags she'd hefted out of the car.

His grin spread as she tried to ward off the desperate affection from the dog.

"How many times do we have to go over this one, simple rule?" she demanded. "You do not jump on people, especially me. Especially me when I'm wearing a suit."

"Great suit," Seth called out. "Better legs."

Her head whipped up, those deep brown eyes widened and showed him the shock, the pleasure, the welcome all in one glance.

"Oh my God!" Heedless of the contents, she tossed the bags through the open car door. And ran.

He caught her, lifted her six inches off the ground and spun her around before setting her on her feet again. Still he didn't let go. Instead, he just buried his face in her hair.

"Hi."

"Seth. Seth." She clung, ignoring the dog that leaped and yipped and did his best to shove his muzzle between them. "I can't believe it. You're here."

"Don't cry."

"Just a little. I have to look at you." She had his face framed in her hands as she eased back. So handsome, she thought. So grown-up. "Look at all this," she murmured and brushed a hand at his hair.

"I meant to get some of it whacked off."

"I like it." Tears still trickled even as she grinned. "Very bohemian. You look wonderful. Absolutely wonderful."

"You're the most beautiful woman in the world."

"Oh boy." She sniffled, shook her head. "That's no way to get me to stop all this." She swiped at tears. "When did you get here? I thought you were in Rome."

"I was. I wanted to be here."

"If you'd called, we would've met you."

"I wanted to surprise you." He walked to the car to pull the bags out for her. "Cam at the boatyard?"

"Should be. Here, I'll get those. You need to get your things."

"I'll get them later. Where's Kevin and Jake?"

She started up the walk with him, glanced at her watch as she thought about her sons. "What day is this? My mind's still spinning."

"Thursday."

"Ah, Kevin has rehearsal, school play, and Jake's got softball practice. Kevin's got his driver's license, God help us, and is scooping up his brother on his way home." She unlocked the front door. "They should be along in an hour, then peace will no longer lie across the land."

It was the same, Seth thought. It didn't matter what color the walls were painted or if the old sofa had been replaced, if a new lamp stood on the table. It was the same because it *felt* the same.

The dog snaked around his legs and made a beeline for the kitchen.

"I want you to sit down." She nodded to the kitchen table, under which Witless was sprawled, happily gnawing on a hunk of rope. "And tell me everything. You want some wine?"

"Sure, after I help you put this stuff away." When her eyebrows shot up, he paused with a gallon of milk in his hand. "What?"

"I was just remembering the way everyone, including you, disappeared whenever it was time to put groceries away."

"Because you always said we put things in the wrong place."

"You always did, on purpose so I'd kick you out of the kitchen."

"You copped to that, huh?"

"I cop to everything when it comes to my guys. Nothing gets by me, pal. Did something happen in Rome?"

"No." He continued to unpack the bags. He knew where everything went, where everything had always gone in Anna's kitchen. "I'm not in trouble, Anna."

But you are troubled, she thought, and let it go for now. "I'm going to open a nice Italian white. We'll have a glass and you can tell me all the wonderful things you've been doing. It seems like years since we've talked face-to-face."

He shut the refrigerator and turned to her. "I'm sorry I didn't get home for Christmas."

"Honey, we understood. You had a showing in January. We're all so proud of you, Seth. Cam must've bought a hundred copies of the issue of the *Smithsonian* magazine when they did the article on you. The young American artist who's seduced Europe."

He shrugged a shoulder, such an innately Quinn gesture, she grinned. "So sit," she ordered.

"I'll sit, but I'd rather you caught me up. How the hell is everyone? What're they doing? You first."

"All right." She finished opening the bottle, got out two glasses. "I'm doing more administrative work these days than casework. Social work involves a lot of paperwork, but it's not as satisfying. Between that and having two teenagers in the house, there's no time to be bored. The boat business is thriving."

She sat, passed Seth his glass. "Aubrey's working there."

"No kidding?" The thought of her, the girl who was more sister to him than any blood kin, made him smile. "How's she doing?"

"Terrific. She's beautiful, smart, stubborn and, according to Cam, a genius with wood. I think Grace was a little disappointed when Aubrey didn't want to pursue dancing, but it's hard to argue when you see your child so happy. And Grace and Ethan's Emily followed in her mother's toe shoes."

"She still heading to New York end of August?"

"A chance to dance with the American Ballet Company doesn't come along every day. She's grabbing it, and she swears she'll be principal before she's twenty. Deke's his father's son—quiet, clever and happiest when he's out on the water. Sweetie, do you want a snack?"

"No." He reached out, laid a hand over hers. "Keep going."

"Okay, then. Phillip remains the business's marketing and promotion guru. I don't think any of us, including Phil, ever thought he'd leave the ad firm in Baltimore, give up urban living and dig down in Saint Chris. But it's been, what, fourteen years, so I don't suppose we can call it a whim. Of course he and Sybill keep the apartment in New York. She's working on a new book."

"Yeah, I talked to her." He rubbed the dog's head with his foot. "Something about the evolution of community in cyberspace. She's something. How are the kids?"

"Insane, as any self-respecting teenager should be. Bram was madly in love with a girl named Cloe last week. That could be over by now. Fiona's interests are torn between boys and shopping. But, well, she's fourteen, so that's natural."

"Fourteen. Jesus. She hadn't had her tenth birthday when I left for Europe. Even seeing them on and off over the last few years, it doesn't seem . . . it doesn't seem possible that Kevin's driving, and Aub's building boats. Bram's sniffing after girls. I remember—" He cut himself off, shook his head.

"What?"

"I remember when Grace was pregnant with Emily. It was the first time I was around someone who was having a baby—well, someone who wanted to. It seems like five minutes ago, and now Emily's going to New York. How can eighteen years go by, Anna, and you not look any older?"

"Oh, I've missed you." She laughed and squeezed his hand.

"I've missed you, too. All of you."

"We'll fix that. We'll round everybody up and have a big, noisy Quinn welcome-home on Sunday. How does that sound?"

"About as perfect as it gets."

The dog yipped, then scrambled out from under the table to run toward the front door.

"Cameron," Anna said. "Go on out and meet him."

He walked through the house, as he had so often. Opened the screen door, as he had so often. And looked at the man standing on the front lawn, playing tug-of-war with the dog over a hunk of rope.

He was still tall, still built like a sprinter. There were glints of silver in his hair now. He had the sleeves of his work shirt rolled up to the elbows, and his jeans were white at the stress points. He wore sunglasses and badly beaten Nikes.

At fifty, Cameron Quinn still looked like a badass.

In lieu of greeting, Seth let the screen door slam behind him. Cameron glanced over, and the only sign of surprise was his fingers sliding off the rope.

A thousand words passed between them without a sound. A million feelings, and countless memories. Saying nothing, Seth came down the steps as Cameron crossed the lawn. Then they stood, face-to-face.

"I hope that piece of shit in the driveway's a rental," Cameron began.

"Yeah, it is. Best I could do on short notice. Figured I'd turn it in tomorrow, then use the 'Vette for a while."

Cameron's smile was sharp as a blade. "In your dreams, pal. In your wildest dreams."

"No point in it sitting there going to waste."

"Less of one to let some half-assed painter with delusions of grandeur behind its classic wheel."

"Hey, you're the one who taught me to drive."

"Tried to. A ninety-year-old woman with a broken arm could handle a five-speed better than you." He jerked his head toward Seth's rental. "That embarrassment in my driveway doesn't inspire the confidence in me that you've improved in that area."

Smug now, Seth rocked back on his heels. "Test-drove a Maserati a couple of months ago."

Cam's eyebrows winged up. "Get out of here."

"Had her up to a hundred and ten. Scared the living shit out of me."

Cam laughed, gave Seth an affectionate punch on the arm. Then he sighed. "Son of a bitch. Son of a bitch," he said again as he dragged Seth into a fierce hug. "Why the hell didn't you let us know you were coming home?"

"It was sort of spur-of-the-moment," Seth began. "I wanted to be here. I just needed to be here."

"Okay. Anna burning up the phone lines letting everybody know we're serving fatted calf?"

"Probably. She said we'd have the calf on Sunday."

"That'll work. You settled in yet?"

"No. I got stuff in the car."

"Don't call that butt-ugly thing a car. Let's get your gear."

"Cam." Seth reached out, touched Cam's arm. "I want to come home. Not just for a few days or a couple weeks. I want to stay. Can I stay?"

Cam drew off his sunglasses, and his eyes, smoke-gray, met Seth's. "What the hell's the matter with you that you think you have to ask? You trying to piss me off?"

"I never had to try, nobody does with you. Anyway, I'll pull my weight."

"You always pulled your weight. And we missed seeing your ugly face around here."

And that, Seth thought as they walked to the car, was all the welcome he needed from Cameron Quinn.

⟡

They'd kept his room. It had changed over the years, different paint for the walls, a new rug for the floor. But the bed was the same one he'd slept in, dreamed in, waked in.

The same bed he'd sneaked Foolish into when he'd been a child.

And the one he'd sneaked Alice Albert into when he'd thought he was a man.

He figured Cam knew about Foolish, and had often wondered if he'd known about Alice.

He tossed his suitcases carelessly on the bed and laid his battered paint kit—one Sybill had given him for his eleventh birthday—on the worktable Ethan had built.

He'd need to find studio space, he thought. Eventually. As long as the weather held, he could work outdoors. He preferred that anyway. But he'd need somewhere to store his canvases, his equipment. Maybe there was room in the old barn of a boatyard, but that wouldn't suit on a permanent basis.

And he meant to make this permanent.

He'd had enough of traveling for now, enough of living among strangers to last him a lifetime.

He'd needed to go, to stand on his own. He'd needed to learn. And God, he'd needed to paint.

So he'd studied in Florence, and worked in Paris. He'd wandered the hills of Ireland and Scotland and had stood on the cliffs in Cornwall.

He'd lived cheap and rough most of the time. When there'd been a choice between buying a meal or paint, he'd gone hungry.

He'd been hungry before. It had done him good, he hoped, to remember what it was like not to have someone making sure you were fed and safe and warm.

It was the Quinn in him, he supposed, that made him hell-bent to beat his own path.

He laid out his sketch pad, put away his charcoal, his pencils. He would spend time getting back to basics with his work before he picked up a brush again.

The walls of his room held some of his early drawings. Cam had taught him how to make the frames on an old miter box at the boatyard. Seth took one from the wall to study it. It showed promise, he thought, in the rough, undisciplined lines.

But more, much more, it showed the promise of a life.

He'd caught them well enough, he decided. Cam, with his thumbs tucked in his pockets, stance confrontational. Then Phillip, slick, edging toward an elegance that nearly disguised the street smarts. Ethan, patient, steady as a redwood in his work clothes.

He'd drawn himself with them. Seth at ten, he thought. Thin, narrow shoulders and big feet, with a lift to his chin to mask something more painful than fear.

Something that was hope.

A life moment, Seth thought now, captured with a graphite pencil. Drawing it, he'd begun to believe, in-the-gut believe, that he was one of them.

A Quinn.

"You mess with one Quinn," he murmured as he hung the drawing on the wall again, "you mess with them all."

He turned, glanced at the suitcases and wondered if he could sweet-talk Anna into unpacking for him.

Not a chance.

"Hey."

He looked toward the doorway and brightened when he saw Kevin. If he had to fiddle with clothes, as least he'd have company. "Hey, Kev."

"So, you really hanging this time? For good?"

"Looks like."

"Cool." Kevin sauntered in, plopped on the bed and propped his feet on one of the suitcases. "Mom's really jazzed about it. Around here, if Mom's happy, everybody's happy. She could be soft enough to let me use her car this weekend."

"Glad I can help." He shoved Kevin's feet off the suitcase, then unzipped it.

He had the look of his mother, Seth thought. Dark, curling hair, big

Italian eyes. Seth imagined the girls were already tumbling for him like bowling pins.

"How's the play?"

"It rocks. Totally rocks. *West Side Story*. I'm Tony. When you're a Jet, man."

"You stay a Jet." Seth dumped shirts haphazardly in a drawer. "You get killed, right?"

"Yeah." Kevin clutched his heart, shuddered with his face filled with pain and rapture. Then slumped. "It's great, and before I do the death thing, we've got this kick-ass fight scene. Show's next week. You're gonna come, right?"

"Front row center, pal."

"Check out Lisa Maxdon, she plays Maria. Total babe. We've got a couple of love scenes together. We've been doing a lot of practicing," he added and winked.

"Anything for art."

"Yeah." Kevin scooted up a little. "Okay, so tell me about all the Euro chicks. Pretty hot, huh?"

"The only way to get burned. There was this girl in Rome. Anna-Theresa."

"A two-named girl." Kevin shook his fingers as if he'd gotten them too close to a flame. "Two-named girls are way sexy."

"Tell me. She worked in this little trattoria. And the way she served pasta al pomodoro was just amazing."

"So? Did you score?"

Seth sent Kevin a pitying look. "Please, who're you talking to here?" He dumped jeans in another drawer. "She had hair all the way down to her ass, and a very fine ass it was. Eyes like melted chocolate and a mouth that wouldn't quit."

"Did you draw her naked?"

"I did about a dozen figure studies. She was a natural. Totally relaxed, completely uninhibited."

"Man, you're killing me."

"And she had the most amazing . . ." Seth paused, his hands up to chest level to demonstrate. "Personality," he said, dropping his hands. "Hi, Anna."

"Discussing art?" she said dryly. "It's so nice of you to share some of your cultural experiences with Kevin."

"Um. Well." The killing smile she was aiming in his direction had always made Seth's tongue wither. Instead of trying to use it, he fell back on an innocent grin.

"But tonight's session on art and culture is now over. Kevin, I believe you have homework."

"Right. I'll get right to it." Seeing his history assignment as an escape hatch, Kevin bolted.

Anna stepped into the room. "Do you think," she asked Seth pleasantly, "that the young woman in question would appreciate being whittled down to a pair of breasts?"

"Ah . . . I also mentioned her eyes. They were nearly as fabulous as yours."

Anna took a shirt out of the open drawer, folded it neatly. "Do you think that's going to work with me?"

"No. Begging might. Please don't hurt me. I just got home."

She took out another shirt, folded it. "Kevin's sixteen, and I'm perfectly aware his major interest at this time is naked breasts and his fervent desire to get his hands on as many as possible."

Seth winced. "Jeez, Anna."

"I am also aware," she continued without breaking stride, "that this predilection—while hopefully becoming more civilized and controlled—remains deep-seated in the male species throughout its natural life."

"Hey, you want to see some of my landscape sketches from Tuscany?"

"I am surrounded by you." Sighing a little, she took out yet another shirt. "Outnumbered, and have been since I walked into this house. That doesn't mean I can't knock every one of your stupid heads together when necessary. Understood?"

"Yes, ma'am."

"Good. Show me your landscapes."

∞

Later, when the house was quiet and the moon rode over the water, she found Cam on the back porch. She stepped out, and into him.

He wrapped an arm around her, rubbing her shoulder against the night's chill. "Settle everyone down?"

"That's what I do. Chilly tonight." She glanced up at the sky, at the ice points of stars. "I hope it stays clear for Sunday." Then she simply turned her face into his chest. "Oh, Cam."

"I know." He stroked a hand over her hair, rubbed his cheek against it.

"To see him sitting at the kitchen table. Watching him wrestling with

Jake and that idiot dog. Even hearing him talking about naked women with Kevin—"

"What naked women?"

She laughed, shook back her hair as she looked at him. "No one you know. It's so good to have him home."

"I told you he'd come back. Quinns always come back to the roost."

"I guess you're right." She kissed him, one long, warm meeting of lips. "Why don't we go upstairs?" She slid her hands down, gave his butt a suggestive squeeze. "And I'll settle you down, too."

TWO

"Rise and shine, pal. This ain't no flophouse."

The voice, and the gleeful sadism behind it, had Seth groaning. He flopped onto his stomach, dragged the pillow over his head. "Go away. Go far, far away."

"If you think you're going to spend your days around here sleeping till the crack of noon, think again." With relish, Cam yanked the pillow away. "Up."

Seth opened one eye, rolled it until he focused on the bedside clock. It wasn't yet seven. He turned his face back into the mattress and mumbled a rude suggestion in Italian.

"If you think I've lived with Spinelli all these years and don't know that means 'kiss my ass,' you're stupid as well as lazy."

To solve the problem, Cam ripped the sheets away, snagged Seth's ankles and dragged him to the floor.

"Shit. *Shit!*" Naked, his elbow singing where it had cracked the table, Seth glared up at his persecutor. "What the hell's with you? This is my room, my bed, and I'm trying to sleep in it."

"Put some clothes on. I've got something for you to do out back."

"Goddamn it, you could give a guy twenty-four hours before you start on him."

"Kid, I started on you when you were ten, and I'm not close to being finished. I've got work, so let's get moving."

"Cam." Anna strode to the doorway, hands on hips. "I told you to wake him up, not knock him down."

"Jesus." Mortified, Seth tore the sheet out of Cam's hands and clutched it around his waist. "Jesus, Anna, I'm naked here."

"Then get dressed," she suggested, and walked away.

"Out back," Cam told him as he strode from the room. "Five minutes."

"Yeah, yeah, yeah."

Some things never changed, Seth thought as he yanked on jeans. He could be sixty living in this house, and Cam would still roust him out of bed like he was twelve.

He snagged what was left of a University of Maryland sweatshirt and dragged it over his head as he stalked from the room.

If there wasn't coffee, hot and fresh, somebody was going to get their ass seriously kicked.

"Mom! I can't find my shoes!"

Seth glanced toward Jake's room as he headed for the stairs.

"They're down here," Anna called back. "In the middle of my kitchen floor, where they don't belong."

"Not *those* shoes. Jeez, Mom. The *other* shoes."

"Try looking up your butt," came the carefully modulated suggestion from Kevin's room. "Your head's already up there."

"No problem finding your butt," was the hissed response. "Since you wear it right on your shoulders."

Such familiar family dynamics would have made Seth smile—if it hadn't been shy of seven A.M. If his elbow hadn't been throbbing like a bitch. If he had had a hit of caffeine.

"Neither one of you could find your butts with your own hands," he grumbled as he sulked down the steps.

"What the hell's up with Cam?" he demanded of Anna when he stalked into the kitchen. "Is there any coffee? Why does everybody wake up yelling around here?"

"Cam needs to see you outside. Yes, there's a half pot left, and everyone wakes up yelling because it's how we like to greet the day." She poured coffee into a thick white mug. "You're on your own for breakfast. I have an early meeting. Don't pout, Seth. I'll bring home ice cream."

The day began to look marginally brighter. "Rocky Road?"

"Rocky Road. Jake! Get these shoes out of my kitchen before I feed them to the dog. Go outside, Seth, or you'll spoil Cam's sunny mood."

"Yeah, he looked real chipper when he yanked me out of bed." Stewing over it, Seth walked out the kitchen door.

There they were, almost as Seth had drawn them so many years before. Cam, thumbs in pockets, Phillip, slicked up in a suit, Ethan, with a faded gimme cap over his windblown hair.

Seth swallowed coffee, and the heart that had lodged in his throat. "This is what you dragged me out of bed for?"

"Same smart mouth." Phillip caught him in a hug. His eyes, nearly the same tawny gold as his hair, skimmed over Seth's ragged shirt and jeans. "Christ, kid, didn't I teach you anything?" With a shake of his head, he fingered the dull-gray sleeve. "Italy was obviously wasted on you."

"They're just clothes, Phil. You put them on so you don't get cold or arrested."

With a pained wince, Phillip stepped back. "Where did I go wrong?"

"Looks okay to me. Still a little scrawny. What's this?" Ethan tugged on Seth's hair. "Long as a girl's."

"He had it in a pretty little ponytail last night," Cam told him. "He looked real sweet."

"Up yours," Seth said, laughing.

"We'll get you a nice pink ribbon," Ethan said with a chuckle and grabbed Seth in a bear hug.

Phillip nipped the mug out of Seth's hand, took a sip. "We figured we'd come by and get a look at you before Sunday."

"It's good to see you. Really good to see you." Seth flicked a glance at Cam. "You could've said everyone was here instead of dumping me out of bed."

"More fun that way. Well." Cam rocked back on his heels.

"Well," Phillip agreed, and set the mug on the porch rail.

"Well." Ethan gave Seth's hair another tug. Then got an iron grip on his arm.

"What?"

Cam only grinned and locked a hold on his other arm. Seth didn't need the gleam in their eyes to understand.

"Come on. You're kidding, right?"

"It's got to be done." Before Seth could begin to struggle, Phillip scooped his legs out from under him. "It's not like you've got to worry about getting that snazzy outfit wet."

"Cut it out." Seth bucked, tried to kick as he was carried off the porch. "I mean it. That water's fucking cold."

"Probably sink like a stone," Ethan said mildly as they muscled Seth toward the dock. "Looks like living in Europe turned him into a wimp."

"Wimp, my ass." He fought against their hold, fought not to laugh. "Takes three of you to take me out. Bunch of feeble old men," he snarled. With grips, he thought, like steel.

That had Phillip's brow quirking. "How far do you think we can throw him?"

"Let's find out. One," Cam announced as they stood swinging him between them on the dock.

"I'll kill you." Swearing, laughing, Seth wiggled like a fish.

"Two," Phillip said with a grin. "Better save your breath, kid."

"Three. Welcome home, Seth," Ethan said as the three of them hurled him in the air.

He was right. The water was freezing. It stole the breath he hadn't bothered to save, chilled him right down to the bone. When he surfaced, spitting it out, shoving at his hair, he heard his brothers howling with delight, saw them ranged together on the dock with the early sun showering down and the old white house behind them.

I'm Seth Quinn, he thought. And I'm home.

⚭

The early-morning dip went a long way toward purging any jet lag. Since he was up, Seth decided he might as well get things done. He drove back to Baltimore, turned in the rental, and after some wheeling and dealing at a dealership, drove toward the Shore the proud owner of a muscular Jaguar convertible in saber silver.

He knew it shouted: Officer, may I have a speeding ticket please! But he couldn't resist.

Selling his art was a two-edged sword. It sliced at his heart each time he parted with a painting. But he was selling very well and might as well reap some of the benefits.

His brothers, he thought smugly, were going to be green when they got a load of his new ride.

He cut back on his speed as he cruised into St. Chris. The little water town with its busy docks and quiet streets was another painting to him, one he'd re-created countless times, from countless angles.

Market Street with its shops and restaurants ran parallel to the dock, where crab pickers still set up tables on weekends to perform for the tourists. Watermen like Ethan would bring the day's catch there.

The town spread back with its old Victorian houses, its saltboxes and clapboards shaded by leafy trees. Lawns would be tidy. Neat, quaint, historic drew in the tourists, who would browse in the shops, eat in the restaurants, cozy up in one of the B and B's for a relaxing weekend at the Shore.

Locals learned to live with them, just as they learned to live with the gales that blew in from the Atlantic, and the droughts that sizzled their soybean fields. As they learned to live with the capricious Bay and her dwindling bounty.

He passed Crawford's and thought of sloppy submarine sandwiches, dripping ice cream cones and town gossip.

He'd ridden his bike on these streets, racing with Danny and Will

McLean. He'd cruised with them in the secondhand Chevy he and Cam had fixed up the summer he turned sixteen.

And he'd sat—man and boy—at one of the umbrella tables while the town bustled by, trying to capture what it was about this single spot on the planet that shone so bright for him.

He wasn't sure he ever had, or ever would.

He eased into a parking space so he could walk down to the dock. He wanted to study the light, the shadows, the colors and shapes, and was already wishing he'd thought to bring a sketch pad.

It amazed him, constantly, how much beauty there was in the world. How it changed and it shifted even as he watched. The way the sun struck the water at one exact instant, how it spread or winked away behind a cloud.

Or there, he thought, the curve of that little girl's cheek when she lifted her face to look at a gull. The way her laugh shaped her mouth, or the way her fingers threaded through her mother's in absolute trust.

There was power in that.

He stood watching a white boat heel to in blue water, its sails snap full as they caught the wind.

He wanted to be out on the water again, he realized. Be part of it. Maybe he'd shanghai Aubrey for a few hours. He'd make a couple more stops, then swing by the boatyard and see if he could steal her.

Scanning the street, he started back for his car. A sign painted on a storefront caught his attention. *Bud and Bloom,* he read. Flower shop. That was new. He strolled closer, noting the festive pots hanging on either side of the glass.

The window itself was filled with plants and what he thought of as whatnots. Clever ones, though, Seth thought, finding himself amused by the spotted black-and-white cow with pansies flowing over its back.

In the lower right-hand corner of the window, written in the same ornate script, was: *Drusilla Whitcomb Banks, Proprietor.*

It wasn't a name he recognized, and since the painted script informed him the shop had been established in September of the previous year, he imagined some fussy widow, on the elderly side. White hair, he decided, starched dress with a prim floral print to go with sensible shoes and the half-glasses she wore on a gold chain around her neck.

She and her husband had come to St. Chris for long weekends, and when he'd died, she'd had too much money and time on her hands. So she'd moved here and opened her little flower shop so that she could be somewhere they'd been carefree together while doing something she'd secretly longed to do for years.

The story line made him like Mrs. Whitcomb Banks and her snobby cat—she'd *have* to have a cat—named Ernestine.

He decided to make her, and the many women in his life, happy. With flowers on his mind, Seth opened the door to the musical tinkle of bells.

The proprietor, he thought, had an artistic eye. It wasn't just the flowers—they were, after all, just the paint. She had daubed, splashed and streamed her paints very well. Flows of colors, a mix of shapes, a contrast of textures covered the canvas of her shop. It was tidy, just as he'd expected, but not regimented or formal.

He knew enough of flowers from the years of living with Anna to recognize how cleverly she'd paired hot-pink gerbera with rich blue delphiniums, snowy-white lilies with the elegance of red roses. Mixed in with those sweeps of color were the fans and spikes and tongues of green.

And the whimsy again, he noted, charmed. Cast-iron pigs, flute-playing frogs, wicked-faced gargoyles.

There were pots and vases, ribbons and lace, shallow dishes of herbs and thriving houseplants. He got the impression of cannily arranged clutter in a limited and well-used space.

Over it all were the fairy-tale notes of "Afternoon of a Faun."

Nice going, Mrs. Whitcomb Banks, he decided and prepared to spend lavishly.

The woman who stepped out of the rear door behind the long service counter wasn't Seth's image of the talented widow, but she sure as hell belonged in a fanciful garden.

He gave his widow extra points for hiring help who brought faeries and spellbound princesses to a man's mind.

"May I help you?"

"Oh yeah." Seth crossed to the counter and just looked at her.

Long, slim and tidy as a rose, he thought. Her hair was true black, cut close to follow the lovely shape of her head while leaving the elegant stem of her neck exposed. It was a look, he thought, that took considerable female guts and self-confidence.

It left her face completely unframed so that the delicate ivory of her skin formed a perfect oval canvas. The gods had been in a fine mood the day they'd created her, and had drawn her a pair of long, almond-shaped eyes of moss green, then added a nimbus of amber around her pupils.

Her nose was small and straight, her mouth wide to go with the eyes, and very full. She'd tinted it a deep, seductive rose.

Her chin had the faintest cleft, as if her maker had given it a light finger brush of approval.

He would paint that face; there was no question about it. And the rest of her as well. He saw her lying on a bed of red rose petals, those faerie eyes glowing with sleepy power, those lips slightly curved, as if she'd just wakened from dreaming of a lover.

Her smile didn't waver as he studied her, but the dark wings of her eyebrows lifted. "And just what can I help you with?"

The voice was good, he mused. Strong and smooth. Not a local, he decided.

"We can start with flowers," he told her. "It's a great shop."

"Thanks. What sort of flowers did you have in mind today?"

"We'll get to that." He leaned on the counter. In St. Chris, there was always time for a little conversation. "Have you worked here long?"

"From the beginning. If you're thinking ahead to Mother's Day, I have some lovely—"

"No, I've got Mother's Day handled. You're not from around here. The accent," he explained when those brows lifted again. "Not Shore. A little north, maybe."

"Very good. D.C."

"So, the name of the shop. Bud and Bloom. Is that from Whistler?"

Surprise, and speculation, flickered over her face. "As a matter of fact, it is. You're the first to tag it."

"One of my brothers is big on stuff like that. I can't remember the quote exactly. Something about perfect in its bud as in its bloom."

" 'The masterpiece should appear as the flower to the painter—perfect in its bud as in its bloom.' "

"Yeah, that's it. I probably recognized it because that's what I do. I paint."

"Really?" She reminded herself to be patient, to relax into the rhythm. Part of the package in the little town was slow, winding conversations with strangers. She'd already sized him up. His face was vaguely familiar, and his eyes, a very striking blue, were frank and direct in their interest. She wouldn't stoop to flirtation, certainly not to make a sale, but she could be friendly.

She'd come to St. Chris to be friendly.

Because she imagined he painted houses, she sorted through her mind for an arrangement that would suit his budget. "Do you work locally?"

"I do now. I've been away. Do you work here alone?" He glanced around, calculating the amount of work that went into maintaining the garden she'd created. "Does the proprietor come in?"

"I work alone, for now. And I am the proprietor."

He looked back at her and began to laugh. "Boy, I wasn't even close. Nice to meet you, Drusilla Whitcomb Banks." He held out a hand. "I'm Seth Quinn."

Seth Quinn. She laid her hand in his automatically and did her own rapid readjustment. Not a face she'd seen around town, she realized, but one she'd seen in a magazine. No housepainter, despite the old jeans and faded shirt, but an artist. The local boy who'd become the toast of Europe.

"I admire your work," she told him.

"Thanks. I admire yours. And I'm probably keeping you from it. I'm going to make it worth your while. I've got some ladies to impress. You can help me out."

"Ladies? Plural?"

"Yeah. Three, no four," he corrected, thinking of Aubrey.

"It's a wonder you have time to paint, Mr. Quinn."

"Seth. I manage."

"I bet you do." Certain types of men always managed. "Cut flowers, arrangements or plants?"

"Ah . . . cut flowers, in a nice box. More romantic, right? Let me think." He calculated route and time, and decided he'd drop by to see Sybill first. "Number one is sophisticated, chic, intellectual and practical-minded, with a soft-gooey center. Roses, I guess."

"If you want to be predictable."

He looked back at Dru. "Let's be unpredictable."

"Just a moment. I have something in the back you should like."

Something out here I like, he thought as she turned toward the rear door. He gave his heart a little pat.

Phillip, Seth thought as he wandered the shop, would approve of the classic, clean lines of that ripening, peach-colored suit she wore. Ethan, he imagined, would wonder how to give her a hand with all the work that must go into running the place. And Cam . . . well, Cam would take one long look at her and grin.

Seth supposed he had bits of all three of them inside him.

She came back carrying an armload of streamlined and exotic flowers with waxy blooms the color of eggplant.

"Calla lilies," she told him. "Elegant, simple, classy and in this color spectacular."

"You nailed her."

She set them in a cone-shaped holding vase. "Next?"

"Warm, old-fashioned in the best possible way." Just thinking of Grace made him smile. "Simple in the same way. Sweet but not sappy, and with a spine of steel."

"Tulips," she said and walked to a clear-fronted, refrigerated cabinet. "In this rather tender pink. A quiet flower that's sturdier than it looks," she added as she brought them over for him to see.

"Bingo. You're good."

"Yes, I am." She was enjoying herself now—not just for the sale, but for the game of it. This was the reason she'd opened the shop. "Number three?"

Aubrey, he thought. How to describe Aubrey. "Young, fresh, fun. Tough and unstintingly loyal."

"Hold on." With the image in mind, Dru breezed into the back again. And came out with a clutch of sunflowers with faces as wide as a dessert plate.

"Jesus, they're perfect. You're in the right business, Drusilla."

It was, she thought, the finest of compliments. "No point in being in the wrong one. And since you're about to break my record for single walk-in sales, it's Dru."

"Nice."

"And the fourth lucky woman?"

"Bold, beautiful, smart and sexy. With a heart like . . ." Anna's heart, he thought. "With a heart beyond description. The most amazing woman I've ever known."

"And apparently you know quite a few. One minute." Again, she went into the back. He was admiring the sunflowers when Dru came back with Asiatic lilies in triumphant scarlet.

"Oh man. They're so Anna." He reached out to touch one of the vivid red petals. "So completely Anna. You've just made me a hero."

"Happy to oblige. I'll box them, and tie ribbons on each that coordinate with the color of the flowers inside. Can you keep them straight?"

"I think I can handle it."

"Cards are included. You can pick what you like from the rack on the counter."

"I won't need cards." He watched her fit water-filled nipples on the end of the stems. No wedding ring, he noted. He'd have painted her regardless, but if she'd been married it would have put an end to the rest of his plans.

"What flower are you?"

She flicked him a glance as she arranged the first flowers in a tissue-lined white box. "All of them. I like variety." She tied a deep purple ribbon around the first box. "As it appears you do."

"I kind of hate to shatter the illusion that I've got a harem going here.

Sisters," he said, gesturing toward the flowers. "Though the sunflowers are niece, cousin, sister. The exact relationship's a little murky."

"Um-hm."

"My brothers' wives," he explained. "And one of my brothers' oldest daughter. I figured I should clear that up since I'm going to paint you."

"Are you?" She tied the second box with pink ribbon edged with white lace. "Are you really?"

He took out his credit card, laid it on the counter while she went to work on the sunflowers. "You're thinking I'm just looking to get you naked, and I wouldn't have any objection to that."

She drew gold ribbon from its loop. "Why would you?"

"Exactly. But why don't we start with your face? It's a good face. I really like the shape of your head."

For the first time, her fingers fumbled a bit. With a half laugh, she stopped and really looked at him again. "The shape of my head?"

"Sure. You like it, too, or you wouldn't wear your hair that way. Makes a powerful statement with a minimum of fuss."

She tied off the bow. "You're clever at defining a woman with a few pithy phrases."

"I like women."

"I figured that out." As she finished up the red lilies, a pair of customers came in and began to browse.

A good thing, Dru thought. It was time to move the artistic Mr. Quinn along.

"I'm flattered you admire the shape of my head." She picked up his credit card to ring up the sale. "And that someone of your talent and reputation would like to paint me. But the business keeps me very busy, and without a great deal of free time. What free time I do have, I'm extremely selfish with."

She gave him his total, slid the sales slip over for his signature.

"You close at six daily and don't open on Sundays."

She should've been annoyed, she thought, but instead she was intrigued. "You don't miss much, do you?"

"Every detail matters." After signing the receipt, he plucked out one of her gift cards, turned it over to the blank back.

He drew a quick study of her face as the blossom of a long-stemmed flower, then added the phone number at home before he signed it. "In case you change your mind," he said, offering it.

She studied the card, found her lips quirking. "I could probably sell this on eBay for a tidy little sum."

"You've got too much class for that." He piled up the boxes, hefted them. "Thanks for the flowers."

"You're welcome." She came around the counter to open the door for him. "I hope your . . . sisters enjoy them."

"They will." He shot her a last look over his shoulder. "I'll be back."

"I'll be here." Tucking the sketch into her pocket, she closed the door.

⚭

It had been great to see Sybill, to spend an hour alone with her. And to see the pleasure she got from arranging the flowers in a tall, clear vase.

They were perfect for her, he concluded, just as the house she and Phillip had bought and furnished, the massive old Victorian with all the stylized details, was perfect for her.

She'd changed her hairstyle over the years, but now it was back to the way he liked it best, swinging sleek nearly to her shoulders with all that richness of color of a pricey mink coat.

She hadn't bothered with lipstick for the day of working at home, and wore a simple and crisp white shirt with pegged black trousers, what he supposed she thought of as casual wear.

She was the mother of two active children, as well as being a trained sociologist and successful author. And looked, Seth thought, utterly serene.

He had reason to know that that serenity had been hard-won.

She'd grown up in the same household as his mother. Half sisters who were like opposite sides of a coin.

Since even the thought of Gloria DeLauter clenched his stomach muscles, Seth pushed it aside and concentrated on Sybill.

"When you, Phil and the kids came over to Rome a few months ago, I didn't think the next time I'd see you would be here."

"I wanted you to come back." She poured them each a glass of iced tea. "Totally selfish of me, but I wanted you back. Sometimes in the middle of whatever was going on, I'd stop and think: Something's missing. What's missing? Then, oh yes, Seth. Seth's missing. Silly."

"Sweet." He gave her hand a squeeze before picking up the glass she set down for him. "Thanks."

"Tell me everything," she demanded.

They talked of his work and hers. Of the children. Of what had changed and what had stayed the same.

When he got up to leave, she wrapped her arms around him and held on just a minute longer. "Thanks for the flowers. They're wonderful."

"Nice new shop on Market. The woman who owns it seems to know her stuff." He walked with Sybill, hand in hand, toward the door. "Have you been in there?"

"Once or twice." Because she knew him, very well, Sybill smiled. "She's very lovely, isn't she?"

"Who's that?" But when Sybill merely tipped her head, he grinned. "Caught me. Yeah, she's got some face. What do you know about her?"

"Nothing, really. She moved here late last summer, I think, and had the store open by fall. I believe she's from the D.C. area. It seems to me my parents know some Whitcombs, and some Bankses from around there. Might be relatives." She shrugged. "I can't say for certain, and my parents and I don't . . . communicate very often these days."

He touched her cheek. "I'm sorry."

"Don't be. They have two spectacular grandchildren whom they largely ignore." As they've ignored you, she thought. "It's their loss."

"Your mother's never forgiven you for standing up for me."

"Her loss." Sybill spoke very precisely as she caught his face in her hands. "My gain. And I didn't stand alone. No one ever does in this family."

She was right about that, Seth thought as he drove toward the boatyard. No Quinn stood alone.

But he wasn't sure he could stand pulling them into the trouble he was very much afraid was going to find him, even back home.

THREE

Once Dru had rung up the next sale and was alone in the shop again, she took the sketch out of her pocket.

Seth Quinn. Seth Quinn wanted to paint her. It was fascinating. And as intriguing, she admitted, as the artist himself. A woman could be intrigued without being actively interested.

Which she wasn't.

She had no desire to pose, to be scrutinized, to be immortalized. Even by such talented hands. But she was curious, about the concept of it, just as she was curious about Seth Quinn.

The article she'd read had included some details on his personal life. She knew he'd come to the Eastern Shore as a child, taken in by Ray Quinn before Ray died in a single-car accident. Some of the story was a little nebulous. There'd been no mention of parents, and Seth had been very closed-mouthed in the interview in that area. The facts given were that Ray Quinn had been his grandfather, and on his death, Seth had been raised by Quinn's three adopted sons. And their wives as they had come along.

Sisters, he'd said, thinking of the flowers he'd bought. Perhaps they had been for the women he considered his sisters.

It hardly mattered to her.

She'd been more interested in what the article had said about his work, and how his family had encouraged his early talent. How they had supported his desire to study in Europe.

It was a fortunate child, in Dru's opinion, who had a family who loved him enough to let him go—to let him discover, to fail or succeed on his own. And, she thought, who apparently welcomed him back just as unselfishly.

Still, it was difficult to imagine the man the Italians had dubbed *il maestro giovane*—the young master—settling down in St. Christopher to paint seascapes.

Just as she assumed it was difficult for many of her acquaintances to imagine Drusilla Whitcomb Banks, young socialite, contentedly selling flowers in a small waterfront shop.

It didn't matter to her what people thought or what they said—any more than she supposed such things mattered to Seth Quinn. She'd come here to get away from the demands and expectations, the sticky grip of family, and the unrelenting upheaval of being used as the fraying rope in the endless game of tug-of-war her parents played.

She'd come to St. Chris for peace, the peace that she'd yearned for most of her life.

She was finding it.

Though her mother would be thrilled—perhaps, stubbornly, *because* her mother would be thrilled at the prospect of her precious daughter capturing the interest of Seth Quinn—Dru had no intention of cultivating that interest. Neither the artistic interest, nor the more elemental and frankly sexual interest she'd seen in his eyes when he'd looked at her.

Or, if she was being honest, the frankly sexual interest she'd felt for him.

The Quinns were, by all reports, a large, complex and unwieldy family. God knew she'd had her fill of family.

A pity, she admitted, tapping the card on her palm before dropping it into a drawer. The young master was attractive, amusing and appealing. And any man who took the time to buy flowers for his sisters, and wanted to make sure each purchase suited the individual style of the recipient, earned major points.

"Too bad for both of us," she murmured, and shut the drawer with a final little snap.

He was thinking of Dru as she was thinking of him, and pondering just what angles, just what tones would work best on a portrait. He liked the idea of a three-quarter view of her face, with her head turned to the left, but her eyes looking back, out of the canvas.

That would suit the contrast of her cool attitude and sexy chic.

He never doubted she'd consent to pose. He had an entire arsenal of weapons to battle a model's reluctance. All he had to do was decide which one would work best on Drusilla.

Tapping his fingers on the wheel to the outlaw beat of Aerosmith that blasted out of his stereo, Seth considered her.

There was money in her background, he decided. Seth recognized designer cut and good fabric even if he was more interested in the form beneath the fashion. Then there was the cadence of her voice. It said high-class private school to him.

She'd tagged James McNeill Whistler for the name of her shop. Which meant, he thought, she'd had a very tony education, or someone pounding poetry and literature into her head as Phil had done with him.

Probably both.

She was comfortable with her looks and didn't fluster when a man made it clear she attracted him.

She wasn't married, and instinct told him she wasn't attached. A woman like Dru didn't relocate to tag along after a boyfriend or lover. She'd moved from Washington, started a business and run it solo because that's just the way she wanted it.

Then he remembered just how far off the mark he'd been regarding the fictional Widow Whitcomb Banks, and decided to hedge his bets by doing a little research before approaching her again.

Seth pulled into the parking lot of the old brick barn the Quinns had bought from Nancy Claremont when the woman's tight-fisted, tight-assed husband had keeled over dead of a heart attack while arguing with Cy Crawford over the price of a meatball sub.

Initially they'd rented the massive building, one that had been a tobacco warehouse in the 1700s, a packinghouse in the 1800s and a glorified storage shed for much of the 1900s.

Then it had been a boatyard, transformed and outfitted by the brothers Quinn. For the last eight years, it had belonged to them.

Seth looked up at the roof as he climbed out of the car. He'd helped reshingle that roof, he remembered, and had nearly broken his neck doing it.

He'd smeared the hot fifty-fifty mix on seams, and burned his fingers. He'd learned to lap boards in the bottomless well of Ethan's patience. He'd sweated like a pig along with Cam repairing the dock. And had escaped by whatever means presented themselves every time Phil had tried to shoehorn him into learning to keep the books.

He walked to the front, stood with his hands on his hips studying the weathered sign. BOATS BY QUINN. And noted that another name had been added to the four that had been there since the beginning.

Aubrey Quinn.

Even as he grinned, she shoved out of the front door.

She had a tool belt slung at her hips and an Orioles fielder's cap low over her forehead. Her hair, the color of burnt honey, was pulled through the back loop to swing at her back.

Her scarred and stained work boots looked like a doll's.

She had such little feet.

And a very big voice, he thought when she let out a roaring whoop as she charged him.

She leaped, boosted herself with a bounce of her hands off his shoulders and wrapped her legs around his waist. The bill of her cap rapped him in the forehead when she pressed her mouth to his in a long, smacking kiss.

"My Seth." With a loud hooting laugh, she chained her arms around his neck. "Don't go away again. Damn it, don't you dare go away again."

"I can't. Too much happens around here when I'm gone. Tip back," he ordered, and dipped her away far enough to study her face.

At two, she'd been a tiny princess to him. At twenty, she was an athletic, appealing handful.

"Jeez, you got pretty," he said.

"Yeah? You too."

"Why aren't you in college?"

"Don't start." She rolled her bright green eyes and hopped down. "I did two years, and I'd've been happier on a chain gang. This is what I want to do." She jerked a thumb toward the sign. "My name's up there to prove it."

"You always could wrap Ethan around your finger."

"Maybe. But I didn't have to. Dad got it, and after some initial fretting, so did Mom. I was never the student you were, Seth, and you were never the boatbuilder I am."

"Shit. I leave you alone for a few years, and you get delusions of grandeur. If you're going to insult me, I'm not going to give you your present."

"Where is it? What is it?" She attacked by poking her fingers in his ribs where she knew him to be the most vulnerable. "Gimme."

"Cut it out. Okay, okay. Man, you don't change."

"Why mess with perfection? Hand over the loot and nobody gets hurt."

"It's in the car." He pointed toward the lot and had the satisfaction of seeing her mouth drop open.

"A Jag? Oh baby." She darted over the stubble of lawn to the lot to run her fingers reverently over the shining silver hood. "Cam's going to cry when he sees this. He's just going to break down and cry. Let me have the keys so I can test her out."

"Sure, when we're slurping on Sno Kones in hell."

"Don't be mean. You can come with me. We'll buzz up to Crawford's and get some . . ." She trailed off as he got the long white box out of the trunk. She blinked at the box, blinked at him before her eyes went soft and dewy.

"You bought me flowers. You got me a girl present. Oh, let me see! What kind are they?" She pulled a work knife out of her belt, sliced the ribbon, then yanked up the lid. "Sunflowers. Look how happy they are."

"Reminded me of you."

"I really love you." She stared hard at the flowers. "I've been so mad at you for leaving." When her voice broke, he gave her an awkward pat on the shoulder. "I'm not going to cry," she muttered and sucked it in. "What am I, a sissy?"

"Never."

"Okay, well, anyway, you're back." She turned to hug him again. "I really love the flowers."

"Good." He slapped a hand on the one that was trying to sneak into his pocket. "You're not getting the keys. I've got to take off anyway. I've got flowers for Grace. I want to swing by and see her on my way home."

"She's not there. This is her afternoon for running errands, then she'll pick Deke up from school and drop him off for his piano lesson and so on and so on. I don't know how she does it all. I'll take them to her," Aubrey added. "Flowers will take some of the sting out of missing you today."

"Tell her I'll try to get by tomorrow, otherwise I'll see her Sunday." He carted the box from his trunk to the snappy little blue pickup.

Aubrey laid her flowers in the cab with her mother's. "You've got some time now. Let's go get Cam and show off your car. I tell you, he's going to break down and sob like a baby. I can't wait."

"You've got a mean streak, Aub." Seth slung his arm around her shoulders. "I like that about you. Now, tell me what you know about the flower lady. Drusilla."

"Aha." Aubrey leered up at him as they walked toward the building. "So that's the way the garden grows."

"Might."

"Tell you what. Meet me at Shiney's after dinner. Say about eight. Buy me a drink and I'll spill everything I know."

"You're underage."

"Yeah, like I've never sipped a beer before," she retorted. "A soft drink, Daddy. And remember, I'll be legal in less than six months."

"Until then, when I'm buying, you drink Coke." He tipped down the bill of her cap, then dragged open the door to the noise of power tools.

Cam didn't break down and weep, Seth thought later, but he had drooled a little. Nearly genuflected. Right before, Seth mused as he parked in front of Shiney's Pub, Cam—being bigger and meaner than Aubrey—snagged the keys and peeled off to take it for a spin.

Then, of course, they spent a very satisfying hour standing around admiring the engine.

Seth glanced at the pickup beside his car. One thing about Aubrey, she was always prompt.

He opened the door to Shiney's and felt yet one more homecoming. Another constant of St. Chris, he thought. Shiney's Pub would always look as if it needed to be hosed down, the waitresses would always be leggy, and it would offer the very worst live bands to be found in the entire state of Maryland.

While the lead singer massacred Barenaked Ladies, Seth scanned the tables and bar for a little blonde in a fielder's cap.

His eyes actually passed over her, then arrowed back.

She was indeed at the bar, urbane and curvy in unrelieved black, her burnt-honey hair spiraling down her back as she carried on a heated conversation with a guy who looked like Joe College.

Mouth grim, body poised for a confrontation, Seth headed over to show College Boy just what happened when a guy hit on his sister.

"You're full of it." Aubrey's voice snapped like a whip and had Seth's mouth moving into a snarl. "You are so absolutely full of it. The pitching rotation is solid, the infield's got good gloves. The bats are coming around. By the All-Star Game, the Birds will be playing better than five-hundred ball."

"They won't see five hundred all season," her opponent shot back. "And they're going to be digging another level down in the basement by the All-Star Game."

"Bet." Aubrey dug a twenty out of her pocket, slapped it on the bar.

And Seth sighed. She might've looked like a tasty morsel, but nobody nibbled on his Aubrey.

"Seth." Spotting him, Aubrey reached out, hooked his arm and yanked him to the bar. "Sam Jacoby," she said with a nod toward the man sitting beside her. "Thinks because he plays a little softball he knows something about the Bigs."

"Heard a lot about you." Sam held out a hand. "From this sentimental slob here who thinks the Orioles have a shot at climbing their pitiful way up to mediocre this season."

Seth shook hands. "If you want to commit suicide, Sam, get a gun. It's got to be less painful than inciting this one to peel every inch of skin slowly off your body with a putty knife."

"I like to live dangerously," he said and slid off the stool. "Take a seat. I was holding it for you. Gotta split. See you around, Aub."

"You're going to owe me twenty bucks in July," she called out, then shifted her attention to Seth. "Sam's a nice enough guy, except for the fatal flaw that encourages him to root for the Mariners."

"I thought he was hitting on you."

"Sam?" Aubrey gazed back toward the tables with a smug and female look in her eye that made Seth want to squirm. "Sure he was. I'm holding him in reserve. I'm sort of seeing Will McLean right now."

"Will?" Seth nearly choked. "Will McLean?" The idea of Aubrey and one of his boyhood pals together—that way—had Seth signaling the bartender. "I really need a beer. Rolling Rock."

"Not that we get to see each other that often." Knowing she was turning the screw, Aubrey continued gleefully. "He's an intern at Saint Chris General. Rotations at the hospital are a bitch. But when we do manage the time, it's worth it."

"Shut up. He's too old for you."

"I've always gone for older men." Deliberately, she pinched his cheek. "Cutie pie. Plus there's only, like, five years' difference. Still, if you want to talk about my love life—"

"I don't." Seth reached for the bottle the bartender set in front of him, drank deep. "I really don't."

"Okay, enough about me then, let's talk about you. How many languages did you score in when you were plundering Europe?"

"Now you sound like Kevin." And it wasn't nearly as comfortable a topic to explore with Aubrey. "I wasn't on a sexual marathon. I was working."

"Some chicks really fall for the artistic type. Maybe your flower lady's one of them, and you'll get lucky."

"Obviously you've been hanging around with my brothers too much. Turned you into a gutter brain. Just tell me what you know about her."

"Okay." She grabbed a bowl of pretzels off the bar and began to munch. "So, she first showed up about a year ago. Spent a week hanging around. Checking out retail space," she said with a nod. "I got that from Doug Motts. Remember Dougie—roly-poly little kid? Couple years behind you in school."

"Vaguely."

"Anyway, he lost the baby fat. He's working at Shore Realtors now. According to Doug, she knew just what she was looking for, and told them to contact her in D.C. when and if anything that came close opened up. Now, Doug . . ." She pointed toward her empty glass when the bartender swung by. "He'd pretty much just started at the Realtor's and was hoping to hook this one. So he poked around some, trying to dig up information on his prospective client. She'd told him she'd visited Saint Chris a couple times when she was a kid, so that gave Doug his starting point."

"Ma Crawford," Seth said with a laugh.

"You got it. What Ma Crawford doesn't know ain't worth knowing.

And the woman's got a memory like a herd of elephants. She recalled the Whitcomb Bankses. Name like that, who wouldn't? But they stuck out more because she remembered Mrs. WB from when *she* was a girl visiting here with her family. Her really seriously kick-your-butt-to-Tuesday rich family. Whitcomb Technologies. As in we make everything. As in Fortune Five Hundred. As in Senator James P. Whitcomb, the gentleman from Maryland."

"Ah. *Those* Whitcombs."

"You bet. The senator, who would be the flower lady's grandfather, had an affection for the Eastern Shore. And his daughter, the current Mrs. WB, married Proctor Banks—what kind of name is Proctor, anyway?—of Banks and Shelby Communication. We're talking mega family dough with this combo. Like a fricking empire."

"And young, nubile and extremely wealthy Drusilla rents a storefront in Saint Chris and sells flowers."

"Buys a building in Saint Chris," Aubrey corrected. "She bought the place, prime retail space for our little kingdom. A few months after Doug had the good fortune to be manning the desk at Shore Realtors when she walked in, that place went on the market. Previous owners live in PA, rented it to various merchants who had their ups and downs there. Remember the New Age shop—rocks, crystals, ritual candles and meditation tapes?"

"Yeah. Guy who ran it had a tattoo of a dragon on the back of his right hand."

"That place lasted longer than anybody figured it would, but when the lease came up for renewal last year, it went bye-bye. Doug, smelling commission, gives the young WB a call to tell her a rental just opened up on Market, and she makes him salivate when she asks if the owners are interested in selling. When they were, and a deal was struck, he sang the 'Hallelujah Chorus.' Then she makes him the happiest man in Saint Chris when she tells him to find her a house, too. She comes down, takes a look at the three he shows her, takes a liking to this ramshackle old Victorian on Oyster Inlet. Prime real estate again," Aubrey added. "No flies on flower lady."

"That old blue house?" Seth asked. "Looked like a half-eaten gingerbread house? She bought *that*?"

"Lock and stock." Aubrey nodded as she crunched pretzels. "Guy bought it about three years ago, snazzed it up, wanted to turn it."

"Nothing much around there but marsh grass and thickets." But it rose over a curve of the flatland river, he remembered. That tobacco-colored water that could gleam like amber when the sun beamed through the oak and gum trees.

"Your girl likes her privacy," Aubrey told him. "Keeps to herself. Courteous and helpful to her customers, polite, even friendly, but carefully so. She blows cool."

"She's new here." God knew he understood what it was like to find yourself in a place, one that had just exactly what you wanted, and not be sure if you'd find your slot.

"She's an outlander." Aubrey jerked a shoulder in a typical Quinn shrug. "She'll be new here for the next twenty years."

"She could probably use a friend."

"Looking to make new friends, Seth? Somebody to go chicken necking with?"

He gestured for another beer, then leaned in until his nose bumped hers. "Maybe. Is that what you and Will do in your spare time?"

"We skip the chicken, and just neck. But I'll take you out in the pram if you've got a hankering. I'll captain. It's been so long since you manned a sail, you'd probably capsize her."

"Like hell. We'll go out tomorrow."

"That's a date. And speaking of dates, your new friend just came in."

"Who?" But he knew, even before he swiveled around on the stool. Before he scanned the evening crowd and spotted her.

She looked sublimely out of place among the watermen with their wind-scored faces and scarred hands and the university students with their trendy shoes and baggy shirts.

Her suit was still crisp and perfect, her face an oval of alabaster in the dull light.

She had to know heads turned as she walked in, he thought. Women always knew. But she moved with purpose and easy grace around the stained tables and rickety chairs.

"Classy" was Aubrey's one-word summation.

"Oh yeah." Seth dug out money for the drinks, tossed it on the bar. "I'm ditching you, kid."

Aubrey widened her eyes in exaggerated shock. "Color me amazed."

"Tomorrow," he said, then leaned down to give her a quick kiss before strolling off to intercept Dru.

She stopped by a table and began speaking to a waitress. Seth's attention was so focused on Dru it took him a moment to recognize the other woman.

Terri Hardgrove. Blond, sulky and built. They'd dated for a couple of memorable months during his junior year of high school. It had not ended well, Seth recalled and nearly detoured just to avoid the confrontation.

Instead he tried an easy smile and kept going until he caught some of their conversation.

"I'm not going to take the place after all," Terri said as she balanced her tray on the shelf of one hip. "J.J. and me worked things out."

"J.J." Dru angled her head. "That would be the lowlife, lying scum you never wanted to see again even if he was gasping his last, dying breath?"

"Well." Terri shifted her feet, fluttered her lashes. "We hadn't worked things out when I said that. And I thought, you know, screw him, I'll just get me a place of my own and get back in the game. It was just that I saw your For Rent sign when I was so mad at him and all. But we worked things out."

"So you said. Congratulations. It might've been helpful if you'd come by this afternoon as we'd agreed and let me know."

"I'm really sorry, but that's when . . ."

"You were working things out," Dru finished.

"Hey, Terri."

She squealed. It came flooding back to Seth that she'd always been a squealer. Apparently, she hadn't grown out of it.

"Seth! Seth Quinn! Just look at you."

"How's it going?"

"It's going just fine. I heard you were back, but now here you are. Big as life and twice as handsome, and famous, too. It's sure been some while since Saint Chris High."

"Some time," he agreed and looked at Dru.

"Y'all know each other?" Terri asked.

"We've met," Dru said. "I'll leave you to catch up on old times. I hope you and J.J. are very happy."

"You and J.J. Wyatt?"

Terri preened. "That's right. We're practically engaged."

"We'll catch up later. You can tell me all about it." He took off, leaving Terri pouting at his back as he caught up with Dru.

"J.J. Wyatt," Seth began as he stepped beside Dru. "Offensive tackle on the Saint Chris High Sharks. Went on to crush as many heads as he could manage at the local university before even his bulldog skill on the football field couldn't keep him from flunking out."

"Thank you for that fascinating slice of local history."

"You're pissed. Why don't I buy you a drink and you can tell me all about it?"

"I don't want a drink, thank you, and I'm getting out of here before my eardrums are permanently damaged by that amazingly loud and untalented band's horrendous version of 'Jack and Diane.'"

He decided it was a point in her favor that she could recognize the mangled song, and pulled open the door for her.

"The flowers were a hit."

"I'm glad to hear it." She took her keys out of a streamlined, buff-colored purse.

He started to suggest they go somewhere else for a drink, but could see by the irritated line between her eyebrows that she'd just shut him down.

"So, you've got a space to rent?"

"Apparently." She moved, dismissively, to the driver's side of a black Mercedes SUV.

Seth got his hand on the handle before she did, then just leaned companionably against the door. "Where?"

"Above the shop."

"And you want to rent it?"

"It's empty. It seems like a waste of space. I can't drive my car unless I'm inside of it," she pointed out.

"Above the shop," he repeated, and brought the building back into his mind. Two stories, yeah, that was right. "Bank of three windows, front and back," he said aloud. "Should be good light. How big is it?"

"Nine hundred square feet, including a small galley-style kitchen."

"Big enough. Let's take a look."

"Excuse me?"

"Show me the space. I might be interested."

She gave the keys in her hand an impatient jiggle. "You want me to show you the apartment now?"

"You don't want to waste space, why waste time?" He opened her car door. "I'll follow you back. It won't take long," he said with that slow, easy grin. "I make up my mind pretty quick."

FOUR

She made up her mind quickly as well, Dru thought as she backed out of the pub's lot. And she had Seth Quinn pegged.

A confident man, and a talented one. Each aspect probably fed into the other. The fact that his rough edges managed to have a sheen of polish was intriguing, something she was certain he knew very well.

And used very well.

He was attractive. The lean, lanky build that looked as though it had been designed to wear those worn-out jeans. All that burnished blond hair, straight as a pin and never quite styled. The hollowed cheeks, the vivid blue eyes. Not just vivid in color, she thought now. In intensity. The way he looked at you, as if he saw something no one else could see. Something you couldn't see yourself.

It managed to be flattering, jolting and just a bit off-putting all at once.

It made you wonder about him. And if you were wondering about a man, you were thinking about him.

Women, she concluded, were like paints on a palette to him. He could dab into any one of them at his whim. The way he'd been snuggled up with the blonde in the bar—a little play she'd noted the instant she herself had walked in—was a case in point.

Then there'd been the way he'd smiled at the waitress, the terminally foolish Terri. Wide, warm and friendly, with just a hint of intimacy. Very potent, that smile, Dru mused, but it wasn't going to work on her.

Men who bounced from woman to woman because they could were entirely too ordinary for her tastes.

Yet here she was, she admitted, driving back to the shop to show him the second-floor apartment when what she really wanted to do was go home to her lovely, quiet house.

It was the sensible thing to do, of course. There was no point in the space staying empty. But it galled that he'd assumed she'd take the time and trouble simply because he wanted her to.

There was no problem finding a parking space now. It was barely nine on a cool spring evening, but the waterfront was all but deserted. A few boats moored, swaying in the current, a scatter of people, most likely tourists, strolling under the light of a quarter moon.

Oh, how she loved the waterfront. She'd nearly howled with glee when she'd been able to snag the building for her shop, knowing she'd be able to step outside any time of the day and see the water, the crabbers, the tourists. To feel that moist air on her skin.

Even more, to feel part of it all, on her own merits, her own terms.

It would have been smarter, more sensible again, to have taken the room above for her own living quarters. But she'd made the conscious and deliberate decision not to live where she worked. Which, Dru admitted as she swung away from Market to drive to the rear of her building, had been a handy excuse to find a place out of the town bustle, someplace on the water again. An indulgent space all her own.

The house in Georgetown had never felt all her own.

She killed the lights, the engine, then gathered her purse. Seth was there, opening her door, before she could do it for herself.

"It's pretty dark. Watch your step." He took her arm, started to steer her to the wooden staircase that led to the second level.

"I can see fine, thanks." She eased away from him, then opened her bag for the keys. "There's parking," she began. "And a private entrance, as you see."

"Yeah, I see fine, too. Listen." Halfway up the stairs, he laid a hand on her arm to stop her. "Just listen," he said again and looked out over the houses that lined the road behind them. "It's great, isn't it?"

She couldn't stop the smile. She understood him perfectly. And it was great, that silence.

"It won't be this quiet in a few weeks." He scanned the dark, the houses, the lawns. And again she thought he saw what others didn't. "Starting with Memorial Day the tourists and the summer people pour in. Nights get longer, warmer, and people hang out. That can be great, too, all that noise. Holiday noise. The kind you hear when you've got an ice cream cone in your hand and no time clock ticking away in your head."

He turned, aimed those strong blue eyes at her. She could have sworn she felt a jolt from them that was elementally physical.

"You like ice cream cones?" he asked her.

"There'd be something wrong with me if I didn't." She moved quickly up the rest of the steps.

"Nothing wrong with you," he murmured, and stood with his thumbs tucked in his front pockets while she unlocked the door.

She flicked a switch on the wall to turn on the lights, then deliberately left the door open at his back when he stepped in.

She saw immediately she needn't have bothered. He wasn't giving her a thought now.

He crossed to the front windows first, stood there looking out in that hip-shot stance that managed to be both relaxed and attentive. And sexy, she decided.

He wore a pair of ragged jeans with more style than a great many men managed to achieve in a five-thousand-dollar suit.

There were paint flecks on his shoes.

She blinked, tuning back in to the moment when he began to mutter.

"Excuse me?"

"What? Oh, just calculating the light—sun, angles. Stuff." He crossed back to the rear windows, stood as he had at the front. Muttered as he had at the front.

Talked to himself, Dru noted. Well, it wasn't so odd, really. She held entire conversations with herself in her head.

"The kitchen—" Dru began.

"Doesn't matter." Frowning, he stared up at the ceiling, his gaze so intense and focused she found herself staring up with him.

After a few seconds of standing there, silent, staring up, she felt ridiculous. "Is there a problem with the ceiling? I was assured the roof was sound, and I know it doesn't leak."

"Uh-huh. Any objection to skylights—put in at my expense?"

"I . . . well, I don't know. I suppose—"

"It would work."

He wandered the room again, placing his canvases, his paints, his easel, a worktable for sketching, shelves for supplies and equipment. Have to put in a sofa, or a bed, he thought. Better a bed in case he worked late enough to just flop down for the night.

"It's a good space," he said at length. "With the skylights, it'll work. I'll take it."

She reminded herself that she hadn't actually agreed to the skylights. But then again, she couldn't find any reason to object to them. "That was quick, as advertised. Don't you want to see the kitchen, the bathroom?"

"They got everything kitchens and bathrooms are supposed to have?"

"Yes. No tub, just a shower stall."

"I'm not planning on taking too many bubble baths." He moved back to the front windows again. "Prime view."

"Yes, it's very nice. Not that it's any of my business, but I assume you have any number of places you can stay while you're here. Why do you need an apartment?"

"I don't want to live here, I want to work here. I need studio space." He turned back. "I'm bunking at Cam and Anna's, and that suits me. I'll get a place of my own eventually, but not until I find exactly what I want. Because I'm not visiting Saint Chris. I'm back for good."

"I see. Well, studio space then. Which explains the skylights."

"I'm a better bet than Terri," he said because he felt her hesitation. "No loud parties or shouting matches, which she's famous for. And I'm handy."

"Are you?"

"Hauling, lifting, basic maintenance. I won't come crying to you every time the faucet drips."

"Points for you," she murmured.

"How many do I need? I really want the space. I need to get back to work. What do you say to a six-month lease?"

"Six months. I'd planned on a full year at a time."

"Six months gives us both an early out if it's not jelling."

She pursed her lips in consideration. "There is that."

"How much are you asking?"

She gave him the monthly rate she'd settled on. "I'll want first and last month's rent when you sign the lease. And another month's rent as security deposit."

"Ouch. Very strict."

Now she smiled. "Terri annoyed me. You get to pay the price."

"Won't be the first time she's cost me. I'll have it for you tomorrow. I've got a family thing on Sunday, and I have to order the skylights, but I'd like to start moving things in right away."

"That's fine." She liked the idea of him painting over her shop, of knowing the building that was hers was fulfilling its potential. "Congratulations," she said and offered a hand. "You've got yourself a studio."

"Thanks." He took her hand, held it. Ringless, he thought again. Long, faerie fingers and unpainted nails. "Given any thought to posing for me?"

"No."

His grin flashed at her flat, precise answer. "I'll talk you into it."

"I'm not easily swayed. Let's clear this all up before we start on what should be a mutually satisfying business relationship."

"Okay, let's. You have a strong, beautiful face. As an artist, as a man, I'm drawn to the qualities of strength and beauty. The artist wants to translate them. The man wants to enjoy them. So, I'd like to paint you, and I'd like to spend time with you."

Despite the breeze that danced through the open door, she felt entirely too alone with him. Alone, and boxed in by the way he held her hand, held her gaze.

"I'm sure you've had your quota of women to translate and enjoy. Such as the buxom blonde in black you were cozied up with at the bar."

"Who . . . ?"

Humor exploded on his face. It was, Dru thought, like light bursting through shadows.

"Buxom Blonde in Black," he repeated, seeing it as a title. "Jesus, she'll *love* that. There'll be no living with her. That was Aubrey. Aubrey Quinn. My brother Ethan's oldest daughter."

"I see." And it made her feel like an idiot. "It didn't seem to be a particularly avuncular relationship."

"I don't feel like her uncle. It's more a big-brother thing. She was two when I came to Saint Chris. We fell for each other. Aubrey's the first person I ever loved, absolutely. She's got strength and beauty, too, and I've certainly translated and enjoyed them. But not in quite the same way I'd like to do with yours."

"Then you're going to be disappointed. Even if I were interested, I don't have the time to pose, and I don't have the inclination to be enjoyed. You're very attractive, Seth, and if I were going to be shallow—"

"Yeah." Another brilliant, flashing grin. "Let's be shallow."

"Sorry." But he'd teased a smile out of her again. "I gave it up. If I were going to be, *I* might enjoy *you*. But as it stands, we're going to settle for the practical."

"We can start there. Now, since you asked me a question earlier, I get to ask you one."

"All right, what?"

He saw by the way her face turned closed-in and wary that she was braced for something personal she wouldn't care to answer. So he shifted gears. "Do you like steamed crabs?"

She stared at him for nearly ten seconds and gave him the pleasure of watching her face relax. "Yes, I like steamed crabs."

"Good. We'll have some on our first date. I'll be by in the morning to sign the lease," he added as he walked to the open door.

"The morning's fine."

He looked down as she leaned over to lock the door behind them. Her neck was long, elegant. The contrast between it and the severe cut of the dark hair was sharp and dramatic. Without thinking, he skimmed a finger along the curve, just to sample the texture.

She froze, so that for one instant they made a portrait of themselves. The woman in the rich-colored suit, slightly bent toward a closed door, and the man in rough clothes with a fingertip at the nape of her neck.

She straightened with a quick jerk of movement, and Seth let his hand drop away. "Sorry, irritating habit of mine."

"Do you have many?"

"Yeah, afraid so. That one wasn't anything personal. You've got a really nice line back there." He stuck his hands in his pockets so it wouldn't become personal. Not yet.

"I'm an expert on lines, nice or otherwise." She breezed by him and down the steps.

"Hey." He jogged after her. "I've got better lines than that one."

"I'll just bet you do."

"I'll try some out on you. But in the meantime . . ." He opened her car door. "Is there any storage space?"

"Utility room. There." She gestured toward a door under the steps. "Furnace and water heater, that sort of thing. And some storage."

"If I need to, can I stick some stuff in there until I get the space worked out? I've got some things coming in from Rome. They'll probably be here Monday."

"I don't have a problem with that. The key's inside the shop. Remind me to give it to you tomorrow."

"Appreciate it." He closed the door for her when she'd climbed in, then he knocked on the window. "You know," he said when she rolled down the window, "I like spending time with a smart, self-confident woman who knows what she wants and goes out and gets it. Like you got this place. Very sexy, that kind of direction and dedication."

He waited a beat. "That was a line."

She kept her eyes on his as she rolled the glass up between their faces again.

And she didn't let herself chuckle until she'd driven away.

⟳

The best thing about Sundays, in Dru's opinion, was waking up slowly, then clinging to that half-dream state while the sunlight shivered through the trees, slid through the windows and danced on her closed lids.

Sundays were knowing absolutely nothing had to be done, and countless things could be.

She'd make coffee and toast a bagel in her own kitchen, then have her breakfast in the little dining room while she leafed through catalogues for business.

She'd putter around the garden she'd planted—with her own hands, thank you—while listening to music.

There was no charity luncheon, no community drive, no obligatory family dinner or tennis match at the club cluttering up her Sundays now.

There was no marital spat between her parents to referee, and no hurt feelings and sorrowful looks because each felt she'd taken the side of the other.

All there was, was Sunday and her lazy enjoyment of it.

In all the months she'd lived here, she'd never once taken that for granted. Nor had she lost a drop of the flood of pleasure it gave her to stand and look out her own windows.

She did so now, opening the window to the cool morning. From there she could admire her own private curve of the river. There were no houses to get in the way and make her think of people when she only wanted to be.

There was the speckled leaves of the liverwort she'd planted under the shade of oaks, its buds a cheery pink. And lily of the valley, with its bells already dancing. And there, the marsh grass and rushes with the little clearing she'd made for the golden-yellow iris that liked their feet wet.

She could hear the birds, the breeze, the occasional plop of a fish or a frog.

Forgetting breakfast, she wandered through the house to the front door so she could stand on the veranda and just look. She wore the boxers and tank she'd slept in, and there was no one to comment on the senator's granddaughter's dishabille. No reporter or photographer looking for a squib for the society page.

There was only lovely, lovely peace.

She picked up her watering can and carried it inside to fill while she started the coffee.

Seth Quinn had been right about one thing, she thought. She was a woman who knew what she wanted and went out and got it. Perhaps it had taken her some time to realize what that thing was, but when she had, she'd done what needed to be done.

She'd wanted to run a business where she could feel creative and happy. And she'd been determined to be successful, in her own right. She'd toyed with the idea of a small nursery or gardening service.

But she wasn't fully confident in her skills there. Her gardening ventures had been largely confined to her little courtyard in Georgetown, and potted plants. And while she'd been very proud of her efforts there and delighted with the results, it hardly qualified her as an expert.

But she knew flowers.

She'd wanted a small town, where the pace was easy and the demands few. And she'd wanted the water. She'd always been pulled to the water.

She loved the look of St. Christopher, the cheerful tidiness of it, and the ever changing tones and moods of the Bay. She liked listening to the clang from the channel markers, and the throaty call of a foghorn when the mists rolled in.

She'd grown accustomed to and nearly comfortable with the casual friendliness of the locals. And the good-heartedness that had sent Ethan Quinn over to check on her during a storm the previous winter.

No, she'd never live in the city again.

Her parents would have to continue to adjust to the distance she'd put between them. Geographically and emotionally. In the end, she was certain it was best for everyone involved.

And just now, however selfish it might be, she was more concerned with what was best for Drusilla.

She turned off the tap and, after sampling the coffee, carried it and the watering can outside to tend to her pots.

Eventually, she thought, she would add a greenhouse so that she could experiment with growing her own flowers to sell. But she'd have to be convinced she could add the structure without spoiling the fanciful lines of her home.

She loved its peaks and foolishly ornate gingerbread trim. Most would consider it a kind of folly, with its fancywork and deep blue color out here among the thickets and marsh. But to her it was a statement.

Home could be exactly where you needed, exactly what you needed it to be, if you wanted it enough.

She set her coffee down on a table and drenched a jardiniere bursting with verbena and heliotrope.

At a rustle, she looked over. And watched a heron rise like a king over the high grass, over the brown water.

"I'm happy," she said out loud. "I'm happier than I've ever been in my life."

She decided to forgo the bagel and catalogues and changed into gardening clothes instead.

For an hour she worked on the sunny side of the house where she was determined to establish a combination of shrubbery and flower bed. The bloodred blooms of the rhododendrons she'd planted the week before would be a strong contrast to the blue of the house once they burst free. She'd spent every evening for a month over the winter planning her flowers. She wanted to keep it simple and a little wild, like a mad cottage garden with columbine and delphiniums and sweet-faced wallflowers all tumbled together.

There were all kinds of art, she thought smugly as she planted fragrant stock. She imagined Seth would approve of her choices of tone and texture here.

Not that it mattered, of course. The garden was to please herself. But it was satisfying to think an artist might find her efforts creative.

He certainly hadn't had much to say for himself the day before, she remembered. He'd whipped in just after she opened the doors, handed over the agreed amount, looped his signature on the lease, snatched up the keys, then bolted.

No flirtation, no persuasive smile.

Which was all for the best, she reminded herself. She didn't want flirtations and persuasions right at the moment.

Still, it would have been nice, on some level, to imagine holding the option for them in reserve.

He'd probably had a Saturday-morning date with one of the women who'd pined for him while he'd been gone. He looked like the type women might pine for. All that scruffy hair, the lanky build.

And the hands. How could you not notice his hands—wide of palm, long of finger. With a rough elegance to them that made a woman—some women, she corrected—fantasize about being stroked by them.

Dru sat back on her heels with a sigh because she knew she'd given just that scenario more than one passing thought. Only because it's the first man you've been attracted to in . . . God, who knew how long?

She hadn't so much as had a date in nearly a year.

Her choice, she reminded herself. And she wasn't going to change her mind and end up with Seth Quinn and steamed crabs.

She would just go on as she was, making her home, running her business while he went about his and painted over her head every day.

She'd get used to him being up there, then she'd stop noticing he was up there. When the lease was up, they'd see if . . .

"Damn it. The key to the utility room."

She'd forgotten to give it to him. Well, he'd forgotten to remind her to give it to him.

Not my problem, she thought and yanked at a stray weed. He's the one who wanted to use the storage, and if he hadn't been in such a hurry to go, she would've remembered to give him the key.

She planted cranesbill, added some larkspur. Then, cursing, pushed to her feet.

It would nag at her all day. She'd obsess, she admitted as she stalked around the house. She'd worry and wonder about whatever it was he had coming in from Rome the next day. Easier by far to take the duplicate she had here at home, drive over to Anna Quinn's and drop it off.

It wouldn't take more than twenty minutes, and she could go by the nursery while she was out.

She left her gardening gloves and tools in a basket on the veranda.

Seth grabbed the line Ethan tossed him and secured the wooden boat to the dock. The kids leaped out first. Emily with her long dancer's body and sunflower hair, and Deke, gangly as a puppy at fourteen.

Seth caught Deke in a headlock and looked at Emily. "You weren't supposed to grow up while I was gone."

"Couldn't help it." She laid her cheek on his, rubbed it there. "Welcome home."

"When do we eat?" Deke wanted to know.

"Guy's got a tapeworm." Aubrey leaped nimbly onto the dock. "He ate damn near half a loaf of French bread five minutes ago."

"I'm a growing boy," he said with a chuckle. "I'm going to charm Anna out of something."

"He actually thinks he's charming," Emily said with a shake of her head. "It's a mystery."

The Chesapeake Bay retriever Ethan called Nigel landed in the water with a happy splash, then bounded up onshore to run after Deke.

"Give me a hand with this, Em, since the jerk's off and running." Aubrey grabbed one end of the cooler Ethan had set on the dock. "Mom may water up," she said to Seth under her breath. "She's really anxious to see you."

Seth stepped to the boat, held out his hand and closed it around Grace's. If Aubrey had been the first person he'd loved, Grace had been the first woman he'd both loved *and* trusted.

Her arms slid around him as she stepped on the dock, and her cheek rubbed his with that same female sweetness as Emily's had. "There now," she said quietly, on a laughing sigh. "There now, that feels just exactly right. Now everything's where it belongs."

She leaned back, smiled up at him. "Thank you for the tulips. They're beautiful. I'm sorry I wasn't home."

"So was I. I figured I'd trade them for some of your homemade fries. You still make the best."

"Come to dinner tomorrow. I'll fix some for you."

"With sloppy joes?"

She laughed again, reached back with one hand to take Ethan's. "Well, that hasn't changed, has it? With sloppy joes. Deke will be thrilled."

"And chocolate cake?"

"Guy expects a lot for a bunch of flowers," Ethan commented.

"At least I didn't swipe them from Anna's garden, then try to blame it on innocent deer and bunny rabbits."

Ethan winced, sent a wary look toward the house to make certain Anna wasn't within hearing distance. "Let's not bring that up again. Damn near twenty years ago, and she'd still scalp me for it."

"I heard you got them from the very pretty florist on Market Street." Grace tucked her arm around Seth's waist as they walked toward the house. "And that you've rented the place above the shop for a studio."

"Word travels."

"Fast and wide," Grace agreed. "Why don't you tell me all about it?"

"Nothing to tell, yet. But I'm working on it."

⟨⟨⟩⟩

She was running behind now, and it was her own fault. There was no reason, no *sane* reason she'd felt compelled to shower, to change out of her grubby gardening clothes. Certainly no reason, she thought, irritated with herself, to have spent time on her precious Sunday fussing with makeup.

Now it was past noon.

Didn't matter, she told herself. It was a lovely day for a drive. She'd spend two minutes on Seth Quinn and the key, then indulge herself at the nursery.

Of course now she'd have to change *back* into her gardening clothes, but that was neither here nor there. She'd plant, then make fresh lemonade and sit and bask in the glow of a job well done.

Feel the air! Brisk with spring, moist from the water. The fields on either side of the road were tilled and planted, and already running green in the rows. She could smell the sharp edge of fertilizer, the richer tones of earth that meant spring in the country.

She made the turn, caught the glint of the sun off the mudflats before the trees took over with their deep shadows.

The old white house was perfect for its setting. Edged by woods, with water hemming its back, and the tidy, flower-decked lawn skirting its front.

She'd admired it before, the way it sat there, so cozy and comfortable with its front porch rockers and faded blue shutters.

While she felt the whimsy and the privacy of her own home suited her perfectly, she could admire the character of the Quinn place. It gave a sense of order without regimentation. The kind of home, she reflected, where feet were allowed to prop on coffee tables.

No one would have dreamed to rest a heel on her mother's Louis XIV. Not even her father.

The number of cars in the drive made her frown. A white Corvette—vintage, she assumed—a sturdy SUV of some sort that appeared to have some hard miles on it. A snappy little convertible, a dented, disreputable-looking hatchback that had to be twenty years old, a manly pickup truck and a sleek and muscular Jaguar.

She hesitated, then mentally assigned the vehicles. The SUV was the family car. The 'Vette was undoubtedly former race-car driver Cameron Quinn's—as would be the truck as work vehicle, giving Anna the convertible and the old hand-me-down to the oldest boy, who must be old enough to drive.

The Jag was Seth's. She'd noticed it, with some admiration, the night before. And if she hadn't, she'd heard all about his recent acquisition from chatting customers in her shop.

She nosed up behind it.

Two minutes, she reminded herself, and grabbed her purse as she turned off the engine.

Instantly, she heard the blast of music. The teenagers, she figured as she started toward the front door, her steps unconsciously timed to the beat of Matchbox 20.

She admired the pots and tubs of flowers on the porch. Anna, she knew, had a clever hand for mixing flowers. She knocked briskly, then bumped it up to a pound before she sighed.

No one was going to hear her over the music, even if she used a battering ram.

Resigned, she stepped off the porch and started toward the side of the house. She heard more than music now. There were shouts, squeals and what she could only describe as maniacal laughter.

The kids must be having a party. She'd just go back, pass off the key to one of Anna's boys and be on her way.

The dog came first, a cannonball of black fur with a lolling tongue. He had a bark like a machine gun, and though she was very fond of dogs, Dru stopped on a dime.

"Hi there. Ah, nice dog."

He seemed to take that as an invitation to race two wild circles around her, then press his nose to her crotch.

"Okay." She put a firm hand under his jaw, lifted it. "That's just a little too friendly." She gave him a quick rub, then a nudge, and managed one more step before the boy streaked screaming around the side of the house. Though he held a large plastic weapon in his hand, he was in full retreat.

He managed to veer around her. "Better run," he puffed out, an instant before she saw a flash of movement out of the corner of her eye.

An instant before she was shot dead in the heart, by a stream of cold water.

The shock was so great that her mouth dropped open but she couldn't manage a sound. Just behind her the boy murmured, "Uh-oh."

And deserted the field.

Seth, the water rifle in his hand, his hair dripping from the previous attack, took one look at Dru. "Oh, shit."

Helpless, Dru looked down. Her crisp red shirt and navy pants were soaked. The splatter had managed to reach her face, making the time she'd spent fiddling with it a complete waste.

She lifted her gaze, one that turned from stunned to searing when she noted that Seth looked very much like a man struggling not to laugh.

"Are you *crazy*?"

"Sorry. Really." He swallowed hard, knowing the laugh fighting to burst out of his throat would damn him. "Sorry," he managed as he walked to her. "I was after Jake—little bastard nailed me. You got caught in the cross fire." He tried a charming smile, dug a bandanna out of the back pocket of his jeans. "Which proves there are no innocent bystanders in war."

"Which proves," she said between her teeth, "that some men are idiots who can't be trusted with a child's toy."

"Hey, hey, this is a Super Soaker 5000." He lifted the water gun but, catching the gleam in her eyes, hastily lowered it again. "Anyway, I'm really sorry. How about a beer?"

"You can take your beer and your Super Soaker 5000 and—"

"Seth!" Anna rushed around the house, then let out a huge sigh. "You moron."

"Jake," he said under his breath and vowed revenge. "Anna, we were just—"

"Quiet." She jabbed a finger at him, then draped an arm around Dru's shoulder. "I apologize for the idiot children. You poor thing. We'll get you inside and into some dry clothes."

"No, really, I'll just—"

"I insist," Anna interrupted, herding her toward the front of the house. "What a greeting. I'd say things aren't usually so crazy around here, but I'd be lying."

Keeping a firm hand on Dru—Anna knew when someone was poised for escape—she guided her into the house and up the stairs.

"It's a little crazier today as the whole gang's here. A welcome-home for Seth. The guys are about to boil up some crabs. You'll stay."

"I couldn't intrude." Her temper was rapidly sliding toward embarrassment. "I just stopped by to drop off the utility-room key for Seth. I really should—"

"Have some dry clothes, some food, some wine," Anna said warmly. "Kevin's jeans ought to work." She pulled a blue cotton shirt out of her own closet. "I'll just see if I can find a pair in the black hole of his room."

"It's just a little water. You should be down with your family. I should go."

"Honey, you're soaked and you're shivering. Now get out of those wet things. We'll toss them in the dryer while we eat. I'll just be a minute."

With this, she strode out and left Dru alone in the bedroom.

The woman hadn't seemed so . . . formidable, Dru decided, on her visits to the flower shop. She wondered if anyone ever won an argument with her.

But the truth was, she was chilled. Giving up, she stripped off the wet shirt, gave a little sigh and took off the equally wet bra. She was just buttoning up when Anna came back in.

"Success." She offered Dru a pair of Levi's. "Shirt okay?"

"Yes, it's fine. Thank you."

"Just bring your wet things down to the kitchen when you're ready." She started out again, then turned back. "And, Dru? Welcome to bedlam."

Close enough, Dru thought. She could hear the shouts and laughter, the blast of music through the open window. It seemed to her half of St. Christopher must be partying in the Quinns' backyard.

But when she snuck a peek out, she realized the noise was generated by the Quinns all by themselves. There were teenagers of varying sizes and sexes running around, and two, no three dogs. Make that four, she noted as an enormous retriever bounded out of the water and raced over the lawn to shake drops on as many people as possible.

The young boy Seth had been chasing was doing precisely the same thing. Obviously, Seth had managed to catch up with him.

Boats were tied to the dock—which explained, she supposed, why the number of cars in the drive didn't match the number of picnickers.

The Quinns sailed.

They were also loud, wet and messy. The scene below was nothing like any of her parents' outdoor social events or family gatherings. The music would have been classical, and muted. The conversations would have been calm and ordered. And the tables would have been meticulously set with some sort of clever theme.

Her mother was brilliant with themes, and dictated her precise wishes to the caterer, who knew how to deliver.

She wasn't certain she knew how to socialize, even briefly, in the middle of this sort of chaos. But she could hardly do otherwise without being rude.

She changed into the Levi's. The boy—Kevin, she thought Anna had said—was tall. She had to roll up the legs a couple of times into frayed cuffs.

She glanced in the pretty wood-framed mirror over the bureau and, sighing, took a tissue to deal with the mascara smudges under her eyes caused by her unexpected shower.

She gathered the rest of her wet things and started downstairs.

There was a piano in the living room. It looked ancient and well used. The red lilies she'd sold Seth stood in a cut-crystal vase atop it, and spilled their fragrance into the air.

The sofa appeared new, the rug old. It was, Dru thought, very much a family room, with cheerful colors, cozy cushions, a few stray dog hairs and the female touches of the flowers and candles. Snapshots were scattered here and there, all in different frames. There had been no attempt at coordination, and that was the charm of it, she decided.

There were paintings—waterscapes, cityscapes, still lifes—that she was certain were Seth's. But it was a lovely little pencil sketch that drew her over.

It was the rambling white house, flanked by woods, trimmed by water. It said, with absolute simplicity: This is home. And it touched a chord in her that made her yearn.

Stepping closer, she studied the careful signature in the bottom corner. Such a careful signature, she recognized it as a child's even before she read the date printed beneath.

He'd drawn it when he was a child, she realized. Just a little boy making a picture of his home—and already recognizing its value, already talented and insightful enough to translate that value, that warmth and stability with his pencil.

Helplessly, her heart softened toward him. He might be an idiot with an oversized water pistol, but he was a good man. If art reflected the artist, he was a very special man.

She followed the sound of voices back into the kitchen. This, she recognized immediately, was another family center, one captained by a female who took cooking seriously. The long counters were a pristine white making a bright, happy contrast to the candy-apple-red trim. They were covered with platters and bowls of food.

Seth stood with his arm around Anna's shoulders. Their heads were close together, and though she continued to unwrap a bowl, there was a unity in their stance.

Love. Dru could feel the flow of it from across the room, the simple, strong, steady flow of it. The din might have continued from outside, people might have winged in and out the back door, but the two of them made a little island of affection.

She'd always been attracted to that kind of connection, and found herself smiling at them before the woman—that would be Grace—backed out of the enormous refrigerator with yet another platter in hand.

"Oh, Dru. Here, let me take those."

Grace set the bowl aside; Anna and Seth turned. And Dru's smile dimmed into politeness.

Her heart might have softened toward the artist, but she wasn't about to let the idiot off the hook too easily.

"Thanks. They're only damp really. The shirt got the worst of it."

"I got the worst of it." Seth tipped his head toward Anna before he stepped forward. "Sorry. Really. I don't know how I mistook you for a thirteen-year-old boy."

The stare she aimed at him could have frozen a pond at ten paces. "Why don't we just say I was in the wrong place at the wrong time and leave it at that."

"No, this is the right place." He took her hand, lifted it to his lips in what she imagined he thought of as a charming gesture. And damn it, it was. "And it's always the right time."

"Gack," was Jake's opinion as he swung through the back door. "Crabs are going in," he told Seth. "Dad says for you to get your ass out there."

"Jake!"

Jake sent his mother an innocent look. "I'm just the messenger. We're *starving*."

"Here." Anna stuffed a deviled egg in his mouth. "Now carry this outside. Then come back, without slamming the door, and apologize to Dru."

Jake made mumbling noises around the egg and carried the platter outside.

"It really wasn't his fault," Dru began.

"If this wasn't, something else was. Something always is. Can I get you some wine?"

"Yes, thanks." Obviously, she wasn't going to be able to escape. And the fact was, she was curious about the family that lived in a young artist's pencil sketch. "Ah, is there something I can do to help?"

"Grab whatever, take it out. We'll be feeding the masses shortly."

Anna lifted her eyebrows as Seth grabbed a platter, then pushed the door open for Dru and her bowl of coleslaw. Then Anna wiggled those eyebrows at Grace. "They look cute together."

"They do," Grace agreed. "I like her." She wandered to the door to spy out with Anna. "She's always a little cool at first, then she warms up—or relaxes, I guess. She's awfully pretty, isn't she? And so . . . polished."

"Money usually puts a gleam on you. She's a bit stiff yet, but if this group can't loosen her up, nothing can. Seth's very attracted."

"So I noticed." Grace turned her head toward Anna. "I guess we'd better find out more about her."

"My thoughts exactly." She went back to fetch the wine.

⬀

The Quinn brothers were impressive examples of the species individually. As a group, Dru decided, they were staggering. They might not have shared blood, but they were so obviously fraternal—tall, lanky, handsome and most of all male.

The quartet around the huge steaming pot simply exuded manhood like other men might a distinctive aftershave. She didn't doubt for a moment that they knew it.

They were what they were, she thought, and were pretty damned pleased about it.

As a woman she found that sort of innate self-satisfaction attractive. She respected confidence and a good, healthy ego. When she wandered around to the brick pit where they steamed the crabs to deliver, at Anna's request, a foursome of cold beer, she caught the end of a conversation.

"Asshole thinks he's Horatio fucking Hornblower." From Cam.

"More like Captain fucking Queed." Muttered by Ethan.

"He can be anybody he wants, as long as his money's green." Delivered with a shrug by Phillip. "We've built boats for assholes before, and will again."

"One fuckhead's the same as—" Seth broke off when he spotted Dru.

"Gentlemen." She never batted an eyelash. "Cold beer for hot work."

"Thanks." Phillip took them from her. "Heard you've already cooled off once today."

"Unexpectedly." Relieved of the bottles, she lifted her wineglass to her lips, sipped. "But I prefer this method to the Super Soaker 5000." Ignoring

Seth, she looked at Ethan. "Did you catch them?" she asked, gesturing to the pot.

"Deke and I, yeah." He grinned when Seth cleared his throat. "We took him along for ballast," he told Dru. "Got blisters on his city hands."

"Couple days in the boatyard might toughen him up," Cam speculated. "Always was puny though."

"You're just trying to insult me so I'll come in and do the hot fifty-fifty work." Seth tipped back his beer. "Keep dreaming."

"Puny," Phillip said, "but smart. Always was smart."

"I wonder if I could come in sometime, take a look around at your work." Cam tilted his head toward Dru. "Like boats, do you?"

"Yes, I do."

"Why don't we go for a sail?" Seth asked her.

She spared him a glance that was on the edge of withering. "Keep dreaming," she suggested and strolled away.

"Classy," was Phillip's opinion.

"She's a nice girl," Ethan said as he checked the pot.

"Hot," Cam commented. "Very, very hot."

"You want to cool off, I'll be happy to stick the Super Soaker 5000 up your ass," Seth told him.

"Got a bead on her?" Cam shook his head as if in pity. "She looks out of your league to me, kid."

"Yeah." Seth gulped more beer. "I'm a big fan of interleague play."

Phillip watched Seth wander off, then chuckled. "Our boy's going to be spending a hell of a lot of money on flowers for the next little while."

"That particular bloom's got some long stems on her," Cam remarked.

"Got careful eyes." Ethan gave the traditional Quinn shoulder jerk when Cam frowned at him. "Watches everything, including Seth, but it's all one step back, you know. Not because she's shy—the girl isn't shy. She's careful."

"She comes from big money and politics." Phillip considered his beer. "Bound to make you careful."

"Saint Chris is a funny place for her to end up, isn't it?" To Cam's mind, family forged you—the family you were born to or the family you made. He wondered how Dru's had forged her.

⚭

She'd intended to stay no more than an hour. A polite hour while her clothes dried. But somehow she was drawn into a conversation with Emily about New York. And one with Anna about gardening. Then there were the mutual acquaintances with Sybill and Phillip from D.C.

The food was wonderful. When she complimented the potato salad, Grace offered her the recipe. Dru wasn't quite sure how to announce that she didn't cook.

There were arguments—over baseball, clothes, video games. It didn't take her long to realize it was just another kind of interaction.

Dogs sidled up to the table and were ordered firmly away—usually after someone snuck food into a canine mouth. The breeze blew in cool over the water while as many as six conversations went on at the same time.

She kept up. Early training had honed her ability to have something to say to everyone and anyone in social situations. She could comment about boats and baseball, food and music, art and travel even when the talk of them and more leaped and swirled around her.

She nursed a second glass of wine and stayed far longer than she'd intended. Not just because she couldn't find a polite way to leave. Because she liked them. She was amused by and envious of the intimacy of the family. Despite their numbers and the obvious differences—could sisters be less alike than the sharp-tongued, sports-loving Aubrey and Emily, the waiflike ballerina?—they were all so firmly interlinked.

Like individual pieces of one big, bold puzzle, Dru decided. The puzzle of family always fascinated her. Certainly her own continued to remain a mystery to her.

However colorful and cheerful they seemed on the surface, Dru imagined the Quinn puzzle had its share of shadows and complications.

Families always did.

As did men, she thought, turning her head deliberately to meet Seth's dead-on stare. She was perfectly aware that he'd watched her almost continuously since they'd sat down to eat. Oh, he was good at the conversation juggling, too; she'd give him that. And from time to time he'd tune his attention fully on someone else. But his gaze, that straight-on and vivid blue gaze, would always swing back to her.

She could feel it, a kind of heat along her skin.

She refused to let it intrigue her. And she certainly wasn't going to let it fluster her.

"The afternoon light's good here." His eyes still on Dru, he scooped up a forkful of pasta salad. "Maybe we'll do some outdoor work. You got anything with a long, full skirt? Strapless or sleeveless to show off your shoulders. Good strong shoulders," he added with another scoop of pasta. "They go with the face."

"That's lucky for me, isn't it?" She dismissed him with a slight wave of her hand and turned to Sybill. "I enjoyed your last documentary very much, the studies and examples of blended family dynamics. I suppose you based some of your findings on your own experiences."

"Hard to get away from it. I could study this bunch for the next couple of decades and never run out of material."

"We're all Mom's guinea pigs," Fiona stated as she handily picked out another crab. "Better watch out. You hang out around here, Seth'll have you naked on a canvas and Mom'll have you analyzed in a book."

"Oh, I don't know." Aubrey gestured with her drink. "Annie Crawford hung around here for months, and Seth never did paint her—naked or otherwise. I don't think Sybill ever wrote about her either, unless I missed the one about societal placement of brainless bimbos."

"She wasn't brainless," Seth put in.

"She called you Sethie. As in, 'Oh, Sethie, you're a regular Michael Dee Angelo.'"

"Want me to start trotting out some of the guys you hung with a few years back? Matt Fisher, for instance?"

"I was young and shallow."

"Yeah, you're old and deep now. Anyway"—he shifted that direct gaze to Dru again—"you got a long, flowy thing? Little top?"

"No."

"We'll get something."

Dru sipped the last of her wine, tilted her head slightly to indicate interest. "Has anyone ever declined to be painted by you?"

"No, not really."

"Let me be the first."

"He'll do it anyway," Cam told her. "Kid's got a head like a brick."

"And that comes from the most flexible, most reasonable, most accommodating of men," Anna declared as she rose. "Anybody got room for dessert?"

They did, though Dru didn't see how. She declined offers of cakes, pies, but lost the battle of wills over a double fudge brownie that she nibbled on before changing back into her own clothes.

She folded the borrowed shirt and jeans, set them on the bed, took one last look around the cozy bedroom, then started down.

Dru stopped short in the kitchen doorway when she spotted Anna and Cam in front of the sink in an embrace a great deal more torrid than she expected from parents of teenagers.

"Let's go upstairs and lock the door," Dru heard him say—and wasn't sure where to look when she noted Cam's hands slide around possessively to squeeze his wife's butt. "No one will miss us."

"That's what you said after dinner last Thanksgiving." There was both warmth and fun in her voice when Anna linked her arms around Cam's neck. "You were wrong."

"Phil was just jealous because he didn't think of it first."

"Later, Quinn. If you behave, I might just let you . . . Oh, Dru."

From the easy grins on their faces, Dru concluded she was the only one of the trio who was the least bit embarrassed. "I'm sorry. I wanted to thank you for the hospitality. I really enjoyed the afternoon."

"Good. Then you'll come again. Cam, let Seth know Dru's leaving, will you?" And damned if she didn't give his butt a squeeze before easing out of his arms.

"Don't bother. You have a wonderful family, a beautiful home. I appreciate your letting me share them today."

"I'm glad you dropped by," Anna said, giving Cam a silent signal as she laid an arm over Dru's shoulder to walk her to the front door.

"The key." Shaking her head, Dru dug into her purse. "I completely forgot the reason I came by in the first place. Would you give this to Seth? He can store whatever he needs to in there for the time being. We'll work out the details later."

Anna heard the kitchen door slam. "You might as well give it to him yourself. Come back," she said, then gave Dru a quick, casual kiss on the cheek.

"Taking off?" A little winded, Seth hurried up to catch Dru on the front porch. "Why don't you stay? Aubrey's getting a softball game together."

"I have to get home. The key." She held it out while he only stood looking at her. "Utility room? Storage?"

"Yeah, yeah." He took it, stuffed it in his pocket. "Listen, it's early, but if you want to split, we can go somewhere. A drive or something."

"I have things to do." She walked toward her car.

"We'll have to try for less of a crowd on our second date."

She paused, looked back at him over her shoulder. "We haven't had a first date yet."

"Sure we did. Steamed crabs, just as predicted. You get to pick the menu and venue for date number two."

Jiggling the car keys in her hand, she turned to face him. "I came by to give you the key, got blasted with a water gun and had a crab feast with your large, extended family. That doesn't make this a date."

"This will."

He had a smooth move—so smooth she never saw it coming. Maybe if she had, she'd have evaded. Or maybe not. But that wasn't the issue as his hands were cupped on her shoulders and his mouth was warm and firm on hers.

He lifted her, just slightly. He tilted his head, just a little. So his lips rubbed hers—a seductive tease—and his hands cruised down her body to add an unexpected punch of heat.

She felt the breeze flutter against her cheeks, and heard the blast of music as someone turned the stereo up to scream again. And when the hard line of him pressed against her, she realized she'd been the one to move in.

The long, liquid tugs deep in her belly warned her, but still she shot her fingers through that thick, sun-streaked hair and let his hands roam.

He'd meant to *suggest* with a kiss, to tease a smile or a frown out of her so he could have the pleasure of watching either expression move over her face.

He'd only intended to skim the surface, perhaps to show them both hints of what could lie beneath. But when she'd leaned into him, locked around him, he sank.

Women were a dazzling array of colors for him. Mother, sister, lover, friend. But he'd never had another woman strike him with such brilliance. He wanted to steep in it, in her until they were both drenched.

"Let me come home with you, Drusilla." He skimmed his lips over her cheek, down to her throat, back up and along the finger-brush indentation in her chin, and to her mouth. "Let me lie down with you. Be with you. Let me touch you."

She shook her head. She didn't like speed, she reminded herself. A smart woman never turned a corner until she'd looked at the map for the entire route—and even then, she went forward only with caution.

"I'm not impulsive, Seth. I'm not rash." She put her hands on his shoulders to nudge him away, but her gaze was direct. "I don't share myself with a man just because there's heat."

"Okay." He pressed his lips to her forehead before he stepped back. "Stay. We'll play some ball, maybe go for a sail. We'll keep it simple today."

With some men, the suggestion would have been just another ploy to persuade her into bed. But she didn't sense that with him. He meant what he said, she decided. "I might actually like you after a while."

"Counting on it."

"But I can't stay. I left a number of things undone to come by, and I've stayed much longer than I intended."

"Didn't you ever ditch school?"

"No."

He braced a hand on the car door before she could open it, and his face was sincerely shocked. "Not once?"

"Afraid not."

"A rule player," he considered. "Sexy."

She had to laugh. "If I said I'd skipped school once a week, you'd have called me a rebel and said *that* was sexy."

"Got me. How about dinner tomorrow night?"

"No." She waved him away from the car door. "I need to think about this. I don't want to be interested in you."

"Which means you are."

She slid behind the wheel. "Which means I don't want to be. I'll let you know if I change my mind. Go back to your family. You're lucky to have them," she said, then closed the car door.

He watched her back out, then drive away. His blood was still warm from the kiss, and his mind too full of her and the possibilities for him to take notice of the car that eased from the shoulder of the road by the trees, then followed after Dru's.

FIVE

She knew he'd moved in. Now and again when Dru went into the back room of the shop, she could hear music through the vents. It didn't surprise her that he played it loud, or that his choices varied from head-banging rock to mellow blues and into passionate opera.

Nothing about Seth Quinn surprised her.

He came and went during the first week of his lease without any rhyme or reason she could see. Occasionally he breezed in and out of the shop, to ask if she needed anything, to let her know he'd be starting on the skylights, to tell her he'd moved some things into the storage space and made a copy of the key.

He was always friendly, never seemed particularly rushed. And never once attempted to follow up on the steamy afternoon kiss.

It irked her, for a number of reasons. First, she'd been set to deflect any follow-up, at least for the time being. She had no intention of Seth, or any man, taking her availability for granted.

That was simply principle.

And, of course, it was expected that he *would* follow up. A man didn't ask to take you to bed one day, then treat you like a casual neighbor the next.

So perhaps he had surprised her after all. Which only irritated her more.

Just as well, she told herself as she worked on the small tabletop arrangements she sold to one of the waterfront's upscale restaurants. She was settling into St. Chris, into her business, into the kind of life she'd always wanted—without knowing she wanted it. A relationship, whether it was an affair, a romance or just no-strings sex, would change the balance.

And she was so enjoying the balance.

The only person who needed anything from her, demanded anything from her, expected anything from her these days was herself. That, in itself, was like a gift from God.

Pleased with the combination of narcissus and sprekelia, she loaded the arrangements into refrigeration. Her part-time delivery man would pick them up, along with the iris and tulips and showy white lilies ordered by a couple of the local B and B's.

She heard Seth arrive—the sound of the car door slamming, the crunch of footsteps over gravel, then the quick slap of them up the back steps.

Moments later came the music. Rock today, she noted with a glance at the overhead vent. Which probably meant he'd be up on the roof shortly, working on the skylights.

She went back into the shop, picked up the plant she'd earmarked, then headed out the back and up the steps. A polite knock wouldn't do, not with the music blaring, so she used the side of her fist to pound.

"Yeah, yeah, it's open. Since when do you guys knock?"

He turned, in the act of strapping on a tool belt, as she opened the door. "Hey." His smile came quick and easy. "I thought you were one of my brothers, but you're a lot better-looking."

"I heard you come in." She would not be a cliché, she promised herself. She would *not* entertain ridiculous fantasies because she'd come upon a long, lanky male wearing a tool belt. "I thought you might like these."

"What? Wait." Amused at himself, he walked into the tiny kitchen where he'd set a tabletop stereo and turned down the volume. "Sorry."

His hammer bounced against his hip. He was wearing jeans that were equal parts holes and denim. His T-shirt was faded gray and splotched with paint and what was probably some sort of engine grease. He hadn't shaved.

She was not, absolutely not, attracted to rough, untidy men.

Usually.

"I brought you a plant." Her tone was sharper, more impatient than she intended. Her own words came back to haunt her. No, she didn't want to be interested in Seth Quinn.

"Yeah?" Despite her tone, he looked very pleased as he crossed over and took the pot from her. "Thanks," he said as he studied the green leaves and little white blossoms.

"It's a shamrock," she told him. "Quinn. It seemed to fit."

"Guess it does." Then those blue eyes lifted, locked on hers. "I appreciate it."

"Don't let it dry out." She glanced up. Two skylights were already installed. And he was right, she mused, they made all the difference. "You've been busy."

"Hmm. Traded some time at the boatyard for some labor here. Cam's going to give me a hand today, so we should finish up."

"Well then." She glanced around. After all, she reminded herself, she owned the place. She could take some interest in what went on there.

He had canvases stacked against two of the walls. An easel with a blank canvas was already set up in front of the windows. She wasn't sure how he'd managed to muscle the enormous worktable up the stairs and through the rather narrow door, but it was plopped in the center of the room and already covered with the detritus of the artist: brushes, paints, a mason jar of turpentine, rags, pencils, chalks.

There were a couple of stools, an old wooden chair, an even older table topped by a particularly ugly lamp.

Shelves, again wood, held more painting supplies.

He'd hung nothing on the walls, she noted. There was nothing but space, tools and light.

"You seem to be settling in. I'll let you get back to it." But one of the propped canvases drew her. It was a wash of purple over green. A riot of wild foxglove under pearly light pulled her in so that she could almost feel the brush of leaves and petals on her skin.

"A roadside in Ireland," he said. "County Clare. I spent a few weeks there once. Everywhere you look it's a painting. You can never really translate it on canvas."

"I think you have. It's wonderful. Simple and strong. I've never seen foxglove growing wild on a roadside in Ireland. But now I feel I have. Isn't that the point?"

He stared at her a moment. The morning sun speared through the skylight and streamed over her, accented the line of jaw and cheek. "Just stand there. Just stand right there," he repeated as he swung to his worktable. "Ten minutes. Okay, I lied. Twenty tops."

"Excuse me?"

"Just stand there. Damn it, where's my—ah." He scooped up a hunk of charcoal, then dragged his easel around. "No, don't look at me. Look over there. Wait."

He moved quickly, snatching up the painting of foxgloves, pulling out a nail from his pouch, then pounding it into the wall. "Just look at the painting."

"I don't have time to—"

"At the painting." This time his voice snapped, so full of authority and impatience, she obeyed before she thought it through. "I'll pay you for the time."

"I don't want your money."

"In trade." He was already stroking the charcoal over the canvas. "You've got that house by the river. You probably need things done off and on."

"I can take care of—"

"Uh-huh, uh-huh. Tilt your chin up a little, to the right. Jesus, Jesus, this light. Relax your jaw. Be pissed off later, just let me get this."

Who the hell was he? she wondered. He stood there, legs apart, body set like a man poised to fight. He had a tool belt slung at his hips and was sketching in charcoal as if his life depended on it.

His eyes were narrowed, so intense, so *focused*, that her heart jumped a little each time they whipped up and over her face.

On the stereo AC/DC was on the highway to hell. Through the open window came the cry of gulls as they swooped over the bay. Not entirely sure why she'd allowed herself to be ordered around, she stood and studied the foxgloves.

She began to see it gracing her bedroom wall.

"How much do you want for it?"

His eyebrows remained knit. "I'll let you know when I've finished it."

"No, the painting I'm staring at while I'm trying not to be annoyed with you. I'd like to buy it. You have an agent, I imagine. Should I contact him or her?"

He only grunted, not the least interested in business at the moment, and continued to work. "Don't move your head, just your eyes. And look at me. That's some face, all right."

"Yes, and I'm certainly all aflutter by your interest in it, but I have to go down and open for the day."

"Couple more minutes."

"Would you like to hear my opinion of people who can't take no for an answer?"

"Not right now." Keep her occupied, keep her talking, he thought quickly. Oh Jesus, it was perfect—the light, the face, that cool stare out of mossy green eyes. "I hear you've got old Mr. Gimball doing deliveries for you. How's that working out?"

"Perfectly fine, and as he's going to be pulling up in back very shortly—"

"He'll wait. Mr. Gimball used to teach history when I was in middle school. He seemed ancient then, as creaky as the dead presidents he lectured about. Once some of us found this big snake skin. We brought it in and curled it up on Mr. G's desk chair before third period."

"I'm sure you thought that was hysterically funny."

"Are you kidding? I was eleven. I nearly cracked a rib laughing. Didn't you ever pull stunts like that on teachers in your private school for girls?"

"No, and why do you assume I went to a private school for girls?"

"Oh, sugar, it's all over you." He stepped back, nodded at the canvas. "Yeah, and it looks good on you." He reached forward, softened a line of charcoal with his thumb before he looked over at her. "You want to call this a sitting or our second date?"

"Neither." It took every ounce of will, but she didn't cross over to look at what he'd drawn.

"Second date," he decided, as he tossed the charcoal aside, absently picked up a rag to clean it off his hands. "After all, you brought me flowers."

"A plant," she corrected.

"Semantics. You really want the painting?"

"That would depend on how much really wanting it jacks up the price."

"You're pretty cynical."

"Cynicism is underrated. Why don't you give me your representative's name? Then we'll see."

He loved the way that short, sleek hair followed the shape of her head. He wanted to do more than sketch it. He needed to paint it.

And to touch it. To run his hands over that silky, dense black until he'd know its texture in his sleep.

"Let's do a friendly trade instead. Pose for me, and it's yours."

"I believe I just did."

"No. I want you in oil." And in watercolors. In pastels.

In bed.

He'd spent a great deal of time thinking about her over the last few days. Enough time to have concluded that a woman like her—with her looks, her background—would be used to men in active pursuit.

So he'd slowed things down, deliberately, and had waited for her to take the next step. To his way of thinking, she had. In the form of a house-plant.

He wanted her personally as much as he wanted her professionally. It didn't matter which came first, as long as he got both.

She shifted her gaze to the painting again. It was always a pleasure, and a bit of a shock, when he saw desire in someone's eyes when they looked at his work. Seeing it in Dru's he knew he'd scored, professionally.

"I have a business to run," she began.

"I'll work around your schedule. Give me an hour in the mornings before you open when you can manage it. Four hours on Sundays."

She frowned. It didn't seem like so very much, when he put it like that. And oh, the painting was gorgeous. "For how long?"

"I don't know yet." He felt a little ripple of irritation. "It's art, not accounting."

"Here?"

"To start, anyway."

She debated, argued with herself. Wished she'd never seen the damn painting. Then because it was a foolish woman who made any agreement without looking at all the terms, she walked to the easel, around the canvas. And studied her own face.

She'd expected something rough and, well, sketchy, as he'd taken no more than fifteen minutes to produce it. Instead, it was detailed and stunning—the angles, the shadows, the curves.

She looked very cool, she decided. A bit aloof and so very, very serious. Cynical? she thought and gave in to the smile that tugged at her mouth.

"I don't look particularly friendly," she said.

"You weren't feeling particularly friendly."

"Can't argue with that. Or with the fact that you have an amazing gift." She sighed. "I don't have a dress with a long, full skirt and a sleeveless top."

And he grinned. "We'll improvise."

"I'll give you an hour tomorrow. Seven-thirty to eight-thirty."

"Ouch. Okay." He walked over, took the painting from the wall, held it out to her.

"You're trusting."

"Trust is underrated."

When her hands were full, he took her arms. He gave her that slight lift again, brought her to her toes. And the door swung open.

"Nope," Seth muttered as Cam strode in. "They never knock."

"Hi, Dru. Kiss the girl on your own time, kid. I don't smell any coffee." Obviously at home, he went toward the kitchen, then spotted the canvas. His face lit with pure delight. "Easiest fifty I ever made. I bet Phil Seth here would talk you into posing before the week was up."

"Oh, really?"

"No offense. Rembrandt here wants to paint something, he finds a way. He'd be a fool to pass up the chance to do that," he added, and the look on his face when he studied the canvas again was so filled with pride, she softened. "He's a pain in the ass half the time, but he's no fool."

"I'm aware of the pain-in-the-ass factor. I'll reserve judgment on whether or not he's a fool until I get to know him better. Seven-thirty," she said to Seth on her way out. "That's A.M."

Cam said nothing, just laid a beat with an open hand on his heart.

"Kiss ass."

"So, are you going to paint her, or poke at her?" Cam hooted out a laugh at Seth's vicious snarl. "What goes around comes around, kid. You spent a lot of time being disgusted at the idea of us poking at girls—as you put it—not so long ago."

"Since it is more than fifteen years that's not so long ago in your mind, it proves you're really getting old. Sure you should go up on the roof? Might have a spell up there and fall off."

"I can still kick your ass, kid."

"Sure. With Ethan and Phil holding me down, you might have a shot at taking me." He laughed when Cam caught him in a headlock. "Oh man, now I'm scared."

But they both remembered a time he would have been, when a skinny, smart-mouthed young boy would have frozen with terror at a touch, rough or gentle.

Knowing it, remembering it, Seth nearly blurted out the trouble he was keeping so tightly locked in the far corner of his mind.

No, he'd handled it, he told himself. And would handle it again, if and when.

He was a man of his word. When the last of the skylights was in place, he followed Cam to the boatyard to put in a few hours.

Once, he'd thought he'd make his living here, working side by side with his brothers building wooden sailing vessels. The fact was, some of his best memories were tucked inside the old brick building, flavored with his sweat, a little blood and the thrill of learning to be a part of something.

It had changed over the years. Refined, as Phillip would say. The walls were no longer bare and patched drywall, but painted a simple, working-man's white.

They'd fashioned a sort of entryway that opened to the stairs leading to Phillip's office and the second-story loft. It separated, in theory, the main work area.

Lining the walls were rough-framed sketches of various boats built by Quinn over the years. They depicted the progress of the business, and the growth of the artist.

He knew, because Aubrey had told him, that an art collector had come in two years before and offered his brothers a quarter million for the fifty sketches currently on display.

They'd turned him down flat, but had offered to build him a boat based on any sketch he liked.

It had never been about money, he thought now, though there had been some lean times during those first couple years. It had always been about the unit. And a promise made to Ray Quinn.

The work area itself hadn't changed very much. It was still a big, echoing, brightly lit space. There were pulleys and winches hanging from the ceiling. Saws, benches, stacks of lumber, the smell of freshly sawn wood, linseed oil, sweat, coffee, the boom of rock and roll, the buzz of power saws, the lingering scent of onions from someone's lunchtime sub.

It was all as familiar to him as his own face.

Yes, once he'd thought he'd spend his life working there, listening to Phillip bitch about unpaid invoices, watching Ethan's patient hands lapping wood, sweating with Cam as they turned a hull.

But art had consumed it. The love of it had taken him away from boyhood ambitions. And had, for a time, taken him from his family.

He was a man now, he reminded himself. A man who would stand on his own ground, fight his own battles and be what it was he was meant to be.

Nothing, no one, was going to stop him.

"You plan on standing there with your thumb up your ass much longer?" Cam asked him. "Or are we going to get some work out of you this afternoon?"

Seth shook himself back to the present. "Doesn't look like you need me," he pointed out.

He spotted Aubrey working on the deck planking of a skiff, her electric screwdriver whirling. She wore an Orioles fielder's cap with her long tail of hair pulled through the back. Ethan was at the lathe, turning a mast with his faithful dog sprawled at his feet.

"Hull of that skiff needs to be caulked and filled."

Grunt work, Seth thought and sighed. "And what are you going to be doing?"

"Basking in the glory of my little empire."

The basking included detailing the bulkhead for the cockpit, the sort of carpentry Cam turned into an art.

Seth did the grunt work; it was hardly the first time. He knew how to plank, he thought, a bit resentfully as Aubrey's drill continued its bump and grind over his head.

"Hey." She bent down to talk to him. "Will's got the night off. We're going to get some pizza, catch a flick after. You want in?"

It was tempting. He wanted to connect with Will again, not only because they'd been friends, but because he wanted to check out any guy who was sniffing around Aubrey.

He weighed that against spending the evening as a fifth wheel.

"Village Pizza?"

"Still the best in Saint Chris."

"Maybe I'll swing in," Seth decided. "Say hi to Will. I'll pass on the flick. I've got to get started early tomorrow."

"I thought you artistic types called your own hours."

Seth worked oakum into a seam of beveled planking on the hull. "Subject's calling these."

"What subject?" She sat back on her heels, then suddenly understood when she noted the expression on his face. "Ooooh, fancy flower lady's going to pose for the famous artist. I got more juice on her."

"I'm not interested in gossip." He managed to hold firm on that for nearly ten seconds. "What kind of juice?"

"Juicy juice, sweetheart. I got it from Jamie Styles, who got it from her cousin who was a Senate page a few years ago. Dru and a certain high-level White House aide were a very hot item back then."

"How hot?"

"Hot enough to burn up the society columns in the *Post* for nearly a year. And to warrant what Jamie's cousin describes as an engagement ring with a diamond the size of a doorknob. Then the diamond disappears, hot goes cold, and the high-level aide starts burning up the newsprint with a blonde."

"She was engaged?"

"Yeah. Briefly, according to my source. It came out that the blonde was a factor *before* the broken engagement. If you get my drift."

"He was cheating on Dru with the bimbo?"

"It so happens that this blonde was—is—a hotshot lawyer, assistant White House counsel or something."

"Must've been tough on Dru, having all that personal business splashed around in the press."

"She strikes me as someone who'd stand up to it pretty well. She's nobody's doormat. And I bet you a month's pay she busted that cheating bastard's balls before she stuffed the ring down his throat."

"You would," Seth said with approval and pride. "Right before you mopped the floor with his lying tongue. But Dru doesn't come off as the violent type. More like she froze him to death with one chilly look and a few icy words."

Aubrey snorted. "A lot you know about women. Still waters, pal of mine. They not only run deep, you bet your ass they can run hot, too."

Maybe, Seth thought as he dropped his filthy, aching body back behind the wheel of his car. But he'd lay money Dru had sliced the guy in two without spilling a single drop of blood.

He knew what it was to have little personal details of your life—embarrassing, intimate details—nibbled on by the press.

It could be she'd come here to get away from all that. He knew just how she felt.

He glanced at the time as he pulled out. He could use that pizza Aubrey had mentioned, and it seemed a waste of effort to drive all the way home to shower off the day's work, then head right back into town.

So he'd just swing by and clean up at the studio. He'd brought over some towels and soap. He even remembered to toss a spare pair of jeans and a shirt into the closet.

He might just find Dru still at the shop and talk her into a friendly pizza. Which would, he thought, pleased with the idea, constitute date number three.

She'd get that cool, I-am-not-amused expression on her face when he called it that, he thought. And that quick light in her eyes that gave her humor away.

He was crazy about that contrast.

He could spend hours—days—contemplating the varieties of shadow and light in her.

But her car was gone from the little lot behind her building. He considered calling her, persuading her to come back into town, before he remembered he didn't have a phone.

He'd have to take care of that, he mused. But since he couldn't call from there, he'd clean up, buzz over to Village Pizza and call her from a pay phone.

Somebody was bound to have her number.

Better, he decided as he started up the steps, he'd get a pizza to go and stop by her house on the way home. With a bottle of Merlot.

What kind of woman would turn a guy away when he had pizza and wine?

Satisfied with the plan, he stepped inside, and felt something skid under his foot. Frowning, he reached down and picked up the folded note that had been slipped under his door.

His stomach pitched as the bottom fell out of his world.

Ten thousand should hold me. I'll be in touch.

Seth simply sat on the floor just inside the studio door and crumpled the paper into a tiny, mean ball.

Gloria DeLauter was back. He hadn't expected her to find or follow him so quickly. He hadn't been prepared, he admitted, to find her nipping at his heels barely two weeks after he'd left Rome.

He'd wanted time to think, to decide. He flipped the little wad of paper across the room. Well, ten thousand would buy him time, if he wanted to piss the money away.

He'd done it before.

When it came to his mother, there was no price he wouldn't pay to be free of her. And more, to keep his family free of her.

It was, of course, exactly what she counted on.

Six

He was sitting on the dock, pole fishing with a smear of Anna's Brie for bait. The sun was summer-hot on his back, with an August weight to it that drenched the skin and set the brain to dreaming.

He wore nothing but cut-off jeans and a pair of wire-rim sunglasses.

He liked looking through them at the way the light beat down from a hazy blue sky and smacked the water. And he thought, idly, that he might just set the pole aside in a bit and slide right in to cool off.

The water lapped lazily against the hull of the little pram with blue sails tied to the dock. A jay was bitching in the trees, and when a stingy little breeze passed by, it carried a hint of roses from a bush that had lived there longer than he.

The house was quiet. The lawn leading to it was lush and freshly mown. He could smell that, too. Newly cut grass, roses, lazy water. Summer smells.

It didn't strike him as odd, though it was still spring.

Something had to be done, and he wished to God he knew what, to keep that house quiet, the air summer-peaceful. And his family safe.

He heard the yip of a dog, then the scrambling of canine feet on the dock. Seth didn't look up, even when the cold nose nudged at his cheek. He simply lifted an arm so the dog could wriggle against his side.

It was always comforting, somehow, to have a dog at your side when your thoughts were heavy.

But that wasn't enough for the dog, whose tail pounded a drumbeat on the dock as its tongue slathered over Seth's cheek.

"Okay, okay, cool it. Thinking here," he began, then felt his heart jump into his throat as he shifted to nudge the dog down.

Not Cam's dog, but his own. Foolish, who'd died in Seth's arms five years before. Speechless, Seth stared as those familiar doggie eyes seemed to laugh into his at the world's best joke.

"Wait a minute, wait a minute." Joy and shock tangled inside him as he grabbed the dog's muzzle. Warm fur, cold nose, wet tongue. "What the hell is this?"

Foolish gave another cheerful bark then flopped adoringly across Seth's lap.

"There you are, you stupid idiot," Seth murmured, as unspeakable love gushed inside him. "There you are, you idiot. Christ, oh Christ, I've missed you." He bobbled the pole, let go of it as he grabbed for his dog.

A hand reached out, snagged the pole before it dropped into the water.

"Wouldn't want to waste that fancy cheese." The woman who sat beside him, legs dangling over the dock, took charge of the pole. "We figured Foolish would cheer you up. Nothing like a dog, is there? For companionship, love, comfort and pure entertainment. Nothing biting today?"

"No, not . . ."

The words slipped back down his throat as he looked at her. He knew that face; he'd seen it in pictures. Long and thin, scattershot freckles over the nose and cheeks. She had a shapeless khaki hat over messy red curls that were streaked with silver. And her dark green eyes were unmistakable.

"You're Stella. Stella Quinn." Stella Quinn, he thought as he tried to make sense of it, who'd been dead more than twenty years.

"You turned out handsome, didn't you? Always thought you would." She gave the stubby ponytail a friendly tug. "Need a haircut, boy."

"I guess I'm dreaming."

"I guess you are," she said easily, but her hand moved from his hair to his cheek and gave it a rub before she tipped down his dark glasses. "You've got Ray's eyes. I fell for his eyes first, you know."

"I always wanted to meet you." You got your wishes in dreams, Seth decided.

"Well, here we are." With a chuckle, she tapped his sunglasses back in place. "Never too late, is it? Never cared much for fishing myself. Like the water—to look at, to swim in. Still, fishing's good for thinking, or not thinking at all. If you're going to brood, might as well have a line in the water. You never know what you'll pull up."

"I never dreamed about you before. Not like this."

The fact was, he'd never dreamed with this kind of clarity. He could feel the warm fur under his hand, and the steady beat of heart as Foolish panted in the heat.

He felt the strength of the sun on his bare back, and could hear, in the distance, the putt and purr of a workboat. The jay never stopped its piercing song.

"We figured it was time I got to play Grandma." She gave Seth an affectionate pat on the knee. "I missed that while I was here. Getting to fuss and coo over the babies when they came, spoiling you and the others. Dying's damn inconvenient, let me tell you."

When he simply stared at her, she let out a long, clear laugh. "It's natural enough to be a little spooked. It's not every day you sit around talking to a ghost."

"I don't believe in ghosts."

"Hard to blame you." She looked out over the water, and something in her face spoke of absolute contentment. "I'd've baked cookies for you, though I was never much of a cook. But you can't have everything, so you take what you can get. You're Ray's grandson, so that makes you mine."

His head was reeling, but he didn't feel dizzy. His pulse was galloping, but he didn't feel fear. "He was good to me. I only had him for a little while, but he was . . ."

"Decent." She nodded as she said it. "That's what you told Cam when he asked you. Ray was decent, you said, and you sure as hell hadn't had much decent up till then, poor little guy."

"He changed everything for me."

"He gave you a chance to change everything. You've done a pretty good job of it, so far. Can't choose where you come from, Seth. My boys and you know that better than anyone. But you can choose where you end up, and how you get there."

"Ray took me in, and it killed him."

"You say something like that and mean it, you're not as smart as everyone thinks. Ray'd be disappointed to hear you say it."

"He wouldn't have been on that road if it hadn't been for me."

"How do you know that?" She poked him again. "If not that road that day, another road another day. Damn fool always drove too fast. Things happen, and that's that. They happen a different way, we'd sit around complaining about it just the same. Waste a lot of living on the ifs and ors, if you ask me."

"But—"

"But hell. George Bailey learned his lesson, didn't he?"

Baffled, fascinated, Seth shifted. "Who?"

Stella rolled her eyes toward heaven. "*It's a Wonderful Life.* Jimmy Stewart as George Bailey. Decides it would be better for everyone if he'd never been born, so an angel shows him the way things would've worked out if he hadn't."

"And you're going to show me?"

"Do I look like an angel to you?" she asked, amused.

"No. But I'm not thinking it'd be better if I'd never been born either."

"Change one thing, change everything. That's the lesson. What if Ray hadn't brought you here, if he hadn't run into that damn telephone pole?

Maybe Cam and Anna wouldn't have met. Then Kevin and Jake wouldn't have been born. You wishing them away?"

"No, Jesus, of course not. But if Gloria—"

"Ah." With a satisfied nod, Stella lifted a finger. "There's the nub, isn't it? No point in saying 'if Gloria,' or 'but Gloria.' Gloria DeLauter is reality."

"She's back."

Her face softened, her voice gentled. "Yes, honey, I know. And it weighs on you."

"I won't let her touch their lives again. I won't let her fuck up my family. She only wants money. It's all she's ever wanted."

"You think?" Stella sighed. "Well, if you do, I suppose you'll give it to her. Again."

"What else can I do?"

"You'll figure it out." She handed him the pole.

He woke sitting on the side of the bed, his hand loosely fisted as if it held a fishing pole.

And when he opened those fingers, they shook a little. When he drew one careful breath, he'd have sworn he smelled the faint drift of summer grass.

Weird, he thought and raked his fingers through his hair. Very weird dream. And he could swear he felt the lingering warmth from his dog stretched across his lap.

∽

The first ten years of his life had been a prison of fear, abuse and neglect. It had made him stronger than most ten-year-old boys. And a great deal more wary.

Ray Quinn's pre-Stella affair with a woman named Barbara Harrow had been brief. He'd put it so completely behind him that his three adopted sons had been totally unaware of it. Just as Ray had been unaware of the product of that affair.

Gloria DeLauter.

But Gloria had known about Ray, and had tracked him down. In her usual style she'd used extortion and blackmail to bleed Ray for money. And had, in essence, sold her son to her father. But Ray had died suddenly, before he found the way to tell his sons, and his grandchild, of the connection.

To the Quinn brothers, Seth had simply been another of Ray Quinn's strays. They'd been bound to him by no more than a promise to a dying man. But that had been enough.

They'd changed their lives for him. They'd given him a home, stood up for him, shown him what it was to be part of a family. And they'd fought to keep him.

Anna had been his caseworker. Grace his first surrogate mother. And Sybill, Gloria's half sister, had brought back the only soft memories of his childhood.

He knew how much they'd sacrificed to give him a life. A life as decent as Ray Quinn. By the time Gloria had stepped back into the picture, hoping to bleed them for more money, he'd been one of them.

One of the brothers Quinn.

This wasn't the first time Gloria had approached him for money. He'd had three years to forget her, to feel safe after his new family had circled around him. Then she'd slithered back to St. Chris and had extorted money from a fourteen-year-old boy.

He'd never told them of it.

A few hundred that first time, he remembered. It was all he could manage without his family finding out—and had satisfied her. For a little while.

He'd paid her off each time she'd come back, until he'd fled to Europe. His time there hadn't been only to work and to study, but to escape.

She couldn't hurt his family if he wasn't with them, and she couldn't follow him across the Atlantic.

Or so he'd thought.

His success as an artist, the resulting publicity, had given Gloria big ideas. And bigger demands.

He wondered now if it had been a mistake to come home, as much as he'd needed to. He knew it was a mistake to continue to pay her. But the money meant nothing. His family meant everything.

He imagined Ray had felt the same.

In the clear light of day, he knew the sensible thing, the *sane* thing would be to tell her to get lost, to ignore her. To call her bluff.

But then he'd get one of her notes, or come face-to-face with her, and he'd clutch. He found himself strangled between his helpless childhood and the desperate need to shield the people he loved.

So he paid, with a great deal more than money.

He knew how she worked. She wouldn't pop up on his doorstep right away. She'd let him stew and worry and wonder, until ten thousand seemed like a bargain for a little peace of mind. She wouldn't be staying in St. Chris, wouldn't risk being seen and recognized by his brothers or sisters. But she'd be close.

However dramatic, however paranoid it was, he'd swear he could all but feel her—the hate and the greed—breathing down his neck.

He wasn't running again. She wouldn't make him deprive himself of home and family a second time. He would, as he had before, lose himself in his work and live his life. Until she came.

He'd wheedled a second morning session out of Dru. From the sitting the previous week he knew she expected him to be prepared when she arrived, precisely at seven-thirty, and for him to be ready to start. And to stop exactly sixty minutes later.

And to ensure he did, she'd brought a kitchen timer with her.

The woman had no tolerance for artistic temperament. That was all right with Seth. In his opinion, he didn't have an artistic temperament.

He was using pastels, just a basic study for now. It was an extension of the charcoal sketch. A way for him to learn her face, her moods, her body language before he roped her into the more intense portraits he'd already planned in his mind.

When he looked at her, he felt all the models he'd used throughout his career had been simply precursors to Drusilla.

She knocked. He'd told her it wasn't necessary, but she kept that formal distance between them. That, he thought as he walked to the door, would have to be breached.

There could be no formality, and no distance, between them if he was to paint her as he needed to paint her.

"Right on time. Big surprise. Want coffee?"

He'd had his hair cut. It was still long enough to lay over the collar of the torn T-shirt that seemed to be his uniform, but the ponytail was gone. It surprised her that she missed it. She'd always felt that sort of thing was an affectation on a man.

He'd shaved, too, and could almost be deemed tidy if you ignored the holes in the knees of his jeans and the paint splatters on his shoes.

"No, thanks. I've had a cup already this morning."

"One?" He closed the door behind her. "I can barely form a simple declarative sentence on one hit of coffee. How do you do it?"

"Willpower."

"Got a lot of that, do you?"

"As a matter of fact."

To his amusement, she set the timer on his workbench, set at sixty. Then went directly to the stool he'd set out for her, slid onto it.

She noticed the change immediately.

He'd bought a bed.

The frame was old—a simple black iron head—and the footboard showed some dings. The mattress was bare and still had the tags.

"Moving in after all?"

He glanced over. "No. But it's better than the floor if I end up working late and bunking here. Plus it's a good prop."

Her brow lifted. "Oh, really?"

"Are you usually so preoccupied with sex, or is it just around me?" It made him laugh when her mouth dropped open. "A prop," he continued as he moved to his easel, "like that chair over there, those old bottles." He gestured toward the bottles stacked in a corner. "The urn and this cracked blue bowl I've got in the kitchen. I pick up things as they catch my eye."

He studied his pastels, and his mouth curved. "Including women."

She relaxed her shoulders. He'd notice if they were stiff, and it would make her feel even more foolish. "That's quite a speech for one 'oh, really.'"

"Sugar, you pack a lot of punch into an 'oh, really.' Do you remember the pose?"

"Yes." Obediently she propped her foot on the rung of the stool, laced her hands around her knee, then looked over her left shoulder as if someone had just spoken to her.

"That's perfect. You're really good at this."

"I sat like this for an hour just a few days ago."

"An hour," he repeated as he began to work. "Before the wild debauchery of the weekend."

"I'm so used to wild debauchery it doesn't have a particular impact on my life."

It was his turn. "Oh, really?"

He mimicked her tone so perfectly, she broke the pose to look toward him, laughing. He always managed to make her laugh. "I minored in WD in college."

"Oh, if only." His fingers hurried to capture the bright, beautiful laughter. "I know your type, baby. You walk around being beautiful, smart, sexy and unapproachable so we guys just suffer and dream."

It was, obviously, the wrong thing to say as the humor on her face died instantly—like flipping a switch. "You don't know anything about me, or my type."

"I didn't say that to hurt your feelings. I'm sorry."

She shrugged. "I don't know you well enough for you to hurt my feelings. I know you just well enough to have you annoy me."

"Then I'm sorry for that. I was joking. I like hearing you laugh. I like seeing it."

"Unapproachable." She heard herself mutter it before she could bite down on the urge. Just as her head jerked around before she could pull back the temper. "Did you think I was so damned unapproachable when you grabbed me and kissed me?"

"I'd say the act speaks for itself. Look. A lot of times when a guy sees a woman—a beautiful one he's attracted to—he gets clumsy. It's easier to figure she's out of reach than to analyze his own clumsiness. Women . . ."

If furious was what he was going to get out of her, then he'd capture fury in pastels. "They're a mystery to us. We want them. We can't help it. That doesn't mean you don't scare the hell out of us, one way or the other, more than half the time."

She would have sniffed if he wouldn't have made such a predictable response. "Do you honestly expect me to believe you're afraid of women?"

"Well, I had some advantage, with all those sisters." He was working now, but she'd forgotten he was working. Sometimes, that was only better. So he continued to talk while she frowned at him. "But the first girl I was ever serious about? It took me two weeks to get up the nerve to call her on the phone. Your kind doesn't know what my kind go through."

"How old were you?"

"Fifteen. Marilyn Pomeroy, a giddy little brunette."

"And how long were you serious about Marilyn?"

"About as long as it took me to work up the nerve to call her. Two weeks, give or take. What can I say? Men are no damn good."

Her lips twitched and curved. "That goes without saying. I was serious about a boy when I was fifteen. Wilson Bufferton Lawrence. The Fourth. Buff to his friends."

"Jesus, where do you guys come up with these names? What do you do with somebody named Buff? Play polo or squash?"

He'd leveled her temper, she realized. It was something else he was good at. Since he didn't appear to mind her being mad, it often seemed a waste of time to *be* mad.

"Tennis, actually. On what you'd call our first official date, we played tennis at the club. I beat him in straight sets, and that was the end of our tender romance."

"You'd have to expect someone who answers to Buff to be an asshole."

"I was crushed, then I was mad. I liked being mad better."

"Me too. What became of Buff?"

"Hmmm. As I was informed by my mother over the weekend, he's going to be married for the second time this fall. His first marriage lasted slightly longer than our long-ago tennis match."

"Better luck next time."

"Naturally," she said, very soberly, "he's in finance, as is expected of a fourth-generation Lawrence, and the happy couple is house hunting for their little fifty-room love nest as we speak."

"It's nice to know you're not still bitter."

"I was reminded, a total of five times, I believe, that I've yet to afford my parents the pleasure of spending lavish amounts of money on a wedding that would show the Lawrences, among others, a thing or two."

"So . . . you and your mother had a nice visit on Mother's Day." Though her expression now all but radiated irritation, he kept working. "Careful, you could spill blood with that sneer."

She took a deep breath, angled her head properly again. "My visits with my mother can rarely be defined as 'nice.' I suspect you spent this past Sunday going to see each one of your mothers—sisters."

"It's hard to pin down just what they are. Yeah, I spent some time with each of them. Took them their presents. And since each one of them cried, I figure they were a big hit."

"What did you get them?"

"I did small family portraits. Anna and Cam and the boys, and so on, for each one."

"That's nice. That's lovely," she said softly. "I got my mother a Baccarat vase and a dozen red roses. She was very pleased."

He set down his pastels, dusted his hands on his jeans as he crossed to her. And took her face in his hands. "Then why do you look so sad?"

"I'm not sad."

In response, he simply pressed his lips to her forehead, keeping them there as he felt her tense, then relax.

She couldn't remember ever having a conversation like this with anyone before. And she couldn't fathom why it seemed perfectly natural to have it with him. "It would be difficult for you to understand a conflicted family when yours is so united."

"We have plenty of conflicts," he corrected.

"No. Not at the core, you don't. I need to get downstairs."

"I still have some time left," he said, holding her in place when she started to slide off the stool.

"You've stopped working."

"I still have some time left," he repeated, and gestured to her timer. "If there's one thing I know about, it's family conflict, and what it does to you inside. I spent the first third of my life in a constant state of conflict."

"You're speaking of before you came to live with your grandfather? I've read stories about you, but you don't discuss that aspect," she said when his head came up.

"Yeah." He waited for the constriction in his chest to ease. "Before. When I lived with my biological mother."

"I see."

"No, sugar, you don't. She was a whore and a drunk and a junkie, and she made the first few years of my life a nightmare."

"I'm sorry." He was right, she supposed, it was something she couldn't see clearly. But she touched his hand, then took his hand, in an instinctive gesture of comfort. "It must have been horrible for you. Still, it's obvious she's nothing to you."

"That's what you got out of one statement from me and a handful of articles?"

"No. That's what I got after eating crab and potato salad with you and your family. Now you look sad," she murmured, and shook her head. "I don't know why we're talking about these things."

He wasn't sure why he'd brought up Gloria himself. Maybe it was as simple as speaking out loud to chase away ghosts. Or as complex as needing Dru to know who he was, all the way through.

"That's what people do, people who are interested in each other. They talk about who they are and where they've come from."

"I told you—"

"Yeah, you don't want to be interested. But you are." He traced a finger over her hair, from the short, spiky bangs to the tender nape. "And since we've been dating for several weeks—"

"We haven't dated at all."

He leaned down and caught her up in a kiss as hot as it was brief. "See?" Before she could comment, his mouth took hers again. Softer now, slower, deeper, with those wonderful hands skimming over her face, along her throat and shoulders.

Every muscle in her body went loose. Every vow she'd made about men and relationships crumbled.

When he eased back, she took a careful breath. And changed her line in the sand. "I may end up sleeping with you, but I'm not dating you."

"So, I'm good enough to have sex with, but I don't get a candlelit dinner? I feel so cheap."

Damn it. *Damn* it. She liked him. "Dating's a circular, often tortuous route to sex. I choose to skip it. But I said I might sleep with you, not that I would."

"Maybe we should play tennis first."

"Okay. You're funny. That's appealing. I admire your work, and I like your family. All completely superfluous to a physical relationship, but a nice bonus all in all. I'll think about it."

Saved by the bell, she thought when the timer buzzed. She got off the stool, then wandered to the easel. She saw her face a half dozen times. Different angles, different expressions. "I don't understand this."

"What?" He joined her at the easel. *Bella donna,*" he murmured, and surprised a shiver out of her.

"I thought you were doing a study of me sitting on the stool. You started it, but you've got all these other sketches scattered around it."

"You weren't in the mood to pose today. You had things on your mind. They showed. So I worked with them. It gives me some insight, and some ideas about what I want in a more formal portrait."

He watched her brow knit. "You said I could have four hours on Sunday," he reminded her. "I'd like to work outside, weather permitting. I've been by your house. It's terrific. Any objection to working there?"

"At my house?"

"It's a great spot. You know that or you wouldn't be there. You're too particular to settle. Besides, it'll be simpler for you. Ten o'clock okay?"

"I suppose."

"Oh, and about the foxgloves? How many more sittings can I get if I frame it for you?"

"I don't—"

"If you bring it back to me, I'll frame it, then you can decide what it's worth in trade. Fair enough?"

"It's down in the shop. I was going to take it to a framer this week."

"I'll stop down and get it before I leave today." He walked his fingers up her arm. "I guess there's no point in asking you to have dinner with me tonight."

"None at all."

"I could just stop by your place later for some quick, cheap sex."

"That's awfully tempting, but I don't think so." She strolled to the door, then glanced back at him. "If and when we go there, Seth, I can promise it won't be cheap. And it won't be quick."

When the door closed, he rubbed his belly that had tightened at that last provocative look she'd sent him.

He glanced back at the canvas. She was, he decided, quite a number of women rolled up in one fascinating package. Every single one of them appealed to him.

~

"Something's troubling him." Anna boxed Cam into the bathroom—one place almost guaranteed to provide space for an uninterrupted conver-

sation in her personal madhouse. She paced the confined area and talked to
his silhouette on the shower curtain.

"He's okay. He's just getting his rhythm back."

"He's not sleeping well. I can tell. And I swear I heard him talking to
himself the other night."

"You do plenty of solo babbling when you're pissed off," Cam mumbled.

"What did you say?"

"Nothing. Just talking to myself."

With an expression between smug and grim—because she'd heard him
perfectly—Anna flushed the toilet. Then smiled in cool satisfaction as he
cursed at the sudden blast of hot water. "Goddamn it, why do you *do* that?"

"Because it irritates you and gets your attention. Now about Seth—"

"He's painting," Cam said in exasperation. "He's working at the boatyard, he's catching up with the family. Give him some time, Anna."

"Have you noticed what he's not doing? He's not going out with his
friends. He's not dating Dru, or anyone else. Though it's clear from the way
he looks at her there isn't going to *be* anyone else for the time being."

Or ever, she concluded.

"He's downstairs playing video games with Jake," she continued. "On a
Friday night. Aubrey told me he's only hung out with her once since he got
back home. How many weekends did you hang around the house when you
were his age?"

"This is Saint Chris, not Monte Carlo. All right, all right," he said
quickly, before she flushed on him again. The woman could be vicious. He
loved that about her. "So he's preoccupied, I'm not blind. I got pretty preoccupied myself when I got tangled up with you."

"If I thought it was infatuation, or interest or just healthy lust where
Dru's considered, I wouldn't be worried. And I am worried. I can't put my
finger on it, but when I'm worried about one of my men, there's a reason."

"Fine. So go hound him."

"No. I want you to go hound him."

"Me?" Cam whisked back the curtain enough to stare at her. "Why me?"

"Because. Mmm, you sure are cute when you're wet and annoyed."

"That's not going to work."

"Maybe I should come in there and wash your back," she said and began
to unbutton her blouse.

"Okay, that's going to work."

SEVEN

Cam jogged downstairs. There was nothing like a spin in the shower with Anna to brighten his mood. He poked a head in the den where his youngest son and Seth were waged in deadly, bloody battle. There were curses, grunts, shouts.

Some of them were from the animation on-screen.

As usual, Cam found himself drawn into the war. Axes swung, blood flew, swords clashed. And he lost track of reality until Jake let out a triumphant cry.

"I kicked your ass."

"Shit, you got lucky."

Jake pumped his joystick in the air. "I *rule*, baby. Bow to the king of Mortal Kombat."

"In your dreams. Let's go again."

"Bow to the king," Jake repeated joyously. "Worship me, lesser mortal."

"I'll worship you."

Seth made his grab. Cam watched them wrestle for a moment. More grunts, impossible threats, a young boy's dopey giggles. Seth and Jake, he thought, weren't so different in age than he and Seth.

But Jake had an innocence Seth had never been allowed. Jake had never had to question who he was, or if the hands reaching for him meant him harm.

Thank God for it.

Cam leaned lazily against the doorjamb and yelled, "Come on, Anna, they're just fooling around."

At the mention of her name, Seth and Jake rolled apart and shot twin looks of panic and guilt toward the doorway.

"Got you," Cam barked with amusement.

"That was cold, Dad."

"That's how to win a battle without a single blow. You." He pointed at Seth. "Let's go."

"Where ya going?" Jake demanded, scrambling up. "Can I go?"

"Have you cleaned your room, done your homework, found the cure for cancer and changed the oil in my car?"

"Come on, Dad," Jake whined.

"Seth, grab some beer and head outside. I'll be right along."

"Sure. Later, kid"—Seth tapped a fist in his palm—"I'm taking you out."

"You couldn't take me out if you brought me flowers and a box of chocolates."

"Good one," Cam commented as Seth snorted out a laugh and left the room.

"I've been saving it," Jake told him. "How come I can't go with you guys?"

"I need to talk to Seth."

"Are you mad at him?"

"Do I look mad at him?"

"No," Jake said after a careful study of his father's face. "But you can be sneaky about that stuff."

"I just need to talk to him."

Jake jerked a shoulder, but Cam saw the disappointment in his eyes—Anna's Italian eyes—before he plopped back on the floor and reached for his joystick.

Cam squatted. "Jake." He caught the scent of bubble gum and youthful sweat. There were grass stains on the knees of Jake's jeans. His shoes were untied.

It struck him unexpectedly, as it often did, that staggering slap of emotion that was love and pride and puzzlement rolled into one strong fist against his heart.

"Jake," he said again and ran his hand over his son's hair. "I love you."

"Jeez." Jake hunched his shoulders and, with his chin tucked, shifted his gaze up to meet his father's. "I know, and stuff."

"I love you," Cam repeated. "But when I get back, there's going to be a bloody coup, and a new king in Quinnland. And believe what I'm saying, you will bow to me."

"You wish."

Cam rose, pleased with the cocky expression on Jake's face. "Your days of rule are numbered. Start praying, pal."

"I'll pray that you don't slobber on me when you're begging for mercy."

He had to admit, Cam decided as he walked toward the back door, he'd raised a bunch of wiseasses. It did a man proud.

"What's up?" Seth asked, tossing Cam a beer as he swung out the back door.

"Gonna take a little sail."

"Now?" Automatically, Seth looked up at the sky. "It'll be dark in an hour."

"Afraid of the dark, Mary?" Cam sauntered to the dock, stepped nimbly into the day sailer. He set the beer aside while Seth cast off.

As he had countless times in the past, Seth lifted the oar to push away from the dock. He hoisted the main, and the sound of the canvas rising was sweet as music. Cam manned the rudder, finessing the wind so they glided, smooth and nearly silent, away from shore.

The sun was low, its beams striking the water, sheening the marsh grass, dying in the narrow channels where the shadows went deep and the water went dark and secret.

They motored through, maneuvering between markers, down the river, through the sound. And into the Bay. Balanced to the sway, Seth hoisted the jib, trimmed the sails.

And Cam caught the wind.

They flew in the wooden boat with its bright work glinting and its sails white as dove's wings. There was salt in the air, and the thrilling roll, that rise and fall of waves as deeply blue as the sky.

The speed, the freedom, the absolute joy of skating over the water while the sun went soft toward twilight drained every worry, every doubt, every sorrow from Seth's heart.

"Coming about," Cam called out, setting to tack to steal more wind, steal more speed.

For the next fifteen minutes, they barely spoke.

When they slowed, Cam stretched out his legs and popped the top on his beer. "So, what's going on with you?"

"Going on?"

"Anna's radar tells her something's up with you, and she nagged me into finding out what it is."

Seth bought some time by opening his own beer, taking the first cold sip. "I've just been back a couple weeks, so I've got a lot on my mind, that's all. Figuring things out, settling in, that kind of thing. She doesn't have to worry."

"I'm supposed to go back and tell her she doesn't have to worry? Oh yeah, that'll go down real smooth." He took another drink. "Look, we don't have to go through all that you-know-you-can-talk-to-me-about-anything crap, do we? Going that route's only going to make us both feel like morons."

"No." But it worked a smile out of Seth. "Just tell her I'm thinking about what happens next. I've got to get a place of my own sooner or later. My rep's bugging me about putting together another showing, and I'm not sure what direction I want to take there. I haven't even finished putting the studio together yet."

"Uh-huh." Cam glanced toward shore, and the pretty old house tucked back on the banks of the river.

When Seth followed the look, he shifted in the bow. He'd been so wrapped up in the sail, he hadn't noticed the direction.

"Sexy flower queen's not home yet," Cam commented. "Maybe she's got a date."

"She doesn't date."

"Is that why you haven't moved on her yet?"

"Who says I haven't?"

Cam only laughed, sipped beer. "If you had, kid, you'd look a hell of a lot more relaxed."

Got me there, Seth thought, but shrugged.

"In fact, I can drop you off here. You can try the 'I was just in the neighborhood so can I come in and get you naked' gambit."

"That one ever work for you?"

"Ah." Cam let out a long, wistful sigh, stared up at the sky as if into deep, dreamy memories. "The stories I could tell. The way I figure it, the more a guy gets sex, the more he thinks about it. And the less a guy gets sex, the more he thinks about it. But at least when he's getting it, he sleeps better."

Seth patted his pockets. "Got a pen? I want to write that one down."

"She's a very tasty morsel."

Amusement fled. "She's not a fucking snack."

"Okay." Having nailed the answer he wanted, Cam nodded. "I wondered if you were really tangled up about her."

Seth hissed out a breath, looked back toward the fanciful blue house tucked among the trees until it was out of sight. "I don't know what I am. I've got to get my life settled, and until I do, I don't have time for . . . tangles. But I look at her and . . ." He shrugged. "I can't figure it out. I like being around her. Not that she's easy. Half the time it's like dealing with a porcupine. One in a tiara."

"Women without spines are fine for a one-nighter, or a good time. But when you're looking for the long haul . . ."

Shock and panic erupted on Seth's face. "I didn't say that. I just said I liked being around her."

"And you got puppy eyes when you said it."

"Bullshit." And the fact that he could feel the heat of a flush working up his neck mortified him. He could only hope the light was too dim for Cam to spot it.

"Another minute, you'd've whimpered. You going to trim that jib, or just let her reef?"

Muttering to himself, Seth adjusted the lines. "Look, I want to paint her, I want to spend some time with her. And I want to get her into bed. I can manage all three on my own, thanks."

"If you do, maybe you'll start sleeping better."

"Dru doesn't have anything to do with how I'm sleeping. Or not much anyway."

Cam came about again and headed toward home. Twilight was falling. "So are you going to tell me what's keeping you up at night, or do I have to pry that out of you, too? You don't tell me, Anna's going to make both of our lives hell until you spill it."

He thought of Gloria, and the words crammed in his throat. If he let the first one out, the rest wouldn't just spill. It would be an avalanche. All he could see was his family buried under it.

He could tell Cam anything. Anything but that.

But maybe it was time to unload something else. "I had this really weird dream."

"Are we going back to sex?" Cam asked. "Because if we are we should've brought more beer along."

"I dreamed about Stella."

The wicked humor on Cam's face drained, leaving it naked and vulnerable. "Mom? You dreamed about Mom?"

"I know it's weird. I never even met her."

"What was she . . ." It was strange how grief could hide inside you. Like a virus, lying low for months, even years, only to spring out and leave you weak and helpless again. "What were you doing?"

"Sitting on the dock in back of the house. It was summer. Hot, sweaty, close. I was fishing, just a pole and a line and some of Anna's Brie."

"You'd better've been dreaming," Cam managed. "Or you're a dead man."

"See, that's the thing. The line's in the water, but I *knew* I'd copped the cheese for bait. And I could smell roses, feel the heat of the sun. Then Foolish plops down next to me. I know he's gone—I mean in the dream I know—so I'm pretty damn surprised to see him. Next thing I know Stella's sitting on the dock beside me."

"How did she look?"

It didn't seem like an odd question while they were gliding along on quiet water in the dimming light. It seemed perfectly rational. "She looked terrific. She had on this old khaki hat, no brim. The kind you just yank down over your head, and her hair was falling all out of it."

"Jesus." Cam remembered the old hat, and the way she'd stuffed her unmanageable hair under it. Did they have a picture of her in that ugly cap? He couldn't recall.

"I don't want to mess you up with this."

Cam only shook his head. "What happened in the dream?"

"Not a whole lot. We just sat there and talked. About you guys, and Ray and . . ."

"What?"

"How they figured it was time she got to play Grandma, since she'd missed out on that before. It wasn't what we said so much as how real it seemed. Even when I woke up sitting on the side of the bed, it seemed real. I don't know how to explain it."

"No, I get you." Hadn't he had a number of conversations with his father, after Ray had died? And hadn't his brothers both had similar experiences?

But it had been so long now. Longer yet since they'd lost their mother. And none of them had ever had that wrenching chance to talk to her again. Even in dreams.

"I always wanted to meet her," Seth continued. "It feels like I have."

"How long ago was this?"

"Last week, I guess. And before you start, I didn't say anything at the time because I figured you might freak. You gotta admit, it's a little spooky."

You ain't seen nothing yet, Cam thought. But that was one of the aspects of being a Quinn Seth would have to find out on his own.

"If you dream about her again, ask her if she remembers the zucchini bread."

"The what?"

"Just ask her," Cam said as they drifted home.

※

When they got home, dinner was cooking. And Dan McLean was standing by the stove, holding a beer and leaning in for Anna to feed him a spoonful of red sauce.

"What the hell's he doing here?" Cam demanded, and fixed a scowl on his face because Dan would expect it.

"Mooching. That's terrific, Miz Q. Nobody makes it like you. It makes having to see his face again easier," he added, and nodded toward Seth.

"Weren't you mooching here two weeks ago?" Cam asked him.

"Nah. I mooched at Ethan's two weeks ago. I like to spread myself around."

"More of you to spread around than there was last time I saw you." Seth hooked his thumbs in his pockets and took a long look at his childhood friend. Dan had filled out in a way that indicated solid gym time.

"Can't men just say, 'Hi, it's good to see you again'?" Anna wondered.

"Hi," Seth echoed. "It's good to see you again."

They moved together in the one-armed hold that constitutes a male hug.

Cam sniffed at the simmering pots. "Christ, I'm tearing up. This is so touching."

"Why don't you set the table," Anna suggested to Cam. "Before you make a sentimental fool of yourself."

"Let the moocher set it. He knows where everything is. I've got to go dethrone and execute our youngest child."

"Make sure you do it within twenty minutes. We're eating in twenty-one."

"I'll set the table, Miz Q."

"No, get out of my kitchen. Take your beer and manly ways outside. I don't know why I couldn't have had just one girl. I don't know why that was too much to ask."

"Next time this one comes over to eat our food, make him put on a dress," Cam called over his shoulder as he headed for the den and his son's date with destiny.

"Cam loves me like a brother," Dan said and, at home, opened the refrigerator to get Seth a beer. "Let us go and sit outside like men, scratching and telling sexual lies."

They sat on the steps. Each took a pull from his beer. "Aub says you're digging in this time. Got yourself a studio over the florist."

"That's right. Aub says? My information is your little brother's after her."

"When he gets the chance. I see more of her than I see of Will. They've got him doing so many double shifts at the hospital he calls out 'stat!' and other sexy medical terms in his sleep."

"You guys still bunking together?"

"Yeah, for now. Mostly I've got the apartment to myself. He lives and breathes the hospital. Will McLean, M.D. Ain't that some shit?"

"He really got off dissecting frogs in biology. You wimped out."

Even from this distance, the thought made Dan grimace. "It was, and continues to be, a disgusting rite of passage. No frog's ever caused me harm. Now that you're back, it screws my plans to visit you in Italy, have the two of us sit at some sidewalk cafe—"

"Trattoria."

"Whatever, and ogle sexy women. Figured we'd catch a lot of action, with you being all artistic and me being so damn handsome."

"What happened to that teacher you were seeing? Shelly?"

"Shelby. Yeah, well, that's another thing that put my little fantasy in the dust." Dan dug in his pocket, pulled out a jeweler's box and flipped the top with his thumb.

"Holy hell, McLean," Seth managed as he blinked at the diamond ring.

"Got big plans tomorrow night. Dinner, candlelight, music, get down on one knee. The whole package." Dan blew out a shaky breath. "I'm scared shitless."

"You're getting married?"

"Man, I hope so, because I love her to pieces. You think she'll go for this?"

"How do I know?"

"You're the artist," Dan said and shoved the ring under Seth's nose. "How's it look to you?"

It looked like a fancy gold band with a diamond in the center. But friendship demanded more than that. "It looks great. Elegant, classic."

"Yeah, yeah." Obviously pleased, Dan studied it again. "That's her, man. That's Shelby. Okay." Breathing out, he put the box back in his pocket. "Okay then. She really wants to meet you. She's into that art crap. That's how I hit on her the first time. Aubrey dragged me to this art show at the university because Will was tied up. And there's Shelby standing in front of this painting that looked like maybe a chimp had done. I mean, what is with that shit that's just streaks and splatters of paint? It's a scam, if you ask me."

"I'm sure Pollock died in shame."

"Yeah, right, whatever. Anyhow, I went up to her and pulled that 'what does it say to you?' kind of line. And you know what she says?"

Enjoying seeing his friend so besotted, Seth leaned back against the step. "What did she say?"

"She said the five-year-olds in her kindergarten class do better work with fingerpaints. Man oh man, it was love. So that's when I pulled out the big guns and told her I had this friend who was an artist, but he painted real pictures. Then I drop your name and she nearly fainted. I guess that's when it really hit me you'd become a BFD."

"You still have that sketch I did of you and Will hanging over your toilet?"

"It's in a place of honor. So, how about you meet Shelby and me some night next week? For a drink, maybe something to eat."

"I can do that, but she may fall for me and leave you brokenhearted."

"Yeah, that'll happen. But just in case, she's got this friend—"

"No." The horror of it had Seth throwing up a blocking hand. "No fix-ups. You'll just have to take your chances on your girl falling under the spell of my fatal charm."

⚭

After the meal, and the noise, Seth let Dan drag him off for a night at Shiney's. It turned into a marathon of reminiscence and bad music.

They'd left the porch and living room lamp on for him, so he made it all the way upstairs before he tripped over the dog sprawled across the bathroom doorway.

He cursed under his breath, limped off to his room and stripped down to the skin where he stood. His ears were still ringing from the last horrendous set when he flopped facedown on the bed.

It was good to be home, was his last thought, and he fell dreamlessly into sleep.

⚭

"Mom?" In the office of the boatyard, Phillip sat heavily in his chair. "He dreamed about Mom?"

"Maybe it was a dream, maybe it wasn't."

Ethan rubbed his chin. "He said she was wearing that old cap?"

"That's right."

"She wore it often enough," Phillip pointed out. "He's probably seen a picture of her wearing it."

"She's not wearing it in any of the pictures we've got sitting around our place." Cam had looked. "I'm not saying he hasn't seen a picture, and I'm not saying it wasn't just a dream. But it's odd. She used to come down and sit on the dock with us like that. She didn't care much for fishing, but if one of us was sitting out there brooding over something, she'd come out and sit until we started talking about whatever it was we had in our craw."

"She was good at it," Ethan agreed. "Good at getting down to the meat of it."

"It doesn't mean this is anything like what happened with us after Dad died."

"You didn't want to believe that either," Ethan pointed out as he hunted up a bottle of water from Phillip's office refrigerator.

"I know this. Something's bothering the kid and he doesn't want to talk about it. Not to me anyway." It stung a little, Cam admitted. "If anybody can get it out of him, it's Mom. Even in a dream. In the meantime, I guess we just watch him. I'm going down before he figures out we're up here talking about him."

Cam started out, then stopped and turned back. "I told him if he dreams about her again to ask her about the zucchini bread."

Both his brothers looked blank. Ethan remembered first and laughed so hard he had to sit on the edge of the desk.

"Christ." Phillip eased back in his chair. "I'd forgotten all about that."

"We'll see if she remembers," Cam said, then started down into the din of the work area. He'd gotten to the last step when the outer door opened, spilling in sunshine just ahead of Dru.

"Well, hello, gorgeous. Looking for my idiot brother?"

"Which idiot brother?"

His grin was pure appreciation. "You catch on. Seth's earning his keep."

"Actually, I wasn't—" But Cam already had her hand and was leading her along.

Legs spread, his back to her, Seth stood on the decking of the boat, stripped to the waist. His back and arms showed considerably more muscle than might be expected from a man who wielded a paintbrush for a living. He guzzled from a bottle of water like a man who hadn't had a drink in a week.

Her own mouth went dry watching him.

Shallow, Dru told herself. Shallow, shallow, shallow, to be interested in a man simply because he looked hot and hard and handsome. She appreciated intellect and strength of character and personality and . . . a really excellent butt, she admitted.

Sue her.

She managed to avoid licking her lips before he turned. He reached up to swipe at his brow with his forearm, then spotted her.

Now, in addition to the long male body clad only in jeans and work boots, her senses were assaulted by the lethal power of his smile.

She saw his mouth move—it was, like his butt, excellent. But the words he spoke were drowned out by the music.

Willing to assist, Cam walked over and turned the stereo down to merely loud.

"Hey!" Aubrey's head popped up from under the deck. "What gives?"

"We've got company."

Dru watched, with some interest, as Seth ran a hand over Aubrey's shoulder as he jumped down from the deck. "We're on for tomorrow, right?" he asked her as he walked over, pulling a bandanna out of his pocket to wipe his hands and face.

"Yes." Dru noted that Aubrey continued to watch, with considerable interest of her own. "I didn't mean to interrupt your work. I was running some errands while Mr. G watches the shop, and I thought I'd come in and have a look at the operation here."

"I'll show you around."

"You're busy." And your blond companion is watching me like your guard dog, Dru decided. "In any case, I'm told it's probably you I want to see," she said to Cam.

Cam gestured at Seth. "I told you that's what all the pretty ladies say. What can I do for you?"

"I want to buy a boat."

"Is that so?" Cam draped an arm around her shoulders and turned to lead her toward the stairs. "Well, sugar, you've come to the right place."

"Hey!" Seth called out. "I can talk about boats."

"Junior partner. We try to humor him. So, what kind of boat are you interested in?"

"Sloop. Eighteen feet. Arc bottom, cedar hull. Probably a spoon bow, though I'd be flexible if the designer has another idea. I want something with good balance, reliable stability, but when I want to move, I want to move."

She turned to study the gallery of sketches and told herself she'd admire the art of them later. For now, she wanted to make her point.

"This hull, this bow," she said, gesturing to two sketches. "I want something dependable, quick to the wind, and I want a boat that lasts."

She obviously knew her boats. "A custom job like that's going to cost you."

"I don't expect it comes free, but I don't discuss terms with you, do I? I believe that's your brother Phillip's area—and if there are any other specific design details, that would be Ethan's."

"Done your homework."

"I like to know who I'm dealing with, and I prefer dealing with the best. That, by all accounts, is Quinn Brothers. How soon can you work up a design?"

Man, oh man, Cam thought, you're going to drive the kid crazy. And it's going to be fun to watch. "Let's go upstairs and we'll figure it out."

⁂

It was Ethan who walked her down and out thirty minutes later. The lady, he'd discovered, knew port from starboard, had very specific ideas about what she wanted, and held her own against a group of men who'd never had their rough edges quite smoothed off.

"We'll have a draft of the design drawn up by the end of next week," he told her. "Sooner if we can browbeat Seth into doing most of it."

"Oh?" She sent what she hoped was a casual glance toward the work area. "Does he do some of the designing?"

"When we can pin him down. Always had a knack. Pretty obvious he draws better than the three of us put together, and then some."

She followed his gaze and looked at the gallery of boats. "It's a wonderful collection, and retrospective, I suppose. You can see his artistic progress very clearly."

"This one here." He tapped his finger against the sketch of a skipjack. "He did this drawing when he was ten."

"Ten?" Fascinated, she moved closer, studying it now as a student might study the early works of a master in a museum. "I can't imagine what it would be like to be born with that kind of gift. It would be a burden for some, wouldn't it?"

In his way, Ethan took his time considering, following the lines of his old skipjack as seen through the eyes and talent of a child. "I guess it would. Not for Seth. It's a joy for him, and what you'd call a channel. Always has been. Well."

He was never long on conversation, so offered her a quiet smile and his hand. "It's going to be a pleasure doing business with you."

"Likewise. Thanks for making time for me today."

"We always got time."

He showed her out, then wandered into the driving beat of Sugar Ray and power sanders. He was halfway to the lathe when Seth shut off his tool.

"Dru up with the guys?"

"Nope. She went on."

"Went on? Well, damn it, you could've said something." He vaulted down from the boat and sprinted for the door.

Aubrey frowned after him. "He's half stuck on her already."

"Seems like." Ethan tilted his head at the look on her face. "Problem?"

"I don't know." She shrugged. "I don't know. She's just not what I pictured for him, that's all. She's all kind of stiff and fancy, with a high snoot factor, if you ask me."

"She's alone," Ethan corrected. "Not everybody's as easy with people as you are, Aubrey. Besides the fact, it's what Seth pictures that matters."

"Yeah." But she was far from sold on Drusilla.

Eight

Since he hadn't told her what to wear for the sitting, Dru settled on the simple, with blue cotton pants and a white camp shirt. She watered her gardens, changed her earrings twice, then made a fresh pot of coffee.

Maybe the hoops had been a better choice, she thought, fingering the little lapis balls dangling from her ear. Men liked women in hoop earrings. Probably had some strange sultry gypsy fetish.

And what the hell did she care?

She wasn't sure she wanted him to make another move on her. One move, after all, invariably led to another, and she wasn't interested in the chessboard of relationships just now.

Or hadn't been.

Jonah had certainly checkmated her, she thought, and enjoyed the little flash of anger. The problem had been she'd believed she was in control of the board there, that all the game pieces were in correct positions.

She'd been completely oblivious to the fact that he'd been playing on another board simultaneously.

His disloyalty and deception had damaged her heart and her pride. While her heart had healed, perhaps too easily, she admitted, her pride remained bruised.

She would never be made a fool of again.

If she was going to develop a relationship with Seth—and the jury was still out on that one—it would be on her terms.

She'd proven to herself that she was more than an ornament for a man's arm, a notch in his bedpost or a rung in the ladder of his career advancement.

Jonah had miscalculated on that score.

More important, she'd proven that she could stand on her own and make a very contented life.

Which didn't mean, she admitted, that she didn't miss a certain amount of companionship, or sexual heat, or the heady challenge of the mating dance with an interesting, attractive man.

She heard his tires crunch on her gravel drive. One step at a time, she told herself, and waited for him to knock.

All right, she thought, so she did feel a rush of heat the minute she opened the door and looked at him. It only proved that she was human, and she was healthy.

"Good morning," she said, as manners had her stepping back to let him inside.

"Morning. I love this place. I just realized that if you hadn't snapped it up before I got back home, I would have."

"Lucky for me."

"I'll say." He scanned the living area as he wandered. Strong colors, good fabrics, he mused. It could've used a little more clutter for his taste, but it suited her with its good, carefully selected pieces, the fresh flowers and the tidy air of it all.

"You said you wanted to work outside."

"Yeah. Oh, hey, your painting." He shifted the package wrapped in brown paper under his arm and handed it to her. "I'll hang it for you if you've picked your spot."

"That was quick." And because she couldn't resist, she sat on the sofa and ripped off the wrapping.

He'd chosen thin strips of wood stained a dull gold that complemented the rich tones of the flowers and foliage so that the frame was as simple and strong as the painting.

"It's perfect. Thank you. It's a wonderful start to my Seth Quinn collection."

"Planning on a collection?"

She ran a finger over the top of the frame as she looked up at him. "Maybe. And I'd take you up on hanging it for me because I'm dying to see how it looks, but I don't have the proper hanger."

"Like this?" He dug the one he'd brought with him out of his pocket.

"Like that." She angled her head, considered. "You're very handy, aren't you?"

"Damn near indispensable. Got a hammer, and a tape measure, or should I get mine out of my car?"

"I happen to have a hammer and other assorted household tools." She rose, went into the kitchen and came back with a hammer so new it gleamed.

"Where do you want it?"

"Upstairs. My bedroom." She turned to lead the way. "What's in the bag?"

"Stuff. The guy who rehabbed this place knew what he was doing." Seth examined the satin finish on the banister as they climbed to the second floor. "I wonder how he could stand to let it go."

"He likes the work itself—and the profit. Once he's finished, he's bored and wants to move on. Or so he told me when I asked just that."

"How many bedrooms? Three?"

"Four, though one's quite small, more suited to a home office or a little library."

"Third floor?"

"A finished attic, which has potential for a small apartment. Or," she said with a glance at him, "an artist's garret."

She turned into a room, and Seth saw immediately she'd selected what suited her best here as well. The windows gave her a view of the river, a sweep of trees and shady garden. The window trim was just fussy enough to be charming, and she'd chosen to drape filmy white gauze in a kind of long swag around them in lieu of formal curtains. It diffused the sunlight and still left the view and the craftsmanship of the trim.

She'd gone for cerulean blue on the walls, scattered a couple of floral rugs on the pine floor, and had stuck with antiques for the furnishings.

The bed was tidily made, as he'd expected, and covered with a white quilt with intricate interlocking rings and rosebuds that seemed to have been crafted specifically for the sleigh bed.

"Great piece." He leaned down to get a closer look at the workmanship of the quilt. "Heirloom?"

"No. I found it at an arts-and-crafts fair in Pennsylvania last year. I thought the wall between these windows. It'll be good light without direct sun."

"Good choice." He held the painting up. "And it'll be like another window, so you'll have flowers during the winter."

Her thoughts, Dru admitted, exactly.

"About here?"

She stepped back, checked the position from several different angles—resisting, only because it was a bit too suggestive, lying down on the bed to see how it would look to her when she woke in the mornings.

"That's perfect."

He reached behind the painting, scraped a vague mark on the wall with his thumbnail, then set it aside to measure.

It was odd, she thought, having a man in her bedroom again. And far from unpleasant to watch him with his tools and his painting, his rough clothes and his beautiful hands.

Far from unpleasant, she admitted, to imagine those beautiful hands on her skin.

"See what you think about what's in the bag," he said without looking around.

She picked it up, opened it. And her eyebrows lifted high as she took out the long, filmy skirt—purple pansies rioting against a cool blue background—and the thin-strapped, narrow top in that same shade of blue.

"You're a determined man, aren't you?"

"It'll look good on you, and it's the look I'm after."

"And you get what you're after."

He glanced back now, his expression both relaxed and cocky. "So far. You got any of those . . ." He made a circle with his finger in the air. "Hoop ear things. They'd work with that."

I should've known, Dru thought, but only said, "Hmm."

She laid the skirt and top on the bed, then stepped back as he fixed the painting on its hook. "Left bottom needs to come up a little—too much. There. That's perfect. Painted, framed and hung by Quinn. Not a bad deal on my side."

"It looks good from my end, too," he said, staring at her.

When he took a step toward her, she considered taking one toward him. Before the phone rang.

"Excuse me." For the best, she assured herself as she picked up the bedside phone. "Hello."

"Hello, princess."

"Dad." Pleasure, distress and, shamefully, a thread of annoyance knotted inside her. "Why aren't you on the seventh green by this time on a Sunday morning?"

"I've got some difficult news." Proctor let out a long sigh. "Sweetheart, your mother and I are getting divorced."

"I see." The pulse in her temple began to throb. "I need you to wait just a minute." She pushed the hold button, turned to Seth. "I'm sorry, I need to take this. There's coffee in the kitchen. I shouldn't be long."

"Okay." Her face had gone blank on him. It was very still and very empty. "I'll grab a cup before I go out to set up. Take your time."

She waited until she heard him start down the steps, then sat on the side of the bed and reconnected with her father. "I'm sorry, Dad. What happened?" And bit her tongue before she could finish the question with: this time.

"I'm afraid your mother and I haven't been getting along for quite a while. I've tried to shield you from our problems. I have no doubt we'd have taken this step years ago if it hadn't been for you. But, well, these things happen, princess."

"I'm very sorry." She knew her job well and finished with, "Is there anything I can do to help?"

"Ah well. I'm sure I'd feel better if I could explain things to you, so I'm sure you're not upset by all this. It's too complicated to discuss on the phone. Why don't you come up this afternoon? We'll have lunch, just you and me. Nothing would brighten my day more than spending it with my little girl."

"I'm sorry. I've got a commitment today."

"Surely, under the circumstances, this is more important."

Her temple throbbed, and guilt began to roil in her stomach. "I can't break this engagement. In fact, I was just about to—"

"All right. That's all right," he said in a voice that managed to be both long-suffering and brisk. "I'd hoped you'd have some time for me. Thirty years. Thirty, and it comes down to this."

Dru rubbed at the tension banding the back of her neck. "I'm sorry, Dad."

She lost track of the times she echoed that phrase during the rest of the conversation. But she knew when she hung up she was exhausted from repeating it.

No sooner had she set the phone down, than it rang again.

Thirty years, Dru thought, might account for the sixth sense her parents had in regard to each other. Resigned, she picked up the phone.

"Hello, Mom."

He'd spread a red blanket on the grass near the bank of the river where there were both beams of sunlight and dappled shade. He added a wicker picnic basket, propping an open bottle of wine and a stemmed glass against it. A slim book with a ragged white cover lay beside it.

She'd changed into the clothes he'd brought, put on the hoop earrings as he'd requested. And had used the time to steady herself.

His table was up, his sketch pad on it. At the foot was a portable stereo, but instead of the driving rock, it was Mozart. And that surprised her.

"Sorry I held you up," she said as she stepped off the porch.

"No problem." One look at her face had him crossing to her. He put his arms around her and, ignoring her flinch, held her gently.

A part of her wanted to burrow straight into that unquestioning offer of comfort. "Do I look that bad?"

"You look that sad." He brushed his lips over her hair. "You want to do this some other time?"

"No. It's nothing, really. Just habitual family insanity."

"I'm good at that." He tipped her head back with his fingers. "An expert on family insanity."

"Not this kind." She eased back. "My parents are getting divorced."

"Oh baby." He touched her cheek. "I'm sorry."

"No, no, no." To his bafflement, she laughed and pressed the heels of her hands to her temples. "You don't get it. They whack the *D* word around like a Ping-Pong ball. Every couple of years I get the call. 'Dru, I have difficult news.' Or 'Dru, I'm not sure how to tell you.' Once, when I was sixteen, they actually separated for nearly two months. Being careful to time it during my summer break so my mother could flee to Europe with me for a week, then my father could drag me off with him to Bar Harbor to sail."

"Sounds more like you've been the Ping-Pong ball."

"Yes, it does. They wear me out, which is why I ran away before . . . before I started to despise them. And still, I wish to God they'd just go through with it. That sounds cold and selfish and horrible."

"No, it doesn't. Not when you've got tears in your eyes."

"They love me too much," she said quietly. "Or not enough. I've never been able to figure it out. I don't suppose they have either. I can't be with them, standing in as their crutch or their referee the rest of my life."

"Have you told them?"

"Tried. They don't hear." She rubbed her arms as if smoothing ruffled feathers. "And I have absolutely no business dumping my mess in your lap."

"Why not? We're practically going steady."

She let out a half laugh. "You're awfully good at that."

"I'm good at so many things. Which one is this?"

"At listening, for one." She leaned forward, kissed his cheek. "I've never been particularly good at asking anyone to listen. I don't seem to have to with you. And for two"—she kissed his other cheek—"you're good at making me laugh, even when I'm annoyed."

"I'll listen some more—and make you laugh—if you kiss me again. And aim for here this time," he added, tapping a finger to his lips.

"Thanks, but that's about it. Let's put it away. There's nothing I can do about them." She eased away from him. "I assume you want me on the blanket."

"Why don't we toss this for today and go for a sail? It always clears my head."

"No, you're already set up, and it'll take my mind off things. But thanks, really, Seth."

Satisfied that the sadness on her face had lifted, he nodded. "Okay. If you decide you want to stop after all, just say so. First, lose the shoes."

She stepped out of the canvas slides. "A barefoot picnic."

"There you go. Lie down on the blanket."

She'd assumed she'd be sitting on it, skirts spread as she read the book. But she stepped onto the blanket. "Face up or down?"

"On your back. Scoot down a little more," he suggested as he walked around her. "Let's have the right arm over your head. Bend your elbow, relax the hand."

"I feel silly. I didn't feel silly in the studio."

"Don't think about it. Bring your left knee up." She did, and when the skirt came with it, smoothed it back down over her legs.

"Oh, come on." He knelt down and had her eyes going to slits when he pulled up the hem of the skirt so it exposed her left leg to mid-thigh.

"Aren't you supposed to say something about how you're not hitting on me, but that this is all for the sake of art?"

"It is for the sake of art." The back of his fingers skimmed her thigh as he fussed with the lie of the material. "But I'm hitting on you, too." He slid the strap of her top off her shoulder, studied the result, nodded.

"Relax. Start with your toes." He rubbed a hand over her bare foot. "And work your way up." Watching her, he ran his hand up her calf, over her knee. "Turn your head toward me."

She did, and glanced over the paint supplies he'd set up by his easel. "Aren't those watercolors? I thought you said you wanted oil."

"This one's for watercolors. I've got something else in mind for oils."

"So you keep saying. Just how many times do you think you can persuade me to do this?"

"As many as it takes. You're having a quiet afternoon by the water," he told her as he began sketching lightly on the paper. "A little sleepy from wine and reading."

"Am I alone?"

"For the moment. You're just daydreaming now. Go wherever you want."

"If it were warmer, I'd slide into the river."

"It's as warm as you want it to be. Close your eyes, Dru. Dream a little."

She did as he asked. The music, soft, romantic, was a caress on the air.

"What do you think of when you paint?" she asked him.

"Think?" At the question his mind went completely blank. "I don't know. Ah . . . shape, I guess. Light, shadow. Jeez. Mood. I don't have an answer."

"You just answered the question I didn't ask. It's instinct. Your talent is instinctive. It has to be, really, as you were so clever at drawing so young."

"What did you want to do when you were a kid?" Her body was a long, slim flow to him. Shape.

"Lots of things. A ballerina, a movie star, an explorer. A missionary."

"Wow, a missionary. Really?" The sun slid through the leaves and lay softly on her skin. Light and shadow.

"It was a brief ambition, but a profound one. What I didn't think I'd be was a businesswoman. Surprise."

"But you like it."

"I love it. I love being able to take what I once assumed was a personal passion and a small talent for flowers and do something with it." Her mind began to drift, like the river that flowed beside her. "I've never been able to talk to anyone the way I seem to be able to talk to you."

"No kidding?" She looked like a faerie queen—the exotic shape of her eyes, the sexy pixie cap of dark hair. The utter female confidence of the pose. A faerie queen drowsing alone in her private glade. Mood.

"Why do you think that is?" he wondered.

"I haven't a clue." And with a sigh, she fell asleep.

The music had changed. A woman with a voice like heartbreak was singing about love. Still half dreaming, Dru shifted. "Who is that singing?" she murmured.

"Darcy Gallagher. Some pipes there. I caught a show she did with her two brothers a couple years ago in County Waterford. Little place called Ardmore. It was amazing."

"Mmm. I think I've heard—" She broke off when she opened her eyes and found Seth sitting beside the blanket with a sketchbook instead of standing behind the table. "What're you doing?"

"Waiting for you to wake up."

"I fell asleep." Embarrassed, she rose on one elbow. "I'm sorry. How long was I out?"

"Dunno. Don't have a watch." He set the book aside. "No need to be sorry. You gave me just what I was after."

Trying to clear her head, she looked over at the table. The watercolor paper was, frustratingly, out of her line of sight. "You finished?"

"No, but I got a hell of a start. Watch or no watch, my stomach's telling me it's lunchtime." He flipped the lid on a cooler.

"You brought a real picnic."

"Hamper was for art, cooler's for practicality. We've got bread, cheese, grapes, some of this pâté Phil swears by." He pulled out plates as he spoke. "And though I had to debase myself and beg, some of Anna's pasta salad. And this terrific wine I discovered in Venice. It's called Dreams. Seemed to fit."

"You're trying to make this a date," she said warily.

"Too late." He poured the first glass, handed it to her. "It already is a date. I wanted to ask why you took off so fast yesterday, when you came by the boatyard."

"I'd finished my business." She chose a chilled grape, bit through its tart skin. "And I had to get back to work."

"So you want a boat?"

"Yes, I do. I like to sail."

"Come sailing with me. That way you can check out how seaworthy a boat by Quinn is."

"I'll think about it." She sampled the pâté, made a sexy little sound of pleasure. "Your brother Phillip has excellent taste. They're very different, your brothers. Yet they hang together like a single unit."

"That's family."

"Is it? No, not always, not even usually, at least in my experience. Yours is unique, in a number of ways. Why aren't you scarred?"

He looked up from scooping out pasta salad. "Sorry?"

"There's been enough information dribbled through the stories I've read about you, and what I've heard just living in Saint Chris, to tell me you had a very hard childhood. You told me so yourself. How do you get through that without being damaged?"

The press articles had barely skimmed the surface, Seth thought. They knew nothing of the young boy who had hidden from or fought off more than once the slick, groping hands of the drunks or druggies Gloria had brought home.

They didn't know about the beatings or the blackmail, or the fear that remained a hard kernel lodged in his heart.

"They saved me." He said it with a simple honesty that made her throat burn. "It's not an exaggeration to say that they saved my life. Ray Quinn, then Cam and Ethan and Phil. They turned their world around for me, and because of it, turned mine around with it. Anna and Grace and Sybill, Aubrey, too. They made a home for me, and nothing that happened before matters nearly as much as everything that came after."

Unspeakably moved, she leaned forward and touched her lips to his. "That's for three. For making me like you. You're a good man. I don't know just what to do with you."

"You could start by trusting me."

"No." She eased back again, broke off a small hunk of bread. "Nothing starts with trust. Trust develops. And with me, that can take considerable time."

"I can probably guarantee I'm nothing like the guy you were engaged to." When her body went rigid, he shrugged. "I'm not the only one who gets written about or talked about."

And when she'd touched on a personal area, she reminded herself, he hadn't frozen up. "No, you're nothing like Jonah. We never had a picnic with his sister's pasta salad."

"Dinner at Jean-Louis at the Watergate or whatever tony French place is currently in fashion. Openings at the Kennedy Center. Clever cocktail parties inside the Beltway, and the occasional Sunday afternoon brunch with co-pacetic friends." He waited a beat. "How'd I do?"

"Close enough." Dead on target.

"You're way outside the Beltway now. His loss."

"He seems to be bearing up."

"Did you love him?"

She opened her mouth, then found herself answering with complete honesty. "I don't know anymore. I certainly believed I did or I'd never have planned to marry him. He was attractive, brilliant, had a deadly sarcasm that often posed for witty—and sometimes was. And, as it turned out, the fidelity of an alley cat. Better I found that out before we were married than after. But I learned something valuable about myself due to the experience. No one cheats on me without serious consequences."

"Bruised his balls, did you?"

"Oh, worse." She nibbled delicately on pâté. "He left his cashmere coat, among other items, at my place. While I was coldly packing up his things, I took it back out of the packing box, cut off the sleeves, the collar, the buttons. And since that was so satisfying, I put, one by one, all his Melissa Etheridge CDs in the microwave. She's a wonderful artist, but I can't listen to her today without feeling destructive urges. Then I put his Ferragamo loafers in the washing machine. These acts were hard on my appliances, but good for my soul. Since I was on a roll, I started to flush my three-carat, square-cut Russian white diamond engagement ring down the toilet, but sanity prevailed."

"What did you do with it?"

"I put it in an envelope, wrote 'For His Sins' on the front, then dropped it into the collection box at a little church in Georgetown. Overdramatic, but again, satisfying."

This time Seth leaned over, touched his lips to hers. "Nice job, champ."

"Yes, I thought so." She brought her knees up, sipped her wine while she looked out over the water. "A number of my acquaintances think I left D.C. and moved here because of Jonah. They're wrong. I've loved it here since that first time we came with my grandfather. When I knew I had to make the break, start fresh, I tried to imagine myself living in different places, even different countries. But I always came back here in my head. It wasn't impulsive, though again, a lot of people think so. I planned it for years. That's how I do things, plan them out. Step by step."

She paused, rested her chin on her knees as she studied him. "Obviously, I've missed a step somewhere with you or I wouldn't be sitting here on the grass drinking wine on a Sunday afternoon and telling you things I had no intention of talking about."

She lifted her head again, sipped wine. "You listen. That's a gift. And a weapon."

"I'm not going to hurt you."

"Healthy people don't step toward a relationship with the intention of hurting each other. Still, they do. Maybe it'll be me who ends up hurting you."

"Let's see." He cupped a hand at the back of her neck, rubbing lightly as he bent down to lay his lips on hers. "No," he said after a moment. "No bruises yet."

Then shifting, he framed her face with his hands to lift it until their lips met again.

Very soft, suddenly deep and wrenchingly gentle, his mouth moved on hers. With silky glides he teased her tongue into a dance as his fingers trailed down the line of her throat, over the curve of her shoulders.

She tasted of the wine that spilled unnoticed when her hand went limp on the glass. He found the quick catch and release of her breath when she drew him closer as arousing as a moan.

He laid her back on the blanket, sliding down with her as her arms linked around his neck.

She wanted his weight. She wanted his hands. She wanted his mouth to go on and on taking from hers. She felt the brush of his fingers on her collarbone, and shivered. They skimmed over the thin material of her top, then slipped down to dance over her breast.

He murmured her name before he grazed his teeth over her jaw. And his hand, so beautifully formed, so rough from work, molded her.

Heat flashed through her, urging her to give and to take. Instead, she pressed a hand to his shoulder. "Wait. Seth."

His mouth came back to hers, hungrier now, and with the dangerous flavor of urgency. "Let me touch you. I have to touch you."

"Wait."

He bit off an oath, rested his forehead on hers while his blood raged. He could feel her body vibrating under his, and knew she was just as needy. "Okay. Okay," he managed. "Why?"

"I'm not ready."

"Oh, sugar. Any more ready, you'd be past me."

"Wanting you isn't the same as being ready." But she was afraid he was right. "I didn't intend for this to happen, not like this. I'm not going to make love with a man who appears to be involved with someone else."

"Involved with who? Jesus, Dru, I just got back home, and I haven't looked at another woman since the first time I saw you."

"You've been involved with this one long before you saw me." He looked so blank, so disheveled, so frustrated she wanted to giggle. But she stayed firm. "Aubrey."

"What about Aubrey?" It took him several jolting seconds to understand her meaning. "*Aubrey?* Me and . . . Christ on a crutch, are you kidding?" He'd have laughed if the idea hadn't left him so shocked. "Where do you get that?"

"I'm not blind." Irritated, she shoved at him. "Move, will you?"

"I'm not involved with . . ." He couldn't even say it, but he sat back. "It's not like that. Jesus, Dru, she's my sister."

"No, she isn't."

"Niece."

"Nor is she that. And maybe you are oblivious to what's between you— though you don't strike me as a dolt—but I doubt very much she is."

"I don't think about her that way."

"Maybe you haven't, on a conscious level."

"At all." The very idea had panic dancing in his throat. "None of the levels. Neither does she."

Dru smoothed down her skirt. "Are you certain?"

"Yeah." But the seed had been planted. "Yes. And if you've got some insane notion that me being with you is somehow cheating on Aubrey, you can forget it."

"What I think," Dru said calmly, "is that I'm not going to have an affair with a man who I suspect is attracted to someone else. Maybe you should work this out with Aubrey before anything goes any further between us. But for now I think we'd better call it a day. Do you mind if I take a look at the painting?"

"Yes." He snapped it out. "I mind. You can see it when it's finished."

"All right." Well, well, she mused, artistic temperament rears its head. "I'll just pack up the food for you. I assume you want at least one more sitting," she said as she began to pack the cooler. "I should be able to give you some time next Sunday."

He stood, stared down at her. "You're a case. Some asshole cheats on you so that means we're all cheats?"

"No." She understood his temper, and since it seemed a reasonable conclusion for him to make, she didn't lose hers. "Not at all. In fact, I think you're as honest as they come. I couldn't consider being with you if I thought otherwise. But as I said, I'm not ready to take this step with you, and I have reservations over your feelings toward someone else—and hers toward you."

She looked up then. "I've been the clichéd victim of the other woman, Seth. I won't do that to anyone else."

"Sounds like instead of you asking me about scars, I should've asked you."

She rose now, nodded. "Yes, maybe you should have. Since you're going to sulk, I'll leave you to it."

He caught her arm before she could breeze by, whipped her around so fast she felt fear burst like a bomb in her throat. "You keep taking those steps one at a time, sugar. It might take you longer to fall on your face, but you'll fall just as hard."

"Let me go now."

He released her, turned his back on her to pack up his gear. More shaken than she wanted to admit, Dru made herself walk slowly into the house.

It was, she admitted, still a retreat.

NINE

Women. Seth tossed the cooler into the trunk of the car, heaved the hamper in behind it. Just when you thought you understood them, they turned into aliens. And those aliens had the power to change a normal, reasonable man into a blithering idiot.

There was nothing a man could do to keep up with them.

He tossed in the blanket, kicked the tire, then yanked the blanket back out again. He stared over at her house and gave it a satisfactory snarl.

His mutters were a combination of curses, pithy remarks and considerable blithering as he stomped back for his folding table and watercolor paper.

And there she was, sleeping on the red blanket in the dappled sunlight. All long limbs and color, with the face of a sleeping faerie queen.

"I ought to know who I'm attracted to," he told her as he carefully lifted the painting-in-progress and carried it to the car. "One guy turns out to be a putz, and damns us all?" He laid the paper on the blanket, scowled at it. "Well, that's your problem, sister."

Sister, he thought and felt an uneasy jittering in his gut. Why the hell had she put that in his head about Aubrey? It was off, that's all. It was way, way off.

It had to be.

He loved Aubrey. Of course he did. But he'd never thought about . . . Had he?

"You see, you *see*?" He jabbed a finger at the painting. "That's what your kind does to us. You confuse everything until we start questioning our own brains. Well, it's not going to work with me."

Because it was more comfortable, he switched back to temper as he finished loading his car. He had nearly made the turn for home when he swung the car around, punched the gas.

"We'll just settle this thing." He spoke aloud and nodded at the painting. "Once and for all. And we'll see who's the idiot."

He pulled up in the drive at Aubrey's house, leaped out of the car and strode to the door with his outrage and temper still leading the way. He didn't knock. No one would have expected him to.

The living room, like the rest of the house, was picture-pretty, cluttered just enough to be comfortable, and ruthlessly clean. Grace had a knack for such things.

Once she'd made her living as a single parent cleaning other people's homes. Now she ran her own business, a cleaning service with more than twenty employees who handled homes and businesses on the Shore.

Her own home was one of her best advertisements—and at the moment it was also entirely too quiet.

"Aubrey?" he shouted up the stairs. "Anyone home?"

"Seth?" Grace hurried in from the kitchen. In her bare feet and cropped pants, her hair pulled carelessly back from her face, she looked entirely too young to have a daughter some wrong-headed woman thought he was attracted to.

Jesus, he'd *baby-sat* for Aubrey.

"Come on back," she told him with a quick kiss. "Ethan and Deke are out back fixing the lawn mower. I was just making some lemonade."

"I just dropped by to see Aubrey about . . ." Oh no, he thought, he couldn't go there with Grace. "Is she around?"

"She plays softball Sunday afternoons."

"Right." Seth jammed his hands in his pockets and scowled. "Right."

"Honey, is something wrong? Did you and Aubrey have a fight?"

"No. No, I just need to . . . talk to her about something."

"She should be back in an hour or so. Emily, too. Em's off with her boyfriend. Why don't you go on out with Ethan and Deke, stay for dinner? We're cooking out later."

"Thanks, but . . . I've got some things . . ." It felt weird, too weird, looking at Grace's face, seeing Aubrey in it and thinking what he was thinking. "I gotta go."

"But—" She was talking to his back as he rushed out the door. Anna was right, Grace thought with a sigh. Something was troubling their boy.

❦

I t was the bottom of the sixth, with two on, two out when Seth arrived at the park. Aubrey's team, the Blue Crabs, was down by a run to their long-time nemesis, the Rockfish.

Spectators munched on hot dogs, slurped cold drinks from paper cups and hurled the expected insults or encouragements at the players. June was coming on with her usual hot breath and moist hands, making spring a fond memory. Sun poured onto the field and drenched it in heat and humidity.

Steam from the concession stand pumped out as Seth passed it to clamber up the stands.

He spotted Junior Crawford, a billed cap shielding his bald head and wrinkled gnome face, with a boy of no more than three perched on his bony knee.

"Hey there, Seth." Junior scooted his skinny ass over an inch in invitation. "How come you ain't down there on the field?"

"Came back too late for the draft." He scanned the field first and noted Aubrey was on deck as the current batter took ball three. Then he winked at the little boy. "Who's this guy?"

"This here's Bart." Junior gave the boy a bounce. "My great-grandson."

"Great-grandson?"

"Yup, got us eight grands now, and this one." Junior's attention swung back to the field at the crack of the bat. "Gone foul," he muttered. "Straighten out that bat, Jed Wilson!" he shouted. "Chrissake."

"Jed Wilson? Is that Mrs. Wilson's grandson?"

"The same. Affable enough boy, right enough, but can't bat worth shit."

"Worth shit," Bart said happily.

"Now, boy." Chuckling, Junior wagged his finger at Bart. "You know you're gonna get me in the doghouse again if you go saying that in front of your mama."

"Worth shit! Pappy!" Bart bubbled out a laugh, then poked his mangled hot dog toward Seth. "Bite?"

"Sure." Grateful for the distraction, Seth leaned down and pretended to take a huge bite.

When ball four was called, the crowd erupted, and Junior let out a whoop. "Walked him. By God. You're in for it now, you stinking Rockfish."

"Stinking Rockfish," Bart echoed joyfully.

"We're gonna see some action now, goddamn it! Now we'll see what's what."

The Blue Crab fans began to croon "Aub-*rey*! Aub-*rey*!" as she swaggered to the plate.

"Knock one out, Aub! That girl can do it," Junior said with such wild enthusiasm Seth wondered he didn't have a stroke on the spot. "You watch!" He stabbed Seth with the razor point of his elbow. "You just watch her slam that bastard."

"Slam that bastard!" Bart shouted, waving his mushed hot dog and dripping mustard.

For both their sakes, Seth nipped the boy from Junior's knee and set him on his own.

She was a pleasure to watch, Seth thought. No question about it. That compact, athletic build. The undeniable femaleness of it despite—maybe because of—the mannish baseball jersey.

But that didn't mean he thought about her . . . that way.

She scuffed at the plate. There was a short exchange with the catcher Seth imagined was derisive on both sides. She took a couple of testing swings. Wiggled her butt.

Jesus, why was he looking at her butt?

And took a hard cut at the first pitch.

The crowd surged to their feet on a roar. Aubrey shot toward first like a bullet banged from its gun.

Then the crowd deflated, and she jogged back to the plate as the ball curved foul.

The crowd began to chant her name again as she picked up the bat and went through the same routine. Two swings, wiggle the bat, wiggle the butt and set for the pitch.

She took it, checking her swing. And when the ump called strike two, she rounded on him. Seth could see her lips move, could hear the bite of her words in his head.

Strike, my ass. Any more outside, that pitch would have been in Virginia. Just how big a strike zone you want to give this guy?

Don't refer to the dubious sexual practices of his mother, Seth warned her mentally. Don't go there and get tossed.

Whether she'd learned some control in the last couple years or his warning got through, Aubrey skinned the ump with one baleful look, then stepped back in the batter's box.

The chant rose again, feet began to stomp on wood until the bleachers vibrated. In Seth's lap, little Bart squeezed what was left of the dog and bun to pulp and shouted, "Slam the bastard."

And she did.

Seth knew the minute the ball met her bat that it was gone. So, obviously, did Aubrey because she held her position—shoulders front, hips cocked, front leg poised like a dancer—as she watched the ball sail high and long.

The crowd was on their feet, an eruption of sound as she tossed her bat aside and jogged around the bases.

"Goddamn fricking grand slam." Junior sounded as if he was about to weep. "That girl is a fricking peach."

"Fricking peach," Bart agreed and leaned over from Seth's arms to plant a sloppy kiss on Junior's cheek.

The Rockfish went scoreless in the seventh, shut down on a strikeout, and a spiffy double play started by Aubrey at short. Seth wandered down toward the dugout as the fans began to drift toward home. He saw Aubrey standing, glugging Gatorade straight from the jug.

"Nice game, Slugger."

"Hey." She tossed the jug to one of her teammates and sauntered over to Seth. "I didn't know you were here."

"Came in bottom of the sixth, just in time to see you kick Rockfish ass."

"Fast ball. Low and away. He should've known better. I thought you were painting the flower girl today."

"Yeah, well, we had a sitting."

She cocked a brow, then rubbed at her nose as Seth stared at her. "What? So, I've got dirt on my face."

"No, it's not that. Listen, I need to talk to you."

"Okay, talk."

"No, not here." He hunched his shoulders. They were surrounded, he thought. Players, spectators, kids. Dozens of familiar faces. People who knew both of them. My God, did other people think he and Aubrey . . . ?

"It's, ah, you know. Private."

"Look, if something's wrong—"

"I didn't say anything was wrong."

She huffed out a breath. "Your face does. I rode in with Joe and Alice. Let me tell them I'm catching a lift home with you."

"Good. Great. I'll meet you at the car."

He shifted the blanket and painting to the backseat. Leaned on the hood. Paced around the car. When Aubrey walked toward him, a mitt in her hand, a bat over her shoulder, he tried to look at her the way he would if he'd never met her before.

But it just wouldn't work.

"You're starting to get me worried, Seth," she said.

"Don't. Here, let me put those in the trunk. I've got my stuff in the back."

She shrugged, passed off her ball gear, then peered into the backseat. "Wow." Transfixed, she yanked open the door for a better look at the watercolor. "No wonder you've been so hot to paint her. This is wonderful. Jeez, Seth, I never get used to it."

"It's not finished."

"I can see that," she said dryly. "It's sexy, but it's soft. And intimate." She glanced up at him, those pretty green eyes meeting his.

He tried to gauge if he felt any sort of a sexual jolt, the way he did when Dru's darker ones leveled on his face.

It was almost too embarrassing to think about.

"Is that what you're after?"

"What?" Appalled, he gaped at her. "Is what what I'm after?"

"You know, soft, sexy, intimate."

"Ah . . ."

"With the painting," she finished, feeling totally confused.

"The painting." The terror in his belly churned into faint nausea. "Yeah, that's it."

Now her face registered mild surprise when he opened the car door for her. "We in a hurry?"

"Just because you hit grand slams doesn't mean a guy shouldn't open the door for you." He bit the words off as he rounded the car, slammed in the other side. "If Will doesn't treat you with some respect, you ought to ditch him."

"Hold on, hold on. Will treats me just fine. What are you in such a lather about?"

"I don't want to talk about it yet." He pulled out, started to drive.

She let him have silence. She knew him well enough to understand that when he had something in his craw, he went quiet. Went inside Seth to a place even she wasn't permitted.

When he was ready, he'd talk.

He pulled into the lot of the boatyard, sat tapping his hands on the steering wheel for a moment. "Let's walk around to the dock, okay?"

"Sure."

But when he got out, she continued to sit until he came around and wrenched the door open. "What're you doing?"

"Merely waiting for you to treat me with the proper respect." She fluttered her lashes and slid out of the car. Then, laughing at him, pulled a pack of Juicy Fruit from her back pocket, offered it.

"No, thanks."

"What's up, Seth?" she asked as she unwrapped a stick of gum.

"I need to ask you for a favor."

She folded the gum into her mouth. "What do you need?"

He stepped onto the dock, stared out at the water, and at the osprey resting on a post before he turned back to her. "I need to kiss you."

She lifted her palms. "That's it? God, I was wondering if you had six months to live or something. Okay. Jeez, Seth, you've kissed me hundreds of times. What's the big deal?"

"No." He crossed his arms over his chest, then ran his hands over his hips and finally stuck them in his pockets. "I mean, I need to *kiss* you."

"Huh?" Shock registered on her face.

"I need to settle something, so I need to kiss you. Like a regular guy would."

"Seth." She patted his arm. "This is weird. Did you get hit on the head or something?"

"I know it's weird," he shot back. "Do you think I don't know it's weird? Imagine how I feel bringing it up in the first place."

"How come you brought it up in the first place?"

He stalked down the dock, back again. "Dru has this idea that I—that we—Christ. That I'm attracted to you in a guy way. And possibly vice versa. Probably."

Aubrey blinked twice, slow as an owl. "She thinks I've got the hots for you?"

"Oh, Jesus, Aub."

"She thinks there's something like that between you and me, so she gave you the boot."

"More or less," he muttered.

"So you want to plant one on me because of her?"

"Yes. No. I fucking don't know." Could it be any worse? he wondered. Could he be more embarrassed, more itchy, more stupid?

"She put this damn idea in my head. I can't work it back out again. What if she's right?"

"What if she's right?" There was a laugh burbling in her throat, but she managed to swallow it. "What if you've got some suppressed fantasy going about us? Get real, Seth."

"Look, look." Impassioned in a way that made her blink again, he took her by the shoulders. "It's not going to kill you to kiss me."

"Okay, okay. Go ahead."

"Okay." He blew out a breath, started to lower his head, then straightened again. "I can't remember my moves. Give me a minute."

He stepped back, turned away and tried to clear his head. "Let's try this." He turned back, laid his hands on her hips to draw her against him. Seconds passed. "You could put your arms around me or something."

"Oh, sorry." She reached up, threaded her fingers together behind his head. "How's this?"

"Fine. That's fine. Come up a little," he suggested, so she rose on her toes. He bent his head. His mouth was a breath from hers when she snorted out a laugh.

"Oh Christ."

"Sorry. Sorry." The fit of giggles forced her to move back and hold her stomach. He stood, scowling, until she controlled herself. "I balked, that's all. Here we go." She started to put her arms around him again. "Shit, wait." Conscientiously, she took the gum out of her mouth, folded it into the old wrapper in her pocket. "If we're going to do this, let's do it right. Right?"

"If you can control the pig snorts."

"Free lesson, sport: When you're about to tangle tongues with a woman, you don't mention pork or swine."

She put her arms around him again, took a good strong hold this time and moved in herself before either of them could think about it.

They stayed locked, the breeze off the water fluttering over them. There was a hum as a car drove by on the road behind them, and the sudden desperate barking of a dog as it chased along behind the fence until the car disappeared.

Their lips separated, their eyes met. The silence between them held for several long seconds.

Then they began to laugh.

Still holding each other, they rocked in a kind of whooping hilarity that would have put either one of them on the ground without the support. He lowered his forehead to hers on a relieved breath.

"So." She gave his butt a friendly pinch. "You want me, don't you?"

"Shut up, Aubrey."

He gave her, his sister, a fierce hug before he eased back. "Thanks."

"No problem. Anyway, you're good at it."

"You too." He rubbed his knuckles over her cheek. "And we're never going to do that again."

"That's a deal."

He started to swing an arm around her shoulders, then stopped as an appalling thought struck. "You're not going to tell anybody about this, right? Like your mom, or Will. Anybody."

"Are you kidding?" Even the idea of it had her shuddering. "You either. Promise." She spat into her palm, held it out.

Seth grimaced down at her hand. "I should never have taught you that one." But resigned, and respectful of the pledge, he spat into his own, then solemnly shook hands.

He was too restless to go home. And, he admitted, he needed a little more time before he faced his family with the kiss incident still fresh in his mind.

He had half a mind to go back to Dru's and let her know just how off the mark, how insulting, how *wrong* she'd been.

But the other half of his mind, the smarter half, warned him he wasn't in the mood to have a rational conversation with her yet.

She'd made him doubt himself, and it stung. He'd worked hard to reach and maintain his level of confidence, in himself, in his work, in his family. No woman was allowed to shake it.

So they'd just move back a step before things went any further. He'd paint her because he couldn't do otherwise. But that would be all.

He didn't need to be involved with a woman who was that complicated, that unpredictable and that damn opinionated.

It was time to slow down, to concentrate on work and family. To solve his own problems before he took on anyone else's.

He parked at his studio, carted his equipment and the painting up the steps. He used his new cell phone to call home and let Anna know he wouldn't be back for dinner.

He turned on music, then set up to work on the watercolor from memory.

As with sailing, worries, annoyances, problems faded away when he painted. As a child, he'd escaped into drawing. Sometimes it had been as dramatic as survival, others as simple as warding off boredom. It had always been a pleasure for him, a quiet and personal one or a soaring celebration.

In his late teens he'd harbored tremendous guilt and doubt because he'd never suffered for his art, never felt the drama of emotional conflict over it.

When he'd confessed all that to Cam, his brother had stared at him. "What, are you stupid?" Cam had demanded.

It had been exactly the right response to snap Seth out of a self-involved funk.

There were times when a painting pulled away from him and he was left baffled and frustrated by the image in his mind that refused to be put on canvas.

But there were times when it flew for him, beyond any height he'd imagined he could achieve.

When the light dimmed through the windows and he was forced to hit the overheads, he stepped back from the canvas, stared at what he'd done. And realized this was one of the times it had flown.

There was a vibrancy to the colors—the green of the grass and leaves, the sunstruck amber of the water, the shock of red from the blanket and the milky white of her skin against it. The garden of flowers on her skirt was bold, a contrast to the delicate way the filmy material draped high on her thigh.

There was the curve of her shoulder, the angle of her arm, the square edge of the blanket. And the way the diffused fingers of light fell over the dreamy expression on her face.

He couldn't explain how he'd done it. Any more than he'd been able to tell Dru what he thought about when painting. The technical aspects of the work were just that. Technicalities. Necessary, essential, but as unconsciously accomplished when he worked as breathing.

But how it was that a painting would sometimes draw out the heart of the artist, the core of the subject and allow it to breathe, he couldn't say.

Nor did he question it. He simply picked up his brush and went back to work.

And later when, still fully dressed, he tumbled into bed, he dropped straight into sleep with the image of Drusilla sleeping beside him.

"What are you calling it?" Stella asked him.

They were standing in front of the painting, studying it in the glare of his studio lights. "I don't know. I haven't thought about it."

"*Beauty Sleeps,*" Stella suggested. "That's what I'd call it."

She was wearing an oversized chambray shirt and baggy jeans with flat canvas shoes that looked as though they'd walked a lot of miles. And when she tucked her arm through Seth's he could smell hints of lemon from her shampoo and soap.

"We're proud of you, Seth. Not for the talent so much. That's God-given. But for being true to it. Being true to what you have and what you are, that's what makes the difference."

She stepped back and looked around. "Wouldn't hurt you to clean up this place some. Being an artist doesn't mean you have to be a slob."

"I'll take care of it in the morning."

She sent him a wry look. "Now where have I heard that one before? That one there." Stella jerked her head toward the painting. "She's neat as a pin. Maybe too neat—which sure as hell isn't your problem. Worries about letting anything shift out of place. Untidiness confuses her, especially when it comes to her own emotions. You've got to figure they're pretty messy where you're concerned already."

He lifted a shoulder in a way that made Stella smile. "I'm putting the brakes on there. She's too much damn work."

"Uh-huh." She twinkled at him. "You keep telling yourself that, boy."

He wanted to leave that area alone. He didn't mind messy emotions, but his own were in such a state he couldn't be sure he'd ever manage to tidy them up again.

"Cam said I should ask you about the zucchini bread."

"He did, did he? Maybe he thinks I've forgotten. Well, you can tell him I may be dead, but I've still got my wits. I wasn't much of a cook. Ray handled that end for the most part. But now and again I stuck my oar in. One day in the fall I got a yen for zucchini bread. We'd planted the stuff, and Christ knows we had more than we could eat in six years. Especially since Ethan wouldn't touch a morsel. So I got out the cookbook and tried my hand at baking some zucchini bread. Four loaves, from scratch, and I set them on a rack to cool. I was damn proud of that bread, too."

She paused a moment, tipped her head up as if looking at the memory. "About a half hour later, I walked back into the kitchen. Instead of four loaves, there were just three. My first thought was, well, those boys have been in here and helped themselves. Felt pretty smug about that one. Until I looked out the kitchen window. What do you think I saw?"

"I've got no clue." But he was sure he was going to enjoy it.

"I'll tell you what I saw," she said with a jut of her chin. "My boys, and my loving husband, out there in the yard using the zucchini bread I'd made from scratch as a goddamn football. Whooping and hollering and tossing that thing around like it was the Super Bowl. I was out that door like a shot, gonna skin the lot of them. About that time, Phil heaved that loaf high and hard, and Ethan loped over to receive. And Cam—he always was quick as a snake—he streaked over the grass, leaped up to intercept. Misjudged, though. The loaf caught him right about here."

She tapped just over her eyebrow. "Knocked him flat on his ass, too. Damn thing was hard as a brick."

She laughed, rocking back and forth on her heels as if her humor had weight. "Ethan snapped up the bread, stepped right over Cam as he sat there with his eyes rolling back in his head, and made the touchdown. By the time I got out to Cam to check him out and give them a piece of my mind, he'd shaken it off and the four of them were howling like loons. They called it the Bread Bowl. Last time I ever baked bread, I'll tell you that. I miss those days. I sure do miss them."

"I wish I'd had time with you. I wish I'd had time with you and Ray."

She moved to him, brushed at the stray tendrils of hair that had fallen over his forehead. The gesture was so tender it made his heart ache.

"Is it okay if I call you Grandma?"

"Of course it is. Sweet boy," Stella murmured. "She couldn't cut that sweet heart out of you, no matter how hard she tried. She couldn't understand it either, that's why hurting you's always been so easy for her."

They weren't talking about Dru now, he thought. But about Gloria. "I don't want to think about her. She can't hurt me anymore."

"Can't she? Trouble's coming. Trouble always does. You be strong, you be smart, and you be true. You hear me? You're not alone, Seth. You'll never be alone."

"Don't go."

"You're not alone," she repeated.

But when he woke with the early sunlight just sliding through his windows, it seemed he was.

Worse, he saw the folded note under the door. He forced himself to get up, to walk over and pick it up.

> *Lucy's Diner, next to the By-Way Hotel on Route 13.*
> *Eleven o'clock tonight.*
> *Make sure it's in cash.*

Trouble's coming. Seth thought he heard the echo of a voice. *Trouble always does.*

TEN

Aubrey stewed about it, picked it apart and put it together again. And the more she fumed and fiddled, the madder she got. Temper made it very clear in her mind that Drusilla Whitcomb Banks needed a come-to-Jesus talk, and Aubrey Quinn was just the one to give it to her.

Since she and Seth had made a pact, she couldn't vent to her mother, her father. She couldn't go by Sybill's and ask for some sort of psychological evaluation of the thing. And she couldn't go to Anna just to spew out her annoyance and resentment.

So it built, layer by layer, until she'd worked up quite a head of steam by the time she left the boatyard at five o'clock.

She practiced what she intended to say as she drove into town. The cool, the controlled, the keen-edged slice of words that would cut Little Miss Perfect down to size.

No one got away with making Seth unhappy.

Mess with one Quinn, she thought as she scooted her pickup into a space at the curb, mess with them all.

In her work boots, dirty T-shirt and well-sprung jeans, she marched into Bud and Bloom.

Yeah, she was perfect, all right, Aubrey thought, and bit down on her ire while Dru wrapped a bunch of daisies for Carla Wiggins. Just perfect in her pink silk blouse and wood-nymph hair. The slacks were stone gray and fluid. Probably silk, too, Aubrey thought, annoyed with herself for admiring the classy, casual look.

Dru's gaze shifted up and over as the door opened. What might have been polite warmth chilled into caution when Aubrey glared at her.

At least that was something.

Carla, bouncy and glowing, turned. "Hi, Aubrey. That was some game yesterday. Everybody's talking about your home run. Bases loaded," she said to Dru. "Aub knocked those Rockfish out of the water."

"Really?" Dru had heard the same, a half dozen times, already that day. "Congratulations."

"I swing to score."

"I about had a heart attack when that ball flew." Carla patted her tidy little breasts to demonstrate. "Jed's still flying. He got walked," she said to Dru, "to load the bases before Aubrey came to bat. Anyway, I'm cooking dinner for his parents tonight—talk about the wedding plans some more—and there I was running around straightening the place up—I took a half day off work—and it hit me I didn't have any flowers for a centerpiece. It's going to be spaghetti and meatballs. That's Jed's favorite. Just fun and cheerful, you know. So Dru said daisies would be nice in that red vase I've got. What do you think?"

Aubrey looked at the flowers, moved her shoulder. "They're pretty. Friendly, I guess. Kind of simple and sweet."

"That's it. That's just exactly right." Carla fussed with her fine blond hair. "I don't know why I get so nervous. I've known Jed's folks all my life. It's just different now that we're getting married in December. I told Dru my colors are going to be midnight blue and silver. I didn't want to go with the red and green, you know, but wanted to keep it Christmassy and festive. Do you really think those colors will work?" Carla chewed on her lip as she looked back at Dru. "For the flowers and all."

"Beautifully." The warmth came back into Dru's face. "Festive, as you say, and romantic, too. I'm going to put some ideas together, then you and your mother and I will go over everything. Don't worry about a thing."

"Oh, I can't help it. I'll drive everyone crazy before December. I've got to run." She scooped up the flowers. "They'll be coming along in an hour."

"Have a nice evening," Dru said.

"Thanks. See you later, Aubrey."

"Yeah. Hi to Jed."

The door closed behind Carla, and as the bells on it stopped ringing, the cheer that had filled the shop faded.

"I don't think you're in the market for flowers." Dru folded her hands. "What can I do for you?"

"You can stop screwing with Seth's brain and putting me in the role of the other woman."

"Actually, I was worried that was my role, and I didn't care for it."

All the cool, controlled, keen-edged words Aubrey had practiced flew out of her head. "What the hell's wrong with you? Do you think Seth would be poking at you if he were interested in someone else?"

" 'Poking at'?"

Aubrey hunched her shoulders. "Family phrase," she muttered. "What do you take him for? He'd never move on you if he was moving on someone else. He's not like that, and if you don't already know it, you're just stupid."

"Calling me stupid is going to end this conversation before it gets started."

"So is punching you in the nose."

Dru lifted her chin—Aubrey gave her points for it, and for the derisive tone. "Is that how you solve your disagreements?"

"Sometimes. It's quick." Aubrey showed her teeth. "And I owe it to you for the 'buxom blonde in black' remark."

Dru winced, but she kept her voice even. "A stupid comment doesn't make me stupid. But it was uncalled for and ill advised. I apologize for it. I suppose you've never had something pop out of your mouth that you've instantly regretted."

"All the time," Aubrey said, cheerful now. "Apology accepted. But that doesn't cover the bases regarding Seth. You messed with his head and you made him unhappy. That's worth a hell of a lot more than a punch in the nose, from where I stand."

"It wasn't my intention to do either." And she felt a flare of guilt. She'd had no trouble making him mad, but she'd never meant to make him unhappy. Still, she'd done what she thought right for everyone.

"I won't be a game piece to a man, even if he doesn't realize that's what he's making me. I've seen the two of you together. I saw the way you looked at me yesterday when I came into the boatyard. I'm standing here right now with you jumping down my throat because of what you are to each other."

"You want to know what we are to each other?" Riled up again, Aubrey leaned on the counter. "We're family. And if you don't know family loves each other and sticks up for each other and worries when one of them looks to be getting in deep where he doesn't belong, then I'm sorry for you. And if the way I look at you makes you unhappy, too bad. I'm going to keep right on looking at you, because I'm not sure you're good for him."

"Neither am I," Dru said calmly and stopped Aubrey in her tracks. "There we have a point of agreement."

"I just don't get you," Aubrey admitted. "But I get Seth. He already cares about you. I've known him . . . I don't remember ever not knowing him, and I can see it when he's gone soft on someone. You hurt him yesterday, and I can't stand to see him hurting."

Dru looked down, saw that her hands were gripping the counter. Deliberately, she relaxed them. "Let me ask you something. If you found yourself getting involved with a man—at a point in your life where it's really the last thing you want, but it's happening anyway—and you see that man has a relationship with another woman—a really attractive, vibrant, interesting woman—that you can't define—all you can see is that it's special and it's intimate and beyond your scope—how would you feel?"

Aubrey opened her mouth, shut it again. She had to take another moment before she answered. "I don't know. Damn it. Damn it, Dru, I love him. I love him so much that when he was in Europe it was like a piece of me was missing. But it's not sexual or romantic or anything like that. He's my best friend. He's my brother. He's my Seth."

"I never had a best friend, or a brother. My family doesn't have the . . . vitality of yours. Maybe that's why it's hard for me to understand."

"You'd have gotten a clue if you'd seen the two of us cracking up after kissing yesterday." Aubrey's lips twitched. "That's Seth for you. You planted that seed and so he worries over it, picks at it. 'Gee, am I screwing around with her, am I messing up people I care about? How can I fix it?' So he tracks me down and gives me the big picture, tells me he needs to kiss me—a real guy-girl smackeroo—so we can make sure there's nothing going on in that direction."

"Oh God." Dru closed her eyes. "And he didn't see that was insulting to you?"

"Nope." Surprised, and rather pleased Dru had seen that angle, Aubrey leaned more companionably on the counter. "I didn't let it bother me that way because he was so stupid about the whole thing, so worried and flustered. So we had our little experiment. He gets major points in the lip-lock department. He knows how to kiss."

"Yes, he does."

"There was relief all around because the earth did not move. It didn't even tremble. Then we laughed ourselves silly, and we're fine. I wasn't going to tell you that part," Aubrey added. "I thought letting it hang would make you suffer more. But since you said I was attractive and vibrant and interesting, I'm cutting you a break."

"Thanks. And I'm sorry. It was beginning to . . ." Dru trailed off, shook her head. "Never mind."

"We've come this far, don't hold back now."

She started to shake her head again, then realized that was one of her flaws. She held back. "All right. What's happening between Seth and me was beginning to worry me a little. I had someone I cared about, very much, cheat on me. I started to see myself as that woman, with some sympathy for her position. I didn't want to have any sympathy for her. I prefer despising her."

"Well, sure." Nothing could have been clearer to Aubrey's way of thinking. "You can relax. The field's all yours. Are we square on that?"

"Yes. Yes, we are. I appreciate your coming in to talk to me, and not punching me."

"Punching you would've pissed off Seth, not to mention my parents, so it's just as well. I guess I'd better get going."

"Aubrey." It was always a terrifying thing for Dru to go with impulse. "I don't make friends easily. It's not one of my skills. I'm terrific at making acquaintances, at social small talk and casual conversation. But I don't have many friends."

She took a long breath. "I'm going to close a little early today. It'll take me a few minutes to close out and lock up. Are you in a hurry, or would you like to go have a drink?"

Seth was a goner, Aubrey realized. He'd never hold out against those hints of vulnerability and need hiding under the polish. "Got any good wine at your place?"

"Yes." Dru's lips curved. "I do."

"I'll swing by home, grab a shower. Meet you there."

⌘

From his studio window, Seth watched Aubrey stride back out to her truck. He'd seen her stride in nearly a half hour before. And though he hadn't been able to see her face, he'd read her body language clearly.

She'd been ready to brawl.

He hadn't gone down. Until he'd seen Gloria, and locked that entire business back in his mental vault, he was keeping a distance from his family.

But he'd listened for the sounds of shouts or breaking glass. If it had come to that, he'd have run down to pull them apart.

But it hadn't come to that, he noted as Aubrey jumped nimbly into the cab of her truck and zipped off without any indication of temper.

One less worry, he supposed, as he walked into the kitchen to look at the clock on the stove. A little more than five hours left to obsess, he thought. Then he'd meet Gloria, give her the cash he'd withdrawn from his account.

And get back to his life.

⌘

Dru had barely walked through the door when Aubrey pulled into the drive. It gave her no time to fuss with the crackers and cheese she'd planned to set out, or to wash the fat purple grapes she'd picked up on the way home.

However casual the invitation, she was accustomed to entertaining a certain way. That certain way wasn't having her guest walk in, push a brown bag into her hand, then look around and whistle.

"Cool. Front page, *House & Garden*." She sent Dru a cheeky grin. "That wasn't really a dig. Man, my mother would love this. She's been itching to get a look at the inside. You got a cleaning service?" Aubrey asked and smoothed a finger over a tabletop. No dust.

"No. It's just me, and I don't—"

"Ought to. Working woman and blah, blah. Mom can give you the whole pitch. Big place." Aubrey began to wander without invitation as Dru stood holding the bag. "I want a big one when I get out on my own. Rattle around a bit, you know? Change from living with what feels like a million people sometimes. Then I'll be lonely and miss them and spend half my time at the house anyway."

She looked up. "High ceilings," she commented. "Must cost you some to heat this place in the winter."

"Would you like to see the bills?" Dru said dryly and made her laugh.

"Maybe later. I'd rather have wine. Oh, those are cookies in the bag. Mom baked some yesterday. Double chocolate chip. Awesome. Kitchen this way?"

"Yes." Dru sighed, then followed, decided to try to go with the flow.

"Nancy Neat, aren't you?" Aubrey said after one glance, then opened the back door. "Man, this is great! It's like your own little island. Do you ever get spooked out here all alone, city girl?"

"No. I thought I might," Dru said as she set the bag on the counter and got out a bottle of Pinot Grigio. "But I don't. I like listening to the water, and the birds and the wind. I like being here. I don't want the city. And I realized the first morning I woke up here, in the quiet, with the sun coming in the windows, I never did. Other people wanted it for me."

She poured the wine. "Do you want to sit out on the patio?"

"That'd be good. I'll bring the cookies."

So they had tart white wine and fat-filled cookies while the sun slid slowly down behind the trees.

"Oh." Aubrey swallowed a mouthful. "I should tell you, Seth and I made a pact not to tell anybody about the big experiment."

"The . . . oh."

"I don't figure you count, since it was your idea. Sort of. But since I spilled it, I've either got to kill you, or you have to swear not to tell anybody."

"Does this oath involve my blood in any way?"

"I usually do it with spit."

Dru thought about it for about two seconds. "I'd rather not involve any bodily fluids. Is my word good enough?"

"Yeah." Aubrey picked up another cookie. "People like you keep their word."

"People like me?"

"Yeah. Breeding," she said with a broad wave of a hand. "You're a fucking purebred."

"I'll assume that's a compliment of some sort."

"Sure. You've got this 'I'm much too cultured and well-bred to make an issue of it' air. You always look perfect. I admire that even when I hate it. It's not like you're all fussy and girly and stuff. You just always look good."

Aubrey stopped, mouth full. Then swallowed fast. "Oh hey, listen, I'm not coming on to you or anything. I like guys."

"Oh, I see. Then I suppose there's no point in us having a big experiment of our own." After two long beats, Dru's laughter burst out. She had to lean back, hold her sides as they ached from the force of it. "Your face. Priceless. It's the first time I've ever seen you speechless."

"That was good." Nodding approval, Aubrey picked up her wine. "That was damn good. I might just like you after all. So, are you going to talk Seth out of the watercolor portrait when he's finished?"

"I don't know." Would he finish it? she wondered. Or was he too angry with her to *see* her as he had? No, he'd finish, she decided. The artist would have no choice.

"If it were me, I'd wheedle it out of him."

"I think I'd feel strange having a painting of myself hanging on the wall. Besides, I haven't seen it. He was too angry to let me."

"Yeah, he gets all tight-assed when he's mad. Okay, here's a tip." Watching Dru, Aubrey rested her elbows on the table. "You don't want to cry. What you want to do is bravely battle back tears. You know, so your eyes get all shiny and wet and your lip quivers a little. Hold on."

She leaned back again, closed her eyes, took a couple of deep breaths. Then she opened them again, stared at Dru with a kind of wide-eyed, pitiful expression as tears swam into her eyes.

"My God," Dru murmured in admiration. "That's really good. In fact, it's brilliant."

"Tell me." Aubrey sniffled. "You can let one spill over if you have to, but that's it." A single tear dripped down her cheek. Then she giggled. "You start to flood, and he's all about patting your head and stuffing a paint rag or whatever in your hand before he goes into full retreat. Then you've lost him.

But you give him the shimmery-eyes, quivery-lip deal, and he'll do anything. It *destroys* him."

"How did you learn to do that?"

"Hey, I work with guys." Aubrey swiped the single tear off her cheek. "You develop your weapons. You can bite the tip of your tongue to get started if you have to. Me, I can turn it on and off. Speaking of guys, why don't you tell me about that creep you were engaged to, then we can trash him."

"Jonah? Assistant communications director. West Wing staff, a man with the president's ear. Brilliant mind, smooth style, gorgeous face and a body made for Armani."

"This isn't making me hate him. Get to the dirt."

"It's not far under the surface. Washington social circles—my grandfather remains a strong force in Washington, and my family is influential. Socially active. We met at a cocktail party, and things moved from there. Smoothly and at a reasonable pace. We enjoyed each other, and we liked each other. Had interests and people and philosophies in common. Then, I thought we loved each other."

It was never anger she felt when she thought of that. But sadness.

"Maybe we did. We became lovers—"

"How was he? In the sack?"

Dru hesitated, then poured more wine. She didn't discuss this sort of thing. Then again, she realized, she'd never had anyone who made her feel able to discuss this sort of thing.

Aubrey made it seem easy.

"What the hell. He was good. I thought we were good—but then again, lovers fall into the same category as friends with me. I don't make them easily."

"That'd make it hurt more when it gets messed up," Aubrey offered.

"Yeah, I guess it does. But I thought Jonah and I were good together, in bed and out of it. I was ready when he asked me to marry him. We'd been moving in that direction, and I was prepared. I'd thought it through."

Curious now, Aubrey tilted her head. "If you had to think it through, maybe you weren't in love with him."

"Maybe not." Dru looked away, watched the fluttering flight of a butterfly, listened to the quiet hum of a boat motor as someone cruised by on the river. "But I need to think things through. The bigger the step, the longer and more carefully I think. I wasn't sure I wanted to be married. My parents' marriage—well, it's not like your parents' marriage. But I felt, with Jonah, it would be different. We never quarreled."

"Never?" Pure shock covered Aubrey's face. "You never had a good shouting fight?"

"No." She smiled a little now as she realized how dull that would seem to anyone named Quinn. "When we disagreed, we discussed."

"Oh yeah, that's how we handle things in my family. We discuss our disagreements. We just do it at the top of our lungs. So you and this guy were good in bed, you didn't fight and you had a lot in common. What happened?"

"We got engaged, we had a round of parties and began making plans for a wedding set for the following summer. July because that was most convenient for our schedules. He was busy with work, and I was busy letting my mother drag me around to bridal shows. We house-hunted—Jonah and me, my mother and me, my father and me."

"That's a lot of hunting."

"You have no idea. Then one night, we were at his apartment. We went to bed. While we were making love, I kept feeling something scrape at the small of my back. Eventually I had to stop. It was funny, really, I made a joke out of it. Then we turned on the lights and I went over the sheets. And came up with another woman's earring."

"Oh." Aubrey's face filled with sympathy. "Ouch."

"I even recognized it. I'd seen her wearing them at some event or other. I'd admired them, commented on them. Which is probably why she made sure to leave it there, where I'd find it at the worst possible moment."

"Bitch."

"Oh yes." Dru lifted her glass in a half toast. "Oh yes indeed. But she loved him, and that was a discreet and surefire way to get me out of the picture."

"No excuses." Aubrey wagged a finger. "She was trespassing on another woman's man, even if the man wasn't worth jack shit. She was as sneaky as he was, and just as guilty."

"You're right. No excuses. They deserve each other."

"Damn straight. So, did you tie his dick in a knot? What?"

Dru let out a long sigh. "God, I wish I could be you. I wish I could, even for one single day. No, I got up, and I got dressed, while he started making excuses. He loved me. This other thing was just physical, it didn't mean anything."

"Christ." Disgust was ripe in her voice. "Can't they ever come up with something original?"

"Not in my experience." The instant, unqualified sympathy and support eased some of the rawness she still carried over it all. "He had needs, sexual needs that I was just too restrained to meet. He'd just wanted to get it out of his system before settling down. Basically, he said that if I'd been hotter, more responsive or creative in bed, he wouldn't have had to look elsewhere for that kind of satisfaction."

"And yet he lives," Aubrey murmured. "You let him turn the thing around on you instead of cutting off his balls and hanging them on his ears."

"I wasn't a complete doormat," Dru objected, and told her about the systematic destruction of Jonah's prized possessions.

"Nuked his CDs. That's a good one. I feel better now. Just as a suggestion, instead of cutting up his cashmere coat? I'd have filled the pockets with, oh, I don't know, say a nice mixture of raw eggs, motor oil, a little flour to thicken it up, maybe a hint of garlic. All easily accessed household items. Then, I'd've folded it up really neat, with the pockets to the inside. Wouldn't he have been surprised when he pulled it out of the box?"

"I'll keep that in mind, should the occasion ever come up again."

"Okay. But I really like the CDs, and the bit with the shoes. If the guy was anything like Phil about his shoes, that one really hurt. What do you say we take a walk, work off some of these cookies? Then we can order some Chinese."

It wasn't, Dru realized, so hard to make a friend after all. "That sounds terrific."

The diner was lit like a runway, and business wasn't exactly booming. Seth sat on the sun-faded red vinyl of the booth in the very back. Gloria wasn't there. She would be late.

She always came late. It was, he knew, just another way for her to show she had the upper hand.

He ordered coffee, knowing he wouldn't drink it. But he needed the prop. The ten thousand in cash was in an old canvas bag on the seat beside him.

There was a man with shoulders wide as Montana sitting on a stool at the counter. His neck was red from the sun, and his hair shaved so sharp and close it looked as if it could slice bread. He was wearing jeans, and the tin of tobacco he must have carried habitually in his pocket had worn a white circle in the fading denim.

He ate apple pie à la mode with the concentration of a surgeon performing a tricky operation.

The Waylon Jennings tune crooning out of a corner juke suited him right down to the ground.

Behind the counter, the waitress wore candy pink with her name stitched in white over the right breast. She picked up a pot of coffee from the warmer, breezed up to the pie eater, and stood, hip cocked, as she topped off his cup.

Seth's fingers itched for his sketch pad.

Instead he drew in his head to pass the time. The counter scene—done in bright, primary colors. And the couple midway down the line of booths who looked as if they'd been traveling all day and were now worn to nubs. They ate without conversation. But at one point the woman passed the man the salt, and he gave her hand a quick squeeze.

He'd call it *Roadside,* he thought. Or maybe *Off Route 13.* It relaxed him considerably to pull it all together in his mind.

Then Gloria walked in, and the painting faded away.

She'd gone beyond thin. He could see the sharp bones pressing against the skin at the sides of her throat, the whip-edge blades of her hips jutting against the tight red pants. She wore open-toed, backless heels that flipped and clicked against her feet and the aged linoleum.

Her hair was bleached a blond that was nearly white, cut short and spiky, and only accented how thin her face had become. The lines had dug deep around her mouth, around her eyes. The makeup she'd applied couldn't hide them.

He imagined that upset and infuriated her when she looked in the mirror.

She hadn't yet hit fifty, he calculated, but looked as though she'd been dragged face first over it some time before.

She slid in across from him. He caught a drift of her perfume— something strong and floral. It either hid the smell of whiskey, or she'd held off on her drinking before the meeting.

"Your hair was longer last time," she said, then shifted to flash her teeth at the waitress. "What kind of pie you got tonight?"

"Apple, cherry, lemon meringue."

"I'll have a slice of cherry, with vanilla ice cream. How about you, Seth honey?"

Her voice, just her voice, set his teeth on edge. "No."

"Suit yourself. You got any chocolate sauce?" she asked the waitress.

"Sure. You want that, too?"

"You just dump it over the ice cream. I'll have coffee, too. Well now." She leaned back, slung one arm over the back of the booth. Skinny as she was, he noted, the skin there was starting to sag. "I figured you'd stay over in Europe, keep playing with the Italians. Guess you got homesick. And how are all the happy Quinns these days? How's my dear sister, Sybill?"

Seth lifted the bag from the seat beside him, watched her focus in on it as he laid it on the tabletop. But when she reached out, he closed his fist around it.

"You take it, and you go. You make a move toward anyone in my family, you'll pay. You'll pay a hell of a lot more than what's in this bag."

"That's a hell of a way to talk to your mother."

His tone never changed. "You're not my mother. You never were."

"Carried you around inside me for nine months, didn't I? I brought you into the world. You owe me."

He unzipped the bag, tilted it so she could see the contents. The satisfaction on her face dragged at his belly. "There's your payment. You stay away from me and mine."

"You and yours, you and yours. Like you got something with those assholes I give two shits about. Think you're a big shot now, don't you? Think you're something special. You're nothing."

Her voice rose enough to have the man at the counter take notice and the waitress give them a wary look. Seth rose, took ten dollars out of his wallet and tossed it on the table.

"Maybe I am, but I'm still better than you."

Her hand curled into a claw, but she fisted it, laid it on the table as he walked out. She snatched the bag, tucked it against her hip on the seat.

Down payment, she mused. Enough to tide her over for a few weeks while she worked out the rest.

She wasn't done with Seth. Not by a long shot.

ELEVEN

He burrowed in his studio. He used painting as an escape, an excuse, and as a channel for his frustration.

He knew his family was worried about him. He'd barely seen them, or anyone else for that matter, for three days. He hadn't been able to go back to them after leaving Gloria.

He wouldn't take any part of her into their homes, their lives. She was the monkey on his back, and he'd do whatever it took to stop her from leaping onto theirs.

Money was a small price to pay to get rid of her. She'd be back. She always came back. But if ten thousand bought a space of peace, it was a bargain.

So, he'd work through his anger until he found that peace.

He'd hauled the big canvas up from storage, and he'd painted what he felt. The messy mix of emotions and images took shape and color and, as they did, emptied out of him.

He ate when he was hungry, slept when his vision blurred. And painted as if his life depended on it.

That's what Dru thought as she stood in the doorway. It was a battle between life and death, between sanity and despair waged with a brush.

He had one in his hand, stabbed at the canvas, sliced at it. Another was clamped between his teeth like a weapon in reserve. Music boomed, a violent guitar riff that was like a battle cry. Paint was splattered on his shirt, his jeans, his shoes. Her floor.

A kind of blood loss, she thought and gripped the vase she carried.

He hadn't heard her knock over the blasting music, but looking at him now, she realized he wouldn't have heard her if the room had been silent and she'd screamed his name.

He wasn't in the room. He was in the painting.

She told herself to back up and close the door, that she was trespassing on his privacy and his work. But she couldn't.

To see him like this was compelling, intimate, oddly erotic. He seduced her with a passion that wasn't simply beyond anything she understood, but was as distant from her world as the moon.

So she watched as he switched one brush for the other, as he swiped and swirled at the paint, then whipped at the canvas. Bold, almost vicious strokes, then delicate ones that seemed to hold a kind of contained fury.

Despite the breeze spilling in through the windows, she could see the dark line of sweat riding up the center back of his shirt, the damp gleam on the flesh of his arms and throat.

This was labor, she thought, and not all for love.

He'd told her he'd never suffered for art, but he'd been wrong, Dru realized. Anything that consumed so utterly came with pain.

When he stepped back from the canvas, she thought he stared at it as if it had appeared out of thin air. The hand that held the brush fell to his side. He took the one he'd clamped between his teeth, set it aside. Then rubbed, almost absently, at the muscles of his right arm, flexed his fingers.

She started to ease back now, but he turned, peered at her like a man coming out of a trance. He appeared to be exhausted, a little shell-shocked and painfully vulnerable.

Since she'd missed her chance to leave unnoticed, she did the only thing she could think of. She walked in, crossed over to his stereo and turned the music down.

"I'm sorry. You didn't hear me knock." She didn't look at the painting. She was almost afraid to. So she looked at him. "I've interrupted your work."

"No." He shoved away the stray strands of hair that fell over his forehead. "I think it's finished."

He hoped to Christ it was, because he didn't have any more to give it. It had, finally, blessedly, emptied him.

He shifted to his workbench to clean his brushes. "What do you think?" he asked with a nod of his head toward the canvas.

It was a storm at sea. Brutal, savage, and somehow alive. The colors were dark and fearful—blues, greens, blacks, vicious yellows that combined like painful bruises.

She could hear the wind screaming, feel the terror of the man who fought a desperate battle to keep his boat from being swallowed by towering walls of waves.

The water lashed, lightning speared out of the turbulent sky. She saw faces—just ghostly hints of them—in the feral clouds that spewed a sharp and angry rain. More, she realized as she was drawn to it, more faces in the sea.

They seemed hungry to her.

The single boat, the single man, were alone in the primal war.

And in the distance, there was land, and light. There, that small piece of the sky was clear and steady blue. There was home.

He was fighting his way home.

"It's powerful," she managed. "And it's painful. You don't show his face, so I wonder, would I see despair or determination, excitement or fear? And that's the point, isn't it? You don't show his face so we look and we see what we'd feel if we were the one fighting our demons alone."

"Don't you wonder if he'll win?"

"I know he will because he has to get home. They're waiting for him." She looked over at him. He was still caught up in the painting, and rubbing his right hand with his left.

"Are you all right?"

"What?" He glanced at her, then down at his hands. "Oh. Yeah. They cramp sometimes when I've been at it too long."

"How long have you been working on this?"

"I don't know. What day is it?"

"That long. Then I imagine you want to get home and get some rest." She picked up the vase of flowers she'd set beside his stereo. "I put this together before I closed tonight." She held it out. "A peace offering."

It was a mix of blooms and shapes in a squat blue vase. "Thanks. It's nice."

"I don't know whether to be disappointed or relieved that you haven't been up here the last few days stewing over our disagreement."

He gave the flowers a quick sniff. Something in the bouquet smelled a little like vanilla. "Is that what we had?"

"Well, we weren't in agreement. I was wrong. I very rarely am."

"Is that so?"

"Very rarely," she acknowledged. "So it's always a shock when I am, and when I am, I like to admit it, apologize and move on as quickly as possible."

"Okay. Why don't you tell me which portion of the disagreement you were wrong about?"

"About you and Aubrey. Not only wrong about the aspect of your relationship, but wrong to make an issue out of something that's your personal business."

"Huh. So you were wrong twice."

"No. That equals one mistake with two parts. I was wrong once. And I am sorry."

He set the flowers down, then rolled his shoulders to try to ease some of the stiffness. "How do you know you were wrong?"

Well, she thought, if she'd expected him to let it go with an apology, she should have known better. "She stopped by the shop the other day and explained things to me very clearly. Then we had some wine and Chinese at my place."

"Back up. I explained things to you, and you kick me out—"

"I never—"

"Metaphorically. Aub explains things to you, and everything's peachy?"

"Peachy?" She chuckled, shrugged. "Yes."

"You just took her word for it, then ate spring rolls?"

"That's right." It pleased her to think of it. The entire evening with Aubrey pleased her. "Since she wasn't trying to get me into bed, she didn't have any incentive, that I could see, to lie about it. And if she had been interested in you in a romantic or sexual way, she'd have no motive for clearing the path where I was concerned. Which means I was wrong, and I apologize."

"I don't know why," he said after a moment. "I can't put my finger on it, but that pisses me off again. I want a beer. Do you want a beer?"

"Does that mean you accept my apology?"

"I'm thinking about it," he called back from the kitchen. "Go back to that 'clearing the path' part. I think that might turn the tide."

She accepted the bottle he handed her when he came back in. "I don't know you, not very well," she said.

"Sugar, I'm an open book."

"No, you're not. And neither am I. But it seems I'd like to get to know you better."

"How about pizza?"

"Excuse me?"

"How about we order some pizza because I'm starving. And I'd like to spend some time with you. You hungry?"

"Well, I—"

"Good. Where the hell's that phone?" He shoved at things on his workbench, rattled items on his shelves, then finally dug the phone out from under a pillow on the bed. "Speed dial," he told her after he pushed some buttons. "I keep all vital numbers— Hi, it's Seth Quinn. Yeah, I'm good. How about you? You bet. I want a large, loaded."

"No," Dru said and had him frowning over at her.

"Hold it a minute," he said into the phone. "No, what?"

"No toppings."

"No toppings?" He gaped at her. "*None?* What are you, sick?"

"No toppings," she repeated, primly now. "If I want a salad, I have a salad. If I want meat, I have meat. If I want pizza, I have pizza."

"Man." He huffed out a breath, rubbed his chin in a way she'd seen Ethan do. "Okay, make that half totally boring and half loaded. Yeah, you got it. At my place over the flower shop. Thanks."

He disconnected, then tossed the phone back on the bed. "Won't take long. Look, I need to clean up." He dug into a packing box and came out with what might have been fresh jeans. "I'm going to grab a shower. Just, you know, hang. I'll be right back."

"Can I look at some of your other paintings?"

"Sure." He waved a hand as he carried his beer into the little bathroom. "Go ahead."

And just like that, she realized, they were back on even ground. Or as even as it ever had been. Just hang, he'd said, as if they were friends.

Wasn't it a wonder that she felt they were. Friends. Whatever else happened, or didn't happen between them, they were friends.

Still, she waited until the door was shut and she heard the shower running before she moved over to the painting propped on the easel by the front windows.

The breath caught in her throat. She supposed it was a typical reaction for someone seeing themselves as a painting. That moment of surprise and wonder, the simple fascination with self, as seen through another's eyes.

She wouldn't see herself this way, she realized. Not as romantic and relaxed and sexy all at once. Made bold by the colors, made dreamy by the light, and sexy by the pose with her leg bare and the bright skirt carelessly draped.

Made, somehow, powerful even at rest.

He'd finished it. Surely it was finished, because it was perfect. Perfectly beautiful.

He'd made her beautiful, she thought. Desirable, she supposed, and still aloof because it was so clear she was alone—that she wished to be alone.

She'd told him she didn't know him well. Now more than ever she understood how true that was. And how could anyone really know him? How could anyone understand a man who had so much inside him, who was capable of creating something so lovely and dreamy in one painting, and something so passionate and fierce in another?

Yet with every step she took with him, she wanted to know more.

She wandered to the stacks of canvases, sat on the floor, set her beer aside and began to learn.

Sun-washed scenes of Florence with red-tiled roofs, golden buildings, crooked, cobbled streets. Another exploding with color and movement— Venice, she realized—all a blur with the crowds.

An empty road winding through luminous green fields. A nude, her eyes dark and slumberous, her hair in untamed splendor around her face and shoulders, and the glory of Rome through the window at her back.

A field of sunflowers baking in the heat that was almost palpable—and the laughing face of a young girl running through them trailing a red balloon behind her.

She saw joy and romance, sorrow and whimsy, desire and despair.

He saw, she corrected. He saw everything.

When he came back in, she was sitting on the floor, a painting in her lap. The beer sat untouched beside her.

He crossed over, picked up the bottle. "How about wine instead?"

"It doesn't matter." She couldn't take her attention away from the painting.

It was another watercolor, one he'd done from memory on a rainy day in Italy. He'd been homesick and restless.

So he'd painted the marsh he'd explored as a boy with its tangle of gum and oak trees, with its wigeongrass and cattails, with its luminous light trapped in dawn.

"That spot's not far from the house," he told her. "You can follow that path back to it." He supposed that's what he'd been doing in his head when he'd painted it. Following the path back.

"Will you sell it to me?"

"You keep coming up here, I'm not going to need an agent." He crouched down beside her. "Why this one?"

"I want to walk there, through that mist. Watch it rise over the water while the sun comes up. It makes me feel . . ."

She trailed off as she tipped her face up to look at him.

He hadn't put on a shirt, and there were still a few stray beads of water gleaming on his chest. His jeans rode low, and he hadn't fastened the top button.

She imagined sliding her finger there, just over that line of denim. Just under it.

"Feel what?" he prompted.

Needy, she thought. Itchy. Brainless.

"Um." With some effort, she shifted to admire the painting again. "A little lonely, I suppose. But not in a sad way. Because it's beautiful there, and the path means you're only alone if you want to be."

He leaned in, closer to the painting. She smelled the shower on him—soap and water—and her stomach muscles tightened even as those in her thighs went loose. "Where would you put it?"

If this was desire, Dru realized, if this was lust, she'd never felt its like before.

"Ah, in my office at home. So when I'm tired of working on the books, I can look at it. And take a quiet walk."

She eased away from him, propped the painting up again. "So, can I buy it?"

"Probably." He straightened as she did, and their bodies brushed. From the glint in his eye she decided he was perfectly aware of her reaction to him. "Did you see your portrait?"

"Yes." It gave her an excuse to put a little distance between them when she walked to it. "It's lovely."

"But you don't want to buy it?"

"It's not for me. What will you call it?"

"*Beauty Sleeps,*" he said, then frowned as the dream he'd forgotten came back to him. "Zucchini football," he muttered.

"Excuse me?"

"Nothing. Just a weird flash. Pizza," he said at the brisk knock on the door.

He snatched his wallet off the workbench and, still shirtless and barefoot, went to the door. "Hey, Mike, how's it going?"

"Hanging loose."

The skinny, pimply-faced teenager handed Seth the pizza box. Then his gaze shifted, and he caught sight of Dru. The way his Adam's apple bobbed, the way surprise, interest and envy sped over his young, bumpy face, warned Dru there would be fresh fruit on the grapevine, and it would have her and Seth clustered together.

"Um, hi. Um. Grandma sent you a bunch of napkins and stuff." He shoved the paper bag into Seth's hands as well.

"Great. Tell her thanks. Here you go, Mike. Keep the change."

"Yeah. Well. Um. See you."

"Looks like Mike's got a little crush on you," Seth commented as he booted the door closed.

"I'd say Mike's double-timing it back to Village Pizza so he can spread the word that the artist and the florist are having hot pizza and hot sex."

"I hope he's right. If we're going to make the first part come true, we'd better dig into this." He dropped the box on the bed. "You need a plate?"

Her heart had given a little lurch, but she nodded. "Yes, I need a plate."

"Now, now, don't get twitchy. I'll get you a glass of very nice Chianti instead of the beer."

"I can drink the beer."

"You could," he commented as he headed into the kitchen again. "But you'd rather have the wine. I'll drink the beer. And, sugar, if you don't like people talking about you, you shouldn't live in a tight-knit little community."

"I don't mind people talking about me so much." Not the way they did here, she thought, that was different, so much less bitchy than the way they gossiped in Washington. "I just don't care for them talking about me doing something before I have a chance to do it."

"Would that be the pizza or the sex?" he asked as he came back with paper plates.

"I haven't decided." She pushed through the clothes in his packing box until she found a denim work shirt. "Put this on."

"Yes 'm. Can you handle sitting on the bed to eat if I promise not to jump you?"

She sat and, using one of the white plastic forks Mike's grandmother had put into the bag, worked a slice free. She plopped it on her plate, then using the same method, lifted a piece of his half.

"You know, we've been dating for a while now—"

"We are not dating. This is not a date. This is a pizza."

"Right. Anyway." He sat down, cross-legged, his shirt carelessly unbuttoned.

It was worse, she realized than no shirt at all.

"We haven't asked some of the essential questions to make sure this relationship has a chance."

"Such as?"

"Vacation weekend. The mountains or the shore?"

"Mountains. We live at the shore."

"Agreed." He bit into the pizza. "Favorite guitar player. Eric Clapton or Chet Atkins?"

"Chet who?"

He actually went pale. "Oh God." With a wince, he rubbed his heart. "Let's skip that one. It's too painful. Scariest movie ever—classic category, *Psycho* or *Jaws*?"

"Neither. *The Exorcist*."

"Good one. Who would you trust, with your life, against the forces of evil? Superman or Batman?"

"Buffy—the vampire slayer."

"Get out." He swigged beer. "Superman. It *has* to be Superman."

"One whiff of kryptonite and he's down for the count. Besides"—she polished off her slice and went for another—"Buffy has a much more interesting wardrobe."

He shook his head in disgust. "Let's move on. Shower or bath?"

"It would depend on—"

"No, no, no." He snagged more pizza. "No depends. Pick."

"Bath." She licked sauce off her finger. "Long, hot and full of bubbles."

"Just as I suspected. Dog or cat?"

"Cat."

He set the slice down. "That is just so wrong."

"I work all day. Cats are self-reliant, and they don't chew your shoes."

He shook his head in deep regret. "This might be the end of things between us. Can this relationship be saved? Quick. French fries or caviar?"

"Really, that's ridiculous. French fries, of course."

"Do you mean it?" As if hope had sprung giddily into his heart, he grabbed her hand in a tight grip. "You're not just saying that to string me along so you can have your way with me?"

"Caviar is fine on occasion, but it's hardly an essential element of life."

"Thank God." He gave her hand a loud kiss, then went back to eating. "Other than a woeful ignorance of music and poor judgment over pets, you did really well. I'll sleep with you."

"I don't know what to say. I'm so touched. Tell me about the woman in the painting—the brunette sitting in front of the window in Rome."

"Bella? Want some more wine?"

She lifted that eyebrow in the way that stirred his blood. "Are you stalling?"

"Yeah, but do you want some more wine anyway?"

"All right."

He got up to get the bottle, topped off Dru's glass before sitting down again. "You want to know if I slept with her?"

"Amazing. I'm transparent as glass to you." She took another bite of pizza. "You could tell me it's none of my business."

"I could. Or I could lie to you. She's a tour guide. I'd see her now and then when I was out and around. We got to know each other. I liked her. I painted her, and I slept with her. We enjoyed each other. It never got any deeper or more complicated than that. I don't sleep with every woman who models for me. And I don't paint every woman I sleep with."

"I wondered. And I wondered if you'd lie to me. That's a habit of mine, assuming someone will give the handy lie instead of the more complicated truth. You're not the kind of man I'm used to."

"Drusilla—" He broke off with a muttered oath when his cell phone rang.

"Go ahead. I'll put this away for you."

She eased from the bed, gathered the pizza box, the plates, while he flipped on the phone. "Yeah? No, I'm okay. I was distracted. Anna, I'm fine. I finished the painting I was working on. As I matter of fact I'm not starving myself to death. I just had pizza with Dru. Uh-huh. Sure. I'll be home to-morrow. Absolutely. I love you, too."

He hung up as Dru came back in. "Anna."

"Yes, I heard." She picked up the phone, set it on a nearby table. "Do you know you have beer, wine, a month's supply of soft drinks and now left-over pizza as the total contents of your refrigerator?"

"There used to be half a meatball sub, but I ate it."

"Oh, well then." She walked to the door. Locked it. The sound of that turning lock might have echoed in her head, but it wasn't going to stop her.

She crossed to him.

"The last time I went to bed with a man it was a humiliating experience for me. That's been nearly two years ago now. I haven't particularly missed sex. It's very possible, on some level, I'm using you to take back something I feel someone else took from me."

Since he was still sitting cross-legged on the bed, she slid onto his lap, hooked her legs around his hips, her arms around his neck. "Do you mind?"

"I can't say I do." He ran his hands up her back. "But here's the thing. You may get more than you bargained for."

"Calculated risk," she murmured and brought her mouth to his.

TWELVE

His hands glided over her skin, and nerves sparked under it. She wanted this, wanted him. The decision to come to his bed had been her own. But she knew the pounding of her heart was as much from panic as from desire.

And so, she realized as those wonderful hands rubbed up and down her back, did he.

"Relax." He whispered it as his lips trailed over her cheek. "It's not brain surgery."

"I don't think I want to relax." Those nerves were a separate kind of thrill, running fast along the tingle of needs. "I don't think I can."

"Okay." And still he stroked, easy hands, easy lips. "Then just be sure."

"I'm sure. I am sure." She eased back. She wanted to see his face. "I never seem to do anything unless I am." She brushed at the strands of hair that fell over his forehead. "It's just . . . been a while."

How could she tell him she'd lost her confidence in this area? If she told him, she'd never be sure that whatever happened between them now was as much her doing as his.

"So we'll take it slow."

She steadied herself. Intimacy, she'd always believed, took courage as well as desire. She'd taken the step. She'd locked the door. She'd come to his bed. Now she'd take another.

"Maybe." Watching him, she unbuttoned her shirt, saw his gaze drift down. Saw the blue of his eyes deepen as she parted the cotton, let it fall off her shoulders. "Maybe not."

He trailed his fingertips along the swell of her breasts, the soft flesh above the fancy white lace of her bra.

"You know one of the really great things about women?" he said conversationally as his fingers danced down over lace and back again. "Not just that they have breasts—which can't be over-appreciated—but all the cool things they put them in."

It made her laugh even as her skin began to shiver. "Like lingerie, do you?"

"Oh yeah." He toyed with the right strap, then nudged it off her shoulder. "On women, that is. I used to swipe Anna's Victoria's Secret catalogues so I could . . . Well." He nudged the left strap. "Probably shouldn't get into that at such a moment. You wearing panty things that match this?"

A quickening of power began to throb under the nerves. "I guess you'll just have to find out for yourself."

"I just bet you are." He leaned in to rub his lips over her shoulder. "You're a coordinated sort of woman. You know what other part—anatomically speaking—I really like about you?"

His lips were gliding along her throat now, rousing and soothing at the same time. "I hesitate to ask."

"This right here." His fingers stroked the nape of her neck. "Drives me crazy. I'll warn you I'm going to have to bite it in just a little while, so don't be alarmed."

"I appreciate you . . . mmmm." His teeth scraped along her jaw, closing lightly over her chin before they nipped at her bottom lip.

"You were starting to relax," he whispered when her breath caught. "Can't have that."

This time his mouth took hers, hot, hard, in a proprietary kiss that was almost a branding. The leap from playful to possessive was so fast, so high she could do nothing but cling while he ravaged.

Steady, she thought as her mind reeled. Had she believed she'd needed to be steady and sure? Oh no, this breathless race was better. So much better.

Her legs tightened around his waist, her body strained. On a jolt of need she answered the demand of the kiss with demands of her own.

No, this wasn't just want, she realized. This was craving.

She shoved at his shirt, pushing it off his shoulders so that her fingers could dig into flesh, could mold muscle.

Her scent was everywhere, as if she'd bathed in wildflowers. The delicacy of it, the silky texture of that fragrant skin misted his mind. The quiet, throaty moans she made when he touched, when he tasted, sprinted through his blood.

The light was changing, softening toward evening. He wanted to see that gentle sunlight glow over her, watch it catch in the green and gold of her eyes.

Her breath trembled out, and she arched back when he feasted on the long line of her throat. Flowed back, as if boneless, when his tongue slid toward her breast.

Struggling not to rush, he lifted his head to look down at her. "Flexible, aren't you?"

"I take"—she shuddered, bowed—"yoga. Twice a week."

"Mother of God," was all he could manage as the long, lean length of her stretched back with her legs still locked around his waist.

Almost reverently now, his hands moved over her, exploring the slope of shoulder, curve of breast, the line of torso. He flipped open the button at her waist and eased the zipper down. Slowly.

"I was right." He tortured them both by slipping his fingers just under the elastic of white lace panties. "Coordinated. In more ways than one."

Tucking his hands under her hips, he lifted them. And nuzzled at her belly. He felt the muscles quiver under his lips, then jerk when he pressed his mouth to the lace between the V of cotton.

The thrill coiled inside her, tight as a fist, then spread, fingers of pleasure that stroked toward an aching. When her legs trembled, he nudged them down, then drew the trim, tailored slacks away.

"I need to work my way up to the nape of your neck." His lips and fingers played over her legs. "It may take a while."

"That's okay." Her breath caught, then released on a sigh. "Take your time."

He didn't rush. As the aches built she fisted her hands in the sheets to stop herself from begging. She wanted to comb her fingers through his hair, to run them over his body, but was afraid if she released her anchor, even for an instant, she would fly out of this pool of swirling pleasures.

She wanted to drown in it.

He nipped lightly at her thigh and had her turning her face into the mattress, choking back a moan. His tongue slipped and slid along the edge of lace, turned moan into sob. Then stroked under it so sob became quick, gasping cries.

Her need was his need, and still his hands were easy as he rolled the lace down, as he brushed his palm over the heat. Watching her rise up, seeing her eyes go shocked, go blind as he urged her up, was glorious.

When she went limp, he moved up her body with lazy kisses. He wanted her to tremble, to call out his name, to clamp around him as if life depended on it.

And she would, he promised himself as he suckled her breast through the lace. Before they were done, she would.

Her heart was thudding under his mouth, and its beat kicked higher when he pulled the lace away and took flesh.

Her fingers tangled in his hair, pressed him closer, then streaked down his back.

"Let me." Her voice was thick and dreamy as she tugged at his jeans. "Let me."

The music was a low, pumping, primal beat, as urgent as her pulse. She rolled as she dragged denim away, pressed her body along the length of his. Found his mouth in a desperate kiss.

She needed, needed to fill herself with him, and took her lips on a wild journey over his face, his throat, his chest.

God, so hard, so lean, so male.

She wanted, wanted him to fill her, to know that shock, that wonder of being invaded, of being joined. But when she would have straddled him, have taken him into her, he reared up.

"Not yet." And flipped her over on her stomach.

"I want—"

"So do I. Christ, so do I."

When he closed his teeth over the nape of her neck, the erotic shock had her crying out. Her hands closed over the iron rungs of the headboard, but there was no anchor this time.

She went wild.

She bucked under him, felt herself hurtling toward something like madness. "God. Oh God. Now."

His hand shot under her, and those clever fingers plunged into her, into the heat and the wet. She came on a violent leap that left her helpless and shuddering.

When her hands unclasped the rungs, he pushed her to her back. "Now," he said, and crushed his mouth to hers, swallowing her scream as he drove into her.

She closed around him, arched to him. A fast rise and fall, flesh pounding damply against flesh. Each time her breath would catch, his blood beat.

So he watched her as the last glints of sunlight glowed on her face, caught in the green and gold of her eyes as they hazed with tears.

She lifted a hand to his cheek, and there was a kind of wonder in her voice when she said, "Seth."

The beauty of it all but drowned him.

He watched her still as everything inside them shattered.

The next best thing to making love, in Seth's opinion, was floating along on the warm river of satisfaction after making love. There was something incredibly soft and lovely about a woman's body after completion that made it the perfect resting place.

They'd lost sunset and were drifting toward dusk. Somewhere along the way, he realized, his last CD had finished playing. Now there was only the sound of wind rising up and Drusilla's breathing.

Rain was coming. He could smell it—could sense the storm dancing on the air.

He'd have to shut the windows. Eventually.

He lifted a hand to stroke it along the side of her breast. "I guess you're relaxed now," he murmured. "Whether you like it or not."

"I guess I am."

He certainly was, she thought. That was a good sign. Wasn't it? She hated herself for being stupid. Hated knowing that now that her mind was clearing again, the doubts were creeping in.

She could hardly ask if it had been good for him without sounding like a ridiculous cliché.

But it didn't stop her from wanting to know.

"Thirsty?" he asked her.

"A bit."

"Hmm." He nuzzled in. "I'll get us something, when I can move again."

She combed her fingers through his hair. He had such soft hair, so straight, so full of lights. "Ah . . . you're all right?"

"Uh-huh. Rain's coming in."

She glanced toward the windows. "No, it isn't."

"I mean rain's coming." He turned his head to look out at the sky. "Storm's blowing in. Your car windows up?"

Why the hell was he asking about her car windows when she'd just had a life-altering experience? "Yes."

"Good."

She stared at the ceiling. "I should go, before it rains."

"Uh-uh." He wrapped her close, then rolled over with her. "You should stay, and we'll listen to the rain when we make love again."

"Again?"

"Mmm. Did you know you have this little dimple right at the base of your spine?" He skimmed his finger there as he opened his eyes, and saw her face. "Something wrong?"

"I don't know. Is there?"

He caught her head in his hands, and considered. "I know that face. You're mildly peeved and working toward seriously pissed. What's wrong? Was I too rough?"

"No."

"Not rough enough, what? Hey." He gave her head a little shake. "Tell me what's wrong, Dru."

"Nothing. Nothing. You're an incredible lover. I've never been with anyone as thorough or exciting."

"Then what is it?" he demanded as she pulled away and sat up.

"I said it's nothing." She could hear the testiness of her own voice. God, she thought, she'd whine in a minute. The first threatening rumble of thunder seemed the perfect accent to her mood. "You might say *something* about me. Even the standard, 'Oh baby, that was amazing.'"

"Oh baby, that was amazing." He might have laughed, but he saw the glint in her eye wasn't just temper. "Hold on." He had to move fast to grab her before she could scoot off the bed. And to avoid a tussle, just rolled on top of her again to keep her in place. "Just what happened between you and that guy you were engaged to?"

"That's hardly relevant now."

"It is when you've just plopped him down in bed with us."

She opened her mouth, prepared to strike out with a sharp, damning reply. And sighed instead. "You're right. You're absolutely right. And I'm absolutely stupid. Let me up. I can't carry on any sort of conversation this way."

He eased back so she could shift. And said nothing when she tugged the sheet up over her breasts, though he recognized the gesture as a lifting of the shield.

She tried to gather her thoughts as thunder rolled again and lightning shuddered through the dark. "He cheated on me, and as he claimed to love me, his reason was the fact that I was unimaginative in bed."

"Were you taking yoga back then?" When she merely stared, coolly, Seth shook his head. "Sugar, if you bought that line, you are stupid."

"I was going to *marry* him. We'd ordered the invitations. I'd had my first fitting for the wedding dress. Then I find out he's been romping between the sheets—ones I bought, for your information—with a *lawyer*."

Wind blew in a gust through the windows, and lightning slashed behind it. But he didn't look away from her. He didn't rush over to shut the windows against the oncoming rain.

"And he expected me to understand his reasoning," she went on. "He expected me to go through with the wedding because it was just sex, which was something I wasn't particularly skilled at."

Prick, Seth thought. The kind of prick that gave regular guys a bad name. "And do you figure a guy who'd go shopping for wedding invitations with one woman and sneak around with another is worth one minute of your time?"

"Hardly, or I wouldn't have walked out on him, causing myself and my family considerable embarrassment. I'm not thinking of him. I'm thinking of me."

She was wrong about that, but he let it go. "Do you want me to tell you what it was like being with you? It was magic." He leaned forward to touch his lips to hers. "Magic."

When he took her hand, she looked down at the way they joined. Then sighing, looked toward the windows. "It's raining," she said softly.

"Stay with me awhile." He brought their joined hands to his lips. "We'll listen to it."

⟨⟨⟩⟩

It was still raining when she rose. The soft, steady patter after the storm turned the room into a cozy nest, one she wished she could wallow in.

"Stay the night. I'll even run out early and hunt up something decent for breakfast."

"I can't." It seemed so intimate, so romantic to talk to him in the dark that her first reaction was disappointment when he turned on the light. The second was shock as she realized she was in full view of the windows. "For heaven's sake." She scrambled with her underwear toward the bathroom.

"Yeah, like there's anyone out there at this time of night, in the rain." Unconcerned with modesty, he got up and, comfortably naked, followed her. He managed to stop the door from slamming in his face. "Look at it this way, you'll only have to walk downstairs to go to work in the morning."

"I don't have any clothes. Any fresh clothes," she added when he gestured to the shirt still in a heap on the bedroom floor. "Only a man could suggest I go to work in the morning wearing the same thing I wore yesterday. Would you mind getting that shirt for me?"

He obliged her, but that didn't mean he couldn't stall. "Bring extra clothes tomorrow. I'll pick up some supplies. We'll have dinner. I can cook," he claimed when she lifted an eyebrow. "Adequately. Or we could hang at your place, and you could fix dinner."

"I don't cook, even adequately."

"We can go out, then come back here. Or your place," he added, easing his arms around her. "I don't care where. A planned date, instead of our usual impromptu."

"This wasn't a date." She wiggled away to button her shirt. "This was sex."

"Excuse me. We had food, alcoholic beverages, conversation and sex. That, baby, is a date."

She could feel her lips quiver into a smile. "Damn. You got me."

"Exactly." He caught her around the waist again when she moved by him, drew her back against him. "Have dinner with me, go to bed with me, wake up with me."

"All right, but we'll have to eat after eight. I have a yoga class tomorrow."

"You're just saying that to torment me. But since we're on the subject, can you actually hook your heel behind your head?"

She laughed and pulled away. "I've got to go. It's after midnight. I'll come back here around eight. I'll risk your cooking."

"Great. Hey, do you want me to frame the watercolor for you?"

She beamed at him. "I can have it?"

"That depends. I'm willing to trade a painting for a painting."

"You've already finished the one of me."

"I want another."

She put on her shoes. "You've done two."

"One day, when I'm a dead, famous artist whose work is studied, and the prices of which are ridiculously jacked up, they'll call this my Drusilla period."

"Interesting. If that's what you want as payment, I'll pose again."

"Sunday."

"Yes, fine. Do you know what you're looking for with this one? What you want me to wear?"

"I know exactly what I'm looking for." He walked over, laid his hands on her shoulders and kissed her. "And you'll be wearing rose petals."

"I beg your pardon?"

"Red rose petals. Seeing as you're a florist, you should be able to get me a supply."

"If you think I'm going to pose wearing nothing but . . . No."

"You want the watercolor?"

"Not enough to be blackmailed."

She turned away, but he only caught her hand, spun her back. "You admire my work enough to want to own it."

"I admire your work very much, but you're not painting me naked."

"Okay, I'll wear clothes, but you're wearing rose petals. Ssh." He tapped a finger on her lips before she could speak again. "Obviously I'm not having you pose nude so I can get you into bed because I've already gotten you into bed. And for the record, I don't use art that way. I've had this image in my head since the first time I saw you. I have to paint it."

He took her hands. "I need to paint it. But I'll make you a deal."

"What's the deal?"

"I won't show it to anyone. When it's finished, you'll decide what to do with it."

He recognized the look on her face—one of mulling and consideration. And knew he had her.

"I decide?"

"I'll trust you to be honest about it. You have to trust me to paint what I see, what I feel. Deal?"

"Red rose petals." She angled her head. "I'm going to order a lot of them."

⁂

Seth walked whistling into the boatyard the next morning. He carried a box of doughnuts, fresh from the bakery.

Cam was already at work, drilling turnbuckles into a hull.

"She's a beauty," Seth called out as he strolled up to the prettily proportioned yawl. "You guys must've busted tail to get her this close to finished so soon."

"Yeah. She's done except for a little brightwork, some details in the cabin. Client wants to pick her up Sunday."

"Sorry I didn't give you a hand the last couple days."

"We managed."

There wasn't a sting in the tone, but there was the implication of one. "Where's everybody?"

"Phil's upstairs. Ethan and Aubrey are checking crab pots this morning. I've got Kevin coming in after school. Another week or so he'll be sprung, put in more time."

"Sprung? School'll be over already? What the hell day is it?"

"You'd keep up better if you checked in at home once in a while."

"I've been busy, Cam."

"Yeah." Cam set another turnbuckle. "So I hear."

"What're you pissed off about?" Seth tossed the bakery box onto the deck. "I'm here, aren't I?"

"You sashay in and sashay out as the mood strikes you. Decide to come swaggering in today because you finally got lucky last night?"

"What's it to you?"

"What's it to me?" Cam set the drill aside, vaulted down to the floor—a quick blur of aggravated male. "You want to know what it is to me, you asshole? It's a hell of a lot to me when you up and disappear for the best part of a week. You go around with some damn black cloud over your head, then hole up in your studio. It's a hell of a lot to me when I have to watch Anna worrying because you can't be bothered to tell us what the fuck's going on. You think you can just walk back in here feeling fine because you finally got Dru's skirt over her head?"

Guilt, which had begun to shimmer, exploded into a red flash of fury. Seth moved before he thought, shoving Cam back against the hull. "Don't talk about her like that. She's not some easy lay I used to scratch an itch. Don't you ever talk about her like that."

Cam knocked Seth back a full step. They were squared off now, nose to nose. Boxers who didn't give a damn about the bell. "You don't treat your family like this. Like a goddamn convenience."

Temper was a vicious dog that snapped at both their throats.

"You want to go a round with me?" Cam invited as fists bunched.

"Hold it, hold it. Jesus Christ, hold it!" Phillip all but leaped between them, pushed them apart. "What the hell's going on here? I could hear the two of you all the way upstairs."

"Kid thinks he can take me," Cam replied hotly. "I'm about to let him try."

"Hell you are. You two want to pound on each other, you take it outside. As a matter of fact, Seth, you go. Cool off." Phillip pointed toward the cargo doors and the dock beyond them. "You've been scarce enough around here lately, another few minutes isn't going to matter."

"This is between me and Cam."

"This is a place of business," Phillip corrected. "Our business, so that brings me into it. Keep it up, and the first one to take a punch at you may be me. I've had enough aggravation from you."

"What the hell are you talking about?"

"I'm talking about keeping promises, remembering your responsibilities. I'm talking about having a client who expects a completed design, which you agreed to do. Where the hell is it, Seth?"

He opened his mouth, closed it. Drusilla's sloop. He'd forgotten it. Just, he remembered, as he'd forgotten he'd told Anna he'd pick up the mulch she wanted for a new flower bed. And the ride he'd promised Bram in his new car.

As his anger turned inward, he stalked out of the cargo doors.

"Pissant," Cam grumbled. "Needs a kick in the ass."

"Why don't you get off his back?"

Baffled, still steaming, Cam rounded on Phillip. "Well, fuck you. You're the one who just finished stomping on him."

"I've been as worried and annoyed as you have," he shot back. "But that's enough. He's old enough to come and go as he pleases. When you were his age, you were racing around Europe and getting your hand up as many skirts as you could manage."

"I never broke my word."

"No." Calmer now, Phillip looked out to where Seth stood on the end of the dock. "And from the look of him, he didn't intend to break his either. How long are you going to let him stand out there feeling like shit?"

"A week or two ought to be enough."

At Phillip's steady stare, Cam hissed out a breath, and felt most of the temper expel with it. "Damn it. I must be getting old. I hate that. I'll go deal with it."

Seth heard the footsteps on the dock. He turned. Braced. "Go ahead and take a shot. But you only get the first one free."

"Kid, I'll only need one."

"Christ, I'm sorry," Seth blurted out. "I'm sorry I let you down. I'll do whatever grunt work you need. I'll get the design finished today. I'll make it up to you."

"Oh hell." This time Cam raked his fingers through his hair. Who felt like shit now? he asked himself. "You didn't let me down. You worried me, you pissed me off, but you didn't let me down. Nobody expects you to give all your time to this place. Or to be at home every spare minute. Damn it, first Anna's nagging at me because you're home too much and she doesn't think it's good for you. Then she's ragging because you're not home at all. How the hell did I get caught in the middle?"

"Just lucky, I guess. I had some things I had to take care of. That's all. And I was working. I got caught up in it and forgot the rest. The family's not a convenience for me, Cam. You can't believe that. It's a miracle. If it wasn't for you—"

"Stop right there. This isn't about old business, it's about now."

"I wouldn't have a now without you."

"You wouldn't have one without Ray. None of us would. Leave it at that." He jammed his hands in his pockets, looked out over the water.

Jesus, he thought. It didn't matter how old a kid got. They were still yours.

"So, you're serious about the sexy florist?"

Unconsciously Seth mirrored Cam's stance, and now they looked over the water together. "It appears that way."

"Maybe now that you've scratched that itch we'll get some work out of you."

"I seem to have some energy to spare this morning," Seth replied.

"Yeah, it always worked that way for me, too. What kind of doughnuts did you pick up?"

They were okay, Seth thought. Somehow, no matter what went on, they came back to being okay. "Variety pack. I got dibs on the Bavarian cream."

"I'm a jelly man myself. Let's go before Phil finds them."

They started back in together, then Seth stopped short. "Zucchini football."

Color drained out of Cam's cheeks. "What the hell did you say?"

"The Bread Bowl. The zucchini bread. She baked bread and you guys used it as a football. She told me."

"When?" Shaken, Cam gripped Seth's shoulders. "When did you see her?"

"I don't know. I don't. I dreamed it. Felt like I dreamed it," he murmured. His stomach jittered, but it wasn't unease he felt. It was, he realized, a kind of joy.

He'd spoken with Stella, he thought. He had a grandmother who'd shared a story with him.

"That's right, isn't it?" That joy leaped out in his voice, filled his face. "And you—you tried to intercept a pass and got hit above the eye. Knocked you down, nearly out. That's right, isn't it?"

"Yeah." Cam had to steady himself. It was a good memory. There were so many good ones. "She came running out the back door, shouting at us just as I was making the jump. I turned, and bam. Fucking galaxy of stars. That bread was like a goddamn brick. She was a hell of a doctor, but she never could cook worth a damn."

"Yeah, she told me."

"So, she bent down, looked at my pupils or whatever, held up fingers for me to count. Said it was just as well I got beaned. Saved her the trouble. Then we all started laughing—me and Dad, Phil and Ethan. Bunch of lunatics. Mom stood there, staring at us, with her hands on her hips. I can still see it. See her."

He let out a long breath. "Then she went back in and got another loaf so we could keep playing. She tell you that part?"

"No." Seth laid a hand on Cam's shoulder as they turned toward the cargo doors. "I guess she wanted you to tell me."

THIRTEEN

When the doughnuts were devoured, and Seth was hunkered down in a corner refining Ethan's basic design for Dru's sloop, Dru stepped outside her shop to snip off any faded blossoms in the whiskey barrel tub of verbena and heliotrope beside the front door.

The night's storm had cooled the air, swept away the dragging humidity and left the morning fresh and bell-clear.

The Bay was rich blue, still kicking a bit from the turbulence of the night. Boats were already rolling over it. The watermen in their workboats, the vacationers in their rented skiffs or motorboats shared the waters. The summer people who moored their boats and stole time to use them were out early. Why waste a minute of a perfect day? Dru mused.

In a few months, she'd be able to spend a pretty morning working on rigging, washing down the deck, polishing the brightwork of her own boat. Owning a boat meant a great deal more than casting off, hoisting sails and riding the wind. It meant pouring time, money, energy into maintenance. But that, she thought, was part of the pleasure. Or would be for her.

She liked to work. It had been one of the many small self-realizations that had come to her over the years. She liked working, producing and the satisfaction of standing back and seeing what she'd managed to do on her own.

She enjoyed the *business* end of running a business. The bookkeeping, the supplies, filling orders, calculating profit. It suited her sense of order just as the nature of her business suited her love of beauty for the sake of beauty.

The boat, when it was finished, would be her personal reward for making it all come together.

And Seth . . . She wasn't entirely sure what Seth was. The night she'd spent with him had been glorious. But like a boat, a relationship with him would never be all smooth sailing, and there was bound to be maintenance.

Just where would they be, she wondered, if the wind that had carried them to this point stalled on them? What would they do if they ran into a serious storm, or ran aground, or simply—as so many did—found the excitement draining from the ride?

And she wished she could do no more than enjoy the moment without looking ahead for problems.

He intrigued her and challenged her. He aroused her and amused her. He stirred up feelings in her no one had—not even, she was forced to admit, the man she'd nearly married.

She was drawn to his solid sense of self, his honesty and his ease. And she was fascinated by the hints of the turbulence and passions she saw bubbling just under the surface of that ease.

He was, she believed, the most compelling man she'd ever met. He made her happy. Now they were lovers, and she was already looking for the trouble ahead.

Because if you didn't look ahead, she reminded herself, you rammed straight into those problems and sank.

She carried the little shears back inside, into the storeroom, where she put it on its place on the shelf. She wished she could talk to someone, another woman, about the thrill and anxiety running so fast inside her. She wanted to be able to sit down with a friend and have a silly conversation where she could ramble on about everything she was feeling.

About how her heart started to flop around when he smiled at her. How it raced when he touched her. How scary and wonderful it was to be with someone who liked and accepted her for who she needed to be.

She wanted to tell someone that she was falling in love.

None of the women in her previous social circle would understand. Not the way she *needed* to be understood. They would be interested, certainly, even supportive. But she couldn't imagine telling any of them how he'd bitten the nape of her neck, then have them groan and sigh in envy.

And *that's* what she wanted.

She couldn't call her mother and tell her she'd had the most incredible sex of her life with a man she was stumbling into love with.

It just wasn't the kind of conversation either of them would be comfortable having.

Though her instincts told her there was nothing she could say to shock Aubrey, and she was dead certain she'd get the exact reaction she was looking for from her new friend, Aubrey's connection to Seth made that possibility just a bit too sticky.

So she was on her own, Dru supposed. Which was exactly where she'd wanted to be in the first place. But now that she had something to share, now that she felt her life shifting under her feet, there was no one to reach out to.

It was her own doing, she admitted. She could either live with it, or begin to change it. Opening up meant more than taking a lover. It meant more than dipping a toe into the waters of a new friendship.

It meant work. So she'd work.

The bells on the front door jingled, signaling her first customer of the day. Dru squared her shoulders. She'd proven she could remake her life once. She could do it again.

Prepared to be more than the polite and efficient florist, she stepped out of the storeroom with a warm smile.

"Good morning. How can I help you?"

"Oh, I'm not sure. I'm just going to look around."

"Help yourself. It's a gorgeous day, isn't it?" Dru walked over to prop open the front door. "Too gorgeous to be closed in. Are you visiting Saint Chris?"

"That's right," Gloria said. "Taking a nice little vacation."

"You picked a perfect time." Dru ignored a frisson of unease at the way she was being studied. "Are you here with your family?"

"No, just me." Gloria flicked fingers over the petals of an arrangement, and kept her eyes on Dru. "Sometimes a girl just has to get away on her own. You know?"

"Yes, I do." She didn't look like the type to spend time or money on flowers, Dru thought. She looked . . . hard, edgy—and cheap. Her shorts were too tight, too brief, and her top too snug. When she caught what she thought was a whiff of whiskey along with the woman's florid perfume, she wondered if she was about to be robbed.

Then she dismissed the thought. Nobody robbed florists, certainly not in St. Chris. And if the woman had any sort of weapon it would have to be very, very tiny to be concealed under that outfit.

And to judge someone because she didn't care for the style of her dress wasn't the way to begin the new phase of becoming more personable with her customers.

"If you're looking for something to cheer up your hotel room while you're here, I have carnations on special this week. They have a nice fragrance and they're very low maintenance."

"That might work. You know, you look familiar, and you don't sound like a local. Maybe I've met you before. Do you spend much time in D.C.?"

Dru relaxed again. "I grew up there."

"That's got to be it. The minute I saw you, I thought . . . Wait a minute! You're Katherine's daughter. Prucilla—no, no, Drusilla."

Dru tried to imagine her mother having any sort of acquaintance with the thin, badly dressed woman who smelled of cheap perfume and whiskey. Then cursed herself for being a snob.

"That's right."

"Well, I'll be damned." Gloria planted her hands on her hips, made her smile large and friendly. She'd done her research. "What the hell are you doing down here?"

"I live here now. So you know my mother?"

"Sure, sure. I worked on several committees with Kathy. Haven't run into her in a while. I guess it's been three or four years. Last time, I think it was a fund-raiser for literacy. Book and author dinner at the Shoreham."

The event had been written up in the *Washington Post,* with enough detail in the archives Gloria had looked up on-line to make her claim smooth. "How is she, and your father?"

No, Dru thought, she wasn't a snob. She was simply a good judge of character. But she spoke evenly. "They're both very well, thank you. I'm sorry, I didn't get your name."

"It's Glo. Glo Harrow," she said, using her mother's maiden name. "Hell of a small world, huh? Seems to me the last time I talked to Kath, you were engaged. She was over the moon about that. Guess it didn't work out."

"No, it didn't."

"Well, men are like buses. Another one always comes along. You know, my mother's friendly with your grandfather." And that was true enough, though "acquainted" would have been more accurate. "The senator, he just keeps trucking along. A regular institution."

"He's an amazing man." Dru spoke coolly now.

"Gotta admire him. A man his age still active the way he is. Then you figure with the family money, he never had to work a day in his life, much less dedicate himself to politics. Tough arena, even for a young man, the way people like to sling mud these days."

"People have always slung mud. My family's never believed that financial advantage means letting someone else do the work."

"Gotta admire that, like I said."

When a man walked in, Dru bit down on her rising irritation and turned toward him. "Good morning."

"Hi. Hey, don't mind me, just finish what you're doing. I'm not in a rush."

"Would you like to look around some more, Ms. Harrow?"

"No." She'd spent more than enough time on this visit. "Why don't I take a dozen of those . . . what was on special?"

"Carnations." Dru gestured to the holding vase where she'd arranged samples in every color. "Would you like any specific color or combination?"

"No, no, just mix them up."

Gloria read the sign under the display and calculated it was a cheap enough price to pay for the up-close look. She took out cash, laid it on the counter.

Now that the contact had been made, Gloria wanted to be gone. She didn't care for the way the guy who'd come in was watching her and trying to pretend he wasn't watching her.

"I hope you enjoy them."

"I already am. Give my best to your mom when you talk to her," Gloria added as she started out.

"Oh, I will." Dru turned to her new customer. Some of the temper that had begun to simmer leaked out on her face.

"Bad time?"

"No, of course not." She readjusted her thoughts. "How can I help you?"

"First, I'm Will. Will McLean." He offered a hand.

"Oh, you're Aubrey's friend." Seriously cute, Aubrey had said. And with perfect accuracy, Dru decided as they shook hands. "It's nice to meet you."

"You, too. I just got off shift, figured on swinging by to see Aub—maybe catch up with Seth, before I go home and crash in a dark room for a few hours. Those flowers Seth got my girl a few weeks back were a really big hit. Can't let him get an edge on me. What've you got that'll knock her out, and make up for me working doubles most of the week?"

"How's your budget?"

"Just got paid." He patted his back pocket. "Sky's the limit."

"In that case, wait right here." She paused, reconsidered. The morning jolt wasn't going to spoil her plans for a more open Drusilla. "Better yet, come on back. If you like what I have in mind, you can sit down, get off your feet for a few minutes while I put them together for you."

"I look that bad?"

"You look exhausted." She gestured him back. "Go ahead, have a seat," she told him while she went to a refrigerated unit. "Delivered fresh this morning," she said as she took out a single long-stemmed rose in cotton-candy pink. "A dozen of these are guaranteed to knock her out."

He sniffed it when she held it out. "Smells great. Maybe I should make it two dozen. I've had to cancel two dates in the last ten days."

"Two dozen will put her in a coma."

"Perfect. Can you put them in one of those fancy boxes?"

"Absolutely." She moved to the work counter. "You and your brother are becoming my best customers. He bought me out of yellow roses about a week ago."

"He got himself engaged."

"Yes, I know. He was floating along about six inches above ground. You and your brother and Seth have been friends a long time."

"Since we were kids," Will concurred. "I can't believe he's been back a month and I haven't been able to catch up with him. Dan says Seth's been pretty tied up himself between his work, the boatyard and you. Whoops." The crooked smile flashed as he rubbed his eyes. "Sorry. Tongue gets loose when I'm brain-dead."

"That's all right. I don't imagine it's a secret Seth and I are . . ." What? "Seeing each other," she decided.

Will did his best to stifle a yawn. "Well, if we ever get our schedules aligned, maybe the six of us can do something."

"I'd like that." Dru laid the roses and baby's breath in the tissue-lined box. "I'd like that a lot."

"Good. Ah, can I ask you something? That woman who was in here before? Was she hassling you?"

"Why do you ask?"

"I don't know, just a feeling. Plus there was something about her. I think I know her from somewhere. Can't put my finger on it, but it doesn't feel right. Do you know what I mean?"

"I know exactly what you mean." She glanced over at him. He was a friend of Aubrey's, of Seth's. The new, more open Dru was going to consider him a friend as well.

"She claimed to know my mother, but she didn't." No one, Dru thought, absolutely no one referred to her mother as Kathy. It was Katherine, and on rare occasions, Kate. But never Kathy, never Kath. "I don't know what she was after, but I'm glad you came in when you did."

"You want me to stick around awhile, in case she comes back?"

"No, but thanks. She doesn't worry me."

"You called her Harrow?" Will shook his head. "Doesn't ring any bells. But I know her from somewhere. When I come up with it, I'll let you know."

"I appreciate it."

⚭

It was a mistake to call her mother. Dru realized it immediately. But she hadn't been able to get the morning customer out of her mind. The only way to check out the story was to ask.

Her mother had breezily told her she knew no one named Glo Harrow, though she did know a Laura Harrow, and a former Barbara Harrow. Dru was lulled by her mother's cheerful mood, and the news that she and Dru's father were reconciled.

For the moment, at least.

But the conversation had soon shot down its usual paths. Why didn't she come home for the weekend—better, for the summer? Why didn't they all go spend a few days at the family enclave in North Hampton?

Reasons were brushed aside, excuses ignored, until when they hung up, Dru had no doubt her mother was just as irritated and unhappy as she herself was.

It reminded her to leave bad enough alone.

But she discovered even that was too little, too late, when her mother walked into the shop ten minutes before closing.

"Sweetheart!" Katherine threw out her arms as she rushed to the counter, then wrapped them like ropes around Dru. "I'm so happy to see you. Just so happy."

"Mom." Dru patted Katherine's back and hated herself for the desire to pull away. "What are you doing here?"

"As soon as we hung up, I realized I just couldn't wait to see you. I miss my baby. Just let me look at you." Katherine eased back, stroked a hand over Dru's hair. "When are you going to grow this back? You have such beautiful hair, and here you go around with it chopped off like a boy. You're so thin! You're losing weight."

"I'm not losing weight."

"I worry about you not eating properly. If you'd hire some household staff—"

"Mom, I don't want household staff. I'm eating very well. I haven't lost an ounce since I saw you last month. You look wonderful."

It was invariably true. She wore a beautifully cut pink jacket over pearl gray trousers, both perfectly draped over a figure she maintained with scrupulous diet and exercise.

"Oh, I feel like a hag these days." Katherine waved a hand in dismissal.

Dru softened. "No, you don't, because you have very keen vision and any number of mirrors."

"You're so sweet."

"Did you drive down alone?"

"Henry," she said, referring to her chauffeur. "I told him to take half an hour, walk around a bit. It's a charming little town, really, for a holiday."

"Yes, it is." Dru kept her voice pleasant. "Those of us who live here are very grateful tourists find it as charming as we do."

"But what do you find to do? Oh, don't get angry. Don't get angry." Katherine waved a hand again as she wandered to the front window. "You're so far away from the city. Everything it offers, everything you're used to. Darling, you could live *anywhere*. Though God knows, I'd go mad if you moved away any farther than you have. But seeing you bury yourself here just hurts my heart."

"I'm not buried. And Saint Christopher isn't the end of the earth. If I wanted whatever the city had to offer, I could be there in an hour's drive."

"I'm not speaking geographically, Dru, but culturally, socially. This area's very picturesque, but you've cut yourself off from your life, your family, your friends. My goodness, darling, when's the last time you had a date with an eligible man?"

"Actually, I had one just last night."

"Really?" Katherine arched her brow much as Dru herself was prone to do. "What did you do?"

She didn't bother to bite her tongue. "We had pizza, and sex."

Katherine's mouth opened into a shocked O. "Well, my God, Drusilla."

"But that's hardly the issue. I wasn't satisfied with my life, so I changed it. Now I am satisfied. I wish you could be happy for me."

"This is all Jonah's fault. I could just strangle him."

"No, he's only one minor pebble in the bowl. I don't want to go over and over this again with you, Mom. I'm sorry we don't understand each other."

"I only want the best for you. You're my whole life."

Dru's head began to throb. "I don't want to be your whole life. I shouldn't be your whole life. Dad—"

"Well, of course, your father. God knows why I put up with the man half the time. But we do have twenty-eight years invested in each other."

"Is that what your marriage is? An investment?"

"How in the world did we get off on such a topic? This isn't at all why I came down."

"Do you love him?" Dru demanded, and watched her mother blink.

"Of course I do. What a question. And however we disagree, we both have one perfect point of agreement. You are the most precious thing in our lives. Now." She leaned over, kissed Dru on both cheeks. "I have a wonderful surprise for you." She gripped Dru's hand. "We'll run over to your little house right now so you can get your passport, pack a few essentials. No need for much, we'll take care of the wardrobe when we get there."

"Get where?"

"Paris. It's all arranged. I had this wonderful brainstorm after we talked this morning. I called your father, and he'll be joining us in a day or so. The plane's waiting for us at the airport. We'll spend some time in Aunt Michelle's flat in Paris, shop—oh, and we'll throw a little dinner party. Then we'll drive south and spend a week at the villa. Get out of the heat and crowds."

"Mom—"

"Then I think you and I should run off and have a nice girls' weekend. We never spend any real time together anymore. There's this marvelous spa not far from—"

"Mom. I can't go with you."

"Oh, don't be silly. It's all set. You don't have to worry about a single detail."

"I can't go. I have a business to run."

"Really, Dru. Surely you can close down for a few weeks, or ask someone to take care of it. You can't let this hobby of yours deprive you of every bit of fun."

"It's not a hobby. It deprives me of nothing. And I can't blithely close down so I can trot around France."

"Won't."

"All right, won't."

Tears sprang into Katherine's eyes. "Don't you see how much I need to do this for you? You're my baby, my sweet baby. I worry myself sick thinking about you down here alone."

"I'm not alone. I'm almost twenty-seven years old. I need to make my life. You and Dad need to make yours. Please don't cry."

"I don't know what I've done wrong." Katherine opened her purse, pulled out a tissue. "Why you won't take a little bit of your time to be with me. I feel so abandoned."

"I haven't abandoned you. Please—" When the bells jingled, Dru looked over. "Seth," she said with desperate relief.

"I thought I'd come by before you . . ." He trailed off when he saw the woman sniffling into a tissue. "Sorry. Ah . . . I'll come back."

"No. No." She had to force herself not to leap in front of the door to block his path of retreat. She knew nothing would dry her mother up as quickly as social introductions. "I'm glad you stopped in. I'd like you to meet my mother. Katherine Whitcomb Banks, Seth Quinn."

"Nice to meet you."

"And you." Katherine gave him a watery smile as she offered a hand. "You'll have to forgive me. I've been missing my daughter, and it's made me overly emotional." Now as she dabbed at her eyes, they began to sharpen. "Seth Quinn. The artist?"

"Yes," Dru confirmed, brightly now. "We've admired Seth's work, haven't we, Mom?"

"Very much. Very much. My brother and his wife were in Rome last year and fell in love with your painting of the Spanish Steps. I was very envious of their find. And you grew up here, didn't you?"

"Yes, ma'am. My family's here."

"It's so important to remember family," Katherine said with a sorrowful look at Dru. "How long will you be in the area?"

"I live here."

"Oh, but I thought you lived in Europe."

"I was staying in Europe for a while. I live here. This is home."

"I see. Will you be having a showing in D.C., or Baltimore?"

"Eventually."

"You must be sure to let me know when. I'd love to see more of your work. I'd be delighted to have you to dinner when it's convenient for you. Do you have a card, so I can send you an invitation?"

"A card?" He grinned, quick and bright. He couldn't help it. "No, sorry. But you can let Dru know. She knows how to get ahold of me."

"I see." And now she was beginning to. "We'll do it very soon."

"Mom's leaving for Paris," Dru said quickly. "When you get back," she told her mother, and nudged her toward the door, "we'll see about getting together."

"Bon voyage." Seth lifted a hand in farewell.

"Thank you, but I'm not sure I'll be—"

"Mom. Go to Paris." Dru gave her a firm kiss on the cheek. "Enjoy yourself. Have a wonderful, romantic holiday with Dad. Buy out Chanel. Send me a postcard."

"I don't know. I'll think about it. It was lovely to meet you, Seth. I hope to see you again, very soon."

"That'd be great. Have a good trip."

He waited, tapping his fingers on his thighs as Dru walked her mother out. More like goose-stepped her out, he corrected. He saw, through the window, her loading Katherine into a cream-colored Mercedes sedan, with uniformed driver.

It reminded him of a small point he'd forgotten. Dru's family was loaded. Easy enough to forget it, he mused. She didn't live rich. She lived normal.

When she came back in, she locked the door, then leaned back against it. "I'm sorry."

"For what?"

"For using you to wheedle out of a very uncomfortable situation."

"What are friends for?" He moved to her, tapped her chin with his finger. "Do you want to tell me why she was crying and you looked so miserable?"

"She wanted me to go to Paris. Just like that," Dru added, lifting her hands, then letting them drop. "She'd made all the arrangements without asking me, then drove down here expecting me to leap with joy, rush out and pack a bag and go."

"I guess some people would have."

"Some people don't have a business to run," she snapped. "Some people haven't already been to Paris more times then they can count anyway. And *some* people don't like to have their lives neatly arranged for them as if they were still eight years old."

"Sugar." Because he could feel her vibrating with anger and frustration, he rubbed his hands down her arms. "I didn't say you should have, but that some people would have. Got you wound up, didn't she?"

"She nearly always does. And I know she doesn't actually mean to. She really thinks she's doing it for me. They both do, and that makes it worse. She makes assumptions she shouldn't make, makes decisions for me she no longer has the right to make, then I hurt her feelings when I don't go along."

"If it makes you feel any better, I got reamed by Cam this morning because I haven't been around and forgot to do some stuff I said I'd do."

Dru angled her head. "Did he cry?"

"He might've gotten a little misty. Okay, no," he said, relieved when her mouth curved. "But we were on the verge of punching each other when Phil broke it up."

"Well, I can hardly hit my mother. Did you work it out with your brother?"

"Yeah, we're okay. I need to go by and grovel to Anna for a while, but I thought I'd drop off the boat design." He nodded toward the large folder he'd set on the counter.

"Oh." She pressed her fingers to her temples. "Can I look at it later? I need to close up or I'll be late for my class."

"Yoga. Oh yeah. You shouldn't miss that. We still on for tonight?"

"Do you want to be on for tonight?"

"I've been thinking about you all day. About being with you."

It warmed her. "I suppose I might have given you a passing thought. Though I've been pretty busy in here today."

"So I hear. Will came by the boatyard and nearly gave Aub a heart attack with that forest of roses."

"Did she like them?"

"She got gooey—and it's not easy to make Aubrey gooey. Will, on the other hand, looked dead on his feet. I figure he's got to be seriously stuck on her to come by here, buy flowers, give them to her when he looked like he hadn't slept for a week."

"I liked him, and his brother. You're lucky to have friends that go back to childhood."

"Don't you?"

"Not really. In any case," she went on to avoid the subject, "I had yet another odd visit just before he came in. Some woman," she continued as she cashed out, locked up her cash from the day. "She claimed to know my mother, but once she started talking, I knew she didn't. Not only from what she said, but how she looked. That sounds like snobbery, but it's just logic."

"How did she look?"

"Hard, cheap and not like anyone who's ever worked on a charity committee with my mother. She was pumping me, feeling me out." Dru shrugged. "Not that unusual when you come from an influential family."

There was ice in the pit of his stomach. "What did she say? What did she do?"

"Nothing much. I think she was laying groundwork for something, but then Will came in. She bought some carnations and left. Funny, he said he thought he recognized her from somewhere."

And now a sickness coated his throat. "She tell you her name?"

"Mmm? Yes." Dru took a last glance around, gathered her purse and keys. "Harrow, Glo Harrow. I've really got to get moving."

She stopped short, surprised when his hand clamped down on her arm. "Seth?"

"If she comes in again, I want you to call me."

"Why? She's just some woman hoping to con me out of some money, or an introduction to my grandfather. Believe me, I've handled that sort of thing all my life."

"I want you to promise me. I mean it. If she comes in, you go in the back, pick up the phone and call me."

She started to tell him she didn't need protection, but there was a fire, an urgency in his voice that had her nodding instead. "All right. I promise."

FOURTEEN

He had to wait until morning, until Dru slipped downstairs to prepare her daily orders. He'd barely slept. Though he'd struggled to lock the turmoil aside, he'd lain awake most of the night.

Even the pleasure of having Dru curled beside him had been tainted.

But he had to be sure.

Though his gut told him Gloria had tromped on yet another part of his life, he knocked on the McLean brothers' apartment door. He had to be sure.

Dressed for work, an enormous cup of coffee in his hand, Dan answered. "Hey, what's up? You just caught me. I've got an early meeting."

"I need to talk to Will."

"Good luck. He's the dead man in the bedroom down the hall. Want coffee? He'll probably pull his resurrection act by noon."

"This can't wait."

"Hey, Seth, really, the guy's wasted." Since Seth was already walking through the debris of the living room, Dan went after him. "No, that's mine." Resigned, Dan jerked a thumb toward a second door. There was a sign tacked to it that advised:

Take two aspirin and go far, far away.

Seth didn't bother to knock, but pushed the door open into the dark. Through the light that spilled in from the hallway, Seth could see blackout drapes were pulled tight over the window. The room itself was barely closet-sized and mostly bed.

Will lay on it, faceup, his arms flung out to the sides as if he'd fallen backward in that position and hadn't moved since. He wore Marvin the Martian boxer shorts and one sock.

He snored.

"Let me get my camera," Dan mumbled. "Listen, Seth, this is his first chance for eight straight in two weeks. He wanted to make up time with

Aubrey, so he didn't get in until after two. He was barely conscious when he came in the door."

"It's important."

"Well, shit." Dan walked over to the window. "He'll probably be speaking in tongues." And ruthlessly whipped the drapes back.

The bright morning sun flashed over the bed. Will didn't twitch. Seth leaned over the bed, shook Will by the shoulder. "Wake up."

"Glumph missitop."

"Told ya." Dan moved to the bed. "Here's how it works." He put his mouth close to Will's ear and shouted, "Code blue! Code blue! Dr. McLean, report to Exam Room Three. Stat!"

"Whazit?" Will sprang into a sitting position as if the top half of his body had been shot from a bow. "Where's the crash cart? Where's . . ." Some part of his brain cleared as he blinked into Seth's face. "Aw fuck." He started to flop back, but Seth grabbed his arm.

"I have to talk to you."

"You bleeding internally?"

"No."

"You will be if you don't get the hell out of here and let me sleep." He grabbed a pillow from behind him, put it over his face to block out the light. "Don't see a guy in years, then you can't get rid of him. Go away, and take the moron who used to be my brother with you."

"You were in Dru's shop yesterday."

"I'm gonna cry in a minute."

"Will." Seth yanked the pillow away. "The woman who was in there when you came in. You said you thought you recognized her."

"Right now I wouldn't recognize my own mother. In fact, who the hell are you and what are you doing in my bedroom? I'm calling the cops."

"Tell me what she looked like."

"If I tell you, will you go away?"

"Yeah. Please."

"Christ, let me think." Yawning hugely, Will scrubbed his hands over his face. He sniffed. Sniffed again. "Coffee." His eyes began to track until they landed on Dan's cup. "I want that coffee."

"This is mine, jerkwad."

"Give me that goddamn coffee or I'm telling Mom you think that yellow dress makes her ass look fat. Your life won't be worth living."

"Give him the damn coffee," Seth snapped.

Dan handed it over.

Will slurped, gulped. Seth waited for him to just dunk his head in the oversized cup and lap with his tongue. "Okay, what was the question?"

Seth fisted a hand at his side, imagined his rage inside it. Trapped and controlled. "The woman you saw in Dru's shop."

"Yeah, right." Will yawned again, tried to concentrate. "Something about her weirded me out. Dressed like she should've been working a corner in Baltimore. Not that I'd know anything about that," he added with a cherubic smile. "Bleached, bony, blond. What my dad would call shopworn. Diagnosis from a quick visual would be serious alcohol abuse, along with some recreational chemicals. Bad tone to her skin. Liver damage, probably."

"How old?" Seth demanded.

"Running toward fifty, but hard years. Could've been younger. Serious smoker's rasp, too. She leaves her body to science, we ain't getting much out of it."

"Yeah." Seth sat heavily on the side of the bed.

"Like I told Dru, there was something familiar about her. Couldn't place it. Maybe it was just the type. Hard, edgy, sort of, I dunno, predatory. What? Did she come back and hassle Dru? I'd've hung around if I'd thought . . ."

Then his jaw dropped as the picture fell into place. "Oh shit. Jesus Christ on a crutch. Gloria DeLauter."

Seth pressed the heels of his hands to his forehead. "Fuck me."

"Wait a minute, wait a minute." Dan held up both hands. "You're saying Gloria DeLauter was in Dru's flower shop? Yesterday? That can't be. She's gone, she's been gone for years."

"It was her," Will stated. "It didn't click until just now. We only saw her that one time," he said to Dan, "but it's a pretty strong memory. Her yelling and trying to get Seth in that car. Sybill knocking her down, Foolish snarling like he was going to take a chunk out of her. She's changed, but not that much."

"No." Seth dropped his hands. "Not that much."

"What the hell's she doing back here?" Will demanded. "You're not a kid now. She can't try to drag you off so she can squeeze your brothers for ransom or some shit. She can't be looking for a sloppy mother-son reunion, so what's the point?"

"Will's a little slow," Dan commented, "especially when it comes to the dark side. Money would be the point, right, Seth? Our pal here's a successful artist, climbing up the shiny ladder of fame and fortune. Whatever hole she's been in, she'd have heard about it. Now she's back wanting her cut of the profits."

"That covers most of it," Seth grumbled.

"I still don't get it." Will shoved at his hair. "You don't owe her a damn thing. She's got nothing on you."

"I've been paying her for years."

"Aw hell, Seth."

"She just kept popping up. I gave her money so she'd go away again. Stupid, but I couldn't see what else to do to keep her from hassling my family. They'd gotten the business off the ground, and the kids were coming along. I didn't want her making trouble for them."

"They don't know?" Will asked.

"No, I never told anybody." He'd put it inside, in the place he tried to keep locked away from what his life had become. "She tracked me down in Rome a few months ago. That's when I figured there wasn't any point in me being three thousand miles away. I wanted to come home. She hit me up again about a week ago. Usually she backs off for longer. A year or two. I thought I'd bought some time. But if she went into Dru's shop, it wasn't because she wanted to buy some fucking daisies."

"What do you want us to do?" Dan asked him.

"Nothing you can do. Just keep a lid on this until I figure it out. Meanwhile, I'll wait. See what she does next."

⟨⟨⟩⟩

But he couldn't just wait. He spent hours driving to hotels, motels, B and B's trying to find her, without a clue what he'd do if and when he did.

He started the search with more fury than plan, thinking only that he needed to confront her, to drive her off by whatever means necessary. But as he drove to and from hotels, he began to cool off. He began to think as she thought. Coldly.

If she thought Dru mattered to him, she would be used. Tool, weapon, victim. Very likely all three. If and when he found her, he would need to take care to paint his relationship with Dru as a casual one. Even a callous one.

If there was one thing Gloria understood, even respected, it was using someone else. Using anyone else for your own purposes.

As long as she thought he was using Dru for sex and studio space, Dru would be safe.

Then at least one person he cared about wouldn't be smeared with Gloria's brush.

He was forty miles outside of St. Christopher before he found an answer.

The motel boasted a pool, cable TV and family suites. The desk clerk was young and perky enough to make Seth decide she'd been hired as summer help.

He leaned on the counter, spoke in a friendly manner. "Hi. How's it going?"

"Just fine, thanks. Will you be checking in?"

"No, I'm here to see a friend. Gloria DeLauter?"

"DeLauter. One moment, please." She caught her bottom lip between her teeth as she began to tap her keyboard. "Um, could you spell the last name?"

"Sure."

When he had, she tapped again, then looked up apologetically. "I'm sorry. There's no DeLauter registered."

"Huh. Oh, you know what, she might've registered under Harrow. That's the name she uses for business."

"Gloria Harrow?" She went back to the keyboard, then frowned. "I'm afraid Miss Harrow checked out."

"She checked out?" Seth straightened, did everything he could to keep his tone mild. "When?"

"Just this morning. I checked her out myself."

"That's weird. Blond? Thin? About this tall." He held up a hand to estimate.

"Yes, that's right."

"Well, hell, I must've messed up the dates. Thanks." He started out, then turned back casually. "She didn't mention heading down to Saint Christopher, did she?"

"No. Seems to me she headed out the other way. Gosh, I hope nothing's wrong."

"Just a mix-up," he said and let himself feel a cautious trickle of relief. "Thanks for your help."

He told himself she was gone. She'd taken the ten thousand and split. She'd checked out Dru, and that was worrying, but Seth imagined Gloria had, once she'd met her, dismissed the idea of him and Dru having any sort of serious relationship she could exploit.

The fact was, he was far from sure where he stood with Dru himself.

She wasn't the type who wore her heart on her sleeve, he thought. Or anywhere else he could get a good look at it. And wasn't part of his fascination with her the very fact that she was so contained?

At least it had been; interest and attraction had melded into something a great deal stronger.

Now he wanted more.

One way he used to see into people was by painting them.

He knew she was far from sold on the idea of posing for him again—particularly in the way he had in mind. But he set up his studio on Sunday morning as if she were in enthusiastic agreement.

"Why won't you just take money for the painting?"

"I don't want money." He arranged the sheets on the bed, ones he'd borrowed from Phil after a raid on his brother's linen closet.

The material was soft, would drape fluidly. And their color, the palest honeysuckle, would be perfect against the bold red of the rose petals and the delicate white of Dru's skin.

He wanted that mix of tones and moods—warm, hot, cool—because she was all of them.

"That's the point of selling your work, isn't it?" She clutched her robe closed at the throat and cast uneasy glances at the bed. "To make money?"

"I don't paint for money. That's a handy by-product, and I leave it to my rep."

"I'm not a model."

"I don't want a model either." Dissatisfied, he shoved, dragged, pushed, until he'd changed the angle and position of the bed. "Professionals can give you a terrific study. But I find using regular people gives me more. Besides, I can't use anyone but you for this work."

"Why?"

"Because it's you."

She hissed between her teeth as he opened the first bag of petals. "What does that *mean*?"

"I see you." He tossed petals on the sheets in seemingly random patterns. "Just relax and leave it to me."

"I can't possibly relax when I'm lying naked on a bed strewn with rose petals and you're staring at me."

"Sure you can." He added more petals, stepped back, considered.

"We made love on that bed a few hours ago."

"Exactly." Now he looked at her, smiled. "It'd help if you thought about that when I'm working."

"Oh, did you have sex with me to put me in the right mood?"

"No, I had sex with you because I can't seem to get enough of you. But the mood's another handy by-product."

"Let me tell you where you can put your handy by-product."

He only laughed, then grabbed her before she could stride into the bathroom. "I'm crazy about you."

"Stop it." She seethed as he nibbled on her earlobe. "I mean it, Seth."

"Absolutely crazy. You're so beautiful. Don't be shy."

"You can't get me to strip with flattery or cajolery."

"Cajolery. Very cool word. How about appealing to your appreciation of art? Just try." He skimmed his lips down to hers. "Give me one hour. If you're still uncomfortable, we'll rethink this. The human body's natural."

"So's cotton underwear."

"It sure is, the way you wear it."

And of course, he made her laugh. "One hour?" She eased back. "And I get the painting?"

"Deal. Now is this music okay with you, or do you want me to put on something to strip by."

"Oh, you're very funny."

"Let's just take this off." He untied the robe, eased it gently from her shoulders. "I love looking at you. I love the shape of you." He spoke softly, easing her toward the bed. "The way your skin looks in the light. I want to show you how you look to me."

"How is seducing me supposed to help me relax?"

"Lie down. Don't think about anything yet. I want you turned on your side, facing me. Your arm like this." He lifted it, draped it low over her breasts.

She did her best to ignore the sensation along her skin where his fingertips, his knuckles brushed. "I feel . . . exposed."

"Revealed," he corrected. "It's different. Slide this knee up. Keep this arm angled down. Palm up, open. Good. Comfortable?"

"I can't believe I'm doing this. This is not me."

"Yes, it is." He reached into the bag, scattered petals over her, letting some drift into her open palm before he placed some more deliberately on her hair, on the slope of her breasts, over her arm, along the line of hip and leg.

"Try to hold that for me." He stepped back, ran his gaze over her in a way that made her skin flush.

"Seth."

"Just try not to move too much. I need your body first. I'm not too worried about the head and face just yet. Talk to me." He retreated behind the canvas.

"About what? How ridiculous I feel?"

"Why don't we go for a sail this evening? We'll bum dinner off of Anna and go out after."

"I can't think about dinner, and I certainly don't want to think about your sister-in-law when I'm . . . People are going to see this, see *me*. Naked."

"People are going to see a painting of a striking woman."

"My mother," Dru said in sudden horror.

"How is she? She and your father still back together?"

"As far as I know. They went to Paris, but they're not happy with me."

"Hard to make everybody happy all the time." He sketched the curve of her shoulder, the stem of her neck, the slender line of torso. "When's the last time you were in Paris?"

"About three years ago. My aunt's wedding. She lives there now—outside of Paris, actually, but they keep a flat in the city."

So he talked to her of Paris, satisfied when he saw the tension draining out of her body. Then he began to paint.

The contrast of the red against white skin, the glint of light, the delicacy of the sheets with their deeper shadows in the soft folds. He wanted the elegance of her open hand and the strong muscles in her calf.

She shifted slightly, but he said nothing to correct her pose. The conversation he carried on to keep her relaxed was in a different part of his mind. The rest was steeped in the image he created with paint and brush.

Here was his faerie queen again, but now she was awake. Now she was aware.

She stopped thinking about the pose, her modesty. It was an incredible thrill to watch him work. An exhilaration. Did he realize, she wondered, how the intensity came over him? The way his eyes changed, took on a certain fierceness of effort that was in direct opposition to the casual flow of his words.

Did he see himself? Surely he must. He had to know the fluidity and focus that were so much a part of his technique. The sexuality of it. And the beauty, the power, that made the subject he took along with him feel beautiful, feel powerful.

She forgot the time limit they'd set. Whatever fantasy he'd created in his mind, she'd become too much a part of it to break the spell.

Did the subject always fall in love with the artist? she wondered. Was it just the nature of things for her to feel this outrageous intimacy with him, and this stupefying need for him?

How had he become the first man, the only man, she wanted to give to? To give anything he asked. It was frightening to know it, to understand that love could mean giving up so much of self.

What would be left of her if she yielded to it?

When his gaze moved over her, as if absorbing what she was, she shivered.

"Are you cold?" His voice was impatient. Then, as if he turned a knob, he spoke more easily. "Sorry, are you cold?"

"No. Yes. Maybe a bit. A little stiff."

He frowned, then glanced down at his wrist for the watch he'd once again forgotten to put on. "Probably hit the hour."

"At least." She worked up a smile.

"You need a break. You want some water? Juice? Did I buy juice?"

"Water's fine. Can I sit up now?"

"Sure, sure." He wasn't looking at her now in any case, but at the work.

"And can I see what you've done so far?"

"Uh-huh." He set down his brush, picked up a rag. And never took his eyes off the canvas.

Dru slipped out of bed, picked up the robe and, wrapping herself into it, walked to him.

The bed was the center of the canvas, with much of the outer space still white and unpainted. She was the center of the bed.

He'd yet to paint her face, so she was only a body—long limbs adorned with rose petals. Her arm covered her breasts, but it wasn't a gesture of modesty. One of flirtation, she thought. Of invitation. Of knowledge.

Only a fraction done, she realized, and already brilliant. Did she ever look and see light and shadow playing so beautifully?

He'd chosen the bed well. The slim iron bars offered simplicity and a timelessness. The delicate tone of the sheets warmed her skin and was yet another contrast to all the rich, bold strokes.

"It's beautiful."

"It will be," he agreed. "This is a good start."

"You knew I wouldn't stop you once I'd seen what you'd done."

"If you'd looked and hadn't seen what I wanted you to see, I'd have failed. Drusilla."

She studied him. Her pulse scrambled when she saw that same narrowed intensity on his face, the strength of focus, of purpose. The need that vibrated around him when he worked.

But now, it was for her.

"I've never wanted anyone like this," she managed. "I don't know what it means."

"I don't give a damn." He pulled her against him, captured her mouth.

He was already yanking off her robe as he dragged her toward the bed.

A part of her—that had been born and bred in luxury, in grace—was shocked at the treatment. Shocked more by her response to it. And the part that responded triumphed.

She tore at his shirt even as they tumbled onto sheets strewn with rose petals.

"Touch me. Oh, touch me." She clawed her way over him. "The way I imagine you touching me when you're painting me."

His hands streaked over her, rough and needy, stroking the flames that had simmered as she'd lain naked for him. It energized her, sparked in her blood until she felt herself become a quivering mass of raw need tangled with reckless greed.

Her mouth warred with his in a frantic battle to give.

He was lost in her, trapped in the maze of emotions she'd wound through him. Steeped in the flood of sensations she aroused by every caress, every taste, every word.

Hunger for more stumbled against a rocky ledge of love.

When he drew her close, held—held tight—he fell over.

Some change, some tenderness eked through the urgency. It swamped her, and she went pliant against him.

Now mouths met, a long, sumptuous kiss. Now hands brushed skin delicately. The air thickened, filled with the scents of roses, of paint, of turpentine, all stirred by the breeze off the water.

She rose over him, and looked down at love.

Her throat ached. Her heart swelled. Unbearably moved, she lowered her lips to his until her throat ached from the sweetness.

This, she knew, was more than pleasure, beyond desire and need. This, if only she could let it, was everything.

If it was consuming, then she would be consumed. And she took him inside her, gave herself over to the everything.

Slow and silky, deep and intent, they moved together. Trembled as they climbed, sighed as they floated. It seemed to her colors, the rich bold tones he'd used in the painting, spread inside her.

He lifted to her, finding her mouth with his again as his arms enfolded her. Wrapped tight, they surrendered.

For a time they didn't speak. She kept her head on his shoulder, looked at the light through the window.

He'd opened a window, she realized. One she'd been so certain needed to remain shut. Now the light, the air was streaming through.

How could she ever close it again?

"I've never made love on rose petals before," she said quietly. "I liked it."

"Me too."

She plucked one from his back. "But now look what we've done." She held it out to him. "The artist is going to be very annoyed with us."

"He should be, but he's not. Besides"—joy, pure joy, was running inside him in long, loose strides—"the artist is very inventive."

"I can verify that."

"Give me another hour."

She leaned back to stare at him. "You're going to paint again? Now?"

"Trust me. It's important, really important. Just—here." She was still gaping at him when he shifted her and gave her a light shove back onto the bed. "Do you remember the pose, or do you need me to set you?"

"Do I . . . oh, for heaven's sake." More than a little miffed, she rolled to her side, flopped her arm over her breasts.

"Okay, I'll set you." Cheerful, energized, he moved her, redistributed rose petals, stepped back, then forward again to make more adjustments.

"It's okay to pout now, but turn your head toward me."

"I'm not pouting. I'm entirely too mature to pout."

"Whatever." He grabbed his jeans, tugged them on. "I need the angle of your head . . . chin up. Whoa, not that far, sugar. That's better," he said, grabbing the brush he needed. "Tilt your head, just a . . . Ah, yeah, that's it. You're amazing, you're perfect. You're the best."

"You're full of shit."

"Now, that's mature." He went to work. "And a little crude coming from you."

"I can be crude when the occasion calls for it." As far as she was concerned, having a man more interested in his work than in holding her when she'd just fallen in love was the perfect occasion.

"Okay, shut up. Just look at me now, listen to the music."

"Fine. I've nothing to say to you anyway."

Maybe not, he thought, but her face had a great deal to say. And he wanted it all. He painted the arrogant angle of it, the strong chin with that lovely shadow in the center, the sculpted cheekbones, the gorgeous shape of her eyes, eyebrows, the straight patrician line of her nose.

But for the rest, for her mouth, for the look *in* her eyes, he needed something more.

"Don't move," he ordered as he came back to the bed. "I want you to think about how much I want you."

"I beg your pardon?"

"Think about how powerful you are, the way you look. As if you're just waking up and you see me looking at you. Craving you. You've got all the power here."

"Is that so?"

"I'm desperate for you." He leaned down, his lips a whisper from hers. "You know it. All you have to do is crook a finger. All you have to do is smile." He laid his lips on hers, took the kiss slow and deep, gave her a taste of his yearning. "And I'm a slave."

He backed up, his eyes on hers as he eased around the canvas. "It's you, Drusilla. You."

Her lips curved, a kind of knowing. In her eyes an invitation shimmered that was both luminous and languid.

He saw everything he wanted in that one moment, the awareness, the confidence, the desire and the promise.

"Don't change."

He saw nothing but her, felt nothing but her to the point where he was almost unaware of his own hand moving. Of mixing the paint, dabbing it, stroking it, all but breathing it onto the paper so that her face bloomed for him.

He caught what he could, knew he would see that light on her face forever. It would be there when he needed to complete the work.

It would be there, in his mind and heart, whenever he was alone. Whenever he was lonely.

"I can do it," he said, and laid aside his brush. "When I do, it'll be the most important thing I've ever done. Do you know why?"

She couldn't speak now, could barely breathe over the tumult of her heart. She could only shake her head.

"Because this is what you are to me. What I knew, somehow, you'd be to me from the first moment. Drusilla." He stepped toward the bed. "I love you."

Her breath shuddered out. "I know." She pressed a hand to her heart, in wonder that it didn't simply burst free in one mad leap of joy. "I know. I'm terrified. Oh God, Seth, I'm terrified, because I love you, too."

She sprang up, scattering rose petals, and leaped into his arms.

FIFTEEN

Hurricane Anna swept through the house and had her men ducking for cover. She blew through the living room, snatching socks, shoes, ball caps, empty glasses. Those who didn't move fast enough to evacuate were forced to catch hurled items, or get beaned.

By the time she reached the kitchen, the survivors had made themselves scarce. Even the dog had gone into hiding.

From what he hoped was a safe distance, Seth cleared his throat. "Um, Anna, it's just dinner."

She rounded on him. He figured he outweighed her by a good forty pounds, and still his belly contracted in something like fear at the kill lights in her dark eyes. "Just dinner?" she repeated. "And I suppose you think food just makes itself?"

"No. But whatever we were having is fine. Is great," he amended. "Dru's not fussy or anything."

"Oh, Dru's not fussy or anything," Anna tossed back as she yanked open cupboards, pulled out ingredients, slammed them shut again. "So it's just fine to give me an hour's notice that we're having company for dinner."

"It's not company, exactly. I thought we'd just grab something, then—"

"Oh, you thought you'd just grab something." She walked toward him with the slow, deliberate steps that struck terror into the very center of his heart. "Maybe we'll just order pizza and have her pick it up on the way."

Cam, hoping her skewering Seth like a bug would keep her attention diverted, tried to sidle in to sneak a beer out of the fridge. He should've known better.

"And you." She bared her teeth at Cam. "You think you can march into my kitchen in your dirty shoes? Don't you even think about plopping your butt down in the living room, sucking on that beer. You're not king around here."

He had the beer, and whipped it behind his back just in case she got any ideas. "Hey, I'm an innocent bystander."

"There are no innocents in this house. Stay!" she ordered when Seth tried to slip out of the room. "I'm not finished with you."

"Okay, okay. Look, what's the big deal? Somebody's always dropping by for dinner. Kevin had that freak friend of his over just the other night."

"He's not a freak," Kevin called out from the safety of the living room.

"Hey, he had a nose ring and kept quoting Dylan Thomas."

"Oh, Marcus. He's a freak. I thought you meant Jerry."

"See?" Seth lifted his hands. "We've got so many people in and out of here we can't even keep them straight."

"This is different." Since Anna had just pulled a large chef's knife out of the block, and Cam, the coward, had deserted the field, Seth decided not to argue.

"Okay. I'm sorry. I'll help."

"Damn right you will. Red potatoes." She stabbed the knife toward the pantry. "Scrub."

"Yes 'm."

"Quinn!"

"What?" Voice aggrieved, Cam eased back into the doorway but kept the beer out of sight. "I didn't do anything."

"Exactly. Shower. Do *not* throw your towel on the floor. Shave."

"Shave?" He rubbed a hand over his chin and looked harassed. "It's not morning."

"Shave," she repeated and began to mince garlic with such violent enthusiasm, Seth tucked his fingers safely in his pockets, just in case.

"Jesus Christ." Cam curled his lip at Seth and stalked away.

"Jake! Pick up your crap on the floor of the den. Kevin! Run the vacuum."

"Why do you want them to hate me?" Seth pleaded.

Anna's only answer was a steely look. "When you've scrubbed those potatoes, I want them cut into chunks. About this size," she said, holding up her thumb and forefinger. "When you finish that, put out the guest soap and towels in the downstairs bath. The first one I catch using the guest soaps or leaving handprints on the towels gets their fingers chopped off," she called out.

She dumped ingredients into a bowl and whisked.

"It's not all my crap on the den floor, I want you to know." Jake stomped in, shot Seth a sneer. "Lots of other people throw crap around this place, too."

"What do you think you're doing?" Anna demanded as Jake pulled open the refrigerator.

"I was just going to get a—"

"No, you're not. I want you to set the table—"

"It's Kev's night to set and clear. I'm on dish duty."

"Tonight you set and wash."

"How come I have to set and wash? I didn't invite some dopey girl to dinner."

"Because I said so. Set the table in the dining room. Use the good dishes."

"How come we're eating in there? It's not Thanksgiving."

"And the linen napkins," she added. "The ones with roses on them. Six place settings. Wash your hands first."

"Jeez. She's just a girl. You'd think the Queen of England or somebody was coming over."

He stalked to the sink, ran water while he curled his lip, exactly as his father had done. "I'm *never* bringing a girl over here."

"I'll remind you of that in a couple of years." Because the idea of her little boy bringing a girl home to dinner made her eyes sting, Anna sniffed and poured marinade over chicken breasts.

"I'll think twice about it myself," Seth muttered under his breath.

"I beg your pardon?"

He winced. "Nothing. It's just, well hell, Anna, I've brought girls over before. Dru even ate here before and you didn't go into a fit over it."

"That's different. She dropped by unexpectedly, and you barely knew her."

"Yeah, but—"

"And you may have brought girls here before, but you never invited the woman you're in love with to dinner before. Men don't understand anything. They understand nothing at all, and I don't know why I've been plagued by a herd of them."

"Don't cry. Oh man. Oh God. Please, don't do that."

"I'll cry if I want to. You just try to stop me."

"Nice going," Jake muttered and fled to the dining room.

"I'll make the chicken." Desperate, Seth abandoned his potatoes and rushed over to stroke Anna's hair. "You just tell me what you want me to do with it. And the rest of it, too. And I'll do the dishes after, and . . ." He stepped back. "I never said I was in love with Dru."

"What, now I'm blind and stupid?" She grabbed the olive oil and Dijon to mix up her special sauce for the potatoes. "Get me the damn Worcestershire sauce."

Instead, he took her hands, then ran his up her arms. "I barely finished telling her. How come you know this stuff?"

"Because, you stupid idiot, I love you. Get away from me. I'm busy."

He laid his cheek on hers, and sighed.

"Damn it." She threw her arms around him. "I want you to be happy. I want you to be so happy."

"I am." He pressed his face into her hair. "A little spooked along with it."

"It's not real if you're not a little spooked." She held tight another moment, then let go. "Now get out of here. Guest soaps, towels. Toilet seats down. And find a pair of jeans that doesn't have holes."

"I'm not sure I have any. And thanks, Anna."

"You're welcome. But you're still doing the dishes."

From the dining room came Jake's enthusiastic *woo-hoo*.

"I appreciate your letting me impose this way. Again."

Anna chose a dark blue vase for the cheerful black-eyed Susans Dru had brought her. "We're happy to have you. It's no trouble at all."

"I can't imagine a last-minute dinner guest, after you've worked all day, is no trouble at all."

"Oh, it's just chicken. Nothing fussy." Anna smiled thinly as Jake rolled his eyes dramatically behind Dru's back. "Is there something you want, Jake?"

"Just wondering when we're going to eat."

"You'll be the first to know." She set the flowers on the kitchen table. "Go tell Seth to come open this lovely wine Dru brought for us. We'll have a glass before dinner."

"People could starve around here," Jake complained—in a whisper—as he trooped out of the kitchen.

"Is there anything I can do to help?" Dru asked. The kitchen smelled fantastic. Something, she assumed it was the chicken, was simmering in a covered skillet.

"We're under control, thanks." With a deft hand, Anna lifted the lid on the skillet, shook it lightly by the handle, poked with a kitchen fork, then set the lid back. "Do you cook?"

"Not like this. I've gotten very adept at boiling pasta, nuking up jarred sauce and mixing it together."

"Oh. My heart," Anna said, and laughed. "Raw clay. I love molding raw clay. One of these days I'll show you how to make a nice, basic red sauce, and see where we can go from there. Seth." Anna beamed at him when he came in. "Open the wine, will you? Pour Dru a glass. You can take her out and show her how my perennials are coming along while I finish putting dinner together."

"I'm glad to help," Dru protested. "I may not cook, but I follow instructions well."

"Next time. Just go out with Seth, enjoy your wine. We'll be ready in ten minutes."

Anna shooed them out, then, delighted with herself, rubbed her hands together before diving into the rest of the preparations.

In fifteen minutes, they were seated in the rarely used dining room, a half dozen tea lights flickering. The dog, Dru noted, had been banished.

"These are beautiful dishes," Dru commented.

"I love them. Cam and I bought them in Italy, on our honeymoon."

"If you break one," Jake put in as he attacked his chicken, "you get shackled in the basement so the rats can eat your ears."

"Jake!" With a baffled laugh, Anna passed the potatoes to her left. "What a thing to say. We don't even have a basement."

"That's what Dad said you'd do, even if you had to dig a basement. Right, Dad?"

"I don't know what you're talking about. Eat some asparagus."

"Do I have to?"

"If I have to, you have to."

"Neither of you have to." Anna prayed for patience.

"Cool, more for me." Kevin reached enthusiastically for the platter before he caught his mother's warning look. "What? I like it."

"Then ask for it, Mr. Smooth, instead of diving across the table. We don't let them out of the kennel very often," Cam told Dru.

"I always wanted brothers."

"What for?" Jake asked her. "They mostly just pound on you."

"Well, you do look pretty well battered," she considered. "I always thought it would be fun to have someone to talk to—and to pound on. Someone to take some of the heat when my parents were annoyed or irritated. When you're an only child, there's no one to diffuse the focus, if you know what I mean. And no one to eat the asparagus when you don't want it."

"Yeah, but Kev swiped half the good Halloween candy last year."

"Jeez, get over it."

Jake eyed his brother. "I never forget. All data is stored in my memory banks. And one day, candy pig, you will pay."

"You're such a geek."

"Thesbo."

"That's Jake's latest insult." Seth gestured with his wineglass. "A play on thespian, since Kev's into that."

"Rhymes with lesbo," Jake explained helpfully while Anna stifled a groan. "It's a slick way of calling him a girl."

"Clever. I enjoyed your school play last month," she said to Kevin. "I thought it was wonderfully done. Are you thinking of going on to study theater in college?"

"Yeah. I really like it. Plays are cool, but I like movies even better. The guys and I have made some really awesome videos. The last one we did, *Slashed*, was the best. It's about this one-armed psycho killer who stalks these hunters through the woods. Carves them up, one by one, in revenge because one of them shot off his arm in this freak hunting accident. It has flashbacks and everything. Want to see it?"

"Sure."

"I didn't know you went to Kevin's play."

Dru shifted her attention to Seth. "I like to keep up with community events. And I love a little theater."

"We could've gone together."

She picked up her wine, smiled at him over it in a way that made Anna's heart swell. "Like a date?"

"Dru has a philosophical objection to dating," Seth said, with his eyes on hers. "Why is that?"

"Because it often involves men who don't interest me. But primarily I haven't had time for that sort of socializing since I moved here. Starting up, then running the shop have been priorities."

"What made you decide to be a florist?" Anna asked her.

"I had to ask myself what I could do—then out of that, what I'd enjoy the most. I enjoyed flowers. I took some courses, and discovered I had a talent with them."

"It takes a lot of courage to start a business, and to come to a new place to do it."

"I'd have withered if I'd stayed in Washington. That sounds dramatic. I needed a new place. My own place. Everything I considered doing, everywhere I considered going, kept circling back around to Saint Christopher and a flower shop. A flower shop puts you right in the deep end of the pool."

"How is that?" Cam wondered.

"You become instantly intimate with the community. When you sell flowers, you know who's having a birthday, an anniversary. You know who's died, who's had a baby. Who's in love, or making up from a fight, who got a promotion, who's ill. And in a small town, like this one, you invariably get details along with it."

She thought for a moment, then spoke in a lazy Shore accent. "Old Mrs. Wilcox died—would've been eighty-nine come September. Came home from the market and had a stroke right there in the kitchen while she was putting away her canned goods. Too bad she didn't make things up with her sister before it was too late. They haven't spoke word one to each other in twelve years."

"That's good." Amused, Cam propped his chin on his hand. More than looks and brains, he thought. There was warmth and humor in there, too. Once you tickled it out of her.

Seth was toast.

"And I thought it was just pushing posies," he added.

"Oh, it's a great deal more than that. When a man comes in, frantic because he just remembered his wedding anniversary, it's my job not to simply put the right flowers into his hands, but to remain discreet."

"Like a priest," Cam put in and made her laugh.

"Not so far from that. You'd be amazed at the confessions I hear. It's all in a day's work."

"You love it," Anna murmured.

"I do. I really do. I love the business itself, and I love being part of something. In Washington . . ." She caught herself, a bit amazed at how easily she'd rambled. "Things were different," she said at length. "This is what I was looking for."

He followed her home, where they sat on her porch steps in the warm summer night, watching fireflies dance in the dark.

"You had a good time?"

"I had a wonderful time. The dinner, getting to know your family a little better. The sail."

"Good." He brought her hand to his lips. "Because Anna's going to pass the word, and you'll be expected to repeat the performance at Grace's, and at Sybill's."

"Oh." She hadn't thought of that. "I'll need to reciprocate. I'll need to have everyone over for . . ."

She'd have to have it catered, of course. And she'd have to determine how best to keep a number of teenagers entertained.

"I'm out of my league," she admitted. "The kind of dinner party I'm used to hosting isn't what's called for here."

"You want to have everyone over?" The idea delighted him. "We'll get a grill and cook out. We'll toss on some steaks and corn on the cob. Keep it simple."

We, she thought. Somehow they'd slid from individuals into *we*. She wasn't quite sure how she felt about it.

"I've been meaning to ask you something." He leaned back on the step so he could study her profile. "What's it like to grow up filthy rich?"

That eyebrow winged, the way he loved. "We preferred the term 'lavishly wealthy' to 'filthy rich.' And obviously, it has its points."

"I bet. We sort of established why the lavishly wealthy society chick is running a flower shop on the waterfront, but how come she doesn't have household help, or a staff of employees?"

"I have Mr. G, who's worked out perfectly. He's flexible, dependable, and he knows and loves flowers. And I plan on hiring someone else, to work part-time in the shop. I needed to make certain there'd be enough business to justify it first. I'm going to start looking very soon."

"But you do the books."

"I like doing the books."

"And the ordering, and the inventory, whatever."

"I like—"

"Yeah, got that. Don't get defensive." It amused him when her shoulders stiffened. "You like manning the rudder. Nothing wrong with that."

"Speaking of rudders, I like the sloop design. I like it very much. I'm going to contact Phillip and have him draw up the contract."

"Good, but you're evading the subject. How come you don't have a housekeeper?"

"If this is a plug for Grace's service, Aubrey's already nagging me about it. I'm going to talk to her."

"It wasn't, but that's a good idea." He ran his fingers down her leg, an unconscious gesture of intimacy. "Spread the wealth, and free up your time. A twofer."

"You're awfully interested in wealth all of a sudden."

"In you," he corrected. "Sybill's the only person I know, really know, who came from money. And I get the drift that her family's pretty small potatoes compared to yours. Your mother comes down to see you, driven by a uniformed chauffeur. Snazzy stuff. You don't even have somebody coming in to scrub the john. So I ask myself how come that is. Does she *like* scrubbing johns?"

"It was a childhood dream of mine," she said dryly.

"Anytime you want to fulfill the dream in the studio bathroom, feel free."

"That's very generous of you."

"Well, I love you. I do what I can."

She nearly sighed. He loved her. And he wanted to understand her. "Money," she began, "great amounts of money solve a lot of problems. And create others. But one way or the other, rich or poor, if you stub your toe, your toe hurts. It can also insulate you, so that you don't meet or develop friendships with people outside that charmed circle. You gain a great deal, you miss a great deal. Certainly you miss a great deal when your parents feel so strongly about shielding you from a variety of things out of that circle."

She turned to look at him now. "That's not 'poor little rich girl' talk. It's just fact. I had a privileged upbringing. I never wanted for a single material thing, and will never have to. I had an exceptional education, was allowed to travel extensively. And if I'd stayed in that charmed circle, I think I'd have died by inches."

She shook her head. "There's that drama again."

"I don't think it's dramatic. There are all kinds of hunger. If you don't get fed, you starve."

"Then I guess we could say I needed a different menu. In the Washington house, my mother runs a staff of sixteen. It's a beautiful home, perfectly presented. This is the first place I've had alone. When I moved to my own place in Georgetown, they—despite my telling them I didn't want or need live-in help—hired a housekeeper for me as a housewarming gift. So, I was stuck."

"You could have refused."

Dru only shook her head. "Not as easy as you think, and it would have created more conflict when I'd just gone through the battle of moving out on my own. In any case, it wasn't the housekeeper's fault. She was a perfectly nice, absolutely efficient and completely pleasant woman. But I didn't want her there. I kept her because my parents were frantic enough at the idea of me no longer living at home, and kept on me about how worried they were about me, how much better they felt knowing I had someone reliable living with me. And I was just tired of the hammering."

"Nobody pushes buttons better than family."

"Not in my experience," she agreed. "It seems ridiculous to complain about having someone who'll cook, clean, run errands and so on. But you give up your privacy in exchange for the convenience and leisure. You are never, never alone. And no matter how pleasant, how loyal, how discreet a household staff may be, they know things about you. They know when you've had an argument with your parents, or your lover. They know what you eat, or don't eat. When you sleep, or don't sleep. They know if you've had sex, or haven't had sex. Every mood, every move, and if they're with you long enough, every thought you have is shared with them.

"I won't have that here." She let out a breath. "Besides, I like taking care of myself. Seeing to my own details. I like knowing I'm good at it. But I'm not sure how good I'll be at putting together a dinner party for the Quinn horde."

"If it makes you feel any better, Anna was a maniac for the hour before you got there tonight."

"Really?" The idea warmed her. "It does make me feel better. She always seems so completely in charge."

"She is. She scares us boneless."

"You worship her. Every one of you. It's fascinating. This is very new territory for me, Seth."

"For me, too."

"No." She turned her head. "It's not. Family gatherings, whether they're casual or traditional, impromptu or planned, are very old territory for you. You don't need a map. You're very lucky to have them."

"I know it." He thought of where he'd come from. He thought of Gloria. "I know it."

"Yes, it shows. You're all so *full* of each other. They made room for me because you asked them to. You care for me, so they'll care for me. It won't be like that with my family. If and when you meet them, you'll be very carefully questioned, studied, analyzed and judged."

"So, they're looking out for you."

"No, not so much for me as themselves. The family name—names," she corrected. "The position. Discreet inquiries will be made as to your financial stability, to ensure you're not after my money. While my mother will be, initially, thrilled that I'm involved with someone with your panache in art circles—"

"Panache. You do use those cool words."

"It's shallow."

"Oh, give her a break." He ruffled her hair as he might have a ten-year-old boy's. "I'm not going to be insulted because someone's impressed with my reputation as an artist."

"You may be insulted when your background is quietly and thoroughly investigated, when the credit line on Boats by Quinn is checked."

The idea of the background check had his blood chilling. "Well, for Christ's sake."

"You need to know. This is standard operating procedure in my family. Jonah passed with high marks, and his political connections were a bonus. Which is why no one was particularly pleased with me for calling off the wedding. I'm sorry. I know I'm spoiling the mood of the evening, but I realized with the way things seem to be moving between us you needed to know this sooner rather than later."

"Okay. Tell me this sooner rather than later." He took her hand, toyed with her fingers. "If they don't like what they find, do things stop moving between us?"

"I pulled myself away from there, from them, because I couldn't live that way." And curled her fingers into his. "I make up my own mind, and heart."

"Then let's not worry about it." He drew her into his arms. "I love you. I don't care what anyone else thinks."

He wanted it to be just that simple.

He'd learned that love was the single most powerful force. It could overcome and overset greed, pettiness, hate, envy. It changed lives.

God knew it had changed his.

He believed in the untapped power of love, whether it showed itself in passion or selflessness, in fury or in tenderness.

But love was rarely simple. It was its facets, its complexities that made it such a strong force.

So, loving Dru, he faced the fact that he would have to tell her everything. He wasn't born at the age of ten. She had a right to know where he'd come from, and how. He had to find the way to tell her of his childhood. Of Gloria.

Eventually.

He told himself he deserved the time to just be with her, to enjoy the freshness of their feelings for each other. He made excuses.

He wanted her to get to know and become more comfortable with his family. He needed to finish the painting. He wanted to put his time and effort into building her boat, so that when it was done it would somehow belong to both of them.

There was no time limit, after all. No need to rush everything. Days passed into weeks and Gloria made no contact. It was easy to convince himself she'd gone again. Maybe this time she'd stay gone.

He bargained with himself. He wouldn't think about any of it until after the July Fourth celebrations. Every year, the Quinns held a huge come-one, come-all picnic. Family, friends, neighbors gathered at the house, as they had since Ray and Stella's day, to eat, drink, gossip, swim in the cool water of the inlet and watch the fireworks.

But before the beer and crab, they were due for champagne and caviar. With obvious reluctance, and after considerable nagging by both her parents, Dru had agreed to attend one of the Washington galas with Seth as her escort.

"Shit, look at you." Cam stood in the bedroom doorway and whistled at Seth in his tux. "All slicked up in your monkey suit."

"You only wish you could look this good." Seth shot his cuffs. "I get the feeling I'm going to be the artist on display at this little soiree. I nearly bought a cape and beret instead of a tux. But I restrained myself."

He began to fuss with the tie. "This rig was Phil's pick. Classic, according to him, but not dated."

"He oughta know. Stop messing with that. Jesus." Cam straightened from the doorjamb and crossed over to fuss with Seth's tie himself. "You've got more nerves than a virgin on prom night."

"Yeah, maybe. I'll be swimming in a lot of blue blood this evening. I don't want to drown in it."

Cam's eyes shifted up, met his. "Money don't mean jack. You're as good as any of them and better than most. Quinns don't take second place to anyone."

"I want to marry her, Cam."

There was a little clutch in his belly. The trip from boy to man, he thought, never took as long as you thought it should. "Yeah, I got that."

"When you marry someone you take on their family, their baggage, the whole shot."

"That's right."

"I deal with hers, she has to deal with mine. I get through tonight in one piece, she makes it though the insanity around here on the Fourth, then . . . I have to tell her about before. About Gloria, a lot more than I have. I have to tell her about . . . all of it."

"If you're thinking she'll run, then she's not the one for you. And knowing women, and I do, she's not the running type."

"I'm not thinking she'll run. I don't know what she'll do. What I'll do. But I have to lay it out for her and give her the chance to decide where she wants to go from there. I've put it off too long already."

"It's history. But it's your history so you have to tell her. Then put it away again." Cam stepped back. "Real slick." He gave Seth's biceps a squeeze, knowing it would ease the trouble on his face. "Oooh, you've been lifting."

"Cram it."

Seth was laughing when he left the house, grinning when he opened his car door. And the panic slammed into his throat like a fist when he saw the note on the front seat.

Tomorrow night, ten o'clock.
Miller's Bar, St. Michael's.
We'll talk.

She'd come here, he thought as he balled the paper in his hand. To his home. Within feet of his family.

Yeah, they'd talk. Damn right they'd talk.

Sixteen

He remembered to tell her she looked beautiful. She did, in the stoplight-red dress that skimmed down her body and left her back bare but for a crisscross of skinny, glittering straps.

He remembered to smile, to make conversation on the drive to Washington. He ordered himself to relax. He would deal with Gloria as he always dealt with her.

He told himself she could take nothing from him but money.

And he knew it was a lie.

Wasn't that what Stella had intimated in the dream? he thought now. It wasn't just money Gloria wanted. She wanted to gouge at his heart until every bit of happiness bled out of it.

She hated him for being whole. On some level, he'd always known that.

"I appreciate your going to all this trouble tonight."

He glanced over, brushed a hand over hers. "Come on. It's not every day I get to mix with the movers and shakers at some spiffy party. Very swank," he added.

"I'd rather be at home, sitting on the porch swing."

"You don't have a porch swing."

"I keep meaning to buy one. I'd like to be sitting on my imaginary porch swing, having a nice glass of wine while the sun sets." And so, she thought, would he.

Whatever he said, something was wrong. She knew his face so well now—well enough that she could close her eyes and paint it, feature by feature, in her mind. There was definitely trouble lurking behind his eyes.

"Two hours," she said. "We'll stay two hours, then we're gone."

"This is your deal, Dru. We'll stay as long as you like."

"I wouldn't be going at all if I could've avoided it. My parents double-teamed me on this one. I wonder if we ever really get beyond the point where a parent can emotionally blackmail us into doing something we don't want to do."

Her words made him think of Gloria, and dread curled in his stomach. "It's just a party, sugar."

"Oh, if only. A party's where you go to have fun, to relax and enjoy the company of people you have something in common with. I don't have anything in common with these people anymore. Maybe I never did. My mother wants to show you off, and I'm going to let her because she wore me down."

"Well, you've got to admit, I look terrific tonight."

"Can't argue with that. And you're trying to cheer me up. So thanks. I'll promise to do the same on the way home when you're glazed and incoherent from being interrogated."

"Does it matter to you, what they think of me?"

"Of course." Amused with herself, she took out her lipstick and missed the way his jaw tightened. "I want all those people who gave me that sticky sympathy over my breakup with Jonah, all the ones who brought it up to my face hoping I'd say or do something they could dine out on the following evening, to take one look at you. I want them to think, Well, well, Dru certainly landed on her feet, didn't she? She bagged herself *il maestro giovane*."

Tension settled on the back of his neck, too weighty to be shrugged off. "So, I'm a status symbol now," he said, and tried to keep it light.

She freshened her lipstick, capped the tube. "Better than a Harry Winston diamond necklace. It's mean, it's petty, it's pitifully female. But I don't care. It's a revelation to realize I've just that much of my mother in me that I want to show you off, too."

"There's no escaping where we come from. No matter how far we run."

"Now that's depressing. If I believed that, I'd jump off a cliff. Believe me, I am *not* going to end up chairing committees and giving ladies' teas on Wednesday afternoons."

Something in the quality of his silence had her reaching over to touch his arm. "Two hours, Seth. Maximum."

"It'll be fine," he told her.

⚭

Seth got his first real taste of Dru's previous life minutes after they entered the ballroom.

Groups of people mixed and mingled to the muted background music of a twelve-piece orchestra. The decor was a patriotic red, white and blue echoed in flowers, table linens, balloons and bunting.

A huge ice sculpture of the American flag had been carved as if it were waving in a breeze.

There was a great deal of white on the female guests as well, which took its form in diamonds and pearls. Dress was conservative, traditional and very, very rich.

Part political rally, he supposed. Part social event, part gossip mill.

He'd do it in acrylics, he thought. All sharp colors and shapes with bright crystal light.

"Drusilla." Katherine swept up, resplendent in military blue. "Don't you look lovely? But I thought we said you'd wear the white Valentino." She kissed Dru's cheek and, with an indulgent *tsk-tsk,* brushed her fingers over Dru's hair.

"And Seth." She held out a hand to him. "How wonderful to see you again. I was afraid you must be stuck in traffic. I was so hoping you and Dru would come stay with us for the weekend so you wouldn't have that terrible drive."

It was the first he'd heard of it, but he rose to the occasion. "I appreciate the invitation, but I couldn't get away. I hope you'll forgive me and save me a dance. That way I'll be able to say I danced with the two most beautiful women in the room."

"Aren't you charming?" She pinked up prettily. "And you can be certain I'll do just that. Come now, I must introduce you. So many people are looking forward to meeting you."

Before she could turn, Drusilla's father strode up. He was a striking man with silver-streaked black hair and hooded eyes of dense brown. "There's my princess." He caught Dru in a fierce and possessive embrace. "You're so late, you had me worried."

"We're not late."

"For heaven's sake, let the girl breathe," Katherine demanded, and tugged at Proctor's arm.

In an instant, Seth had the image of Witless trying to wedge his way in between Anna and anyone who tried to hug her when he was nearby.

"Proctor, this is Drusilla's escort, Seth Quinn."

"Good to meet you. Finally." Proctor took Seth's hand in a firm grip. Those dark eyes focused on Seth's face. Studied.

"It's good to meet you." Just when Seth began to wonder if he was about to be challenged to Indian-wrestle, Proctor released his hand.

"It's a pity you couldn't make time to come down for the weekend."

"Yes, I'm sorry about that."

"Dad, it's not Seth's fault. I told you—both of you—that I couldn't manage it. If I—"

"Dru's shop is terrific, isn't it?" Seth interrupted, his tone cheerful as he took champagne from a tray offered by a waiter, passed flutes to Katherine, to Dru, to Proctor before taking one for himself. "I'm sure the business aspects are complicated and challenging, but I'm speaking aesthetically. The use of space and light, the evolving blend of color and texture. One artist's eye admiring another," he said easily. "You must be incredibly proud of her."

"Of course we are." Proctor's smile was sharp, lethally so. *She's my girl*, it said as clearly as Katherine's tugging had done. "Drusilla is our most cherished treasure."

"How could she be anything but?" Seth replied.

"There's Granddad, Seth." Dru reached down, gripped Seth's hand. "I really should introduce you."

"Sure." He shot a beaming smile at her parents. "Excuse us a minute."

"You're very good at this," Dru told him.

"The tact and diplomacy department. Probably get that from Phil. You might've mentioned the weekend invite."

"Yes, I'm sorry. I should have. I thought I was saving us both, and instead I put you in the hot seat."

They were stopped a half dozen times on the way to the table where Senator Whitcomb was holding court. Each time, Dru exchanged a light kiss or handshake, made introductions, then eased away.

"You're good at it, too," Seth commented.

"Bred in the bone. Hello, Granddad." She bent down to kiss the handsome, solidly built man.

He had a rough and cagey look about him, Seth thought. Like a boxer who dominated in the ring as much with wit as with muscle. His hair was a dense pewter, and his eyes the same brilliant green as his granddaughter's.

He got to his feet to catch her face in two big hands. His smile was magnetic. "Here's my best girl."

"You say that to all your granddaughters."

"And I mean it, every time. Where's that painter your mother's been burning my ears about? This one here." Keeping one hand on Dru's shoulder, he sized Seth up. "Well, you don't look like an idiot, boy."

"I try not to be."

"Granddad."

"Quiet. You got sense enough to be making time with this pretty thing?" Seth grinned. "Yes, sir."

"Senator Whitcomb, Seth Quinn. Don't embarrass me, Granddad."

"It's an old man's privilege to embarrass his granddaughters. I like your work well enough," he said to Seth.

"Thank you, Senator. I like yours well enough, too."

Whitcomb's lips pursed for a moment, then curved up. "Seems to have a backbone. We'll see about this. My sources tell me you're making a decent living off your painting."

"Quiet," Seth told Dru when she opened her mouth. "I'm lucky to be able to make a living doing something I love. As your record indicates you're a strong patron of the arts, you obviously understand and appreciate art for art's sake. Financial rewards are secondary."

"Build boats, too, don't you?"

"Yes, sir. When I can. My brothers are the finest designers and builders of wooden sailing vessels in the East. If you visit Saint Chris again, you should come by and see for yourself."

"I might just do that. Your grandfather was a teacher. Is that right?"

"Yes," Seth said evenly. "He was."

"The most honorable of professions. I met him once at a political rally at the college. He was an interesting and exceptional man. Adopted three sons, didn't he?"

"Yes, sir."

"But you come from his daughter."

"In a manner of speaking. I wasn't fortunate enough to have my grandfather for the whole of my life, as Dru's been fortunate enough to have you. But his impact on me, his import to me, is every bit as deep. I hope he'd be half as proud of me as I am of him."

Dru laid a hand on Seth's arm, felt the tension. "If you've finished prying for the moment, I'd like to dance. Seth?"

"Sure. Excuse me, Senator."

"I'm sorry." Dru turned into Seth's arms on the dance floor. "I'm so sorry."

"Don't be."

"I am. It's his nature to demand answers, however personal."

"He didn't seem to want to roast me over an open fire, like your father."

"No. He's not as possessive, and he's more open to letting me make my own decisions, trust my own instincts."

"I liked him." That, Seth thought, was part of the problem. He'd seen a shrewd and intelligent man who loved his grandchild, and expected the best for her. Who obviously concluded that she'd expect the best for herself.

And the best was unlikely to be a stray with a father he'd never met and a mother with a fondness for blackmail.

"He's usually more subtle than that," she said. "And more reasonable. The situation with Jonah infuriated him. Now, I suppose, he'll be overprotective where I'm concerned for a while. Why don't we just go?"

"Running away doesn't work. Believe me, I've tried it."

"You're right, and that's very annoying."

She eased back when the music stopped, and saw Jonah over his shoulder. "If it's not one thing," she said quietly, "it's two more. How's your tact and diplomacy holding up?"

"So far, so good."

"Lend me some," she said, then let her lips curve into a cool and aloof smile.

"Hello, Jonah. And Angela, isn't it?"

"Dru." Jonah started to lean in, as if to kiss her cheek. He stopped short at the warning that flickered in her eyes, but his transition to a polite handshake was silky smooth. "You look wonderful, as always. Jonah Stuben," he said to Seth and offered a hand.

"Quinn, Seth Quinn."

"Yes, the artist. I've heard of you. My fiancée, Angela Downey."

"Congratulations." Well aware dozens of eyes were on her, Dru kept her expression bland. "And best wishes," she said to Angela.

"Thank you." Angela kept her hand tucked tight through Jonah's arm. "I saw two of your paintings at a showing of contemporary artists at the Smithsonian last year. One seemed a very personal study in oil, with an old white house, shady trees, people gathered around a big picnic table, and dogs in the yard. It was lovely, and so serene."

"Thanks." *Home*, Seth thought. One he'd done from memory and his rep had shipped back for the gallery.

"And how's your little business, Dru?" Jonah asked her. "And life in the slow lane?"

"Both are very rewarding. I'm enjoying living and working among people who don't slide into pretense every morning along with their wing tips."

"Really?" Jonah's smile went edgy. "I got the impression from your parents that you were moving back shortly."

"You're mistaken. And so are they. Seth, I'd love a little fresh air."

"Fine. Oh, Jonah, I want to thank you for being such a complete asshole." Seth smiled cheerfully at Angela. "I hope you're very happy together."

"That was neither tactful nor diplomatic," Dru admonished.

"I guess I get the calling an asshole an asshole from Cam. The restraint for not busting his balls for calling your shop 'your little business' is probably Ethan's influence. Want to go out on the terrace?"

"Yes. But . . . give me a minute, will you? I'd like to go out alone, settle down. Then we can make the rest of the rounds and get the hell out of here."

"Sounds good to me."

He watched her go, but before he could find someplace to hide, Katherine swooped down on him.

Outside, Dru took two steadying breaths, then a sip from the champagne she'd taken before stepping onto the terrace.

This town, she thought, looking out at the lights and the landmarks, smothered her. Was it any wonder she'd bolted to a place where the air was clear?

She wanted to sit on her porch, to feel that quiet satisfaction after a long day's work. She wanted to know Seth was beside her, or would be.

How strange it was that she could see that image so clearly, could see it spinning on, day after day. Year after year. And she could barely make out the shape and texture of the life she'd led before. All she knew was the weight of it at moments like this.

"Drusilla?"

She glanced over her shoulder, managed to suppress the sigh—and the oath—when Angela stepped up to her. "Let's not pretend we have something to say to each other, Angela. We played for the crowd."

"I have something to say to you. Something I've wanted to say for a long time. I owe you an apology."

Dru lifted an eyebrow. "For?"

"This isn't easy for me. I was jealous of you. I resented you for having what I wanted. And I used that to justify sleeping with the man you were going to marry. I loved him, I wanted him, so I took what was available."

"And now you have him." Dru lifted a hand, palm up. "Problem solved."

"I didn't like being the other woman. Sneaking around, taking whatever scraps he had left over. I convinced myself it was your fault, that was the only way I could live with it. All I had to do was get you out of the way and Jonah and I could be together."

"You did do it on purpose." Dru turned, leaned back against the railing. "I wondered."

"Yes, I did it on purpose. It was impulse, and one I've regretted even though . . . well, even though. You didn't deserve to find out that way. You hadn't done anything. You were the injured party, and I played a large role in hurting you. I'm very sorry for it."

"Are you apologizing because your conscience is bothering you, Angela, or because it'll tidy up the path before you marry Jonah?"

"Both."

Honesty at least, Dru thought, she could respect. "All right, you're absolved. Go forth and sin no more. He wouldn't have had the guts to apologize, to come to me this way, face-to-face, and admit he was wrong. Why are you with someone like that?"

"I love him," Angela said simply. "Strong points, weak points, the whole package."

"Yes, I think you do. Good luck. Sincerely."

"Thank you." She started back in, then stopped. "Jonah's never looked at me the way I saw Seth Quinn look at you. I don't think he ever will. Some of us settle for what we can get."

And some of us, Dru realized, get more than we ever knew we wanted.

∽

He was worn out when they got back to Dru's. From the drive, from the tension, from the thoughts circling like vultures in his mind.

"I owe you big."

He turned his head, stared at her blankly. "What?"

"I owe you for tolerating everything. My grandfather's interrogation, my ex-fiancé's smugness, my mother's prancing you around for over an hour like you were a prize stallion at a horse show, for all the questions, the intimations, the speculations. You had to run the gauntlet."

"Yeah, well." He jerked his shoulders, shoved open the car door. "You warned me."

"My father was rude, several times."

"Not especially. He just doesn't like me." Hands in his pockets, Seth walked with her toward the front door. "I get the impression he's not going to like any guy, particularly, who touches his princess."

"I'm not a princess."

"Oh, sugar, when your family's got themselves a couple of business and political empires, you're a princess. You just don't want to live in an ivory tower."

"I'm not what they assume I am. I don't want what they persist in believing I want. I'm never going to please them in the way they continually expect. This is my life now. Will you stay?"

"Tonight?"

"To start."

He stepped inside with her. He didn't know what to do with the despair, with the sudden, urgent fear that he was going to lose everything he'd tried so hard to hold on to.

He pulled her close, as if to prove he could hold on to this. And could hear the mocking laughter rising in his brain.

"I need . . ." He pressed his face into the curve of her neck. "Goddamn it. I need—"

"What?" Trying to soothe, she stroked her hands over his back. "What do you need?"

Too much, he thought. More, he was sure, than fate would ever let him have. But for now, for tonight, all needs could be one.

"You." He spun her around, shoved her back against the door in a move as sharp and shocking as a whiplash. His mouth cut off her gasp of surprise in a kiss that burned toward the savage.

"I need you." He stared down into her wide, stunned eyes. "I'm not going to treat you like a princess tonight." He dragged her dress up to the waist, and his hand, rough and intimate, pressed between her legs. "You're not going to want me to."

"Seth." She gripped his shoulders, too dazed to push him away.

"Tell me to stop." He stabbed his fingers into her, drove up her hard and fast.

Panic, excitement, burst inside her with the darkest of pleasures. "No." She let herself fly, vowed to take him with her. "No, we won't stop."

"I'll take what I need." He snapped one of the thin jeweled straps so the material slithered down to cling to the tip of her breast. "You may not be ready for what I need tonight."

"I'm not fragile." Her breath clogged in her throat. "I'm not weak." Though she shuddered, her gaze stayed on his. "You might not be ready for what I need tonight."

"We're about to find out." He whipped her around, pressed her against the door and fixed his teeth on the nape of her neck.

She cried out, her hands fisting against the door as his raced over her.

They had loved urgently, with great tenderness, even with laughter. But she'd never known the kind of desperation he showed her now. A desperation that was ruthless, reckless and rough. She hadn't known she could revel in it, could feel that same whippy violence herself. Or that she could rejoice in the snapping of her own control.

He assaulted her senses, and left her writhing on the wreckage.

He yanked the second strap, broke the elegant jeweled length in half so the dress slid down into a red puddle on the floor.

She wore a strapless bra and a garter of champagne lace, sheer, sheer hose and high silver heels. When he turned her, looked at her, his fingers dug into her shoulders.

She was quivering now, her skin flushed and damp. And that power, that knowledge were in her eyes. "Take me to bed."

"No." He molded her breasts. "I'm going to take you here."

Then his hands were on her hips, lifting her up, bringing her to him. He ravaged her mouth while he took his hands on an impatient journey over lace and flesh and silk. While his blood pounded, he ran the same hot trail with his mouth.

He wanted to eat her alive, to feed on her until this grinding hunger was finally sated. He wanted to lose his mind so he could think of nothing but this driving primal need.

The delicacy of her skin only made him mad to possess it. Her fresh female scent only stirred feral appetites.

When she exploded against him, he knew only a bright and burning triumph.

She dragged at his jacket, her fingers fumbling in her rush, her choked cries muffled against his mouth. Dizzy, desperate, she yanked at his tie.

"Please." She no longer cared that she was reduced to begging. "Please. Hurry."

He was still half dressed when he pulled her to the floor. And she was arching up in demand when he drove himself into her.

Her nails raked over his shirt, under it to dig into flesh gone hot and damp. Racing with him now, she met him thrust for frantic thrust.

Their breath in rags, their hearts slamming to the same primal beat, they surrendered to the frenzy.

Rider and ridden, they plunged off the edge together.

She lay spent, and used, and blissful on the bare, polished floor with the light from her prized Tiffany lamp spreading jewels in the air. As the pounding of blood in her ears faded, she could hear the night sounds coming through her open windows.

The water, the lazy call of an owl, the song of insects.

The heat still pumped from him, and spread through her like a drug. She rubbed her foot indolently against his ankle.

"Seth?"

"Hmm."

"I never thought I'd hear myself say this, but I'm so very glad we went to that tedious, irritating party tonight. In fact, if they put you in this kind of mood, I think we should go to one at least once a week."

He turned his head, saw the bright pool of red on the floor. "I'll pay to have your dress fixed."

"Okay, but it might be awkward to explain the damage to a tailor."

He came from violence, he thought. He knew how to control it, channel it. He recognized the difference between passions and punishments. He knew sex could be mean, just as he knew what had just happened between them was a world away from what he'd known and seen during the first years of his life.

And still . . .

"There's a lot you don't know about me, Dru."

"I imagine there's a lot we don't know about each other yet. We've both been with other people, Seth. We're not children. But I know I've never felt like this about anyone else. And for the first time in my life, I don't seem to need to plan every detail, to know every option. That's . . . liberating for me. I like discovering who you are, who I am. Who we are together."

She stroked her fingers through his hair. "Who we will be together. For me, it's a wonderful part of being in love. The discovery," she said as he lifted his head to look down at her. "The knowing there's time to discover more."

He was afraid time was the problem, and that it was running out.

"You know what I'd like you to do now?" she asked him.

"What would you like me to do now?"

"Carry me up to bed." She hooked her arms around his neck. "Here's something you didn't know about me. I've always, secretly, of course, fantasized about having some strong, gorgeous man carry me up the stairs. It goes against my sense of intellect, but there you are."

"A secret romantic fantasy." Determined to have this one night of peace, he laid his lips lightly on hers. "Very interesting. Let's see if I can fulfill that for you."

He rose, then glanced down at himself. "I'm going to lose the shirt first. It's a pretty silly image, some guy wearing nothing but a tuxedo shirt, carrying a naked woman upstairs."

"Good idea."

He dealt with the studs, the cuff links, then tossed the shirt over by her dress. He reached down for her; she reached up for him.

"How's it going so far?"

"Perfectly," she said, nuzzling his neck as he carried her toward the stairs. "Tell me something I don't know about you."

It broke his stride, but he shifted her and continued up the stairs. "I've been dreaming about my grandfather's wife. I never met her. She died before I came to Saint Chris."

"Really? What kind of dreams?"

"Very detailed, very clear dreams where we have long conversations. I used to listen to the guys talk about her and wish I'd gotten a chance to know her."

"I think that's lovely, and loving."

"The thing is, I don't think they're dreams. I think I'm having these conversations with her."

"You think that when you're dreaming?"

"No." He laid Dru on the bed, stretched out beside her, then drew her against his side. "I think that right now."

"Oh."

"That got you."

"I'm thinking." She shifted until her head rested comfortably in the nook of his neck. "You think they're some sort of visitation? That you're communicating with her spirit?"

"Something like that."

"What do you talk about?"

He hesitated, and evaded. "Family. Just family stuff. She told me things I didn't know, stuff that happened when my brothers were kids. Stuff that turned out to be true."

"Really?" She snuggled against him. "Then I suppose you'd better listen to her."

⚶

"That's a smart woman you've got there," Stella commented. They walked through the moist, heavy night air near the verge of Dru's river. The lamp in the living room window sent pretty colored light against the glass.

"She's got a strong, complicated brain. Everything about her's on the strong and complicated side."

"Strong's sexy," Stella said. "Don't you think she looks to you for the same? Strength of mind, of character, of heart? All the rest is just glands—not that there's anything wrong with glands. Makes the world go round."

"I fell for her so fast. One minute I'm standing up, the next I'm flat on the ground. I never thought it would be the same for her. But it is. Somehow."

"What're you going to do about it?"

"I don't know." He picked up a stone, skipped it out over the ink-black river. "You take somebody on, for the long haul, you take up their baggage, too. My baggage is damn heavy, Grandma. I have a feeling it's about to get a lot heavier."

"You've handcuffed yourself to that baggage, Seth. You've got the key, you always have. Don't you think it's time to use it and pitch that load overboard?"

"She'll never go away and stay away."

"Probably not. What you do about it is what makes the size of the load. Too damn stubborn to share it. Just like your grandfather."

"Really?" The idea simply warmed his heart. "Do you think I take after him in some ways?"

"You got his eyes." She reached up, touched his hair. "But you know that already. And his stubborn streak. Always figured he could handle things himself. Irritating. Had a calm way about him—until he blew. You're the same. And you've made the same damn mistakes he made with Gloria. You're letting her use your love for your family, and for Dru, as a weapon."

"It's just money, Grandma."

"Hell it is. You know what you have to do, Seth. Now go on and do it. Though being a man, you'll find a way to screw it up some first."

His jaw set. "I'm not dragging Dru through this."

"Hell. That girl doesn't want a martyr." She planted her hands on her hips and scowled at him. "Stubborn to the point of stupid. Just like your grandfather," she muttered.

And was gone.

SEVENTEEN

The bar was a dive, the sort of place where drinking was a serious, mostly solitary occupation. The blue curtain of smoke, thick enough to part with your hands, turned it all into a poorly produced black-and-white movie scene. The lights were dim, encouraging patrons to mind their own, with the added benefit of hiding the stains when someone decided to mind his neighbor's.

It smelled of last year's cigarettes and last week's beer.

The recreation and socializing area consisted of a stingy strip of space along the side where a pool table had been jammed. A bunch of guys were playing a round of eight ball while a few more stood around sucking beers, the expressions of bored disgust on their faces showing the world what badasses they were.

The air-conditioning unit was framed in a window with a sheet of splintered plywood, and did little more than stir the stink and make noise.

Seth took a seat at the end of the bar and, playing it safe, ordered a Bud in the bottle.

He supposed it was fitting she'd dragged him out to a place like this. She'd dragged him into them often enough when he was a kid—or if she'd had transportation, he'd slept in the car while she'd gone in.

Gloria might have been raised in a solid upper-class environment, but all the benefits and advantages of that upbringing had been wasted on a spirit that continually sought, and found, the lowest level.

He'd stopped wondering what it was inside her that drove her to hate, to despise anything decent. What compelled her to use anyone who'd ever had reason to care for her until she'd sucked them dry or destroyed them.

Her addictions—men, drugs, liquor—didn't cause it. They were only one more form of her absolute self-indulgence.

But it was fitting it would be here, he thought, as he sat and listened to the sharp smack of balls, the rattling whine of the failing AC, and smelled the smells that pulled him back into the nightmare of his childhood.

She'd have come in to pick up a john, he remembered, if she needed cash. Or if she'd had money, to drink herself drunk—unless booze hadn't been her drug of choice for that night. Then she'd have come in to score.

If the john was the target, she'd take him back to whatever hole they were living in. Sex noises and wild laughter in the next room. If it was drink or drugs, and they put her in a good mood, there would've been a stop at some all-night place. He'd have eaten that night.

If the mood had turned nasty, there would have been fists instead of food.

Or so it had been until he'd been big enough, fast enough, mean enough to avoid the punches.

"You gonna drink that beer?" the bartender demanded, "or just look at it all night?"

Seth shifted his gaze, and the cold warning on his face had the bartender easing back a step. Keeping his eyes level, Seth pulled a ten out of his pocket, dropped it on the bar by his untouched beer.

"Problem?" His voice was a soft threat.

The bartender shrugged and got busy elsewhere.

When she walked in, a couple of the pool players looked over, checked her out. Seth imagined Gloria considered their leering smirks a flattering assessment.

She wore denim cutoffs that hugged her bony hips and frayed at the hem just below crotch level. The snug top was hot pink, left several inches of midriff bare. She'd had her belly button pierced and added a tattoo of a dragonfly beside the gold bar. Her nails, fingers and toes were coated in a glitter polish that looked black in the ugly light.

She slid onto a stool, then sent the pool players one long, hot look.

It only took one look at her eyes for Seth to realize at least a portion of the money he'd given her had gone up her nose.

"G and T," she told the bartender. "Easy on the T."

She took out a cigarette, flicked on a silver lighter, then blew a slow stream of smoke at the ceiling. She crossed her legs, and her foot jiggled in triple time.

"Hot enough for you?" she said and laughed.

"You've got five minutes."

"What's your hurry?" She sucked in more smoke, tapped her glittery nails in a rapid tattoo on the bar. "Drink your beer and relax."

"I don't drink with people I don't like. What do you want, Gloria?"

"I want this gin and tonic." She picked up the glass the bartender set in front of her. Drank long and deep. "Maybe a little action." She sent the pool players another look, licked her lips in a way that curdled Seth's stomach. "And just lately I've been thinking I need a nice little place at the beach. Daytona maybe."

She took another drink, left lipstick smeared on the rim. "You, now, you don't want a place of your own, do you? Still living in that same house, crowded in with those kids and dogs. You're in a rut."

"Stay away from my family."

"Or what?" She sent him a smile as glittery and black as her nails. "You'll tell your big brothers on me? You think the Quinns worry me? They've all gone soft and stupid, the way people do when they hang around some dead-ass town their whole fucking, useless lives, breeding noisy kids and sitting around the TV every night like a bunch of goddamn zombies. Only smart thing they did was take you in so they could get the old man's money—just like that asshole married my spineless sister for hers."

She tossed back the rest of her drink, rapped it hard twice on the bar to signal for another. Her body was in constant motion—the jiggling foot, the tapping fingers, the swivel of her head on her neck. "The old man was my blood, not theirs. That money should've been mine."

"You bled him for plenty before he died. But it's never enough, is it?"

"Fucking A." She fired up another cigarette. "You got yourself some smarts, after all these years. Hooked yourself up with a live one, didn't you? Drusilla Whitcomb Banks. Woo-hoo." Gloria threw back her head, let out a hoot. "Fancy stuff. Rich stuff. Bagging her's the only smart thing you ever did. Set yourself up for life."

She snatched the glass the minute the bartender set it down. "'Course you've been doing pretty well for yourself drawing pictures. Better than I realized." She crunched down on ice. "Can't figure why people'd piss away all that money on something to hang on the wall. Takes all kinds."

He laid a hand on her wrist, slowly closed his fingers around it in a grip mean enough to make her jolt. "Understand this: You go near my family or Dru, you go around anyone who matters to me, and you'll find out exactly what I'm capable of. It'll be a hell of a lot worse on you than Sybill knocking you on your ass the way she did years ago."

She leaned her face into his. "You threatening me? *Son?*"

"I'm promising you."

Through the drugs and alcohol, she caught some hint of that promise. And eased back, as the bartender had done. "That your bottom line?" She picked up her drink with her free hand, and her thin, used face went cagey. "You want me to steer clear of your nearest and dearest?"

"That's my bottom line."

"Here's mine." She jerked her hand free, reached for her cigarette. "We've been playing nickel and dime long enough, you and me. You're raking in the dough with your pictures, and you're screwing your way into a big, fat pile of it. I want my cut. One-time deal, lump-sum payment, and I'm gone. That's what you want, right? You want me gone."

"How much?"

Satisfied, she took another deep drag, let the smoke stream into his face. He'd always been the easiest of marks. "One million."

He didn't even blink. "You want a million dollars."

"I've done my homework, sweetie pie. You get big bucks when the suckers plunk it down for your paintings. You pulled in a pile over there in Europe. Who knows how long you can run that con? Add to that the fancy piece you're busy banging."

She shifted on the stool, recrossed her legs. The mix of drugs and alcohol raging through her system made her feel powerful. Made her feel *alive*.

"She's rolling in it. Lots of money there. Old money, too. The kind of money that doesn't like scandal. Mess things up for you if it got out in the press that the senator's purebred granddaughter was spreading her legs for a mongrel. One that was ripped from his mother's arms when she came to the father she'd never known for help. I can play it all kinds of ways," she added. "You and the Quinns won't come out clean in any of them. And the dirt'll stick to your girlfriend, too. She won't hang around once the shit starts to fly."

She signaled for a third drink, shifted again. "She'll dump you, and fast, and maybe people won't be so willing to shell out for your pictures once they hear my side of things. Oh, I bought him his first little paint kit. Sniff, sniff."

She threw back her head and laughed, the sound so full of malice and glee, the pool players stopped smacking balls to look over. "Press'll lap it up. Fact is, I could sell the story, make a nice little bundle. But I'm giving you a chance to buy it first. You can consider it an investment. You pay me, and I'm out of your life once and for all. You don't, and someone else will."

His face was blank, had stayed blank throughout her rant. He wouldn't give her even his disgust. "Your story's bullshit."

"Sure it is." She laughed and gulped gin. "People can't get enough bullshit, not when it's piling up on somebody else. I'll give you a week to come up with it—cash. But I want a down payment. We'll just call it good-faith money. Ten thousand. You bring it here, tomorrow night. Ten o'clock. You don't show, then I start making some calls."

He got to his feet. "Spend another ten on nose candy, Gloria, you'll be dead in the back room of some dump like this long before you can enjoy any part of that million."

"Just let me worry about me. Pay for the drinks."

He simply turned his back on her and walked toward the door.

⚛

He couldn't go home, not when he intended to sit in the dark and get quietly and thoroughly drunk.

He knew better. He knew it was an escape, self-pity, a one-way trip.
Steady, deliberate drinking was a crutch, an illusion, a trapdoor.

He didn't give a damn. So he poured another shot of Jameson and studied its deep amber glow in the single light he'd turned on in his studio.

His brothers had given him his first taste of whiskey on his twenty-first
birthday. Just the four of them, Seth remembered, sitting around the kitchen
table with the kids and the women gone.

It was one of those solid, rich-toned memories that he knew would never
leave him. The sharp scent of the cigar smoke after Ethan had passed them
around. The sting of the whiskey on his tongue, down his throat, mellowing
out as it reached his belly. The sound of his brothers' voices, their laughter,
and the absolute certainty he'd felt of his own belonging.

He hadn't cared much for the taste of the whiskey. Still didn't. But it was
what a man reached for when his single intention was oblivion.

He'd long since stopped questioning what Gloria DeLauter was, and
how she became. Part of her was inside him, and he accepted that as he
would a birthmark. He didn't believe in the sins of the father—or mother.
He didn't believe in tainted blood. Each one of his brothers had come from
some sort of horror, and they were the best men he knew.

Whatever there was of Gloria inside him had been drowned out by the
decency and pride and compassion given to him by the Quinns.

Maybe that alone was part of the reason she hated him—hated all of them.
It didn't matter why. She was part of his life, and he had to deal with her.

One way or the other.

He sat drinking by that single light in a room filled with his paintings
and the tools of the work he loved. He'd already made his decision, and he
would live with it. But for tonight, he'd cloud his future with Irish whiskey
and the throb of the mournful blues he'd chosen as his drinking music.

When his cell phone rang he ignored it. Picked up the bottle, poured another shot.

⚛

Dru hung up and paced her living room. She'd tried Seth's number half a
dozen times, had worn a path on the floor over the last two hours. Since
Aubrey had called, looking for him.

He wasn't with Aubrey, as he'd told Dru he would be that evening. Nor was he with Dru—as he'd told Aubrey and his family he would be.

So where the hell was he?

He'd been off. *Something* had been off, she decided, since the night before. Even before the party, she thought now. Before the drive. There'd been some kind of repressed violence in him—viciously repressed, she realized. It had, eventually, taken its form in rough sex.

And even then, after they'd exhausted each other, she'd sensed an underlying turbulence. She'd let it go, Dru admitted. It wasn't in her nature to pry. She resented the way her parents questioned and picked apart her every mood. Moods, she liked to think, were often private matters.

Now he'd lied to her. That, she felt strongly, was not his nature.

If something was wrong, she needed to help. Wasn't that part of the duty of love?

She checked her watch, barely stopped herself from wringing her hands. It was after midnight. What if he was hurt? What if he'd been in an accident?

And what if he'd simply wanted an evening to himself?

"If he did, he should have said so," she mumbled and marched to the door.

There was one place she imagined he could be. She wasn't going to rest until she checked.

On the drive into town she lectured herself. Her relationship with Seth didn't mean he had to account to her for every minute of his time. They both had lives, interests, obligations of their own. She certainly wasn't the sort of woman who couldn't be content and productive with her own company.

But that didn't give him the right to lie to her about his plans for the evening. If he'd just answer his goddamn phone, she wouldn't be driving into town in the middle of the night to look for him like some clichéd, nagging sitcom wife.

And she was going to ream him inside out for making her feel like one.

She'd worked up a good head of steam by the time she turned toward the rear lot and saw his car parked. The insult of it nearly had her driving right past and back home again. He couldn't have told her, and everyone else, that he'd wanted to work? He couldn't just pick up the phone and . . .

She slammed on the brakes.

What if he couldn't get to the phone? What if he was unable to answer because he was unconscious, or ill?

She whipped the car into the lot, leaped out and charged up the stairs.

The image of him lying helpless on the floor was so strong that when she burst in, saw him sitting on the bed pouring liquor from a bottle into a short glass, it didn't register.

"You're all right." The relief came first, made her knees weak. "Oh, Seth, God! I was so worried."

"What for?" He set the bottle down, studied her out of bleary eyes as he drank.

"Nobody knew where . . ." Realization came next, made her blood boil. "You're drunk."

"Working on it. Got a ways to go yet. What're you doing here?"

"Aubrey called looking for you hours ago. Your stories got crossed. Since you didn't answer your phone, I was foolish enough to worry about you."

He was still much too sober. Sober enough to consider her mood could make it easier on both of them. "If you came running in here hoping to catch me in bed with another woman, I'm sorry to disappoint you."

"It never occurred to me that you would cheat." Nearly as baffled as she was angry, she walked toward the bed, noted the level of whiskey in the bottle. "Then again, it never crossed my mind that you'd need to lie to me either. Or that you'd sit here alone drinking yourself drunk."

"Told you there's a lot you don't know about me, sugar." He jerked a thumb at the bottle. "Want one? Glasses in the kitchen."

"No, thank you. Is there a reason you're worrying your family and having a drinking marathon?"

"I'm a big boy, Dru, and I don't need you crawling up my ass because I want a couple drinks. This is more my style than a couple polite belts of champagne at some boring political gala. You can't deal with it, it's not my problem."

It stung, and had her chin lifting. "I was obliged to go. You weren't. That choice was yours. You want to drown yourself in a whiskey bottle, that's certainly your choice as well. But I won't be lied to. I won't be made a fool of."

He gave a careless shrug and, riding on the whiskey, decided he knew what was best for her. A few more jabs to the pride, he thought, and she'd be gone.

"You know the problem with women? You sleep with them a few times, you tell them what they want to hear. You show them a good time. Right away, they start crowding you. Take a little breather, and they're all over you like lice on a monkey. Jesus, I knew I should never've gone to that deal with you last night. Told myself it'd give you ideas."

"Ideas?" she repeated. She felt her throat fill and burn. *"Ideas?"*

"Can't just let things be, can you?" He shook his head, poured another drink. "Always got to be looking ahead. What's the deal for tomorrow, what's going to happen next week? You're plotting out a future, sugar, and that's just not what I'm about. You're a hell of a lot of fun to be with once you loosen up, but we'd better quit while we're ahead."

"You—you're dumping me?"

"Aw now, don't put it like that, sweetheart. We just need to throttle back some."

Grief rolled up, and numbed her. "All this, all this was just for, what, for sex and art? I don't believe that. I don't."

"Let's not make a big thing out of it." He reached for the bottle again. Poured whiskey onto whiskey. Anything to keep from looking at her, at the tears swimming in her eyes.

"I trusted you, with my body and my heart. I never asked you for anything. You always gave it before I could. I don't deserve to be treated this way, discarded this way, only because I fell in love with you."

He looked at her then, and the combination of pride and sadness on her face destroyed him. "Dru—"

"I love you." She said it calmly, while she could still be calm. "But that's my problem. I'll leave you alone with yours, and your bottle."

"Goddamn it. Goddamn it, don't go," he said when she spun toward the door. "Dru, don't walk out. Please don't." He shoved the glass onto the table, dropped his head in his hands. "I can't do this. I can't let her steal this from me, too."

"You think I'm going to stand here and cry in front of you? Even *speak* to you when you're drunk and insulting?"

"I'm sorry. Christ, I'm sorry."

"You are that. You're very sorry." The hand that gripped the doorknob trembled, and a tear spilled over. The combination infuriated her. "I don't want your pathetic guilty male conscience because you hurt me enough to bring on a few tears. What I really want right now is for you to go straight to hell."

"Please don't walk out the door. I don't think I could stand it." Everything inside him—grief, guilt, loathing and love—clamped his throat like strangling hands. "I thought I should shove you out before you got pulled under. I can't do it. I can't *stand* it. I don't know if it's selfish or if it's right, but I can't let you go. For God's sake, don't walk on me."

She stared at him, at the naked misery on his face. Her heart, already cracked, split in two. "Seth, please tell me what's wrong. Tell me what's hurting you."

"I shouldn't have said those things to you. It was stupid."

"Tell me why you said them. Tell me why you're sitting here alone, drinking yourself sick."

"I was sick before I bought the bottle. I don't know where to start." He raked his hands through his hair. "The beginning, I guess." He pressed his fingers to his lids. "I got about halfway drunk. I'm going to need some coffee."

"I'll make it."

"Dru." He lifted his hands again, then just let them fall. "Everything I said to you since you walked in the door was a lie."

She took a deep breath. For now, she thought, she would tuck the anger and hurt away, and listen. "All right. I'll make you coffee, then you can tell me the truth."

⟫

"It goes back a long time," he began. "Back before my grandfather. Before Ray Quinn married Stella. Before he met her. Dru, I'm sorry I hurt you."

"Just tell me. We'll deal with that later."

He drank coffee. "Ray met this woman, and they got involved. They had an affair," he corrected. "They were both young and single, so why not? Anyway, he wasn't the type she was looking for. You know, a teacher, one who leaned toward the left while she leaned right. She came from a family like yours. What I mean is—"

"I know what you mean. She had a certain social position, and certain social aspirations."

"Yeah." He let out a breath, drank more coffee. "Thanks. She broke it off, left. She was pregnant, and not too pleased about it from the way I've heard it. She met another guy, one she clicked with. So she decided to go through with the pregnancy, and she married him."

"She never told your grandfather about the child."

"No, she never told him. Little ways down the road, she had a second daughter. She had Sybill."

"Sybill, but . . . oh." Dru let it sift in her mind until it fell into place. "I see. Ray Quinn's daughter, Sybill's half sister. Your mother."

"That cuts through it. She—Gloria. Her name's Gloria. She's not like Sybill. Gloria hated her. I think she must've been born hating everyone. Whatever she had growing up, it never seemed to be enough."

He was pale, and looked so drawn and ill, Dru had to bank down on the urge to simply gather him close and comfort. "For some, nothing is ever enough."

"Yeah. She took off with some guy at some point, got knocked up. That would be me. Turns out he married her. That's not important. I've never met him. He doesn't come into this."

"Your father—"

"Sperm donor," Seth corrected. "I don't know what happened between them. I don't lose sleep over it. When Gloria ran out of money, she went back home, took me with her. I don't remember any of that. They didn't kill the fatted calf for her. Gloria's got an affection for the bottle, and various chemical enhancements. I think she came and went for a few years. I know when Sybill had a place of her own in New York, she dumped me there. I don't remember much about it. Didn't remember Sybill at all when I first met her again. I was a couple years old. Sybill gave me this stuffed dog. I called it Yours. You know, when I asked whose it was she said . . ."

"Yours," Dru finished, and touched, brushed a hand over his hair. "She was kind to you."

"She was great. Like I said, I don't remember much, except feeling safe when I was with her. She took us in, bought us food, clothes, took care of me when Gloria didn't show up for a few days. And Gloria paid her back by stealing everything she could fence when Sybill was out, and taking off with me."

"You didn't have a choice. Children don't."

"I'm not taking on responsibility for it. I'm just saying. I don't know why she didn't leave me and head out on her own. I can only figure it was because Sybill and I had made a connection, because we . . ."

"Because you'd started to love each other." Dru took his hand, let his fingers grip tight on hers. "And she resented you both, so she couldn't have that."

He closed his eyes a moment. "It helps that you get it."

"You didn't think I would."

"I don't know what I thought. She fucks me up; that's the only excuse I've got."

"Save the excuses. Tell me the rest."

He set the coffee aside. It wasn't doing anything for his headache or queasy stomach but making him more awake and aware of them. "We lived a lot of different places, for short amounts of time. She had a lot of men. I knew about sex before I could write my own name. She'd get drunk or high, so I was on my own a lot. She ran low on money, couldn't get high, she'd take it out on me."

"She hit you."

"Jesus, Dru. However perceptive you are, you don't know that kind of world. Why should you? Why should anybody?" He pulled himself in. "She'd beat the shit out of me if she felt like it. I'd go hungry if she didn't feel like feeding me. And if she paid for drugs with sex, I'd hear them going at it in the next room. There wasn't much I hadn't seen by the time I was six."

It sickened her. It made her want to weep. But if Seth needed anything from her now, it was strength. "Why didn't Social Services do something to help you?"

He just looked at her for a moment, as if she'd spoken in a language he didn't recognize. "We didn't hang around in places where concerned adults call the authorities on junkie mothers and their abused kids. She was mean, but she's never been stupid. I thought about running away, started to save up for it. A nickel here, a quarter there. When I was old enough, she dumped me in school—gave her more time to cruise. I loved it. I loved school. Never admitted it, couldn't be so uncool, but I loved it."

"None of your teachers realized what was going on?"

"It never occurred to me to tell anybody." He shrugged. "It was life, that's all. And under it, I was just so fucking scared of her. Then . . . I guess I was about seven the first time. One of the men she brought back with her . . ."

He shook his head, pushed to his feet. Even after all the years between, the memories could slick his skin with sweat. "Some of them had a taste for young boys."

Her heart simply stopped, then jolted again to pound in her throat. "No. No."

"I always got away. I was fast, and I was mean. I found places to hide. But I knew what it meant when one of them tried to put his hands on me. I knew what it meant. It was a long time before I could stand anyone touching me. I couldn't stand being touched. I can't get through this if you cry."

She willed back the tears that threatened to overflow. But she rose, crossed to him. Without a word she wrapped her arms around him.

"Poor baby," she crooned, rocking him. "Poor little boy."

Undone, he pressed his face to her shoulder. The smell of her hair, of her skin was so clean. "I didn't want you to know about this."

"Did you think I would love you less?"

"I just didn't want you to know."

"I do know, and I'm so awed by who you are. You think this is beyond my scope, because of my background. But you're wrong." She held tight. "You're wrong. She never broke you, Seth."

"She might have, but for the Quinns. I have to finish." He drew himself away. "Let me finish it."

"Come sit down."

He went with her, sat on the side of the bed again. "During one of her scenes with her mother, Gloria found out about Ray. It gave her someone else to hate, someone else to blame for all the injustices she liked to think were aimed at her. He was teaching at the university here when she found him. This was after Stella had died, after my brothers were adults and had moved out of the house. Cam was in Europe, Phil in Baltimore and Ethan had his own place in Saint Chris. She blackmailed Ray."

"For what? He didn't even know she existed."

"Didn't matter to her. She demanded money; he paid. She wanted more, went to the dean and spun some lie about sexual harassment. Tried to pass me off as Ray's kid. It didn't fly, but it started planting seeds here and there. He made a deal with her. He wanted to get me away from her. He wanted to take care of me."

"He was a good man. Every time I've heard his name mentioned by anyone in Saint Chris, it's with affection and respect."

"He was the best," Seth agreed. "She knew he was a good man. That's the kind of thing she despises, and needs to use. So she sold me to him."

"Well, that was a mistake," Dru said mildly. "And the first decent thing she ever did for you."

"Yeah." He let out a long breath. "You get it. I didn't know who he was. All I knew was that this big old man treated me . . . decent, and I wanted to stay in that house on the water. When he made promises, he kept them, and he never hurt me. He made me toe the line, but, hell, you wanted to when it was Ray's line. He had a puppy, and I never had to go hungry. Most of all, I was away from her, for the first time away from her. I was never going back. He said I'd never have to, and I believed him. But she came back."

"Realized her mistake."

"Realized she'd sold off cheap. She wanted more money or she was taking me. He gave her more, kept giving it. One day, he had an accident on the way back from paying her. It was bad. They called Cam back from Europe. I still remember the first time I saw him, the first time I saw the three of them together, standing around Ray's hospital bed. Ray made them promise to take care of me, to keep me with them. He didn't tell them about Gloria or the connection. Maybe he wasn't thinking about that. He was dying, and he knew it, and he just wanted to make sure I was safe. He trusted them to take care of me."

"He knew his sons," Dru said aloud.

"He knew them—better than I did. When he died, I figured they'd ship me off, or I'd have to run off. I never figured they'd keep me around. They didn't know me, so what did they care? But they kept their promise to Ray.

They changed their lives around for him, and for me. They made a home—
pretty wild one at first with Cam running it."

For the first time since he'd begun, some of the misery lifted. Humor slid
into his voice. "He was always blowing something up in the microwave or
flooding the kitchen. Guy didn't have a clue. I pushed at them, gave them—
Cam mostly—as much grief as I could dish out. And I could dish out plenty.
I kept waiting for them to kick me out, or smack me senseless. But they
stuck with me. They stood up for me, and when Gloria tried to hose them
like she'd done with Ray, they fought for me. Even before we found out I
was Ray's grandson, they'd made me one of them."

"They love you, Seth. Anyone can see it's as much for your sake as it is
for their father's."

"I know it. There's nothing I wouldn't do for them. Including paying off
Gloria, the way I've been doing on and off since I was fourteen."

"She didn't stay away."

"No. She's back now. That's where I was tonight, meeting her to discuss
her latest terms. She came into your shop. Guess she wanted to get a close-
up look at you while she was figuring her angles on this one."

"The woman." Dru stiffened, rubbed suddenly chilled arms. "Harrow,
she said. Glo Harrow."

"It's DeLauter. I think Harrow's a family name. She knows about your
family. The money, the connections, the political implications. She's added
that to the mix. She'll do her best to hurt you, the way she'll do whatever she
can to hurt my family if I don't give her what she's after."

"It's just another form of blackmail. I know something about this kind
of blackmail, the kind that uses your feelings to squeeze you dry. She's using
your love as a weapon."

A chill danced over his skin at the phrase, and he heard the echo of
Stella's voice in his mind. "What did you say?"

"I said she's using your love as a weapon, and you're handing it to her. It
has to stop. You have to tell your family. Now."

"Jesus, Dru, I haven't figured out if telling them's the right thing to do.
Much less telling them at two in the morning."

"You know very well it's the right thing, the only thing to do. Do you
think what time it is matters to them?"

She crossed to the workbench where he'd tossed his phone. "I'd say
Anna would be the one to call first, and she can contact the others." She held
out the phone. "Do you want to call her and tell her we're on our way, or
shall I?"

"You're awful damn bossy all of a sudden."

"Because you need to be bossed just at the moment. Do you think I'm going to stand by and let her do this to you? Do you think any of us will?"

"The point is, she's the monkey on my back. I don't want her taking swipes at you, my family. I need to protect you from that."

"Protect me? You're lucky I don't knock you senseless with this phone. Your solution was to let me go. Do you think I want some self-sacrificing white knight?"

He nearly smiled. "Would that be the same thing as a martyr?"

"Close enough."

He held out his hand. "Don't hit me. Just give me the phone."

EIGHTEEN

The kitchen had always been the place for family meetings. Discussions, small celebrations were held there; decisions and plans were made there. Punishments were meted out and praise was given most often at the old kitchen table no one had ever considered replacing.

It was there they gathered now, with coffee on the stove and the lights bright enough to push away the dark. It seemed to Dru there were too many of them to fit in that limited space. But they made room for one another. They made room for her.

They had all come without hesitation, dragging themselves and their sleeping kids out of bed. They had to be alarmed, but no one peppered Seth with questions. She could feel the tension quivering in the sluggish, middle-of-the-night air.

The younger ones were shuffled upstairs and back to any available bed, with Emily in charge. Dru imagined there was quite a bit of whispered speculation going on up there by anyone who'd managed to stay awake.

"I'm sorry about this," Seth began.

"You drag us all out of bed at two in the morning, you've got a reason." Phillip closed his hand over Sybill's. "You kill somebody? Because if we've got to dispose of a body this time of night, we'd better get started."

Grateful for the attempt to lighten the mood, Seth shook his head. "Not this time. Might be easier all around if I had."

"Spit it out, Seth," Cam told him. "The sooner you tell us what's wrong, the sooner we can do something about it."

"I met with Gloria tonight."

There was silence, one long beat. Seth looked at Sybill, understanding she'd be the most upset. "I'm sorry. I was going to try to find a way not to tell you, but there isn't one."

"Why wouldn't you tell us?" There was strain in Sybill's voice, and her hand tightened visibly on Phillip's. "If she's in the area and bothering you, we need to know."

"It's not the first time."

"It's going to be the last." Fury snapped into Cam's voice. "What the hell is this, Seth? She's been back around before and you didn't mention it?"

"I didn't see the point in getting everyone worked up—the way you're going to be worked up now."

"Fuck that. When? When did she start coming back around you?"

"Cam—"

"If you're going to tell me to calm down," he said to Anna, "you're wasting your breath. I asked you a question, Seth."

"Since I was about fourteen."

"Son of a bitch." Cam shoved back from the table. Across from him, Dru jumped. She'd never seen that kind of rage, the kind with a ready violence that threatened to smash everything in its path.

"She's been coming around you all this time, for years, and you don't say a goddamn word?"

"No point yelling at him yet." Ethan leaned on the table, and though his voice was calm, there was something in his eyes that warned Dru his manner of fury would be every bit as lethal as his brother's. "She get money from you?"

Seth started to speak, then just shrugged.

"Now you can yell at him," Ethan muttered.

"You paid her? You've been paying her?" Shock vibrated as Cam stared at Seth. "What the hell's the *matter* with you? We'd've booted her greedy ass to Nebraska if you'd said one goddamn word about it. We took all the legal steps to keep her away from you. Why the hell did you let her bleed you?"

"I'd've done anything to keep her from touching any one of you. It was just money. For Christ's sake, what do I care about that as long as she went away again?"

"But she didn't stay away," Anna said quietly. Quietly because her own temper was simmering under the surface. If it boiled over, it would make Cam's seem like a little boy's tantrum. "Did she?"

"No, but—"

"You should've trusted us. You had to know we'd be there for you."

"Oh God, Anna, I knew that."

"This isn't the way to show it," Cam snapped.

"I gave her money." Seth held out his hands. "Just money. It was all I knew how to do, to protect you. I needed to do *something*, anything I could to pay you back."

"Pay us back? For what?"

"You *saved* me." Emotions swelled in Seth's voice and the almost desperate flood of them silenced the room. "You gave me everything I've ever had that was decent, that was clean, that was fucking *normal*. You changed your lives for me, and you did it when I was nothing to you. You made me family. Goddamn it. Goddamn it, Cam, you made me."

It took a moment before he could speak, but when he did Cam's voice was rough, and it was final. "I don't want to hear that kind of crap from you. I don't want to hear about fucking checks and fucking balances."

"That's not what he meant." Struggling with tears, Grace spoke softly. "Sit down now. Sit down now, Cam, and don't slap at him that way. He's right."

"What the hell does that mean?" But Cam dropped back in his chair. "Just what the hell does that mean?"

"He never lets me say it," Seth managed. "None of them ever let me—"

"Hush now," Grace said. "They did save you, and they started it when you were nothing more than a promise to their father, because they loved him. Then they did it for you, because they loved you. All of us loved you. If you weren't grateful for what they did, for what they've never stopped doing, there'd be something wrong with you."

"I wanted to—"

"Wait." Grace only had to lift a finger to stop him. "Love doesn't require payment. Cam's right about that. There are no checks and balances here."

"I needed to give something back. But that wasn't all. She said things about Aubrey." He stared at Grace as the color ran out of her face.

Aubrey, who'd been silently weeping, found her voice. "What? She used me?"

"Just things like wasn't she pretty, and wouldn't it be a shame if anything happened to her. Or her little sister, or her cousins. Christ, I was terrified. I was fucking fourteen. I was scared to death if I said anything to anybody she'd find a way to hurt Aubrey, or one of the kids."

"Of course you were," Anna said. "She counted on that."

"And when she said I owed her for all the trouble I'd caused her, how she needed a few hundred for traveling money, I figured it was the best way to get rid of her. Jesus, Grace was pregnant with Deke, and Kevin and Bram were just babies. I just wanted her gone and away from them."

"She knew that." Sybill let out a sigh, rose to go to the coffeepot. "She knew how much your family mattered to you, so that's what she used. She was always good at finding just the right button to push. She pushed mine often enough when I was a lot older than fourteen." She laid a hand on his shoulder, squeezed as she topped off mugs. "Ray was a grown man, but he paid her."

"She'd go away, months at a time," Seth continued. "Even years. But she came back. I had money. My share from the boatyard, what you gave me from Ray, then from some paintings. She hit me twice when I was in college, then came back for a third. I'd figured out she wasn't going anywhere, not for long. I knew it was stupid to keep paying her. I had the chance to go to Europe to study, to work. I took it. Wasn't any point in her coming around here if I was gone."

"Seth." Anna waited until he looked at her. "Did you go to Europe to get away from her? To get her away from us?"

The look he sent her was so fierce, so full of love it made Dru's throat hurt. "I wanted to go. I needed to find out what I could do with my work, on my own. That was just another door you opened up for me. But in the back of my mind . . . Well, it weighed in, that's all."

"Okay." Ethan turned his mug in slow circles. "You did what you thought you had to do then. What about now?"

"About four months ago, she showed up on my doorstep in Rome. She had some guy with her she was stringing along. She'd heard about me—read stuff—and figured the pot was a whole lot richer now. She said she'd go to the press, to the galleries, and give them the whole story. Her story," he amended. "The way she'd twisted it around. Dragging Ray's name through the dirt again. I paid her off, and I came home. I wanted to come home. But it turns out I brought her back with me."

"You never brought her anywhere," Phillip corrected. "Get that through your thick head."

"Okay, she came back. Only this time the money didn't send her off again. She's been staying around, somewhere. She came into Dru's shop."

"Did she threaten you?" Temper fired into Cam's face again. "Did she try to hurt you?"

"No." Dru shook her head. "She knows Seth and I are involved. So she's added me to the mix, using me as another weapon to hurt him. I don't know her, but from everything I've heard, everything I'm hearing, she wants that as much as she wants money. To hurt him. To hurt all of you. I don't agree with what Seth did, but I understand why he did it."

Her gaze traveled around the table, from face to face. "I shouldn't be sitting here at this table while you talk about this. This is family business, and as personal as it gets. But no one questioned my being here."

"You're Seth's," Phillip said simply.

"You can't know how special you are. All of you. This . . . unit. Whether Seth's trying to protect that unit was right or wrong, smart or stupid doesn't much matter at this point. The point is he loved you all too much to do otherwise—and she knew it. Now it has to stop."

"There's a woman with brains," Cam said. "Did you pay her tonight, kid?"

"No, she set new terms. She'll go to the press, tell her story. Blah blah." He shrugged, and realized a great deal of the weight on his shoulders had already lifted. "But she's got a new spin, pulling Dru into it. Senator's granddaughter in sex scandal. It's bull, but if she does it, it's going to pull everybody in. Reporters hounding her at the flower shop, hounding all of you, turning her family upside down. All of us, too."

"Screw her," Aubrey said, very clearly.

"Another girl with brains." Cam winked at Aubrey. "How much she want this time?"

"A million."

Cam choked on the coffee he'd just sipped. "A million—a million fucking dollars?"

"She won't get a penny." Face grim, Anna patted Cam on the back. "Not a penny this time, or ever again. Is that right, Seth?"

"I knew when I sat with her in that dive she had me meet her in, that I had to cut it off. She'll have to do whatever she's going to do."

"We won't be sitting on our hands," Phillip promised. "When are you supposed to meet her again?"

"Tomorrow night, with a ten-thousand-dollar down payment."

"Where?"

"This redneck bar in Saint Michael's."

"Phil's thinking." Cam grinned a wide, wide grin. "I love when that happens."

"Yeah, I'm thinking."

"Why don't I start some breakfast." Grace got to her feet. "And you can tell us all what you're thinking."

⌘

Dru listened to the ideas, the arguments and, incredibly from her point of view, the laughter and casual insults as a plan took shape.

Bacon sizzled, eggs were scrambled and coffee was brewed. She wondered if the lack of sleep had made her dull-witted, or if it was just impossible for an outsider to keep up with the dynamics.

When she started to get up, to help set the table, Anna laid a hand on her shoulder, rubbed. "Just sit, honey. You look exhausted."

"I'm all right. It's just I don't think I really understand. I suppose Gloria hasn't committed an actual crime, but it just seems as if you should talk to the police or a lawyer instead of trying to deal with it all yourselves."

Conversation snapped off. For a few seconds there was no sound but the gurgle of the coffeepot and the snap of frying meat.

"Well now," Ethan said in his thoughtful way, "that would be one option. Except you have to figure the cops would just tell Seth how he was a moron to give her money in the first place. Seems we've already covered that part here."

"She *blackmailed* him."

"In a manner of speaking," Ethan agreed. "They're not going to arrest her for it, are they?"

"No, but—"

"And I guess a lawyer might write a whole bunch of papers and letters and what-all about it. Maybe we could sue her or something. You can sue anybody for any damn thing, it seems to me. Maybe it goes to court. Then it gets ugly and it drags out."

"It isn't enough to stop the extortion," Dru insisted. "She should pay for what she's done. You work in the system," she said to Anna.

"I do. And I believe in it. I also know its flaws. As much as I want this woman to pay for every moment of pain and worry and unhappiness she's brought Seth, I know she won't. We can only deal with now."

"We deal with our own." Cam spoke in a tone of flat finality. "Family stands up. That's all there is."

Dru leaned toward him. "And you're thinking I won't stand up."

Cam leaned right back. "Dru, you're as pretty as they come, but you're not sitting at this table for decoration. You'll stand up. Quinn men don't fall for a woman unless she's got a spine."

She kept her eyes on his. "Is that a compliment?"

He grinned at her. "That was two compliments."

She eased back, nodded. "All right. So you handle it your way. The Quinn way," she added. "But I think it might be helpful to find out if, considering her lifestyle and habits, she has any outstanding warrants. A call to my grandfather ought to get us that information before tomorrow night. It wouldn't hurt for her to realize we play hard, too."

"I like her," Cam said to Seth.

"Me too." But Seth took Dru's hand. "I don't want to drag your family into this."

"Not wanting to drag yours into it or me into it is why we're sitting here at four in the morning." She took the platter of eggs Aubrey passed, scooped some onto her plate. "Your bright idea was to get drunk and dump me. How'd that work out for you?"

He took the platter, tried a smile. "Better than expected."

"No thanks to you. I wouldn't advise you going down that path again. Pass the salt."

While his family looked on, he reached over, took her face in his hands and kissed her. Hard and long. "Dru," he said. "I love you."

"Good. I love you, too." She took his wrist, squeezed lightly. "Now pass the salt."

∞

He didn't think he would sleep, but he dropped off like a stone for four hours. When he woke in his old room, disoriented and soft-brained, his first clear thought was that she wasn't beside him.

He stumbled out of the room and downstairs to find Cam alone in the kitchen. "Where's Dru?"

"She went into work, about an hour ago. Borrowed your car."

"She went in? Jesus." Seth rubbed his hands over his face, tried to get his brain to engage after too much whiskey, too much coffee, too little sleep. "Why didn't she just close for the day? She couldn't have gotten very much sleep."

"She looked like she handled it a lot better than you did, pal."

"Yeah, well, she didn't down half a bottle of Jameson first."

"You play, you pay."

"Yeah." He opened a cupboard to search for the kitchen aspirin. "Tell me."

Cam poured a glass of water, handed it to Seth. "Down those, then let's take a walk."

"I need to clean up, get into town. Maybe I can give Dru a hand in the shop. Something."

"She'll hold for a few minutes." Cam opened the kitchen door. "Let's take it outside."

"If you're planning on kicking my ass, it won't take much this morning."

"Thought about it. But I think it's been kicked enough for now."

"Look, I know I fucked up—"

"Just shut up." Cam gave Seth a shove out the door. "I've got some things to say."

He headed for the dock, as Seth had expected. The sun was strong and hot. It was barely nine in the morning, and already the air had a mean, threatening weight that promised to gain more muscle before it was done.

"You pissed me off," Cam began. "I'm mostly over it. But I want something made clear—and I'm speaking for Ethan and Phil. Get that?"

"Yeah, I get it."

"We didn't give up a goddamn thing for you. Shut up, Seth," he snapped out when Seth opened his mouth. "Just shut the hell up and listen." He let out a breath. "Ha. Looks like I'm still pissed off after all. Grace has some points, and I'm not going to argue about them. But none of us gave up jack."

"You wanted to race—"

"And I raced," Cam snapped out. "I told you to shut up. Now shut the fuck up until I'm done. You were ten years old, and we did what we were supposed to do. Nobody wants a fucking obligation from you, nobody wants payment from you, and it's a goddamn insult for you to think other-wise."

"It's not like that."

Cam stepped closer. "Do you want me to tie your tongue in a knot or are you going to shut up?"

Because he *felt* ten again, Seth shrugged.

"Things changed for you the way they were supposed to change. Things changed for us, too. Ever stop to think that if I hadn't been stuck with some smart-assed, skinny, pain-in-the-ass kid I might not have met Anna? I might have had to live my whole life without her—and without Kevin and Jake. Phil and Sybill, same deal. They found each other because you were in the middle. I figure Ethan and Grace might be getting around to dating just about now, almost twenty years after the fact, if you being part of things hadn't nudged them along."

He waited a beat. "So, how much do we owe you for our wives and chil-dren? For pulling us back home, for giving us a reason to start the busi-ness?"

"I'm sorry."

Pure frustration had Cam dragging at his own hair. "I don't want you to be sorry, for sweet Christ's sake! I want you to wake up."

"I'm awake. I don't feel much like George Bailey, but I'm awake. *It's a Wonderful Life*," Seth added. "Grandma—Stella told me I ought to think about it."

"Yeah. She loved old movies. I should've figured if anybody could put a chip in that rock head of yours, it would be Mom."

"I guess I didn't listen to her either. I think she's pissed off at me, too. I should've told you right along."

"You didn't, and that's done. So we start with now. We'll deal with her tonight."

"I'm looking forward to it." Seth turned with a slow smile. "I never thought I'd say it, but I'm looking forward to meeting her tonight. It's been a long time coming. So . . . you want to kick my ass, or slap me around?"

"Get a grip on yourself. Just wanted to clear the air." Cam slung a friendly arm around Seth's shoulder. Then shoved him into the water. "I don't know why," Cam said when Seth surfaced, "but doing that always makes me feel better."

"Glad I could help," Seth sputtered and let himself sink.

⬥

"You're staying here. That's the end of it."

    "And when did we come to the point where you dictate where I go and what I do? Play it back for me, I must have missed it the first time around."

"I'm not going to argue about this."

"Oh yes," Dru said, almost sweetly, "you are."

"She's not getting near you again. That's number one. The place I'm meeting her is a dive, and you don't belong there. That's two."

"Oh, I see. Now you decide where I belong. That's a tune I've been hearing all my life. I don't care for it."

"Dru." Seth paused, then paced to the back door of the family kitchen, back again. "This is hard enough without me going in there worrying about some asshole hassling you. The place is one step up from a pit."

"I don't know why you think I can't handle assholes. I've been handling you, haven't I?"

"That's real funny, and I'll bust into hilarity over it later. I want this done and over. I want it behind me. Behind us. Please." He changed tack, laid his hand gently on her shoulder. "Stay here and let me do what I have to do."

It was turmoil in his eyes now rather than temper. And she responded to it. "Well, since you ask so nicely."

His shoulders relaxed as he laid his forehead on hers. "Okay, good. Maybe you should stretch out for a little while. You didn't get much sleep last night."

"Don't push it, Seth."

"Right. I should go."

"You know who you are." She turned her head to brush her lips over his. "And so do I. She doesn't. She never could."

⬥

She let him go, and stood on the front porch with the other Quinn women as the two cars drove away.

Anna lowered the hand she'd lifted in a wave. "There go our strong, brave men, off to battle. And we womenfolk stay behind, tucked up safe."

"Put on the aprons," Aubrey mumbled. "Make potato salad for tomorrow's picnic."

Dru glanced around, saw the same look in her companions' eyes she knew was in her own. "I don't think so."

"So." Sybill rolled her shoulders, glanced at her watch. "How much lead time do we give them?"

"Fifteen minutes ought to be about right," Anna decided.

Grace nodded. "We'll take my van."

Seth sat at the bar, brooding into his untouched beer. He figured the dread in the pit of his stomach was natural. She'd always put it there. The venue, he supposed, was the perfect place for this showdown with her, with his early childhood, with his own ghosts and demons.

He intended to walk out of it when he was finished, and leave all of that misery behind, just another smear on the dirty air.

He needed to feel clean again, complete again. He wondered if Ray would have understood this nasty tug-of-war between fury and grief.

He liked to think so. Just as he liked to think some part of Ray was sitting beside him in the bar.

But when she walked in, there was only the two of them. The drinkers, the pool players, the bartender, even that nebulous connection with the man who'd been his grandfather faded away.

It was just Seth, and his mother.

She relaxed onto a stool, crossed her legs and sent the bartender a wink.

"You look a little rough around the edges," she said to Seth. "Tough night?"

"You look the same. You know, I've been sitting here thinking. You had a pretty good deal growing up."

"Shit." She snagged the gin and tonic the bartender put in front of her. "Lot you know about it."

"Big house, plenty of money, good education."

"Fuck that." She drank deep. "Bunch of jerks and assholes."

"You hated them."

"My mother's a cold fish, stepfather's pussy-whipped. And there's Sybill, the perfect daughter. I couldn't wait to get the hell out and live."

"I don't know about your parents. They don't have anything to do with me either. But Sybill never hurt you. She took you in, took both of us in when you landed on her doorstep, broke and with nowhere else to go."

"So she could lord it over me. Goddamn superior bitch."

"Is that why you stole from her when we were in New York? Cleaned her out and took off after she'd given you a place to stay?"

"I take what I need. That's how you get ahead in life. Had to support you, didn't I?"

"Let's not bullshit. You never gave a damn about me. The only reason you didn't take off without me, dump me on Sybill, was because you knew she cared about me. So you took me away, you stole her things because you hated her. You stole so you could buy drugs."

"Oh yeah, she'd've loved it if I'd left you behind. She could've gone around feeling righteous, telling everybody how worthless I was. Fuck her. Whatever I took out of her place, I was entitled to. Gotta look out for number one in this life. Never could teach you that."

"You taught me plenty." When Gloria rattled the ice in her glass, he signaled the bartender for another drink. "Ray didn't even know about you, but you hated him. When he found out, when he tried to help you, you only hated him more."

"He owed me. Bastard doesn't keep his dick zipped, knocks up some idiot coed, he oughta pay."

"And he paid you. He didn't know Barbara was pregnant with you, he never knew you existed. But when you told him, he paid you. And it wasn't enough. You tried to ruin him with lies. Then you used his decency against him and sold me to him like I was a puppy you were tired of."

"Fucking A I was tired of you. Kept you around for ten years, cramping my style. Old man Quinn owed me for giving him a grandson. And it all worked out pretty well for you, didn't it?"

"I guess I owe you for that one." He lifted his beer in a toast, sipped. "But it worked out pretty well for you, at least when he was alive. You just kept hitting him up for more money, using me as the bait."

"Hey, he could've tossed you back anytime. You were nothing to him, just like I was nothing."

"Yeah, some people are just stupid, weak, natural marks, believing a promise made to a ten-year-old boy needs to be kept. The same type who think that same kid deserves a shot at a decent life, a home, a family. He'd have given you the same, if you'd wanted it."

"You think I wanted to be stuck in some backwater bumfuck town, paying homage to an old man who picks up strays?" She gulped her gin. "That's your scene, not mine. And you got it, so what're you bitching about? And if you want to keep it, you'll pay. Just like you've always paid. You got the down payment?"

"How much you figure you've gotten from me over the years, Gloria? Between what you bled out of Ray, what you've been bleeding out of me? Must be a couple hundred thousand, at least. Of course, you never got anything out of my brothers. You tried—the usual lies, threats, intimidation—but they didn't bleed so easy. You do better with old men and kids."

She smirked. "They'd've paid if I'd wanted them to pay. I had better things to do. Bigger fish to fry. You wanna fry your own fish now, keep that fancy art career you've got going from getting screwed up, wanna keep sticking it to the senator's granddaughter, you pay for it."

"So you said. Let me get the terms clear. I pay you, one million dollars starting with the ten-thousand-dollar down payment tonight—"

"In cash."

"Right, in cash, or you'll go to the press, to Dru's family, and spin another web of lies about how you were used and abused by the Quinns, starting with Ray. You'll smear them and me and Dru along with it. The poor, desperate woman, girl really, struggling to raise a child on her own, begging for help only to be forced to give up the child."

"Has a nice ring. Lifetime Movie of the Week."

"No mention in there of the tricks you turned while that child was in the next room—or the men you let touch him. No mention of the drugs, the booze, the beatings."

"Bring out the violins." She leaned in, very close. "You were a pain in the ass. You're lucky I kept you around as long as I did." And lowered her voice. "You're lucky I didn't sell you to one of my johns. Some would've paid top dollar."

"You would have, sooner or later."

She shrugged. "Had to get something out of you, didn't I?"

"You've been tapping me for money since I was fourteen. I've paid you to protect my family, myself. Mostly I've paid you because the peace of mind was worth a hell of a lot more than the money. I've let you blackmail me."

"I want what's due me." She snatched the third drink. "I'm making you a deal here. One lump-sum payment and you keep your nice, boring life. Screw with me, and you'll lose it all."

"A million dollars or you'll do whatever you can to hurt my family, ruin my career and destroy my relationship with Dru."

"In a nutshell. Pay up."

He nudged his beer aside, met her eyes. "Not now, not ever again."

She grabbed his shirt in her fist, yanked his face close to hers. "You don't want to fuck with me."

"Oh yeah, I do. I have." He reached in his pocket, pulled out a mini recorder. "Everything we've said is on here. Might be a problem in court, if I decide to go to the cops."

When she grabbed for it, he cuffed her wrist with his hand. "Speaking of cops, they'll be interested to know you jumped bail down in Fort Worth. Solicitation and possession. You go public and some hard-ass skip tracer is going to be really happy to scoop you up and haul you back to Texas."

"You son of a bitch."

"Truer words," he said mildly. "But you go right ahead and try to sell your version of things. I figure anybody who wants to write a story about all this will be really interested in this informal interview."

"I want my money." She shrieked it, tossed what was left in her glass in his face.

The quartet playing pool looked over. The biggest of them tapped his cue against his palm as he sized Seth up.

She leaped off the stool, and fury had her practically in tears. "He stole my money."

The four men started forward. Seth rose from the stool.

And his brothers walked in, ranged themselves beside him.

"That seems to even things up." Cam tucked his thumbs in his front pockets and gave Gloria a fierce grimace. "Been a while."

"You bastards. You're all fucking bastards. I want what's mine."

"We've got nothing of yours." Ethan spoke quietly. "We never did."

"I take anything from her?" Seth asked the bartender.

"Nope." He continued to wipe the bar. "You want trouble, take it outside."

Phillip scanned the faces of the four men. "You want trouble?"

The big man tapped his cue twice more. "Bob says he didn't take nothing, he didn't take nothing. None of my never mind."

"How about you, Gloria? You want trouble?" Phillip asked her.

Before she could speak, the door opened. The women came in.

"Goddamn it," Cam muttered under his breath. "Should've figured it."

Dru walked directly to Seth, slid her hand into his. "Hello again, Gloria. It's funny, my mother doesn't remember you at all. She isn't the least bit interested in you. But my grandfather is." She took a piece of paper out of her pocket. "This is the number to his office on the Hill. He'll be happy to speak to you if you'd like to call him."

Gloria slapped the paper from Dru's fingers, then retreated quickly when Seth stepped forward.

"I'll make you sorry for this." She shoved through them, pausing briefly to snarl at Sybill.

"You shouldn't have come back, Gloria," Sybill told her. "You should've cut your losses."

"Bitch. I'll make you sorry. I'll make you all sorry." With one last bitter glance, she shoved through the door.

"You were supposed to stay home," Seth told her.

"No, I wasn't." Dru touched his cheek.

NINETEEN

The house and the yard were crowded with people. Crabs were steaming, and a half dozen picnic tables were loaded with food.

The Quinns' annual Fourth of July celebration was well under way.

Seth pulled a beer from the keg, grabbed some shade, and took a break from the conversations to sketch.

His world, he thought. Friends, family, slow Shore voices and squealing kids. The smells of spiced crabs, of beer, of talcum powder and grass. Of the water.

A couple of kids were out in a Sunfish with a bright yellow sail. Ethan's dog was splashing in the shallows with Aubrey—old times.

He heard Anna's laugh and the cheerful clink of horseshoes.

Independence Day, he thought. He would remember this one for the rest of his life.

"We've been doing this here since before you were born," Stella said from beside him.

The pencil squirted out of Seth's fingers. No dream this time, he thought in a kind of breathless wonder. He was sitting in the warm, dappled shade, surrounded by people and noise.

And talking to a ghost.

"I wasn't sure you were speaking to me."

"Nearly made a mess of it, and that ticked me off. But you figured things out in the end."

She was wearing the old khaki hat, a red shirt and baggy blue shorts. Without any real thought, Seth picked up the pencil, turned the page in his book and began to draw her as she looked, sitting contentedly in the shade.

"Part of me was always scared of her, no matter what. But that's gone now."

"Good. Stay that way, because she'll always cause trouble. My God, look at Crawford. How'd he get so old? Time just goes by, no matter what the hell you do. Some things you let go. Some things are worth repeating. Like this party, year after year after year."

He continued to sketch, but his throat had tightened. "You're not coming back again, are you?"

"No, honey. I'm not coming back again."

She touched him, and he would never forget the sensation of her hand on his knee. "Time to look forward, Seth. You don't want to ever forget what's behind you, but you've got to look ahead. Look at my boys." She let out a long sigh as she gazed over at Cam, and Ethan, and Phillip. "All grown up, with families of their own. I'm glad I told them that I loved them, that I was proud of them, while I was still breathing."

She smiled now, patted Seth's knee. "Glad I got a chance to tell you I love you. And I'm proud of you."

"Grandma—"

"Make a good life for yourself or I'm going to be ticked off at you again. Here comes your girl," she said, and was gone.

His heart wrenched in his chest. And Dru sat down beside him. "Want company?" she asked.

"As long as it's you."

"So many people." She leaned back on her elbows. "It makes me think Saint Chris must look like a ghost town right now."

"Just about everyone swings by, at least for a while. It whittles down by nightfall, and the rest of us stay here and watch the fireworks."

Some things you let go, he remembered. Some are worth repeating.

"I love you, Drusilla. Just thought that was worth repeating."

She angled her head, studied the odd little smile on his face. "You can repeat it whenever you like. And if you come home with me afterward, we can make our own fireworks."

"That's a date."

She sat up again, examined his drawing. "That's wonderful. Such a strong face—and a friendly one." She glanced around for the model. "Where is she? I don't remember seeing her."

"She's not here anymore." He took a last look at the sketch, then gently closed the book. "Wanna go for a swim?"

"It's hot enough, but I didn't think to bring a suit."

"Really?" Grinning, he stood up, pulled her to her feet. "But you can swim, right?"

"Of course I can swim." As soon as the words were out, she recognized the gleam in his eye. "Don't even think about it."

"Too late." He scooped her up.

"Don't—" She wiggled, shoved, then began to panic as he jogged toward the dock. "This isn't funny."

"It will be. Don't forget to hold your breath."

He ran straight down the dock and off the end.

∞

"It's a Quinn thing," Anna said as she handed Dru a dry shirt. "I can't explain it. They're always doing that."

"I lost a shoe."

"They'll probably find it."

Dru sat on the bed. "Men are so strange."

"We just have to remember that in some areas, they're really just five years old. These sandals ought to fit you well enough." She offered them.

"Thanks. Oh, they're fabulous."

"I love shoes. I lust for shoes."

"With me it's earrings. I have no power against them."

"I like you very much."

Dru stopped admiring the sandals and looked up. "Thank you. I like you very much, too."

"It's a bonus. I would have made room for any woman Seth loved. All of us would. So you're a very nice bonus. I wanted to tell you."

"I . . . I don't have experience with families like yours."

"Who does?" With a laugh, Anna sat on the bed beside her.

"Mine isn't generous. I'm going to try to talk to my parents again. Seeing what Seth's been through, what he faced down last night, made me realize I have to try. But whatever understanding we reach, we'll never be like yours. They won't welcome him the way you're welcoming me."

"Don't be so sure." She wrapped an arm around Dru's shoulders. "He has a way of winning people over."

"Certainly worked with me. I love him." She pressed a hand to her stomach. "It's terrifying how much."

"I know the feeling. It'll be dark soon." Anna gave Dru a quick squeeze. "Let's go get a glass of wine and get a good spot to watch the show."

When she stepped outside, Seth met her with one very soggy canvas slide and a sheepish grin. "Found it."

She snatched it, set it beside the back door where she'd put its mate. "You're a baboon."

"Mrs. Monroe brought homemade peach ice cream." He brought his hand out, with a double-scoop cone in it, from behind his back.

"Hmm." She sniffed, but she took the cone.

"Want to sit on the grass with me and watch fireworks?"

She took a long lick. "Maybe."

"Gonna let me kiss you when nobody's looking?"

"Maybe."

"Gonna share that ice cream?"

"Absolutely not."

⋙

While Seth was trying to cadge his share of a peach ice cream cone, and excited children were bouncing in anticipation of that first explosion of light and color in the night sky, Gloria DeLauter pulled into the parking lot of Boats by Quinn.

She jerked to a halt and sat stewing in the messy juices of her fury laced with a pint of gin.

They'd pay. All of them would pay. Bastards. Thought they could scare her off, gang up on her the way they had and go back to their stupid house and laugh about it.

They'd see who laughed when she was finished with them.

They *owed* her. She beat the heel of her hand on the steering wheel as rage choked her.

She was going to make that son of a bitch she'd given birth to sorry. She'd make all of them sorry.

She shoved out of the car, stumbling as the gin spun in her head. She weaved her way to the trunk. *God!* She loved being high. People who went through life sober and straight were the assholes. World was fucking full of assholes, she thought as she stabbed her key at the trunk lock.

You need to get into a program, Gloria.

That's what they told her. Her worthless mother, her spineless stepfather, her tight-assed sister. The sainted sucker Ray Quinn had tried that with her, too.

It was all bullshit.

On the fourth try, she managed to get the key in the lock. She lifted the trunk, then hooted with delight as she dragged out the two cans of gasoline.

"We're gonna have some motherfucking fireworks, all right."

She stumbled again, stepped right out of one of her shoes but was too drunk to notice. Limping now, she carted the cans to the door, then straightened up, caught her breath.

It took her a while to uncap the first can, and as she fought with it she cursed the gawky kid at the gas station who'd filled them for her.

Just another asshole in a world of assholes.

But her good humor returned when she splashed gasoline on the doors and the sharp, dangerous smell of it stung the air.

"Stick your wood boats up your ass. Fucking Quinns."

She splashed it on the brick, on glass, on the pretty barberry bushes Anna had planted along the foundation. When one can was empty, she started on the second.

It was a thrill to heave it, still half full, through the front window. She danced in the dark to the sound of breaking glass.

Then she hobbled back to the trunk and retrieved the two bottles she'd filled with gas earlier and plugged with rags. "Molotov cocktail." She giggled, swayed. "I got a double for you bastards."

She fumbled out her lighter and flicked. And was smiling when she set the flame to the rag.

It caught faster than she'd expected, burned the tips of her fingers. On a little shriek, she heaved it toward the window, shattered it on brick.

"Shit!" Flames leaped along the bushes, ate down to the ground and crept toward the doors. But she wanted more.

She edged closer and, with the heat soaking her face, lit the second rag. Her aim was better this time, and she heard the boom of glass and flame as the bottle crashed on the floor inside the building.

"Kiss my ass!" She screamed it and gave herself the pleasure of watching the fire sprint before she ran to her car.

⁂

The rocket exploded across the sky in a fountain of gold against black. With Dru nestled between his legs, his arms around her waist, Seth felt almost stupidly content.

"I really missed this when I was overseas," he told her. "Sitting in the backyard on the Fourth of July and watching the sky go crazy." He turned his lips to the nape of her neck. "Do I still get the fireworks later?"

"Probably. In fact, if you play your cards right, I might let you . . ."

She trailed off, glancing over as Seth did at the sound of raised voices. He was on his feet, pulling Dru to hers even as Cam raced toward them.

"Boatyard's on fire."

⁂

The fire department was already fighting the blaze. The doors and windows were gone, and the brick around them blackened. Seth stood, hands fisted, as water pumped through the openings and smoke billowed out.

He thought of the work inside that old brick barn. The sweat and the blood that went into it, the sheer determination and family pride.

Then he bent down and picked up the high-heeled backless shoe at his feet. "It's hers. Stay with Anna and the rest," he told Dru, and went to his brothers.

"Couple of kids heard the explosion and saw the car drive away." Cam rubbed his hands over eyes that stung from smoke. "Not much doubt it was arson since she left the gas cans behind. They got the make and model of her car, and a description. She won't get far."

"She'll see this as payback," Seth said. "Fuck with me, I'll fuck with you more."

"Yeah, well, she's got a surprise coming. This time she's going to jail."

"She messed us up real good first."

"We're insured." Cam stared at the blackened brick, the trampled bushes, the stream of smoke still belching out of the broken door.

The pain in his heart was a physical stab. "We put this place together once, we can do it again. And if you're planning on taking any guilt trips—"

"No." Seth shook his head. "That's done." He held out his hand as Aubrey walked to them.

"We're okay." She squeezed his fingers. "That's what counts." But the tears on her cheeks weren't all from smoke.

"Hell of a mess," Phillip said as he walked up. His face was smeared with soot, his clothes filthy with it. "But it's out. Those kids who called nine-one-one saved our asses. Fire department responded in minutes."

"You got their names?" Cam asked him.

"Yeah." He let out a breath. "Ethan's over talking with the fire marshal. He'll let us know when we're clear to go in. It's gonna be a while with the arson investigation on top of it."

"Which one of us is going to talk the women into taking the kids home?"

Phillip stuck his hand in his pocket, pulled out a coin. "Flip you for it. Heads it's your headache, tails it's mine."

"Deal. But I flip. Your fingers are a little too sticky to suit me."

"You saying I'd cheat?"

"Over this? Damn right."

"That's cold," Phillip complained, but handed over the coin.

"Damn it." Cam hissed through his teeth when he flipped heads.

"Don't even think about saying two out of three."

Scowling, Cam tossed Phillip the coin, then stalked over to argue with the women.

"Well." Phillip folded his arms and studied the building. "We could say screw it, move to Tahiti and open a tiki bar. Spend our days fishing until we're brown as monkeys and our nights having jungle sex with our women."

"Nah. Live on an island, you end up drinking rum. Never had a taste for it."

Phillip slapped a hand on Seth's shoulder. "Then I guess we stick. Want to break it to Ethan?" He nodded toward his brother as Ethan crossed the muddy lawn.

"He'll be okay. He doesn't like rum either." But the optimism Seth was fighting to hold on to wavered when he saw Ethan's face.

"They picked her up." Ethan swiped a forearm over his sweaty brow. "Sitting in a bar not five miles out of town. You all right with that?" he asked Seth.

"I'm fine with that."

"Okay then. Maybe you ought to go talk your girl into going on home. It's going to be a long night here."

⬿

It was a long night, and a long day after. It would be, Seth thought, some long weeks before Boats by Quinn was back in full operation.

He'd tromped through the wreckage and the stink of the building, mourned with his brothers and Aubrey the loss of the pretty, half-built hull of a skiff that was now no more than scraps of blackened teak.

He grieved over the sketches he'd drawn from childhood on, which were nothing but ashes. He could, and would, reproduce them. But he couldn't replace them, nor the joy each one had given him.

When there was no more to do, he went home, cleaned up and slept until he could do more.

It was nearly dusk the next evening when he drove to Dru's. He was tired down to the bone, but as clearheaded as he'd been in his life. He hauled the porch swing he'd bought out of the bed of the truck he'd borrowed from Cam, got his tools.

When she stepped out, he was drilling in the first hook.

"You said you wanted one. This seemed like the place for it."

"It's the perfect place." She walked over, touched his shoulder. "Talk to me."

"I will. That's why I'm here. Sorry I didn't get in touch today."

"I know you've been busy. Half the town's been in and out of my shop, just like half the town was there at the fire last night."

"We got more help than we could handle. Fire didn't spread to the second level."

She knew. Word spread every bit as quickly as flame. But she let him talk.

"Main level's a wreck. Between the fire, the smoke, the water, we'll have to gut it. Lost most of the tools, toasted a hull. Insurance adjuster was out today. We'll be okay."

"Yes, you'll be okay."

He stepped over to drill for the second hook. "They arrested Gloria. Kids made her car, and the kid who sold her the gas ID'd her. Plus she left her fingerprints all over the gas can she dumped outside the building. When they picked her up for questioning, she was still wearing one shoe. Losing shoes seems to be going around."

"I'm so sorry, Seth."

"Me too. I'm not taking it on," he added. "I know it's not my fault. All she managed to do was mess up a building. She didn't hurt us. She can't. We've built something she can't touch."

He looped the chain, hooked a link. Tugged to test it. "Not that she'll stop trying."

He walked around, looped the other chain. "She'll go to jail." He spoke conversationally, and she wondered if he thought she couldn't see the fatigue on his face. "But she won't change. She won't change because she can't see herself. And when she gets out, it's a pretty sure bet she'll come back this way, sooner or later, make another play for money. She's in my life, and I can deal with that."

He gave the swing a little nudge, sent it swaying. "It's a lot to ask someone else to take on."

"Yes, it is. I plan on having a long heart-to-heart with my parents. But I don't think it'll change anything. They're overly possessive, discontent people who will, most likely, continue to use me as a weapon against each other, or an excuse not to face their own marriage on its own terms. They're in my life, and I can deal with that."

She paused, tilted her head. "It's a lot to ask someone else to take on."

"Guess it is. Want to try this out?"

"I do."

They sat, swung gently as dusk thickened and the water lapped the shore. "Does it work for you?" he asked her.

"It certainly does. This is exactly where I would've hung it."

"Dru?"

"Hmmm?"

"Are you going to marry me?"

Her lips tipped up at the corners. "That's my plan."

"It's a good plan." He took her hand, lifted it to his lips. "Are you going to have children with me?"

Her eyes stung, but she kept them closed and continued to swing gently. "Yes. That's the second stage of the plan. You know how I feel about stages."

He turned her hand over, kissed her palm. "Grow old with me, here, in the house by the water."

She opened her eyes now, let the first tear spill down her cheek. "You knew that would make me cry."

"But just a little. Here." He drew a ring out of his pocket, a simple gold band with a small round ruby. "It's pretty plain, but it was Stella's—it was my grandmother's." Slipped it on her finger. "The guys thought she'd like me to have it."

"Oh-oh."

"What?"

Her fingers tightened on his as she pulled his hand to her cheek. "It may not be just a little after all. It's the most beautiful thing you could have given me."

He laid his lips on hers, drawing her in as she wrapped her arms around him. "Somebody really smart told me you've got to look ahead. You can't forget what's behind you, but you got to move forward. It starts now. For us, it starts now."

"Right now."

She laid her head on his shoulder, held his hand tight in hers. They rocked on the swing in the heavy night air while the water turned dark with night, and the fireflies began to dance.